Oath & & Shadow

Book ONE of
The Catalyst

Oath & & Shadow

Book ONE of
The Catalyst

Frank Morin

CONTENTS

1.	Bloodset	1
2.	The Most Epic Break-Up Fight of All Time	13
3.	An Uneasy Alliance	22
4.	Be Careful What You Worship	31
5.	The Song of Savas	38
6.	The Futility of Containment	47
7.	A Little Loyalty Taken Too Far	52
8.	A Temporary Reprieve	59
9.	The Right Answers For the Wrong Questions	65
10.	The Timbered Rest	72
11.	Plots Within Plots	81
12.	Things That Go Bump In the Night	91
13.	Two Out of Three is Not a Win	99
14.	Some Bad News	107
15.	The Cleansing Power of Darkness	114
16.	A Crazy Choice	121
17.	The Importance of Good Shoes	129
18.	A Step Down a Slick Road	133

19.	Complications	138
20.	Spinning The Wheel Can Be a Bad Habit	142
21.	No Way Out	148
22.	Even The Cunning Can Doubt	154
23.	Facing a Legend	157
24.	The Steward	164
25.	A Glimmer of Light in a Moment of Darkness	168
26.	Taking The Path Less Traveled Often Sucks	176
27.	Another Unexpected Road	187
28.	A Path of Darkness	194
29.	Are We There Yet?	197
30.	Unexpected Allies	206
31.	Making Friends	216
32.	Cryptic Answers	224
33.	The Deadliest of Weapons	235
34.	Painful Lessons	247
35.	Unexpected Consequences	252
36.	Surprise Connections	255
37.	Conflicting Memories	264
38.	Buttering Toast With Your Feet	271
39.	Playing Catch-up	280
40.	Bad News Comes in Packs	285
41.	Dealing With Grief	288
42.	Sword Brothers	290

43. Unexpected Company   301

44. Kidneys in the Mind   307

45. Choices   318

46. A Friend of a Friend   321

47. With Allies Like These . . .   326

48. A Taste of Battle Magic   337

49. An Unexpected Power of Healing   346

50. The Path of Dangers   350

51. The Path to Glory   359

52. The Weight of Power   364

53. Continuing The Chase   366

54. The Choosing   376

55. A Point of No Return   386

56. Doing Magic   390

57. A New Kind of Journey   397

58. Setting the Board   403

59. The Pain Behind the Laughter   410

60. The Rhythm of Life   417

61. Power Reserves Exist for a Reason   421

62. A New Master   432

63. A Bit of Insight   438

64. A Glimpse   446

65. Allies   448

66. A New Angle   453

67.	Changing Forecasts	459
68.	Elemental Carnage	464
69.	The Man With The Plan	469
70.	Bridges	470
71.	Meeting Your Worst Nightmare	476
72.	Into the Breach	482
73.	Well-Timed Faith	485
74.	Heroes Come in All Sizes	492
75.	The Song of Savas	500
76.	A Name For Death	509
77.	Mess With One Brother, Mess With Them All	515
78.	One Good Shield	527
79.	An Open Door Is An Open Invitation	530
80.	The Race Is On	533
81.	Perfect Time For A Bit Of Drama	542
82.	Desperate Choices	547
83.	The Point Of No Return	553
84.	Fires of Change	558
85.	Unleash The Hound Of Justice	567
86.	A Devious Quarry	572
87.	Group Hug	579
88.	The Devils We Serve	580
89.	Fates And Chances	586
	About the Author	592

Afterword 593

Other Works by Frank Morin 594

1

BLOODSET

Kevlin slipped between a pair of small trees, careful to avoid their long thorns. His thick, boiled-leather armor protected his torso, but his left hand still stung from having run into one of those cursed little trees earlier. Thankfully most of the heavily-forested part of Hallvarr was covered in less painful species, like oak and purple netwood.

Warblers and other birds he could not hope to identify chirped in the branches above in a final defiant chorus as twilight descended over the world. The forest felt alive, and for once he did not feel uncomfortable under the towering trees.

He glanced back the way he'd come, but could see no trace of the hidden clearing where Dathan and his half-dozen thugs were setting up camp. Barely a quarter mile from the highway, it was well concealed from passing travelers. Kevlin had only managed to find it by applying one of the few bits of woods lore he knew and following a small stream back into the forest.

Dathan had railed at the delay, but the risk paid off. Had the attempt to find a good hiding spot failed, the delay could easily have turned fatal. Piran's mercenaries were not far behind and they had proven to be determined pursuers.

The lucky break carried its own debt, though. Kevlin did not like owing anything to Akillik. He'd be sure to leave some coins with the next Karakol Stalwarts to square his account.

Even so, he wanted to be sure all trace of their passing was eradicated before Piran's men passed by. He and his party had barely avoided the mercenaries in Ingolf, just hours north of where he now crouched. That lucky escape was another credit owed to Akillik. The more the fickle god's Wheel spun in one's favor, the more likely it would spin against them when they really needed it.

"Four more days," Kevlin whispered to himself as he slipped between thick oaks.

They just had to elude the mercenaries long enough to reach Tamera. In the imperial capital, Dathan could seek injunction from the Salawin Stalwarts. He might even gain enough respite to barter a truce with Piran. Either way, Dathan's fate would no longer rest in Kevlin's hands, and he could move on and find a better job.

In the next heartbeat, just as Kevlin skirted a huge bush dripping with poisonous riffle berries, the forest fell silent. The warblers quieted and the myriad other little noises of the forest ceased. Kevlin was not much of a woodsman, but even he could not miss the signs.

Danger walked the woods with him.

He slipped a hand to the hilt of his sword and listened. In the heavy forest he trusted his ears more than his eyes. Nothing moved and even the creaking of trees seemed to still. His breathing sounded loud in the hush. Kevlin inched forward, seeking a better vantage, and cringed at every rustling leaf and snapping twig.

After pushing through a screen of heavy brush, he finally gained an unobstructed view of the imperial highway. It cut through the thick forest, straight as the path from Dathan to his strongbox, and wider than three logging wagons abreast. The hard-packed gravel surface lay empty, their tracks from earlier invisible. No one could tell they had turned off the road. Their secret campsite would remain hidden.

Kevlin glanced westward, then blurted out, "Sherah's Teeth!"

The sun hung low above the trees, and crimson clouds stained the horizon. Unlike those evenings when a beautifully painted sky soothed the eye, tonight the clouds hung scarred and bleeding. Long, jagged sections, like shards of broken glass, ripped free and drifted down in tortuous, twisted patterns before shredding into what looked like bloody rain that fell beyond the western hills.

A Bloodset. A big one.

He avoided staring at those dying shards that flowed from one shape into another every few seconds, often resembling agonized faces. Seeing one's own face bleeding in the heavens was a very bad omen.

The profound silence made sense. No birds flitted among the trees, no squirrels darted through the drifts of autumn leaves. The forest huddled under the crimson sky as if bracing for disaster.

Kevlin had only seen two bloodsets in the quarter century of his life. Both had occurred in the past five years, but neither had stretched so far across the horizon. In each previous occasion, he had faced those times of conflict sanctioned by Savas, god of war, with battle-hardened legions at his command. Kevlin had welcomed the conflicts and led his troops to victory.

No longer. Kevlin now fled across Hallvarr, leading Dathan and the half-trained bullies who guarded him in a wild dash toward the promised safety of Tamera. If it came to a real fight, they'd be slaughtered.

'By the Lady's fickle winds, I don't need this,' he thought.

How could there be a bloodset? He doubted there were sufficient people in the sparsely-populated region to bleed enough to satisfy such an omen.

We should have taken our chances in Diodor. Better to have faced Piran's mercenaries than walk into a conflict sanctioned by Savas.

He'd offer a prayer to the Lady if he thought it might do any good, but he hadn't paid the goddess of the sea more than lip service for years. Trying it might just anger her, since her favor was as contrary as the seas she ruled. Not as fickle as Akillik and his infamous Wheel, but Kevlin refused to trust his fate to luck again so soon.

Kevlin crouched behind some scraggly pine and made a point of not looking west again as he watched for pursuit. The shadows lengthened into early evening, but every second seemed to last forever. He fought to keep his breath even and ignore the itch between his shoulder blades.

Ten minutes later the sun slipped beneath the horizon, finally ending the bloodset. Kevlin stood and blew out a breath. Maybe they could escape before the bloodletting started.

A brilliant flash of light blossomed up the road to his right. It dwarfed the trees and drove the darkness back like the sudden return of the sun. Thunder shattered the air, and a blast of hot wind howled past as it fled the light, flattening nearby grass and bending trees so far over that a couple snapped with ear-splitting *cracks.*

The forest groaned under the abuse. Leaves whipped into the air, forming a whirling, multicolored blanket, heavy with the scent of decay. Kevlin dropped to one knee and raised an arm to shield his face.

As the echoes from the thunder faded, people started to scream. Above him?

Kevlin looked up through the fluttering leaves and gasped. Four figures tumbled through the air, high above the trees, starkly backlit by the brilliant white light.

He surged to his feet, one hand half-raised in an instinctive attempt to help. But he could do nothing but watch in open-mouthed dismay as those screaming people reached the height of their arc and plummeted back toward the ground, arms and legs flailing in a vain attempt to stave off the inevitable. They tumbled into the trees not far from where he crouched.

Images of splintered bones and burst organs flashed through his mind. He'd witnessed the results of falling from great heights, and his stomach knotted in horror as he imagined what happened to those unfortunates.

The screaming stopped.

Kevlin winced and ran a hand across his face.

The screaming started again.

No longer the panic-driven screams of mortal terror, the shouting seemed more angry than fearful.

By the bearded foam of the Lady's wrath, what's going on? How could anyone survive that fall?

The brilliant light faded and shadows eagerly reclaimed the surrounding area. The wind died to a low moan and the leaves settled to the ground. It had to be sentinels. Only they could light the night like ten thousand tempest lanterns and shake the entire forest.

Another blast of light shattered the dimness. Unlike the pure-white brilliance of the first flash, this one stained the night burgundy, and illuminated everything in a way that made Kevlin's eyes water.

The crimson light came from across the highway immediately to the north, only a few hundred yards away. Again, thunder ripped the air and he ducked. Another blast of air fled past, although not as powerful as the first.

He muttered a curse. Bloodsets and sentinels. Bad things were piling up like rogue waves in the Gohban Straits.

The voices presented a new risk and he needed to know what was going on. He was responsible for Dathan's safety, no matter how he felt about the fat merchant.

Staying ignorant might prove fatal, so Kevlin drew his sword and jogged toward the voices. His eyes darted to every shadow, searching for any threat, half afraid he might find one.

Within seconds, another blast of white light eclipsed the fading red glow and lit up the forest. He would rather have stumbled through the darkness than walk through that unnatural light. The nearby shouting settled into a heated argument between a man and a woman, punctuated every few seconds by a second woman's panic-filled wail.

Rounding a heavyset oak, Kevlin paused at the edge of a small clearing just as another flash of red light pushed the shadows back. The light illuminated the unmoving forms of three people lying a few feet apart, each facing a different direction. They argued with a lot more strength than they should have after falling so far.

Kevlin crouched beside the old oak and studied the scene as the light faded again. He spotted only three people, but there had been four in the air a moment ago. Where was the last one?

"I told you I can't move," the man was saying.

"What good is it having you along then, Strength?" said one woman. "The first time we need you, you're helpless."

"It's not my fault! I can't compete with magic."

"Why'd he do it?"

"I don't know. Answering questions like that is your responsibility, Cunning."

"Why give us cryptic titles just to throw us away like an unused dress?"

"I'm not a dress," the man growled. "And we can't live up to that prophecy he's always muttering about if we're not around to help."

"Maybe it was Bajaran," the woman said. "All I know is after he stabbed Antigonus, something threw us over the trees."

Kevlin leaned forward. Much of the conversation made no sense, but he recognized the name Antigonus, as would anyone in the Six Kingdoms.

"I didn't even get a hand to my sword," the man muttered.

The second woman, who lay closest to where Kevlin crouched, shrieked wordlessly, then shouted, "Mistress! Mistress, save us! Oh, please!"

Could they really be talking about *The* Antigonus? Awe-inspiring legends told how the mighty sentinel had battled shadeleeches and their Grakonian armies in several wars over the past century.

Unable to hold his tongue, Kevlin called from the shadow of the oak, "What's going on?"

"Who's there?" demanded the man. In the fading light, Kevlin could see little of him. He lay farther away than the other two.

The woman lying closest to him cried out shrilly, "Help. Oh, help, please!"

Kevlin rose and took a slow step forward. Even without sentinels tearing up the night, the situation seemed wrong. Why did they not move, and where was the fourth person? He studied the bloody shadows that were fading to black, but saw nothing threatening. He closed his eyes and listened for several heartbeats.

Nothing moved. No sounds betrayed a concealed enemy.

"Are you still there?" the closest woman called. "Please don't leave us. Please oh please oh please. . ." Her voice trailed off into a soft, pleading litany.

The helplessness of that woman's voice finally convinced him to risk approaching. He advanced, every sense alert for danger, and knelt beside her.

"Are you hurt? Did you break any bones?"

She laughed hysterically. Maybe she had knocked her head against one of the trees as she fell?

"Leave her alone," snapped the other woman. "Who are you?"

Still no one moved. Kevlin stepped past the first woman and dropped to one knee beside the second, nerves tensed for any tricks.

The white light flashed again, dimmer than before and filtered by the trees, but bright enough to briefly see. The woman looked young, with a slender frame and pretty, heart-shaped face framed by dark hair. She wore a dark vest over a white blouse that glowed in the strange light, a skirt split for riding, and tall leather riding boots. Surprisingly, she wore a sword belted to her hip. Her hand lay only inches from the hilt, but made no move to grasp it.

She did not look injured. Again the light dimmed, replaced by that disturbing red glow.

"Are you hurt?" Kevlin asked.

"No."

"Then why are you lying there?"

"Because I can't get up," she said slowly, as if the answer were obvious.

"So you *are* hurt."

"No. I'm stuck."

"Like stuck to the ground?" Kevlin asked.

"Just like that," she snapped. "Can't you see?"

The man lying a few feet away interrupted in a voice ringing with authority. "We don't have time for this. You, sir, what is your name?"

"Kevlin."

"I'm Terach, and the lady is Ceren." He spoke with the formal accent of Tamera, the imperial seat and capital of Tamarr.

"Are you stuck too?"

"Aye."

"How is that the worst thing that happened to any of you after falling so far?"

"Magic, obviously," Ceren interjected.

"Listen," Terach said, "we are bound by some spell, so you must find out what's going on."

"I don't think so." Kevlin picked up his sword and took a step back. "In case you hadn't noticed, some sentinels are going crazy not far from here."

"There are only two of them," Terach said. "We were members of their party until Bajaran stabbed Antigonus."

"Do you mean *the* Antigonus?"

"Yes."

"He's been fighting shadeleeches for generations," Kevlin said. "He doesn't need help."

"He shouldn't," Terach agreed, "but something's wrong. The fight's taking too long. You've got to go see what's happening."

"No. Look what they did to you, and you know them."

"Listen," Ceren interrupted sharply. "If anything happens to Antigonus. . ."

She did not need to finish. Antigonus was the bearer of the mighty talisman that acted as the key to the empire's magical defenses. Known simply as Oris, the famous relic should make Antigonus untouchable. And yet, if anything happened to Antigonus . . . Kevlin's mind shied away from the thought.

There was nothing he could do. Anyone stupid enough to get caught in the middle of a sentinel duel would be annihilated.

"If you're so sure he needs help, you go help him," Kevlin suggested.

"What do you think I want to do?" Ceren snapped. "Did you forget already that I can't move?"

That problem, maybe he could deal with. Stand her up, and let her run off and get killed. He placed his sword on the ground, grasped her narrow waist and pulled, trying to lift her to her feet. With her slender build, he should have been able to lift her easily.

She did not budge. Grunting with the effort, he slid his hands a little lower down her hips to get a better hold, and tried again. She remained stationary, as if glued to the forest floor.

The soft cotton of her blouse felt warm against his hands, and the tight muscles of her stomach hardened as she strained to move.

"Get your hands off me!" she snarled. "What do you think you're doing?"

"You want to go help him. I'm trying to get you up."

"Keep your hands off."

Another flash of the sentinels' white light allowed him to see her face. Her green eyes blazed like emeralds, but her expression was suspicious.

Sherah's Teeth. He snatched his hands from her waist and stifled a groan. With the world turned upside down by crazy sentinels and omens of doom, he should have realized she'd misinterpret his intentions.

Then again, she didn't know him from a canavar.

"Don't worry, miss. I'm the least of your problems right now."

Terach spoke before Ceren could. "Listen, Kevlin. We can't do it, so you have to. I need to know why Bajaran would betray Antigonus."

Kevlin stood and ran a hand through his hair. It caught on a tangle and he bit back a curse. He hadn't had a bath in the past few days and the constant itching brought back memories of campaigns from a time when he'd been a leader of men. Those memories made him feel responsible, and Terach had used the one word that resonated through his soul and tugged at him to intervene.

Betrayed.

Kevlin took a deep breath to steady his thoughts. Drawing closer to the sentinels would be suicide.

"Kevlin," Terach tried again. "We're not asking you to join the fight. That would be madness. We just need you to go look, and then bring us word."

"Besides," said Ceren, "Rhea will be able to help Antigonus."

"Who's Rhea?"

"Antigonus' mistress," Ceren said flatly. "She's a sentinel too. She was caught in the spell like the rest of us, but was able to get up. She left just before you arrived."

That explained the missing fourth person.

"Why didn't she free you?"

"I don't know."

"Sounds like Rhea knows that anyone who isn't a sentinel should stay away. I think she's right."

"I can't believe this," Ceren spat. "We're stuck like flies in a spiderweb, and the only person who can help is a coward."

"There's nothing brave about committing suicide." Kevlin knew she was goading him, but the insult still burned.

"Listen," Terach began, but his voice trailed off into a muttered curse.

The white light had faded, replaced again by that disturbing reddish glow. This time the crimson light took on a sickly green tinge. It brightened and congealed into pale mist.

Kevlin spun and found the mist forming all around the clearing. It swirled and thickened into long, twisting fingers of glowing fog that crawled through the air toward them. The sight made him shiver with dread. He wanted to run, but the mist already encircled them in an unbroken wall.

"What is it?" he whispered, his voice dry.

"Shush," Ceren whispered back, voice tight with fear.

Terach remained silent, and even the hysterical woman quieted. A fearful silence descended over the clearing as tendrils of glowing mist clawed at the air and drew ever closer.

As it neared, its movements became surer. Then a thick tendril lashed forward and curled around Ceren's legs. She shrieked with fear, but could not move as the mist rolled up her legs.

The sound of her cry seemed to encourage the glowing, emerald fog. It pulsated as other tendrils reached Terach and the hysterical woman. Terach muttered a curse and the woman shrieked.

Kevlin's every muscle quivered with the need to flee as the jade colored mist encircled them with its greedy fingers. A tendril separated from the rest and reached for him.

"By the seven gods, leave me alone," he snarled and slashed at it with his sword.

The blade passed through, but came away with tendrils clinging to it. The mist continued up the blade and flowed from there onto his hand. He shook his arm in a vain attempt to dislodge it and tried to retreat.

The mist closed in.

It ran up his arm and curled around his legs and torso. Fear pounded through him and he had to bite his tongue to keep from shrieking like the hysterical woman had. His flesh burned with cold. Starting with his arms, then everywhere else the mist made contact, a deep chill settled into his flesh and stabbed inward.

He writhed in its hold, trying to break free. Although the mist looked ethereal like vapor, its strength grew every second. With grasping fingers, it dug into his limbs and clawed its way toward his face.

On the ground, Ceren screamed as the mist crawled over her cheeks and dug into her eyes. The air became heavy and difficult to breathe. It smelled like a cesspit had opened nearby. Kevlin would have gagged on the stench if he were not so nearly panicked.

Just as one curling finger of vapor caressed his face with its icy touch, a fresh explosion of white light erupted through the forest. The mist recoiled as if burned by its brilliance, and a high-pitched wail echoed through the clearing.

Then it disappeared.

The white light subsided within seconds, but it had dispelled the killing mist, at least for a moment. Kevlin shook from that icy touch.

Dark memories of bondage bubbled to the surface of his mind, but he ruthlessly pushed them back down. On the ground Ceren wept, while the other woman wailed the urgent, continuous cry of someone pushed to the brink of madness. Terach lay silent, his face covered in a sheen of sweat.

Kevlin spun, searching for any remaining sign of the mist, but saw nothing. "What was that?" he whispered. He wanted to run, but his legs shook so bad he could barely stay upright.

"A curse," Ceren said through sobbing breaths. "A forbidden spell."

Kevlin had never heard of forbidden spells, and the concept terrified him.

"It's known as the Sentinel Fog," Ceren explained, recovering her composure.

"If it's forbidden, how was it cast?" Terach asked.

"Obviously Bajaran is beyond fear of censorship. He has already betrayed the fundamental sentinel oaths."

"What does Sentinel Fog do?" Kevlin asked, even though he already suspected the truth.

"It's a killing spell. It was used to ferret out hidden enemies."

"Bajaran must be trying to shatter the prophecy," Terach said.

"Murdering us would be one more step toward victory," Ceren agreed.

"What are you talking about?" Kevlin cried, his terror turning to anger. "I don't have anything to do with any prophecy and it tried to kill me too."

"Do you think he cares?" Terach asked.

"Then it's time for me to go." Kevlin turned to leave. "I'm sorry I can't help you."

"You cannot outrun the spell," Ceren said. "You've been marked. If Bajaran wins this contest, he'll complete the spell and you'll die along with us, wherever you try to hide."

The crimson light blossomed again, throwing everything into bloody shadow. Kevlin cringed, his fear returning, but the green mist did not materialize again.

"We three are powerless," Ceren said softly. "Only you can act."

"It sounds like I'm dead either way," Kevlin growled.

"At least you can choose how you'll die."

"The only chance you have now is to find Rhea and help Antigonus," Terach said.

"Time to spin the Wheel," Ceren declared.

Kevlin grunted. The last thing he wanted to do was rely on Akillik's luck again tonight, but Ceren was right. He had no other choice.

The next words nearly stuck in his throat and came out as little more than a hoarse rasp.

"I'll go."

2

The Most Epic Break-Up Fight of All Time

Kevlin approached the highway and the sentinels' conflict on the far side. Flashes of light came faster. White, red, white, like some crazy, gigantic firefly. They were also dimmer, and thunder no longer rumbled with each flash, leaving the woods blanketed in an eerie quiet.

Just a couple of old friends quarreling. If only he could believe that! The memory of the sentinel fog dogged his steps and set his skin crawling.

Surely Antigonus must be all right. He'd survived a century of battle against the shadeleeches. It would be worse than unfair for him to die in this forsaken wilderness. Kevlin thought again of the bloodset. Then he paused to close his eyes and breathe deeply, even though he hated inhaling the magic-laden air.

Focus, he told himself, and reached for the calm he always sought before a fight. *The battle lines are drawn. Just. . .treat it like a night assault on a fortified position.*

He might be about to die at a sentinel's hand, but he wouldn't blunder in and make it easy for them.

After a moment, he felt centered again and pushed through the brush to the edge of the highway. There he crouched in the shadows to scan the road. In the dim, flickering light, he could not see far along the wide expanse of hard-packed gravel.

Nothing moved, so he started across.

Before he reached the midpoint, two columns of fire – one green and one gold - erupted upward from beyond the trees. They twisted into a writhing, multicolored pillar that reared a hundred feet into the sky. Trees all around the flames ignited into giant torches. Flames leapt high, then leaned toward the blazing column in their center, creating a firestorm that blasted scorching air in all directions.

Sap from several huge pine trees exploded. One giant toppled into the forest with a thunder of cracking wood that shook the ground and hurled flaming debris in every direction. The trees seemed to scream as fire ripped through them and dense smoke obscured the crowns like funeral veils.

Kevlin ducked and raced for the far edge of the road. Despite being closer to the conflagration, it offered better concealment. Burning leaves swirled around him, fading to ash before settling to the ground, and filling the air with tendrils of soft smoke.

Crouched beside a wide tree, Kevlin stared in awe at the towering flames. More trees ignited until a wall of fire blocked his path. The heat blistered his exposed skin, and he raised a hand to shield his face.

This is as crazy as sailing the Gohban Straits on a moonless night. If he drew any closer, he'd be just another piece of fuel to be immolated.

In the next heartbeat, the pillar of fire at the center of the inferno winked out, and the flames subsided around the trees. Kevlin pushed forward for a better view even as another burst of red light flared beyond the wall of burning timber and painted everything a deep, sinister crimson.

The flames flickered toward the source of that light as if driven by an unseen wind. Every bit of fire licking along every nearby tree pulsed together, as if part of a single, giant heartbeat.

Then they all winked out in the blink of an eye. The sickly light of the sentinel's magic intensified, and a booming shockwave thundered through the woods and knocked Kevlin back a pace.

A man shouted, but his cry cut short.

All light vanished, and darkness rushed in to fill the void, drawing with it a heavy blanket of absolute silence.

Kevlin inched forward, hating the thought of breaking that unnatural silence with even a tiny sound. He breathed a soft prayer of thanks to the Lady that the heavy winds had scoured the ground clean. He'd been trained to move silently in a darkened building or city street, but not in a dense forest. Those were the only skills he had, so he tried to apply them.

It was legendarily stupid to draw closer to the magical confrontation, but he had no choice. Forward or back, he might die tonight but, by the Lady, he'd face his fate with sword in hand.

As the dense smoke settled around him like a shroud, he covered his nose and mouth with the cuff of his shirt and breathed shallow to avoid coughing. A wan yellow light, about as bright as a campfire, appeared just ahead. Kevlin crept around a stocky old pine tree that a moment before had burned like a torch, but now stung his fingers with icy cold.

Beyond the bole, a man in the white robes of a sentinel stood in the center of a charred circle of ground about thirty paces across. Kevlin couldn't tell if it had been a natural clearing, or if the magic had just vaporized the trees.

The figure was turned away, so Kevlin could only see a head of brown hair streaked with gray. The man stood panting, with a ball of glowing yellow light hovering over one upturned palm.

Another white-robed sentinel lay at the man's feet, cocooned neck to toe in a web of red energy. His long gray hair and beard were disheveled, and a wide bloodstain darkened the front of his robe. Despite the wound, his eyes glowed with inner light like a partially-shuttered tempest lantern.

Kevlin grimaced. That looked like a lung wound, and those were always ugly. Terach had said Bajaran stabbed Antigonus, so he assumed the prone sentinel must be the great man.

"How did you manage to conceal the mark of evil from me?" Antigonus spoke into the silence.

Bajaran barked a laugh. "You see nothing but the future you hunt. How many years has it been since you've thought of me as anything but a tool to use on this journey?"

"Is that why you're doing this? Because I offended you?"

Bajaran snorted. "Your place is only to die. I need Oris."

"You cannot wield it. You can't even touch it."

"I don't need to touch it. I just need to transport it."

Antigonus regarded Bajaran for several seconds. "You mean to deliver it to the Sigrun? They would destroy the Six Kingdoms."

"They might. What matters is that Oris will guarantee my seat on the Sigrun council. It's time for *me* to taste a little power."

"You were raised to Elite not a dozen years ago."

"So what? How many decades, or centuries, would I have to wait to sit on the High Council? With Oris, the Sigrun will accept me immediately."

Kevlin leaned a hand against the tree to steady himself and tried not to gasp. He refused to think about the Sigrun. Saying that word, even to oneself, brought bad luck.

"You would destroy the Six Kingdoms for your ambition?"

"Yes." The calm way Bajaran spoke made the declaration all the more terrible.

Antigonus' expression turned sorrowful. "Then you are already worse than dead."

"You first," Bajaran said, and he raised a hand that burst into red fire.

Kevlin stepped out from behind the tree. He had to do something. The sight of Antigonus lying helpless, about to be murdered, triggered dark memories of suppressed terror. It compounded the lingering fear that Bajaran might again unleash the sentinel fog after destroying Antigonus. If only Kevlin hadn't left his bow in camp.

He crouched to charge, but then paused.

Almost directly across the clearing from him, a woman stepped out of the forest and walked calmly into the light of Bajaran's magic. Tall and shapely, with long, honey-blond hair cascading past her shoulders, she seemed completely out of place in the wilderness.

She dressed simply, but elegantly, in a pearl-gray silk bodice and deep green riding skirt, and moved with a sensual grace that made Kevlin's pulse race. The sway of her hips, the tilt of her chin, and her inviting smile with slightly parted lips seemed perfectly orchestrated to capture a man's attention.

"Rhea," Bajaran said, his eyes glued to her.

Antigonus' mistress? Terach had said she was a sentinel, so why wasn't she wearing the traditional sentinel white? Was she so confident in her power that she could walk up to Bajaran without striking first? Would he merely surrender?

The way she moved, many men would be happy to.

Kevlin gripped his sword tighter. He could cover the dozen paces to Bajaran in a few seconds. With Rhea creating a distraction, he might just make it.

Rhea stopped close to Bajaran and looked down at Antigonus' bound form. The fallen sentinel stared back at her, a question in his eyes.

"Good work," she said to Bajaran in a warm, sultry voice. "I wasn't sure you'd be able to take him yourself."

"Little good you did. Why did you even come along, if not to help me tonight?"

Rhea shrugged. "You both caught me by surprise."

"I hadn't expected him to last so long."

"I came back as quickly as I could, but it looked like you had everything under control."

"You watched but didn't intervene?"

"Why ruin the victory for you?" she purred, stepping closer and sliding a hand along one of Bajaran's arms.

Kevlin barely suppressing a growl. Images of remembered betrayal, shaken loose by Rhea's treachery, clouded his thoughts and filled him with fury.

Why does a person do that?

Although it was another woman's face that burned in his mind, he focused his rage on Rhea. He needed to smash something, but rushing out into the open would just get him killed. He picked up a fist-sized rock, but nearly laughed to consider it. Insanity was piling upon insanity tonight, with no end in sight. Attacking two sentinels was usually a guaranteed way to return to the eternal embrace of the Lady, and the only ranged weapon at hand was a rock.

The searing agony of having had his heart, his very life, shattered by one he had trusted returned with undiminished force. He had spent a lot of effort to banish those emotions, but they ignited in his soul with full potency, as if eager for a reunion.

Those two sentinels had completely wrecked his evening.

In the clearing, Bajaran was saying, "Once I've dispatched him, I'll take Oris and we can be gone."

"I'm proud of you." She leaned closer and brushed his lips with her own. One hand wrapped around the back of his neck, while the other slid off his arm and fell to her side. Her palm opened and a long, thin poniard appeared in it.

It appeared she was not going to wait as long to betray him as she had Antigonus.

Bajaran did not notice the weapon as she kissed him once more, then pulled away a little, a seductive smile on her lips.

"Now's not the time," he said, his voice so soft Kevlin could barely make out the words. "I have to finish this."

"So do I."

She clutched his hair with one hand, while slamming the poniard into his eye.

Bajaran screamed and convulsed away, the movement ripping the poniard out of her hand. He twisted as he fell, giving Kevlin a clear view of the hilt of her blade protruding from his face. He toppled to the ground, twitching.

Rhea immediately turned and raised a hand over Antigonus. The web of magic holding him had begun to fade, but she restored it before he could move.

Antigonus glared at her, his eyes reflecting the same remembered rage burning in Kevlin's heart. "I can't believe I loved you."

Kevlin was starting to wonder how anyone could live long enough around her to even try.

Rhea looked away, her eyes drawn to Bajaran's still-twitching form. Without warning, she doubled over and vomited.

She had killed with such flair, it surprised Kevlin to see her affected by death. Rhea knelt for several seconds, her breath loud in the quiet. Only after a few steadying breaths did she wipe her mouth with the back of one hand and stand up.

She met Antigonus' gaze and whispered, "I am so sorry." A tear slid down one cheek, and her body shook as if with suppressed sobs.

She was one twisted piece of work. Was she in league with Bajaran or not? The woman who had roasted Kevlin's heart on the spit of her betrayal hadn't wasted time with second-guessing.

"Rhea," Antigonus pleaded gently. "Release me."

She placed one hand over her mouth and cried openly. "I can't, but I want you to know I really do care for you."

She needed someone to explain to her what caring for someone really meant.

"Then why do this?"

"I have to. . .I have to take Oris." She spoke in a voice so soft Kevlin barely heard. "My master commands it."

"You have a choice."

"No, I have to do it."

"I can protect you."

She shook her head. "He's marked me. I can't break free."

"What is your master's name?"

After several gulping breaths, she twice opened her mouth to speak before finally managing to say, "Masego."

Then Rhea shrieked and clutched at her head. She stumbled, her face glistening with sweat and her lovely features twisted in fear.

"I will. I will!" she shouted hysterically. "I'll do it."

Whatever crazy episode she was having passed and she regained some of her lost composure. "I have to do it," she repeated through her sobs. Her body still shuddered from whatever ordeal she'd just suffered. "Goodbye."

Her words galvanized Kevlin into action. He'd watched the spectacle in mute astonishment. What an idiot. In those seconds while she was distracted, he could have put her out of her misery.

He didn't need to understand her. In fact, he doubted he ever could. It didn't matter, though. She was going to murder a man she professed to love. That was more than enough.

Good thing he had a rock handy.

Kevlin threw it far out over the clearing. It landed on the far side, at the edge of the trees. Rhea spun at the dull sound it made, and pointed. Fire erupted all along the edge of the glade, igniting trees and flooding the air with heat and light. And sound.

Flames roared through the trees like a hungry animal. Under that concealing din, Kevlin sprinted from the shadows toward Rhea. He covered four paces, then six. His sword rose to deliver the killing blow.

Somehow Rhea sensed his presence. She spun around when only four leaping strides still separated them. Despite the surprise on her face, she did not hesitate. She raised a hand, palm out, and the three remaining strides might as well have been half a mile.

Her eyes were hard, no longer showing any doubt. Her hand glowed with brilliant light as she called forth her magic.

He was a dead man.

Kevlin threw himself to the side as a bolt of ugly red magic shot from her palm. There was no way she could miss. But as the bolt reached out with the promise of instant, violent death, it seemed to slow, as if struggling to pass through the air.

That split second of delay was enough. Kevlin tumbled to the ground on top of Bajaran's body, and the fiery bolt singed his armored shoulder instead of blasting a hole through his chest.

The acrid smell of Rhea's vomit burned in Kevlin's nose and his heart pounded with fear. He tried to gather his feet under him to spring across the gap toward her, but his legs became tangled in Bajaran's robes, and he wasted a vital second.

Rhea cursed and kicked Antigonus in the head, as if he had somehow interrupted her magic bolt. She raised one hand over the fallen sentinel and the magical prison flared with renewed strength. Then she pointed her free hand at Kevlin.

He could not move, had not regained his balance, and was still hopelessly entangled with Bajaran's corpse. He would not escape death a second time.

A silvery spear of magic appeared in her hand and leaped toward his chest. He did not even have time to blink.

It flared as it touched him.

Then it disappeared.

Kevlin stared first at Rhea, then at Antigonus. She seemed just as surprised, and fearfully took a step back.

I should be dead, twice over.

This was not the time to dwell on why. If he didn't *move*, his miraculous second life would be short-lived. He kicked his legs free of Bajaran's robes, leaped to his feet, and raised his sword. Rhea retreated another step, her hand outstretched to cast another spell.

In that second, the magic web binding Antigonus splintered with a *boom* and a shockwave that knocked Kevlin and Rhea apart.

Antigonus struck. White-hot magic flashed from his eyes and slammed into Rhea's torso. She screamed and staggered from the impact. Her blouse blackened, and charred flesh showed through a gaping hole that exposed her midriff.

"I have to do it," she wailed.

"So do I," Antigonus replied sadly. He threw his head back and roared, his eyes blazing with power.

Kevlin braced himself. This sentinel love spat was about to turn very, very ugly.

3

AN UNEASY ALLIANCE

Blinding light shattered the darkness, and a peal of thunder tumbled Kevlin to the ground. Rhea's scream floated distant and unreal at the edge of his consciousness.

The double-blow to sight and sound overwhelmed Kevlin's senses. He shouted, a guttural cry of primal fear, and clutched at his head, struggling to regain his scattered thoughts and blink away the blinding afterimage of what had to be a lightning strike. If Rhea was still out there, she'd kill him.

Move, soldier!

He rolled to his hands and knees, forced his eyes open, and blinked to clear his fuzzy vision. An odd silence surrounded him, as if his ears were packed in a barrel of wool. His head pounded with a tremendous headache, and he gripped the charred earth to steady himself against the feeling of the ground swaying. Bile rose in his throat and he spat out a few drops.

It seemed to take forever, but his vision slowly focused. After a long moment, he took a deep breath and looked up.

Rhea was gone. The ground where she had been standing was scarred with a deep, black gouge a span wide. He scanned the shadowed clearing.

Nothing.

Either she'd been obliterated by the lightning strike, or she'd fled. His thoughts were as scattered as his senses, but he still lived. Not bad, all things considered.

He crawled over to Antigonus. The sentinel lay with eyes closed, one hand clutching weakly at his chest. For the first time, Kevlin noticed the silver hilt of a dagger protruding from the center of the large bloodstain. How had he missed seeing that before?

That was the least of the questions he needed answering. Why hadn't Rhea's magic killed him? Had Antigonus managed to block her spell? If he could do that, why hadn't he just attacked her sooner?

If Antigonus survived, Kevlin might find some answers, but he didn't know what to do. His hands shook as he considered the powerful old man.

Antigonus, bearer of Oris, was one of the best-known names in the Six Kingdoms. He was a man out of legend, but now he lay dying. His face was pale and drawn, and his chest barely moved.

The last thing Kevlin wanted to do was touch a sentinel, so instead he leaned close and whispered, "Antigonus?"

The old man blinked open bloodshot eyes. His skin sagged from his frame and his mouth hung slightly open.

"Who are you?" Antigonus' voice sounded like a far off whisper.

"My name is Kevlin." It sounded like he was talking underwater. "Terach sent me to help."

Antigonus smiled. "Then help. Remove the dagger."

Kevlin glanced at the sentinel's chest, but had to concentrate to bring the bloody weapon into focus. Antigonus should already be dead. Perhaps his magic kept him alive, but if Kevlin removed that dagger, the shock might kill the old man.

Antigonus gestured weakly at the hilt. "Remove it. I cannot heal myself until it is gone."

By the Lady, he could be a fool sometimes. Kevlin grasped the dagger's hilt. "This is going to hurt."

Then he snatched the dagger free with a single, smooth pull.

Antigonus ground his teeth together and moaned, his body arcing up off the ground in a spasm of pain. A heartbeat later a soft, white glow appeared and enveloped the old man in a gentle embrace.

I can handle this, Kevlin told himself as he fought the impulse to back away.

The scent of herbs filled the air and Kevlin's tension drained away as he reluctantly breathed the aroma. A faint thrumming emanated from the white light, and for a dozen heartbeats the magic flared, obscuring the wound. The thrumming intensified until it sounded like a thousand invisible hummingbirds flitting around the aged sentinel.

When the magic faded, the result was a little disappointing. Kevlin had expected the wound to vanish completely. Sentinels possessed healing abilities, although not as powerful as the stalwarts. Still, a sentinel as experienced as Antigonus should be able to heal even a punctured lung. The gaping, bloody hole in his chest had closed, but it still looked ragged and raw, as if on the verge of breaking open again.

The old man groaned and opened his eyes. His pale face didn't seem to sag as much as before.

"Are you going to be all right?" Kevlin asked.

Antigonus grimaced and blinked a few times, his cobalt blue eyes clearing. "I have delayed death for a time."

"What do you mean?"

"The wound is. . .difficult." For a second it looked like he might elaborate, but instead he raised a hand. "Help me up."

Kevlin eased him to a sitting position. A globe of amber light appeared above Antigonus' head and lit the clearing far better than the guttering remnants of Rhea's fires. Antigonus looked at Bajaran's body and sighed. Some of his newfound strength faded.

Antigonus gestured toward the betrayer. "Go to him. He has an amulet around his neck. Take it."

The amulet proved to be a large, jeweled stone set in a heavy steel chain. Kevlin let out an appreciative whistle. It was about a quarter of the size of an egg and strangely cool to the touch, with flat sides and faceted edges. Its opaque color did not reflect any light. It must have been worth a fortune. Kevlin unclasped the chain and lifted the amulet away from the fallen sentinel.

Antigonus said, "Put it on. It will offer some protection."

Protection from what? The old man looked half-dead, so Kevlin didn't bother to ask. He clasped the heavy chain around his neck and settled the stone under his shirt. He shivered to think it was probably tainted with magic.

"Keep the dagger."

He found the sheath for the blade on Bajaran's belt. Silver runes in eye-twisting patterns ran the length of the black leather. Impressed, Kevlin studied the silver dagger more closely. Slender and well balanced, it felt comfortable in his hand.

Silver made poor fighting weapons, but this blade was no mere decoration. Whatever the metal, it unnerved him more that he had so much trouble focusing on it. It was probably tainted with magic too, but he wiped it clean on Bajaran's robes and sheathed it.

He lifted two heavy purses containing a fortune in gold and silver coins from the corpse's belt and whistled again. When he turned back to Antigonus, the old man had settled back to the ground, asleep. The globe of light above his head dimmed and pulsed in rhythm with his breathing.

Kevlin slipped off his small burglar pack. He'd confiscated it from a very clever thief whose allergies had given him away when trying to steal from one of Kevlin's previous employers. Slow thieves did not live long.

Small and shaped like a teardrop, the pack hung so neatly between Kevlin's shoulder blades that he always wore it and often forgot about it. He slipped the purses and silver dagger inside, alongside his travel rations. He would pass the items on to Antigonus later.

A branch snapped in the darkness.

Kevlin leapt to his feet, drew his sword, and scanned the shadows. If Rhea had returned, they were dead.

Two shapes carrying drawn swords separated from the surrounding gloom, followed shortly by a third.

Kevlin shifted into a defensive stance. He had not risked his life saving the sentinel only to have someone else kill him. The newcomers slowed as they advanced, but kept their weapons ready. When they stepped into the circle of Antigonus' light, Kevlin recognized the woman, Ceren.

The sword in her hand was slender, like its owner, with a slight curve to its single-edged blade. Ceren held it low, with the point angled away from her, and the blade facing Kevlin in the standard Ayvoltec style. She moved gracefully, and the thick braid of her auburn hair hanging halfway to her waist swung into view as she walked. She was young, probably not yet twenty, but bore herself with confidence.

She was proving to be a study in contradictions. The Ayvoltec style was Nedikan, rarely used in the Six Kingdoms. She spoke with a Freyarri accent, but didn't look like a native of Freyarr. Her olive skin fit, but she lacked the blond hair and curvaceous physique common in that southern kingdom.

Freyarr produced the best knights and archers in the empire, but its women rarely trained to fight. Kevlin had traveled widely enough that he could usually identify people's origins, but Ceren proved difficult. The last thing he needed was another mystery.

No mystery shrouded Terach. He exactly matched the classic image of a warrior from Tamarr. Average height and medium build, thick black hair cut short, and dark eyes set in a solid face. He moved with the fluid control of an athlete and wore chainmail under a maroon coat that bore the insignia of a noble house Kevlin did not recognize.

His sword, known as a pala, confirmed his heritage. Long and narrow, its single-edged blade ran straight from the pommel to an abrupt, sharp point. A flat, perpendicular guard separated the blade from the long hilt. Terach carried it high across his body in the standard Harci style.

Behind Ceren and Terach crept the other woman. She appeared to be in her late twenties, and she was not one of those women who looked alluring when terrified. Her long, brown hair was tangled and half-covered her tear-streaked face.

Terach lowered his pala with a nod toward Bajaran's body. "Did you kill him?"

"Rhea did."

"Where's my mistress?" The hysterical woman scurried into the clearing. When she caught sight of Bajaran's corpse, she shrieked and covered her face with her hands.

Ceren put a comforting arm around her. "Take it easy, Haisyl," she whispered as the woman sobbed into her shoulder. Haisyl did not appear dangerous, but as Rhea's servant, she might be just as deceptive.

"Rhea betrayed Antigonus," Kevlin said. "She nearly killed both of us."

Haisyl backed away, shaking her head. "No, it can't be true. Not Mistress Rhea."

To Ceren, Kevlin said, "Keep an eye on her."

"So I just get dismissed so you *men* can deal with the real problems? Is that it?"

What was it with her? Maybe she wasn't really from Freyarr, but just affected the accent to confuse people.

"I just thought you could comfort her best."

Ceren looked like she wanted to say more, but thankfully turned her attention to Haisyl and whispered more soothing words to her.

"What happened?" Terach asked.

"Why can you move now?" Kevlin asked instead.

Ceren said, "The spell vanished a few minutes ago. We don't know why."

Which of the sentinels had been holding them down? There were still too many unknowns to trust these people. Kevlin carefully watched their reactions as he recounted what had happened.

When he finished, Terach muttered a curse and scanned the trees. "So she could be watching us right now?"

"Aye, she could be. It'd be stupid to assume she's dead."

"I can't believe it," Haisyl wailed. "I have to find her." She pulled away from Ceren and headed toward the trees.

"I wouldn't," Kevlin warned

Perhaps her distress was an act. He definitely didn't want her lurking unseen in the shadows. Any of the three might have been in on the plot to kill Antigonus. Why would the sentinel have hurled them far away when the fighting started? It might have been to remove potential assassins he wasn't sure he could trust.

Or maybe he found Haisyl as annoying as Kevlin already did.

"Why not?" Haisyl asked.

"You don't know where Rhea went. Besides, if she's still alive, she might just kill you."

"She wouldn't do that!"

Kevlin shrugged. "If you say so, but a minute ago you claimed she'd never betray Antigonus, and you were wrong about that."

She hesitated, and Kevlin considered his options. He could let her go, but it was easier to watch the three of them together. He could detain her, perhaps bind her, but that might spark a fight with the others, and he was not ready to risk that yet.

Ceren said, "Stay with us. It's not wise to wander into the darkness alone, Haisyl." After another long look at the forest, Haisyl nodded and wandered back to stand beside Ceren.

Terach stepped toward Antigonus, but Kevlin held up a hand. "Hold. I don't want you near Antigonus with a drawn sword."

"But we're in his party," Ceren snapped and advanced a step. Terach tensed, just a tightening of the fingers around the pommel of the pala.

"So were the two people who just tried to kill him," Kevlin said.

"Listen," Terach said, his expression hard. "I appreciate what you did to help Antigonus. You did more than we expected, but don't presume to take command."

"I don't want command, but I nearly got killed helping Antigonus, so I have a right to be concerned. And you're not getting near him with bared steel."

Terach frowned. "I am a captain of the elite imperial guard, and I'm ordering you to stand aside."

He bore himself like a leader, but Kevlin had known a lot of men who claimed to be many things they were not. He was not sure how to validate the man's claim. Since he was not wearing the uniform of the elite guard, he could be lying. If he was telling the truth, Kevlin didn't want to fight him.

"Where are your men?" Captains were usually assigned command of a thousand men, one of five columns in a legion.

"Elsewhere. Stand aside, Kevlin. You've just about spent the debt of gratitude you earned helping Antigonus. Don't interfere with me."

Ceren moved to Terach's left, her sword at the ready.

"You really want to fight over this?" Kevlin asked. He held up his left hand in a sign of peace. "You're the one who convinced me to get involved. I don't know you, so allow me a little suspicion. All you have to do is lay down your weapon first."

Ceren opened her mouth to make an angry reply, but Terach nodded. "This once, I'll concede the point. Don't interfere with me again."

In a single, fluid motion Terach slid the long pala into the sheath strapped to his back, then slipped the belt over his shoulder and laid it on the ground. He drew his dagger and placed it next to the pala.

Holding his empty hands out, he asked, "Good enough?"

Kevlin nodded and stepped aside.

Terach dropped to one knee beside Antigonus and placed a hand on the sentinel's forehead. Kevlin hovered nearby, prepared to intervene if Terach made any threatening move. If he really was skilled in the Harci style, the man could kill with his bare hands as effectively as with his blade. Kevlin didn't know how to prove Terach's intentions without incurring a little risk, and his gut told him to trust the dark-haired man.

Antigonus blinked open his eyes and smiled a greeting.

"You shouldn't have sent us away," Terach said.

"You would have died. What good would that have done?" Antigonus asked softly, then lapsed back into sleep.

"Convinced?" Terach asked.

Kevlin nodded. Hopefully Antigonus' trust was well founded.

"Cunning, I need you," Terach said. "Take a look at his wound."

"You guys into pet names a lot?" Kevlin asked.

"Ask Antigonus about it," Ceren said as she dropped to her knees on the other side of the unconscious sentinel. She pulled back the bloody robe and inhaled sharply. "Oh my."

Ceren probed the wound with careful fingers. After a moment, she glanced up, "It looks fairly stable, but it could easily break open again."

"It was a lot worse," Kevlin said. At least she seemed to know what she was doing. "He tried to heal himself, but couldn't finish the job."

"Maybe when he's rested he can try again," she said. "We'll bind it for now to help protect it."

"Good idea because we can't stay," Kevlin said.

"Why not?" Ceren asked.

"If Rhea survived, she'll look for us here. Anyone else in the area would've seen the lights and might come to investigate." In his weakened condition, Antigonus was all but helpless, and Kevlin was not about to let him get killed tonight, especially not by Rhea.

Despite Rhea's claims of continuing affection, her betrayal was the foulest treachery. Kevlin felt motivated to help the old sentinel get out of his current mess. Maybe that would help Kevlin feel better about how much of an idiot he'd been once too.

"What do you suggest?" Terach asked.

"Join my party tonight. In the morning, we can decide what to do next."

"You're not alone?" Ceren asked.

"No, I'm part of a small group camped off the road just to the south."

"How many?" Terach asked.

"Eight. Come on and I can tell you more while we're moving."

Terach exchanged glances with Ceren, who nodded. He turned back to Kevlin. "Very well."

"Any sign of our horses?" Ceren asked.

"None."

"Perhaps they'll return in the morning," Terach said with a noted lack of conviction.

"Let's pray for a positive spin of the Wheel," Ceren said.

Maybe she really was from Freyarr. She clearly liked to spin the Wheel as much as any Freyarri he'd known. Akillik, god of luck, enjoyed a wide following across the empire, but the Freyarri had the closest ties to the fickle god. Kevlin did not like relying on Akillik or His Wheel. The Wheel spun against one as often as for them, and it always seemed to pick the worst possible times to come up black.

They fashioned a litter for Antigonus, and Ceren bandaged the partially-healed wound with a strip of cloth cut from the old man's robe. The two men hefted the litter and, with Kevlin leading the way, started out with Antigonus' dim, pulsing light holding the darkness back just enough for them to see where to place their feet.

4

BE CAREFUL WHAT YOU WORSHIP

Kevlin awoke with a start and tried to figure out what had awakened him. Clouds covered the stars and the only light came from the eastern sky that hinted at the approaching dawn.

Something moved in the grass nearby. The embers of the campfire around which Antigonus and the others of his party camped offered little light. Dathan, Kevlin's employer, had been less than pleased when he brought the refugees to the secluded clearing. Worse, the horses Dathan's men had found earlier belonged to Antigonus' company, and he hadn't concealed his disappointment at losing the valuable mounts. The two groups had settled on opposite ends of the clearing to pass a tense night.

Kevlin flicked off the blanket and slipped a hand to the hilt of his sword. He had slept fully dressed, willing to endure the discomfort in order to respond quickly to any threat.

A shadow moved, and Kevlin's hand tightened around the hilt. He'd posted two of Dathan's guards to keep watch, so why hadn't they sounded the alarm?

"Haisyl, is that you?" Ceren called from her position near Antigonus, across the fire from Kevlin.

"Yes, milady." Haisyl's form became clear as she approached.

"What were you doing?"

"Just visiting the privy." Haisyl giggled and settled back onto her blankets.

Kevlin sighed. With a little luck, he might catch a little more sleep.

Luck was not with him.

Before he could close his eyes, a spiraling tail of white fire arced up into the air from the western end of the clearing closest to the road. It plummeted back to the ground on the far side, leaving a trail of clear flame burning in the air.

Kevlin sprang to his feet, sword in hand, and shouted, "Awake! To arms!"

Terach surged off his blanket, pala in hand. He too had slept fully dressed and armored. Ceren responded almost as quickly, but Haisyl shrieked and cowered in her blankets.

"What *is* that?" Terach pointed at the spiraling arc of fire.

"An early warning signal I set," Kevlin said. "Someone or something just tripped it." He'd hesitated to use the valuable photophor, but it might have just paid off.

Across the clearing, Dathan's men scrambled to respond to Kevlin's shout and Dathan called, "What is the meaning of this?"

Kevlin scanned the darkness for a threat. For a dozen heartbeats they waited, hardly breathing.

"Maybe it was an animal," Ceren said finally.

An agonized scream sounded from the lower end of the clearing, then cut off abruptly. A couple of seconds later, one of Dathan's guards, a greasy-haired, skinny fellow named Nyx, dashed to Dathan's campfire, shouting incoherently. He collapsed at Dathan's feet, his bloody face panic-stricken.

"They killed Lugs," Nyx wailed.

The shouting of many voices rolled out of the darkness and across the clearing from three sides. With the voices began a rhythmic metallic banging sound, like the flats of swords being struck together.

"Mercenaries," Kevlin decided. Piran's men must have found them. "Come on, let's join Dathan."

As he turned to lift Antigonus, a wall of fire erupted out of the ground and split the clearing between the two groups. It rose fully a dozen feet and seemed to snap hungrily at the empty air. The tall grass carpeting the clearing ignited all along the edges of the wall of fire, but the flames did not spread. Smoke tickled Kevlin's nose and the crackling of the flames seemed unusually loud in the pre-dawn stillness.

"What's happening?" Ceren cried as Haisyl screamed again.

"Rhea," Kevlin guessed.

They were in trouble.

"Ceren, wake him up," Terach ordered.

She dropped to the ground beside Antigonus and started shaking him and calling his name, but his eyes remained closed.

Kevlin scanned the clearing for Rhea. Why didn't she just burn them all with that fire? She could have killed them already.

Maybe that lightning bolt earlier had addled her brain, or maybe she still struggled against her mysterious master's command. Whatever the reason, if they could keep her distracted until Antigonus awoke, the old sentinel could surely deal with her.

The clanging of the mercenaries on the far side of the wall of fire stopped. Through the pulsing flames, Kevlin could dimly make out the shapes of a dozen men converging on Dathan's fire from three sides.

Dathan, surrounded by his remaining five guards, called out, "We surrender."

Kevlin grunted in disgust and hoped Dathan's cowardice would buy the fat merchant some time. More pressing was the question of how Piran's men fell in with Rhea? Or were those even Piran's men? Perhaps they were some other force she had secreted nearby. That seemed unlikely, but at this point he would believe anything.

"You don't seem surprised to find a bunch of mercenaries attacking in the dead of night," Terach said.

"No, they're not entirely a surprise."

"Why didn't you warn us?"

"I thought we lost them."

"What do they want?"

"I'll tell you later." *If there is a later.*

Kevlin breathed a sigh of relief when he saw Antigonus stirring. With the sentinel awake, they might just survive until sunrise.

"Kevlin," Terach called, voice tense.

He turned and studied a figure that approached out of the darkness shrouding the lower end of the clearing. It was not Rhea, but a big man who approached with an easy, confident stride. He passed close to the wall of fire, which illuminated his dark face and set his coat of scaled armor alight like a thousand candles.

Kevlin's heart sank. That was just not fair.

"Terach, beware. Ceren, stay close to Antigonus, and watch for Rhea."

"What's going on?" Ceren asked nervously.

Terach said, "Listen to him. Let Strength deal with this."

"Who is it?" Her voice cracked with fear at the sight of the approaching armored man.

"A Blade Stalwart," Kevlin stated.

He stared at the dark-skinned man and fought to control memories of desperate struggle. Fear chilled him. Why would Piran spend the vast sums needed to secure a Blade Stalwart only to unleash him on Dathan?

Blade Stalwarts were a totally different class of hired warrior. Disciples of Savas, they *worshipped* war, and lived for battle. Excellent tacticians and devastating warriors, they were sometimes hired to lead entire legions. Kevlin had never heard of one employed to resolve a dispute between a couple of merchants.

He could not beat this man.

In the past couple of years, the low profile security jobs that kept Kevlin inconspicuous had pitted him against little more than cutthroats and common thieves, most with no formal training. The sharp edge of his skills had dulled, but one could not face a Blade Stalwart with any weakness and hope to survive.

Memories he'd kept locked away for years swept into his mind, and for a moment Kevlin was again staring at a different Blade Stalwart. He'd been bound while the woman he loved prepared to slit his throat.

What a miserable memory.

Kevlin drove it away. If he lost focus, the Blade Stalwart would remove his head.

Beside him, Terach regarded the advancing Blade Stalwart with a mixture of concern and interest, but no sign of abject terror. Either he was confident, or just ignorant. Hopefully it was the former. As a captain of the elite imperial guard, Terach should be a master fighter. If they worked together, they might stand a chance.

About as much chance as standing atop the mainmast of his father's ship with an upraised sword during a thunderstorm.

"Did you know about this too?" Terach asked without looking at Kevlin.

"No." If he had known about a Blade Stalwart, he would have started running hours ago.

"Then there's more going on than we thought."

The Blade Stalwart halted ten paces away and folded his arms across his armored chest. Kevlin fought an overwhelming urge to sheath his own sword and do the same. To his left, Terach's sword slid home in its sheath with a click.

"Resist him," Kevlin hissed.

"What?" Terach blinked rapidly as if struggling to focus his thoughts.

"Fighting a Blade Stalwart starts before you cross swords with him. Don't let his influence control you."

The Blade Stalwart watched them impassively.

Terach spared a glance at Kevlin. "I've never faced one of his order, but there's no dishonor in being polite."

"There is tonight. If he reaches full rapture, we're dead."

The risk was dire. Blade Stalwarts fully immersed in the trance-like state they sought during battle received powerful endowments from Savas that made them nearly unstoppable.

With a bloodset having already declared Savas' willingness to favor chosen warriors, it would be even easier for the Blade Stalwart to reach that state. They could not allow him to perform the ritual opening ceremony before the fight began and slip into his religious trance, or he would slaughter them.

"I am Dhanjal," the Blade Stalwart announced in a surprisingly gentle voice. "To you who dare compete for Savas' favor, I greet you as brothers." He faced Terach. "Honor to you, son of Salawin. May the justice of your god never waver."

Terach inclined his head. "And honor to your blades, son of the Eternal Storm."

"Stop it," Kevlin hissed.

Undeterred, the Blade Stalwart continued, "After you die, I will inter you deep in the earth, with hands and face clean for your journey to Salawin's council."

He turned to Kevlin but he paused and his eyes narrowed. "It is rare I cannot place an opponent. Will you make your heritage known?"

It wasn't the first time someone had struggled to figure out Kevlin's birth. It wasn't that he looked all that different from a typical citizen of Meinarr. His chestnut hair hanging to the base of his neck was fairly common, as were his hazel eyes. But he'd traveled the Six Kingdoms, and each culture had left its mark.

Kevlin struggled to remain silent and bite back the flowery response that came to his lips under Dhanjal's influence, but was not entirely successful. "I was born in the hand of the Lady."

The man's influence was so strong!

Dhanjal nodded solemnly. "We are too far from the sea for burial in the Lady's embrace, but I will wash your body with saltwater before laying you to rest."

The man's armor began glowing brighter, the light shifting slowly through various muted hues, an outward sign of his deepening reverie.

With a growl of defiance, Kevlin swallowed the words that came to mind and said instead, "When you die, I'll bury you face down, stripped of armor, with your own broken blades thrust through your heart."

"Cheapen not the contest of arms with harsh words and insults."

"I'll cut off your hands. You'll grovel at Savas' feet like a dog instead of feasting with his favored ones. Maybe he'll let you wash dishes for eternity."

The glow faded from the armored scales and the dark-skinned warrior dropped his hands to the hilts of his twin scimitars. His face flushed and his stony calm faded to a look of annoyance.

Good, Kevlin thought. *Keep him unsettled.*

The scale-clad warrior removed the close-fitting knit cap from his head. *Sherah's Teeth!* Kevlin hadn't thought things could get worse.

At least a score of tattoos shone white against the dark skin of Dhanjal's shaven head. The brands were images. A pala, a ship, a horse, and others, representing the heritage or chief skill of Dhanjal's enemies defeated in battle.

Kevlin had seen the head of only one other Blade Stalwart bared for battle, and that one's pate had displayed fewer than half the number of tattoos.

The man facing him was a senior stalwart, perhaps even a Fist-Forged High Captain. Kevlin had to rattle the man's confidence or they were dead.

Dhanjal smiled, once more calm. "I will take your heart-skill and honor your memory through the eternal councils."

"Kill him or die clean," Kevlin said quietly to Terach, "or he'll steal part of your soul. That's what the tattoos mean."

"I've heard they do that, but I thought the tale a lie."

"It's real. Every brand makes him stronger."

Dhanjal stepped forward a single pace. "Tell me your name."

Time to shake the man.

"I am Kevlin, and I'm going to kill you like I did Shaemal."

Dhanjal's eyes widened in surprise and his confidence cracked. "You." He did not even seem to notice that he broke the formality of his own pre-battle ritual.

Unnerving the man was necessary, but Kevlin would have preferred not opening the door to questions the others would later want to ask. That chapter of his life was over, and he did not want to revisit it.

"Time to kill him." Kevlin advanced before Dhanjal regained his composure.

Terach drew his pala and paced Kevlin a few steps to his left.

"I know you, Trueson of Savas," Dhanjal snarled as he drew his heavy scimitars and rolled his shoulders.

"Enough," Kevlin shouted to drown out Dhanjal's words. The man seemed willing to talk forever.

Kevlin charged.

Dhanjal beckoned him on.

"Come. Let us dance the Song of Savas."

5

THE SONG OF SAVAS

Kevlin charged through the tall grass. The wall of fire to his right lit the clearing in a pulsing glow, while the fresh scent of crushed grass mixed with a sharp tang of sulfur in the air. Fear evaporated and his arm tingled with the need to drive his sword through Dhanjal's heart.

Dhanjal raised both scimitars as Kevlin struck. Their blades slashed silver-white through the dimness and met with a clash. The two traded rapid blows and the staccato sounds of steel striking steel shattered the early morning stillness.

Terach joined the fray by leaping over a swinging scimitar and kicking Dhanjal in the side of the head. The Blade Stalwart tumbled to the ground and rolled away. His armored scales shredded the long grass and scattered it in his wake. He leapt to his feet in a single, fluid motion, his back to the wall of fire.

Terach moved to Dhanjal's left, so Kevlin moved the other way. He spared Terach a glance. Even on his best day, he wouldn't have tried a move like that. Maybe they had a chance after all.

The three came together again, trading fast blows. Kevlin caught the full impact of one scimitar on his sword and the shock nearly numbed his arm. He suppressed a new tingle of fear.

He'd faced a Blade Stalwart before and knew what to expect. Dhanjal fought with the heavy strokes of the Muscadele style favored by stalwarts, with forms that maximized their supernatural strength.

For his part, Terach fought with the fluid moves of a master of the Tamarri Harci discipline. His pala flicked out, knocking the stalwart's scimitars just wide of the mark. He flowed around the bigger man, seeking an opening for his own blade.

Kevlin followed Terach's lead and adjusted his stance to avoid taking the full force of Dhanjal's blows. The Taiseluz fighting style he favored was a hybrid of various forms and provided tremendous flexibility, although he struggled to match Terach's fluid grace.

Had he faced Dhanjal alone, Kevlin would have already died. Together, he and Terach barely held their own.

The three shifted along the wall of fire, and Kevlin soon dripped with sweat from the intense heat. He threw himself into the fight, drawing deep from the well of his experience, reaching for forms he hadn't used in years.

Dhanjal lunged and Kevlin twisted, letting the heavy blade scrape along his side. He stepped in close and slammed the hilt of his sword into Dhanjal's face. The blow rocked the man's head back hard enough that it would have stunned or incapacitated most men.

Not Dhanjal. The Blade Stalwart shrugged it off and elbowed Kevlin in the side of the head. He reeled and barely blocked the next scimitar, but the force of the blow staggered him back several steps. Terach leaped in to take advantage of the opening, but Dhanjal was ready for him.

When they broke a moment later and circled one another, Kevlin was ready to rejoin the fight. He was amazed no one was dead yet. Most sword fights ended within seconds, despite what the ballads claimed.

He stepped close to Terach. "I'll take the blades high."

At Terach's nod, Kevlin lunged to draw Dhanjal's attention and then left his sword low. As expected, Dhanjal took the opening and slashed for his throat with both blades.

Kevlin was already ducking, and deflected the swords high.

Terach dove under all three blades in a tumbling roll, slamming a booted foot into Dhanjal's left knee. The knee snapped back with an audible *crack,* and Dhanjal staggered, bellowing in pain. Even he could not ignore an injury like that, and for a second it stunned him.

That was all the time Terach needed. The Tamarri captain surged to his knees and drove the pala up through the scale armor into Dhanjal's stomach.

Dhanjal grunted, but swiped at Terach's neck. Terach rolled back out of reach, forced to withdraw his pala before he could drive it up into Dhanjal's heart.

The Blade Stalwart stumbled back, but managed to keep from falling. The effort cost him four hopping steps back toward Rhea's wall of fire.

Kevlin and Terach watched as Dhanjal took one last faltering step backward into the magical flames that hungrily enveloped his armored form.

Yes! Kevlin shared a triumphant look with Terach. Then he met the Blade Stalwart's gaze as flames licked at the big man's torso.

Dhanjal smiled.

He stood unaffected by the flames that surrounded him like a demonic, full-body halo. After taking a deep breath, he placed a hand over his wounded stomach, closed his eyes, and started to chant in a deep, low tone. As he did so, his hand began to glow softly white.

Kevlin fought to catch his breath and swallowed a curse. His foolish hope that Dhanjal would be consumed by the flames died and fluttered away like ash in his heart. Dhanjal was a stalwart.

Stalwarts of the various gods, despite often dramatic differences, all shared a common endowment from their patron deities, a shield of Faith. That faith, if strong enough, protected them from magical harm.

Kevlin reached for a dagger. He and Terach could not enter the flames but, with Dhanjal's eyes closed in his healing chant, a well-thrown blade might still kill him.

A flash of light caught his eye, and Kevlin turned to glimpse a bolt of magic disappearing into the sky above Antigonus, who sat next to Ceren with one glowing hand raised.

A bolt of silver-streaked, black magic blasted out of the trees and bored through the air with a heavy rumbling sound, like a growling panther. It too deflected off Antigonus' defenses and careened up into the sky.

Rhea stepped out of the trees, one hand raised to cast another spell. Her face glowed with health, and her long, lustrous hair shimmered like quicksilver in the dim light. Only her tattered garments gave evidence of the earlier conflict.

"Hold," Dhanjal commanded.

The Blade Stalwart, still immersed in billowing flames, scowled at her. "Do not interrupt the dance. You may have the old man when I am finished."

"Kill those two if you must, but don't interfere with me. I cannot wait."

"You should have stayed away," Antigonus said.

He surged to his knees and lifted both arms high. Magic arced between his palms like lightning. The air of the clearing became heavily charged. A deep rumbling began below their feet and the ground shook. Trees all around the clearing thrashed and filled the air with the sharp cracking of splintering limbs.

Rhea looked around, her expression confused. The ground beneath her feet burst upward in an eruption of splintered stone. It formed a rough pillar a full eight feet in diameter and lurched up with startling speed. It reared twenty feet above the clearing and tossed Rhea so high she disappeared into the darkness.

Rhea's scream echoed back to them as the ground settled. The clearing shook again with the movement of the heavy earth. Billowing dust filled the air in a choking cloud that tasted like clay and decaying plants.

Rhea plummeted back toward the ground, but the air beneath her began to glow, and her descent slowed. About three feet above the ground, the air condensed around her until it looked like a large crystal sphere. Inside it, she appeared distorted, as if seen through thick glass. Kevlin wasn't sure if she or Antigonus had cast the spell.

The harsh red light from the wall of flame dimmed, and Kevlin spun around to look. It burned lower, barely five feet high, and Dhanjal stood with his scaled armor reflecting the flames like a thousand burning tears. Dhanjal held one hand over his injured knee, still softly chanting his healing litany, undoing everything they had accomplished.

Before Kevlin could again reach for his dagger, Dhanjal charged out of the fire and the three met with ringing swords. As they battled, a slow beat began throbbing in Kevlin's heart, unfamiliar yet compelling. At first, it seemed nothing more than his heartbeat distorted through the strain of battle, but it grew in strength until a pounding cadence like heavy drums reverberated through his chest.

Terach launched a furious attack, and the stalwart pivoted to fend him off. As Kevlin drove for an opening in Dhanjal's defenses, the cadence became clearer, pounding in his veins. It was something alien, welling up inside him. Not exactly a song, it rang with a powerful tempo, and he hesitated, sword raised, and missed his chance. Dhanjal spun away.

Deep-throated horns, the likes of which he had never heard, joined the drums and increased the power of the cadence. Kevlin tried to force the music from his mind, but it would not disappear. It swelled in intensity until the distraction nearly caused him to miss a block. He stumbled back and struggled to focus.

Serve Me.

Between the beats of the disturbing cadence, the words came like a voice whispering in his ear. He shuddered and poked the finger of his free hand into his left ear. Nothing.

Glory everlasting.

The same voice came again and the drums drowned out all thought as they rumbled through his chest, down his limbs, and set his muscles quivering with the need to move in response. Kevlin suppressed the urge, but his focus wavered and Dhanjal nearly sliced him open. On heavy scimitar knocked his sword aside and the flat of the blade smacked him across the chest.

What was happening to him? A thrill of cold fear trickled down his spine. Was he going crazy? He'd heard of men cracking in battle or going berserk. His pride cringed at the thought of going mad, but berserk might not be a bad idea.

Heed Me, the voice called.

With the words, an image flashed into his mind of his sword striking Dhanjal.

I might be going crazy, but at least I'm still focused on what's important. The voice, though soft, rang with power, and he could not ignore it.

Beat.

The alien horns blared again, and once more the sound burned through Kevlin, demanding action. He responded, moving with the beat, and was surprised when his sword slipped past Dhanjal's scimitar and struck a glancing blow across the scales protecting the man's side.

How did I do that?

Dhanjal struck in turn, but Kevlin deflected.

Beat.

A hundred drums thundered together, and the power of the cadence increased. It rang through his mind, driving out thought and pushing his growing fears aside.

Heed Me, the voice whispered, and a new image appeared, an unfamiliar form that still felt right.

Beat.

Horns again. The sound raced through his very marrow. His muscles quivered with renewed strength and yearned to follow the mysterious form.

Serve Me.

Another impression, a lunging strike between Dhanjal's blades that was breathtaking in its simple audacity.

Beat.

Drums rolled like thunder. Kevlin leaned forward, barely suppressing the urge to throw himself ahead. He felt an overpowering conviction that to do so would bring victory even while plunging his soul into oblivion.

Kill, said the voice.

Another image. He *knew* without understanding how that if he gave in to the compelling voice, the blows would fall exactly as they played out in his mind.

It was invigorating.

It was terrifying.

Beat.

Alien horns trumpeted so loud that his ears ached. The image intensified, burned into his vision and obscured all else from view. His body lurched forward, his muscles caught between the need to move with the beat and to obey his instinct to retreat and regain control.

He ground his teeth and tried to push the voice of madness away. After staring insanity in the eye, he didn't want to go berserk. Berserkers didn't live long. His sword wavered as he fought to maintain control of his mind.

Dhanjal knocked aside his blade with a dazzling backhand blow that sliced deep into the leather armor over Kevlin's stomach. Pain exploded in his midsection and he staggered. He touched the wound and his hand came away smeared with blood. Dhanjal's blade had not cut deep, but the pain was still sharp and distracting.

Life and glory are yours.

The voice again rang in his mind along with images of Dhanjal lying dead at his feet.

Beat.

Drums and horns sounded together in a unique harmony as frightening as it was wonderful. The force of the cadence rattled him to the core and he swayed, momentarily forgetting who he was and where.

Then Terach stumbled back from a ferocious onslaught, overwhelmed and unable to slip away from Dhanjal's brutal scimitars. Time seemed to slow, while Kevlin strove to control his quivering limbs. As Dhanjal's blades flashed in for the kill, the scene burned into Kevlin's mind by the next overwhelming beat.

As Kevlin struggled to stay focused, he understood with a clarity that chilled him to his soul. He could not fight the madness and Dhanjal both at the same time.

Terach was going to die.

Kill Dhanjal first.

He let go of all restraint and the cadence swept his mind away. Pounding drums replaced his conscious will, and blaring horns overwhelmed self-control, leaving Kevlin little more than the witness to a living nightmare.

His body leapt back into the fight, knocked the enemy's scimitar aside, and slammed a shoulder into Dhanjal. The bigger man stumbled under the unexpected attack.

They faced off as new forms, unlike any he'd known, rolled into Kevlin's mind. His body responded with startling skill, as if he'd practiced the forms hundreds of times. It was like some foreign being had invaded his soul and usurped control.

It was an excellent swordsman.

In a matter of seconds, Kevlin beat past Dhanjal's defenses, landing two glancing blows against the man's scale armor. He met Dhanjal's surprised gaze and held it for a single beat.

Dhanjal spun away and, using both scimitars, knocked Terach's pala aside, then kicked the captain in the chest. Terach tumbled backward onto grass packed low from their struggle.

Instead of leaping forward to finish his fallen opponent, Dhanjal turned back to Kevlin. He smiled, white teeth contrasting sharply with the darkness of his face.

"The Song of Savas sings in your veins," Dhanjal said with a reverent nod.

Kevlin frowned and tried to think through the thunder of the drums. His mind did not work well in that dreamlike state. Everything felt ethereal. Could it really be the elusive Song of Savas the Blade Stalwarts sought in battle? They were crazy to worship war, but he'd never realized they walked around with voices whispering in their heads.

It explained a lot.

Why would Savas try to influence him as well as Dhanjal? Wasn't that a conflict of interest? The god would end up with two pawns facing off using moves He dictated, leaving the outcome up to His whim. With that terrifying thought, Kevlin decided he didn't want to play Savas' game any more.

He could not stop.

He tried shaking his head, but it would not move. He struggled to slap himself to shock his mind awake, but his hand obeyed a new master.

He tried to scream. Silence.

Terach rolled back to his feet but paused to watch them.

Dhanjal beckoned to Kevlin with one hand, his expression exultant. "Come, my brother, let us dance the Song of Savas and contend for the favor of our god. War's blessing be upon us."

Suddenly Kevlin's mouth worked again, but the beat pulsed through his soul, swallowing his fear and replacing it with desire for battle.

"You talk too much," Kevlin said, and lunged.

Still smiling, Dhanjal met his attack, and the ringing of their blades made a beautiful counterpoint to the song burning in Kevlin's soul. The next beat washed all care aside, and he stepped to a dance unlike any other. Dhanjal moved in perfect counterpoint, and their blades rang again and again.

Terach, excluded from the full experience, fought alone, his movements adding an extra harmony to the rhythm. Kevlin and Dhanjal shifted to accommodate the new score, and the battle raged on.

Time ceased to have meaning for Kevlin. With the song ringing in his limbs, he lived only to reach the final crescendo where one of them would sheath a blade in the other's heart. It did not matter who won or lost, so long as they honored the song.

Deep within the recesses of Kevlin's mind, a tiny voice of reason screamed in terror and watched in rising horror as the influence of the alien song consumed him.

6

THE FUTILITY OF CONTAINMENT

"**D**on't kill my mistress!"

Antigonus spared a glance at Haisyl as she dropped to her knees beside him, her face lined with worry and her hands clutching at her skirt. He knew her soul. She was innocent of guile and most surely terrified. She would have to wait, though. His strength was fully tapped and he barely held on.

Excruciating pain throbbed in his chest where Bajaran's cursed dagger had struck. The dagger might have been removed, but the taint of its evil magic remained undiminished. It tore at his flesh like a living thing.

That dagger could kill in seconds with a simple scratch, and only reflexes honed from a century of fighting shadeleeches had staved off death for a time. Still, it required a staggering amount of power to contain.

Imprisoning Rhea had cost him dearly and his wards had slipped, allowing the curse to expand its hold. It ate at the flesh of his chest, gaining strength while weakening the area to the point where the original wound could burst open again at the barest touch, like a rotting melon.

The sacrifice had been necessary, for he needed to question Rhea. Was her love a lie? Who was that Masego she called master? Given a little time, he could free her of her master's influence.

Ceren crouched beside him, her eyes darting from Rhea's cocooned form to the battle against the stalwart. It was a testament to her discipline that she maintained her post instead of throwing herself into the fray as she clearly wanted.

"Please," Haisyl begged. She grabbed his shoulder to get his attention.

Under the bandage, the wound broke open. Pain spiked from the torn flesh all the way down into his lung. He gasped and nearly lost control of the two spells.

"Get away!" Ceren cried and knocked Haisyl back.

"I didn't mean it." Haisyl scurried back, then ran toward Rhea's hovering form.

Antigonus closed his eyes against spasms of pain as he struggled to calm his mind and control his racing heart. The relentless curse exploited his temporary weakness, expanded its hold, and tore at newly exposed flesh in his chest. He barely had the strength to reinforce the walls containing the curse. The sacrificed flesh burned in unimaginable agony as the curse eagerly consumed it.

Rhea strained against the weakened crystal prison, and the air surrounding her began to fade from pure white to a light gray. Her hand twitched, looking large and deformed through the prism-like air. Last night, she had claimed reluctance in obeying her new master, but her actions belied her words.

"Can you hold her?" Ceren asked. "Or kill her?"

He needed answers, but if Rhea escaped she might kill them all.

"I cannot."

Ceren nodded. She was Cunning, so he expected her to understand. The prophecy was clear. Without Strength and Cunning, he would fail. It was being proven in ways he had never expected, so he felt doubly glad he had chosen his companions wisely.

"You must do it," Antigonus said.

Her expression grave, Ceren rushed toward the crystal prison. Haisyl was already pounding against the glowing light. Each blow sank a little deeper. The prison was failing.

Ceren drove her sword into the crystallized air, opposite Rhea's heart. It sank deep, but slowed just short of contact. Antigonus lacked the control needed to create an opening for her blade, so she would have to cut through.

Ceren pressed harder, and the blade inched forward till it pierced Rhea's blouse. Blood stained the pearl silk as the sword drove half an inch into the captive's chest.

Haisyl shrieked and shouldered Ceren aside. The sword remained embedded in the crystal prison.

"Get out of my way," Ceren cried as she climbed back to her feet.

"No," Haisyl shouted with tears streaming down her haggard face. "Why do you want to kill her?"

"I don't *want* to kill her. I *have* to." Ceren knocked Haisyl aside and reached for the hilt of her sword to drive it home.

Antigonus moaned in pain and lost control of the magic.

The prison shattered.

Shards of magical crystal knocked Ceren backward. Rhea landed gracefully on her feet. Her eyes blazed green with power.

Antigonus could do nothing. All of his strength was focused on shoring up the walls of magic around the curse. He needed a few seconds.

Ceren did not have that much time.

Rhea pointed at Ceren as she snatched up her fallen sword. "I'll deal with you in a minute."

She flicked her wrist as if brushing away a fly. An invisible force threw Ceren over the wall of fire. She tumbled into the tall grass on the far side of the clearing.

Antigonus groaned and opened himself to so much magic that his body burned. The power roiled his very soul, threatening to burst all constraints and destroy him in a catastrophic wave of devastation.

He held on. Barely.

The risk was extreme. Another moment of weakness or a heartbeat of hesitation and the magic would break free from his control and annihilate him. It would probably level the forest for miles around. The air crackled with flashes of magical energy, arcing like mini lightning bolts.

It would kill him eventually, but for the moment he could leverage that new influx of strength. Antigonus sealed the walls around the curse and centered his mind. His eyes flashed with white light, and blood stopped oozing from his wound.

His senses turned preternaturally sharp until he could see clearly in the wan light. The scent of raw earth mingled in his nostrils with smoke and crushed grass. The coppery tang of blood and the reek of sweat from the men fighting across the clearing overlay everything. The seductive aroma of Rhea's hair tugged at his heart.

"Mistress." Haisyl beamed as she dropped to her knees at Rhea's feet.

"You did well, Haisyl." Rhea spared her a glance. "Now, hide until I'm finished."

Haisyl scampered away into the darkness.

Exulting in the clarity of his enhanced senses, Antigonus turned his gaze on the three men still fighting. He had done well in choosing Terach to fill the role of Strength. Most men would have succumbed to the power of the stalwart by now.

A brilliant light, visible only to sentinels, surrounded the servant of Savas. Its intensity testified to how deep the man had succumbed to the will of Savas and been imbued with his patron god's battle prowess.

Antigonus' breath caught in his throat. The very same multicolored aura of power surrounded the one called Kevlin.

Remarkable.

The man was no stalwart, but there could be no mistaking the glow of Savas' power. No one received such an endowment without first dedicating their lives to Savas and becoming a stalwart.

Not unless Savas had a reason for claiming them.

Behold, Light will fill a vessel not of power. The favor of Gods shall declare him and their enmity shall hedge up the way.

The obscure lines of prophecy leaped to mind and set Antigonus' heart racing. Could Kevlin's involvement be more than happenstance? Was the entire expedition based on incorrect assumptions?

He could not afford to get distracted. Antigonus buried the questions and focused on Rhea again. Only after dealing with her could he contemplate other matters.

Rhea raised both hands, and fire erupted all around him, crackling as it licked at his clothing and scorched his exposed skin.

Antigonus twitched from the searing heat, but quickly cast a counter spell and *pushed* the air away from his body, creating a glowing void through which her flames could not pass. He reached out with fingers of power and *pulled*.

The tall grass nearby wilted, and the earth dried to dust as he drained the moisture from it and used it to extinguish the flames.

Time to finish this.

Antigonus surged to his knees and threw both arms wide, his face glowing like a beacon. With a voice that shook the clearing, he bellowed a single word of powerand unleashed the magic hammering within his soul.

Wind ripped through the forest behind Rhea and drove a blizzard of splintered branches into the clearing. It whipped the airborne missiles into a whirlwind that enveloped Rhea. She screamed and convulsed under the onslaught. The fire wall fluttered, then winked out altogether.

The insane wind raged through the clearing, clawing at everyone, ripping grass out of the ground and hurling it into the air with the stinging debris. From within the depths of the cyclone, Rhea screamed again, visible only as a vague shape amidst the madly tumbling vortex.

7

A LITTLE LOYALTY TAKEN TOO FAR

Ceren groaned as she pushed herself to a sitting position in the tall grass and groped for her sword. Every muscle ached from being tumbled across the clearing. If the grass hadn't been so thick, she'd have broken some bones.

I've got to get back to Antigonus. Without him, none of them would survive.

Something moved through the tall grass nearby. She froze and probed the gloom for the source of the sound, but it was dark and all the shadows seemed to be moving. Her heart pounded so loud she could hear nothing over the thundering in her ears.

Even as she huddled closer to the ground, a rough hand grabbed her right arm and yanked her to her feet. She spun to face a hard-eyed man in leather armor. A scraggly beard half-heartedly covered his face, and greasy, unwashed hair lay matted against his skull. She yelped in pain and he smiled, revealing several missing teeth.

I don't have time for this.

She jabbed her knee into his groin. He moaned and, as he lurched forward, she grabbed a length of his greasy hair with one hand and slammed her other palm into the base of his jaw. It broke with an audible crack.

The mercenary howled and clutched his mouth with one hand. With the other, he twisted her head down savagely.

Unable to pry his hand free, she yanked the dagger from his belt. Twisting her neck to the uttermost against his grasp, she reared high enough to bash the hilt against his temple.

He dropped like a stone.

Ceren panted while massaging her bruised neck. She'd practiced that palm-strike many times, but had never expected to use it. Her hand hurt and she trembled from the shock of the short, terrifying fight.

She had dreamed of standing strong in a real fight, but reality did not fit her dreams. Her body ached, her clothes were filthy, and her hands began to shake. Still, she could not suppress a surge of pride.

I really did it.

If only her father could see her, he'd never again say her training had been a diversion, a simple rebellion against her other duties. He'd finally take her seriously.

None of the other mercenaries came to investigate, so she slipped into deeper shadows, and only then realized the wall of fire had gone out. Across the clearing, Kevlin and Terach still fought the Blade Stalwart. She watched, spellbound, and tried to reconcile her fantasies about battle with the grim reality. The three men fought with brutal savagery, intent on murdering each other. Her tutors had been right. Despite all the training, she hadn't really understood.

Beyond the three combatants, a dark whirlwind raged where Rhea had stood. Antigonus knelt with hands outstretched. He glowed with magic, seemingly oblivious to a wide bloodstain that spread across the front of his robe.

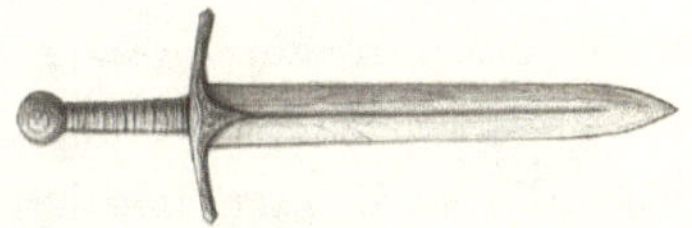

Focused on the whirlwind, Antigonus did not notice Haisyl until she grabbed his shoulder with both hands and wrenched it. His wound tore open again and he toppled to the ground with a moan. He lost control of the whirlwind.

"Don't hurt my mistress," Haisyl cried as she beat at his bloody chest. "Just stop. Everyone, just stop!"

The girl was not strong, but each blow felt like a dagger stabbing his chest. He struggled to think against the waves of pain.

A blast of fire from within the whirlwind disintegrated the flying wood. For three heartbeats, a blazing tornado roared around Rhea. Then the wind died and the fire winked out.

Antigonus pushed weakly at Haisyl from his prone position. Blood was pouring from the open wound, soaking his robes.

She backed away, wringing her hands together. "I'm so sorry. I didn't mean it."

She turned and fled into the darkness.

Antigonus groaned and tried to gather his thoughts. Haisyl was probably telling the truth. She had no idea how much damage she'd done. The girl was normally a pacifist who, back in Tamera, ran a nursery for wounded animals. She was fanatically loyal to Rhea for having saved her father from a life-long illness. That spell had cost Rhea dearly and it had taken her weeks to recover. That act of kindness had so impressed Antigonus that he'd sought her out. He wondered if the whole scenario had been orchestrated to seduce him.

Rhea stood on a patch of scorched earth. Her clothing hung about her in tatters, and hundreds of wooden shards punctured her bleeding torso. Her hair was tangled, with large chunks missing. She swayed, surrounded by a dim glow of crimson magic. After a single deep breath, she dropped hands impaled in a dozen places from her face and screamed with rage.

"Why are you making this so difficult?" she shouted. "I have to do this, so just die." She raised both arms high, ignoring the blood dripping from her palms.

Red-green tendrils of magic ripped through the air between them and struck Antigonus in ten places. His thoughts scattered as the magic scorched his flesh and burned his psychic senses like living fire.

"You will scream for every splinter," Rhea shouted as he howled with pain. He tried to speak a word of power, but her magic ripped the words from his mind.

Haisyl ran toward Rhea, tears streaming down her face. "Please, mistress, can't we just leave?"

Rhea snarled. At a wave of her hand, an invisible force threw Haisyl screaming back into the darkness.

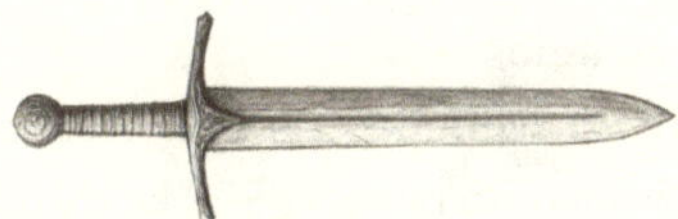

Still immersed in the Song, Kevlin stumbled in a knot of twisted grass. Dhanjal lunged and struck him across the shoulder, slicing through the heavy boiled leather and into flesh. The flash of pain jolted Kevlin out of the trance.

He nearly toppled to the ground. Every muscle trembled with fatigue, and his mind clouded with the need for rest. He fought to center his mind but the cadence, still beating softly, set his limbs shaking in fits and starts.

Terach stepped in before Dhanjal could strike again and plunged his pala into Dhanjal's thigh. The big man grimaced and slashed at Terach's exposed neck.

Drawing deep from the nearly empty well of his strength, Kevlin stepped forward to deflect the fatal blow.

Sacrifice him, the voice commanded in his head. *Strike down your enemy*. With the voice, an image of his sword stabbing through Dhanjal's throat burned into his thoughts.

All he had to do was let Terach die.

He could not do it.

He blocked the scimitar. Barely.

Something snapped inside of him, and the cadence faded away. His mind came fully awake for the first time since the terrible song began.

Terach drove the palm of his hand into Dhanjal's sternum in a classic Harci straight-arm deathblow.

Dhanjal's breath whooshed from his lungs and he staggered back. His armor must have prevented the blow from stopping his heart, but even his supernatural strength could not shrug it off entirely. As Dhanjal lurched away, he swung his scimitars clumsily at Terach. The flat of one heavy blade clipped the Tamarri captain in the side of the head.

The two men fell together. Terach dropped to the side while Dhanjal stumbled backward several steps before falling in a heap with a resounding crash of armor.

Terach twitched on the ground, stunned. Dhanjal rolled to his knees but fell back again, his mouth open wide as he tried to regain his breath.

Finally, he was vulnerable.

Kevlin raised his sword.

Antigonus screamed.

Kevlin glanced at the old sentinel. The last thing he remembered, Rhea had been encased in a whirlwind. Now, Antigonus writhed on the ground, tortured by red-green lightning. Rhea stood barely twenty feet away, covered in blood, her body riddled with wooden shafts.

Dhanjal managed to roll onto his hands and knees, a perfect setup for a killing blow, but Antigonus screamed again. Kevlin could not both kill Dhanjal and save the sentinel.

Nothing about sentinels was ever easy.

Kevlin made his choice and took two quick steps toward Rhea. He drew his heavy belt dagger, and threw it. The blade spun once and plunged to the hilt between Rhea's ribs, knocking her several paces to one side.

She screamed and pawed at the dagger. The magic torturing Antigonus winked out. Rhea fell to one knee, cried out again, and the red halo surrounding her pulsed, faded, then strengthened again.

Served her right. Psycho.

"Kevlin!" Terach shouted.

He dove to one side, and a blade whistled past his ear, so close the air vibrated against his skin. Kevlin rolled and came to his feet just as Dhanjal kicked Terach aside and turned to face him.

The Blade Stalwart lowered his scimitars and smiled. His eyes drifted past Kevlin to stare at something beyond him. Although it was one of the oldest tricks, Kevlin could not resist the urge to glance back over his shoulder.

He gasped, but had no more time than to register the huge ball of fire bearing down on him. The heat singed his face as death crashed into his chest.

It didn't kill him, but disappeared with a little popping sound.

Rhea shouted a vile curse and staggered. He couldn't imagine how she managed to remain standing.

When Kevlin turned back to Dhanjal, the Blade Stalwart stared at him with eyes wide. "The Song of Savas rings in your soul, and magic does you no harm. Has some god accepted your service as stalwart and granted their shield of faith?"

Kevlin had no idea, but snarled, "You'll never know, coward." Dhanjal's dark face reddened and he again raised his scimitars.

"Dhanjal, I need you," Rhea called.

The big man hesitated.

"Dhanjal, remember our purpose."

The stalwart sighed and retreated a step. After sheathing his heavy blades, he bowed to Kevlin and Terach in turn. "Brothers, rest well and prepare to meet your gods. We will dance the song again."

Dhanjal whistled a single, shrill note and declared, "We go."

Then he strode across the clearing toward Rhea, who staggered into the distant trees, still clutching at the dagger that protruded from her side.

Terach, his face dripping with sweat, made to follow, but Kevlin held him back.

"We can take him," Terach said through labored breaths. A bloody lump stood out from his thick black hair, and his surcoat had been slashed in several places, but he seemed willing to carry on the fight.

"Perhaps, but I don't know if we can kill Rhea and the rest of the mercenaries too."

"Good point."

Ceren joined them, streaked with dirt, and with grass clinging to her disheveled clothing. Slender and barely as tall as Kevlin's shoulder, she stood proud and defiant.

"Are you all right?" Kevlin asked.

She nodded, sheathed her sword, and tried to smooth her hair.

"Are you all right?" Terach repeated.

She nodded, then threw her arms around Terach's neck and hugged him tight. The Tamarri captain was clearly surprised, but just as clearly pleased, and wrapped his arms around her in return.

Kevlin turned away and shrugged. Let the nobles have their fun. The last woman he let himself love had destroyed his life and nearly killed him.

Even though he wanted nothing more than to lie down and sleep for a year, he jogged over to Antigonus to see if the old man still lived. Maybe the sentinel had some answers.

8

A Temporary Reprieve

Kevlin dropped to the ground beside Antigonus, who lay face down and unmoving next to the dead coals of the campfire. His chest barely stirred, and when he coughed, bloody foam dripped from the corner of his mouth.

Kevlin gently turned him over. Blood and dirt caked the front of his robe. Since Kevlin's dagger was still sheathed between Rhea's ribs, he swung his arm down sharply and twisted his wrist. A stiletto popped out from its hidden sheath between the layers of his leather wrist guard, and he caught the slender blade with a practiced move.

He cut open the front of Antigonus' robe to find the makeshift bandage had come undone. The wound from Bajaran's dagger gaped open, ragged and bleeding heavily.

Ceren joined him on the other side of the prone sentinel. With efficient precision, she cut a large section from Antigonus' robe, balled the cloth, and pressed it against the old man's chest. She looked worried.

"I'm going to follow those mercenaries," Terach said.

"Be careful," Ceren told him.

"Always." He smiled, then loped off toward the trees. The man's stamina was amazing.

Ceren turned to Kevlin. "I need water to clean this wound. Hot if you can."

It took only a few minutes to light another fire and set a pot over it. Meanwhile, Ceren tied off the bandage and rushed to her bags. She returned a minute later carrying a small green leather case about as long as Kevlin's forearm and several inches thick.

"How's that water?" Ceren asked.

"Warm, but not hot."

"It'll have to do."

The interior of the case was lined with green velvet, and its various compartments held a wide assortment of healing supplies. Three rows of small glass bottles were nestled into recesses on one side, while the other held bandages, several bags of herbs, and a row of wickedly curved needles for stitching flesh.

"Are you a Healer?" he asked. Some Healers were gifted with powerful magic like stalwarts, while others, though lacking magic, could still work amazing cures with their herbs and tonics. Those Healers carried similar green cases.

"My father gifted it to me before I left on my journey."

"But you know how to use it?"

"I do."

Another puzzle. Healers often apprenticed for years. Why train and then not follow the path? Even stranger that she was also trained in the sword.

Ceren scanned the vials and selected one with an indigo-colored stopper. Holding the bottle far from her face, she worked the stopper free and waved it under Antigonus' nose.

"What's that?" Kevlin asked.

"Spirit of Hartshorn."

Antigonus grunted and jerked awake, but then cried out in pain. Ceren put the bottle away, then placed a hand on the sentinel's brow and asked, "Do you recognize me?"

His eyelids drooped, and his mouth moved a couple of times before he finally whispered, "Water."

As Kevlin fetched a cup of cool water, Ceren produced a bottle with a copper-colored stopper, measured several drops of thick, clear liquid into the cup, and mixed it with one finger. Kevlin raised Antigonus' head while she held the cup to his lips.

Antigonus managed several sips before pushing the cup away and closing his eyes. A soft white glow enveloped his body and a faint scent of herbs rose around them. Kevlin inhaled deeply, and his aching muscles relaxed. A sound like a hummingbird's thrum intensified, as it had the first time Antigonus healed himself.

Ceren smiled and pulled the blood-soaked bandage from his chest. The magic flared, obscuring the wound for a dozen heartbeats before fading again.

Antigonus seemed to deflate and sagged against the ground. His skin looked as gray and brittle as old parchment, webbed by a series of shallow cracks as if it could flake away at the gentlest touch. It hung loose on his frame and he seemed smaller. It looked like the magic had burned away some of the flesh underneath.

Ceren frowned over the wound. Kevlin leaned closer for a better view. It no longer bled freely but looked only partially closed. Ceren used a clean cloth and tarm water to carefully clean the wound, then smeared a vile-smelling paste onto it. She covered it with some soft cotton padding.

"I can't heal this," she said as she tied the bandage in place. "I'd hoped he could."

Antigonus' eyelids fluttered open. His gaze was clear, but weak, and his cobalt eyes were sunk deep in their sockets. He smiled at Ceren, and she leaned close.

"Can you heal yourself?" Ceren asked.

"The wound. . .difficult. . .Bajaran's magic." He spoke faintly, his breathing shallow. Kevlin and Ceren exchanged a concerned look.

"Not much time," Antigonus whispered.

"For what?" Ceren asked

"Die," he breathed. "A few days. Less than a week."

He grimaced and closed his eyes, and in a moment drifted off to sleep. Ceren stared at Antigonus, her face stricken.

The grass nearby rustled and Kevlin sprang up, his sword half-drawn before he recognized Haisyl stumbling toward them. She stared with a haunted, despairing look, her face grimy and streaked with tears.

She stopped near the fire and complained, "I think I twisted my wrist."

With a cry of rage, Ceren launched herself at the woman, grabbed her by the throat, and began slapping her across the face. Haisyl's head whipped from side to side and she screeched and clawed at Ceren's arm. Ceren only tightened her grip until her fingers shone white against Haisyl's dirty skin. Blood sprayed from the corners of Haisyl's mouth at each blow.

Kevlin pushed between them and pried Ceren off. Haisyl fell to the ground, clutching at her face and sobbing.

Ceren turned on Kevlin, her face a mask of rage, and struck at him. He caught her wrist and shook her by the shoulders until her teeth clacked together.

"Control yourself," Kevlin snapped. "Why are you doing this?"

Ceren shrugged free and took a moment to regain her composure. Her long, auburn hair had escaped its braid and hung loose across her face and shoulders. She brushed it aside and glared.

"Didn't you hear Antigonus? He's going to die in a few days, and it's her fault."

"How is it Haisyl's fault?"

Ceren opened her mouth to reply, but paused. "I guess you didn't see."

"I guess not. I was kind of busy." The corners of her mouth lifted in a hint of a smile. It was a good sign. Her crazed anger seemed to have broken.

"What did she do?" Kevlin asked.

"She distracted Antigonus while he was holding Rhea prisoner, interfered with me until Rhea could destroy that crystal prison, and when Antigonus caught Rhea in that cyclone, she attacked him. That's how Rhea broke free. She'd have killed him if you hadn't thrown that knife."

Kevlin struggled to picture the timid Haisyl accomplishing all that. He'd dismissed her as a rather empty-headed, overly devoted servant, a bit on the crazy side.

"Really?" he said finally.

Ceren thrust her face close to his. "Are you calling me a liar?" Her eyes flashed with anger. They were lovely eyes if one could get past the belligerent attitude.

"It's her fault," Ceren repeated, "and she's got to be punished for it."

"Leave her alone," Antigonus murmured from where he lay. "I will cast Truth. Tomorrow. We will know her guilt then."

Kevlin shuddered and backed up a step. Truth was a powerful spell which denied anyone under its power the ability to speak falsehood. Under its influence, conflicting accounts of events could be resolved, and spells of darkness dispersed. Kevlin had experienced the power of Truth, and the memories still haunted his sleep.

Today they did not need Truth. Haisyl's actions clearly marked her a traitor.

Antigonus spoke again, more strongly. "Where are we?"

Ceren briefly recounted their trek to the clearing the night before, explained a little about Dathan, and the sudden attack. At the mention of Kevlin's early warning device, Antigonus said, "So that must be what lies burning at the edge of the clearing."

Kevlin stood and noticed for the first time the small fire burning near the trees. He jogged over and found the leather ball, about the size of a newborn's head, lying in a patch of burned grass with fire still spouting from the opening at the top. He turned it over with his foot and pressed it into the ground to smother the flames, then screwed the cap closed to prevent the fire from starting again.

When he returned to the others, Antigonus regarded the leather ball with interest.

"Is that photophor?"

"Aye. I'm surprised you know it."

"In the past hundred years, I have learned the secret, despite how closely the Meinarri sailors guard it. How is it that you carry photophor so far from the sea?"

"I'm from Meldan." Kevlin had not been there in years, and he didn't think about it often. For him, the past was better left alone.

"Ah," Antigonus said, as if that were somehow important. "In the hand of the Lady."

"Aye, I sailed aboard my father's ship as a boy."

"Is that what they use in tempest lanterns?" Ceren asked. "How does it work?"

Since she'd already seen it in action, he didn't see any harm in explaining it. "The ball's packed with crystals that burn in water. Those mercenaries tripped a line that released a bent sapling I had it tied to. That tossed it into the air and shattered a small tube of water inside that could mix with the crystals."

"I am glad you thought to use it," Antigonus said before settling back. "Very cunning."

"I suppose." Kevlin glanced up and found Ceren scowling again. She'd get premature wrinkles if she kept that up.

Together, they changed Antigonus into his spare robe, careful to jostle him as little as possible. From a silver chain fastened around his neck hung a soft leather pouch covered with silver runes that glowed in the early morning light. Whatever it contained looked to be about the size of a large egg. They were careful to avoid touching it.

As they finished, Terach returned to the clearing. He nodded toward Dathan and his other guards, who had nearly finished breaking camp, and growled, "Return to your master, Kevlin. I want you gone."

9

THE RIGHT ANSWERS FOR THE WRONG QUESTIONS

"I don't like your tone." Kevlin rose to face Terach. "I risked my life to help you."

"And you endangered our lives bringing us here."

"I didn't think the mercenaries would find us."

"And the Blade Stalwart? You didn't think we'd like to know about him?"

"I never saw him before."

"You've faced one before, so don't pretend you know nothing."

"I know nothing about Dhanjal. I did face a Blade Stalwart once, but it had nothing to do with this. There's no reason one of their kind should be chasing Dathan."

"So the mercenaries will follow him and leave us alone?" Ceren asked hopefully.

"No," Antigonus spoke, surprising them by joining the discussion. "For some reason, they have allied with Rhea, and she will pursue us until she destroys me, or is killed in the attempt."

"Why is she doing it?" Terach asked.

"She revealed that her master commands it, but I do not know him or his plans. Bajaran was planning to take Oris to the Sigrun, so perhaps that is her master's ultimate goal."

Ceren gasped and Terach's face drained of color. Haisyl let out a terrified moan and fainted.

Another shiver of fear crawled down Kevlin's spine at the mention of the Sigrun. Bad enough to think about the shadeleeches without considering the Sigrun council that ruled them. Masters of Sthenic magic, the evil lords of darkness inspired endless tales of horror.

None of those enemies had plagued the Six Kingdoms of the Tamerlane Empire since the last great war. To Kevlin, like many born decades after the last war, the Sigrun had always been more legend than reality.

Not anymore.

Over two hundred years ago, while the empire was young, the combined might of the High Council of sentinels had barely held the Sigrun at bay. The clash of titanic powers had devastated the western border. Mountains had been torn down and all life drained from miles of earth, leaving it a barren wasteland. Bottomless fissures crisscrossed the land like eternal wounds, and poisonous gasses hung like a death shroud over everything.

"You have Oris with you?" Kevlin asked, thinking of the rune-covered pouch strung around Antigonus' neck.

"It can never leave my side," Antigonus said. "I see you all understand how grave the situation is. Rhea cannot gain possession of Oris. The consequences for the empire would be catastrophic."

He held out his hands to Ceren and Terach, and the two of them dropped to their knees beside him, each clasping a hand. "The prophecy spoke truly. Without Strength and Cunning, I will fail. Believe in yourselves. You were chosen for a reason and must not falter."

They both nodded. Ceren's eyes shone bright with emotion. Antigonus held their hands for several heartbeats, then his hands began to glow. The glow spread to the other two, and flared. As it dissipated, Ceren and Terach shared a look of wonder.

"I cannot fully heal myself, but this small gift I can give you." Antigonus beckoned to Kevlin to approach.

Terach backed out of the way with a glare and Kevlin took his place. Antigonus clasped his hand. "You are bound to me now. You will serve me until I release you."

"You don't really have to do that," Kevlin said. The fewer spells directed at him, the better.

"It is done," Antigonus said. His cobalt eyes bored into Kevlin's hazel ones. "Do not fail me."

"I'll see you safe wherever you need to go," Kevlin assured him. As he spoke, an unexpected feeling of purpose flooded through him. For the first time in years, he had actually allied with what appeared to be a worthy cause.

Why did it have to be sentinels?

Terach didn't want him around, and the thought of Rhea and Dhanjal pursuing them frightened him more than he wanted to admit. Then again, he needed answers that only Antigonus could give. With any luck, they could get Antigonus healed quickly and he could be on his way.

Antigonus settled back and closed his eyes again.

"We have work to do," Terach said.

"First I need to patch Kevlin's wounds," Ceren said.

Under her direction, Kevlin unlatched his armor, dropped the battered leather to the ground, and slipped out of his bloodstained padded jerkin. The slash across his stomach was painful but shallow. The gash on his shoulder was more severe.

Ceren refilled the cup and measured out a few thick drops of the painkilling liquid. It turned out to be very bitter. Muttering to herself, she pulled some waxed thread from her green case along with a wickedly curved needle.

"Sit," she ordered, and he complied with a nervous glance at the needle.

She snorted. It was a singularly unbecoming habit for a pretty young woman, but he decided not to mention it until she finished. "You fought a Blade Stalwart, so don't tell me my little needle makes you nervous."

Kevlin held still while she pierced the skin of his shoulder and began efficiently stitching him up.

Terach crouched beside him. "Tell us how you faced Dhanjal like that. You moved like he did, and he said you heard the Song of Savas. What did he mean?"

Kevlin shuddered at the memory, and his muscles tingled with remembered power. But his heart quailed at recalling the loss of control. He hated the feeling of helplessness he felt around magic and those who wielded it.

"I don't know how it happened. I need to talk with Antigonus about that. Maybe it had something to do with the bloodset."

Terach considered that. "Perhaps, but how did Rhea's magic not harm you?"

"I don't know." That was an even greater mystery. Kevlin should be dead twice over from her. "Maybe it's tied to whatever made me hear Dhanjal's song."

"That doesn't make sense," Ceren said with a frown.

Kevlin shrugged. "I know."

"Keep still."

"Sorry. It's one more question for Antigonus."

"What happened the last time you faced a stalwart?" Terach asked, shifting the topic back to painful memories Kevlin didn't want to think about. "Did you hear the song then too?"

"No, I heard nothing."

"Then how did you survive?"

Kevlin braced himself against the tide of memories flooding his mind. Memories of battle, of pain, and of love raced past, leaving him grappling with the residue of bitter betrayal that always clung to him like ash. *Chayah.* The name sent a chill through him. Even spoken within the silence of his mind, it carried such power. Conflicting emotions raged as he thought about her.

"Shaemal." He grasped that memory to avoid thinking about the rest. "The stalwart's name was Shaemal. I fought him two years ago."

"I've heard of no Blade Stalwarts hired in the Six Kingdoms over the past couple of years," Ceren said.

How would she know? Few would, but she seemed confident that she should have.

Kevlin said, "I doubt you'd have heard of Shaemal. His presence in Donarr was a secret."

"Donarr?" Terach asked.

"Aye. Shaemal was plotting with General Stigandr to betray the Donarri." Kevlin's hatred for the general still burned hot despite the passage of time. "I killed Shaemal before they could set their plot in motion."

To avoid any more questions, he changed the topic. "Antigonus named you Strength and Cunning. You said he likes assigning nicknames, but it sounds like there's more to it than that."

Terach did not seem ready to change the topic, but Ceren made the transition smoothly. "It has something to do with an old prophecy he's always muttering about."

"He said you were chosen to bear those titles. How? Who are you?"

Terach said, "I am of House Elsdon, stationed at the Imperial Palace in Tamera. I was assigned to accompany Antigonus as Strength. We'd met a few times, and I guess I impressed him."

"I am of House Iarbonel in Agoraeun," Ceren said. "My cousin runs the city's intelligence service, and I work with him." With a little smile, she added, "At first, Antigonus wanted my cousin to go, but instead he chose me to fill the role of Cunning."

Kevlin tried not to wince as Ceren jabbed her wicked needle into his stomach. The pieces fit. Terach certainly fought with the skill of the legendary Elite Guard, and Ceren was a noblewoman. Did she actually gather intelligence? Agoraeun was one of the great trading centers of Freyarr, and the city was governed by Lord Baris of House Iarbonel. How were they related?

Ceren continued, "Since it's Antigonus' expedition, we decided not to object to the titles. They started rubbing off on us. He's got one too, you know."

"What is it?"

"They call him the Catalyst, although he's only mentioned it once."

"How is it that Antigonus leads the party?" Kevlin asked. "I've never heard of sentinels being given command when imperial troops are involved. Shouldn't you be leading, Terach?"

Terach nodded. "Normally, yes, but the whole expedition is tied to Antigonus and his prophecy, so he was given permission to lead."

Bloodsets, Blade Stalwarts, prophecies, and sentinels who wanted to ally themselves with the Sigrun. All better left alone. Could it get any more complicated?

"What about you?" Terach asked, interrupting his thoughts.

"I am Kevlin. Security expert and sometimes mercenary, at your service."

Ceren snorted again and pulled the waxed cord. He winced, but she continued stitching without looking at all apologetic. Maybe if he punched her in the jaw while she was biting her lip in concentration like that, she'd feel his pain.

"We'll leave it at that for now," Terach decided, then rose to his feet. "We've already taken more time than we can afford."

Ceren completed her ministrations, tied off the last stitch, and smeared some of the vile-smelling paste on the wounds before tying bandages over them.

"Do you think they'll come back soon?" she asked with a glance at the trail.

"Sooner than I'd like. I trailed them close to the highway, where they stopped in a small glade to heal. They'll be a while. Dhanjal's going to have a hard time keeping Rhea alive. She barely made it that far. It'll probably be hours before he recovers enough to finish the job."

"You saw all that? How close did you get?" she asked.

Terach smiled. "They posted two men as lookouts, but they were sloppy." He pulled a dagger from his belt and tossed it to Kevlin. "Dhanjal was just extracting your knife from Rhea's ribs, so I brought you one of the guards'. It seems a decent blade."

Indeed, it was a close match to Kevlin's own, with a good balance and keen edge, and it fit well in the empty sheath.

Terach rose. "Come, we need to find another trail to the highway."

"Which way should we go?" Ceren asked.

"North."

She jumped up and placed a hand on his arm. "Terach, Antigonus told us his wound will kill him, and he's only got a few days left. We're a week south of Diodor."

"We came from there too," Kevlin said. "Pushing hard, it still took five days."

Terach considered the motionless sentinel. "How far is it to Tamera?"

"Probably a little closer than Diodor, But not by much," Kevlin said.

Ceren said, "Maybe we should head south then. Can we find a stalwart to heal him?"

"Maybe," Kevlin said with a shrug. "I haven't passed through this part of Hallvarr in a long time. Every town has a shrine to Serigala, but with the harvest nearly over, the Pemburu Stalwarts will be traveling. Most of the Jagen Stalwarts are concentrated farther north, near the capital and Chandravernan lands."

"We ride north," Terach said. "The closest town is Ingolf, and we can be there by afternoon. Hopefully we can find a stalwart."

Ceren frowned. "What if there aren't any? It'll take days to reach the next big town."

"Then pray we get a positive spin of the Wheel."

Kevlin stifled a groan. Calling on Akillik again was the last thing he wanted to do.

10

THE TIMBERED REST

It didn't take long to pack their meager supplies and saddle the horses. Dathan welcomed Kevlin's decision to join Antigonus' party when Kevlin explained that by doing so he could best lead the mercenaries away. So eager was he to be away that he paid Kevlin's wages without even trying to cheat him, then led his men south into the woods.

With Terach's help, Kevlin fashioned a more durable stretcher. They hoisted it and headed into the forest, with the ladies leading the horses behind. Since the mercenaries blocked the direct route back to the highway, they forded the stream and headed northwest. By the time they reached the road, an hour later, Kevlin's arms quivered under the strain of carrying Antigonus, and his injuries burned despite Ceren's painkilling medicine.

They secured the stretcher between a couple horses. Terach mounted his own stallion and took the lead lines. Ceren's horse had not been recovered, so she rode behind Kevlin. They moved at a fast walk to avoid jostling Antigonus.

When Haisyl mounted her horse, Ceren said, "You're no longer part of this company, Haisyl. Find your own way."

She paled. "But Antigonus said."

"He said not to punish you for your treachery, but he didn't say we had to trust you. Your mistress is in the woods not far from here. Go find her."

They left her sitting her horse, staring after them as they moved north. She looked pathetic, but Kevlin didn't fall for the act. The journey would be difficult enough without babysitting the annoying woman and worrying if she would turn on them again.

Kevlin decided to enjoy the rare peace as they rode. The morning was turning out better than he had expected. They had survived Dhanjal's attack, which alone merited celebration. On top of that, he was free of Dathan, with money in his pouch and a pretty girl on his horse.

They moved together, her weight a steady pressure against his back, and her arms lightly holding his waist. She smelled nice, like springtime. She was too polite to mention how badly he stank. It was nice to have someone with good manners around for a change.

They rode north through the morning, pushing against a flood of travelers fleeing south from the expected conflict promised by the bloodset. None of the travelers felt inclined to stop and chat, so Kevlin gained little useful information.

The highway ran straight north, with only the occasional gentle curve. Part of an extensive highway system linking all the major cities of the Six Kingdoms, this section connected Diodor, the capital city of Hallvarr in the north, to Tamera, the imperial seat and capital of Tamarr in the south.

The sun shone bright in a cloudless blue sky, making it an unusually beautiful autumn day. Woods flanked the highway, a thick wall already brilliant with the reds, golds, and purples of leaves changing with the season. At noon, they stopped to rest the horses and eat a meager lunch while Ceren checked on Antigonus.

"How is he?" Terach asked as he inspected the horses' hooves.

"Unchanged," Ceren said.

Terach frowned. "Earlier, his face seemed to be glowing. I'd hoped he was healing."

"Why didn't you tell me?"

"What would you have done?"

"I don't know. I could have checked on him."

"I didn't want to stop."

They continued at the same steady walk, and Kevlin started to feel impatient with the pace. He tried passing the time talking with Ceren, and she spoke at length about Agoraeun. She'd lived there her whole life and loved the bustling metropolis.

Ceren possessed a quick mind and surpised him with the depth of her understanding of the complex economy driving the city. She refused to clarify exactly what she did in the intelligence service, but Kevlin didn't mind. He enjoyed listening to her speak. When she wasn't yelling or snorting, she had a lovely voice.

A couple hours after noon they reached Ingolf, a large town straddling the Nagendra River near its mouth on the Tamerlane Sea. A tributary of the mighty Ujutus River, the Nagendra was narrow but deep, and used for moving freight from southern Hallvarr all across the Six Kingdoms.

Stacks of timber lay in muddy lots on the south side of the river. Rough piles of iron and copper ore were piled in massive heaps nearby. They were extracted from the Straton Mountains to the east. Mountains of coal reared farther from town, while sturdy crates of produce were stacked on the north shore awaiting shipment.

The center of town lay on the north side of the river, which they crossed via a wide, arcing stone bridge. The few people on the streets hurried about their business with worried expressions.

The shrine of Serigala was a simple, single-story building set back from the road at the edge of the central market square. It looked serene, with a small, manicured lawn flanked by vegetable gardens. A white-painted picket fence ran along the road, with a wide gate that stood open.

The wooden roof was closed, which was a little unusual. The Pemburu Stalwarts, disciples of Serigala in her form as goddess of the harvest and moon, cared for most of her shrines, and were avid star gazers. They preferred to prop the roofs open whenever the weather permitted.

A woman wearing a wide straw hat and a smock of heavy, unbleached wool worked in the garden, harvesting late-season spice beans. She didn't look up until they dismounted.

"Pardon, miss," Terach called.

The woman smiled, her broad face tanned from long hours in the sun, and etched with lines of mirth and hard work. Her eyes shone merry and blue. She noticed the stretcher bearing Antigonus and her smile faded.

"Can I be of service?" she asked.

"We hope so. We have an injured man. Are you a stalwart?" Terach asked.

She laughed. "Oh goodness, no. I have some little skill, but no endowment from Serigala. I help tend to the shrine."

"Are there any stalwarts here?"

"I'm afraid not. After the bloodset last night, things got pretty busy."

"What do you mean?" Kevlin asked.

"Didn't you see it?"

"Aye, but why would that force the stalwarts away?" Terach asked.

"They spent the whole night trying to calm the council and guild masters. People panicked, and those who haven't fled have barricaded themselves in their homes. The stalwarts left this morning to visit the surrounding villages."

Terach swore softly but sincerely, and the woman's face blanched. "I'm sorry," he said. "Our friend will die without the aid of a stalwart. Will they return soon?"

"Not for several days, at least."

He turned from her to survey the deserted marketplace. His lips moved, but he kept his curses silent.

Ceren's face lit up. "Wait. A ship. We can take a ship for Tamera!"

"I'm sorry," the woman said. "The docks are empty. Every vessel that could float was sailed downriver to the sea at first light."

Ceren stamped her foot in frustration.

"Where exactly did the stalwarts go?" Kevlin asked. "Maybe we could catch up with them."

The woman shrugged. "I cannot say for sure. The villages are scattered throughout the countryside. They could be anywhere."

Terach said, "We have to push north. How far to the next town with a stalwart?"

Glancing at the litter-bearing horses, the woman said, "Walking, it'll take you two or three days."

"Thank you," Terach said, and they withdrew to discuss their next move. It didn't take long, for there was really only one option. They had to press on.

Ceren said, "We need some supplies. I'll see what I can find."

"Be quick. Kevlin, go with her," Terach ordered.

Kevlin sighed. Riding with Ceren was nice, but she'd better not start thinking of him as her errand boy.

Many shops were closed, but Ceren proved an aggressive shopper. She had Kevlin pound on doors until reluctant merchants answered, then she haggled like a horse trader. In less than an hour, she acquired most of what they needed. She used Kevlin as her pack mule.

As she passed a low barn, she stopped and grinned. Her eyes fixed on a handsome open carriage parked inside. Behind the high driver's seat, two plush benches faced each other, with a large compartment for baggage in the rear.

Using funds from one of Bajaran's purses, they purchased the carriage, and within ten minutes were hitching a couple horses to it.

"Brilliant," Terach said after they settled Antigonus on one of the plush benches. "We'll cover a lot more ground this way."

Ceren climbed aboard and settled on the other seat with her green healer's case. Kevlin climbed up to the driver's seat while Terach flanked the carriage on his stallion. The sun was halfway to the western horizon by the time they headed north out of town. The road ahead lay empty, so they pushed the horses into a rolling canter that ate up the miles.

Kevlin smiled as he drove, his hopes buoyed by their rapid progress. They'd find a stalwart for sure. Once restored to health, Antigonus could take care of Rhea, and Kevlin's oath to see him safe would be fulfilled. Antigonus might even answer some of the questions he yearned to ask.

They paused a little before dusk to rest the horses and eat.

"We'll push on into the night if it's clear enough to see," Terach said. "I want as much distance between us and Rhea and those mercenaries as possible."

They made very good time for another hour, but as night fell, heavy clouds rolled in from the west, and thunder rumbled with the promise of a deluge.

"We have to find shelter," Ceren called out. "We can't expose Antigonus to that storm. It might kill him."

Terach said, "If we find a good place, we'll stop. If not, we'll rig some blankets over him."

A chill wind picked up and a few fat drops of rain splattered onto Kevlin's face. A minute later, lightning flashed in the distacne. The pealing thunder seemed to unlock the heavens and the rains began in earnest.

Kevlin caught sight of a light visible ahead through the gathering darkness. Shouting to Terach to follow, he whipped the horses and raced for the promised shelter as the wind rose to a howl, and rain slashed his face in stinging sheets.

"We've got to get out of this," Ceren shouted while trying to hold a spare blanket over Antigonus.

The lights belonged to a long, two-story inn built close to the highway. A sign above the door, rocking in the wind, showed a tree sheltering a bed. Kevlin had never felt happier to see an inn, and decided not to dwell on the lucky spin of the Wheel.

He drove around the near side of the building to a huge barn set perpendicular to the north end of the inn, with doors wide enough to drive the carriage inside. Two hostlers took the horses and called another man to help with their baggage.

One of the men then led the way through a covered walk to the back door of the inn. They entered a large common room flooded with cheery light and shimmering with warmth.

A massive fireplace filled most of the wall to their left. Dozens of candles burned in sconces along the walls, and the light reflected from polished wooden surfaces everywhere. The oak tables shone and the floor, made of closely fitted purplish-brown walnut planks, sparkled. At the far end of the room, near the front door, a gleaming cherry bar ran the full length of the wall.

A handful of other travelers sat scattered among the tables. Several were eating, and Kevlin savored the aroma of roasted pork. Most of the other customers stood talking near the fire, and paused to stare at the stretcher.

A heavyset, middle-aged woman in a starched white apron hurried over as they crossed the room. Her hair and eyes were a deep brown, and her ruddy face warm and friendly.

"Welcome to the Timbered Rest." She frowned at the stretcher. "Is your friend ill?" It was early for the winter skin rot, but with the bloodset spooking everyone, it was clear she did not want to take any chances.

"He is injured." Ceren clasped the woman's arm and added, "You have such a beautiful inn. The woodwork is gorgeous."

"Thank you, milady." By the time they reached the bar, Ceren and the innkeeper were chatting like old friends. Two minutes later, after dipping again into Bajaran's purse, the innkeeper led them from the common room and down a short hallway.

They stopped at a door paneled in gleaming cherry and carved with intricate patterns of vines and candle fruit. It opened into a comfortable study. Several books, a rare luxury, sat on a high shelf to their right. Padded chairs faced a cheery fire in a large hearth under a mahogany mantel. An oak table and chairs filled the rest of the room, with a candelabra glowing in the center. A large window was shuttered against the storm.

"Very nice," Ceren observed, removing her sodden cloak and hanging it on a peg near the fire.

The innkeeper's teenage son brought in a small trundle bed and placed it near the fire for Antigonus. The sentinel looked weak. He rolled his head from side to side and muttered to himself, but did not awaken.

Ceren checked his bandages while a serving girl set a full meal on the table. The roasted pork was cut into medallions and covered with delicious gravy. Other dishes included mashed potatoes dripping with butter, steamed carrots, spice beans, and mulled cider that quickly chased away the cold.

They ate ravenously, and the solid, hearty meal tasted delicious. Soldiers know to eat when they can, so Kevlin polished off three helpings, then waddled over to one of the plush chairs. He stretched his feet toward the fire and stared into the flames with half-closed eyes, enjoying the simple pleasure of feeling stuffed, warm, and dry.

Ceren dropped into another chair with a contented smile, and cocked her head to listen to the drumming of the rain. "Better than sleeping on the road, don't you think?" she asked Terach.

He had lingered at the table over a glass of wine, which he raised in a toast. "Absolutely."

Antigonus groaned and opened his eyes. Ceren sprang up and brought him a cup of mulled cider. "Drink," she ordered. He managed a few small sips before pushing it away.

"Where are we?" he whispered.

"An inn north of Ingolf. We're looking for a stalwart to heal you," Ceren explained.

He nodded and closed his eyes. For a minute it looked like he had fallen asleep, but he stirred and reopened them. "I have contacted Harafin."

"Harafin? How?" Ceren asked.

"Mindlink. I was too weak to hold the connection long, but I think he understood I had been betrayed and need help."

"When?" Terach asked.

"This morning."

"Where is he?"

"Tamera." He clenched his eyes against a fresh wave of pain. "Need to rest."

"We'll watch over you," Ceren promised, wiping his brow with a cloth. His face began to glow with a soft, silvery light and his breathing deepened.

"That's what he was doing earlier," Terach said. "Is he healing?"

Ceren checked under the bandages, but the soft glow did not extend past his face.

"Harafin." Terach slammed one fist into his open palm. "He's in Tamera, and we're going the wrong way."

Kevlin decided not to point out that it was Terach's choice to take the northern road.

"Do you think he'll ride north to meet us?" Ceren asked.

"Undoubtedly."

"Maybe we should head south tomorrow."

"If Harafin *doesn't* come, Antigonus will never make it to Tamera," Kevlin said.

"It's not worth the risk of running into Rhea or Dhanjal again," Terach decided. "We stick to the original plan."

The choice made sense, although it luffed Kevlin's sails to think they were continuing away from their best help.

The thought of meeting Harafin was thrilling, and terrifying. Harafin of the ruling council in Tamera, was an even greater living legend than Antigonus. His exploits dated back over two hundred years to before the creation of the empire. He had been one of the mightiest defenders of the Six Kingdoms through all the wars against the Grakonians.

Hopefully Harafin rode fast. Once he caught up with them, they'd be safe.

Within a couple of minutes, the glow faded from Antigonus' face and he settled into a deep sleep. They all headed to their rooms.

Ceren directed them to place Antigonus on a hastily-prepared bed in the parlor attached to her suite at the end of the upstairs hall. Terach urged her to let them help watch over Antigonus, but she shooed them out and ordered them to get some sleep.

Kevlin was impressed. Ceren was smart, resourceful, and willing to make hard decisions. He'd known few women who could claim all those qualities. Of course, one of them had turned out to be a lying murderer.

Kevlin and Terach shared a cramped little room near Ceren's suite, but Kevlin didn't mind. It was better than sleeping outside in the rain.

Both rooms looked out over the back courtyard. A maid who had been assigned to attend Ceren mentioned that one of the buildings outside was a bathhouse. Ceren grabbed a change of clothing and headed for the bath faster than a legionnaire rushing to dinner.

Kevlin didn't stink so bad that he couldn't sleep, so he dropped onto his bed. Terach drew the first watch and went to check on Antigonus. Kevlin fell asleep before the door even closed behind him.

11

PLOTS WITHIN PLOTS

Wayra followed a servant down a wide marble hall in the palace of Diodor. Although substantial, the building felt rather provincial to her. The Hallvarri penchant for straight lines and solid, simple design made the palace functional but not very inspiring. Had she been heading for the throne room, she wouldn't have needed a guide. It took determination to get lost in the main corridors.

She wasn't headed for the throne room, however. Only an hour in Diodor and already summoned to meet King Leszek. They may not have been imaginative but the Hallvarri were efficient. A little too efficient for her taste today. Events were moving fast and she was late. The king's summons did not bode well.

Rain pounded the city and the palace halls were mostly empty. They passed a pair of enormous windows that usually offered panoramic views of the harbor but tonight revealed only sheets of rain streaming down the glass in undulating waves.

The shifting water reflected her face poorly but even perfect mirrors could do little for her. She had given up pretending to worry about her appearance years ago. Her brown hair, when she bothered to wash it, hung limp to her shoulders. Her distorted reflection looked even more pinched and skeletal than normal, although her eyes stood out clearly.

Unusually large, those pale blue orbs shone with inner fire, reflecting her unwavering conviction in her mission. The future of the Six Kingdoms would be decided soon and she was destined to play a pivotal role in directing that future.

A gentle tickle at the back of her neck startled her. The precursor to a mindlink connection, the feeling returned tentative, as if the sentinel trying to contact her knew she did not wish to be disturbed. If the message was important enough to bother her, they shouldn't have hesitated. Not breaking stride, she shielded her mind and opened herself to the contact, expecting to hear the voice of one of the kestrels in her party.

Wayra.

Weak and distant, she didn't recognize the voice. She buttressed her mental shields and prepared to strike if the unknown sentinel proved hostile.

Who is this? She threw the thought across the psychic connection.

Antigonus.

She gasped. *Where are you?*

Hurt. The connection wavered, his mindvoice barely above a whisper. She threw her own strength into the link, trying to sense his location. It helped only a little since mindlink connections were sustained by the sentinel who initiated contact. *Bajaran. . . betrayed . . . dying.*

Then he was gone.

Wayra's thoughts raced as she stared unseeing at an intricate tapestry hanging on the wall. She had sensed he was far to the south but that was not precise enough.

The effort required to establish and maintain a mindlink connection increased exponentially with the distance between sentinels. Even fully rested, she could not stretch her mind so far. That Antigonus could do so when gravely injured only underlined the importance of her mission. She needed more power to shape the empire's future the right way.

His words haunted her. Hurt. Betrayed.

Bajaran had already struck. *It's not supposed to happen this way.* If Bajaran succeeded, the disaster would sweep away everything she'd worked for. But Antigonus was wounded, not dead. Had he killed Bajaran? Or did the betrayer still hunt him?

Did Antigonus know about Rhea?

Wayra didn't have enough information. She had to act and act quickly if she was to have any chance of salvaging the situation. She forced her doubts aside. *I am ready. I will not fail.*

"It *is* a beautiful tapestry, ma'am." The servant's voice pulled her from her reverie.

Light preserve me from fools.

"Lead on," she ordered. The man resumed walking, although he cast furtive glances at her every dozen paces or so.

She ignored him as she considered the best way to track down Antigonus. They turned off the main halls, climbed a long stair, and finally halted at the end of an elaborate hallway before a pair of tall double doors engraved with the crest of the royal House Dalagan.

Interesting that a pair of Outriders flanked the doors instead of the traditional palace guard. The elite Chandravernan soldiers wore their trademark suits of close-fitting chain and leather armor under cloaks of mottled forest hues.

The guards opened the double doors and the attendant announced her before motioning her into the expansive study. Unlike the simple, functional decor of the rest of the palace, this room was richly decorated in polished mahogany, thick carpets and gilt-edged furniture. Leather-bound books filled shelves spanning the length of the wall to her right, while to her left a fire crackled in a deep hearth. Above the mantel hung pennants bearing the heraldic emblems of the various houses that had ruled Hallvarr over the past two centuries.

King Leszek sat in a tall padded armchair behind an enormous mahogany desk. A window took up most of the wall behind him, although tonight it revealed nothing but sheeting rain.

The king greeted her with a polite smile as he set aside the parchment he had been reading. Leszek was past his prime, but still handsome. Captivating hazel eyes shone out from his broad, rugged face. His thick, raven hair was graying around the temples, giving him an additional air of distinction.

Solidly built but not yet run to fat, he cut an impressive figure in his gold, sleeveless doublet over a forest green silk shirt. A finely tailored russet coat hung over the back of his chair.

"Wayra, thank you for coming."

"I was honored to receive the invitation, Your Majesty," she replied with a curtsy.

Although not technically a subject of Hallvarr, as an adept sentinel and adjutant to the gerent of Il'Aicharen, she had represented the enclave in Diodor on a handful of occasions.

"I have a message for you from Antigonus," Leszek said.

"Antigonus? When did you see him?" she asked, taking a step forward.

Leszek raised an eyebrow and she regretted her lapse in self-control. If only Antigonus had contacted her after the audience instead of before. The recent mindlink had left her rattled.

"You were expecting to see him, I take it."

"Yes." It was a fact she wished he didn't know, but she couldn't deny it.

"You're late then. He stopped here six days ago, and then headed south. What are your plans?"

Although not a sentinel, the king possessed a piercing gaze that undoubtedly proved effective on those not used to wielding actinic magic. Wayra considered how best to downplay the significance of Antigonus' visit but the king was no fool.

Under the king's intense stare she said, "I was to accompany him on part of his journey."

He leaned back in his chair and steepled his fingers, his expression grave, eyes distant. After a moment, he muttered, "Too early. It's too early."

His gaze snapped up to meet hers again as he leaned forward. "But it *is* happening, isn't it?" His face paled. "And it involves Antigonus?"

"Don't jump to conclusions, Your Majesty."

"No one said anything about Antigonus. What's really going on?"

"I don't know yet. I need to find him."

"This changes things."

"No, it doesn't." She refused to show the dismay his words caused. If King Leszek decided to intervene, it could destroy the plan, and in the ensuing chaos, the enemy might just succeed in escaping with Oris.

"It does," the king shot back, rising to his feet. "I was misled. The timing is wrong and Antigonus is involved. *Antigonus!* If anything happens to him. . ." His voice trailed off as his thoughts followed that line to its likely conclusion. He sank back into his seat. "I can't do it."

"Do?" Wayra stepped closer and leaned over the desk, her gaze boring into his. "You must *do* nothing. I will deal with the situation. These are sentinel matters and if you meddle in them you could destroy everything: your kingdom, your reign. . .everything. I have a dozen sentinels with me, all battle-trained kestrels."

The kestrels in her party were all experienced sentinels, either proven or adept. Bajaran may have slipped past her, but he could not escape.

"How am I supposed to believe that?"

"You have to trust me," she said in her most confident voice.

The king regarded her for half a dozen heartbeats before nodding. She let out a slow breath but before she could congratulate herself on averting a disaster he added, "I'm sending Nikias with you."

She rolled her eyes and swallowed a curse. Nikias, that young fool! He had no idea how to wield the awesome power entrusted to him. He was like a berserker at a tea party, totally unpredictable and more likely to damage their efforts than help.

She forced calm into her voice. "That's a mistake, Your Majesty. We can--"

"No," he cut her off. "You want me to trust you. I will, but not blindly. If my stalwart were here, I'd send him. But he's not, so Nikias will do. He will accompany you and follow your lead but he reports to me."

She opened her mouth to object again but he raised a hand.

"I have spoken." Leaning forward, he added in a soft voice. "Consider this a partnership, the kingdom and the sentinels working together." His eyes narrowed and he continued, "If you deny me this, I will be forced to seal off the kingdom, marshal all of my troops, and flood the kingdom with them."

He had her and he knew it. "It will be as you command, Your Majesty. I leave within the hour."

"Very well. Nikias will be ready. You are dismissed."

She turned to go but before she reached the door he called after her. "Wayra, keep me posted. If I don't hear from you regularly, I'll assume you've failed and will be forced to act."

She nodded without turning and strode from the room, dismissing the king from her thoughts as she laid her plans. There was much to do and more than the fate of one little kingdom hung in the balance.

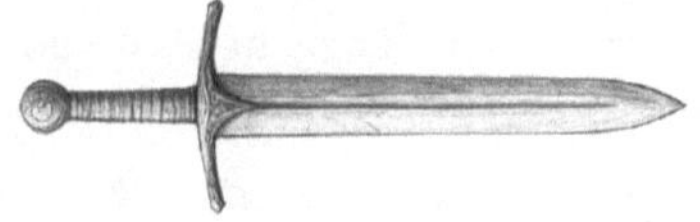

Twenty minutes later, the double doors to the king's study banged open and Nikias swaggered into the room. Nineteen years old, he was of average height. Trim, with broad shoulders, he dressed in tan leather breeches and a tight-fitting black leather jerkin cut to accentuate his muscular torso. His blond hair hung down to his shoulders, pulled back from his face with a rawhide cord. The coat of arms of House Dalagan was emblazoned in red over his heart.

In his right hand he carried the Bladestaff.

One of the six weapons of power, it had been entrusted to Hallvarr over two centuries ago during the Great War that resulted in the formation of the empire. Intricate inlaid silver runes ran the length of its five-foot shaft of rare and deeply-polished white waxwood, capped at both ends with broad, eighteen-inch blades of the same silvery metal as the runes.

Nikias bowed deeply. "You sent for me, Your Majesty?"

"Yes. We have a crisis on our hands and the kingdom needs you."

Nikias' smile widened and he swelled with pride. Raising the Bladestaff in salute, he declared, "I am ready!"

Blue flame ignited along the blades and crackled down the silvery lengths. Nikias spun the weapon around his body and the twin blades trailed streams of blue fire in their wake. As bearer of the Bladestaff, Nikias was endowed with uncommon speed, while the magic of the Bladestaff protected and strengthened him.

King Leszek fought to suppress an irritated frown as he watched with alarm the magical flames licking the air close the bookcase.

"That is enough."

"Oh." Nikias cringed and the flames winked out. "Sorry."

"We don't have much time. You leave in half an hour."

"Where am I going?" His excited grin returned.

"You will accompany Sentinel Wayra and her party south. You will rendezvous with Sentinel Antigonus and escort him safely to Diodor or to Tamera, whichever he prefers."

"Really?" Nikias bounced on his toes. "Is Antigonus in trouble?"

"Perhaps. Something is going on and Wayra is leaving to determine the extent of the threat."

"Thank you, Your Majesty!" Nikias cried. He spun and rushed for the door.

"Nikias," the king called after him, rising to his feet.

Nikias spun in midstride. "Yes, Your Majesty?"

"Be very careful. The enemy could be anywhere."

Nikias grinned even wider, his eyes sparkling with excitement.

"You represent me personally on this mission," the king continued. "No matter what Wayra or anyone else says, you will follow my orders and see that nothing happens to Antigonus. He is your responsibility. Is that clear?"

"Yes, my king!" Nikias saluted, then dashed from the room.

King Leszek groaned and fell back into his chair, one hand over his eyes.

"Are you sure it's a good idea to send that fool?" A voice asked.

The king removed his hand as Commander Tekla rose from an overstuffed chair facing the fire, where he had remained hidden from view. The commander was a lean, grizzled soldier with white hair and steel-gray eyes. He stood tall, his broad shoulders unbent by six decades of hard life.

He strode around the chair, his movements smooth and powerful. As commander of the Wolves, the elite of the Outriders, he was the living exemplar of everything his forces stood for.

"No, I'm not sure," the king admitted, "but I need someone in that party who won't be totally helpless when things go bad."

"I don't think he can handle it. He's been bearer for less than a year. He's headstrong and reckless."

"I know, but he serves the purpose I have set for him. His death would be unfortunate."

"Every death serves a purpose," Tekla replied automatically, repeating the mantra of the Outriders.

King Leszek nodded. "Perhaps the next bearer would be easier to manage." He shrugged and added, "I had expected the Blade Stalwart to handle things but the timing is wrong. I'm afraid we've been misled."

"It was unwise to lend the stalwart to Piran."

"Perhaps."

"This could prove disastrous."

"Perhaps," the king said again and rubbed a hand across his face. "The kingdom is in grave danger and we must prepare to defend our interests. For the good of the Chandravernan, the kingdom, and the empire. But we must tread cautiously or everything we've planned will be destroyed."

"Do you trust Wayra?"

King Leszek leaned back in his chair and stared at the large pennant bearing the coat of arms of his house as he considered his recent conversation with the sentinel. He did not like Wayra but she held a prominent position in the enclave at Il'Aicharen so she had to be capable.

She seemed confident in her ability to prevent disaster but she was late. The plan he'd agreed to was a good one and should ensure the perpetuation of his kingdom, but that plan seemed to be at risk. There was too much at stake for anything to go wrong.

Meeting Commander Tekla's gaze he said, "No, I don't trust her. What is the current disposition of our forces?"

"In Diodor we have one full legion of regulars, three hundred Outriders, and three Jagen Stalwarts."

"How many more Outriders can we marshal within a week?"

"If we strip the nearest Chandravernan outposts, we can assemble at least a column. If we had longer, we could raise a full legion."

"I don't think we have that much time. Muster those you can and see if you can call in any more Jagen Stalwarts."

"As you command."

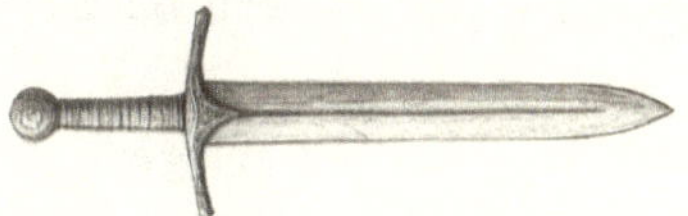

All of them?

Yes, Wayra hurled the thought at Ruggiero. *This is an emergency. We need them all. Strip Il'Aicharen of every kestrel and make haste for Diodor. I'll send you further instructions later.*

Despite the gravity of the situation, a thrill of excitement raced through her. With the ten kestrels at Il'Aicharen added to the dozen already at her disposal, she'd be commanding the most powerful force of battle-ready sentinels assembled in the past half-century. She would not fail.

The gerent will be angry. He'll be left with no more than a couple competent sentinels in the enclave, Ruggiero cautioned.

Don't argue with me.

Ruggiero was a strongly gifted sentinel and a dedicated kestrel but sometimes he worried too much.

Tell him you act on my command. He rules Il'Aicharen, but I lead the kestrels. After a calming breath she added, *Tell him I will contact him soon and explain further. That should placate him.*

Very well. We will leave at first light.

Wayra broke the connection and wiped her sweating face. Reaching nearly two hundred miles across Hallvarr to Il'Aicharen to establish the mindlink connection with Ruggiero had taxed her strength to the limit. As she steadied her heavy breathing, she smiled with fierce pride. Few sentinels could reached so far.

Turning to the mirror in the small room she had commandeered to initiate the mindlink, she smiled at her skeletal reflection, not minding in the least how unnatural her wide eyes looked.

She was ready.

Opening the door, she beckoned the kestrels into the room. With their power augmenting her own, she could cast her thoughts even greater distances. The connection would be difficult, but they had to make the attempt.

Her master needed to know what was going on.

12

THINGS THAT GO BUMP IN THE NIGHT

Kevlin awoke slowly under Terach's insistent shaking. Fighting down the urge to punch the captain and go back to sleep, he mumbled, "What time is it?"

"Around midnight."

As soon as Kevlin sat up, Terach dropped onto his own bed and instantly fell asleep.

Kevlin dressed and buckled on his armor. He slipped into the parlor of Ceren's suite. She was curled up in a fat, cushioned chair beside Antigonus' bed, cheek resting on one palm, wearing a robe over her night dress.

Kevlin would have taken the huge bed in the next room. Ten paces away wouldn't have hurt Antigonus, and she would have slept better. Still, her dedication was impressive.

Antigonus lay quiet as a corpse, and looked almost as bad. His shallow, rasping breaths made Kevlin want to cough to clear his own lungs. The wounded man's skin was hot and cracked in places as if all the moisture in his body had burned away.

"Hold on," Kevlin whispered to the old man. They'd find a stalwart tomorrow to heal him. They had to.

Ceren shifted in the chair, so Kevlin slipped out and returned to his own room. Outside, rain still pounded the inn, although the wind had died down. Lightning flashed occasionally, but the thunder seemed weaker. With any luck the storm would blow itself out before sunrise so they could get an early start.

As he stood staring out the window into the darkness, a flash of lightning lit up the yard behind the inn for just a second.

It was enough.

In that second, several shapes were clearly illuminated as they moved toward the rear of the inn.

"Can't they let us get one night's sleep?" Kevlin muttered. He had no doubt who the approaching forms were.

Time to run.

"Terach," he called sharply. The man muttered and rolled over. Kevlin called again and kicked him in the leg. Terach rolled onto his back and groaned before finally opening his eyes.

"What's going on?"

"We've got enemy forces closing on the inn," Kevlin said with a nod toward the window.

Terach cursed, jumped up and began buckling on his armor. Kevlin stepped over to the next room, pushed open the door, and called loudly, "Ceren."

She started and nearly fell out of the chair.

"Get up. We have to leave. Now."

She rose, brushing strands of hair from her face. "Rhea?"

"Most likely. Hurry."

She rushed into the bedroom and Kevlin returned to the other room to grab his things. Terach was already fully armored and packed.

Kevlin blinked in surprise. By the Lady's temper, that was fast. If they survived the day, tomorrow he'd kick Terach awake and order an omelet. That kind of speed needed to be put to good use.

They transferred Antigonus to the stretcher in the parlor and tied him down. He didn't move. Kevlin was tempted to wake him.

Terach noted his gaze and shook his head. "Wait until it's absolutely necessary. He lacks the strength to stay awake for long."

"I hope we have time later."

They slung packs over their shoulders, hoisted the stretcher, and headed out into the hall. Ceren emerged, still stuffing items into her bag. She had not found time to secure her hair, and it hung around her face like a halo, accentuating her olive complexion and emerald eyes. She appeared calm as she held her naked sword ready.

Kevlin took the lead, heart pounding and hands clammy on the handles of the stretcher. They had reacted quickly, but even the two minutes they'd already consumed might have been too long.

He wished for another set of stairs at the far end of the inn, but hadn't bothered to search that area earlier and couldn't risk the time to look. He paused at the top of the main stairs and glanced down to the closed door at the bottom. It opened into a corner of the common room, near the bar. They would be exposed as they crossed toward the exit. No choice.

Taking a deep breath, he started down, treading close to the wall to reduce the chances of a loose board squeaking. Terach and Ceren followed suit, and they made it to the bottom with hardly a sound.

Maybe they had a chance after all.

At first he thought the common room was empty. The fire burned low, a handful of dying candles guttered along the walls, and the chairs all rested upside down on the tables. As he headed across the room toward the door to the barn, the fire popped and a woman started upright from behind a table where she had been sleeping.

"Haisyl?" Kevlin asked.

"Oh, I'm so glad I caught up with you," she cried, rushing across the room toward them. On the way, she bumped a table and knocked four chairs to the floor with a crash.

"I'll kill her," Ceren growled.

Kevlin didn't usually like to hit women, but he was tempted to race Ceren for the chance to beat Haisyl.

Before either of them could move to strangle the annoying woman, the door to the barn was flung open, and several leather-armored mercenaries rushed inside with swords drawn.

"The front door," Kevlin yelled.

Too late.

More mercenaries flooded in from that direction, shouting triumphantly.

"Back!" Kevlin shouted. "To the study."

The group turned and raced for the hall leading to the study where they had eaten the night before, with mercenaries closing in behind. In the rear, Kevlin felt particularly exposed. A well-thrown dagger could drop him in his tracks.

He pushed Terach faster.

Haisyl outran them all. One thing she did well was run away. Another mercenary appeared in the doorway, blocking the way. She screamed and tried to skid to a halt, but she was too close and moving too fast.

The grinning mercenary aimed his sword at her stomach. She slid onto it with a scream that became a gurgling wail of agony, cut short by a fountain of blood spewing from her mouth. Haisyl slid off the sword and onto the ground, clutching at her bloody stomach.

"Mistress," she moaned as blood pooled around her. Her entire body shuddered.

Ceren stopped, staring in horror at the gore, her face white and her sword arm shaking. Two more mercenaries appeared behind the one who had impaled Haisyl.

Terach and Kevlin lowered the stretcher and drew their swords. Ten mercenaries closed in around them, weapons ready and eyes cold with the promise of violent death.

"Wait."

At the gentle command, the mercenaries halted. Dhanjal entered the room through the door leading from the barn. His scale armor ignited like a thousand torches, reflecting the dying fire and guttering candles. He approached with the same unhurried, confident stride that had carried him into the clearing early the previous morning.

Dark circles ringed his eyes, and his tired face looked haggard. His armor seemed to hang a little loose, and the bones of his hands stood out against his skin.

Healing Rhea had drained him, if he'd managed to save her at all. Stalwarts were endowed with marvelous gifts of healing, but not with unlimited energy for exercising those gifts. It looked like Dhanjal had exceeded those limits and sacrificed some of his own strength to feed his gift.

The ring of mercenaries parted and Dhanjal passed through, stopping four paces from Kevlin. The Blade Stalwart nodded as he crossed his arms. Kevlin had no trouble ignoring the impulse to do the same.

"Well met, brothers," Dhanjal declared. "The Song of Savas sings loud this night. We will compete for His favor again."

"Well met, brother," Terach said. He stepped up next to Kevlin and slid the pala home in its sheath.

"What are you doing?" Kevlin hissed, not taking his eyes off Dhanjal. "Don't encourage him."

Terach ignored him. "Son of Savas, I challenge you to fight for the favor of your god."

Dhanjal smiled. "Very well, son of Salawin. I accept your challenge." The scales of his armor glowed brighter, then shifted slowly through the colors of the rainbow, signaling his growing rapture.

"We can beat him," Kevlin whispered fiercely, "but not this way."

Dhanjal reached for his twin scimitars, but Terach held up one hand. "Allow me a moment to make peace with my god."

"Very well."

Dhanjal crossed his arms and tilted his head back. He stared at the ceiling in some sort of ritual prayer, leaving his neck exposed. Kevlin reached for his dagger, but Terach grabbed his hand.

"No," Terach whispered. "If we kill him, the others will slaughter us. We can't win that way."

"What other choice do we have?"

"I can keep him busy for a while. You figure out how to get us out of here."

Ceren stepped over to them, her eyes darting from Haisyl's still-twitching, bloody form to the mercenaries, then to Dhanjal.

"What are you doing?" she asked, her voice tight with fear.

"I will fight him," Terach said.

"He'll kill you."

Terach placed a hand on her shoulder and replied in a whisper, "We're surrounded. Dhanjal wants to fight, so I'll fight."

"But--"

"No," he cut her off. "I must do this or we all die. It's the only hope I can give you."

She embraced him and kissed him hard on the mouth.

Breaking away, Terach drew his pala and stepped toward Dhanjal. The mercenaries retreated and dragged tables out of the way to give the fighters space.

"What's going on down there?" a woman's voice called from upstairs. It sounded like the innkeeper. Dhanjal snapped his fingers and two of the mercenaries slipped past Kevlin's group and through the door that led to the second floor.

"Run," Kevlin yelled in warning.

The innkeeper shrieked and her footsteps retreated down the hall. The mercenaries climbed the stairs but remained stationed at the top. Silence reigned once more. If any of the other guests heard the commotion, they wisely remained in their own rooms.

"Come," Dhanjal beckoned, drawing his scimitars with a flourish. "Let us dance the Song of Savas."

The two closed, their swords flickering through the soft light, slashing the air like flashes of muted lightning. They moved around each other like twin cyclones of deadly steel.

Ceren took an involuntary step forward, but Kevlin caught her arm. "We need to figure out how to get out of here. It's the only way to help him." He didn't bother to mention that the chances of any of them escaping were slim, but for Terach they were almost nonexistent.

Kevlin forced himself to tear his eyes off the two fighters and study the rest of the room. His heart sank. Too many men blocked both doors. They might have a chance against the three clustered in the hallway leading to the study, but the others would cut them down from behind before they could get through.

"Ceren." He caught her eye and flicked his gaze toward Antigonus. She nodded and slowly stepped back to the sleeping sentinel. None of the mercenaries seemed to notice. They were all focused on the battle raging in the center of the room.

Ceren nudged Antigonus with her foot. He didn't move. She tried again, harder. He rolled his head and muttered something unintelligible that was lost amid the sharp ringing of swords.

She looked like she wanted to kick him hard, and Kevlin silently urged her on. They needed Antigonus awake.

Instead of booting the sleeping man, she glanced at her pack where her healer's case rested. It was unlikely she'd be allowed to open the case and revive Antigonus with her medicines, but she was clearly considering taking the chance.

Kevlin ran his gaze around the room again, but found nothing useful. The only possibility he kept coming back to was finding a way past those three mercenaries in the hallway and retreating to the study.

The front door opened, and Kevlin stared at the figures entering, hoping crazily that the mighty Sentinel Harafin had somehow covered the hundreds of leagues between them and come to help.

It was not Harafin.

The first person through the door was a man of medium height and build, who was heavily cloaked against the rain. He pushed the hood back to reveal dark brown hair and a face that would have been unremarkable if not for his eyes.

Shifting darkness filled the eye sockets, and pure evil emanated from them, so strong it rippled across Kevlin's skin like clinging tendrils of a frozen web. Those were the eyes of a creature whose soul belonged to EnKur, Lord of Darkness, whose flaming chains consumed forever the dead who fell into His snares.

Those terrifying eyes swept across the room and paused to focus on Kevlin. Fear immobilized him and his breath caught in his throat. All sound faded in the moment he stared into the roiling blackness of those eyes.

With an effort, Kevlin broke away from that gaze and shuddered with terror. No one needed to identify the creature of darkness for him.

A shadeleech.

Tales of the shadeleeches, recounted to him all his life, suddenly seemed laughable. They utterly failed to convey the abject terror this servant of evil projected.

Kevlin's mind reeled as he tried to process the staggering turn of events. A shadeleech in Hallvarr? How was it possible? No shadeleeches had been seen in the empire for half a century, and Hallvarr lay on the far side of the empire from the Grakonian border.

Beside him, Ceren gasped, her hands trembling. The sound pulled Kevlin back from the brink of panic. He glanced down at Antigonus, but the sentinel hadn't moved, nor did it look like he planned to. The terrible, brutal truth slammed into Kevlin so hard he wanted to throw up.

They were going to die.

There might have been a chance, however slim, to escape Dhanjal and the mercenaries, but with a shadeleech, death was a surety. It would be ugly, too. Panic flitted at the edges of his mind, and he wasn't sure he wanted to resist it any more.

Behind the shadeleech, other figures entered the inn. The first through the door was Rhea. The sight of her was a welcome relief after seeing the shadeleech.

She limped and seemed more dead than alive. What was left of her hair hung in limp, ragged clumps around her head. Her eyes lurked deep in their sockets, and the dark circles around them seemed impossibly wide. Her skin looked rough and scabrous, like the bark of an old sycamore tree.

She and Dhanjal might have preserved her life, but only barely.

Kevlin stared at her and tried to reconcile reality with the nightmare they were living. How could she stand with a shadeleech? She had said she needed to kill Antigonus to obey her master, and she'd seemed genuinely tormented by it. Now she stood in open rebellion against every oath she'd ever taken.

Maybe the shadeleech was her master? Did her treachery run so deep? His mind whirled as he grappled with the horrible thought.

Behind Rhea came a dozen heavily cloaked men who were probably the shadeleech's bodyguards. They towered over everyone else in the room, easily among the biggest men Kevlin had ever seen. They threw back the hoods of their cloaks, and Kevlin could not suppress a cry of fear. Ceren cried out and pressed against him, her entire body trembling with terror.

They were not men.

They were Makrasha.

13

TWO OUT OF THREE IS NOT A WIN

Ceren fainted, toppling backward, and Kevlin barely caught her.

"Let me go, blockhead," she hissed, her lips barely moving as she sagged against him. "You'll ruin my fall."

Kevlin stared, mouth agape.

"Let go," she insisted.

He dropped her.

Ceren crumpled to the ground, as loose as a ragdoll. She lay limp on the floor next to Antigonus, but then one hand snaked out to shake the sleeping sentinel.

Kevlin forced himself to look away, not wanting to draw attention to what she was doing. He noted that although the mercenaries pulled away from the makrasha, they didn't attack or run.

Makrasha were the shock troops of Grakonian armies. Their size, brute strength, and monstrous appearance were legendary. Kevlin stared at one of them in fearful fascination.

Built like a giant, its head looked wrong. Shorter and much wider than a man's, it sat on a short, powerful neck covered sparsely by bristly hairs that poked from its gray, leathery skin. The creature's mouth cut across that wide, flat head and was filled with sharp teeth and a pair of long fangs.

Two narrow slits formed its nose, and nothing could be seen of its ears. Three large, dark green eyes, spaced evenly across the creature's wide forehead, stared flatly across the common room. With no lids or whites, they resembled the eyes of some giant insect.

A second set of arms, trisegmented like a spider's, sprouted from its torso. Known as *hengaruk*, they were long and thin, but supposedly very strong, and tipped with three stubby fingers capped with hooked claws. In each hengaruk, the makrasha carried small crossbows that they pointed indiscriminately at everyone in the room.

The creature was disgusting.

Rhea sidled slowly away from both the makrasha and the shadeleech, her face frozen in a grimace. Maybe the shadeleech wasn't her master, the mysterious Masego. It didn't matter, though. Kevlin would be dead soon, either way.

All of the newcomers were soaking wet.

The fact seemed important, somehow. Puddles of water spread out from beneath the newcomers, and water dripped off their clothing. Kevlin frowned, grasping for an idea that flitted just out of reach. The mercenaries were soaked too, and water pooled across the inn's tightly fitted floor.

Rhea caught sight of Kevlin, snarled with rage, and hurled an ugly red bolt of magic at him. The crimson bolt of death leaped across the room to destroy him.

He lacked time to dodge, and he was ashamed that his final thought wasn't a scream of defiance, but relief that he'd get to die quick, and not linger at the hands of the shadeleech.

The magic bolt slammed into his chest, but instead of splattering him across the room, it flared, then disappeared like her magic had done the previous times she'd tried to kill him.

For a raging, traitorous, sentinel, she had a lot of performance issues. For once, Kevlin didn't mind that magic didn't make sense.

Rhea shrieked in rage. Another drop of water slipped from her outstretched arm and splashed into the puddle at her feet.

In that second, the beginning of a desperate plan formed in Kevlin's mind. It was crazy, but he had no other ideas. So he let his mind loose on it like a hound after a rabbit.

And he stepped to one side, just in case lightning decided to strike him twice.

Dhanjal crossed his scimitars in front of his chest and retreated a step from Terach. Terach backed away and leaned his hands on his knees, panting. As spent as Dhanjal seemed, Terach was no better off. He hadn't slept since that dawn battle in the clearing, and the heavy fighting was taking a visible toll.

Dhanjal glared at Rhea. "You will not insult my god again. The dance must be honored."

Rhea opened her mouth to reply, but the shadeleech raised a hand and she cringed.

"Hurry then," the shadeleech said in a low, menacing voice. "We will wait, but not for long."

"Son of EnKur, I fear you not." Dhanjal turned to the shadeleech. "Servants of the burning chains seek Savas' favor, as do all who yearn for power. Do not interfere with me."

The shadeleech waved a dismissive hand, but made no other move.

During the exchange, Terach seemed to realize who the newcomers were for the first time. His face paled and he glanced at Kevlin, as if to confirm he wasn't going crazy.

Kevlin smiled and winked. They might be crazy, but they weren't dead yet. Terach raised a questioning eyebrow, and Kevlin held up a single finger. Terach nodded and straightened.

Dhanjal raised his scimitars, and the two launched themselves back into the fight.

Ceren pulled herself to a sitting position. Antigonus still hadn't stirred. "I can't wake him up," she whispered.

"It's all right," Kevlin said. "Slide my pack over here."

Ceren snaked a hand onto his pack and dragged it across her lap, shielding it from view of both the shadeleech and Rhea. Kevlin slipped a hand inside, rummaging around until he found the item he sought. He breathed a sigh of relief and extracted it.

Kevlin stood, keeping his hand by his side, and watched the fight. Within seconds, Terach managed to spare a glance in his direction, and he nodded. Terach worked his way around Dhanjal until his back was to Kevlin. Under Dhanjal's next heavy blow, Terach stumbled all the way back to Kevlin.

"You carry Antigonus," Kevlin whispered to Terach. "I'll lead the way."

Not waiting for a response, he turned to face the shadeleech and shouted, "Take your pets and go, before I'm forced to kill you!"

The shadeleech sneered, but Kevlin moved before the servant of darkness could rip out his soul, or worse. He threw the leather ball concealed in his hand.

His last container of photophor.

As ball sailed across the common room, the sentinel pointed a finger at it. A bolt of pure darkness leapt from his hand and intercepted it in the center of the room.

It exploded.

Kevlin was already charging for the door leading to the study. Stinging particles pelted him in the back as the photophor crystals blasted across the room and covered everyone with a thin layer of powder. The three mercenaries in the doorway cursed and wiped at their eyes.

The momentary distraction was all Kevlin needed. He snapped his left arm down, twisting his wrist, and the hidden stiletto popped into his hand. He threw it at the first mercenary from ten feet away, catching the man in one eye.

He leaped Haisyl's prone form. Two quick slashes of his sword dispatched the other mercenaries. With the way clear, he spun back to the common room. Ceren was right behind him, carrying several of the bags. Terach staggered after her, awkwardly bearing Antigonus, stretcher and all. Kevlin met Haisyl's eyes and she opened her mouth in a silent plea.

He could do nothing for her.

Everyone else in the room was still wiping their eyes clear of photophor dust. The shadeleech locked Kevlin in his terrifying gaze and smiled, as if amused by the attempt to flee. The servant of darkness raised a hand to cast a spell.

He burst into flame.

The photophor reacted to the wet clothing, skin, and hair of the intruders, and ignited. White fire raced over their bodies and burned along the puddles on the floor.

Pandemonium broke out.

Mercenaries and makrasha howled and thrashed. Several of the gigantic beasts fired their crossbows, and at least one mercenary was hit. His scream added to the tumult.

It actually worked!

Kevlin wanted to whoop with relief and exultation, but the photophor was spread so thin that it wouldn't last long. He bolted down the short hallway to the study.

Terach deposited Antigonus on the floor, and Ceren slammed the door closed. He wedged a ladder-back chair under the latch. Kevlin helped him maneuver a couple of the heavy, padded chairs against the door. The makeshift barricade wouldn't hold for long, but they only needed a few seconds.

"Well done," Terach said.

"We're not out of here yet," Kevlin reminded him.

The door shuddered under a heavy blow, and both of them leaped to brace it. "Ceren," Kevlin yelled. "The window."

She raced to the window and spent a few seconds struggling to twist open the lock to raise the window and access the outer shutter, but it remained stuck.

More blows slammed into the door till the latch splintered. The door slid open a fraction of an inch.

"Hurry!" Kevlin shouted.

Ceren ran to the table, grabbed a chair, and hurled it at the window. It shattered the glass but splintered against the shutter. She caught up a broken table leg, cleared the glass away and began wrestling with the catch to the shutter.

The pounding on the door intensified, then the tip of a sword split the wood right next to Kevlin's head.

They were out of time.

"Go!" Terach shouted. "Help her."

Kevlin raced to the window, drew his dagger, and slammed the hilt against the latch. It snapped free, and he pushed the shutter wide, then turned back to the room. Terach left the door and bent to lift Antigonus.

Before Kevlin could move to help, the door burst open. Dhanjal loomed in the doorway, flanked by half a dozen mercenaries.

The Blade Stalwart threw one of his scimitars.

It tumbled across the room and slammed into Terach's back, punching through his armor and sinking deep into his torso. The blow drove Terach forward onto his knees, arms outstretched, eyes widening with shock.

Blood spewed from his mouth, and he locked eyes with Kevlin. His mouth worked as if he were trying to speak. Then the light faded from his eyes and, a single heartbeat later, his body became an empty, lifeless husk.

Kevlin stared in mute horror. He'd witnessed many comrades die in battle, but that split second when life departed always shook him.

In the common room, he'd accepted the fact that they were probably going to die, but hope had pushed that certainty aside when they reached the study. They had been so close to escaping! The open window and concealing darkness mocked him with promised safety.

"No!" Ceren screamed, echoing the cry ringing in Kevlin's mind. She tried to run past, but he caught her shoulder and pulled her to a stop.

Mercenaries boiled into the room around Dhanjal.

"Let me go," Ceren hissed, pushing Kevlin's arm aside and reaching for her sword.

Terach began to burn. The photophor reacted with his blood, and white flames licked across his torso and face.

Kevlin choked down the bile that rose in his throat at the sight. He grabbed Ceren by her sword belt and collar and threw her out the window. Her scream of protest was lost as she tumbled into the darkness.

Sparing one last glance at Terach's burning body still sagging on his knees above Antigonus' prone form, Kevlin dove headfirst out the window after her. He rolled right into Ceren who was already struggling to stand. The two of them collapsed in the mud in a tangle of arms and legs.

Kevlin surged to his feet. Ignoring Ceren's complaints, he spun back to the window, wiping rain out of his eyes just as a mercenary appeared in the window, peering into the night. Kevlin drew a long throwing dagger from its hidden sheath under his collar and threw it. It took the mercenary in the throat.

Ceren leaped to her feet, and Kevlin grabbed hold of her.

They both burst into flame.

Photophor.

Ceren yelped and tried to run, but Kevlin tackled her and hissed, "Roll. The mud will put out the fire."

For once, Ceren obeyed and the two of them wallowed around like pigs until they had covered themselves with a thick layer of cold mud. The flames were doused as clinging muck smothered the photophor dust.

By the time they pulled themselves back to their feet, two mercenaries were clambering out the window with swords drawn. Others emerged from a nearby door, carrying a torch. Kevlin grabbed Ceren's elbow and pulled her toward the forest. The rainy darkness made it impossible to see more than a couple of feet, and it cloaked their movements. The mercenaries moved cautiously around the near side of the inn. Two of them caught fire as vestiges of photophor ignited under the rain, and they hopped around, cursing and beating at the flames.

Kevlin didn't slow until they slipped through the first screen of trees and crouched down behind some thick brush. The darkness enveloped them, blocking out all light. When Ceren shook her arm free of his grasp, he feared she would race back to the inn and get herself killed, but she only huddled next to him, crying.

With the immediate danger gone, the shock of what had just happened crashed in on him too. His stomach lurched and the bitter taste of failure clung like vomit to his mouth.

He really hated that feeling.

Terach was dead. Despite the captain's willingness to sacrifice himself to enable their escape, his death had been anything but noble. Dhanjal had struck him down from behind like a coward. After all his high-sounding words, Dhanjal had proven himself nothing but a murderer.

Kevlin had seen too many comrades die too young. He focused on anger at Dhanjal to cover the insidious sense of guilt that threatened to distract him. It wasn't easy. This wasn't the first time he had failed in a big way, but this time the consequences might prove irreversible.

Antigonus was dead. If Rhea hadn't already finished him, the shadeleech would have consumed his soul by now.

That thought was nothing short of depressing. The old man had depended on them, and they'd left him to die. Had they tried to get to Antigonus, they'd have died too, but that stark reality did little to help.

Kevlin tipped his head back, letting the downpour course down his face. The water washed away the muddy photophor powder and left his skin clean, but did nothing to ease the heavy thoughts clinging to his mind.

The enemy had Oris. The memory of that rune-covered bag around Antigonus' neck burned in his mind. Now a shadeleech had it.

About all he knew about magic was to avoid it. He didn't even know exactly what Oris was. The powerful talisman and its bearer were key to the empire's defenses against the Sigrun. That defense was now gone. What would prevent the enemy from sweeping across the empire with their armies, destroying the Six Kingdoms?

Not good.

Kevlin scratched the three-day stubble on his chin as he considered the mess they were in. He'd known it was a mistake to get involved with sentinels, but somehow here he was. He'd sworn an oath to see Antigonus to safety, but he'd failed.

Moping over the situation wouldn't help, so Kevlin leaned closer to Ceren and asked, "Are you injured?"

She didn't answer for a minute, but finally murmured between sobs, "He's dead."

Kevlin wrapped an awkward arm around her shoulders. At first she remained rigid in the crook of his arm, but after a moment she fell against him and buried her head in his shoulder and sobbed like her heart had broken.

It probably had.

It was obvious she'd cared for Terach, and took her responsibilities as one of Antigonus' companions very seriously. Kevlin was on intimate terms with both the thrills of victory and the bitter misery of failure, so he could cope.

He doubted she'd ever faced life-and-death situations like this before. The first time was always rough. He said nothing but silently held her as they knelt together in the mud and the rain, surrounded by impenetrable darkness.

14

SOME BAD NEWS

Sitara paused in the concealing darkness and listened. She pressed her hand lightly against the wooden panel of a secret door blocking her way and carefully probed the room beyond with her mind.

Empty.

A gentle push on a hidden latch swung the door open. Sitara slipped from the narrow passageway into Emperor Tegnazian's lavishly decorated bedroom.

The door swung shut behind her with a soft click while she surveyed the room with her natural eyes. She struggled to calm her nerves and slow her breathing. She had ventured through the secret passage several times before, but only once without knowing in advance who she would be eavesdropping on. That venture had nearly ended in disaster.

On that occasion, Bajaran had seemed very agitated when he asked her to take the risk of listening in on the council chamber in the emperor's inner tower. Despite not knowing who would be in the room, he had urged her to come, with one warning.

"Sitara, use extreme caution. If Harafin is there, get out. Get out immediately."

His desperate need had given her the courage to go. She had done it for him, and she smiled at the memory. She had been strong, for him.

It'd been the least she could do. He had given her so much, taught her so much. He'd opened her eyes to a vision of what the world could be, of the peace all would enjoy when the pair of them ruled together.

For the revolution to succeed, she risked her life to gather critical information. Should she ever be discovered, she would hang.

Death was the punishment for treason. Bajaran had warned her they would call it treason to eavesdrop on the words of the emperor as he sat in secret council. They were wrong. His throne was a sham, an appointment made by a king who sought only the greatest political advantage for himself. Such power belonged to those better suited to rule.

The revolution would sweep the corrupt, complacent fools from power. When Bajaran took his place at the head of government, with her by his side, the people would know true leadership. What she did wasn't treason but the truest form of patriotism.

To think, at eighteen, she would soon rule the empire. The thought gave her confidence and helped focus her thoughts on the dangerous task at hand.

After listening for another long moment, she crept forward through the silence. She crossed the huge bedroom with no more than a passing glance at its opulent furnishings.

Like a flickering shadow, she slipped out of the bedroom and down a short hallway. After another pause to listen, she crept into the private dining room and hurried across. This was the most dangerous part, the most likely place to encounter someone. As usual, she held her breath until she reached the small closet cleverly concealed under a polished wooden staircase that spiraled up into the emperor's tower.

The closet was the key. She slid a barrel and a stack of linen out of the way and crawled into the tiny space behind them. A panel of wood slid aside under her fingers, revealing a small opening just wide enough for her to squeeze through. Anyone not possessing her petite frame would find it far too narrow.

Sitara paused in the cramped space that smelled of dust and stale air and cast a thought, ever so gently, up to the next level. She'd practiced the maneuver with Bajaran until she could float a wisp-thin thought past his shielded mind without alerting him to her presence.

Her heart pounded in her chest as she struggled to keep her breathing calm. It had seemed so easy in the comfort of the bedchamber where they used to meet. Crouched in the darkness, not knowing who might be waiting for her above taxed her limits. She bit her trembling lip and used the resulting sharp pain to focus.

In her mind's eye, the walls and furniture of the council room, situated one level up, looked ethereal. She didn't dare expend the extra power necessary to draw them into sharper detail, for any other gifted mind in close vicinity would surely sense her presence.

The council room stood empty, meaning the emperor would be meeting at the very top of the tower, in his private study.

Why can't it ever be easy?

The winding stair circled the tower all the way to the top floor. Doors opened into each level so staff could move up and down the tower without disturbing the emperor or eavesdropping on him. It also provided the unseen passage for Sitara's secret infiltrations.

Sitara opened her soul to her gift, allowing only a tiny spark of power to seep into her torso. She directed that power into her hands and feet, and concentrated on what she wanted.

Her hands tingled and glowed softly green. Sitara hated the sickly color, but it was the only light she dared allow as she carefully ascended the underside of the staircase. Her hands and feet, coated with a thin, sticky substance Bajaran had taught her to conjure, easily gripped the rough wood.

After three steps, Sitara pushed through her first cobweb and barely stifled a shriek. She cursed herself for being a fool, even as she fought to calm her racing heart.

I hate spiders.

If only she could send fire boiling up through the recesses of the stairwell and cleanse it from those disgusting creatures. Of course, that would guarantee discovery, but every time she crept into that dark world the tempting thought arose.

Instead, after another mental sweep of the area, Sitara concentrated, hardening the air around her body and forming it into a tiny layer of armor to repel spiders. That saved her from feeling them creep along her skin, but she'd found one in her hair after her last mission and nearly screamed.

Sitara resumed climbing and quenched her gift after sealing the armored air around herself. It would last for twenty minutes and, unless a sentinel was actively searching for her, no one would sense the miniscule amount of power she consumed.

Three minutes later, Sitara pulled herself up to the top level and slipped her slender frame under an enclosed reading bench. She then focused on the mind-clearing exercise Bajaran had taught her. She couldn't shield, for any sentinels with the emperor would sense her shields the next time they swept the room.

Instead, Sitara calmed her mind and body and drew around herself layer after layer of mental illusion. She filled herself with dark, musty air, dust, and even a wooden support beam. Any sentinel's thoughts would be gently diverted around her, seeing her as nothing but empty space.

As long as she did nothing to alert them to her presence, she would remain virtually invisible. Of course, once alerted, an active search would peel away the layers of illusion in seconds.

Sitara listened.

A moment later, voices sounded from the emperor's study. At first, they were muted and difficult to make out. This was as far as she had penetrated the last time she ventured here without knowing who the emperor was meeting with.

That time, just as she had crouched to listen, the emperor had spoken, "Harafin, my old friend. Thank you for coming."

Harafin. That name had plunged an icy dagger of fear into her heart. He was one of the most powerful sentinels alive. He would undoubtedly have discovered her and unleashed terrible vengeance had she remained hidden.

A master sentinel, Harafin was lauded as one of the greatest defenders of the empire and its people, but she knew the lies behind the façade of his nobility. He used his power to guarantee the emperor and other corrupt leaders remained in power. He would never allow peace with their Grakonian neighbors to the west, for war and aggression kept the masses distracted from the real evils that governed them.

Harafin would have to die, as would everyone else who stood in the way of progress. That had been a difficult truth for her to accept, but Bajaran had been patient in explaining it. Over time, she had come to see the necessity of cleansing the empire of these enemies of peace.

But the time was not yet, and instead she had fled for her life, keeping her mind void of all thought so as to not draw his attention. She had returned to Bajaran so shaken that he'd put her into a deep sleep, calming her so she wouldn't make a mistake and give them away.

Now Bajaran was gone. He had left several weeks ago to strike the first blow for the revolution. He hadn't told her any specifics, only that she would know when it was done. Everyone in the empire would know. From the deep forests of Hallvarr to the wide plains of Einarr, the news of his deeds would shake the empire.

Today she'd heard rumors of disaster, of some dire threat to the empire. It had to be him. She was so proud of him.

He embodied everything she considered a great man to be. He was handsome and noble, and sometimes when he looked at her, her devotion to him burned so hot, it threatened to melt her soul. Powerfully gifted, he dedicated his life to bringing much-needed change to the world.

So she took the risk to find out for herself, to find out before anyone else save the emperor. It was the best way to share his victory, since he could not return until the revolution destroyed the emperor. Then Bajaran would come in power and glory, and all would bow before him. He could finally declare publicly their love, the love they had kept secret for so long.

"Sentinel Felix, thank you for coming so quickly." Emperor Tegnazian's voice reached her clearly.

Sitara cringed and began to withdraw, her heart pounding so loud she worried they would hear. But she paused, her need to know about Bajaran struggling against her fear. Curiosity finally won out.

"Any news of Antigonus?"

She nearly jumped in shock, for the emperor's voice sounded from directly above. He must have sat on the very bench underneath which she crouched. Sitara pressed herself to the floor, willing herself to complete silence.

"In his last report, Harafin said they were headed to Ingolf."

"We should inform King Leszek and mobilize the legions, Your Excellency," spoke someone with a deep voice she didn't recognize.

"No, Ankur," the emperor said. "We don't know yet what has happened, and without clear information rumors will spread. We could create a panic if we're not careful."

Field Marshall Ankur? What else but Bajaran's revolution could draw the supreme commander of the empire's legions at this hour of the night?

"If we react too late?" Ankur pressed.

"What is the worst-case scenario?" the emperor asked.

"Antigonus has indeed been attacked, or even killed," said Sentinel Felix.

"And Oris stolen," added Ankur gravely.

"The very possibility makes me shudder." Emperor Tegnazian said it so softly that, had she not been lying at his feet, she never would have heard.

"You must consider it," Ankur said. "If it should come to pass, our mightiest weapon might fall into the hands of the enemy."

"And doom would lie at the door," Sentinel Felix added.

Oris? So that was Bajaran's mighty blow. Sitara had never imagined anything so bold, but immediately understood the audacity of it. She could think of no greater victory for the revolution than acquiring the powerful weapon.

Its very name made her shiver. A talisman of unmatched magical power, it had been the centerpiece of the empire's defenses for over two hundred years. Wielded by exceptionally gifted sentinels, it United the Six, which was a force never defeated. Their power had broken every attack by enemies of the empire, and protected its people from being overrun.

Or so the story was told. Sitara knew better.

Oris was used neither for good nor for defense, and always it brought death and destruction to the nations neighboring the empire. And Bajaran had stolen it! The boldness of his action overwhelmed her, and she very nearly forgot where she lay. The emperor's voice startled her back to awareness.

"That will never happen," he said forcefully. "Harafin himself is accompanying Gabral's force, which we dispatched to investigate Antigonus' alarming message."

"Very true," Felix said. "I myself offered to help, but Harafin insisted he go."

"If anyone can find out what happened and prevent Oris from being lost, it's Harafin," the emperor agreed.

A stab of fear once more chilled her: fear for Bajaran. He was in terrible danger if Harafin hunted him.

Run Bajaran! she thought fervently. *Be swift, my love.*

The men continued talking about strategies and eventualities, but she had heard enough. She scampered back down the staircase to the hidden closet, replacing everything as it had been. Every second she spent close to that sentinel increased the chances that she would be discovered.

She paused, struck by the magnitude of Bajaran's actions. They were no longer talking of revolution in the comfortable darkness of the bedchamber where they met. It was no longer merely a distant eventuality that thrilled her with the promise of romance and adventure.

With his action, Bajaran had risen in open rebellion against the empire. He had crossed a line of no return. He must either achieve victory, or die.

She would share his fate.

Feeling chilled and a little sick, she left the closet, crossed the parlor, and stepped into the hallway leading to the bedroom and the secret door.

Someone stood in the hall directly in front of her.

15

THE CLEANSING POWER OF DARKNESS

Sitara yelped, and an old woman, dressed in the colors of the emperor's personal staff, stumbled back with a cry of surprise. Terror flooded through Sitara. Discovery meant death.

She again reached for her gift of magic. Normally it came instantly, like a sunburst in her heart. This time it came slowly, reluctantly, a disturbing trend that had started in recent weeks.

Sitara drank in the power and lashed out with an invisible blow. She struck the old woman's head, dropping her like a stone to the carpeted floor.

She crouched over the woman and listened. Silence. Apparently no one had heard her small cry.

As she surveyed the unconscious form, her power bled away. She tried to hold onto it, but it slipped from her grasp like water. How was it possible? Her commitment to the cause had only grown, as had her skill at deceiving her employer and in ferreting out the many secrets Bajaran needed. Why then would her powers desert her when she needed them most?

Terrified to think she might be losing her gift, she had shared the disturbing trend with Bajaran shortly before he departed. He had explained how the sentinels had corrupted magic, making it increasingly difficult for the patriots of the revolution to access their power. Then he had taught her a different way.

As Sitara leaned over the old woman, she knew what she must do, and reached for that other source of power. It crawled into her eagerly, despite her reluctance.

The first time she had tried it, it had left her feeling tainted. Bajaran had assured her it was natural, that she was being cleansed of the sentinels' corruption. Usually the truth of his teachings was obvious, but that time she'd hesitated and not ventured to use the alternate power again.

As she embraced it now, driven by desperate need, she cringed and wanted to pull away. Bajaran had described it as the strength of the night, but that explanation didn't seem right. She often walked alone at night and enjoyed the clean, fresh darkness. This new power dirtied her as it seeped into her soul. She gritted her teeth against her own sense of revulsion and drew it in until it filled her with sickening strength.

She wanted to vomit.

Instead, she gazed at the woman with magic-enhanced vision. Now she could see the woman's life force encircling her like a dimly glowing light. Sitara took a deep breath, grabbed that glow of life, and began leeching it away.

The spell wasn't difficult, but she struggled with it. The only other time she had practiced it, the same night Bajaran had first taught her, she'd used a stray cat as the subject. She had held the spell for only a short time, but that had been long enough.

The experience of stealing even part of another being's life repulsed her at some fundamental level. She had hidden her revulsion from Bajaran, ashamed at her weakness, but unable to change the way she felt. Still, he had sensed her discomfort.

"It is the nature of life," he explained as he held her in a long, comforting embrace. "This animal is fulfilling the purpose of its creation by surrendering its strength to us so we can use it in our struggle to make the world a better place."

Although Sitara had strengthened her resolve to accept that deeper truth, it hadn't worked yet. In this moment, she could afford no doubts.

Standing over the old woman's unconscious body, she stripped away all doubt, all thought, until nothing remained but the churning corruption of magic. The glowing aura of life slowly dimmed around the woman as her life bled away, reluctantly feeding Sitara's soul. It was more difficult than she remembered with the cat, and she had to concentrate to keep the spell from slipping out of her control.

In sharp contrast with the lurking darkness Sitara used to steal it, the pure essence of the woman's life force filled her with clean vitality. She could sense qualities possessed by her victim even as she leeched the life from her.

Honesty and loyalty were clearly evident, for the old woman was innocent of any evil. The pure goodness of it was so welcome and refreshing that Sitara absorbed it greedily, making it part of herself.

She wanted to shout for joy.

She wanted to scream in horror.

It felt as though two distinct beings vied to possess her. One was pure and clean and glowing with strength; the other dark and menacing, slowly corrupting and consuming the first. In the very act of embracing the purity of the old woman's life, she destroyed it.

From the dark recesses of her being rose a part of her that reveled in the glory of the moment. It was a piece of her normally sealed and hidden. She could convince herself most of the time that it didn't really exist.

Not now. It rose up and forced her to recognize it. Although she wanted to cringe away, it held sway, willing to do what must be done.

Reverently Sitara placed a hand over the old woman's chest and drove her power through the body like extensions of her fingers. Within those fingers of power, the old woman's heart pumped valiantly despite her age and frailty.

Sitara hesitated for several counts of the woman's heartbeat. She had never killed before.

With darkness filling her soul, she saw with a clarity she had never before possessed that it had only been a matter of time. She reflected in amazement at how long she had dreamed of ascending to power at Bajaran's side, of ruling the empire and seeing all those she had served kneeling before her. Only she had never accepted that she would have to kill to achieve that goal.

Staring at the nameless old woman, who would die for no greater fault than running into her, Sitara wanted to laugh at her own naiveté, and to weep at its loss.

Faced with the need to kill, she found herself desperately seeking another way. The old woman's face looked peaceful, and her heartbeat vibrated against the power Sitara held around it. *Thump-thump. . .thump-thump.* Sitara fought against the darkness directing her actions, and began to ease her hold.

Bajaran will die if she lives and I am captured.

The thought flashed through her mind, returning her to clarity and firming her resolve.

"Your sacrifice will bring you everlasting reward," she whispered, gently stroking the old woman's hair. Something deep inside her turned cold and dark.

She squeezed.

The heart beat futilely against the force of her power. Once, twice, a third time.

Then it stopped.

Tears streamed down Sitara's cheeks. Filled with her victim's life force, she slowly rose to stand over the dead woman. Exultant joy surged through her, and the dark corner of her soul that held sway made her want to throw her head back and shout out her victory. She reveled in the sheer *power* of the moment, and finally understood what Bajaran had been trying to teach her. She had been a fool to have doubted him. This was true power, and she deserved it.

Then shame, held temporarily at bay, seared her conscience and mocked her strength. Through the eyes of the darkness that ruled her, it seemed a childish response, one she needed to outgrow.

She no longer needed that darkness, however, for the deed was done. Sitara suddenly felt an overwhelming need to hide that sinister part of herself. With a great effort she drove it back into the chill corner of her mind where it normally lurked. It went reluctantly, and she wasted a long moment regaining her composure. She would never again be able to pretend that part of her being didn't exist.

Revulsion rose up within her and threatened to make her physically ill. Her head spun, and she felt like ripping at her hair and screaming in impotent rage at the woman who lay dead at her feet.

Bajaran, she cried within the depths of her mind, *what have you forced me into?*

Then another mind touched hers, just a feather-light caress for a fraction of a second. Sitara tensed, senses alert. Bajaran had reached out to her that way many times.

It was not Bajaran.

She waited, poised to strike. She wouldn't let herself be taken alive. There could be no mercy for her. She had joined Bajaran in the revolution. This murder had sealed her fate to his.

He would be proud of her.

After an anxious moment in which nothing happened, Sitara fled through the bedroom and the secret door, not pausing until she exited the other end of the passageway. She couldn't explain how she had escaped detection. Whoever had touched her mind must have sensed her power.

Why had they not attacked? Who else had been in the emperor's apartment? Had they also been eavesdropping on the conversation? Had they recognized her?

She had no answers, and that terrified her. She took a deep breath and forced her fear down. She couldn't surrender to it. She lived in constant danger of discovery and couldn't allow herself the luxury of wallowing in such fears. So she buried the questions until they could be addressed later.

Sitara continued through the bedroom. It was empty, as expected, so she returned to her own small room at the foot of a narrow stair and locked the door. Slumping against it, she let her tension seep away.

As she glanced across the room, she noticed her reflection in the mirror suspended above her desk. Tears had streaked the smooth skin of her face, and her shoulder-length hair hung in terrible disarray. Most alarmingly, her eyes, normally the same light brown as her hair, glittered like obsidian.

It took a long moment of concentration to dispel the dark power that clung to her. It left slowly, reluctant to relinquish its hold. Finally she scraped it off and her eyes again looked normal, although haunted by the horror of what she had done.

Shuddering, she was nearly overpowered by the sudden urge to strip off all her clothes and scrub herself clean. It would do no good. No amount of water could remove the filth that lurked in her soul.

She staggered to the bed and fell onto it, clutching her head and fighting to suppress the sobs that threatened to burst forth. She shook uncontrollably. If she succumbed to the shame of what she had done, she would be a wreck for hours.

Too much time had passed already. She would soon be missed. She forced herself to rise and make herself presentable. She straightened her dress, brushed her hair, and splashed some scented water on her face. More importantly, she locked the fearful memories away. They could only be allowed to surface again when she had time to deal with them safely.

She was a sentinel, after all. She had to be strong.

Satisfied with her new appearance, Sitara put on a bright smile and left the room. She climbed to the uppermost floor of the Keisara's Tower, the twin of the tower she had just escaped. The ladies were still talking over their evening repast while admiring the twilight glowing on the western horizon.

Sitara loved the comfortably appointed sitting room where the keisara invited close friends, particularly the eight windows that circled the tower, providing unbroken vistas in every direction.

"Oh, Sitara, perfect timing as usual," said her mistress. "I was just telling Lady Elva about your amazing massages. She has a terrible knot in her back no one has been able to relieve. I told her you'd be happy to work on it."

"Of course, my lady," Sitara said, moving around to Lady Elva's chair.

As usual, her voice set everyone at ease. Although not magical, it was one of her greatest gifts. She had never met anyone she couldn't charm with her voice. Its exceptional sweetness, coupled with her youth, disguised her with a cloak of innocence few ever penetrated.

Tonight she was doubly grateful for its effect, as it shielded her from close scrutiny. These ladies would be stunned when she revealed her true self on the day she began her rule.

That daydream, one of her favorites, was now tinged with darkness. She dropped her gaze to the thick carpet to avoid looking any of them in the eye as she began working on the muscles of Lady Elva's back.

Before she assumed the throne, she would have to kill these women.

Sitara glanced across the room toward her mistress, the emperor's wife, the empress-consort Fideima Tamar Tegnazian. Never one to accept the status quo, Fideima had assumed the far more grandiose title of keisara, despite lacking the full authority of the station. Even though the title had never been officially ratified, no one openly challenged her, and Sitara doubted anyone would until the emperor's death.

By then, it would not matter. Bajaran had struck, so Sitara must begin her own careful assault in the very heart of the empire.

The keisara must be the first to fall.

16

A Crazy Choice

Several minutes passed in the cold rain as Kevlin held Ceren while she wept. She started shivering in his arms, but he lacked anything else with which to shelter her, and they dared not move.

He frowned at nothing in particular. The best way to get over a major setback was to move on to something else, but they were stuck, immobile for now. That made it the perfect time to wallow in depressing memories.

He'd gotten good at avoiding thinking about past failures in the last couple years. He'd buried them deep, but in the chill, rainy darkness, his new failure unearthed them like reeking, rotted corpses. Again he recalled kneeling, bound, while the woman he loved prepared to butcher him like a pig. His entire life had crashed down around him as he learned how he'd set up an entire kingdom for destruction.

Until today he would have sworn nothing could topple that day from the number one worst day of his life. At least back then, Donarr had not actually fallen and he'd escaped alive, if destitute and hunted.

He preferred to focus on the positive.

A door banged nearby and he eagerly focused on it. Finally, something to do besides whining.

Slipping his arm from Ceren's shoulder, he whispered, "Wait here."

He pushed through the brush to the edge of the forest. The inn loomed ahead, a huge, dark shadow. At least the photophor hadn't torched the structure.

As he watched, several mercenaries exited, two of them carrying lanterns, while two others bore between them a large bundle wrapped in heavy canvas. Three more carried shovels. Dhanjal followed.

The Blade Stalwart walked with his normal, confident stride. Ignoring the rain, he directed his men toward the trees close to where Kevlin crouched.

He doubted they had any idea he was hidden there, and stayed to watch. The brush beside him rustled and he pulled Ceren down beside him.

"Quiet, or they'll hear," he whispered.

"What is it?"

"I don't know yet."

The group of mercenaries stopped nearby, and those with shovels began to dig. It took only a few minutes to excavate a hole three feet deep in the soft loam. Two of the men then dumped the canvas-wrapped bundle into the hole.

Dhanjal stood at the edge of the pit and spoke in a solemn tone. "Son of Salawin, you were not chosen by Savas, but you were a worthy adversary. Return to your god with honor."

Beside Kevlin, Ceren gasped. He put a hand on her shoulder to remind her to be quiet.

"It's Terach," she whispered.

"Aye. Dhanjal promised to bury him."

A murderer who kept his word. The man had to review his priorities.

The mercenaries filled the hole and headed back toward the inn. When Dhanjal turned away, Kevlin glimpsed for the first time a sword strapped to the Blade Stalwart's back.

Terach's Pala.

The Blade Stalwart had failed to steal Terach's essence, so he'd stolen his heritage. He'd never be able to use the sword effectively. It required too much finesse. Kevlin wondered if Dhanjal had a room in his home where he kept all of his murder souvenirs.

"I'm going to have to kill that man," he said softly.

"Good." Ceren's voice was harsh, if soft. He hadn't thought anyone could hear.

A door banged from the far side of the inn, and a couple of shouts rang out in the darkness. "Come on," Kevlin said. "I think they're leaving."

They skirted the woods to reach the back of the barn. From there, they found a good view of the north wall of the inn, illuminated by a single torch in a covered bracket. Cloaked makrasha were marching north on the highway past the inn.

The small pool of light cast by the torch shone on each pair for a second before they passed into darkness. After a score of the giant beasts passed, a pair of mercenaries bearing lanterns appeared. Rhea came next, then two more men carrying a stretcher covered by a length of canvas.

"Is that Antigonus?" Ceren asked.

"I can't tell. We need to get closer."

They sidled along the wall of the barn, mere shadows moving in the darkness. The stretcher-bearers passed beyond the small pool of light and Kevlin took a chance, running forward to the wall of the inn with Ceren close on his heels.

They arrived just as the shadeleech strode past, and both cringed back out of sight. Kevlin's heart pounded and he welcomed the surge of strength. When he risked another look, the shadeleech was already gone. It was even more terrifying not knowing his location.

Two more makrasha passed next, bearing a second stretcher covered in canvas. A gust of wind caught the front edge of the canvas, giving them a glimpse of what lay beneath.

Antigonus.

As pale as death, the old sentinel twitched as rain slashed at his face. His eyes remained closed, but Kevlin's heart sang with renewed hope.

Apparently the legends about how tough the old sentinel was contained some truth. Kevlin was as surprised as he was pleased to realize Antigonus still breathed.

Beside him, Ceren clutched his arm tight in restrained glee, her emerald eyes shining with hope. He covered her hand with his as he continued to watch the road.

Dhanjal passed through the pool of light next.

Kevlin leaned against the wall of the inn. He had memorized Dhanjal's features and didn't need to look at the man again until he was ready to kill him. Pressed against the rough timber, he heard the smashing of glass inside. Puzzled, he glanced around the corner again, just as a handful of mercenaries jogged past, laughing.

Kevlin and Ceren waited half a minute, but no one else passed. Just as Kevlin was preparing to head onto the road, Ceren grabbed his arm.

"Look!"

Flickering yellow light shone from the windows of the common room. The inn was burning.

"Come on."

Kevlin drew his sword and pushed through the door to the common room to find an inferno raging inside. Most of the tables and chairs had been piled in the center of the room and set alight. The fire had spread rapidly, fueled by the polished wood paneling. A wave of heat forced Kevlin back outside.

He ran to the back door, with Ceren close behind, and stepped inside. The heat was intense and smoke billowed around them, but the fire hadn't yet spread across the inn.

"There are people upstairs," Ceren cried.

"Fire!" Kevlin bellowed at the top of his lungs. "Get out of the building!"

There were no sounds of running feet, no screams. The crackling flames seemed to mock him.

Kevlin had Ceren wait a moment while he retrieved his stiletto from a body in the doorway to the burning common room. They then jogged down the hallway, opening doors and looking for another staircase.

When they reached the study, Ceren said, "See if you can salvage any of our gear. I'll try to find a stair."

"Hurry."

She stifled a cough and moved further along the hallway while Kevlin entered the study, bending double to stay beneath the heavy smoke. As soon as he found the packs Ceren had been carrying earlier, he tossed them through the window and jumped out.

Ceren met him outside a minute later. In the ruddy light of the blaze, she wept openly. "They're all dead."

Kevlin pulled her away from the burning building. The senseless slaughter was a sign of unprofessionalism, and that stoked his anger higher.

He looked from the burning inn to the darkness of the road where the enemy had disappeared. He and Ceren were in a worse mess than any he had ever seen. The enemy might not have killed Antigonus yet, but that was probably just because they wanted to take the time to enjoy the process.

The enemy had captured Oris. Would they launch an invasion before the snows or wait till spring? Either way, the empire could not hope to stop them.

Part of him wanted to turn and run the other way, but he had been running for years and it hadn't helped. He was tired of living only with the consequences of failure. If he left now, he'd never regain his honor.

And millions of people would die. He'd bear some of the responsibility.

The flames roared like a living thing as they consumed the inn. The still-falling rain reflected the light, glittering like amber diamonds before hissing onto the flames. In any other situation, it would have been beautiful.

"Kevlin, help me," Ceren cried as she tugged at the heavy barn doors. "Antigonus is still alive. We have to help him."

So much for agonizing over the decision of what to do next.

Kevlin muttered, "I hate you."

"What?"

"Nothing."

By the Lady's endless wrath, he was an idiot. Was he really contemplating going after the shadeleech? If they didn't die before dawn, the shadeleech would probably rip out their souls or inflict some other unmentionable torture on them.

He might be a fool, but he couldn't fool himself. He was going after Antigonus. He'd complain about it and rail against the chains of fate, but he'd go. And as much as he hated to admit it, he welcomed the feeling of having purpose again, of being part of something greater than himself.

His time as a mercenary should have taught him to be less sentimental.

Together they pulled open the barn doors. Inside, the ostlers were dead and all the animals slaughtered in their stalls. The fire hadn't yet spread there, so they took a minute to take stock of their supplies: Ceren's healing case, some clothing, blankets, and a few provisions.

While Kevlin searched the barn for anything useful, Ceren changed out of her wet clothes in one of the empty stalls. He found a few apples in a bin, a well-shielded lantern, and a couple of rain slickers. He too changed into dry clothes, then they donned the slickers and took up their packs. He lit the lantern and led the way back into rain, now slackened to a steady drizzle.

They had only spent a few minutes in the barn, but clouds of smoke billowed from its wet thatch roof. A moment later, it burst into flame.

Back on the highway, the half-shuttered lantern gave off enough light to track the war party north, so they followed the muddy footprints.

After a few minutes, Kevlin asked the question that bothered him most. "Ceren, how can a shadeleech be in Hallvarr?"

"I don't know. I don't know what's going on." Tears shone in her eyes. She was clearly struggling to stay in control.

"You work with information. Could a war have started we don't know about?"

"No, but it looks like one's about to."

"What do you make of it? First Bajaran and Rhea, then Dhanjal and the mercenaries, and now a shadeleech and makrasha. All here, all now. All united to kill Antigonus."

"But they didn't kill him."

"Why not?" He decided it was a bad time to mention his theory about torture.

"I don't know." They walked in silence for a few minutes.

"It can't be a coincidence," Ceren said finally. "I can't imagine how they smuggled a shadeleech across the empire with a band of makrasha."

"Why take such a risk?"

"Oris." Meeting his eye, she said with conviction, "It has to be. Antigonus said Bajaran planned to deliver it to the Sigrun."

"Rhea was trying to get it for her master."

"So maybe the shadeleech came to make sure the Sigrun got it."

"Maybe." Kevlin thought about that, but something still didn't fit.

They walked on in silence for another twenty minutes but came up with no new ideas. Antigonus was in terrible shape, had already admitted he'd die within days, so maybe the shadeleech was holding him prisoner, a bonus prize for his masters to kill?

"We can't beat them," Ceren said at last in a small voice.

"No, we can't. But we can find out where they're going. They can't move around much during the day. There aren't a lot of people, but there are enough. Stealth is their only defense against discovery."

"Or murder," Ceren said with a shudder, glancing back toward the inn, still visible as a glowing beacon in the darkness.

"Aye, but they can't kill everyone. They have to hide, at least until they start for the border."

Ceren nodded. "If we can find where they're hiding, we can figure out what to do next."

"Let's hope we have enough time."

It wasn't much of a plan, but it was a start. Even if they discovered where the enemy hid, he wasn't sure of the next step. The enemy was very well organized. They had managed to ship a shadeleech with his makrasha across the empire in time to coordinate an attack against Antigonus. They must have also planned how to escape.

How could he and Ceren hope to stop them? Even if they did convince the local authorities, the sparsely populated land lacked a host of trained warriors and sentinels sufficient to confront the invaders. It would take far too long to call for reinforcements from Tamera or Diodor. Il'Aicharen, the Myrrdin enclave, could send sentinels, but it lay far to the northeast.

Kevlin trudged along, chewing on the problem out of pure obstinacy. Any force that engaged an enemy of superior strength without a plan lost. Actually even with a plan, chances of losing were pretty high.

Ceren was supposed to be Cunning, but she was walking right along with him. That helped him feel a little less like an idiot.

They continued in silence for mile after weary mile. The rain subsided into sporadic showers, and finally stopped altogether. Just as dawn began to lighten the eastern horizon, the tracks turned east and disappeared into the forest.

That didn't make sense. The Tamerlane Sea lay a couple of days' ride to the west. That was the most likely escape route, so why go east?

All they could do was follow. In the gray light of early morning, they pushed into the trees. Kevlin glanced back once, but the highway was already lost to view. Hopefully they would emerge from that wilderness again, and not fall in the trackless expanse that lay ahead.

17

THE IMPORTANCE OF GOOD SHOES

The tracks led northeast through the heavy, sodden forest. Kevlin extinguished the lantern and they moved warily. After leaving the highway, the enemy would probably camp and post sentries.

The enemy did not stop.

The sun finally appeared by mid-morning. They paused at the top of a low hill only sparsely covered with trees. To the east, a high bluff reared up a thousand feet or more above the forest in a sheer cliff. The escarpment, perhaps twenty miles east, ran north as far as they could see, its shadow stretched long across the forest, as if trying to block the coming of the sun.

"I don't know where they're going, but they can't get past that," Kevlin said.

Half an hour later, the tracks emptied onto a game trail that ran straight east toward the bluff.

"It doesn't make sense," Ceren said. "They need to make a run for the border. Why waste time in the forest?"

Kevlin shrugged and kept walking. They followed the trail all morning, and he grew jumpier with every mile. The stress of watching for an ambush wore on him, magnified by lack of sleep and the constant burning of his injuries.

The day again turned overcast and grim, accompanied by a constant chill wind. The forest grew thicker on both sides of the trail, and raindrops regularly splashed down onto them from the overhanging leaves.

At least wet leaves were quiet, and pretty soft. Still, his feet began to ache. He'd have blisters soon.

Just what I need, one more problem.

They paused around noon near a bubbling stream and ate some of their meager provisions. As Kevlin rummaged through his small, tear-shaped burglar pack, he discovered Bajaran's silver dagger. He had forgotten about it, and studied it while they ate. Ceren didn't seem to notice the weapon, but sat staring up into the cloudy sky.

The blade looked silver. When he tested the edge on a piece of wood as thick around as his wrist, it sliced clean through in one stroke. Definitely infested with magic, but of a kind he could appreciate. The eye-twisting silver runes on the scabbard gave him a headache. Since he hadn't retrieved the dagger that usually hung at the base of his neck, he secured the new one in its place.

The forest to the east grew thick over the trail. The path was tight, and rarely could they see more than a dozen yards ahead. Fear of an ambush kept Kevlin on edge.

The bluff loomed ahead, and he reckoned they'd reach the foot of it by nightfall if the trail didn't change direction. It started to rain again at dusk, and within half an hour it poured down. With great difficulty, Kevlin lit the lantern and opened the shutter just wide enough to show the way.

"Do you think we should stop?" Ceren asked as darkness became complete, the first words she'd spoken in hours. Her voice sounded thin and tired.

"Not yet." Kevlin yearned for sleep, but he didn't want to risk losing the trail. The rain would wash away even the makrasha's heavy tracks. "I doubt they can see any better in this mess than we can, so I want to find where they camp tonight."

"What if they don't stop?"

"I don't know." He hoped they would. He was exhausted and already felt at least one blister on each foot. Neither he nor Ceren were going to make it much farther, but they couldn't stop yet.

"Where are they going?" Ceren asked.

"I have no idea."

This appeared to be an untracked piece of wilderness, but the trail still ran east, straight for the towering bluff. The enemy should be running for the sea.

With the degree of sophisticated planning they'd demonstrated, it would have been a simple matter to have a ship standing ready to pick them up in a quiet cove. They could then set sail for the western shores closest to Grakonia.

Kevlin and Ceren trudged on, fighting to stay alert and stave off their growing exhaustion. Two hours later, Kevlin was on the verge of calling a halt when the trail suddenly widened.

Ceren stepped up beside him and they stared vainly into the darkness. They crept forward and, within a hundred yards, the trail widened further to become a narrow road.

"Wherever they're going, I think we're nearly there," Ceren murmured.

Kevlin nodded and shuttered the lantern to allow only a single, tiny beam of light to fall at their feet. They pushed on silently over the muddy road, with rain cascading down around them.

A quarter of a mile farther, the road turned left, and after fifty paces they felt rather than saw the trees falling away to either side. They seemed to have reached a clearing, although its size remained a mystery. Kevlin reckoned it must lie very close to the base of the cliff. He blew out the lantern and they crouched together, striving to hear anything over the constant drumming of the rain.

Nothing.

They ate a little food and waited.

Still nothing.

"Come on," Kevlin said, pulling Ceren to her feet. "Let's go a little farther."

"Should we light the lantern to see the tracks?"

"No."

"We could lose them, or the rain could wash them away."

"I know, but I have a feeling they're close."

"How do you know?"

"Just a feeling."

He didn't mention that it was a feeling of growing dread, of certainty that they were approaching deadly evil.

"If I'm wrong, we'll return here and use the lantern," he added.

They walked out into the clearing, trying their best to hold a straight line in the darkness. The open space was level but dotted with tree stumps, and it was huge. After walking at least a quarter mile, they heard a low *boom*.

Ceren held to his arm and they stopped to listen. Leaning close, Ceren whispered, "That sounded like a gate closing."

"Let's keep going, but be careful." He led the way forward, cautiously feeling each step, and arranged his slicker to better reach his sword.

The rain slackened as they crossed another hundred yards or so, then both stopped together. The flickering light of a torch had appeared high above the ground, perhaps two hundred yards ahead. It moved slowly left to right for about fifty feet before disappearing.

"They're up on a wall," Ceren said. "Carrying a torch along the top of a wall."

He had been hoping for some good news for a change. With all the bad spins of the Wheel they'd had in the past day, they were due for a change of luck.

They really should turn and run, but instead he said, "We need to get closer."

With hands outstretched, they crept forward in the darkness, feeling their way one step at a time. After half an hour, Kevlin touched wood. It felt like the trunk of a tree lying horizontal. Beside him, Ceren inhaled sharply.

The wall.

They had blindly walked right up to a wall of rough-hewn logs rearing higher than he could reach.

They had found the enemy.

Kevlin did not feel like celebrating.

18

A Step Down a Slick Road

Sitara stood behind Keisara Fideima, brushing her mistress' beautiful golden hair. The keisara sat in her private parlor, directly beneath the sitting room where she often entertained her closest friends.

She faced a huge window with a breathtaking view over the western cliffs that dropped far below to the wide expanse of the Tamerlane Sea. Sitara preferred the view from the other side of the tower with its panoramic vista of Tamera.

The keisara was very talkative today, and Sitara tried to seem attentive, but she struggled to focus. Her thoughts kept turning to her harrowing experience in the emperor's tower the previous night. The old woman's death had been ruled a heart attack, so it appeared Sitara could remain safely concealed in the heart of the enemy stronghold.

The mysterious gifted mind that had briefly touched hers hadn't returned. All day, Sitara had fought the urge to embrace her power and scan the keisara's tower and its lower apartments for hints of the other mind. Not only might she have given herself away, but what would she do if she found it? She was barely trained, and if they had so far failed to identify her, she would only be playing into their hands.

What if they *had* identified her? The thought sent a chill of fear creeping up her spine. What would they do? Who would they tell?

"Sitara," the keisara said, interrupting her thoughts, "tell me about that woman who died in Zuberi's apartments last night."

Terror seized Sitara for a second, freezing every muscle in a spasm of fear. Did the keisara know what she had done? But Keisara Fideima calmly gazed out the wide windows rather than staring at her accusingly.

Sitara managed to stammer out the sparse details she had heard about the death.

The keisara frowned. "What a shame. I'll have to speak with Zuberi about it tomorrow."

Sitara resumed brushing the keisara's hair and breathed a silent sigh as she fought to regain her composure. Attending to the keisara strained Sitara's nerves and her will even on uneventful days.

If she didn't guard her thoughts, the keisara's very presence could chip away at her confidence and leave her feeling hopelessly inferior. The keisara didn't do it on purpose, but she couldn't help having that effect. She lived on a different plane than anyone Sitara had ever met, be they gifted or not.

Keisara Fideima Tamar Tegnazian was the living jewel of the empire. Her beauty and grace were legendary, and her wisdom renowned. Sitara had detected few chinks in the woman's seemingly perfect image, and most were inconsequential.

She couldn't help but compare herself to the one she planned to supplant, and she fought a daily battle to convince herself she was worthy of taking the throne.

Tonight Sitara drove away those daily worries. She needed to focus on maintaining her normal façade while preparing to strike the first blow in her secret conquest of the great lady. Her heart raced with anticipation, despite her efforts to remain calm.

After all, she'd influenced the keisara before. She must focus on the one weakness that could topple the woman and destroy her.

Barely two months ago, Sitara had first grasped the significance of the keisara's remarkable loneliness, her deep yearning that somehow the emperor had failed to fill. Sitara had explored that weakness and gently manipulated the keisara's yearnings by *pushing* thoughts, little more than temptations, into the woman's mind.

The resulting experiment had startled her by its near success. The keisara had proven surprisingly susceptible to gentle urgings to consider a dalliance with the dashing young Lord Naitingael. Unfortunately, Lord Naitingael was ordered to take command of one of the far outer fortifications before the experiment could be concluded.

Shortly before Bajaran had left on his bold mission, he had persuaded Sitara to make another attempt, timed to coincide with his first strike. Bajaran insisted she choose a more humble target for the keisara's affection. If she could drive the keisara to act upon her temptations, the scandal would rock the throne at the worst possible moment.

Thinking back on those memories filled Sitara with a sense of unease. She had not wanted to pursue that avenue of attack, but Bajaran had insisted they exploit every potential weakness.

He had offered to choose the target, but Sitara insisted she do it. She must take responsibility for what she did next. It was the only way she could feel right about it.

The choice had proven extremely difficult. She couldn't choose any of the nobility the keisara regularly interacted with, but on the other hand she refused to choose a servant. Forcing the keisara to fall for a mere servant would be too barbaric. Besides, if the scandal were too outrageous, suspicion might be roused.

She had agonized over the choice. Even though Bajaran had left weeks ago, only yesterday, shortly before hearing rumors of Bajaran's bold attack, had Sitara found the perfect target.

His name was Junian.

She had been attending her mistress in the formal audience hall while the emperor heard a particularly tiresome petition. While letting her eyes wander the room, she spotted him.

Junian had slipped into the room through a side door, carrying several documents in both hands, intent on his task. She first saw him as an amusement. He was a middle-aged man who might have been considered moderately handsome at a younger age. His face now bore the marks of age, and his paunch seemed intent on graduating into a full-blown ale gut.

He delivered the documents to a nearby official, accepted several others in return with an air of great formality, and departed. No one else seemed to notice him or pay him any attention. The man was perfect: completely obscure, and yet self-important.

It surprised her just how easily she had made the decision, and a burgeoning sense of her own power exhilarated her to the core. She could destroy that man, and she watched him leave with a satisfied smile on her lips. But it froze and wilted under the full gravity of what she intended. The satisfaction turned sour in her gut.

Sitara pushed aside the memory of those feelings just as her mistress began to speak of the day's happenings at court. Sitara had trained herself to seem interested in those running monologues from her mistress, though gossip did not interest her much. However, Bajaran had helped her to understand just how much information she could glean from the keisara's idle musings.

So she usually paid attention, filing away useful bits of information to share with him later, and even gently prodding for more details on occasion. It was an art at which she had proven adept. Over time, Sitara had developed a clear picture of the personalities, dispositions, and means of all the major players at court.

Keisara Fideima said, "What was Zuberi thinking when he ruled on that petition?" Her mouth twisted into a surprisingly childish pout. "He must not have been listening at all."

"A lot of people seemed interested in it."

"Did you think so?" The keisara paused as if to think back on who she remembered seeing there. Perfect.

Junian was looking unusually good today.

Sitara gently *pushed* the thought into the keisara's mind. She'd found in her previous attempt that if the keisara's thoughts were already running in the direction she wanted, she could easily toss in a whispered thought.

The keisara gave a start and shuddered in her seat.

Sitara cursed herself. What a stupid thought to have started with. Why spend so much effort choosing the right person but then not prepare the right thought to initiate the temptation?

"Are you all right, Your Majesty?"

"Yes." The keisara rolled her shoulders and shuddered again. "Just a rather surprising thought."

As soon as the keisara dismissed her, Sitara retired to her small room and dropped onto her bed. What had gone wrong? The keisara had quickly succumbed to thoughts implanted about Lord Naitingael.

After pondering for a while, Sitara decided the keisara must have already felt attracted to Lord Naitingael. Most of the ladies at court had, for he was still rather young, dashingly handsome and charming. The fact that his dearly loved wife had died in childbirth added a twist of tragedy to him that many women found deliciously attractive. Even the keisara herself could harbor fantasies about such a man.

She would never fantasize about Junian. Sitara frowned and hugged her pillow while she considered the best way to proceed. Should she choose a different target?

No, Junian was perfect. She felt it so deep that she refused to reconsider. How to proceed then?

The keisara would clearly never dwell on thoughts of Junian, which would make implanting the thoughts far more difficult. If she pushed too hard and overcame the keisara's natural mental defenses, the woman might well realize someone was tampering with her thoughts and seek help.

Even those non-actinopathic with no gift still possessed natural mental defenses. The weak-willed might languish all but defenseless, but a strong mind could withstand all but a concerted sentinel attack.

The keisara possessed a strong will, but lacked discipline. Sitara could exploit that, especially when pushing simple thoughts, or thoughts that paralleled what the woman was already thinking.

Sitara lay on her back and stared unseeing at the ceiling for hours as she considered the best way to make the next assault on the keisara's mind.

She sat upright in a single, convulsive movement. The truth illuminated her mind like the unshuttering of a covered tempest lantern.

Of course.

Sitara smiled, knowing what to do.

19

COMPLICATIONS

Kevlin and Ceren crept along the side of the wall, where bark still clung to the wood and the stubs of branches jabbed at their fingers. A moment later, a sentry approached along the top. The flickering light of his torch revealed that the wall reared a dozen feet into the air and curved away in a gentle arc.

They dropped to the wet ground and Kevlin whispered, "Keep your face hidden under your slicker."

Despite the temptation to look up and see if the sentry noticed them, Kevlin kept his gaze locked on the muddy soil in front of his face. The dark slickers would be difficult to spot, but light reflecting off their faces, particularly their eyes, would give them away.

The guard passed on, his footsteps never slowing, and the light faded. Kevlin got to his feet and helped Ceren up.

"We need to get out of here," she said.

They moved away from the wall for about a hundred yards before breaking into a careful jog. When they reached the trees, Ceren asked, "Which way?"

Kevlin took her hand and turned left, along the edge of the trees, searching for the trail. They followed the curving edge of the clearing for about a hundred yards until his hand touched stone.

With his fingers, he explored the obstacle in the darkness. It was the bluff. So the enemy had indeed led them all the way to its base.

They turned back and eventually found the trail a hundred and fifty yards from the cliff. Once they retreated well into the trees, Kevlin risked lighting the lantern. They crouched beside its welcome light.

"They have a fort," Ceren said.

"They don't need a fort to grab Oris and run," Kevlin said. Then he had another thought. "You know, I've been thinking how difficult it'd be for them to get the shadeleech across the empire just in time to intercept Antigonus. They didn't do it that way."

"They were already here."

"Aye."

"So, it isn't just about stealing Oris," Ceren said. "Something else is going on."

"What?"

She shrugged. "Your guess is as good as mine."

So much for being Cunning. Of course, she hadn't been a soldier for years either.

"There's more of them," Kevlin said, and his hopes for saving Antigonus fell.

"How do you know?"

"We saw a small force. That's not enough to build or defend a fort. It only makes sense if you have a larger force."

"How is that possible?"

"I don't know. I was impressed they could smuggle a dozen makrasha across the empire. I can't imagine how they managed more."

"Maybe they're using mercenaries."

Kevlin shrugged. If only he could believe that. He knew how mercenaries thought. They'd have a chance if the fort was full of soldiers for hire, but he doubted it.

He hadn't been able to figure out how to save Antigonus from the original war party. Add a hidden fort and some unknown number of additional enemy forces, and conventional wisdom dictated he run screaming in the other direction.

"There's only a few reasons someone builds a fort in enemy territory."

"This makes less and less sense," Ceren said. "Even if they had ten thousand troops hidden in the forest, once the empire discovers them, they'll marshal the legions and wipe them out."

"I know."

They crouched together in the trail, huddling in their slickers, with only a single tiny beam of light from the lantern holding back the darkness.

Kevlin was starting to feel depressed. He really needed to hit someone.

After a few minutes, Ceren bowed her head. "It's not supposed to be like this."

That was one of the first rules new recruits learned.

Shuffling closer, he placed an arm around her shoulder. She leaned against him, her body quivering with suppressed sobs.

"It's not supposed to be like this," she repeated. "He said I was Cunning. I should know what to do, but I don't."

Kevlin tipped her chin up until he could look her in the eye. She wiped rain and perhaps a tear from her face. "No one could've expected this. No one would have answers."

She took a deep breath. "We need to decide what to do."

"We need help."

"Who?"

"I don't know." He tried to come up with a plan, but his mind remained as dark as the night. He kept seeing the image of himself on a horse, galloping fast in any other direction. The situation had spiraled beyond their ability to deal with it.

Then he remembered.

"Harafin. Harafin is coming! If anyone can handle this situation, it's him."

"Of course. We need to find him and bring him back."

Kevlin shook his head. "*We* can't do that."

"What do you mean?"

"They might leave. It'll take a few days to find Harafin and return. Rhea, and whoever else is in that fort, could be anywhere by then."

Kevlin squeezed her shoulder. "You have to go. Get Harafin and come back as fast as you can."

Her face paled. "Kevlin, that's not a good idea."

"No, it's not. But it's the only idea we have, so it's what we have to do."

"No," she repeated. "I'm not good in the woods. I grew up in a city. I'll get lost."

"You won't," he reassured her. "I'm not a great woodsman either. All you have to do is follow that trail back the way we came."

"There's got to be a better way."

"I can't think of one. Can you?" He waited.

She studied the ground, biting her lip. After a minute she grimaced and whispered, "No."

"You can do it." Time for coddling her was over. "You're stronger than you think."

She smiled a little, and pushed a sodden length of hair back from her face. "I'll do it."

Then she leaned forward and kissed him full on the lips.

He was surprised, but not stupid. When a lovely young woman with warm, soft lips, decided to kiss a man, it wasn't time to think. It was time to act.

So he kissed her back.

When she pulled back a moment later he asked, "What was that for?"

She smiled and stood. "I'd better go."

He really liked how she said good-bye.

Kevlin handed her the lantern and fished one of Bajaran's heavy purses from his burglar pack. She hugged him, turned, and marched up the path. Darkness swallowed her in seconds, but he stared after her for several minutes, struggling to understand the complex young woman.

What a waste of time. He'd proven he couldn't understand women.

The kiss had been nice, but he wasn't a complete fool. Forget the fact that she seemed to have been falling for Terach just yesterday. She was still a noblewoman and he was not noble.

He turned and headed back toward the clearing.

With Ceren safely away, he could act.

20

SPINNING THE WHEEL CAN BE A BAD HABIT

Kevlin worked along the southern edge of the clearing until he reached the cliff.

"I'm crazy," he muttered.

Sentinels, shadeleeches, magic. Life had gotten messy. His honor and his very soul hung in the balance, and that was the craziest part. All his life he'd tried to stay as far away from anything to do with magic. How had he gotten lashed into this mess?

The image of Terach kneeling in a pool of his own burning blood haunted him, and he shivered.

No choice.

He concealed his extra gear in the heavy underbrush, taking only his burglar pack and a length of rope. Following the cliff, he headed north toward the fort. He suspected its wall formed a half-circle built right up against the cliff face.

Eyes open or closed, it didn't matter. He couldn't see anything. But then, neither could the enemy. He and Ceren had already proven that, and he couldn't pass up the chance to scout their position.

He refused to think about how insane it was to try sneaking up on a shadeleech and a bunch of makrasha. Sanity was not going to save Antigonus and, unless he moved fast, insanity wouldn't help much either.

Walking close to the cliff turned out to be difficult, with loose rock littering the ground and threatening to twist an ankle or rattle and give him away. So he moved farther into the clearing, hoping to hold a course parallel the rock face. If he lost his way, he could end up wandering around for a long time in that huge open space, but didn't see any better option.

Kevlin counted each step as he walked. The minutes ticked by, and the chill and the incessant rain ate at his resolve. His mind turned to Ceren.

Was she all right? Was she still on the trail? Would he ever get to kiss her again?

I'm a leech-brained worrier.

Ceren would be fine. They hadn't run into any patrols on the way in, so the trail was clear. All she had to do was follow it.

He thought of that kiss. He was a fool to dwell on it, but couldn't make himself push the memory away. His blood warmed, and the memory of her soft lips set his tingling. Her motivation didn't matter. Her rank and birth, and the impassable gulf they created didn't matter. All that mattered tonight was that brief moment.

After he'd covered about half a mile, and without any warning, he walked straight into the rough logs of the fort wall. Sucking on a sore finger, he followed the wall to the right until he reached its juncture with the cliff.

So far so good.

He waited several minutes while the rain slackened to a steady drizzle. The air smelled of rain and wet earth, but all other scents had been washed away, taking with them every sound.

Just as he was preparing to move out along the wall, the darkness began to fade under the light of an approaching torch, and he saw the wall inches from his face.

Crouching low, he huddled close to the ground and waited for the sentry. The light brightened, but the guard never noticed him hiding in the mud. The man or makrasha, he did not know which, reached the end of the wall and turned back the other way.

Kevlin settled in to wait. It took fifteen minutes for the guard to return, but without the torch this time. Only the regular tread of boots gave him away.

Was the guard a makrasha, and could they see in the dark better than men? He had assumed they couldn't since no one had seen him and Ceren approach earlier, but now he wondered if he'd made a serious mistake.

What a stupid question. Of course he'd made a mistake. The entire plan was a mistake, but it was too late to back out now.

After the guard's footsteps retreated, Kevlin stood and turned to the rough cliff. The narrow gaps between the end of the wall and the cliff were too small to slip through, so he found handholds in the stone and started to climb. The strain tugged at the stitches in his stomach and shoulder, but it felt like they were holding.

A fall could alert a guard, or injure him and make it difficult to retreat to the safety of the forest before sunrise. But he couldn't very well knock on the front gate and ask them to let him in.

At least he didn't have to climb far. It took only a few minutes to scale the cold, wet rock to a level above the top of the wall.

Sherah's Teeth, I'm such an idiot.

He saw nothing. Not a glimmer.

He clung to the cliff face for a minute, with rainwater trickling down his arms and pooling at his elbows inside the slicker. His fingers ached from the strain and cold, and his shoulder burned.

He couldn't leave. He'd never get another chance to peek over the wall and see. . .well, whatever was in there.

Time to spin the Wheel.

Kevlin climbed above the palisade of sharpened logs and worked his way down to the rampart. Crouching low, he shook out his numb fingers, massaged feeling back into them, and stared at darkness. He closed his eyes, and the view did not change.

For several minutes he remained crouched on the rampart, leaning against the cliff face, hoping to catch a glimpse of something useful. Finally, he pulled the rope from his shoulder and looped it over one of the sharpened spikes of the palisade, letting the two ends drop to the ground outside the fort. He would wait as long as possible before slipping down the rope and out of sight.

Turning back to the interior of the fort, he caught his breath. A glimmer of hope warmed his soul.

A light.

A single flicker appeared in the otherwise empty blackness. It grew, its source obscured by the shadow of a building about fifty yards away. Kevlin stood too close to the cliff to see around the building.

The guard was due again any minute, and didn't seem to be carrying a torch this time. Kevlin would have little warning, but he had not come so far only to quit.

He ghosted along the wall to get a better view. Ten feet. . .twenty. . .fifty. At each step, the tension within him grew until he felt he would burst.

Just a few more feet.

Then he could see beyond the corner of the building, to the source of light. It was an open door set in the center of the building's front wall. Three hulking figures bearing torches exited the building and the greater light revealed that the edifice stood two stories tall, although he could not clearly see its full dimensions.

The makrasha crossed a narrow porch, descended a short flight of steps, and marched into a large open space, like a parade ground in the center of the fort. There they separated. One of the creatures headed north away from Kevlin toward a long, low building with wide double doors, which was probably their stable.

The other two turned south and their approaching torches revealed the silhouettes of two additional buildings built close to the wall where Kevlin crouched. A moment later, light seeped out of those buildings through gaps in the rough log walls. The glow revealed each building was a single story about fifty paces long, paralleling the wall.

Other hulking beasts began exiting both buildings. Many bore torches, providing ample light for Kevlin to watch the ranks of makrasha assembling. The milling creatures growled and jostled each other, while several others climbed to the top of the wall.

Their light gave Kevlin a good view of its structure. The gate in the center of the wall was shielded by two small buildings, about ten paces in length, built right up against it. They formed a narrow alley leading to the gate, wide enough for four or five riders abreast.

Kevlin's assumption proved accurate about the shape of the wall. It continued around the simple compound in a half circle from the cliff. The fort was bigger than he has first assumed, but he saw no other buildings. The large building at the back, built close to the cliff, would be the command structure, with the barracks buildings and stables framing the central parade ground. Simple but effective.

Soon a dozen torch-wielding makrasha had reached the top of the wall, and began to spread along the curving defenses. Even crouching, Kevlin wouldn't remain concealed much longer. He was shocked to count two hundred makrasha, but still memorized the layout.

He wasn't sure what they were doing, but it didn't look like a mobilization to hunt him down. If he'd been discovered, they wouldn't flood the compound with light and assemble out in the open. They'd attack under the cover of darkness.

A pair of makrasha bearing torches drew near. He was still far outside their circle of light, but retreated toward the cliff anyway.

He'd seen enough. Time to leave.

Kevlin glanced back at the interior of the fort, trying to burn the scene into his memory. Half of the makrasha filled the center of the parade ground, drawn up in four equal columns, while the rest lined the perimeter. Some held torches aloft, while others scurried around on unknown errands. The compound vibrated with their growling and disgusting clicking sounds. Their heavy, musky scent filled the air.

A huge makrasha that towered over the others exited the command building and roared a deep, piercing bellow that drove terror into Kevlin's heart.

"Silence," the creature ordered, its rasping tone clear above the din.

Kevlin stared in disbelief as the massive creature shouldered through the ranks of makrasha. He had never considered they might talk, and that fact made them all the more horrible.

A couple of makrasha led saddled horses from the stable, and Kevlin paused to watch. The thought that they might be leaving chilled him. Even though he had stayed behind for just such an eventuality, he finally saw the flaw in their plan. He could follow them if they left, but could not notify Ceren.

The dull thud of footsteps reminded him of his current situation. The guards had drawn closer, their circle of torchlight almost touching him. When he turned to look at them, one of them grunted and held its torch higher.

Kevlin spun away to hide his face from the light. Hoping the patter of rain would mask his footfalls, he ran back toward the cliff. Behind him, the guards advanced more quickly, but did not run. It seemed they weren't sure if they'd glimpsed anything or not.

That was way too close.

Hurrying along the darkened wall, he nearly collided with the cliff. The guards were still coming at a trot, and their disgusting insectlike second arms carried small crossbows cocked and ready to fire. They might not be sure they saw something, but they were taking no chances, hengaruk weaving the weapons in the air in front of them.

It took only a couple of seconds to find his rope. He grasped the twin lines and prepared to slip over the wall, but paused.

They might be leaving.

He looked back toward the parade ground, much of which was obscured by buildings, but he could still see one of the horses waiting in front of the assembled makrasha.

I have to know.

Making a snap decision, he pulled up the rope and dropped it to the ground *inside* the wall. Not pausing to let reason interfere, he jumped over the side and slid down.

21

No Way Out

As soon as his feet touched the ground, Kevlin yanked on one end of the rope with panic-driven strength. The other end snaked up over the wall and fell at his feet. He grabbed the rope, turned, and bolted away from the wall and the torch-bearing makrasha on top.

In his haste, he forgot that the ground at the base of the cliff was littered with stone. One foot slipped, sending him sprawling amid a clatter of rocks.

The makrasha rushed to the end of the wall and held the torch high, peering into the darkness. Kevlin rolled onto his stomach and pulled his hood down over his face, hoping the dark slicker would shield him from view in the poor light.

When no crossbow bolts slammed into his back, he risked a glance up. One of the makrasha still stood, its freakish hengaruk poised to fire the deadly crossbow.

The other was gone.

Coming to investigate, most likely.

Kevlin was tempted to hit himself in the head a few times with a rock. He could have been safely outside the wall, but had to spin the Wheel just one more time. Akillik was surely laughing.

Kevlin might be a fool, but dying wasn't a short term goal. Very slowly he rose to a crouch, painfully aware that any noise would be fatal. The distant torch didn't quite reach where he stood, but it was close enough that the thin veneer of concealment could part all too easily. He moved one foot and set it down only after feeling for loose rocks.

Shuffling forward like that proved difficult and the seconds ticked by with terrifying swiftness. He was stuck crawling along like a slug while the makrasha could appear at any time.

After a dozen agonizingly slow steps, he risked another glance behind. The Makrasha, still poised to strike, had turned its head to the side. Kevlin followed its gaze and noticed a faint flickering light that grew steadily brighter.

Someone was coming.

Time to move.

Holding his breath, as if that would somehow make him lighter, Kevlin increased his pace. He headed for the rear of the command building, angling away from the cliff face and the perilous rocks at its base. He cringed at each footstep, fearing the rattle of stone that would seal his fate.

He covered fifty feet before a dozen makrasha rounded the end of the nearest barracks and headed toward the end of the wall.

Kevlin was still too close.

With no alternative, he broke into a jog. Tension knotted his insides so tight he could hardly breathe. The makrasha drew closer and he ran faster, angling away. They would pass within twenty or thirty paces of him.

As they neared, he crouched low to the ground but kept moving, not daring to breathe until he leaned against the wall of the building. He sagged against the rough wood, struggling to keep from gasping for breath.

The makrasha began examining the ground along the base of the cliff. It had felt rocky, but if he'd left any tracks, they'd find him.

Only one possibility came to mind. Despite his panic-driven desire to run the other way, he crossed behind the command building and headed toward the outer wall and the rear of the barracks where the makrasha had passed. If any more of them came that way, he would be finished, but he could run into more of the beasts anywhere. That was the only place he was sure to find other tracks.

He paused at the corner of the barracks to glance down its length. It stood only ten feet from the wall and the gap was pitch dark. He jogged the length of the opening, hoping any tracks he might leave would be lost among the heavier footprints of the makrasha that had just passed through.

Kevlin reached the far end of the building without incident, crept around the corner and through the alley between the two barracks. He paused near the front corner where he could see the parade ground and four columns of makrasha assembled less than fifty paces away.

They stood quietly, ignoring the rain, watching their leader with their triple green eyes. Crouched so close to nearly two hundred of the disgusting creatures, the insanity of Kevlin's situation crashed home.

What was I thinking?

They might not be able to see any better than he, but could they hear him? Or smell him? It wasn't hard to smell *them*. The scent of the assembled creatures hung heavy in the air despite the rain: a cloying, musky scent that made him want to sneeze.

He breathed shallow and tried to convince himself he was well hidden. Creeping forward, he peered around the corner toward the command building and nearly jumped out of his skin.

A makrasha stood at the corner, not a pace away.

Kevlin slipped back around the corner and pressed against the rough log wall, fighting to remain silent. It took several seconds for the rush of fear to ebb enough for his brain to start working again

After a moment, he risked edging back, leaning out just far enough to see the door of the command building. As he watched, four figures exited onto the narrow porch.

Their crimson robes had no hoods. They were not makrasha. Staring at them, fear spiked through Kevlin like a frozen blade.

Shadeleeches.

Four of them.

Despite their hulking size, the makrasha all bowed their heads in silent obeisance. A fifth man stepped onto the porch, and the others made way for him. Kevlin didn't have to see his face to know him. The icy chill of evil emanating from the man was enough.

The shadeleech from the inn. Their leader.

Kevlin shrank deeper into the shadows, but couldn't tear his eyes away from the five on the porch. Blood pounded in his ears and panic threatened to send him racing blindly away. Only with a supreme effort did he hold still.

I'm dead.

One shadeleech was more than he ever wanted to see. Five were beyond reason.

Just slip into a fort with a couple hundred makrasha and five shadeleeches? No problem. He fought down a burst of crazed laughter.

Two of the shadeleeches bowed to their leader. As the leader gestured toward the massed makrasha, his words carried to Kevlin through the deep silence. "Be prepared to strike on my order."

The pair of shadeleeches bowed again and descended the stairs.

The leader turned to one of the other two, "Haraz, find me a bear."

The shadeleech Haraz, an unremarkable man of medium height with sandy hair, bowed and left. The two shadeleeches who had already left the porch moved to the head of the four columns and mounted the waiting horses.

One of them gestured toward the wall and the main gate began to open with a heavy creaking. The two rode out of sight toward the gate, followed by the gigantic makrasha leader, with the hundred creatures under its command trailing behind.

Kevlin watched from the shadows, indecision adding another twist to the knots in his stomach. The enemy wasn't supposed to split up. He could not track them all.

The leader had captured Antigonus, so that was the shadeleech Kevlin had to watch. Besides, he had seen nothing of Rhea or Dhanjal in the party leaving the fort. Whatever that other group was up to, he couldn't worry about it. One more mystery added to the growing list of things to deal with later.

At least fewer remained in the fort. But then a terrible thought brought him up short. What if that departing force took the same trail as Ceren? If she stopped for the night, they would find her.

No one would ever alert Harafin.

He'd be left well and truly alone.

Hurry, Ceren, he thought. Hopefully she'd prove to be as cunning as Antigonus believed.

Settling back into the deepest shadows, he huddled under his slicker, cold and haunted by dark thoughts. A moment later the gates creaked ominously closed.

He had survived some pretty dangerous situations, but nothing like this. Kevlin waited several more minutes while most of the milling makrasha extinguished their torches and returned to the barracks with much growling and jostling. Welcome darkness returned, but the rain slowed to a barely perceptible mist, no longer shrouding him with its protective cloak.

He had waited long enough. This was the perfect time to slip away. Levering himself to his feet, he peeked around the corner closest to the outer wall and swallowed a curse along with the bile that threatened to spew from his too-tightly clenched stomach.

No more than twenty paces away, and approaching along the side of the building, were the same dozen makrasha that had been sent to investigate the noise Kevlin had made when slipping over the wall. They were advancing slowly, studying the ground. As he watched, one of the hulking creatures leaned down and touched its wide, fanged mouth to the mud. Then it looked up.

Right at Kevlin.

For a second, Kevlin gazed full into the three hideous green eyes that stared flatly out of the creature's wide skull. He froze in terror and time seemed to stop.

His heart beat once. Then again.

The makrasha stood and the group proceeded forward at the same measured pace as before.

By the Lady's blessed temper, it hadn't seen him. Relief turned his knees to rubber and he sagged against the building. He savored it for a single heartbeat. They would reach the corner in a minute or two and notice his tracks or smell his scent.

He breathed deep to loosen his clenched muscles and forced calm on his racing thoughts. Fear could no longer help, so he pushed it away. He had to act, and act fast. There was too much at stake for him to fall tonight. He had to find a way out.

He jogged to the far end of the alley facing the empty parade ground. A single torch burned at the base of the far stair, leading up the perimeter wall, but a dozen makrasha still patrolled on top of it.

Kevlin walked out to the middle of the parade ground. The shadows were thick and only the most careful observer would notice his dark form. When no one challenged him, he spent a moment walking in random circles, backtracking and crisscrossing the muddy parade ground.

It was hard to breathe.

Despite the concealing shadows, his shoulders itched, expecting a crossbow bolt to slam home between them at any second. He willed himself to keep moving. Mixed with the hundreds of other footprints across the parade ground, the confusing trail might throw off his pursuers for a while.

Time to spin the Wheel.

Kevlin jogged to the command center, the squishing of his boots sounding loud in the darkness. Just as he reached the stairs, a high-pitched howl shattered the stillness and nearly stopped his heart.

The dozen makrasha who had been tracking him poured into the open space, growling and making those disturbing clicking sounds. Their weapons were drawn.

They knew.

The barracks doors banged open and more makrasha spilled into the parade ground in a disorganized mass, weapons drawn and teeth bared. Few carried torches, resulting in a confused mass of huge monsters rushing around without direction. Several started fighting among themselves, filling the parade ground with growls and yelps of pain.

There was only one place to go.

Kevlin dashed up the steps to the command building, crossed the porch, pulled open the door, and slipped inside.

22

EVEN THE CUNNING CAN DOUBT

Ceren paused to rest at the top of a small hill and gave her tiny lantern a shake. She grimaced at the pitiful amount of oil remaining.

Not long after leaving Kevlin, she had opened the shutter wide, but it generated only a small pool of light in the rainy darkness. Kevlin would have chided her for taking such a risk, but they had already walked this trail once and she had enough to worry about without imagining monsters lurking in the shadows.

She adjusted her slicker and pulled the hood lower over her face. Despite its protection, her clothes were damp from the pervasive moisture and the deep chill had settled into her bones. Still, it was a favorable spin of the Wheel that Kevlin had found the slickers. She wouldn't have made it so far otherwise.

Ceren sank down onto a fallen log, her body aching with fatigue. Trudging through the wilderness for the past twenty-four hours had taxed her strength.

Her body craved sleep, but she could not give in yet. She had to keep walking until the lantern consumed the last of the oil or dawn arrived to drive back the darkness. Stifling a yawn, she munched on an apple and a handful of nuts and thought of Kevlin.

What was he up to? She did not doubt he had some plan he didn't want to tell her about. Whatever it was, she trusted him to be safe, or as safe as anyone could be in that insane situation.

That trust surprised her a little. Kevlin was clearly more than the simple mercenary he pretended to be. When she returned with Harafin, she'd insist on learning the truth about him.

Did he even understand why she had kissed him?

She smiled at the memory of his lips against hers. He'd proven himself to be very clever, so hopefully he wouldn't read too much into it.

It was clear Kevlin was going to risk his life again. The situation was difficult. She wanted him to be safe but, if he succeeded, would they still need her?

I can do this, she thought, repeating the phrase for the hundredth time that night. It had become the mantra by which she'd trudged for hours through the spooky darkness, the one she'd relied on to hold her terror and worries at bay.

Very cunning. She winced at the memory of Antigonus' words to Kevlin. The old sentinel had been right. Kevlin had proven his cunning. As she thought back to each time he had saved them, she asked herself a painful question: *What did I do?*

What had she contributed? For her, the past couple of days had been a string of failures. She had failed to prevent Haisyl from hurting Antigonus, failed to kill Rhea. She shuddered at the memory of her blade slowly piercing Rhea's flesh.

She'd never killed anyone before and needing to execute the woman in cold blood had been horrible. It had taken every ounce of will to attempt it, but it still hadn't been enough.

She had failed to heal Antigonus, failed to think of a way to escape the inn. Failed to save Terach. The memory of his brutal death tore at her heart. He had been such a good man and he'd trusted her to save them.

She'd failed.

Terach had been so strong, but he was gone. She had impulsively embraced him that one time, drawing strength from him. He'd seemed invincible, like a rock, but he was gone, dead because she failed.

Tears ran down her cheeks and she didn't bother to stifle the sobs that racked her slender frame. Kevlin was not here to see.

"I can do this," she shouted out loud. Throwing the apple core aside, she rose, took up the lantern, and stomped up the trail.

I am Cunning. Antigonus chose me, not Kevlin.

She would prove herself worthy of the title. She would show them all: Kevlin, Antigonus. . .her father.

She could not let her father down. He doubted her enough already. If she failed again, all of her training and preparation would be a lie, a diversion, a hobby like he'd always claimed.

He had only allowed her to accompany Antigonus when he thought there would be three sentinels in the party to keep her safe. If he knew what had happened, he'd have half the armies of Freyarr tramping through the wilderness to save her.

How embarrassing.

No, she would be strong. She'd make him proud.

"I can do this," she whispered into the uncaring rain.

She trudged for another hour, despite the deep weariness that clung to her body and soul. She would not stop until she found Sentinel Harafin and warned him of the danger.

Or until her lantern went out.

It began to flicker twenty minutes later and she used the last moments of light to scout for a place to stop. At the prospect of rest, the weariness she'd been holding at bay through sheer willpower crashed in on her, nearly toppling her to the ground in the middle of the trail.

Biting her lip to stay focused, she spied a large deadfall just off the trail. On closer inspection, it was a thick pile of brush grown up against a tree leaning steeply against its neighbors. She pushed some of the brush aside, crawled under the tree and found a spot that, although not exactly dry, was far less wet than anything else she'd seen.

Curling up in her slicker and hugging the still-warm lantern close, she fell asleep in seconds.

23

FACING A LEGEND

Kevlin found himself in a large room crowded with tables and benches, dimly lit by the dying embers in a huge fireplace. A stairway to his left led toward the second floor where the shadeleeches had probably gone.

Kevlin slipped off his boots to avoid leaving muddy footprints, then padded across the room, wincing at each step. Hopefully the blisters would be the most painful thing he'd have to endure.

Someone with a light started descending the stair, so Kevlin slipped under one of the tables. It wasn't much cover, but they'd be focused on the racket outside.

He drew the heavy dagger from his belt, along with one of his stilettos. If they found him, it would be better to die fighting than to be captured.

That always sounded better when it was someone else making that choice.

The footsteps reached the bottom of the stair and proceeded across the room. Kevlin could see only the man's shoes and the hem of his crimson robes, but that was enough.

More shoes clattered on the stairs as someone else hurried down. The exterior door was thrown open and a rush of cold air set the candle guttering.

"What's going on?" the shadeleech demanded.

A makrasha entered and spoke in a gravelly voice. "Intruder."

The creature chopped the word short and clicked its teeth together at every other syllable.

"Find this intruder," the shadeleech ordered. As a second shadeleech entered the room from the stairs, the first said, "Merab, rouse Tanathos. Then join the search."

Tanathos must be the name of the leader. So the shadeleech wasn't Rhea's mysterious master.

"You're not my senior, Haraz," said the newcomer.

"Do as I say or challenge me now. Don't waste my time."

Kevlin didn't dare breathe in the same room with two squabbling shadeleeches. As much as he'd love for them to destroy each other, in this confined space they'd probably kill him too.

He was getting tired of holding his breath so much.

"Later," Merab said.

"Go," Haraz said in a smug voice. "I will check the prisoner."

Merab left and the makrasha lumbered back through the door. Haraz crossed the room, passing less than six feet from where Kevlin crouched under the table and exited the far side.

Kevlin clenched his eyes, the only gesture he could think to relieve a little tension without making any noise.

Maybe this wasn't such a good idea.

Still, this was the last place they'd look for him. They would've caught him in seconds if he'd stayed outside. Besides, the only prisoner he knew of was Antigonus. Maybe they hadn't started the torture killing yet.

Kevlin slipped from under the table and shoved his boots through the straps of his burglar pack to keep his hands free. If he could wake Antigonus, maybe the powerful old man could free them both.

Maybe.

Kevlin peeked around the edge of the door the shadeleech Haraz had passed through. It opened into an empty hallway where Haraz's light was already fading.

Kevlin ghosted along the hall and mouthed a silent prayer to Asherah. She was goddess of the sea and patron of Meinarr. He wasn't very religious, but tonight he'd take any help he could get.

Around the corner, the next hallway was empty, but a heavy oak door, banded with iron, hung open twenty paces away. Candlelight shone dimly from within. Kevlin slipped down the hall. Crouching, he risked a peek around the doorframe.

Another hallway. It stretched about thirty feet to a room with a small table holding a couple of burning candles. Haraz stood profile to Kevlin, looking at something beyond Kevlin's view.

Antigonus. It had to be.

Kevlin pulled back from the door and glanced around. Two other heavy wooden doors stood closed. He stepped to the nearest one and pressed his ear to it, but heard nothing. The door was secured by a simple lock.

Footsteps. Haraz was coming back.

Kevlin wasn't crazy enough to try ambushing a shadeleech, so he peeled back the top layer of his wristguard to reveal a set of lock picks. Old Tog, the sergeant responsible for his earliest military training, had been the most corrupt individual he'd ever met. He'd taught him more than just how to defend himself on the battlefield.

Ye nev'r know when the 'unsavory' skills is what's will save yer life, Tog had said.

Few words had proven truer.

Slipping the picks into the lock, Kevlin explored its simple mechanism. The footsteps drew nearer and it took all of his will to keep his fingers from shaking. With careful, precise movements, he prodded the tumbler back until it clicked.

With Haraz but seconds away, Kevlin yanked the door open, leaped inside, and pulled it closed.

It creaked. Just a little.

He pressed his ear to the wood and listened, barely breathing. The crash of a heavy, ironbound door closing thundered through the stillness and he jumped. A lock clicked, then footsteps approached. His muscles tensed so tight it was amazing his blood could flow.

The footsteps continued past, not slowing, till they faded around the corner leading back to the main room. Kevlin sank to the floor and wiped sweat out of his eyes. He was drenched with it.

Let's not do that again.

His body ached as if he'd just spent half an hour fighting Dhanjal. After a deep breath, he slipped back into the hallway.

Kevlin picked the simple lock on the ironbound door that had stood open earlier, which Haraz had closed and locked on his return. He slipped down the darkened hall beyond. In the small room where he'd seen Haraz in profile earlier, he felt his way to the table and lit the candles with his flint and steel.

The warm glow didn't help the desolate room look better. It was round, with two wooden chairs facing each other across the rough tabletop. Five reinforced doors were set in the circular wall, each locked and secured with a heavy deadbolt. High in each door was a small, hinged panel.

Kevlin opened the panel in the first door and peered through a little barred window. Inside the bare, wooden room lay Antigonus on a crude bunk.

He looked dead.

Unbelievably emaciated, with loose skin sagging from his frame, as if all of the muscle and tissue had melted away, leaving him little more than a skeleton. Limp strands of hair hung around his head and only scraggly remnants of his beard clung to his chin. A wide bloodstain marred the front of his filthy robe.

Kevlin's fingers trembled so bad it took several seconds to unlock and open the door. He entered, placed the candle on the floor, then reached out and touched Antigonus' forehead. It burned with fever.

The old man's eyes fluttered open and Kevlin breathed a sigh of relief. Antigonus stared at him for a moment, his cobalt eyes dim and clouded.

"It's me, Kevlin."

After what seemed an eternity, Antigonus blinked and smiled. His eyes cleared and he whispered, "How?"

"Long story. I'll tell you once we're away."

Antigonus shook his head, just a twitch.

"We have to go," Kevlin repeated, not sure if the old man understood.

"No, I cannot."

"Of course you can."

If Antigonus was too weak to wield his powers, they'd never get out.

Kevlin lifted the old man to a sitting position and barely suppressed a shudder at how weightless the sentinel felt. A web of fine cracks etched across Antigonus' exposed skin and as he turned his head, the skin cracked wide and began oozing a pale yellow puss.

A stomach-turning odor clung to him, reminding Kevlin of half-rotted corpses he'd helped bury after his first battle. It was the stench of death.

"No," Antigonus repeated, his voice a little stronger. "I am going nowhere." He leaned against the stone wall.

"Why didn't they just kill you?"

"For now, I serve their purpose better alive."

"What can I do for you?"

It was clear Kevlin could not bring the old man with him when he tried to escape. After everything he'd done to help, he did not want to kill Antigonus but that might be the most merciful gift he could give.

"Are you a stalwart?"

That was not what Kevlin expected. "No." He recalled the song of Savas ringing through his soul and the terror of losing control to that soft, compelling voice.

"Beware," Antigonus said. "Gods do nothing without a reason. Guard against favors given too easily. There is always a price."

"You saw?"

"Yes."

"What does it mean?"

"I cannot say for sure, but know that Savas' favor is no blessing."

Tell me about it.

"Know that I was wrong." Antigonus frowned and repeated softly. "I was wrong about everything."

That would've been good to know before embarking on a suicidal mission.

"Your arrival offers hope," Antigonus continued. "We can still prevent disaster."

Here it comes.

Although Kevlin had longed for an excuse to kill a sentinel for much of his life, he shrank from the need to do it now. Instead of asking for the mercy of a swift death however, Antigonus pulled a heavy gold ring from one finger and held it out.

"Put it on."

Kevlin took the ring. A dark stone was set in its face and silver runes traced six-pointed stars along the band. Perhaps it was a family crest, or some heirloom the old man wanted returned to his kin.

Kevlin slid it onto the third finger of his right hand, expecting it to get stuck at the first knuckle. It slid home as if crafted for him.

Strange, since his fingers were thicker than Antigonus'. A creeping feeling of unease set the hairs of his arms standing on end.

Antigonus reached a shaking hand up to his throat and pulled the rune-covered pouch from inside his robe. Kevlin stared in disbelief. If that was what he thought it was, surely the shadeleeches would have taken it.

The sentinel pulled the silver chain over his head and held the pouch out to Kevlin. It dangled before him like a forbidden fruit.

"Take it."

Over the past couple of days, Kevlin had been immersed in so much magic that his nerves might never recover. He shrank from the pouch.

"Take it," Antigonus repeated stronger.

The old man's hand began to shake, so Kevlin grabbed the pouch before he could drop it. He shuddered and cursed himself for a fool.

I'm kneeling in a dungeon in the center of a fortress filled with shadeleeches and makrasha. I can handle one rune-covered bag.

"Open it." Antigonus said. "Into your hand." His cobalt eyes glistened with emotion. Whatever was going on, it meant a lot to him.

As Kevlin untied the leather thong, the import of what he was doing brought him up short. He was about to set eyes upon Oris, the great talisman.

Only the most powerful sentinels were chosen as its bearers and their exploits were legendary. Despite all the legend, power, and prestige surrounding Oris, he had no idea what it looked like. It was only ever spoken of in general terms.

He was about to see it, touch it.

Glancing up at Antigonus, he asked, "Is this really. . .?"

"Yes."

Kevlin's hand shook as he upended the pouch. Images flashed through his mind of what he might be about to see: a priceless jewel, a beautiful figurine, even the mummified heart of a great sentinel from times of old. It had to be something incredible.

It spilled into his hand, a solid weight surprisingly warm to the touch. Struggling to appear calm, he tilted his hand toward the candlelight. The guttering glow washed over it and he stared, dumbfounded.

It was a rock.

24

THE STEWARD

"**A**re you sure this is the right pouch?"

It had to be a mistake. Kevlin shook the empty bag. The rock wasn't even pretty. Dark gray, it was about the size of a large egg that had been half squashed. Its edges were rough, although the side facing him was fairly smooth and curved.

"Absolutely," Antigonus said.

Kevlin glanced up and choked back his next retort. The old man's face was red and his eyes blazed with anger. Frail and half-dead though he might be, he was still a powerful sentinel.

He's gone mad, Kevlin decided.

The shadeleeches had taken Oris and left the rock in its place. Antigonus was so far gone, he couldn't tell the difference. Kevlin would humor the old man. He'd dump the sentinel's pet rock and see if he could escape from the fort before sunrise.

Kevlin sighed, filled with bitter disappointment. For a moment, he'd actually thought he'd get to see it. He should have known better.

Never trust magic or those who wield it.

He couldn't remember who had told him that, but the phrase rang true like never before.

Antigonus coughed and clutched at his chest. His anger subsided and he settled back against the stone wall. "Appearance has nothing to do with power."

"If you say so," Kevlin replied.

He decided not to point out that it wasn't a good analogy. Look at Antigonus. He looked like the walking dead and that's about as much power as he seemed to have left.

In an attempt to look interested in the rock, Kevlin flipped it over in his hand. The opposite face was almost flat, with a raised emblem in the center, in the shape of a six-pointed star that reflected the light like crystal.

Twisting the stone round to straighten the star, Kevlin started in surprise. The curved underside of the stone fit his palm like it had been molded for him and some rough protrusions along the top fit neatly between his fingers. It was as if the stone had melted to fit a man's hand.

My hand?

He shivered. That was a creepy thought.

The crystal emblem flashed bright blue, temporarily blinding him, surprising him so much that he nearly dropped the rock. After his eyes cleared, he found the six-pointed star gone, replaced by a sword emblem with flames radiating out in six lines toward his fingers and wrist. The candle flared and the flames seemed to dance, as if alive.

Maybe it really was more than just a rock.

He looked up at Antigonus to find the sentinel staring at him with wide eyes, an expression of wonder on his face. That made Kevlin suddenly nervous. Magic was not supposed to surprise Antigonus.

He extended the rock to Antigonus. "I don't think I should take this."

Antigonus shook himself, as if emerging from a trance. His smile was triumphant, even though his eyes looked sad.

"No," the sentinel said. "I cannot take it back."

"Why not?"

"I name you Steward," Antigonus intoned, his expression grave. "Guard Oris well until the Chooser commands."

Kevlin nodded, trying to mimic the grave expression on Antigonus' face. *Great,* he thought with a sigh, *more riddles. Who's the chooser?* But then the rest of what Antigonus said sank in.

I'm the steward?

His mind raced as he tried to remember tales he'd heard of Oris. Only the mightiest sentinels were called as bearers, but when one of them died and another chosen, a steward was involved. Exactly how, he had no idea.

"What do I do?" Kevlin asked, his voice cracking a little. He licked his lips and tried to swallow but found his mouth dry.

"Leave this place," Antigonus said. "Find Harafin. He'll know what to do."

Harafin. Kevlin had forgotten about the powerful sentinel hopefully riding to their aid. He grabbed Antigonus' arm. "Ceren's on her way to meet him. She'll bring him back."

"Good. Without Cunning, you will fail." He sagged, and Kevlin helped him lie back down.

"Can you use your magic?" Kevlin had to ask. "Can you help me get out of here?"

"No." He barely heard the old man's faint whisper. "The shadeleeches consume my strength. I am weak, useless."

"Why didn't they kill you?"

Antigonus coughed, his body convulsing with pain. When he recovered enough to speak, he said, "Must get the stone away."

"Why haven't they taken it?"

"They can't. It would destroy them. Only the steward can hold it unharmed."

Kevlin glanced down nervously at the misshapen rock he held. Shouldn't Antigonus have done the whole steward naming thing before telling him to dump the rock into his hand? Oversights like that got people killed.

"They hope to break my mind," Antigonus said. "And force me to name one of them steward."

At least that part make a twisted kind of sense. Kevlin rose to his feet. "Rest. I'll keep it safe. We'll return for you."

He tucked the rock into its pouch and drew the cord tight. Uncomfortable with the idea of placing it around his neck, he slipped it into the burglar pack on his back. He turned to say goodbye to Antigonus but the old man was already sleeping, his scrawny chest barely moving.

His mind whirling, Kevlin left the room, locked the door, and extinguished the candles. He padded to the end of the hallway, pushed open the far door and slipped into the hall beyond.

A makrasha that had been standing behind the open door, howled right in his face.

25

A Glimmer of Light in a Moment of Darkness

Before Kevlin could react, the makrasha seized him with hands and hengaruk and smashed him into the heavy door. The first impact rattled him with pain. The second drove his mind into welcome darkness.

Some time later his thoughts slowly coalesced out of the fog. The first thing he became aware of was that his feet were cold. Kevlin struggled to focus while his senses returned. Why would his feet be cold?

With a start he came fully awake and lurched up, his arms and legs thrashing. Something struck him in the side of the head so hard it rattled his teeth.

He sagged back, groaning as existing bruises joined together in a sadistic chorus, reminding him how much his head already hurt. Only when that clamor faded to a constant throbbing ache did it register how much his arms hurt. He was being dragged backward along the floor by the arms.

He glanced to one side, then the other, and his heart fell. Two makrasha were dragging him backward along a dark hallway with their hengaruk. The stubby-fingered appendages dug into his muscles and he had no doubt they could rip his arms off if they chose.

He looked back and his heart fell further, taking up permanent residence in his chilled toes. He could just make out an ironbound door. They were taking him back to the cell block.

The foul taste of defeat choked him, tasting like bile. After everything he'd achieved, he had failed. His head pounded and a slow trickle of wetness ran down his face. Hopefully he wasn't bleeding too much, although he'd be dead soon anyway, so it probably didn't matter.

He was such an idiot. Sure, he'd had a lot on his mind, but that was no excuse for getting sloppy.

Antigonus gave me Oris and told me to keep it safe. I lasted about thirty seconds.

They'd kill him and break Antigonus' mind soon. Once the old man named one of them steward, they'd vanish with the mighty talisman, leaving the empire defenseless. For several seconds, Kevlin wallowed in misery. It didn't help, but he was finding it hard to scrape up any optimism.

They reached the small circular room. The makrasha slammed him into one of the chairs but did not release their iron-like grip on his arms. A third creature deposited Kevlin's sword belt and gear on the table in front of him.

The sword was so close, that had to be the first torture. Dying fighting would be the best possible outcome for him now but he couldn't imagine how to get his hands on the weapon.

Haraz, holding a torch high, turned from where he had been peering into Antigonus' cell. "The beast posted by the door was supposed to keep intruders from entering. I had not expected someone to be leaving."

"Well, with how you treat visitors, are you surprised?"

Haraz glared and the look burned out Kevlin's false bravado. Up close, the shadeleech looked cruel, with a haughty stare and no sense of humor. Kevlin could smell evil on him, clinging to his nostrils like burned toast.

The door at the far end of the hall opened and footsteps approached. The newcomer bore no light, so he remained invisible until he entered the room. The palpable chill of evil emanating from him left no doubt as to his identity.

Tanathos.

The shadeleech studied Kevlin silently. Kevlin met his gaze for just a second but had to look away from the roiling darkness that cloaked those eyes. He'd thought the effect was scary enough back in the inn. Now that evil aura nearly overwhelmed him.

This shadeleech could never appear unremarkable. Indeed, he had to struggle to look human, for he clearly had surrendered his soul to EnKur, Lord of Darkness.

"You." Tanathos sounded surprised. "Impressive."

"You, not so much," Kevlin said. He couldn't hurt anything but the man's pride, so why not?

Tanathos gave a low chuckle. "You haven't lost your spirit yet. This will prove more interesting than I had feared." Then he commanded, "Shackle him."

The makrasha dragged Kevlin out of the chair and hauled him into a cell constructed of rough-cut lumber, with loose straw scattered on the floor. The creatures pushed Kevlin onto the low bunk and clasped a set of shackles around his wrists. The shackles were attached to chains that ran up the wall, through a set of iron rings, then back to the far corner of the room, ending in a series of gears attached to a large wheel.

That can't be good.

Haraz entered the cell and placed the torch in a bracket near the door.

Tanathos entered last and said to Haraz. "See if the other prisoner has been disturbed." Haraz left immediately and the leader stepped closer to Kevlin. "It is good to have your company. We have some time on our hands, so we will talk."

"I'd rather not."

"You will," Tanathos said with a fake smile. "You will talk, you will scream, you will tell me everything I wish to know." He continued in a whisper, "And then you will die and I will feed on your soul."

Kevlin shuddered as every horror story he'd ever heard about what shadeleeches did to people ran through his mind. Killing someone was only the beginning. He had no doubt that in real life they could do far worse.

Sitting in that dungeon, shackled and facing a shadeleech, his sense of helpless terror unearthed memories he'd fought for years to suppress. They now burst from the dam that held them prisoner in a dark corner of his soul. In that second, he was again a boy of seven who'd made the mistake of sneaking into the cabin of a sentinel who'd booked passage on his father's ship.

He hadn't known the sentinel was there and couldn't remember what he'd seen the man doing. That memory had been burned from his mind. He'd just wanted to see a sentinel, see a little magic. He'd gotten more than he'd ever wanted.

His body screamed with remembered pain that his throat couldn't vent. His mind reeled with shame and terror as a sentinel stood over him in that tiny cabin. Kevlin had tried to call out for help, to scream in pain, to run, but the sentinel's magic held him there, a silent captive.

Then the sentinel had used Truth to rip knowledge from him despite everything he did to hold his tongue. "What did you see, boy?"

He'd told the man everything, knowing it would only lead to more pain.

He'd been right.

The memory of what he'd seen was gone, but the memory of that torture remained, as bright and undimmed by the passage of years as if it had happened only yesterday.

After what seemed an eternity, the man had asked, "What did you see?"

"Nothing."

"Will you speak of this to anyone, boy?"

"Yes."

Magic burned through his soul, torturing him to the brink of insanity. He could not scream, could not move, could not cry his mother's name.

After another eternity, the pain eased and the sentinel asked again, "Will you speak of this to anyone, boy?"

"I don't know what you're talking about."

The man smiled. "You will stop crying. You will remain silent about our visit. Is that clear?"

"Yes," Kevlin had sobbed, his tiny frame shuddering with the effort to suppress the screams of pain and terror that threatened to burst forth.

"Leave me," the sentinel had commanded.

Kevlin had staggered to his feet and stumbled from the cabin. He'd hidden from the sentinel for the rest of the voyage, but it had been months before he could sleep soundly again and years before he'd managed to bury the pain and terror.

Kevlin now struggled to calm his breathing under the flood of those memories. Sweat broke out across his forehead and turned his hands clammy against the chill of the iron shackles.

"Tell me your name," Tanathos commanded.

Kevlin remained silent. Even he knew giving up that information was a bad idea.

"My name is Tanathos. I will know yours."

"How about giving me the tour first?"

Surprise flickered across Tanathos' inhuman face. He leaned close and extended an arm, his clenched fingers less than a foot from Kevlin's chest.

"You disappoint me." He spread his fingers wide and a bolt of pure darkness, so deep it burned the eyes, leapt out to strike Kevlin's breastplate, just above his heart.

Kevlin barely registered what was happening before the bolt winked out as fast as it had appeared.

By the seven gods, how can I not be dead?

It couldn't be Antigonus protecting him. The man barely had enough power to stay alive.

Tanathos frowned, reflecting Kevlin's confusion. Then the shadeleech lashed out toward Kevlin's throat.

He's going to throttle me?

The thought seemed ridiculous. Kevlin had envisioned many horrible tortures. Common strangulation seemed insulting.

Instead of choking him, Tanathos grabbed the heavy steel chain around his neck and yanked it, slicing it into the back of Kevlin's neck until the clasp snapped and it came free. Tanathos stepped back, holding up the large, dark amulet Antigonus had made Kevlin take from Bajaran.

Kevlin stared at it in surprise. He'd forgotten he was even wearing it. That stone looked more like he had imagined Oris should. Tanathos seemed to think it was important.

For a moment he savored the idea of Tanathos taking it instead of the real talisman. They'd kill him without realizing where the real talisman was. He'd get the last laugh after all.

Holding the amulet high, Tanathos spun it in the torchlight and laughed when no light reflected off its faceted edges.

"I wondered where this ended up." He made a mock bow to Kevlin. "Thank you for bringing it to me."

"Since you like it so much," Kevlin said, "consider it a gift."

"You intrigue me. I'm surprised you didn't try to murder us tonight. With the amulet nullifying our magic, you might have succeeded."

Realization struck Kevlin like a sledgehammer between the eyes. The amulet? All along it had been the amulet protecting him? *It will offer some protection,* Antigonus had said. If only the old man had stayed conscious long enough to explain.

The bitter disappointment must have reflected on his face because Tanathos smiled, a snakelike ripple of his lips. "You didn't know?"

This conversation was getting embarrassing, so Kevlin sulked and said nothing.

"Let's start with those devilish little crystals you used at the inn," Tanathos said. "Tell me about them."

"Sorry." Kevlin forced the words past the lump of dread in his throat. "It's a trade secret. If I tell you, I'll have to kill you."

He'd love nothing better than to kill Tanathos, but he wasn't fooling anyone. The first thing to remember when being interrogated was to never give them what they wanted. Of course, that led to the second thing which was that things were about to get ugly.

One of the hovering makrasha slammed a fist into Kevlin's stomach. Pain exploded where Dhanjal's blade had sliced him two days before and he spewed out the pathetic remains of the little he'd eaten.

He aimed for Tanathos, but the makrasha stood in the way. It ignored the bile dripping down its torso and looked to Tanathos for permission to strike again.

Kevlin closed his eyes and tried to calm his screaming midsection. His padded tunic felt damp and he had no doubt the blow had torn the stitches open. He tried to spit the vile-tasting residue of vomit out of his mouth, but it only dribbled down his chin, filling his nostrils with the stench of his own guts.

He hadn't screamed. It was a small triumph, one that would be taken away all too soon.

Haraz entered the cell, "He has taken it."

Tanathos nodded. "As I expected." He then spoke a word in a harsh, guttural dialect.

The second makrasha started cranking the geared wheel. The chains tightened, lifting Kevlin off the bunk by the wrists, pulling him so high his toes barely touched the top of the bunk. The weight on his injured shoulder sent searing waves of pain all the way down his arm.

Definitely ugly. He hated being right so often.

Tanathos eyed him like a butcher examining a hog he was about to slaughter. "He named you steward, didn't he?"

Even as Kevlin struggled to think of an appropriate reply, Haraz said, "He wears the old man's ring."

Tanathos glanced at Antigonus' ring on Kevlin's right hand. Then he did a double-take and stepped closer, peering intently. His smile faded.

"It's not the old man's ring." He sucked in a quick breath. "The Flaming Sword."

Haraz leaned closer. "How is that possible?"

Tanathos rounded on Kevlin. "That's what you're going to explain right now."

"I'm the last person you want to ask."

Kevlin instantly regretted saying that for two reasons. First, it was the truth and the cardinal rule when being interrogated was to always lie. Second, that answer *really* triggered Tanathos' temper. Another rule was to not get them too angry too fast.

Too late.

"Enough," Tanathos shouted, his veneer of cordiality burned away. "I know the symbols of the Six and of Oris, but none have proclaimed the Flaming Sword. Who is your master? Who dares carry this symbol?"

He screamed the last words. Fire burned in the depths of the darkness cloaking his eyes and he reached out to snatch the ring from Kevlin's finger.

It exploded.

Or rather, a blue-white sphere of power exploded *out* of the ring. It hurled Tanathos across the cell and sent the others tumbling to the floor.

The incandescent blast stabbed into Kevlin's eyes and the concussion deafened him. The shockwave from the explosion wrenched his shoulders and he ground his teeth against the agony.

Despite the chaos, he refused to close his eyes and miss the sight of Tanathos slamming into the wall before collapsing into an unmoving heap on the floor.

The chain holding the shackle around his right wrist snapped, freeing his arm. The blast had driven the chain into the wall in the middle of a charred spot, roughly the size of his hand. Thinking fast, Kevlin raised his hand again, placing the shackle over the end of the chain. If no one looked closely, they would not notice it had broken.

No one noticed. Haraz rushed to the unmoving Tanathos. The two makrasha drew their weapons and positioned themselves between Kevlin and the shadeleeches, as if expecting him to burst his bands and attack them.

Haraz grasped Tanathos' temples and, after a moment, the man slowly opened his eyes and groaned. He tried to sit up but slumped sideways. With help from a couple of the guards, they dragged Tanathos to his feet. His eyes remained unfocused and his head lolled around as they moved him. His entire right side sagged, as if nothing worked properly.

Tanathos muttered something Kevlin could not hear and the makrasha carried him from the room. Haraz followed and the thick oak door slammed shut behind him.

Kevlin had no idea what had just happened, but loved it. His whisper echoed through the now-empty room.

"That was awesome."

26

TAKING THE PATH LESS TRAVELED OFTEN SUCKS

Slow seconds ticked by while Kevlin held the awkward position against the wall until he was sure his captors would not return. He glanced down at the seemingly harmless ring on his finger. How had it blasted Tanathos?

He had no idea what the flaming sword meant, but one thing was crystal clear: Tanathos would butcher him when he returned. Best to be long gone by then.

It took a little twisting, but he finally extracted the lock picks concealed in his wristguard and freed his other hand. His shoulders ached and his stomach still burned, but it felt like the bleeding had stopped. He didn't bother to inspect it.

His captors had been rather careless in removing his weapons. They'd entirely overlooked the silver dagger in its hidden sheath. Haraz probably hadn't expected him to live very long, and his carelessness gave Kevlin a chance.

He crossed the cell to where Tanathos had fallen, smiling at the memory. A glint of light caught his attention. He pushed aside a clump of straw and laughed in triumph.

Bajaran's amulet.

Tanathos must have dropped it when he struck the wall. Kevlin frowned as he inspected it. The blast that had disabled Tanathos had altered the amulet. It was now a light blue stone on a silver chain.

Hopefully it wasn't damaged. The stone spun on the chain, revealing the tiny flaming sword symbol etched in silver.

With its promised protection, maybe he had a chance. Kevlin slipped the silver chain over his neck and tucked the amulet inside his tunic. He knew without a doubt now that it was a magical item, but that knowledge did not even make him flinch. With shadeleeches planning to rip out his soul and suck it dry, his perspective of what constituted bad magic had changed.

He turned to the door and pressed his ear against the little shuttered window set into it, but heard nothing. It took less than a minute to pick the simple heavy lock. The tumbler fell back with what seemed a terribly loud *click*.

He threw his weight against the door.

It did not budge.

The deadbolt.

Kevlin bit back a curse and listened again. Nothing. Maybe they hadn't heard. It didn't really matter.

By the Lady's temper, I need a break.

Leaning his head against the unyielding oak, he considered his options. He drew the silver dagger from its hidden sheath. The blade had sliced clean through a wrist-sized chunk of wood just yesterday, although that seemed a lifetime ago.

It proved just as effective against the hardened oak of the doorframe, and he soon carved away enough of the frame to reveal the deadbolt and the anchor bolts holding the bracket to the door. He struck the blade against one of the anchor bolts, hoping to wiggle it free of the restraining wood. Instead, the blade sheared clean through.

The edge of the blade appeared unaffected by the abuse. Bajaran might be a betrayer, but he had excellent taste in weapons. Then Kevlin thought of how easily the blade must have plunged into Antigonus' chest, and shuddered.

He changed tactics and drove the dagger against the back of the deadbolt, scarring it deeply. It cut through on the third strike.

He'd made some noise with those cuts. Surely anyone standing guard outside would know something was up. Time to find out. Kevlin threw his weight against the door, driving it open hard in case someone was lurking right outside.

It flew open without resistance, and he barely caught it before it slammed against the wall. The effort pulled him off-balance, into the room.

Not only was the room empty, but his belongings were still sitting on the table.

"There's no way they could be so stupid," he muttered as he stepped toward the table.

"You're right."

He spun to see Haraz leaning back in a chair beside one of the other cell doors, where no chair had stood a moment ago.

Haraz clapped his hands slowly, mockingly, as Kevlin's hopes for escape, for life, crumbled. The shadeleech had just been playing with him all along.

The shadeleech rose. "You are a puzzle. Your resourcefulness suggests extensive training, but simple tricks seem to surprise you."

"How did you. . .?"

"Remain unseen?" The shadeleech sneered. "It's a simple trick to take one's surroundings and bend them around one so as to remain unseen."

"I'll remember that," Kevlin said, in an attempt to keep the man talking.

Haraz snarled, "No, you will die." He raised one hand and a bolt of black magic streaked across the space between them, striking Kevlin in the chest.

Kevlin looked down, expecting to see a gaping hole, but his armor was unmarked.

It looked like the amulet was working, but that hadn't been the way he'd hoped to test it. Actually, he felt great. A throbbing warmth spread through his chest, and with it returned his strength, as if he'd slept for hours. Even the pain in his stomach faded.

Haraz cursed and lifted both hands. A rolling ball of fire materialized and spun toward Kevlin, crackling with lethal magic and growing until it filled the room. The sharp tang of sulfur stung his nostrils as the air became searing hot.

Kevlin backed away, but could not escape. The fire struck, but was sucked into his chest with a blue-white flash.

He laughed and blew Haraz a kiss.

A blue glow emanated from under his jerkin, and light spilled out his open collar. The warm sensation in his chest intensified. This new strength was too similar to what he'd experienced under the influence of the song of Savas, like a foreign power invading his soul.

I won't surrender again.

Instead of trying to drown his mind, the power pushed against him, struggling to escape. It roared through his veins like liquid fire, burning away his aches and pains and filling him with boundless energy.

Haraz shouted in rage, drew a dagger from beneath his robes and charged.

Steel on steel. That was a threat Kevlin knew how to deal with.

Kevlin threw the silver dagger at Haraz and focused all his new energy on the dagger as it left his hand, willing it to be gone.

It obeyed.

Somehow that energy transferred to the blade. He could not explain it, but as soon as he formed the thought in his mind, it happened. Blinding white light enveloped the dagger as it flew across the room.

Haraz's shout of fury turned into a cry of surprise, and he raised his hands to ward off the attack.

Too slow.

The silver dagger slashed through Haraz's upraised hand without slowing, then drove deep into his chest. The energy encasing the blade exploded, blasted the shadeleech off his feet and left him a smoking, bloody ruin.

What a mess.

For a double heartbeat Kevlin stood transfixed, mouth agape. He stared at his own hand, wonder mixed with fear at what he'd done.

He was alive. That was all that mattered.

Of course, if he didn't get moving fast, he might not be alive for long. Haraz's cries were sure to have roused others. He had no idea what he'd just done to Haraz or how to do it again. No, he didn't *want* to do it ever again. He just needed to run.

Running he could do.

Grabbing up the silver dagger from the mess that used to be Haraz, Kevlin ran back to the table. He found the rune-covered bag still in the burglar pack, with the rock inside it.

"Thank the Light and the Lady."

Kevlin slipped on the pack, buckled on his sword belt and grabbed his boots. He paused to listen outside Antigonus' cell, but heard nothing. He wanted to throw open the door and give the old sentinel the chance to escape. The hard truth was that he couldn't save Antigonus, not today.

To save him, Kevlin had to get away and return with reinforcements. Placing a hand on the door, he mouthed a farewell before turning and racing down the corridor toward the exit. He kicked open the door at the end of the hallway where he'd been ambushed last time, sword ready, expecting to be met by armed makrasha.

The hallway was deserted.

Maybe the walls surrounding the holding cells had been muffled with more than thick wood to block the screaming of prisoners. He ghosted down the hall and returned to the front room. The fire was dead, the whole room cloaked in darkness. He crossed to the main door and slipped on his boots. His blisters hurt less than he expected. At this point, he'd take every little mercy he could get.

Out on the porch, he paused to survey the darkened parade ground. The sky was already beginning to change from black to pre-dawn gray. Most of the fort lay quiet and dark, but in the glow of the two remaining torches fixed to the wall, he caught glimpses of guards passing in turn. Getting out over the wall was going to be tricky, so he spent several precious seconds considering his next move.

Although it was no longer raining, the ground was still muddy and his tracks could be easily followed once they discovered he was gone. That meant no tracks in new places.

He descended the steps and crossed the parade ground at a loping run. His boots squished in the mud and he breathed deep the fresh air scrubbed clean by heavy rain.

After jogging down the dark alley between the barracks, he surveyed what he could of the outer wall. No torches burned nearby, and he heard no footsteps on the walk. He only needed a few more minutes. His tracks would hopefully blend in with those he'd left earlier, and make it harder for them to determine if he'd returned that way.

Kevlin skirted the outer edge of the barracks, heading back to where the wall ended against the cliff. Time was slipping away. Already he could see more clearly.

"Here we go," he breathed, reaching for handholds. Just at that moment, a shout rang from the command building.

They knew he'd escaped.

Even as the echoes of the shout faded, the blast of a horn raised the alarm. The fort erupted into a maelstrom of activity as makrasha boiled from their barracks to assemble in the parade ground. Many others raced up onto the top of the wall. Torches sprang to life all along it as the guards stationed there spread out.

Black despair sapped Kevlin's strength like poison, and he slammed a fist against the uncaring wood that blocked his escape.

With terrible efficiency, the makrasha mobilized. Orders were shouted and torches lit as the creatures began splitting into squads to hunt him down. On the wall, several beasts raced for the cliff above where he crouched. He'd never get over the top before they spotted him.

Kevlin slipped back along the edge of the cliff to stay clear of their torchlight. There he stopped and leaned back against its rough surface in despair. If he went any further, the fresh tracks he made would give him away and the hunt would be over in seconds.

There was nowhere left to run.

Hiding anywhere in the fort would just delay the inevitable. They would find him.

He'd come too far, learned too much, and now carried the hope of the empire in his pack. Thrusting aside despair, he racked his brain, searching for a plan, an idea.

Wherever I walk, they can track me. The thought mocked him.

He looked up.

Deep shadow obscured everything more than a few feet up the face of the cliff. If he couldn't see up there, they probably couldn't either. Although almost vertical as it soared high into the darkness, the cliff face was rough, climbable.

Lights were approaching. Time to move.

Kevlin found promising handholds and pulled himself off the ground. The rock was cold and wet but offered good purchase, and the first several feet were easy.

He climbed as fast as he dared through the near-darkness while several makrasha approached below. They paused and appeared to be arguing over something on the ground, giving him another precious minute to continue his ascent.

He found a narrow ledge about forty feet up the cliff and settled onto it with his back against the rock. He rested while the patrol continued moving along the base of the cliff, still studying the ground.

Then Merab strode into the torchlight. With the shadeleech directly below him, Kevlin felt terribly exposed. If only he had a really big rock to drop.

The group searched methodically, but none of them looked up. Merab struck one of the beasts and shouted something in a harsh language. The makrasha all cowered away from him, then returned to their search while Merab strode away into the darkness.

A clatter of hooves drew Kevlin's eyes to the gate. A mounted column of riders, followed by scores of makrasha on foot, left the fort, split into two groups, and rode slowly along the outside of the wall.

Had he climbed over, they would have found his tracks and run him to ground before he could cover the half mile to the shelter of the forest. At least out on open ground he'd have a fighting chance.

The light of the coming day would eventually reveal him on the cliff, but he couldn't risk descending. The patrol had moved on, but they'd surely return.

Only one way to go.

Deep shadow prevented him from seeing much higher, but the memory of that towering cliff set his heart pounding. It was a very long way to climb.

Lady have mercy.

Not giving himself time to reconsider, he began climbing again. In the near-complete darkness, he felt his way up, concentrating on making every movement count while not making a sound. His wounds ached, but the stitches held, and he made a point of not thinking about it.

The rock face was rough, cold, and wet, with small pockets of lichen and moss that he avoided for fear of slipping and plummeting to his death. After a time he glanced down and found himself high above the treetops.

Seeing the land spread out in the early morning light, with nothing supporting him but his toes and the tips of his fingers, was dizzying. He'd heard of brave men suddenly going weak when faced with a long drop. As a youth, scaling the masts of his father's ship had never bothered him, but somehow this was different.

He decided not to look down again.

At least the cliff faced west, away from the rising sun. Even though the early morning light shone across the trees far out in the forest, shadow still ruled the cliff face and would continue to hide him until noon. All he had to do was get to the top.

Like scaling ten ship's masts, stacked atop each other, but without the handy rope ladders.

He really started wishing for those rope ladders when he reached a stretch of blank stone face that prevented further progress. Glancing down, he bit back a curse. He couldn't go back. Rising panic threatened to overwhelm him.

He was stuck.

Pressing himself against the cliff, he reached out as far as he could with one hand, searching for a way around. Nothing.

Shifting his grip, he tried with the other hand.

There. At the very farthest reach of his fingers he felt something that might be a handhold, but he couldn't be sure. He wasn't quite tall enough.

He'd have to jump to reach it.

For half a minute, he clung there, fighting fear and searching for a different way. Stone dust coated his lips and he fought down a cough that might shake him loose.

There was no other way.

Time to spin the Wheel.

Kevlin kicked off with both feet, lunging up and to the right. He grabbed for the handhold, and at the apex of his leap, his fingers slipped around a knob of stone.

For a terrifying heartbeat he hung, feet scrabbling for purchase against the cliff while he clawed at the stone with his other hand. The strain on his injured shoulder set the muscles screaming in protest. His fingers trembled and his hand began to cramp.

One foot found purchase, a tiny crack barely enough for his toes. It took a little of the strain off until he found a hold for his left hand and pulled himself higher.

A few minutes later, he reached a rougher section of the cliff, with a small ledge he could stand on. Breathing heavily, he wiped sweat from his eyes and fought the urge to give up. His muscles quivered from the strain, and he felt shaky with fear. He could not go back down, but doubted he'd make it all the way up. What a stupid way to die.

He had no other choice.

So he climbed.

In the past couple of days, he'd walked many miles, battled a Blade Stalwart and shadeleeches, and watched comrades die. His strength was beginning to fail. His equipment dragged him down, and his feet hurt. He yearned to drop extra weight, but that would give him away.

He eventually found another small ledge to stand on, barely four inches wide, that allowed him to relieve his aching fingers. His body trembled with exhaustion and he panted for breath. Craning his head back, he looked for the top of the cliff, but could see nothing but unending stone above. How high was it anyway?

Action for Honor, for Life.

The slogan of his mercenary legion reverberated through his mind. He hadn't allowed himself to even think it for years, but the power of that slogan rang within his soul with undiminished force.

His men used to chant it before battle, uniting them in purpose and brotherhood. Repeating the phrase to harden his resolve, he reached up and grabbed the next handhold. He climbed for several minutes, trying to drive himself up the cliff face by sheer force of will.

If wishes were cargo, he never would have left the life of a merchant as a youth.

He had to slow down as the pain in his fingers and arms grew severe. His legs shook from the strain, and his stomach started to cramp.

Still he climbed. Hours dragged by as he focused entirely on the next handhold, then the next. Nothing else mattered. So focused was he on the struggle to move forward that he nearly climbed right past a wide ledge.

Once he confirmed it wasn't a delusion crafted by his exhausted mind, he climbed onto it. He lay gasping for breath, exulting in the simple pleasure of relaxing, past caring how precariously close to the edge he might be.

Had his position not been so dangerous, he would have gladly drifted off to sleep. He closed his eyes for several moments, willing his muscles regain their strength, and slowly became aware of sunlight streaming over his face. At first he welcomed its warmth, then sat up with a start.

He was no longer in the shadow.

Kevlin looked around and, for the first time in hours, really took stock of his position.

"Light preserve me," he whispered.

The ledge upon which he rested was positioned high up the massive cliff. Far below lay the fort, looking like a child's toy, with miniature figures barely discernible. He had to be at least a thousand feet above the forest floor, and could see for miles over the forest under the clear noonday sun.

Noonday sun? He'd spent the entire morning scaling the cliff.

Looking back at the route he'd traveled, he could scarcely believe he'd managed it. He twisted around to look up, and his heart leaped with joy.

Above his little perch, the slope became much gentler, and the top wasn't far off. Staggering to his feet, he finished the ascent with a final burst of energy and fell exhausted behind the first screen of thick brush clustered along the top of the cliff.

After a minute of blissful relaxation, he peered back through the screen of greenery, and froze. Something came flying up across the cliff face, circling as it rose along a current of air. It looked like a hawk, but seemed to be formed from glowing red light.

Kevlin ducked behind the thick brush. He didn't know what the spectral bird might be, so he assumed it came from Tanathos. Who else but a shadeleech would conjure such a thing directly over the fort?

Had he remained any longer on the cliff face, it would have spotted him. Would it have ripped him from his precarious perch or just summoned Tanathos? It wouldn't have offered him a ride, that was for sure.

Every sense alert, Kevlin waited in tense silence for any indication that he had been seen. After five long, uneventful minutes, he peeked out between the bushes, but saw no sign of the spectral bird. He'd have to stay within the thickest cover for the remainder of the day to avoid being spotted.

With the immediate threat gone, he sagged back and took off his boots to massage his feet. The blisters were worse, and he even had a couple on his toes. One had popped, and it burned in the air. Walking was going to be torture.

Kevlin removed his burglar pack, checked the rock in the rune-covered pouch, and munched some of his meager rations. Only one apple remained, along with a couple handfuls of nuts and some hard bread. He jingled Bajaran's purse and smiled ruefully. He had plenty of money but nothing to buy.

After pulling on his boots, he stood with a grimace and headed south along the cliff edge. From what he remembered, the cliff ended a few miles farther south. Hopefully there would be a way down, and hopefully Ceren had found Harafin.

While he was making wishes, hopefully Harafin thought to bring a cook who loved to grill steaks.

At least the shadeleeches and makrasha were stuck at the bottom of the cliff. They'd have a hard time catching him. Since he wasn't much of a woodsman, he couldn't easily live off the land, and in such a deep forest he could easily get lost. Keeping close to the cliff made the most sense.

As he started what was bound to be a long hike, he wondered how Ceren was doing.

27

ANOTHER UNEXPECTED ROAD

The whinny of a horse woke Ceren.

She sat up with a start and banged her head on the roof of her shelter. Her body ached from the strain of the past couple of days. She shivered with cold but was glad to see the rain had stopped. The gray light of pre-dawn had replaced the darkness, and the air was crisp. Her breath clouded in front of her face when she exhaled.

She peered through the brush to see two men riding up the trail past where she lay concealed. That was a lucky spin of the Wheel. She was saved.

Even as she opened her mouth to call out to them, the words froze on her lips. The two men wore crimson robes.

Shadeleeches.

A gigantic makrasha marched into view behind them, followed by many more, all marching in silence, their breath billowing around them in steamy clouds.

Ceren pressed herself down to the damp earth, biting her lip to suppress a whimper of fear. Questions multiplied in her mind but she lacked the information to answer them. One rose to the fore.

Had they killed Kevlin?

The creatures marched past without slowing. Ceren was amazed at the number of the beasts, but she did not spot the shadeleech from the inn, or Rhea, or Dhanjal.

It had to be a separate group. Were they an advance guard, clearing the way for the rest to make their escape? She frowned as she considered the possibilities, none of which were encouraging.

The trail led toward the highway, but she doubted that company would risk the open road. Even if they killed every traveler they encountered, they would be discovered eventually.

Several minutes after they all passed, Ceren crawled out of her hiding place and moved to the middle of the trail to look after them. She drew her sword and considered her options.

A growl behind her made her spin. Three paces away, filling the trail with its terrifying bulk and making horrible clicking sounds with its teeth, stood a makrasha. Its sword was already raised and it stared at her with flat green eyes.

It opened its huge maw and roared, giving her a clear view of rows of sharp teeth and two long fangs glinting with poison. Its heavy, musky scent filled the air, and its breath smelled like a cesspit.

The creature lunged for her, both hengaruk extending to grab her with their stubby, clawed fingers. Ceren scuttled to the side and slashed at one grasping hengaruk, slicing the disgusting hand from the end of the tri-segmented limb. The makrasha howled and swung a heavy overhand blow that would have split her like a melon.

She dodged again, and the sword thundered into the ground next to her, burying itself a foot into the soft earth. The creature stumbled forward, so close its stench made her want to vomit.

It tried grabbing her again, but she slashed her sword across its insect-like eyes. They burst, spurting green liquid into her face, and she couldn't suppress a shriek of disgust as she backed away.

Unable to see, it howled in pain, then barreled forward, arms outstretched. The crippled beast raced past her and collided with a tree.

Ceren gulped as it crashed to the ground. If she'd been standing a little closer, it might have grabbed her and killed her even when blinded.

Loud grunting noises from farther up the trail spun her around. More makrasha appeared around the distant corner and howled when they caught sight of her. They fired crossbows, then charged.

With a scream, Ceren dove off the trail and sprinted into the forest. Driven by terror, only one thought beat in her mind.

Run!

The entire forest shook behind her as makrasha crashed through the heavy brush. They growled and clicked and shouted, and the sounds of pursuit drove her on faster. She flew through the woods like a deer, flowing around trees and brush that her pursuers had to trample or hack through to follow.

She ceased to think. Nothing mattered but running farther and faster than the creatures hunting for her blood. Gradually the makrasha fell behind, unable to match her breakneck pace. She smiled, a feral grin of victory.

The forest to her right erupted in flame and the heat blasted her exposed skin. After the deep chill from earlier, the difference felt wonderful, and she laughed aloud.

The danger was all too clear. Shadeleeches had joined the pursuit.

As an intelligent, educated noblewoman, she had been taught to scoff at the wild tales of horror told of the shadeleeches. Racing through the early morning wilderness, pursued by a hundred makrasha and a pair of shadeleeches intent on turning the forest into her funeral pyre, she no longer doubted even the wildest stories.

Another blast of fire ignited the forest to her left, so close that moisture evaporated from her slicker in a puff of steam. Sweat poured down her reddened face, but she could do nothing but run harder still.

Smoke blinded and choked and burned in her lungs. The taste of ash filled her mouth, and the fire roared like thunder as it crackled on both sides, consuming the wet forest till all was obscured in heavy, black smoke.

Then she ran off a cliff.

Ceren screamed, arms and legs flailing, as she plummeted toward the churning surface of a river thirty feet below. She struck the fast-moving water, sinking deep, her sweating body assaulted by the brutal cold of the water.

She struggled upward, desperate to reach the surface and escape the river's icy embrace. Though hampered by the weight of her sword, she would never consider letting it go.

A few seconds later she surfaced, the force of her last kick driving her half out of the water. She gulped for air and rolled onto her back to sheath her sword. She slipped off her pack while it still retained some buoyancy.

This section of the river flowed rapidly through the deep cut in the earth she had run off of. It was already sweeping her around a bend that blocked her view of the thick smoke rising into the early morning sky. The intense cold leeched the warmth from her overheated muscles. The near shore was too steep to climb, and the far shore looked little better.

Growing up in the coastal city of Agoraeun, she was an accomplished swimmer. If the water wasn't so cold, she could stay afloat as long as she needed to, but if she didn't escape its icy embrace soon, the uncaring river would finish what the makrasha had failed to do.

The pack wouldn't stay afloat for long, so she salvaged what she could. She slipped a couple of apples into the pockets of her slicker, along with the purse of coins Kevlin had given her. If she survived to Ingolf, she could purchase whatever else she needed.

The only other item worth saving was the healer's case. Its tight seal guaranteed it would float. She scavenged a strap from the larger pack and used it to secure the case over one shoulder. Then she floated on her back, trying to conserve her waning strength.

A minute later she spotted a huge pile of brush jammed against some large rocks, and kicked in that direction. Timing was crucial as she angled across the current to intersect the jam. She needed to get close enough to grab hold of something without getting dragged under.

She lined herself up carefully, but an unexpected eddy swept her in closer, threatening to drive her into the center of the pile. She struggled to swim clear, but the current proved too strong.

Despite her frantic clawing at the slippery wood along the edge of the pile, the water swept her under a heavy branch and into darkness. She raised one arm to prevent her head from crashing into the logs as the water rolled her under the mass of branches.

The current drove her onward, smashing her into the thick end of another log, and the impact knocked the breath from her lungs. Stars sparkled in the darkness around her, and she barely held on to consciousness.

I can't die like this!

She was an excellent swimmer, but that didn't matter. As a girl, she'd seen a friend drown when waves drove her under an overhanging rock.

The current tumbled Ceren past the log and drove her deeper under the log jam. Her lungs screamed for air, panic threatening to overwhelm her.

Helpless against the force of the river, she crashed into the face of a large boulder. She hung there, pressed against the solid rock for three heartbeats. One wildly kicking foot pushed against another rock below her. She pushed off and slid up the boulder face.

With the slight change of position, the water caught her differently and shot her up along the sloping face of the stone. She collided with the massed tangle of wood, her head smacking into a protruding branch.

The branch snapped and her head burst through the surface of the water. She gulped a sweet mouthful of air before coughing up water. She gripped the branches to maintain her precarious position. The force of the current was less there, but if she went under again, she doubted she'd ever surface.

Only her head rose out of the water. The intertwining branches blocked further access. She had to climb higher before her strength failed, but the gap was too narrow even for her slender shoulders.

She fumbled for her dagger with numb, sluggish fingers and almost dropped it. Finally, with the blade firmly in hand, she hacked at the branches blocking her way, but they seemed made of iron.

"I can do this!" she screamed, hacking at the wood with desperate strength.

A branch broke. She struck again, and another gave way. It took several more minutes to widen the gap enough to worm her way through. Weeping with exhaustion, and ignoring the scratches from the branches, she hauled her body out of the water until she lay in the midst of the log jam.

As she lay shivering from cold and the emotional drain of nearly drowning in the nameless river, she closed her eyes, just for a second, to gather her strength.

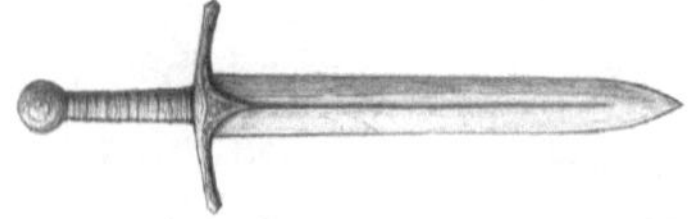

Ceren awoke several hours later, cramped and shivering. The river roared just below, and her soaked clothing dripped from the constant spray. The tiny den smelled of fish and rotting wood. The dense tangle blocked most of the light, leaving her in a constant twilight. She spit out bits of bark that left a taste like acorns in her mouth.

Her battered body ached, but she forced herself to explore the wooden prison. It took half an hour, and a lot of hacking with her dagger, before she broke free of the brush and climbed out onto the top of the pile. She rested for a few minutes, gnawing on one of the apples still in her pocket with a jaw so numb she could barely close it over the icy fruit.

She opened the green leather healer's case with fingers shaking from cold. The seal had held, and no water penetrated inside, so at least she'd gotten one positive spin of the Wheel.

She pulled out the small jar with the copper-colored stopper and worked the cork free. Lacking a cup, she measured several drops of the thick liquid into her palm and licked it into her mouth with a grimace. It tasted terrible, but it would dull the pain.

Next she extracted another, smaller bottle with a bright red stopper. She carefully measured a single drop of golden liquid into her palm and licked that too.

A wave of heat shivered through her, and she gasped with ecstasy. Energy coursed through her, burning away fatigue and pain as if the past few harrowing days had never happened. Her senses sharpened and she felt more alert than ever.

Re-stoppering the bottle, she smiled and tucked it away. Extract of Zindagi was a powerful stimulant, but extremely dangerous. The addictive potion might induce the feeling of strength, but the effect was only a mask. Zindagi allowed one to push their body far beyond its normal limit. If abused, a person could literally run themselves to death.

Given the situation, it was worth the risk.

With renewed strength, Ceren clambered over the brush pile and in less than an hour assembled a cluster of large branches. Using skills she learned as a girl, she wove the branches together into a raft.

She pushed the makeshift craft into the current, leapt aboard, and lay in the center. The river whisked her downstream. The raft shuddered in the current, but held.

This river should empty into the Nagendra, which would carry her to Ingolf. If Harafin hadn't already passed through the town, she'd ride south to meet him.

As the river bore her around the next bend she grinned with fierce pride.

"I can do this."

28

A Path of Darkness

Sitara waited until the quiet hour before dawn to begin her new assault. She probed beyond her room, extending tentacles of thought through the keisara's apartments, then up the narrow stair to the woman's bedroom. The keisara's mind beckoned like a dim light, drawing Sitara's thoughts unerringly toward her.

Sitara caressed the keisara's mind, gently touching her thoughts. Even while sleeping, Keisara Fideima's will proved formidable, like a thick bubble protecting her thoughts.

Proceeding with extreme caution, Sitara first wrapped the keisara's mind with her own thoughts, maintaining a gentle connection. Over a period of several minutes, she increased the pressure until she felt resistance. Then she projected only thoughts of the emperor, of quiet moments Sitara had witnessed them share during her past year of service.

Those thoughts flowed around the outer shell of the keisara's will, a gentle caress that eased the resistance with familiar images. The sleeping woman's thoughts took up the pattern, and Sitara wormed through the barrier, probing deeper, still masked with thoughts of Zuberi.

It took nearly half an hour of careful manipulation that left Sitara trembling with fatigue and drenched with sweat. Finally the keisara's defenses weakened sufficiently. All the while, Sitara monitored the keisara's breathing, watching for signs she might begin waking.

Ever so slowly, Sitara altered the focus from quiet moments spent with Zuberi to more formal events. From there she adjusted again to memories of audiences the emperor had held with his wife in attendance. From there,

Sitara guided the sleeping woman's thoughts to all the times the emperor had been absent, called away to fulfill his duties to the realm instead of his duty to her.

She encountered increasing resistance as the keisara, even in sleep, tried to avoid such disturbing thoughts. Sitara could delay no longer. The drain was proving too great to maintain, and even a momentary lapse in concentration would break the tenuous connection, wasting all the evening's hard work.

She risked planting a thought of Junian into the mix.

That was the dangerous part. Something so foreign to the keisara's normal mental process might trigger a defensive rejection and snap her awake.

The image she *pushed* into the woman's mind was not an exact likeness. She could not use truth to destroy the keisara. Instead, she painted Junian as a slightly younger man, a more handsome one. She eliminated the lines from his face and slightly altered his features to convey a sense of solid dependability.

With the image, she *pushed* whispers of feelings. Junian would appeal to the secret loneliness that tormented the keisara. Sitara crafted Junian into the answer to the keisara's longings. There stood a man whom a woman could count on, who would make his love the center of his life rather than his duty or position. That man would never allow a woman to feel lonely.

The keisara's resistance flared, and Sitara's tenuous connection snapped. She withdrew and returned to her own exhausted body. For several minutes she lay panting, massaging a pounding headache, wondering if the message had been received.

Despite her exhaustion, she didn't drop instantly asleep. She'd barely slept all night, and the effort to infiltrate the keisara's mind had taken a terrible mental toll. When she did eventually slip into a fitful slumber, her dreams were dark and troubling.

Over breakfast later that morning, the only indication that her efforts had proven successful was a passing comment by the keisara that she had not slept well.

It was a start, if a humble one.

Pride warmed Sitara and helped stave off her own exhaustion, quelling the queasiness that had lurked in the pit of her stomach all morning. She embraced it, for she could not afford any weakness. This battle would be fought in the dead of night, in the recesses of the keisara's deepest secrets.

29

ARE WE THERE YET?

Kevlin traveled steadily all afternoon, periodically peering out over the top of the cliff for signs of pursuit. A thin line cutting along the far horizon might be the highway, but nothing else broke the heavy expanse of forest. On top of the cliff, the forest grew thick enough to provide excellent cover without blocking his path.

For the first hour or two, his spirits remained high and he made good progress, but soon the aching of his feet became impossible to ignore. By mid-afternoon, he had acquired a new crop of blisters that formed just as the older ones began to pop.

Before sunset, his feet were covered in bleeding, oozing sores that flared painfully at every step. His feet had always blistered easily, but never so bad.

I wish Ceren were here.

He doubted she could carry him far, but he could really use some of that painkiller. Another kiss might have helped a lot too. He used the pleasant memory of the first to ward off the pain of his feet.

He plodded on until he could no longer see and started blundering into bushes and trees. When he found a bubbling stream, he collapsed to the ground for the night.

He munched a handful of nuts and washed them down with icy water from the stream. His blanket was in the pack he'd left behind in the woods outside the fort, but at least he had his flint and steel. With a thick branch, he dug a pit and lit a small, well-shielded fire to huddle beside. The temperature fell, and his nose started to drip. It was going to be an uncomfortable night.

Leaning against a tree, he tried to sleep, but between the chill air and his throbbing feet, he managed little more than a doze.

Eventually he gave up and sat cross-legged next to the fire where he passed the night feeding the tiny blaze to keep warm. As the temperature dropped almost to freezing, the little fire couldn't produce nearly enough heat, but he didn't dare build it higher. His mind eventually settled into a half-dozed stupor as the seconds ticked slowly by.

At the first gray light of morning, he awakened to a cacophony of noise. Birds greeted the coming day, and small animals scurried through the forest in their incessant hunt for food to hoard against the coming winter. A breeze picked up, smelling of moss and pine, and the forest seemed to glow with the first rays of morning light.

One squirrel started chirping angrily at him from a nearby tree and he began looking for a rock. Roasted squirrel sounded pretty good.

Kevlin rose then nearly pitched forward onto his face.

"Sherah's teeth," he muttered at the stabbing pain from muscles contracted during the cold night. For several minutes, he worked feeling and flexibility back into his aching limbs. Only then did he risk standing again and shambling slowly south.

The squirrel disappeared after a final, chittering outburst that sounded far too much like mocking laughter.

Kevlin's breath misted the air in front of him, and within the first dozen steps the pain in his feet flared to a roar. It was going to be a long day.

About midmorning, he crossed a small stream and drank greedily from the pure water before sitting to rest. He pulled his boots off and gritted his teeth against the sharp sting of the fresh air against his open sores.

That sight was as disgusting as most mercenaries' table manners.

He inspected the bleeding, oozing mess, then cut a piece off the bottom of his tunic and bathed his feet with the icy water. He grunted from the searing pain at first contact, but after a few minutes the cold water soothed some of the ache away.

After working his boots back on, he set his jaw and stumbled on. A short while later he again stepped out onto the edge of the cliff. The ground didn't look so far away, confirming his suspicion that he had been walking a gentle downslope for the past hour.

He scraped lunch from the last crumbs of food in the bottom of his burglar pack, and some water from another stream. His stomach complained loudly about the abuse, and it was a relief to focus on that discomfort for a while rather than his feet. If he didn't reach some sort of village soon, or run across other travelers, he was going to have serious problems.

While he walked, he mulled over the situation. Again and again he played out in his mind the events of the past few days, amazed at how deeply his fate had become tangled with Antigonus'. Had he not lived it himself, he wouldn't have believed the tale.

Magic terrified him. Even those who professed to serve the empire and protect the helpless from others were too easily seduced by it, too ready to abuse it. He'd learned young to maintain a wary distance.

Despite his best efforts, he now wore an enchanted amulet that scared him as much as it protected him. Antigonus had named *him* steward. Unbelievable. No steward had ever carried Oris through the Hallvarri wilderness with a bunch of shadeleeches and makrasha in pursuit.

It seemed undignified.

What was a steward supposed to do anyway? Antigonus had said he should give the rock to Harafin, so that's what he'd do. Let the other sentinel figure out what to do with it.

No wonder no one talked about Oris in detail. It'd lose a lot of its grandeur if everyone knew it was just a rock.

How did it work?

Most rocks were only good for throwing at people, or annoying squirrels. Oris was supposed to be a mighty talisman.

If only he knew how it worked, he'd turn it on Tanathos in a heartbeat. He was so far in over his head, he didn't know what to think anymore.

The rock was supposed to be tied to the empire's defenses, and the Six, the bearers of the magical weapons of the Six Kingdoms. The power of the Six somehow combined with Oris, transforming into a force the enemies of the empire had never been able to withstand.

None of those legends ever detailed exactly what powers the rock possessed. That had never been a concern before, because of the great stories about the exploits of the individual champions who bore the six weapons of power.

Each weapon chose a champion, its bearer, from among the people of the kingdom it protected. They held that honor throughout their lives. When they died, a new champion was chosen. They might work independently, or fight within the armies of their kingdoms, but the ultimate power of the Six was only unleashed together, united through Oris.

Each weapon was as unique as the kingdom it protected, and the tales of their bearers were many and varied. As he trudged along, Kevlin recounted his favorite tale to help pass the time.

It was the century-old adventure of Cothric Laistran, the famously colorful bearer of the Bladestaff, and Hakan Dubhara, bearer of the Spear. Those two men, renowned heroes from the last war against the Grakonians, had been sent to negotiate a treaty with Nedikat, the kingdom south of Einarr that often allied with the Grakonians.

Nedikan raiders had been spotted in Einarr, stealing horses and capturing people to be sold as slaves. The two kingdoms had agreed to send ambassadors to the Nedikan border fortress of Albajorg to form a treaty. Hakan had been assigned to represent Einarr, with Cothric an eager companion.

It hadn't gone well.

The peace delegation had been attacked and everyone but the two bearers killed. Hakan and Cothric had fought their way free, although Hakan had been badly injured. The two heroes returned two days later to the surprise of the Nedikans still hunting them.

After sneaking into the fortress, Cothric boldly assaulted the main keep, supported by the wounded Hakan, who despite his injuries managed to climb to the top of one of the towers overlooking the central fortress.

Safely ensconced in that strategic position, he hurled the Spear, unleashing explosive elemental magic upon those attempting to stand against Cothric. The Spear's power had returned it to the hand of its bearer within seconds, and he threw it again, and again.

Cothric, his speed enhanced by the Bladestaff, fought his way into the keep and killed the lord of the city, the king's ambassador, and most of the other nobles. So overwhelming was the attack that the entire population of Albajorg fled. The two heroes then returned to Einarr to inform the king that no treaty had been signed.

Such power, such amazing exploits, were the legacy of the bearers of the Six.

Kevlin stumbled, driving one foot onto a jagged rock and generating a wave of pain that shot all the way up his thigh. He gasped and leaned on a tree until the throbbing subsided. He spat a couple fresh curses at Tanathos. Thinking of the story of Cothric and Hakan had helped him keep his mind off the discomfort for a while, but the afternoon was still far from spent.

With a grunt of determination, he resumed his difficult journey. He soon cut a couple of walking sticks to help ease the pressure on his feet, so he no longer had to hunch over like a cripple. Desperate for distraction, he again turned his thoughts to the bearers of the Six, and tried to remember as many of their stories as possible.

Cothric and Hakan had accumulated the most but, as a group, bearers of the Axe and the Mace generated even more than bearers of the Bladestaff. The Axe of Donarr and the Mace of Tamarr were powerful weapons that could launch blasts of energy and endow their bearers with tremendous battle prowess. The Bow of Freyarr rarely played as crucial a role, even though its arrows, imbued with elemental magic, often turned the tide of battle from its support position.

After a couple more hours of painful hiking, Kevlin paused to rest on a fallen log where he could look out over the cliff to watch for signs of pursuit. While he sat, he considered the final weapon, the Pike of Meinarr. The kingdom of Meinarr, his homeland, produced few noteworthy warriors, and those chosen to bear the Pike were often humble and unassuming.

They didn't generate lots of stories. The Pike usually held the center of the empire's lines, radiating a shield of energy that protected the entire front line of a phalanx.

With an effort, Kevlin rose and resumed walking. There were other powers and capabilities accredited to the Six, but the legends were often contradictory. He had no idea if some were just wrong, or if the Six really did adjust to the skills of their bearers.

Too bad he couldn't use Oris to destroy Tanathos and his secret band, but that was fantasy. Only the most powerful sentinels ever wielded the rock's power, and Antigonus alone had done so for most of the last hundred years.

At least I get to deliver it to Harafin. Maybe I'll get to watch the next bearer rip Tanathos to pieces.

He'd enjoy that.

With those thoughts keeping him occupied, he limped painfully on through the rest of the afternoon, leaning more and more heavily on the walking sticks. As darkness settled over the land, he took one last look over the edge of the cliff that rose a mere thirty feet, a pale shadow of its earlier mighty height.

Not far ahead, the ridge descended abruptly to meet the ground below. He'd have to be more careful in the morning. His pursuers could come at him from any direction.

Just as he was searching for a place to pass another miserable night, a flash of light drew his attention. He scanned the darkness, ready to flee if it glowed red, the hallmark color of shadeleech powers.

There. A torch was shining through the trees a little to the southwest. It didn't move, and after a moment another torch flared into view nearby, followed closely by several more.

Kevlin grinned in relief. They were being lit along the street of a town. Kevlin rushed forward, grateful the cliff no longer blocked his route.

He hurried through the darkness, staggering past trees and bushes that seemed intent on barring his path, until he stumbled out onto a road at the edge of a town. Ten days ago, he'd been living in Diodor and this nameless town would have looked insignificant.

Tonight, it seemed a godsend.

A large building with a sign of a frothy mug hanging over the door beckoned him on. Inside, a wave of heat enveloped him in its welcome embrace, rooting out the stubborn chill that clung to him. He breathed deep the delicious aroma of roasting beef, and barely suppressed the urge to laugh with joy.

Tables and chairs filled the large rectangular common room, only sparsely filled with patrons. An open fireplace filled most of the wall under the balcony that led to the upstairs rooms. An astonishing array of hooks and pots and ovens were suspended over the coals, and the wonderful smells that had first greeted him rose from those coals in a nearly tangible wave.

A polished oak bar ran the length of the wall to Kevlin's right. Half a dozen men clustered there, all sparing a moment or two to stare at him as he pushed past them. The innkeeper nodded a greeting. The heavyset, balding fellow's gut bulged out around the apron that tried unsuccessfully to hold it in place.

"What kin I do for you, good sir?" the innkeeper asked.

"I need a room, a bath, and a meal, but in reverse order."

"We kin help with all them. We take fur, credit from the lumber purchaser, or coin."

"Coins. I'll pay with coins."

That earned Kevlin a happy nod. He then had to hide his surprise at the ridiculously low price the innkeeper charged. In Diodor, he'd have spent ten times as much.

For another laughably small fee, he arranged for the innkeeper's daughter to purchase supplies for him so he could get an early start in the morning. Hopefully the local stables could provide a decent mount.

Kevlin took a seat in a chair close to the fire, relaxed, and absorbed the heat. The waitress brought him a huge platter of roast beef, potatoes, spice beans, and half a loaf of fresh bread, along with a mug of mulled cider. Food had never tasted so good.

The innkeeper's daughter, a dark haired girl named Alva, stopped by as he finished his meal. He gave her the list of supplies he needed.

"Tell me about the town, Alva," he said before she left.

"Baldev be the biggest town on the road to Fiachra from the highway." She spoke with obvious pride. "Lots of trappers an' hunters an' loggers bring goods here. The miners bring in a lot of ore from the mountains down south. They float stuff down the river to Ingolf. We got ten merchants living in town."

"How far is it to the highway?"

"I been told it be about a day's ride." She attempted a curtsy before leaving on her errand.

Kevlin followed the innkeeper's directions to the bathhouse situated in a small courtyard to the rear of the inn. The water was already hot over a glowing bed of coals, and it took only a moment to pour a steaming tub. He enjoyed a long soak before washing as best he could with the rough, homemade soap.

By the time he reached his room, Alva had returned and piled all his purchases at the foot of the bed. He gratefully donned a fresh set of clothing. He'd still have to wear the heavy, padded jerkin that went under his armor, but it felt great to have clean clothes against his skin.

Alva had done well. He smiled while inspecting the pile of foodstuffs, heavy cloak, and new blanket. It took only a few minutes to organize it in the new pack. As long as he could buy a decent horse in the morning, he'd be well on his way to finding Ceren.

After everything was in order, he extracted the rune-covered pouch holding Oris. He'd thought about it a lot that day and worried about its safety. He felt uncomfortable wearing the pouch around his neck like Antigonus did, but he also disliked the idea of it swinging at his belt or remaining in his pack. It would be too easy to lose.

Finally, he'd had an idea. He wrapped the pouch in a piece of soft linen, pulled off his right boot, and tucked the small bundle up under its overhanging top.

Knee-high when raised, he normally kept the boots turned down several inches. The folded top flared and easily concealed the presence of the rock. Using needle and thread Alva had purchased for him, he stitched the package in place and surveyed his handiwork. He smiled. Only rarely did anyone look closely at a person's shoes.

He was warm and fed, but he'd already spent two days reaching the town. Hopefully Ceren had found Harafin and warned him of the danger. Time was short. Tanathos could be days gone by the time they returned with reinforcements.

Kevlin's room was at the rear of the inn, on the second floor, with a window overlooking the bathhouse, which didn't seem heavily used. Kevlin carefully barred the door and propped the single chair against. He then barred the window. The bed was small but clean, and it felt wonderful.

As he drifted off to sleep, he mouthed a prayer to whichever god might deign to listen. All they needed was a few days and they could restore Antigonus. Surely that wasn't too much to ask.

30

Unexpected Allies

*B*ang.

The door to Kevlin's room shuddered under a heavy blow.

Kevlin awoke instantly, yanked on his boots, and grabbed his sword belt. The door splintered under another blow and several makrasha tore at the frame to get into the room. Kevlin yanked the blanket off the bed and flung it into the doorway.

Thwok! Crossbows fired, and one whisked past his cheek, missing him by a finger's breadth.

Kevlin ripped the bar from the window, letting the soft light of dawn flood the shadowed room. He threw it back into the mass of bodies jammed in the doorway. One monster grunted in pain.

Another pushed through the door and lunged for him. He leaped through the window, barely escaping its grasping hengaruk, and fell to the flat roof of the bathhouse.

As he rolled off the far side, he wanted to howl with frustration. He had been so close to getting safely away. Maybe he should have paid the gods more respect before asking for favors.

At least the makrasha's Grakonian handlers hadn't thought to station anyone in the courtyard. He raced for the door that led into the common room. He had to get away.

Several makrasha leapt from the window after him. They landed on the bathhouse roof, and their combined weight shattered the tiny building. They fell into a pile of tangled bodies and splintered wood. He didn't look back, but sprinted through the common room, overturning tables and alarming early patrons.

"Get down. Assassins!" Kevlin shouted.

It was a useless gesture. No one would understand what he was talking about until it was too late. Even as he ran for the outside door, the makrasha charged out of the upstairs hallway and raced for the stairs to cut him off.

One of the terrified patrons screamed, "Makrasha!"

The hideous creatures hadn't bothered to hide their telltale hengaruk or cover their faces. People scattered from the foot of the stairs, forcing Kevlin to push through them as the monsters came hurtling down.

It was going to be a close race for the main door.

To block his escape, the lead makrasha jumped the last eight steps. An old man nearby shouted a battle cry in a thin, reedy voice,

"For Land and Lady!"

He threw his chair at the creature, striking it midair.

Knocked off-balance, the beast sprawled across the bottom step. Kevlin vaulted through the doorway just as the old man shrilled another ancient war cry.

That old guy was crazy. If he didn't interfere, the makrasha would probably ignore him.

Shouting chased Kevlin up the street, and he slowed. He couldn't let the villagers get slaughtered. When he turned, he saw makrasha pouring into the street after him. The best thing he could do now was to draw them away.

Great. They're chasing me. So how in the name of the seven gods do I get out of here?

Shouts of alarm were spreading through town, but it would do little good. There was no militia to come to Kevlin's aid.

He had to get away.

Kevlin ran down the street, driving his legs as fast as possible. The sores on his feet reopened and pain flared all the way up his legs at each step. He gritted his teeth and cursed the makrasha for not giving him more time to rest. His only chance was to find a horse.

A quick glance back spurred him on. Strung out along the street behind him were at least thirty makrasha. He didn't spot the telltale robes of the shadeleeches yet, but they would be close by.

Hopefully no other enemies lurked in town. He'd been spinning the Wheel a lot lately, and it'd turned in his favor many times. If it spun against him today, he was doomed.

Arms and legs pumping, he ducked out of the main street into a narrow lane with buildings packed close together on either side. It was barely wide enough for wagons to pass, and an ominous foreboding raised goose-bumps on his arms.

This was a bad idea.

With no time to turn around, Kevlin continued up the narrow street, searching for a horse.

Nothing. Not even a mule.

In fact, the lane was empty except for a white-haired man in the unbleached woolen trousers and tunic common to several orders of stalwarts. In the early-morning shadows, the old man's hair and neatly trimmed beard seemed to glow.

It figured. He'd been looking for stalwarts for days. Now he finally found one and didn't have time to stop.

He closed on the man, yelling, "Get away! For your own safety, run." He was going to add "hide," but the shuttered buildings were built right up against each other. The only option was to run.

The old stalwart smiled widely, as if spotting a long-lost friend. He raised a hand. "Hold, my son."

Kevlin attempted to run past, but the old man stepped into his path, nearly tripping him. The stalwart grabbed his shoulder in a surprisingly strong grip and dragged him to a halt.

"Are you crazy?" Kevlin shouted. "Run before we're both killed." He attempted to shake off the old man's hand.

Still smiling, the stalwart held Kevlin firmly. "When flight will not free you, it is often better to stand and face darkness."

Kevlin looked back to see the first of the makrasha already turning the corner, only fifty paces away. Seeing him standing unmoving in the street, they shouted in triumph.

"Fighting those odds is suicide," Kevlin protested, pointing at the approaching enemy.

"I share faith with you that you may see clearly."

A wave of calm washed over Kevlin, enveloping his panic with a blanket of peace. He took a deep breath.

"Your faith must be blind, old man. I can't defeat them all. You could never heal me fast enough."

The stalwart laughed heartily. "You have more allies than you expect, even in this tiny village."

The old man let go of his shoulder and faced the onrushing creatures. Kevlin took a step away, again intent on fleeing.

"You wouldn't allow an old stalwart to die alone protecting your back, would you, my young friend?"

Kevlin needed to run, to escape, to deliver the rock and fulfill the mission Antigonus had assigned to him. But the stalwart's words seared his conscience and shamed him into holding his ground. He muttered a curse, glowering at the old man.

The stalwart called out loudly to the makrasha. "My children, you have a final opportunity to forsake darkness and turn to the Light. Will you be saved?"

The monsters slowed and clustered together about thirty paces away. Their leader bellowed, "Kill him."

A dozen crossbows fired in unison.

Kevlin tried to grab the old man to pull him to one side, but the stalwart didn't budge. Instead he grinned as if enjoying himself immensely, and snapped his fingers.

A deadly war hammer appeared in his hand, and he took a step toward the bolts streaking straight for him.

He's insane, Kevlin decided. *He's committing suicide.*

The old man began swinging his hammer with blinding speed, and knocked the bolts out of the air. The whirling hammer left a blue glow in its wake.

Already half-turned to flee, Kevlin paused and stared in awe. He'd never seen such a feat.

One bolt broke through the old man's defenses and punched deep into his thigh. He grunted in pain and threw his empty hand into the air. A streak of blue light shot from his fingertips and exploded in a brilliant flash high above the town.

Then he cocked back his arm and *threw* his hammer at the mob of makrasha. It shot from the stalwart's hand like a ballista bolt, spinning once before smashing into one of the makrasha, shattering its ribs and hurling its body back. Blood splattered the group and the monsters recoiled in shock.

"You should've hit the leader," Kevlin said as he strapped on his sword belt. They might just survive after all.

"I first had to administer justice for the bolt that struck my leg."

"You knew who that came from?" Kevlin hadn't been able to track the flights of each bolt, having been focused on getting out of the way.

The angry makrasha leader roared, a singularly disturbing sound from its insect-like mouth, and the entire crowd of monsters charged.

The hammer reappeared in the old man's hand, and he threw it again. The deadly missile crushed the makrasha leader and bowled over several others, but didn't break the charge.

Kevlin drew his sword and heavy dagger, preparing to face the onrushing horde. The old man's prowess was impressive, but too many of the creatures remained. Kevlin's mouth went dry, and he fought an urge to wipe his palms as he stared at the charging beasts.

He focused on the lead makrasha and the thrill of impending struggle set his arms tingling and his heart pounding. He raised his sword, but the ground began to shake with the unmistakable thunder of galloping horses.

Kevlin spared a glance behind to see the new threat.

Charging into the far end of the narrow street came row after row of mounted horsemen. After a frozen heartbeat of dread, he realized that they weren't Grakonians, but men wearing the colors of the Elite Imperial Guard.

"How. . .?" Kevlin breathed. It must all be a dream, a crazy dream.

Four abreast, the horsemen pounded forward in perfect formation, lances lowered, bearing down on the makrasha. Kevlin had never seen a more glorious or welcome sight. In the lead rode a compact warrior in silver-trimmed armor. Rather than a lance, he carried a wicked-looking mace with unusually long spikes.

The makrasha halted their charge and formed a line across the street, pulling small, round shields from their backs.

Kevlin grabbed the old stalwart and dragged him bodily to one side to avoid being crushed by charging horsemen.

The Grakonians loosed another volley of crossbow bolts, aimed mostly at the lead rider. The man shouted and extended his weapon. A blue nimbus gathered around it and expanded in front of him like a giant shield that deflected the bolts aside.

Shouting battle cries, the horsemen smashed into the makrasha with a crash of splintering wood. The center of the Grakonian line collapsed as the first rank of horsemen trampled over the creatures, leaving the remainder pressed back against the walls on each side as the horsemen galloped past.

Rank after rank of horsemen charged between the two lines of Grakonians, but only the riders at either end of each rank could engage the beasts as they thundered past. With more horsemen charging in behind, they couldn't stop.

Sound reverberated between the close-packed buildings, magnified by the echoes until it beat at Kevlin's head like a living thing. The thunder of hooves, loud war cries, the crack of lances against iron shields, and screams of pain rolled together in a nearly overwhelming din. Dust rose like a cloud to choke him. He tasted dirt, and the coppery stench of hot blood filled the alley.

It seemed an eternity before the last of the horsemen galloped past and disappeared around the corner. A third of the Grakonians lay trampled and pierced after the initial charge. Most of the rest gathered into tight groups along either wall and turned to face the next charge.

A handful of them broke away and raced toward Kevlin and the stalwart, intent on fulfilling their duty before the riders could return.

The stalwart's hammer returned again to his hand and he threw it, taking down one of the beasts while they were still a dozen paces away.

Kevlin stepped in front of him.

My turn.

Despite the deadly power of the makrasha, the din of battle stirred his blood, and strength surged through his body. He snarled in defiance, though each of the makrasha stood easily a head taller, and probably weighed twice as much.

Their hengaruk reached longer than his arms, but were burdened by their spent crossbows and shields. In their human-like hands, they each wielded a heavy, single-edged sword. One solid blow from one of those would probably cut him in half.

Battle fury swept away fear and Kevlin leaped forward to meet the closest monster.

It raised its sword high to strike, but an arrow slammed into the middle of its chest, punching through the chain armor. It stumbled and fell dead to the ground.

Kevlin sidestepped the fallen makrasha, unable to spare time to look around for his unexpected ally. The second beast charged, but he deflected its swiping blade high, then jumped aside to avoid being trampled. As it skidded past, he slashed at the creature's legs, cutting deep into the unprotected flesh behind its knees.

It roared in pain and tumbled to the earth with a crash that shook the ground. A heavy blow from the old stalwart's hammer silenced the beast. Kevlin twisted to avoid a strike from the next enemy. It sliced the air so close, that it scraped against his shirt.

Before he could return the blow, the creature shield-smashed him in the face. He stumbled back a step with lights dancing before his eyes, and knees that felt suddenly weak. He struggled to clear his vision, only dimly aware that the narrow street was once more filled with the heavy pounding of a cavalry charge.

The makrasha lunged forward again, striking at his sword arm. He tried to block, but his body responded sluggishly, as if moving under water. Time slowed to a crawl as the creature's heavy blade swung toward his arm.

It was going to cut his arm off.

The stalwart's hammer swept around him and knocked the blade wide with a clash of ringing steel. The sound cleared his head and Kevlin rolled forward under the creature's arms. He lunged to his feet beside it and drove his sword through its chain-link armor with every ounce of strength.

As the blade plunged deep into its chest, its body shuddered and it screamed in agony, a terrible high-pitched shrieking.

Before he could withdraw his sword, another beast grabbed him with its hengaruk and hoisted him off the ground. In that instant, Kevlin saw two long columns of horsemen charging up either side of the street, lances lowered toward the remaining creatures. Behind them followed soldiers on foot to engage in close combat whatever enemies remained.

None of that mattered to Kevlin. They wouldn't be able to help him. He struggled mightily, but the hengaruk were too strong. The creature opened wide its horrible maw, revealing all its sharp teeth and long fangs coated with poison. It pulled him close to rip out his throat.

An arrow slammed into one of its three eyes, exploding it in a splash of liquid before punching through the creature's brain.

Kevlin dropped to the ground as the makrasha reeled away from him. Even as he regained his balance to face the two remaining creatures, a wave of arrows swept across them, riddling them with long, wooden shafts.

They were dead before they hit the ground.

Kevlin spun to see a group of archers, standing fifty paces away, dressed in the rough clothing of local hunters, each carrying long ash bows. In the center of their line stood a short blond woman carrying a bow taller than herself. She continued launching arrows even while sidestepping to make way for the charging horsemen.

Kevlin turned back to the fighting as the horsemen pounded past. The second charge had felled a few more of the Grakonians, but most of them had succeeded in deflecting the soldiers' lances, and had turned to face the men on foot.

Movement across the street caught Kevlin's attention, as a man in flowing red robes rose to stand on the rooftop.

Merab.

The shadeleech stood well above the fighting, positioned to wreak deadly havoc among the imperial troops. He wasted no time in raising his staff and throwing a large ball of crimson fire down at the soldiers below.

Kevlin started forward, trying to put himself between the unprotected men and the blazing death hurtling toward them. Their only chance was for him to use the power of the amulet to block the attack.

He'd never make it in time.

A bolt of blue-white lightning ripped the air over their heads. It struck the ball of fire, shattering it into a thousand glittering shards of light and shaking all the nearby buildings with the thunderclap.

Kevlin whirled to find the latest unexpected ally. An old man in sentinel white robes stood in the street. Beside him stood a woman in the hooded green robes of a Healer.

Behind her, rushing to catch up, was Ceren.

The sentinel's hands were still raised from casting his spell, his eyes locked on Merab. The shadeleech shouted and pointed his staff at the newcomer, but before he could unleash his power, the old stalwart hurled his hammer. The shadeleech shouted a foreign word, and a shimmering shield of red energy materialized in the air in front of him, deflecting the hammer.

Merab spun his staff back toward the sentinel, just as another bolt of energy flashed through the air. It cut cleanly through the staff, which exploded into a cloud of splinters, then struck him in the chest. Merab rocked backward, his arms windmilling. Then he froze in place, surrounded by a nimbus of blue light.

The soldiers, led by their mace-wielding officer, charged into the ranks of remaining makrasha. Barely a score of the monsters still lived, but they fought savagely against the greater numbers of men. They towered over the soldiers, like bears among a pack of hunting dogs.

Despite his short stature, the leader of the men tumbled makrasha to the ground with his mace burning with blue fire. It smashed through shields and armor like they were made of clay.

Another volley of arrows streaked past Kevlin as the local hunters rejoined the fray. The missiles dropped half of the remaining creatures. The battle degenerated into a formless brawl, with each of the monsters surrounded by several soldiers, fighting in unison to bring them down.

Eventually only one creature remained. With two of its eyes gone and its tough hide covered with its own blood, it howled a ringing cry of defiance. Shouldering past two soldiers, it lunged at the mace-wielding officer. The little man calmly met it with an overhand blow that shattered the creature's head and smashed its ruin into the dust.

31

MAKING FRIENDS

The soldiers surveyed the dead makrasha with open amazement. The many questions they must have been asking themselves were surely the same ones Kevlin had been asking for days. From Ceren they'd have been warned of the threat, but being told about it was different than experiencing it.

Ceren.

She was standing beside the healer. She wore a teal-colored, linen dress. It hung a little loose on her slender frame, but still looked attractive.

Ceren noticed Kevlin at the same time. She shouted his name and rushed toward him. Kevlin moved to meet her, and for a second it looked like she was going to throw her arms around him. Maybe that kiss in the forest had meant something after all.

Or maybe not.

Two paces away she slowed and, instead of hugging him, started peppering him with questions.

"What are you doing here? Why aren't you watching the fort? Did the Grakonians leave? Is Antigonus dead?"

"Slow down," he said when she paused for breath. "How did *you* get here? This isn't exactly the road back to the fort."

"I take it you are Kevlin," the old stalwart interrupted.

"Aye."

"I am Leander," he said with a warm smile, his bright blue eyes sparkling as if with suppressed laughter.

"Thanks for your help this morning, sir. You saved my life more than once."

"Well, my boy, why don't you help me down so I can deal with this leg?"

"Oh. Of course."

The sentinel joined them as Leander settled to the ground, his injured leg thrust out before him. Where Leander's white hair was close cropped, the sentinel's hung halfway to his shoulders. Leander wore his beard neatly trimmed, but the newcomer's hung to his chest.

He stood taller than Leander, and his deep-set eyes were a unique steel-gray. Leander radiated a solid, honest strength, but the sentinel's shaggier hair and narrower face gave the impression of a predator. Kevlin got the uncomfortable feeling that the old man could read all his secrets.

Despite his dangerous aura, the sentinel asked in a concerned voice, "Is the wound serious, Leander?"

"Nothing to worry about, my old friend," replied Leander calmly. "But I am getting rusty."

"I don't see how that's possible considering how busy you keep your Pallian Stalwarts."

Pallian Stalwarts. That explained the hammer. Sort of.

Pallians were commonly known as Hammer Stalwarts and were dedicated to the seemingly contradictory tenets of both justice and mercy. Kevlin wasn't sure what god they served, but they were highly respected. Given the old fellow's prowess with the hammer, he could see why.

The sentinel turned to Kevlin and extended a hand. "I am Harafin."

Harafin! Kevlin eagerly clasped hand-to-wrist with the old man. *Thank the Lady, something's finally going right.*

Meeting Harafin so soon was a good omen. "I need to talk with you."

"You and I both have questions."

"Let me fix my leg first," Leander said.

The green-robed healer pushed back her hood and bent over the old stalwart to inspect the injury.

Kevlin stared, transfixed.

She was young, maybe twenty, and her shoulder-length sable hair shone like satin in the morning light. It seemed to caress her face and neck as she moved.

Breathing suddenly became difficult.

Her face was flawless. That was the only word to describe it. Her features were perfectly formed. From the high cheekbones to the curve of her lips, to her creamy white skin, it was as though she had been sculpted by a master artist. Beyond her heart-stopping beauty, she radiated purity, like a glow embedded in her smooth skin.

Kevlin had to focus to finally register the tail end of what she was saying to the old stalwart. ". . .help you with that."

"I can deal with this just fine, my dear," Leander said. "There are wounded soldiers who need you far more than I."

"Who will take the bolt out of your leg?"

"My young friend can help me," Leander replied, gesturing at Kevlin.

She turned to Kevlin and asked, "Do you have experience with this sort of thing?" He met her gaze and the midnight pools of her eyes captured his soul. His mind went completely blank.

"What?" he finally managed to stammer.

Ceren snorted and glared at him. "He's a little thick-headed," she explained to the healer.

Kevlin tried to protest, but the green-robed healer's gaze stopped his tongue again. She smiled shyly and repeated the question. He had to concentrate to not be distracted by the movement of her lips or the sweet gentleness of her voice.

The words finally registered, and he managed to say, "I'm not a healer, not like Ceren, but I've treated battlefield injuries before."

"Good," said Leander. "Indira, go see to the other wounded. Take Ceren with you. I'm sure she will prove very helpful. I'll be fine with Kevlin's help."

"All right, but I'll be back soon to check on you," Indira said with a final warm smile before heading for the rows of wounded. Ceren unstrung her healer's case and hurried after. Kevlin watched them go, his emotions an indecipherable knot.

"Did you fall asleep standing up?" Harafin asked, poking Kevlin.

"Excuse me?" Kevlin blinked, having forgotten for a moment that he had found Harafin.

"Just daydreaming," Harafin said, one bushy eyebrow raised.

Leander chuckled. "Indira is my ward. Her compassion is so strong, it's impossible not to respond to it."

It wasn't her compassion that left Kevlin breathless.

He glanced back at the women. Indira stood a little taller than Ceren, and although both women moved gracefully, Indira seemed soft and vulnerable next to Ceren's more athletic gait. No woman had affected him so powerfully in a long time and that made him very nervous.

"Give me a hand here, my boy," Leander said.

Kevlin crouched beside him, wincing at a fresh twinge from his feet.

"Are you injured too?" Leander asked.

"Nothing new. I've been running from those brutes for a few days and my feet haven't held up well to the punishment."

"I'm sure we can help you feel better," Leander said. He then directed Kevlin to cut away the fabric of his trousers to get at the bolt embedded deep in his thigh.

Kevlin grimaced as he surveyed Leander's injury. *The old guy must be tough as granite. With a wound like that, I don't think I could've stayed on my feet and kept fighting.*

Leander placed his hands on either side of the bolt, closed his eyes, and started chanting softly. Both hands glowed with a gentle white light, but without the hummingbird sound that had accompanied Antigonus' attempt to heal himself. After a moment, Leander took a deep breath, slowly let it out, and opened his eyes.

"Now, cut that bolt out," Leander said.

Kevlin drew his dagger. "This is going to hurt."

"I have numbed the flesh around the wound, so have no concerns about that. I just need an efficient extraction. I'll deal with what's left of my leg."

Kevlin sliced into the flesh of the old man's thigh, wincing at how deep he was forced to cut. Then with a firm, steady tug, he pulled the bolt free. Blood flowed thick from the wound. It was a good thing the pain was blocked, or Leander would have screamed and most likely passed out before the operation was complete.

As soon as the bolt came free, Leander pressed the wound closed and resumed chanting. His hands again began to glow with the same soft white light. A full minute slowly ticked by. Kevlin was afraid to move.

When Leander removed his hands, his skin was as clean and unmarked as that of a child's.

"Well done," commented Harafin.

Kevlin couldn't help but think of Antigonus' partially closed wound after he'd tried to heal it. If only he'd succeeded, things would have turned out so differently.

Leander closed his eyes and blew out a long breath.

"You need rest, my friend," said Harafin.

"I know, but not yet."

"Do not push yourself too hard. That healing took more out of you than you like to admit."

Leander laughed. "Don't preach to me. I'm the stalwart."

Harafin turned to Kevlin. "Now that it appears Leander will live, let us find a suitable place to talk."

Kevlin suppressed his impatience while Harafin turned and made a beckoning motion. The shadeleech Merab, still imprisoned by Harafin's magic, began drifting slowly toward them.

The leader of the horsemen approached. Short and thin, he stood barely five and a half feet, even in thick-heeled boots. His large mace looked too big for him to wield effectively. Sweat plastered his straight black hair to his skull when he pulled off his helm. His face was smooth and his gray eyes burned with excitement.

The man's slender build and dark features declared him a citizen of Tamarr. His silver-trimmed armor bore the rank of colonel as well as the personal crest of the emperor. He seemed young for such a rank. Colonels generally assisted legion commanders. How had he ended up in the middle of the Hallvarri wilderness with a command of a hundred lances?

"When Harafin saw your signal, he ordered the charge before we knew what was going on," the newcomer said to Leander. "How did you manage to flush those creatures?"

"It was not my doing."

"Thanks for responding so fast," Kevlin interrupted. "I thought we were dead. . .although, seeing Leander's prowess with his hammer, maybe I shouldn't have worried so much."

"I am Colonel Gabral Aradjan," said the soldier proudly, "Bearer of the Mace and champion of the emperor and of Tamarr." As he spoke, he straightened to his full, diminutive height.

"Bearer of the Mace? I'm honored to meet you." Kevlin held out his hand. Gabral hesitated a second before clasping it. "I am Kevlin."

Kevlin was impressed, but not surprised that one of the Six should have appeared. He had never met any of the bearers of the Six in person, but with the amazing events of the past days it seemed only appropriate that they should be among those who responded to the threat. It was interesting that the Mace from Tamarr and not the Bladestaff from Hallvarr found him first.

Gabral dropped the handshake and frowned. "You are the man Lady Ceren left watching the enemy fortress?"

"Aye."

"Why have you deserted your post?"

"What?" Kevlin demanded, surprise quickly turning to anger.

"You were left with a specific assignment," Gabral said stiffly. "And yet we find you here. I don't like repeating myself, so answer my question."

After everything Kevlin had been through in the past few days, the accusation stung. He clenched his fists, but managed to keep from going for his sword.

"Men who make stupid assumptions die young," Kevlin said.

"Enough," said Harafin. "We will speak inside and learn exactly what has happened."

Two more soldiers approached and Gabral turned to them, dismissing Kevlin. Both of the newcomers bore the rank of captain. Generally a captain would command a thousand men, leading one of the five columns of a legion. Hopefully that meant there were more troops in town.

Beyond their rank and uniforms, the two captains could not have been more different. The first was a giant of a man, whose shoulders and chest strained the limits of his armor. He towered over everyone, arguably the biggest man Kevlin had ever met.

He bristled with weapons. A huge battle axe hung on his back and a broadsword swung from his belt, along with a dagger and small throwing axe. His curly brown hair hung in thick braids past his shoulders and a dense russet beard sprang out from under his helmet.

No doubt he was from Donarr. Kevlin had known many Donarri in his career and he liked most of the tough, loyal stock who lived in the rugged Donarri highlands.

The second captain was tall, but as trim as his companion was broad, and he walked with a swaying grace that bespoke a life spent in the saddle. He carried a spear capped with an unusually long, thin head, while a quiver of short javelins hung on his back, flanked by intricately-carved handles of two long-knives.

His face was clean-shaven, his eyes a bright, piercing blue, and his hair completely concealed by his helm. The man had to be from Einarr, whose wide plains produced the premier horses in the world, along with riders to match.

"Sir," the second captain spoke crisply to Colonel Gabral, "we have reports of the situation."

"Ukko's beard, that was a good little fight," interrupted the towering Donarri captain with a grin.

"Too bad there weren't more of them," the Einarri captain said.

Gabral ignored the remark and ordered curtly, "Proceed."

The lanky Einarri captain replied, "All enemy forces have been destroyed."

"Casualties?"

"Five dead, twelve wounded. Indira is working with them."

"Excellent. Thank you, Drystan." Gabral ran a hand over his head and frowned at the sweat that clung to his fingers. "Assign patrols of the area and arrange for burial of our dead."

He turned to the huge Donarri. "Jerrik, find us a place to interrogate the prisoner and speak with this man." He nodded at Kevlin.

A minute later, Kevlin sat between Leander and Harafin on crates in an empty warehouse, with Merab floating in his prison across the room. Jerrik stood between them and the exit and Gabral paced nearby. Piles of crates filled the rest of the huge room and dust hung heavy in the air.

The colonel planted his feet and faced Kevlin. "Explain why those creatures attack openly in the light of day. From what Lady Ceren told us, they were trying to avoid being seen."

Ceren appeared in the door. "They were, last I knew."

"I thought you were helping Indira," Kevlin said.

"She has an amazing gift," Ceren said in an awed voice. "The things she can do. . .she doesn't really need me, and I wanted to find out what happened to you."

"Yes, come in," Leander said with a warm smile.

When Ceren had seated herself, Kevlin said, "They were chasing me." Although still angry at Gabral's earlier words, he forced calm into his voice. He needed these men.

"So they discovered you watching their fort?" Gabral prompted. "And exposed their presence just to prevent you from doing so?"

"Not exactly." Kevlin turned to Harafin. "Can we trust everyone here? I have word from Antigonus, but he commanded me to speak with you. He said nothing about anyone else."

Gabral opened his mouth to protest, his expression outraged.

Harafin said, "I vouch for these men. They are aware of the danger and details of what has happened."

"You talked with Antigonus?" Ceren asked.

Kevlin nodded. Then he pulled off his right boot, barely suppressing a groan of pain. He sliced the stitches holding Oris in place, extracted the bundle, unrolled the rune-covered bag from the linen cloth and dumped the rock into his palm.

"Master Harafin," he said. "I have Oris."

32

CRYPTIC ANSWERS

Harafin glanced from the rock to Kevlin, the sentinel's expression unreadable. "This is unexpected."

"That's all you have to say?" Gabral cried.

Leander smiled, as if he understood a joke none of the rest of them did.

Ceren gasped, "How did you get that?"

"He named me steward," Kevlin added nervously under Harafin's gaze.

Harafin nodded and scratched his beard, his eyes never leaving the rock in Kevlin's hand. Kevlin looked down and realized it was upside down. He flipped it in his hand to reveal the emblem.

A sharp, blue light flashed from the emblem as the rock spun, surprisingly bright in the dim warehouse. The stone settled perfectly into his palm. His fingers curled around it, slipping between the protrusions on its rough upper edge, and it felt disturbingly *right*.

Harafin leaped to his feet, shouting something that sounded like a curse, but in a language Kevlin didn't understand. Leander joined him.

"The Flaming Sword," Harafin declared in an awed tone.

"Aye," said Kevlin, wishing he'd left the rock facing the other way. "Tanathos seemed pretty upset about that too."

"Tanathos?" Harafin asked.

"The shadeleech in charge. He was trying to break Antigonus' mind so he could be named steward. Antigonus said that was the only way Tanathos could touch the rock."

"We call it a stone, not a rock," Harafin said.

"Aren't they the same thing?"

"It is a matter of style. Calling it a rock makes it sound common."

"I suppose."

They were all crazy. Rock or stone, didn't matter. All Kevlin cared about was Harafin assigning a bearer to it so they could get to the important business of killing Tanathos.

"When did the emblem change?" Harafin asked.

"When I snuck into Antigonus' cell and he gave it to me."

"I knew you were going to try something stupid," Ceren said.

"I'm here, aren't I?"

"Tell us everything," said Harafin. "Leave nothing out."

The air felt suddenly heavy and charged, like just before a storm. Kevlin's palms began to sweat. He stared down at the rock and marveled at the exquisite details of the flaming sword emblem. It was surprisingly warm to the touch. A deep calm settled over his mind and thoughts fled.

"Kevlin." Harafin's voice shook him from his reverie. "Put it away while you tell us your story."

Kevlin obeyed, despite a surprisingly strong reluctance to do so. Beginning with the startling explosions of magic the night of the bloodset, he related his story.

Gabral tried to ask questions, but Harafin shushed him. As Kevlin recounted the fight with Dhanjal and Rhea, he left out everything to do with the song of Savas. He was nervous enough in the presence of the legendary Harafin without trying to describe something he didn't really understand. Thankfully, Ceren did not point out the omission.

He also said nothing of the amulet, and skipped details of how he had defeated the shadeleech Haraz to avoid questions that might lead back to the amulet. Harafin didn't challenge him on it.

When Kevlin finished, he held up the rune-covered bag. "So here I am." He extended the pouch. "And here's the stone, like I promised."

"I cannot take it," Harafin said.

"Antigonus said to get it to you."

Harafin nodded. "That you made it so far is a great victory."

"So, why won't you take it?"

"I cannot. You are steward."

"What does that mean?" Normally Kevlin wouldn't dare push a sentinel, but he was in no mood for cryptic answers.

"It means time is short, and events are spiraling out of control."

Leave it to a sentinel to complicate a simple question. He wondered how the old man ever ordered breakfast at the inns he stayed in.

"Then we'd better get back to the fort and rescue Antigonus before they escape," Kevlin said. "If you don't want it, I'll give the rock back to him."

Harafin shook his head. "No. The time for Antigonus to bear Oris is past."

"He's dead?" Ceren asked. "How do you know?"

"Antigonus may yet live, but another bearer must be chosen."

"I don't understand," Kevlin said. "Tanathos' forces are pretty strong, but we can't just give up."

"No one is going to give up," Harafin said. "I must choose a new bearer of Oris and, as steward, you must accompany me."

"Okay," Kevlin said, running a hand through his hair. "Fine. We can do that. Let's go save Antigonus, and then I'll help you find someone else to carry the rock."

"There is not enough time to do both."

"Why not?"

Harafin frowned, his face a mask of frustration. "Timing could not be worse. We must race for Tamera with all speed."

"I swore an oath to save Antigonus," Kevlin said. Legendary sentinel or not, Harafin's evasive answers stoked his frustrated impatience to anger. "There's no way I'm running the other way."

Gabral rose to his feet. "You will stand down or I'll have you whipped for insubordination."

Kevlin ignored the colonel, refusing to break eye contact with Harafin. The old sentinel seemed surprised at first, then irritated. Kevlin had been pushed too far and stubbornly refused to look away, despite the terror shaking his hands.

After a dozen heartbeats of silent scrutiny, Harafin said, "I like your spirit, young man."

"You still haven't told me why you want to abandon Antigonus and run away."

Gabral growled and stepped toward Kevlin, but Harafin held up a hand to forestall him. "Know this," Harafin said. "Antigonus has been my friend for more than a century."

"So let's go save him."

"There's more at stake than the life of one friend."

"If we throw away the lives of our friends, what do we have left?"

"I throw away no life," Harafin snapped, his voice shaking the room, eyes flashing like lightning. Kevlin retreated a step despite his resolve to hold firm. Maybe he'd goaded the old man a little too much.

"I believe Kevlin has a right to know," declared Leander.

"Very well," Harafin conceded after a moment, still frowning.

Leander explained, "The problem we face is one of timing and location. We don't have enough time to reach the fort where Antigonus is held. A new bearer of Oris must be chosen before sunset six days hence."

"Why?" Kevlin and Ceren asked together.

"The autumn equinox, when night and day are equal in length, occurs in six days," Harafin said. "It is the last day before darkness commands more of each day than light, until the vernal equinox next spring."

"Why's that important?" Ceren asked.

"Because Oris is the key to an aegis, or shield, of magic blocking the Sigrun from unleashing their full might against us. If we pass the autumn equinox with no bearer of Oris, the aegis will weaken and eventually fail. The power woven into the aegis is enormous and it would rebound against Oris, destroy the stone, and lay waste to everything for miles around," Harafin said.

Kevlin stared at the rune-covered bag, wondering what other details Antigonus had left out when he assigned Kevlin's mission. It didn't matter. He now knew more than enough. He held the pouch out to Harafin. "Take it. I don't want it."

"Antigonus named you steward. You alone can touch it until the next bearer takes possession of it," Harafin said.

"I don't want it."

"That is irrelevant," Harafin said. "Now you understand. Time is too short to both save Antigonus and find a new bearer."

This stupid rock was going to be the death of him.

"So we race for Tamera," Kevlin said slowly, hating every word, "and then who do I give the rock to?"

"Stone."

"Fine, stone. Who gets it?"

"I do not know."

Kevlin blinked. "Excuse me?"

"I don't." Harafin shrugged. "I won't until the moment of choosing, when Oris itself reveals the next bearer."

"So how do you know it'll choose someone in Tamera?" Ceren asked.

Harafin frowned. "I do not, but that's where the greatest concentration of sentinels is to be found."

Kevlin groaned. "So even if we leave Antigonus to die and let Tanathos escape, we could still fail?"

"And destroy the imperial seat too," Leander added.

"That's not helping," Harafin said.

"None of this is helping." Kevlin sank onto a crate. "I can't believe it. You're supposed to help me save Antigonus."

"Us," Ceren said. "Help *us* save him. We both swore to get him back."

Harafin said, "We will do what we can, but you and I must leave for Tamera. Colonel Gabral, accompanied by Leander, will cut off Tanathos' escape until reinforcements can be marshaled."

Gabral swallowed, looking a little pale, but said nothing.

"That is not a good plan," Leander remarked. "Gabral is well protected as bearer of the Mace and I have nothing to fear from shadeleech magic, but the rest of the company will be exposed."

"I know, but it is the only plan we have." Harafin stood. "The flaming sword, Leander. It's the flaming sword, and we're stuck in the wilderness."

Kevlin rose too. "There is another option."

"Oh?" Harafin asked.

"We have five days. It'll only take two to get to Antigonus and free him. I'll give the rock back to him, and he'll be bearer again. Catastrophe averted. Tanathos dead."

And Kevlin would settle the score with Dhanjal with a hundred imperial lancers at his back.

Harafin shook his head. "Antigonus cannot take up the stone."

"Why not?"

"It is complicated."

"Not as complicated as you're making it," Kevlin shot back.

Leander rose and held up his hands to calm them. "Let us think on this further. In the meantime, we can interrogate the shadeleech to see what he knows."

Gabral sent Jerrik off to prepare the company to ride out, then approached Merab's floating form. "Master Harafin, can you alter that shield so we can communicate with him?"

"Yes, but I must caution you to choose your words carefully," Harafin said. "Shadeleeches are masters of lies, half-truths, and manipulation. Although he is within my power, he is not helpless."

"I'm not afraid of this man," Gabral said. "He will answer my questions, willing or no."

Harafin joined Gabral beside the floating prisoner and gestured with one raised hand. Merab blinked and looked around. When he noticed Harafin, he snarled with hatred burning in his eyes.

"You are a prisoner of the empire," said Gabral. "Your days of treachery and darkness are ended."

Merab addressed Harafin. "You were lucky today, sentinel. But for the distraction of the old man's hammer, you would be burning in the dark lord's chains."

"An optimist," Harafin said with a little smile. "Unusual in one of Angrama's slaves."

"You will answer me, prisoner," said Gabral. "I'm in charge and will ask the questions."

"Sentinel, why do you allow this pup to speak? Is that how the torture begins?"

Gabral's face reddened. "I am bearer of the Mace and champion of the emperor. I have power over your life."

Merab sneered down at him. "You don't understand power. You think that toy you carry makes you a man?"

Gabral raised a hand to strike.

"Beware," Harafin cautioned. "I warned you he is adept at turning you from your questions. Do not fall into that trap."

Harafin turned his back on the prisoner and returned to his seat. Merab's angry gaze never left him.

With an obvious effort, Gabral calmed himself. "Your games will not save you today, Shadeleech Merab. We know a great deal about you and your plot to steal Oris."

Merab glowered at him, but made no reply.

"I want to know how you came to be here. What are your numbers, and what was your plan?"

Merab laughed. "You want to know many things, but you will learn nothing, little man. You are a child and cannot understand the workings of men."

The shadeleech glanced around the room and caught sight of Kevlin for the first time. "You will not escape. You are marked. Ophisurus will own your soul, and you will suffer endless torment."

Kevlin shuddered. The god of darkness was not true-named often. Most people referred to him as EnKur for fear of cursing themselves. The sentinels called him Angrama, but only the dark god's followers named him true. Hearing a shadeleech invoke the name Ophisurus raised the hair on Kevlin's arms and sent a shiver of fear through his soul.

"You seem to forget that you are the prisoner," remarked Harafin from where he sat. "You are in no position to make threats. Concern yourself with your own life and how much pain you are willing to bear before it ends."

"Such idle threats," Merab mocked. "You sentinels deny real power when you could take it."

"The power of darkness has never been real," interjected Leander. "Its illusion serves only to enslave you. In the end, it abandons all who follow it."

"Stalwart of the hammer," spat Merab in Leander's direction. "You stand among the paramount hypocrites. You preach mercy, but are the first to strike down those who oppose you. Have you considered how well you truly serve darkness?"

Leander chuckled, unperturbed. "You have a way with words, but I don't have the time to explain truth to you, nor do I believe you would accept it."

Gabral stepped directly in front of Merab to draw the prisoner's gaze. "You cannot avoid our questions. You will give me the information I seek."

"You have no power over me."

"You want to see power? I'll show you real power!"

Enraged, Gabral grasped the handle of the Mace. The curious leather sheath that held it on his back *melted* away, allowing him to pull the weapon up over his shoulder.

Merab scoffed. "You think I fear--"

With a snarl, Gabral drove the long spike at the top of the Mace into the center of the shadeleech's chest. Merab's eyes widened in surprise and he opened his mouth in a silent scream.

Kevlin jumped to his feet. Leander gasped.

"What are you doing?" Harafin shouted. "I warned you to be careful. We can't get anything useful from him if he's dead."

Gabral held the Mace steady with its long spike piercing Merab's heart. The weapon glowed with a dark blue light which seeped into Merab's chest and began to pulsate in time with his heartbeat.

Heartbeat? How could he still have a heartbeat?

Gabral spoke over his shoulder. "He is in my power. His life will remain for a time and he will be forced to speak the truth. I know what I'm doing."

To Merab, he asked, "What is Tanathos' plan?"

"He has not shared it with me."

"Who in the empire is helping you," demanded Gabral.

As the shadeleech hesitated, the pulsating energy surrounding his chest slowed. They were running out of time.

"Bajaran," Merab whispered.

"We know that one" Gabral's voice was tight with the strain of holding the Mace's power in place. "Who else?"

Merab howled like an animal. As he screamed, his features twisted and stretched beyond their natural boundaries. His eyes filled with malevolent darkness.

A deep, guttural voice issued from his throat. "You dare force truth from the mouth of a servant of darkness?"

Dread shivered through Kevlin. That voice did not belong to Merab. Something new spoke through his lips.

"Gabral, get back," shouted Harafin.

The sentinel leapt to his feet in unison with Leander as Merab began a terrifying wail that sounded like it was ripping out his vocal chords.

"You will obey me," shouted Gabral, increasing his pressure on the Mace, as if by brute force he could regain control of the shadeleech, who was obviously under some other power.

The energy binding the shadeleech exploded, shattering the spell. Harafin stumbled back, as if struck an invisible blow. Merab settled to the floor and grabbed Gabral by the throat. He pulled the colonel close, trapping the soldier's arms between them and ignoring the Mace still piercing his heart.

Gabral struggled to free the Mace, but he was pressed too close against the shadeleech. He beat futilely against Merab's arm as his face began to turn purple from lack of air.

Not relaxing his grip around Gabral's neck, Merab glanced up at Harafin, who was running toward him.

"You have defied us for the last time," a different voice snarled through Merabl's lips.

A wave of pure blackness swept from his eyes toward the sentinel. Just before the evil tide engulfed Harafin, piercing white light exploded out of him. Shadow and light swirled around Harafin, becoming a blur of magic, a terrible struggle beyond physical comprehension.

Kevlin felt an icy blast of fear as he looked into the empty depths that had once been Merab's eyes. Had Enkur risen to possess his servant?

A third voice, more sinister than the others, spoke through Merab's lips. "You are marked. Your death is certain. The prophecy will fail."

A bolt of magic so dark it drew the light from the air erupted from those inhuman eyes. It struck Kevlin directly in the chest.

It disappeared, sucked in by the amulet's protective spell.

Kevlin's knees shook with terror. The amulet had stopped the bolt, but the air around him felt cold. A stomach-wrenching odor, like a long-dead corpse exhumed from the earth hung around him.

The amulet poured the captured magic into him. It strengthened him and eased the pain of his feet, but he wanted to scream. If he could have expelled it by driving hands into his own flesh, he would have done so in a heartbeat.

Leander stepped in front of Kevlin. "Begone, creature of hell!"

As the old stalwart advanced on the shadeleech, another wave of darkness swept out from Merab, but it dissipated when it reached Leander. He snapped his fingers and his war hammer appeared in his fist.

"Begone," Leander commanded again in a thunderous voice, then slammed the hammer into Merab's forehead.

Merab collapsed to the ground and his body began to smolder and burn, emitting greasy black smoke. Gabral stumbled away from the shadeleech, struggling to breathe through his bruised neck. Kevlin grabbed the man's arm and pulled him from the smoky room, followed by the others.

Harafin turned to Leander. "Thank you, my old friend. I was barely holding on."

They stopped on the street, coughing the vile smoke out of their lungs. Kevlin trembled from what he had witnessed. Gabral's vicious interrogation had resonated too powerfully with memories of torture. The helplessness of being compelled to speak Truth despite ensuing pain made him shiver with remembered terror.

He managed to bury those memories only because of the panic bubbling just under the surface as he thought of the evil magic trapped inside him.

How did I get rid of it last time?

Beside him, Ceren dabbed at her face and tried to catch his eye, but he ignored her.

The dagger. I threw the dagger.

Harafin turned angrily to Gabral. "Colonel, what did you think you were doing?"

"We needed answers, and I thought that was the best way to get them."

"No," countered Leander. "You ignored Harafin's advice and played straight into the shadeleech's hand."

"I suspect he knew much," said Harafin.

"Now we shall never know. We have wasted a rare opportunity," said Leander.

Gabral stood mutely for a moment, struggling to come to grips with the fact that his prisoner had manipulated him. Finally, he said, "I cannot take back what was done, but I will pay better heed to your counsel in the future."

"I hope that proves sufficient," said Harafin. He glanced toward Kevlin, and cried out in surprise.

Kevlin glanced behind him, but saw nothing that would cause the sentinel's alarm. He turned back to Harafin, intending to ask what was wrong, but paused to stare. Light poured into Harafin from all around, building inside of him until the old man shone like a beacon.

He's drawing upon the power of magic, and I can see it.

Kevlin had never imagined it could be so beautiful. He smiled at the wonder of it.

Harafin pointed one hand at Kevlin, and a bolt of blue-white magic leaped from it and lanced toward Kevlin's heart.

33

THE DEADLIEST OF WEAPONS

The bolt struck before Kevlin could react, but once again the amulet hidden under his shirt absorbed the magic and poured it into him. Coupled with the power it had already stolen from Merab, it became a torrent that surged through his body, filling him with strength and terror.

He wanted to scream with frustration. Why would Harafin do this? He needed to get rid of it before it corrupted him or killed him from the inside.

"What are you doing?" Ceren yelled, echoing Kevlin's thoughts.

Harafin ignored her, his eyes fixed on Kevlin. "I don't know how you annulled my power, but I will not allow you to possess the steward. I'll destroy the vessel first."

Kevlin back-pedaled, and the truth hit him. *Harafin can see the magic in me, like I can see it in him. He thinks. . .Oh, no.*

The Leander frowned. "I'm not so sure--."

Gabral showed no hesitation. As the little man lifted the Mace, it burst into blue fire.

"Wait a minute." Kevlin forced the words through suddenly dry lips. "They're not possessing me. Let me explain."

He pushed at the magic, trying to get rid of it, but it wouldn't leave. Instead, it seeped deep into his bones, filling him with strength. It was like a river raging inside his body, and every muscle thrummed with the need to use the marvelous power.

He didn't know how.

His senses sharpened to unbelievable clarity. He could count the hairs in Harafin's beard, hear the creak of Gabral's grip tightening on the haft of the Mace, and smell the gentle perfume Ceren wore.

"You don't get a minute to work your devilry," Gabral said. The Mace bearer raised his flaming weapon and pointed it at Kevlin.

The spike shot off the top.

It sliced through the air faster than an arrow, straight for Kevlin's heart. Time slowed, along with everything else around him.

The missile should have pierced him before he even registered the danger, but he reacted faster than he'd ever imagined possible, throwing himself backward and extending a hand to ward off the blow.

Even as he envisioned the spike deflecting away, the magic inside him *responded*. It flowed out of his hand and hardened the air in front of him, knocking the spike off course.

"You can't do that," Gabral shouted.

Harafin pointed again, and fire erupted all around Kevlin. It licked to within a hair's breadth of his body, but didn't burn him.

The amulet poured even more magic into him, until he felt he might burst. Heat from the flames seared his lungs, and fire encircled him like a burning tomb. He tasted ash, and the smell of cinders filled his nostrils.

The single beat of a drum sounded in his soul.

He cringed, and the fear blossomed into full-blown panic.

The song of Savas.

A fanfare of horns rang through him and his body tried to react. He suppressed the urge, barely.

I can't let that happen! They'll kill me for sure.

It had to stop.

"Stop!" He screamed and threw his hands wide. The air *cracked* with a thunderclap, and magic blasted from him in all directions in a single, tremendous wave. It slammed into his companions, tumbling Gabral and Ceren across the street and shaking the buildings on both sides.

It deflected away from Harafin, who stood with light encircling him like an impenetrable halo. It rolled past Leander without effect. Leander half-raised his hammer, but did not attack.

Drained of magic, Kevlin's senses contracted back to normal. He felt half-blind and his body sagged with weariness as if he'd just run for miles.

"I've got to stop doing that," Kevlin muttered. "I'm not a sentinel."

Across the street, Gabral leapt to his feet. The magic fire burning around the Mace rolled down over his arm, then enveloped him. "Let's see you do that again," he shouted angrily. Raising the Mace, he charged.

"Hold." Harafin's voice cracked like a whip and the colonel skidded to a stop. The sentinel stared at Kevlin with a frown on his face.

"Please," Kevlin said, raising his hands in the universal sign of surrender. "Just stop for a minute."

"Where are those who possessed you?" Harafin demanded.

"They were never here," Kevlin shouted. "If you'll just wait a minute, I'll explain."

"Let's kill him," Gabral said, "just to be safe."

"No," said Harafin. "Not yet."

Gabral cursed under his breath and lowered the Mace. The blue fire winked out, but he didn't put the weapon away.

Harafin approached. "How can you explain it?"

Kevlin reached into his shirt and lifted the amulet on its silver chain. "With this."

"That looks like Bajaran's amulet." Harafin frowned and leaned closer. "But it's not, is it?"

"It used to be."

They all drew closer, and Leander declared, "The flaming sword."

He pointed to the small silver emblem embedded in the face of the blue amulet, which was a miniature reflection of the one on Oris.

Something was going on that Kevlin lacked any ability to grasp. Hopefully Harafin could provide some answers, or he'd throw the rock at the next squirrel he saw and be done with it.

Harafin nodded slowly and met Kevlin's eye. "I think it's time you tell us the rest of your story."

Kevlin explained about the amulet, how he came to possess it, and how it changed after striking down Tanathos.

"You lied to us," Gabral spat.

"No. I spoke no lies. I just didn't tell you the whole truth."

Harafin moved a few paces away. Turning, he slammed a fist into his open palm. "There isn't enough time."

"What do you mean?" Ceren asked. She'd been studying Kevlin with an unreadable expression. Kevlin was grateful when she turned from him to look at the sentinel.

"I need to question this Tanathos," Harafin said. "With the Sigrun united and focused on events here, we need more information."

"The Sigrun?" Ceren asked, glancing around with the same nervousness Kevlin felt.

Harafin nodded. "They are the ones who attacked us through Merab. They are masters of the Sthenic arts, but only the united power of the Sigrun council could have achieved so much."

"It is no simple thing to unite the Sigrun," Leander said.

"No, it is not," Harafin agreed. "But I recognized at least three of them, and I believe the entire quorum was involved."

Kevlin wasn't sure if he should be relieved to know that Enkur himself hadn't possessed Merab, or terrified that it was the Sigrun council.

"How could you recognize them?" asked Gabral. "You've actually met them?"

"I knew them well," Harafin said with a wry smile. "I was close friends with two before they pledged their service to Angrama and led the uprising that overthrew the reign of the sentinels before the empire was founded. We were all very young then."

Harafin sighed, two centuries of grief on his face. "Kyllikki and Nyyrikki were twins, and my sworn brothers. They succumbed to the allure of power offered through service to the Lord of Darkness, despite my best efforts to dissuade them."

"When I stood against them, they swore to kill me for betraying them when it was they who betrayed everything we had all lived for. That was in the early days of the war, and they became the cause of much suffering and death among the people."

Kevlin shared a look of amazement with Ceren. Harafin was living proof of all the legends. Harafin had lived those legends. The thought made Kevlin feel very small.

"I need answers to many questions now raised," Harafin said. "But we don't have time to reach their fort and still make it back to Tamera."

"We might," Ceren interjected, her eyes bright with an idea. She turned to Kevlin. "Ingolf. Remember the boats?"

"Of course."

"Boats?" Leander asked.

"Yes," Ceren said excitedly.

She explained how they had hoped to take ship from Ingolf to Tamera, but the boats were all gone due to the bloodset. "At least some of them are bound to be back. If we can't return the stone to Antigonus, we could sail from Ingolf and still make it to Tamera. I think."

"It's risky," Leander said. "But it may be worth trying."

Harafin paced away, his head bent in thought. He glanced at Kevlin once, then continued pacing. Half a minute later, he turned.

"The idea has merit, but our duty is clear. We must leave for Tamera immediately. Finding the rightful bearer of Oris is our most important task."

Kevlin's heart fell. Harafin scared him, and he didn't want to anger the powerful old man, but he had no choice.

"I'm not going," Kevlin said.

"Listen, Kevlin," Harafin said, "I understand your frustration."

"I don't think so." Kevlin needed to explain, but how could he put it into words?

He hated magic. The thought of being named steward, of carrying around the most powerful artifact he'd ever heard of, rattled him to the core. And yet, his sworn duty to Antigonus offered a chance to break the shackles of his memory, to become whole for the first time ever.

He didn't need to love magic, but he could face it without terror. Abandoning Antigonus would leave him broken, and he wasn't sure he'd ever find the strength to attempt reconciling his past again.

Kevlin couldn't explain all of that, but he had to say something. "I swore an oath to save Antigonus, but ever since I met him, I've been immersed in magic. It's like. . .it's like all the forces of light and darkness have swarmed around me, and I'm stuck in the middle of a whirlwind."

Harafin rocked back as if he'd been struck. He glanced at Leander, and the two old men shared a meaningful look that compounded Kevlin's nervousness. Scheming old men were best avoided.

So of course, he was surrounded by them.

Harafin studied Kevlin closely, like a butcher trying to decide on a cut of meat. Kevlin's heart pounded, his hands sweaty. How did he manage to set the old man off so fast?

"This is unexpected," Harafin said softly. "So be it."

He turned to Gabral. "Assemble your men. We leave for the fort with all speed."

Despite the confusion evident on his face, Gabral saluted. "It will be done." He hurried up the street toward a pair of soldiers standing guard at the corner.

"I agree," Leander said to Harafin. "It must be done."

"What did I just miss?" Kevlin asked. Harafin's sudden, inexplicable change of heart made him as nervous as that intense stare a moment earlier.

"We have much to discuss," Harafin said.

More riddles. That was getting old really fast.

Harafin fixed him with a serious gaze. "The Sigrun have marked you. They do not do that lightly." Then he turned and headed up the street after Gabral.

Kevlin cursed under his breath. That was a rotten way to end a conversation. He already felt out of his depth, and now he had to worry about the Sigrun hunting him?

They killed sentinels.

The belligerent and perhaps not very bright part of him rose in defiant rage to hold back the fear. He was tempted to face west toward Grakonia where the Sigrun ruled and make an obscene gesture in their direction.

All he needed to do was get the rock to Antigonus. After that, he was done.

Leander clapped him on the shoulder and smiled. "Don't worry, my boy. All will become clear in time."

"That's not very helpful."

Kevlin glanced past the stalwart to Ceren. She was watching him again. Did noblewomen just instinctively do that, or was it part of their training?

He turned from her and noticed Healer Indira approaching. He couldn't tear his gaze from the beautiful young woman. She moved gracefully, but looked extremely tired, with dark circles around her lovely eyes.

Maybe she was enchanted to beguile travelers and lull them into accepting Harafin's cryptic words without question. He decided to guard himself around her and not fall for the trick.

Indira smiled warmly at Leander. "Are you feeling better? Is there anything I can do to help?"

"We're all fine. Thank you, my dear," said Leander. "How are the men?"

"One of the wounded died before I could reach him," she replied with a deep frown. "Three of the others will require bed rest for several days to fully recover. The rest have already joined the company and are preparing to ride."

"Excellent work, as always. You didn't overtire yourself, did you my dear?"

"I'm fine."

"Then will you see to Kevlin's feet? I'm sorry, but I don't have the energy to deal with it myself."

"Of course." Indira motioned for Kevlin to take a seat. He did so, and painfully pulled off his boots and stockings. He'd forgotten about the blisters during all the talk of Sigrun. He slipped the amulet from around his neck and dropped it in a pocket.

"Oh my," Indira breathed as she surveyed the patchwork of broken blisters and raw sores. "I'm impressed you were able to walk at all."

The compliment made him feel good, but Kevlin pushed it away. She was being too nice. What was her angle?

Indira placed her hands over his feet, and her alluring fragrance drifted to his nostrils. She smelled like spring, an enticing mix of wildflowers and clover.

She started to chant in a sweet, musical voice, and her hands glowed softly white. The light flowed over his feet, and a wonderful feeling swept through him, first draining away the pain, then extending up his legs and into his torso.

The constant burning of his wounds washed away under the gentle balm of Indira's magic, leaving him refreshed and whole. Unlike the raging strength of the magic the amulet had captured, her power was wholesome and peaceful.

He tried to find a reason not to trust it, but couldn't. That made him all the more suspicious. He'd never encountered anything magical that was simply good. He'd learned as a youth the dark underbelly of magic and wouldn't be taken unawares again.

After another minute, Indira sat back with a sigh. She swayed, and it looked like she might faint. He reached out a steadying hand.

"I'm all right," she said with a weak smile. "You've had a rough time."

"Thank you." He pulled on his boots and jumped to his feet. Indira rose to stand beside him and he added, "You have no idea how good that feels."

He decided to test her act of simple goodness. Before she could respond, he lifted her off the ground by the waist and spun her around. She cried out in surprise and clutched at his arms.

When he set her back down, she laughed and tossed her hair back. Their eyes met and a spark of pure heat rippled down to his heart. Standing so close, holding each other, and with her face flushed with excitement, he couldn't help it.

He kissed her squarely on the lips.

Indira stiffened in shock, and he broke off. She stepped away and he stared after her, watching for a crack in her perfect façade. He ignored the burning of his lips from the brief contact and stood fast against the urge to chase after her and kiss her again.

"I'm sorry," he said. "It's been a while since I've had a good kiss. I guess I'm out of practice."

Indira turned away and pulled up the hood of her cloak to cover her flushed cheeks. "You surprised me. I didn't expect you to do that."

Still sweet, not railing at him. Either she was extremely well trained, or maybe she really was the good-hearted woman she seemed. Either way, she scared him as much as she attracted him.

Ceren punched him in the shoulder hard. "You're such a brute."

"Where I come from, kissing is a sign of deep gratitude," he said.

"And where do you come from?" she asked, hands on hips, anger pouring off of her.

Her anger seemed disproportionate until he realized he had just insulted her recent kiss. He had never expected Ceren to want to kiss him again, particularly after they found safety. It looked like he wouldn't have to wonder about that any more.

Leander interrupted. "Perhaps you should consider which customs of your home might cause problems before you share them?" He looked more amused than angry, but Kevlin didn't miss the warning.

He didn't want the powerful old stalwart mad at him. At least Gabral was gone. The little colonel probably would have seen it as an excuse to try to kill him again.

"I need to fetch my pack from the inn," Kevlin said. He needed some time alone to think too.

"Hurry," Leander said. "We need to leave right away."

"Where should I meet you?"

"In the square at the center of town."

Kevlin headed for the inn while the others followed Harafin. He blew out a long breath. What a morning. Harafin had agreed to lead the expedition against the fort, but Kevlin couldn't shake the feeling that he was farther than ever from escaping his current entanglement with magic.

It would've been helpful if Harafin had thought to bring a bigger army. Kevlin still felt optimistic about their chances of defeating Tanathos' forces. With the Mace leading the charge, Harafin's powers ready to block the shadeleeches, and Leander's incredible battle prowess, they fielded a mighty force.

Kevlin half expected the Grakonians to surrender when they learned Harafin led the assault. The stories written about Harafin's exploits against the Sigrun filled volumes.

Harafin scared Kevlin. His motives were unfathomable, and he seemed willing to sacrifice anything to the demands of his duty. He'd already shown that he'd sacrifice Kevlin in a heartbeat. Their paths lay in the same direction for the moment, but how long would that continue?

Now they had this autumn solstice to worry about too. Killing Tanathos should be enough for anyone. Once they got the rock back to Antigonus, the solstice would take care of itself.

He liked Leander. There was a man to be trusted. Of course, it didn't hurt having the powerful stalwart close by when confronting Tanathos. . .and the Sigrun.

Gabral was another story. The irritating little man's motives were clear. He wanted respect, and his pride seemed easily affronted. Being bearer of the Mace didn't seem to be enough, despite its tremendous power.

Gabral's methods worried Kevlin. The soldier had gone too far in his interrogation, had been too quick to unleash deadly force. Kevlin had seen others with that same reckless disregard for control. Without mastering it, they tended to die young, and got a lot of their companions killed in the process. Gabral could prove as much a danger to them as Tanathos.

Then again, Indira was proving to be a threat of an entirely different sort.

The common room of the inn lay in shambles, with broken furniture scattered around. The fat innkeeper stood beside a table on which lay a prone figure covered by a tablecloth.

"I see ye survived," the big man remarked.

"I'm sorry about your inn. They were after me."

"Aye. They left everyone else alone but old Dwyn." He gestured at the shape on the table.

"Dwyn?" The man had spoken as if Kevlin should recognize the name.

"Aye, he be the one wot threw his chair at the beasts on the stairs as ye ran by."

"I was afraid he'd gotten himself into trouble with that."

"Don't feel sad for him. He was the oldest fellow in Baldev. He fought the Grakonians in the last war, and he died fighting them just like he wanted. His soul'll go to Serigala bearin' yew an' stone."

"Aye," Kevlin nodded solemnly.

The Hallvarri burial customs were interesting. Dwyn's hands would bear to the grave yew, representing a bow to signify death in battle, and stone, representing the earth. Serigala, goddess of the hunt and the harvest, would welcome him home as a cherished son, the greatest honor for Hallvarri dead.

As they spoke, a very short young woman whom Kevlin recognized as one of the archers from the battle entered the room and joined them.

"I never got a chance to thank you and your friends for saving my life," Kevlin said.

The innkeeper smiled proudly. "This be Adalia, my niece. Best hunter in Baldev."

Kevlin took her hand. "A pleasure to meet you, Adalia."

"By Jagen, I wish I'd gotten there sooner," Adalia said hotly. "I'd like ta kill more of the brutes fer killin' Dwyn."

"You defended your town and your family with honor today. You should be proud of that."

"Why was they after you anyway?" the innkeeper asked.

"Because I'm going to destroy them."

"There be more of 'em?"

"Aye, and we're leaving to hunt them down."

Adalia grabbed his arm. "Kin I go with ye?" Her bright green eyes lit with fierce determination.

She's got spirit.

"If you bring along those other archers, you can. We're going to need all the help we can get."

"Aye," Adalia exclaimed. "I kin git the whole bunch of 'em. I pledge me honor to it, sir."

"Good, then assemble your men and meet me in the town square. Bring supplies for several days in the forest. And be quick. We leave within the hour."

"Aye, sir."

"Check in with your father afore you go," the innkeeper said to her.

"I will." Adalia raced from the room, her long blond braid flying out behind.

"Thank ye for taking her," said the innkeeper. "It be important to the folk in Baldev to know we kin defend our town."

Kevlin had a thought. "Are there any woodcutters and miners in town with as much will to fight as your archers?"

"Aye, but why?"

"I have an idea for how they could help turn the tide of battle for us. Can you find me half a dozen of the best woodsmen in town, and an equal number of good miners? And quick?"

"Aye," replied the innkeeper. "I know just who ye need. I'll get 'em to the square quick-time."

Kevlin clasped wrists with the innkeeper. Then he jogged upstairs to what was left of his room. He picked through the shattered remains of his bed to find his possessions, then buckled on his leather breastplate. After donning his pack, he hung the amulet around his neck with a silent reminder never to take it off again.

When he reached the town square, he had to do some fast explaining to Gabral before the impetuous colonel sent the eager miners and woodcutters away. The colonel finally agreed to Kevlin's plan.

Then Adalia and her archers arrived.

Gabral nearly refused to allow the fiery woman to accompany the group. She was the captain of the archers however, so he reluctantly agreed.

Before the sun stood directly overhead, the grim force rode out of town.

34

PAINFUL LESSONS

Tanathos' world burned with pain.

With every breath, every movement, it flared up in staggering waves. A lesser man would have been overwhelmed and incapacitated by it.

He was not a lesser man.

He did not fear pain. He understood it and gloried in administering it to others, subjecting them to unbearable torment before ripping their souls from their broken bodies.

That was just the beginning.

Once he possessed their souls, he fed upon them, stealing their life force. He corrupted them and consumed the strength of their souls. He was strong enough to take it, so it was his right to do so.

He deserved it.

Staggering to his feet, Tanathos paced his room in the second floor of the fort's command building. Though larger than any of the other rooms, this one was barely large enough for a crude desk and chair, a bed, a closet, and small window that faced the front gate. As he considered the situation, the darkness cloaking his eyes roiled like ebony thunderclouds.

Fear, the aftereffect of his just-concluded interview with the angry Sigrun council, chilled him with its unwelcome weakness. Even though their voices had been but distant whispers due to the vast distance, their rage at his failure was undiminished. The pain they inflicted was awe-inspiring. It was a necessary gesture, though meaningless in itself.

No, the pain was but an incentive to drive him on, and a reminder not to fail again. Those who failed were tortured in Ophisurus' fiery chains long after the Sigrun had broken their bodies and fed upon their souls.

It was no less than they deserved.

That thought sent a new thrill of fear creeping across his scalp. It wasn't unusual for servants of the Sigrun to feel afraid, although he usually converted such fear to anger or excitement as he contemplated the incredible power they wielded. He hungered for a chance to join them and share in their glory.

One more test and the coveted seventh seat at the council table would be his. In the last seconds before the tenuous connection with his far-distant masters failed, they informed him that the fool Kevlin was bringing Oris back to him. Tanathos smiled as he contemplated the tortures he'd inflict on the man.

Kevlin was returning with reinforcements. The strength of the sacrificed soul they had used to power the communication spell had failed before the Sigrun could share more information.

Tanathos was not worried, nor would he risk contacting his masters again without first completing his primary mission. In such a remote location, who could Kevlin have rounded up to help? The fool was desperate and playing into Tanathos' hands.

Destroying Kevlin's little strike force, coupled with Tanathos' triumphant return of Oris to Grakonia, would guarantee his elevation to the Sigrun council. Tanathos feared only one sentinel, but Harafin was ensconced in his seat of power in Tamera.

Then again, Kevlin and his unknown allies had defeated Merab and his makrasha. Tanathos thought on that for a moment before making a decision. He had not survived so long without planning for worst-case scenarios. He always ensured other shadeleeches who lacked his forethought were the ones sacrificed instead of himself.

First he needed to restore his strength. He extended his senses beyond the room, reaching out with his mind until he touched the nearest makrasha. The creatures were all slaves to his will, their souls shackled to him, so it was a simple matter to feel for the ethereal conduit that linked them.

The beast he chose was one of two stationed at the head of the stairs. The creature was strong and healthy, its life force pulsing down his sthenic senses in inviting waves. Tanathos reached through the conduit, grasped the power of that life force, and *pulled*.

Life flooded into him, filling him with strength and washing away the pain inflicted by the Sigrun. Tanathos shuddered in ecstasy and frantically sucked every last vestige of life out of the creature, greedily drinking it into his own soul. Intense pleasure suffused his being as he basked in the warmth of another's life essence surrendered to his whim.

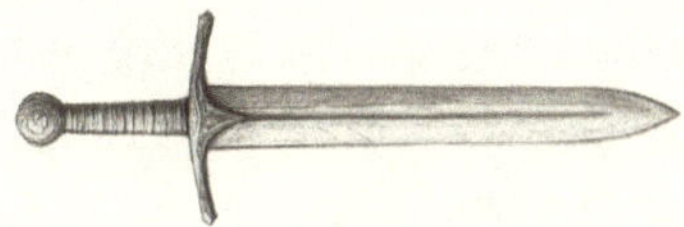

At the head of the stairs, a black cloud enveloped one of the makrasha standing guard. It opened its mouth to scream, but only a choking gasp escaped its withering lips. Its entire form shriveled, collapsing in on itself as its life and strength drained away.

It took only a couple of seconds.

The darkness dissipated as the skeletal remains of the once hulking creature toppled down the stairs. Bones cascaded through the brittle skin and shattered into pieces that broke into dust. Wisps of shadow settled to rest at the bottom of the stairs, the only remains of what had been a living creature.

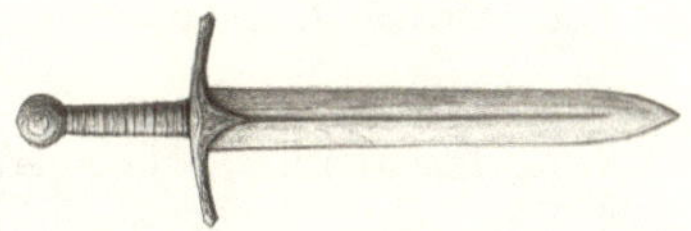

The makrasha served Tanathos well, restoring his vigor and filling him with the power he needed. Taking the soul of even one makrasha was a glorious experience, although it paled next to the ecstasy of ripping out the soul of an enemy while they still resisted.

A soul thus taken could be held captive in Tanathos' power while he tortured it and drained its energy, only to be released after he had taken everything. The shade that remained would be but a pale shadow, barely recognizable as a person's soul.

Casting the shattered remains of such a shade loose was pure delight, for those souls lacked the strength to reach the eternal worlds. Instead, Ophisurus would encircle the victims with his burning chains and torture them forever.

"Slave," Tanathos called. The other makrasha stationed at the top of the stairs entered the room immediately. "Summon Neasa."

An ugly, fat toad of a woman, his second-in-command Neasa entered the room a moment later. Her black hair shone greasily in the scant sunlight penetrating the curtained window and fell straight from her head to her broad shoulders.

In stark contrast with Tanathos' own, Neasa's eyes were milky white, staring out over a large nose. She rarely blinked, and few liked to meet her gaze. Tanathos despised her for more than her ugliness, but couldn't afford to kill her. Yet.

"So, they left you alive," Neasa said, not masking her disappointment.

"Don't push me today," Tanathos hissed.

"You can't afford to destroy me, Tanathos," Neasa said, echoing his thoughts disturbingly well. "Both of your little disciples are dead, so I'm all you've got. You should not have kept me from the man Kevlin."

He didn't show how much her words rang true. Had he sent her after Kevlin instead of Merab, he'd be rid of her already. It didn't matter. When the time was right, he would take her life and use her strength to further his own ends.

He only said, "We have no time for this. Kevlin is returning with reinforcements."

"They mean to rescue Antigonus?"

"I don't care what they *mean* to do. They serve only to return the stone to me."

"He still has it?"

"Yes. He lacks even the sense to run."

"What is your plan?"

"I will create a halimaw. The fools think to take us by surprise, but we'll slaughter them."

Neasa grinned. "Yes. The halimaw will shatter their resistance and we can take the souls of the rest."

"See to the defenses," Tanathos said. "I will take Kevlin myself."

"Let me create the halimaw," Neasa begged, her eyes alight with anticipation. "It has been a long time, and the woman Rhea is a perfect candidate."

Rhea's arrogance would make such a fate so much more satisfying. He considered his overweight second for a moment before nodding. "Very well. She is yours."

Let her feel needed, even appreciated. . .until he killed her.

Neasa smiled, revealing perfect white teeth that only served to make the rest of her face seem all the more hideous. "I'll do it now."

Striding from his room, he headed for Antigonus' cell. He had work to do.

35

UNEXPECTED CONSEQUENCES

Keisara Fideima sat listless at the breakfast table, dark rings under her eyes, her shoulders slumped. She hadn't slept well the past couple of nights.

Neither had Sitara. She awoke feeling exhausted and unsettled each morning after completing a fresh wave of whispered attacks on the keisara's mind. The physical toll was becoming so great that she barely functioned well enough to avoid detection. When she did doze, unsettling dreams tormented her sleep and left her feeling unrested.

Still, she caught glimpses of progress. Yesterday the keisara had visited the audience hall while the emperor and ruling council held court. Outwardly she appeared normal, but Sitara noticed her scanning the crowd more intently than usual.

Had she been looking for Junian?

Luckily the man was not in attendance, for actually seeing him would have shattered the carefully crafted illusion Sitara had built around him in the keisara's mind. Sitara hadn't considered that risk, and she wondered if she should try to influence the keisara into avoiding the audience hall.

If only Bajaran were there to guide her. He'd trained her thoroughly in how to infiltrate the emperor's tower, but she was exploring aspects of her power she'd barely touched before. She needed his help to plan for consequences she hadn't anticipated.

That morning, the keisara seemed unusually withdrawn. She frowned into her tea and snapped commands at Sitara. She never even glanced out the window, despite the dramatic vista of the inner palace and the northern flank of the Great Dome.

Sitara maintained her place near the keisara's left shoulder and watched. The woman was clearly struggling to withstand the effects of Sitara's secret assault, but could she? The agony of anticipation kept Sitara tense, filled with doubts.

The door opened and a maid entered the private breakfast room, situated on the same level of the tower as the keisara's bedchamber. The maid curtsied, "Pardon, my lady, but Healer Ithai has come to visit."

Keisara Fideima's face lit with a smile. "Please, show her in."

Sitara clasped her trembling hands over her stomach. She forced her expression to remain calm despite the panic bubbling in her heart.

Ithai was the keisara's personal healer, who had served her since her childhood. She possessed a remarkably powerful healing gift, and none boasted her experience. Would Ithai sense Sitara's manipulations?

The thought set Sitara's already knotted stomach twisting further until she felt she might vomit. *I should have planned for this*, she wailed silently. Only with great effort did she remain in her appointed place.

Despite her great age, Ithai still walked with a firm stride. She stood somewhat shorter than Sitara, but her bright blue eyes made her appear taller, and wispy gray hair floated around her head like a tarnished halo.

Keisara Fideima rose from her seat and hugged Ithai warmly. "It is so good to see you. How are you?"

Ithai smiled as she gazed intently at the keisara. "I am fine, my dear. But the question is, how are you?"

Fideima managed a rather forced laugh. "I'm fine." She returned to her seat and motioned Ithai to sit as well. Sitara set a plate in front of the old healer and offered tea and an assortment of breakfast pastries. Ithai accepted the cup without taking her eyes off the keisara.

"Young lady," Ithai said a little sternly, "you are clearly not fine. Lady Elva mentioned you were looking a little peaked yesterday. I am glad she did. Now tell me what is bothering you."

The keisara shrugged, but tears gleamed in her eyes. "Just some troubling dreams."

Sitara found it difficult to breathe. Her legs felt weak and she leaned against the table to keep from staggering. Luckily no one noticed.

"Dreams, eh?" Ithai frowned and shuffled her chair closer. "We'll see about that." She reached out and touched the keisara's forehead with a hand that began to glow with a soft, pure white light.

Sitara forced herself to stand straight, despite a tremor that shivered up her legs all the way to the base of her skull. Bile rose in her throat till she could barely keep it down. Still, she watched Ithai's glowing hand with hungry intensity. Her own magic used to feel like that: pure, white, and beautiful.

Ever since it had fled from her in the emperor's apartments, forcing her to embrace the power of darkness, she had difficulty calling upon it. It came slower and didn't penetrate to her core like it used to.

Instead of filling her with bounding joy, it seemed reluctant and tarnished, hovering just under her skin as if unable to penetrate deeper. The sentinels must be corrupting the magic at a faster rate than Bajaran had suggested.

Ithai gasped and surged to her feet. "What in the name of the accidental gods?" She placed both hands on the keisara's head.

"What's wrong?" the keisara asked.

"Hush, child." The glow of Ithai's gift flared bright, and blinding. Sitara glanced aside and blinked away tears. Fear burned unfettered through her soul.

Ithai *knew*.

36

Surprise Connections

A dalia and her hunters led the assault force out of town and onto a narrow road heading north and slightly west of the base of the cliff. "We'll be able ta foller this here road fer about five miles afore it turns west. We'll have ta go through the forest from there," she explained to Kevlin.

"Have your men scout ahead," Kevlin instructed. "Keep a sharp eye out for any more Grakonians."

"Aye, m'lord." Adalia banged one fist over her heart in a rough imitation of the soldier salute.

"Call me Kevlin. I hold no rank among these men."

"I thought ye was a captain with givin' us orders about wot ye wants us ta do."

"I agree," said Leander, who rode beside Kevlin. "Now that we're on the road, tell us how you come to have the bearing of a leader of men."

"You're always looking for a good story," the huge Donarri Captain Jerrik rumbled.

"Of course, my big friend," replied Leander with another of his ready smiles. "Knowledge is power. I never pass up an opportunity to learn something new."

"To give power over oneself to another takes a lot of trust," said Kevlin.

"I do not seek power over anyone, my young friend. I merely seek knowledge, for with that knowledge we can know better how to work together."

"That's really all you're after?"

"Of course. Using knowledge against my allies is against my religion." Leander grinned and Kevlin couldn't help but smile in return. The old man's good humor was infectious, and for the first time in far too long, Kevlin felt he had met a person he could actually trust.

"You still owe me your story," Ceren called from where she rode at the head of the column alongside Gabral.

"All right." Kevlin thought for a moment, his eyes drifting up to the trees. A strange mood settled over him and words came unbidden to his lips. "I was born upon the waters of the sea, was forged to manhood in the heat of battle, and I've shed blood in all six kingdoms."

Harafin, riding just ahead of Leander, said, "An interesting choice of words."

"Sorry, just waxing poetic, I guess."

He hadn't planned to say it that way. Maybe spending so much time around cryptic sentinels was starting to rub off. Instead of annoying Harafin, the old man was studying Kevlin closely, far too interested.

"I really was born upon the waters of the sea," Kevlin added. Or rather *in* the waters of the sea."

At his companions' questioning looks, he explained, "I was born into a merchant family. It's a long-held belief among seafaring Meinarri that a child born in the waters of the Tamerlane Sea may be blessed by the touch of the Lady and accomplish great things. So my mother gave birth to me while hanging from the side of one of our ship's boats, far out at sea."

"I have heard of that custom," Harafin said. "Although I've never met anyone born that way."

"It never seemed to help. We weren't very successful traders. For the first fourteen years of my life, I rarely spent more than a few days ashore at a time. We traded all through the empire, but never seemed to profit. I hated it."

"So I picked an interesting port and jumped ship."

That sounded pretty good, and completely skipped the real reason he had finally fled his father's ship. The memories of that sentinel had haunted his dreams for years. The day he jumped ship was the day he learned another sentinel had booked passage for their next journey.

"I didn't have any plans about what to do next, but then I ran into a group of mercenaries. I thought at the time that the Wheel had spun in my favor. I'd seen little of fighting men on my father's ship, and was very impressed. One old sergeant noted my interest and invited me to join them. With nothing better to do, I agreed."

"Ye was a mercenary?" asked Adalia.

"Aye. It turned out they were recruiting to swell their ranks for some upcoming skirmish. I was given a spear and some rudimentary training, and placed in the front lines with the other new recruits."

Kevlin paused, remembering that terrible day for the first time in many years. He clearly recalled the laughing face of the old sergeant who said, "If ye survive lad, ye might just make a decent soldier."

It seemed the entire company was leaning closer to hear the story over the steady clopping of their horses' hooves.

"That battle was terrifying, but I survived," Kevlin said. "I had to kill for the first time."

"You were lucky," said Captain Drystan, the lanky Einarri. "Throwing you to almost certain death like that tells a lot about the leaders of that troop."

"Aye," agreed Kevlin. "Although it was quite a while before I realized that. I found I made a decent soldier, and for the next six years I crossed the empire from one skirmish to another. I gained some small promotions, convincing myself I had accomplished what I'd set out to do. Then about seven years ago, I was sent with the first mercenary company to Donarr."

Jerrik surprised Kevlin by exclaiming, "I don't believe it. You're Kevlin the mercenary?"

"I just said so."

Kevlin liked Donarri soldiers, but sometimes they were a little slow. He personally suspected it had something to do with the long winters and high altitudes.

"Tell me," Jerrik said. "What are your thoughts about General Stigandr?"

So much for avoiding painful subjects.

"I'd kill General Stigandr on sight," Kevlin said, trying to keep his memories bottled up. He failed and they came flooding back in a painful wave. "He betrayed us as much as he did your people. I just wish I'd been able to finish him when I had the chance."

Jerrik whooped, a mighty yell that echoed through the forest, causing several of the horses to shy in surprise. He jumped from his horse and wrapped huge arms around Kevlin's torso in a crushing grip.

Kevlin had met a lot of friendly people, but this was ridiculous. The big man lifted him bodily from the saddle. Kevlin couldn't breathe, couldn't move. He was completely helpless.

Kevlin tried to shout to Jerrik to let go but only managed, "Ack, gurk!"

"Sorry." Jerrik dropped him to the ground and pounded him on the back so hard, Kevlin stumbled into his horse.

"What's going on?" Gabral demanded.

Jerrik ignored him and clapped big hands on Kevlin's shoulders so hard he nearly drove Kevlin to his knees. "By the Light," Jerrik grinned, "To be the one to find you."

"I'm glad we met," Kevlin said, hoping the giant captain would let him go before killing him with friendliness.

Jerrik wasn't finished.

"By my honor, I name Kevlin Swordbrother and Truefriend of Donarr."

Kevlin had no idea how to respond to that.

"Well, well," muttered Harafin.

Leander laughed heartily.

"Captain, I demand an explanation," Gabral snapped, obviously confused and just as obviously upset about being confused.

Jerrik said, "Sir, this is Kevlin, commander of the first mercenary legion, and sworn truefriend of the Donarri people."

"Hey, I'm the one telling the story," Kevlin said.

"You hardly know this man," Gabral protested, "and Truefriends can only be named in the presence of a king."

"That's usually the way of it, sir. But I do know this man, and our king commanded us not to miss the chance to name him truefriend when we found him."

Kevlin really didn't want to continue this conversation. He had hoped to gloss over a few things from his days in Donarr. "I think I would've remembered meeting you, Jerrik."

"You know my brother," Jerrik replied. "Our surname is Treyger."

That shook Kevlin, triggering another flood of memories and exhuming a long-buried fear.

He spoke slowly. "So your older brother is Jannik Treyger, commander of the first Donarri legion?"

"Aye."

Jerrik hadn't tried to kill him, so Kevlin dared to ask, "And he's all right?"

"By your warning, aye. If not for that, even Kamen's Fury wouldn't have saved the kingdom."

Kevlin breathed a deep sigh of relief, hardly believing he could finally let that worry go. Too many memories from those days were painful. It felt so good to find a glimmer of hope filtering through the universal blackness.

"Would you mind sharing the good news with the rest of us?" asked Gabral evenly.

"Aye, sir," replied Jerrik. "After the swordbrother ceremony."

"You mean to conduct it here? Now?"

"Aye, sir. We can't complete the truefriend appointment until we get to Tirloch and the king's court, but the debt due my brother's life demands I name him swordbrother immediately."

Kevlin stared in stark amazement as Jerrik rolled back the sleeve of his jerkin to the elbow, revealing the corded muscles of his right forearm. He motioned Kevlin to do the same. Kevlin did so, his motions slow as he tried to grasp the abrupt change of fortune.

The company formed a circle around them, silently witnessing the unusual event unfolding in the middle of the forest road.

"Your blade," said Jerrik solemnly.

On impulse, Kevlin drew Bajaran's silver blade from the base of his neck. Jerrik stared at it for a moment, as if he had trouble seeing it, just as Kevlin had when he'd first picked it up.

Maybe this wasn't such a good idea.

Too late. Jerrik was already extending his arm, palm up. With two deft slashes, Kevlin cut into Jerrik's palm and forearm, leaving trails of blood in the blade's wake. A powerful tingling sensation ran up Kevlin's arm from the blade, then down through his body to his right boot where Oris lay hidden.

This definitely wasn't a good idea.

Jerrik made no move, so Kevlin ignored the ominous feeling.

Please let me have something go right without the cursed magic interfering, he wished.

Jerrik took the blade and cut Kevlin's palm and forearm. Though it didn't hurt much, again he felt the strange tingling sensation. It spread up his arm from the wound but did not extend further. He accepted the blade and flexed his hand. Everything worked, so he pushed aside his growing concern.

He and Jerrik clasped palms to forearms, locking their arms in a powerful grip and mixing their blood.

Jerrik recited the ancient oath. "I, Jerrik Treyger, son of Liron Treyger, Lord of the Yochanan, recognize Kevlin of Meinarr as swordbrother and truefriend to Donarr, and kin of my kin. My Brother."

Kevlin responded, the words flowing from his mouth smoothly as if he had practiced the ceremony a hundred times. "I, Kevlin of Meinarr, recognize Jerrik Treyger, son of Liron Treyger, swordbrother. Kin of my kin, my brother. I swear to defend and honor Donarr as my own kingdom and people."

Those words, older than the empire itself, bound them as brothers in a bond as close as blood. As Kevlin spoke, a feeling of relief washed through him. Perhaps his life hadn't been such a complete failure. Maybe he had been remembering only the wrong parts of it for too long.

Before they broke their grip, Drystan stepped forward, pulling back his own sleeve. The Einarri captain extended his arm over theirs, palm up. "I've heard what you did, Kevlin, and would like to honor it. May I add my oath to yours?"

"Back off," Jerrik growled. "This isn't about you."

"I wasn't talking to you."

Kevlin groaned inwardly. The last thing he wanted was his new brother angry at him. It would probably be best to deny Drystan's unusual request.

Although not exactly rare, swordbrothers weren't common. He'd never heard of three families uniting across different kingdoms when at least two came from noble houses.

Before Kevlin could respond, Jerrik broke the hold and rounded on Drystan. "You can't resist, can you? Can't stand for anyone else to be honored?"

"You really are as dumb as they say," Drystan said.

Jerrik grabbed for his sword. Drystan grinned and swung his long spear around to the ready, his hawk-like eyes shining with eagerness to fight.

Just my luck. I'll be the first man in history to get a swordbrother killed within minutes of swearing the oath.

Gabral pushed between the captains before they could start a duel. "Stand down. This will not happen."

"Why not?" one of the soldiers called from the encircling ranks. "Let them fight. Contest match rules."

"It won't take long," Jerrik said.

Drystan laughed. "I love it when they're optimistic."

"No," Gabral said. "That's an order. You two are not to fight each other until the mission is over. Then you can kill yourselves for all I care."

Jerrik slammed his sword home, still scowling, while Drystan turned to Kevlin and held out his arm. Despite the furious glare from Jerrik, Kevlin nodded. He didn't know the man, but it felt right to accept his oath. He might be sailing unfamiliar waters with everything to do with sentinels and magic, but he'd learned to trust his instincts.

Kevlin cut Drystan's palm and forearm like he had Jerrik's, and again that odd tingling coursed through him. *I wish this stuff would stop happening.*

As the two clasped palms to forearms, the lanky Einarri captain proclaimed, "I Drystan Aldacosia, son of Birger Aldacosia, Herdmaster and Lord of the Chandana, Rider of the Einarr plains, recognize Kevlin of Meinarr swordbrother. Kin of my kin, my brother."

Kevlin responded with the proper words and, hoping to break some of the tension, added, "Thank you, brothers. I am honored that you would mix your noble blood with that of a commoner."

Jerrik growled to Drystan, "You may be Kevlin's brother, but you're not mine."

Harafin pushed through the crowd. "Kevlin, show me your blade."

He held up the silver dagger.

"Quick," Harafin commanded. "Your wounds."

The three men turned up their arms and Kevlin was amazed to see the cuts nearly healed. As they watched, the healing process completed, leaving only thin white scars to testify of the oaths they had just taken.

"How'd you manage that?" Kevlin asked.

"I did nothing," Harafin said softly. "Nothing at all. I have seen a blade like that only once in my life, carried by the betrayer, Bajaran. One cut from that blade would kill a grown man in seconds. For a moment, I thought this was his cursed blade."

"That would explain your concern," remarked Drystan dryly.

"But does not explain what just happened," Harafin said.

"Well, I'm glad Bajaran wasn't the one wielding a blade today," said Kevlin carefully. He hadn't mentioned the silver dagger when relating his tale earlier, and still felt a great reluctance to do so.

Poisoned magic? That would explain why Antigonus couldn't heal himself. And he'd just cut himself and his brothers with the same blade. The thought made his knees weak. He remembered how easily the dagger had cut through wood, and even metal.

So why weren't they dead?

"I must give this further thought," Harafin said softly.

"Later. We're wasting time." Gabral gave a stern look to Drystan and Jerrik, then ordered, "Mount up." As they all obeyed, he added to Jerrik, "You will explain as we ride."

"Aye, sir," the big man said, still glowering.

That could have gone better, Kevlin thought. Despite the near violence, however, he felt happy. There was obviously more going on between his two new brothers than he knew, and they would have to work that out. At the moment, he felt confident they could do so.

Much remained to consider, but at least one thing was certain. His life had just changed. He was formally allied with two powerful families from different kingdoms. If he didn't get either of them killed, for once the change might be a good one.

As he swung into the saddle, he caught Ceren staring at him, a thoughtful expression on her face as she nibbled on a lock of her auburn hair. She noticed him looking and glanced away quickly.

At least she wasn't glaring anymore.

He studied her as the column moved forward, watching her sway in time with her mount, and his mind wandered back to that dark night when she'd kissed him. The fact that it wouldn't ever happen again didn't matter. It was a nice memory.

That memory led him to another, and his eyes drifted toward Indira. She'd rejected his kiss, but hadn't slapped him. She was a puzzle. Could anyone really be that good and still live in this world? The very sight of her stirred powerful emotions that he couldn't dare trust. The last time he allowed a woman into his life nearly killed him.

Some would say that death by a lover was the best kind.

They were idiots.

37

Conflicting Memories

As the group rode, Jerrik continued the interrupted tale. "I named Kevlin swordbrother and truefriend because he saved our kingdom from destruction."

Kevlin stared at the big man, dumbfounded. That's not how he remembered it at all. He'd failed. He'd lost his livelihood and the woman he loved. His entire life had proven to be a lie.

"This, I have to hear," Ceren said. "That doesn't sound like the Kevlin I know."

"That's not fair," Kevlin said.

She gave him that I'm-better-than-you-because-I'm-noble look.

He wanted to stick out his tongue at her, but Indira was watching and he hesitated. Now that they were surrounded by soldiers and powerful magic, Ceren didn't need to rely on him. It looked like she planned to make that fact very clear.

Jerrik spoke before Kevlin could think of a suitable retort. "It was a tough time in Donarr. We'd never hired mercenaries before and a lot of people hated the idea." Talking seemed to ease his anger at Drystan. "We're a nation of warriors, with enemies on two borders. We've been fighting the Grakonians and the Ragnheidur since the empire was founded, and we've never needed help."

"So what changed?" asked Leander.

"Well," said the big man slowly, "my father said we had too much peace. We didn't have anyone to fight for a generation, and people started thinking there wouldn't be another war. For a while, they were right."

"But about ten years ago the Ragnheidur and their Canavars attacked without warning from across the northern mountains. They razed two towns before our legions drove them out. There weren't a lot of them, but we weren't prepared. We'd gotten lazy."

"Instead of uniting, people argued about how to respond. Some even suggested sending a peace delegation to the Ragnheidur, and using mercenaries."

Jerrik shook his head in disgust. "The king's no fool. He didn't bother with a peace delegation, but activated the third legion for the first time in twenty years. The Ragnheidur kept attacking every year in greater numbers, and people kept arguing about what to do."

"The king finally made a deal to try to settle things down. The fourth legion was activated and he ordered the repair of three mountain forts that had been abandoned. He also hired a column of a thousand mercenaries. Kevlin was one of them."

"We didn't know anything about the situation," said Kevlin.

"Aye," said Jerrik. "The mercenaries were in a tight spot. If they failed, they'd be kicked out for good, but none of our commanders wanted to work with them. My brother Jannik finally agreed to. He didn't like the idea, but wouldn't leave those men to die."

"Jannik couldn't protect us from the stupidity of our own captain," said Kevlin.

"I take it things didn't go very well," said Gabral.

"Nay, but that gave Kevlin a chance to shine," replied Jerrik. "Timaeus, the mercenary leader, led his force into a trap on their first campaign. Most of them died, but Kevlin salvaged some of the force and wiped out their attackers."

"The Wheel spun in my favor," Kevlin said.

"How so?" asked Harafin as the rest of the troop bunched up around them, straining to hear.

"I was a sergeant then and overheard Jannik explain to Timaeus about the forces we might face. That information proved critical. Our mission was to secure a mountain pass, and Timaeus led us into a canyon where the Raghneidur trapped us and attacked. It was a slaughter."

Kevlin stared up at the sky through overhanging branches and thought of that terrible day. "Timaeus was one of the first to fall, taken by an arrow. He died before he ever realized what he'd done."

"There were only about a hundred Raghneidur, but all of them were Canavar handlers. They unleashed the monsters on us from both sides of the canyon. Our men were already in disarray and the sight of those beasts shattered all discipline."

"They're twelve feet tall, with skin as thick as plate armor. They reared up on two legs to fight, and many carried uprooted trees as clubs. They obliterated half our force in minutes, then started feeding on the dead and wounded."

"What?" exclaimed Ceren. "They eat men?"

"Aye," said Jerrik. "'Tis a terrible sight. Worst thing is when they start on the wounded. Those screams stay with a man."

Kevlin nodded. "The Canavars began to feast, and the Raghneidur came down into the canyon to rouse them. During the lull, I took command as the senior living officer and rallied the men."

"We didn't have enough pikemen to fight the Canavars the way Jannik had advised, so I ordered each four-man squad to fight one Canavar, with an archer in support. With arrows distracting the beasts, we slashed the backs of their knees where the hide was soft. Once they fell, we finished them with a heavy stroke to the neck, or stabbed them through an eye, into the brain."

"It's tough fighting a Canavar close up like that," said Jerrik.

"It was either that or get eaten," Kevlin said. "We broke through, and from the rim of the canyon our archers finished off the Raghneidur, turning their trap back on them."

"The Canavars came after us again, but only in small groups. We knew how to fight them by then, so we killed them all. Only seventy-five of us survived."

"You were lucky any of you got out," Jerrik said. "Kevlin's success against the Canavars was why the mercenaries got to stay on another season, with Kevlin in command. Over the next two years, he won every battle and became commander of the first full mercenary legion authorized by the king."

"Each year, the enemy kept attacking, and in greater numbers, despite everything we did to hold them. The year after Kevlin became commander, the king authorized a second mercenary legion. And that year, General Stigandr came to Donarr to lead his forces.

"By then, thanks to Kevlin's success, people had started trusting the mercenaries and thinking they were a good idea. The king was even planning to authorize a third mercenary legion. With that many men, we were going to take the battle over the mountains to the Raghneidur."

"That's when everything fell apart," said Kevlin. "I discovered that General Stigandr was playing both sides of the conflict. He had contracted with the Raghneidur to betray Donarr the next season and support a massive invasion they were preparing."

"If he'd done it, the kingdom would've been destroyed," said Jerrik. "The empire couldn't have come to help in time."

"I made a huge mistake," said Kevlin. "I spoke of what I had learned with the leader of the second mercenary legion."

"Commander Chayah," said Jerrik.

"Aye. Commander Chayah." Kevlin paused for a moment as the memories he'd struggled to bury burst into his mind like floodwaters through a breached hull.

He had been with Chayah almost a year then. They were both commanders, so what could be more natural? She'd been beautiful, brilliant, and his equal in combat. Completely smitten, he had expected to marry her when the campaign ended. He'd never considered she might be part of the plot to destroy Donarr, and kill him.

"She betrayed me."

For the first time in years, he relived the anguish of Chayah's betrayal, a memory that still burned him to the core. She had mocked him, laughed in his face, and said she was happy to see him die. She claimed that he had been nothing but an amusement to her.

It couldn't have hurt more had she literally ripped his heart from his chest. Despite the passage of time, he still fumed at his stupidity in having fallen for her.

"She and the general knew I'd never betray Donarr," he said, trying to keep the pain from his voice. "So they planned to kill me and use my death to motivate my men to join the attack on Donarr. They were orchestrating the whole thing with a Blade Stalwart."

"*That's* when you fought the stalwart," Ceren said.

"Aye. His name was Shaemal."

The anguish of that betrayal faded under other memories. Unexpected freedom, the explosion of action, and the desperate struggle against Shaemal and the general.

"I wounded the general in my escape, slashing his knee in a stroke similar to those we used against the Canavars."

"He limps still," said Jerrik with a vicious grin. "The healers could never fix it up right."

"I'm glad to hear that," Kevlin said. "I warned your brother of the danger and escaped the encampment."

"Aye. When you took off, half the mercenaries in the camp were sent after you. Jannik's legion fought their way free and raised the alarm across the kingdom. General Stigandr was last seen fleeing across the Meinarr border at the head of what was left of his army."

"Why didn't you pursue him into Meinarr?" asked Drystan. "I'd have thought the king would've wanted the general's head on a pike."

Jerrik nodded. "That he did, but Meinarr wouldn't let our army cross the border. They said they'd take care of it."

"Do you have any idea where General Stigandr is now?" Kevlin asked.

"Last I heard he was still in Meinarr, working for them."

"That's madness," said Kevlin. "Meinarr is a kingdom of merchants and farmers. If General Stigandr's given any hold, it'll be impossible to get him out. Sherah's teeth, there aren't enough soldiers in the whole kingdom to run him off."

"The use of mercenaries in Meinarr has been discussed by the ruling council," remarked Harafin, "although I never heard the details as you explained them. This must be brought to the attention of the emperor once we return to Tamera."

"Will the council act?" asked Leander.

"That I cannot say."

"So what have you been doing for the past two years since all of that fell apart, Kevlin?" asked Ceren.

"Trying to forget about it," he said, unable to keep the bitterness from his voice. "And trying to keep a low profile. General Stigandr swore to hunt me down."

"Why didn't you return to Donarr?" asked Drystan. "Sounds like they'd have welcomed you back a hero."

"I would have, but I wasn't aware of the king's decree, and I honestly didn't think of it. I wanted to bury everything to do with my past life. Returning to Donarr would've made that impossible."

"Well, you've got to come back now," said Jerrik. "King Odovacar wants to talk with you."

"That sounds like a good idea."

"After we're finished," Gabral said, bringing them all back to the present.

The men drifted back to their positions in the column, leaving Kevlin with his own thoughts. He had much to think about, and old memories to reconcile with Jerrik's point of view.

None of it mattered until he got the rock back to Antigonus. He couldn't afford to fail again. Despite what Jerrik said, he'd played an important role in pushing Donarr to the brink of destruction. He wouldn't be responsible for the destruction of the empire.

They followed the road steadily northward for an hour until it turned sharply to the west. There they plunged into the forest. For the rest of the afternoon, they continued north. The heavy forest seemed intent on barring their way. At dusk they found a sizable clearing next to a bubbling stream and made camp.

The men set about their various duties, displaying the efficiency of long experience. In short order, the cooking fires were lit, the horses tended to, and guards posted. The air was clear and heavy with the scent of pine trees and late-season gandrel flowers.

Harafin drew Kevlin aside. "There are a few things the two of us need to discuss."

"What sorts of things?" Kevlin asked uneasily. He'd rather not deal with Harafin right then. He felt emotionally exhausted after unearthing those painful memories, and just wanted to get some sleep.

"Magic."

38

Buttering Toast With Your Feet

"I've seen enough magic lately," Kevlin said. "I actually prefer less magic, honestly."

"We are facing a time of dire conflict," Harafin said. "You are steward of Oris while its bearer yet lives. This is a unique situation that requires study."

Study all you want. Just leave me out of it.

Before Kevlin could answer, Harafin made a sweeping gesture with his right hand. A globe of amber magic appeared and encircled them. Kevlin jumped in surprise, knocked his head against the sloping roof, and tripped.

The warm floor smelled slightly of cinnamon. As soon as he touched it, it flared and cracked, and he fell through to the ground beneath. He scrambled up onto his knees and stared around nervously.

"What is this thing?" he asked.

"Do not worry. It won't harm you." Harafin sat on the floor of the round magical room. "Although that amulet of yours makes it as hard to protect you as it is to harm you." He snapped his fingers and the floor retreated away from Kevlin.

"Warn me next time," Kevlin growled. Gentle warmth began flowing into his chest, and he shuddered.

Magic.

The amulet must have captured magic from Harafin's sphere when he touched it. Not good. The song of Savas was triggered last time the amulet did that. He had to get rid of that power before the song tried to take control again.

He drove his fist into the ground, willing the magic away.

Amazingly, it obeyed. The feeling of warmth condensed into a line of intense heat that flowed down his arm and out his fist. Light burst from his fingers as the magic drilled into the ground, leaving a smoking hole two feet deep.

Relieved, he glanced up at Harafin and found the old man watching him, stroking his white beard, and nodding.

"I am sorry for startling you." Harafin gestured at the glowing sphere. "This shield will offer protection while we talk."

Protect who, from what?

"All right, let's talk," Kevlin said.

"I believe we should start with that amulet of yours."

"What about it?" *There's no way I'm giving it to you.*

"To my knowledge, no sentinel has ever found a way for a non-actinopathic person to wield magic. Yet, for some unknown reason, Oris has chosen to alter Bajaran's amulet and provide exactly that capacity to you."

"What do you mean, Oris *chose* to alter it? It can't think. It's just a rock."

"Stone."

"Stones don't think or act on their own." Kevlin glanced down at his boot. *Do they?*

"As you should have guessed by now, Oris is no ordinary artifact. Did you know it has another name? Or rather, a more complete name? Oris, the Fatebreaker."

"Um, that sounds terrifying. What does it mean?"

"I know of several potential interpretations, but none are pertinent to our current discussion. I felt it important that you know the stone's full name, since you are its steward. Do not share it with others."

"Okay." It wasn't like he chatted about Oris with anyone but Harafin anyway. Mostly, he just tried to forget about it.

"I believe we must start your training by covering some of the basics."

"What basics?"

"What is magic?" Harafin asked.

"What are you talking about?"

The old sentinel regarded him sternly. "You've been lucky so far, but you need to learn to control the magic provided to you, or you could destroy yourself and those around you."

Kevlin frowned. He didn't want to deal with magic, and part of him wanted to hand the amulet over to Harafin. But the old man had already said he wouldn't take Oris, and Kevlin would need the amulet's protection until he returned the rock to Antigonus. Besides, having a safeguard against magic relieved some of the constant fear that knotted his stomach around sentinels.

"I think I know how to get rid of it," Kevlin said. "Isn't that enough?"

Harafin chuckled. "You have no idea. Now tell me, what is magic?"

Kevlin sighed. The old man wasn't going to let him out of this little round prison until he played along.

He could just walk through the wall. Wouldn't that tie Harafin's beard in a knot?

Then again, did he want Harafin angry? The amulet seemed powerful, but who knew what the sentinel could do if he lost his temper? Images of explosions, burning trees, and towering pillars of multicolored fire came to mind, followed by memories of helpless terror.

Definitely not a good idea to upset a sentinel. Not without a solid escape route already mapped out.

Kevlin sighed and thought back to all the magic he'd witnessed in the past week, and how it had felt burning in his chest. Despite all his exposure to magic, Kevlin had no idea what it really was.

Harafin was waiting, so he finally managed to say, "Ah, magic is a power used by sentinels and shadeleeches to do things."

What a stupid answer.

"You are partially correct," Harafin said. "It is power. It is also more than that, and we will leave the discussion of shadeleeches for later. What is light?"

"Light? I don't know," Kevlin said, nervousness turning to frustration. "Light comes from the sun. It gives us, well, light."

"All correct. What most people do not realize is that light and magic are intimately connected. You see, at its most fundamental level magic *is* light. . .and light is magic."

"You mean when the sun is shining, I'm really seeing magic, not light?"

"Not exactly. The relationship between light and magic is simple, yet so profound that most people have a hard time understanding it at first. But that understanding gives sentinels tremendous power."

"I asked you those two questions to help you open your mind to important truths. Magic is the lifeblood of the planet and of all living things. It can be found all around us, and is replenished daily by sunlight. We can see rays of light, but what is not seen, and what most people cannot sense, is that with the light comes power, and that power is what we call magic."

"The true term for it is actinic energy. It is in the air, in the ground, permeating the earth to its core. Sentinels, those who we call gifted, or actinopathic, are persons who for some unknown reason have the ability to sense that energy and to command it, to control it, to bend it to their will."

Harafin paused while Kevlin considered his words. Kevlin thought of the forest, the cliff, and everything that made up the landscape. All of it infected with magic? Could it be possible?

Kevlin gestured to the sphere of softly glowing magic. "Is that why magic always gives off light?"

"Yes. Most of the time, the use of magic discharges some form of visible light. Some spells may discharge light not visible to us, but those require much more control and experience."

"What about the shadeleeches? When Merab was possessed by the Sigrun, they attacked you with pure darkness. How did they do that?"

"That is an excellent question, and the answer to it lies at the root of the power the Sigrun wield. As servants of Angrama, they are enemies of the light, their goal being the domination or destruction of all living things. They cannot wield actinic energy like sentinels do, for it is foreign to them. They have no part in it. Their power, although often referred to as magic, is an abomination. Its true name is sthenic energy."

"What's the difference? I've seen both shadeleeches and sentinels throw balls of fire and things like that."

"True. But actinic magic is part of the fabric of life on the planet. Sentinels can draw upon the power within them, as well as the latent magic all around. Shadeleeches, on the other hand, gain power only through destruction. Their sthenic magic is an abomination, wielded by sucking the very life out of something else."

"I don't understand," Kevlin said. "A ball of fire thrown by a sentinel is destructive too."

"Yes, but a sentinel's fire is formed from latent magic available to them. Fire created by a shadeleech uses power stolen from another living thing: a tree, a rock, water in a stream, almost anything can be exploited."

"But shadeleeches gain the most power by sacrificing a living being, particularly humans. Shadeleech is a very accurate name. Taking a person's life force gives a shadeleech tremendous power for short periods of time, and they use this to justify their actions."

"If they kill a person with their sthenic powers, they can feed on the life force of that individual's soul after they die, sucking its very essence until it is spent. Souls destroyed in that way are easily overcome by Angrama's fiery chains and endure eternal torment."

"That's horrible." Kevlin had thought he was afraid before, but it was worse than he'd imagined.

"It is," Harafin agreed, again stroking his beard. "Time to move from theory to practice. I will teach you a basic but important spell that could very well save your life."

Kevlin glanced around the little prison globe and considered breaking out again. "I'd rather not."

"Do you really think you can remain safe from the Sigrun if you refuse to use the power you have been given?" Harafin asked. "Would you go into battle against armed foes not knowing how to wield a sword?"

"Not if I want to live."

"We are battling the forces of evil," Harafin said, fixing Kevlin with his penetrating gaze. "This is a battle of magic and unseen powers. If you refuse to learn to fight this battle, you will die."

Kevlin swallowed. He'd rather fight Dhanjal again than learn how to wield magic, but could think of no way to refute Harafin's argument. So he nodded.

Gesturing at the blackened hole in the ground, Harafin said, "You have gained a modicum of control already, which is a good sign."

Kevlin shrugged. "I just willed it to go away."

"Then you understand a core principle, for magic is a tool, wielded like any other, with dangers and risks inherent in its use. But unlike your sword, this tool is wielded by your thoughts."

"What dangers?"

Harafin ignored the question. "Instead of driving the magic away, I want you to create the image of a shield."

"What kind of shield?"

"That is up to you. Any shield you feel comfortable with. The bigger the shield, the more power required to form it."

Kevlin thought about it. He had used shields at times in the past, and in close fighting they were invaluable. The thought of a shield made of magic intrigued him. He formed the image of a simple round shield in his mind.

"What now?" he asked.

"Now you need magic." Harafin raised a hand, palm up. It began to glow with a faint golden light. He pointed, and the light rolled through the air toward Kevlin, touched his chest, and disappeared. Instantly a warm sensation spread through Kevlin's body.

Magic.

He recognized it as it pooled in his chest and flowed down his arms and legs, strengthening him. He took a shuddering breath and forced down the urge to drive the magic away.

"What do I do?" Kevlin asked.

"Hold the image in your mind, and envision the magic flowing into it and becoming the shield."

That sounded easy enough, so Kevlin focused on the image of the shield and willed the magic into it. The power condensed in his chest, pressing against his skin. His muscles quivered with energy until he struggled to hold still.

Become the shield, he commanded.

Nothing happened.

Make a shield. He imagined the magic hardening into a shield.

The power in his chest churned and roiled and hardened inside of him. Pain blossomed and he gasped and clutched at his ribs. He lost focus, and the energy slipped from his control and rolled around through his body like water sloshing in a bucket.

"What just happened?" he asked. *This was a bad idea.*

"Shields are more effective *outside* of your body," Harafin explained. Although he spoke with a straight face, Kevlin got the sense that the old man was secretly laughing at him.

"You didn't tell me to do that," Kevlin snapped.

Harafin smiled. "I didn't think I had to."

"Of course you have to. I don't know anything about magic."

"But you have used shields before, yes? How effective is a shield in your stomach?"

Kevlin glowered at him, embarrassed and frustrated.

"Watch me," Harafin said.

Light coalesced around him, flowing into the old man until he glowed with it. Then it rolled back out of him like a tangible thing and condensed in the air. In the span of a couple of heartbeats, the light shaped into an unusual triangular shield.

"Why didn't you just show me that first?"

Harafin only smiled and waved his hand. The shield of light disappeared. "Now, you try."

Kevlin again formed the image of a shield and concentrated, imagining it forming in the air in front of him, flowing out of him the same way it had from Harafin. He focused his will and commanded, *Do it.*

Again the magic condensed inside his chest, but this time it moved, a visible wave of light rolling out to hang in the air a foot in front of him. The light swirled and contracted into a rough sphere.

It's really working.

Shaping magic felt strange, like trying to butter toast with his feet. It was possible, but used muscles he'd never trained for that particular chore.

Do it, he commanded the magic again, imagining a complete glowing shield.

The light flared, but slipped from his mental fingers. The partially-formed shield shattered into a thousand glowing fragments of light that shot in all directions. Kevlin instinctively ducked as splinters of light collided with the walls of the little room and disappeared with green flashes.

That's why he locked us in here, so I won't kill anyone.

Kevlin wiped a hand across his sweaty face, feeling as exhausted as if he'd run for miles.

"Very good," Harafin said calmly.

"Right," Kevlin replied sarcastically. "I bet you say that to all your students."

Harafin smiled. "You may not believe it, but for a man who touched magic for the first time only days ago, what you just did was remarkable."

"Thanks."

"Try again."

Kevlin sighed. It was going to be a long night.

He managed to get it right on his fourth attempt. He stared at the construct of magic he'd created, and between labored breaths asked, "How's that?"

Harafin pointed at the shield, and a miniature arrow made of coppery light shot from his finger. It struck the shield and punched through with barely a pause. Kevlin ducked just in time to avoid being skewered.

"What do you think?" Harafin asked.

Kevlin stared at the shield with the small hole in its center. He'd *felt* the bolt strike, in his mind, like someone had poked him in the head with a finger. And he'd *felt* it pass through his shield, but it had all happened so fast he hadn't had time to react.

"One more time," Kevlin said, determination growing to get it right. He'd show the old man he wasn't a useless fool.

Releasing the previous shield, he pulled the magic back, then willed it out again. It formed in a heartbeat, and Kevlin willed it to be thicker, stronger.

"Try that again," Kevlin challenged.

Harafin shot a little magic arrow at the shield. It struck, and again Kevlin felt the jab, but it deflected, striking the glowing wall with a flash of green light.

"Very good," Harafin observed.

Kevlin grinned. Then a single drum beat in his soul, and distant horns blared.

Savas.

He panicked and threw the magic away. The shield disintegrated and light burst from Kevlin in all directions in a formless wave.

"What are you doing?" Harafin asked with a disapproving frown.

A single drum beat again, as if mocking him. Then it was gone. Kevlin breathed a sigh of relief, his elation at forming the magical shield swallowed up by fear of Savas.

Could he trust the sentinel with that secret?

Not yet.

"I just couldn't do it anymore," Kevlin lied.

"Very well. You have made significant progress tonight. Remember the things you have learned. The ability to form an effective shield is a critical tool in a sentinel's arsenal."

"I'm not a sentinel."

Harafin smiled, again looking aged and mysterious. Kevlin decided he really didn't want to know what Harafin was thinking.

The old sentinel waved a hand and the little amber room dissipated, leaving them once again sitting at the edge of the clearing. Kevlin breathed deep the fresh air and savored the smell of pine and wood smoke. Maybe next time he could convince Harafin not to enclose them like that. It made him nervous.

I can't believe it. He's already got me accepting the fact we've got to do it again.

Full night had fallen and most of the men were already rolled in their blankets. A discordant chorus of snoring rumbled around the clearing.

Kevlin headed for his own blankets before Harafin could think of some other way to torment him with magic. He lay on his back, staring at the chill night sky. His mind whirled with the things he'd learned. He'd actually done it. He, Kevlin, had used magic.

The thought was strangely exciting, and very scary.

What is happening to me?

That thought chased him into the welcome release of deep sleep.

39

Playing Catch-up

Wayra reined in before the shrine to Serigala in the town of Ingolf and swung down from the saddle. Turning to her company, she pointed at the late-afternoon marketplace.

"Spread out. Five minutes."

The sentinels dispersed through the square. They would glean any information about Antigonus worth having. Wayra pushed through the gate and crossed to the porch of the simple wooden shrine, trailed by her two closest aides.

A woman wearing a wide straw hat and a smock of heavy, unbleached wool met them at the door. Her eyes widened at seeing three sentinels on the step. She flung the door open and bowed low.

"How may I help you?" she asked.

"We're looking for an elderly man," Wayra said. "A sentinel. Wounded. He would have passed through in the past week."

"We have seen many wounded during that time. With the stalwarts gone, it has been difficult. There were no wounded sentinels. Besides, couldn't a sentinel have healed himself? In fact, while you are here, will you come see to a few of my patients who are very ill?"

"We have no time for that." Wayra turned to go.

"Wait," the woman said. "I just remembered something that might help."

Wayra scowled. She didn't have time for games. The race south from Diodor had been arduous and frustrating, and they had found no trace of Antigonus. Ingolf was the largest town in the area, so she had hoped for news.

The woman took an involuntary step back from Wayra's glare, unnerved like most people by the power of her huge eyes. But squaring her shoulders, she said, "Will you at least have one of your companions see what they can do about my patients while we talk?"

Wayra advanced a step. The woman cringed, but did not retreat.

"It will not take them long," the woman added quickly. "Surely a few minutes spent saving lives is worth what I can tell you?"

Wayra suppressed the urge to cast Truth upon the woman. She might get what she wanted, but unless she was sure, it wouldn't be worth the risk. The woman was pledged to Serigala and therefore under the protection of the stalwarts. Angering the stalwarts without good cause would only slow her down.

She forced calm on herself and said to the sentinel on her left, "See to them."

He strode past the woman and disappeared inside the shrine.

"Now, tell me what you know," Wayra demanded.

"A woman stopped here the day after the bloodset. She was also looking for an injured old man. Only one man fit the description, an old fellow who had passed through earlier that day. He was in a very bad way, although his friends wouldn't let me treat him. They purchased a carriage and raced north to find a stalwart to heal him."

"Was the old man a sentinel?" Wayra asked. She grasped the woman's arm, her gaze so intense that sparks of fire danced in her eyes. "We came from the north and saw no one like that."

"I don't know," the woman croaked, trying to back away. "They had him covered with a blanket."

"Describe this woman."

"She dressed like a lady, although her clothes were tattered. Fine features, but something about her made me uncomfortable."

Wayra raised a glowing hand and placed it on the woman's head. "Envision her in your mind, and I will see her."

"You're not supposed to do that," the woman stammered.

"We are healing your precious patients," Wayra said in a whisper, her face inches from the other woman's. "This is the price you must pay for our aid."

The woman swallowed and closed her eyes. As Wayra concentrated, an image came to her mind. Rhea. There could be no mistake. She gasped and tightened her grip until the woman cried out.

"Show me the wounded man and his companions."

Another image. Antigonus. She memorized every detail of his face, and those of his party.

"It was him," Wayra exulted and released the woman, who stumbled back, rubbing at both her bruised wrist and her head.

"I am afraid your friend may be dead," the woman said.

It cannot be. She was so close.

"You didn't see them on your ride south. They went north, so you should have. The night after they passed, an inn north of town burned to the ground. The dead were so disfigured that we could not identify them, but we did find the remains of a carriage in the barn like the one they purchased."

Dread curdled Wayra's stomach. She glanced at Thyra, her second. "We passed that inn earlier. Nothing left but some stones of the chimney and part of the barn."

They hadn't stopped, but pressed ahead toward Ingolf. Wayra thought back to the charred rubble and couldn't shake a chill of dread. If Rhea had caught up with Antigonus and killed him at the inn, she would have Oris and several days' head start.

And they hadn't passed her on the road.

Without a word, Wayra returned to her horse and raised a fist. A thin column of blue fire shot into the air to signal the kestrels to return. Not waiting for them, she wheeled her horse north and drove her heels into its flanks.

As soon as she reached the charred remains of the inn, she leaped from her lathered mount and approached a solitary figure digging through the rubble. It was a man dressed in simple woodsman garb, covered in ash, except where tears had streaked his cheeks.

He turned to Wayra, his eyes dead with grief. Upon seeing her white robes, he mumbled, "M'lady."

"You lost relatives here?"

He nodded. "All dead."

"Do you know if anyone got out alive?"

He shrugged. "It were raining that night, so tracks was all wiped out. We saw the one grave, but nothing more." He nodded toward the tree line, then turned back to his hopeless digging.

Wayra strode toward the trees while the rest of her party straggled into the inn yard. Wayra pointed to the grave.

"Thyra, have someone dig that up. I need to know who's down there."

Thyra pushed her brown hair, tangled from the ride, out of her eyes, then gestured at one of the Kestrels in the party. He was a young man with heavy gray eyes, named Keld. He dismounted and raised a hand above the grave.

Wayra noted the skill with which Keld manipulated the light, directing it into the earth, which boiled and cascaded upward. In seconds, a corpse rose through the inverted avalanche before settling gently back to the ground. Without being bidden, Keld leaned over the body and wiped the dirt from its face.

Wayra studied the features and her heart fell. That man had led Antigonus' party in the memory she'd seen. The certainty of it shattered her hopes of an easy victory.

She sighed but thrust the despair aside. She had to be strong. She couldn't allow Rhea to escape with Oris. Everything Wayra had trained for had prepared her for this mission. She would not fail.

"This man was in Antigonus' party," Wayra said. "We can assume Rhea caught up with them here."

"Do you think she killed Antigonus?" Thyra asked.

Wayra considered the question. Rhea would have taken Oris, but would she have killed Antigonus first, or taken him prisoner? With Antigonus wounded, it was a possibility.

"I don't know, but we start the search here." She nodded toward the charred timbers of the inn. "I want that wreckage excavated and every body recovered. Now."

As the group of Kestrels turned to the grisly task, she held out a hand to Keld. "You have the best touch with animals, correct?"

"Yes," he said with a happy wag of his head.

"Good. Find a hawk and sweep the area. Search for anything unusual. We need to know where Rhea's gone."

"At once."

He turned to face the forest and his eyes went blank. A soft yellow glow enveloped his face as he sought out a suitable bird to link his mind to. Using its senses, he could guide it far and see through its eyes. If Rhea was anywhere nearby, he would locate her.

Turning to Thyra, who alone remained by her side, Wayra said, "Go. Join them. We need to know if Antigonus lies dead here."

The ash-covered man who had been poking hopelessly at the rubble moments earlier stared with open-mouthed awe as timbers and ash floated up and away from the rubble, revealing the devastation lying underneath.

It wouldn't take long to find the bodies.

Wayra watched, impassive, already planning her next move.

40

BAD NEWS COMES IN PACKS

Sitara looked up from where she sat at a simple wooden table in the corner of the kitchen in the keisara's apartments. When the cook, a heavyset woman with graying brown hair, stepped into the room, her face, usually creased with laugh lines, looked solemn. Sitara began to stand, but the cook waved her back down.

"I am not summoned?" Sitara asked.

"Not yet." The cook fetched a pot of water that had been simmering over a small fire, along with fixings for tea. "Sentinel Felix left a moment ago, but the emperor said he wished some quiet time alone with his wife."

"Of course."

While they waited for the tea to steep, the cook said, "I can still hardly believe it. If our lady herself can be attacked, and in her own quarters, none of us are safe."

"It's terrifying."

Sitara *was* terrified, more than ever in her life. She could barely contain the constant urge to retch. Only the fear that one of the healers might then offer to help gave her the strength to force an outward appearance of calm. If Ithai could detect her tampering with the keisara's mind, what might they discover if they touched Sitara with their power?

As soon as Ithai had realized someone had been tampering with Fideima's mind, she had sent Sitara to fetch the emperor. Felix, a senior sentinel, had come with him.

Sitara tried to keep her mind void of thought around him. She wanted to wrap herself in illusion, but he would know. She suspected he could read her mind if he wished, and she focused on not giving him any reason to want to.

If only Bajaran had taught her more about the full range of sentinel powers. He had begun her training, but she barely understood the basics. She knew the specific skills required to fulfill her task, but little else. Her ignorance might prove her destruction.

The emperor's fury upon learning his wife's mind had been tampered with had terrified Sitara. She expected to be confronted at any moment, and it was clear the emperor would reserve the worst possible tortures for whoever was found responsible.

She couldn't even run, or they would discover her all the sooner. Her greatest defense had always been a façade of sweet innocence, so she clung to it with all her might.

Sentinel Felix, a fat, jolly fellow, had examined the keisara. Ithai had hovered nearby, muttering to herself that he had all the deftness of a mule ox. After confirming Ithai's findings, he stood with hands raised, fingers spread wide, and eyes closed.

Sitara felt his will slip around her as he scanned the area. She struggled to calm her racing heart, focusing on her worries for the keisara's well-being.

Felix found nothing, but the emperor demanded he erect magical shielding around the keisara's apartments. He also ordered Felix to alert the sentinels to begin a search for the secret attacker.

Then he had dismissed the cook and Sitara, who was all too glad to leave. The last thing she wanted to do was face the keisara. She was surprised to feel hot shame mingling with her fear of discovery. The thought that soon the keisara might know she had betrayed her made her want to swoon.

The emperor had also ordered all of the other servants away from the keisara's apartments with strict orders to mention nothing of what they might have heard or seen to anyone, on penalty of death. So stern was the emperor that Sitara expected he would be obeyed. Thus he had robbed her of even the hint of a scandal.

Sitara nearly laughed at the foolishness of the thought. Any moment she would likely be discovered, tortured, and executed, and she was worried simply that scandal had been averted. If only Bajaran could know that she'd tried. A tear slid down her cheek despite her efforts to restrain it.

The cook noticed and placed a gentle hand over hers. "Now don't worry yourself, dear. They'll find who did this."

Sitara managed a weak smile.

They drank their tea in silence for a few minutes and it helped calm Sitara's overwrought nerves a little. The cook set down her empty cup. "With all the terrible things happening, I almost forgot. Sentinel Felix has shared some good news."

"I would love some good news."

The cook leaned forward. "Word came just today that the traitor, that sentinel Bajaran, died attacking Antigonus."

"What?" Sitara gasped.

"Didn't you hear, dear? There's been rumors for days that Antigonus was attacked somewhere in Hallvarr. Harafin himself led the relief party."

Sitara's thoughts whirled so fast, she couldn't think. "What did you say about Bajaran?"

"He's dead."

The world tilted around Sitara as screaming agony exploded through her mind. She toppled from her chair and her head struck the tiled floor.

Oblivion took her.

41

DEALING WITH GRIEF

Sitara awoke with a start. The cook knelt beside her, holding a bottle of something vile under her nose. The smell triggered memories of working on her parents' farm in the countryside of Freyarr, and the ghastly stench she had waded through every day as a child.

As soon as she stirred, the cook heaved a great sigh of relief. "You gave me such a start." She helped Sitara sit up. "What happened?"

Sitara tried to force her mind to work, but one thought burned so hot she could think of nothing else.

Bajaran is dead!

When she didn't speak, the cook continued, "Now that you're awake, I'm going to fetch Ithai. I'm sure she can help."

Sitara wanted to both scream with terror and laugh hysterically at the same time. She clutched the cook's arm.

"No. Don't bother her. She is busy with the keisara."

"Nonsense. The emperor is with the keisara."

"I'm all right," Sitara insisted. "Please, just help me to my room. My nerves got the better of me. I was so worried about the keisara, and then when you spoke of people dying. . ." Her voice failed her.

The cook patted her arm. "I am so sorry, dear. I didn't realize how deeply all this had affected you."

Sitara maintained her composure until the cook left her alone in her room. Then she threw herself onto the bed and let the torrent of emotion explode through her, unchecked.

She only managed to keep from screaming by burying her face deep in a pillow. Tears burned her eyes and her throat constricted until she could barely breathe. Great sobs racked her body, and her limbs trembled violently.

Bajaran is dead.

It was unbelievable, so horribly wrong! In one terrible instant, her world had shattered.

Bajaran could not be dead. Ever since he had found her four years ago among the ranks of the newly accepted in her small village, he had remained a constant in her life. At fifteen years old, she had been so innocent, so blinded by the lies of her teachers.

Then Bajaran came and explained her glorious destiny. He'd rescued her, trained her in secret, and revealed the important and dangerous role she would play in the revolution.

He became her secret lover. He brought her to the palace and his subtle influence, coupled with her gifts, obtained for her the coveted position serving the keisara. There she gained critical access to those who held the highest seats of power and the secrets they kept.

He was gone. Her heart torn with grief, Sitara lay there, unable to think. Only after a long time did a new thought penetrate her storm of anguish.

Someone killed him.

She might have failed in her attempt to destroy the keisara, but Bajaran could not fail. He was too great a man for the revolution to falter. The mere thought triggered a wave of rage that burned away some of her overwhelming grief. She wanted to scream in defiance and wreak terrible vengeance on whoever was responsible.

She would discover their name.

If she survived, if she remained undiscovered, she would hunt down the one responsible for his death, and she would kill them. Slowly. She would be strong, for him.

If only she could turn to someone for information.

Sitara sat up and rubbed savagely at her burning eyes.

There *was* someone.

42

SWORD BROTHERS

The strike force ate breakfast under a chill gray sky. They might be elite soldiers, but they didn't cook much better than the mercenaries Kevlin had commanded.

As they finished tying their gear onto the backs of their mounts, Drystan approached Kevlin. "How about a little exercise?"

"Exercise?"

"Aye, I'd like to cross blades with you before we go into battle together."

"Me too," Jerrik said. "No brother of mine's going to embarrass us tomorrow. Besides, nothing like a good fight in the morning to get the blood pumping."

Kevlin followed the two of them away from the camp to the open end of the clearing. Jerrik settled against a nearby tree while Kevlin faced Drystan.

"Leave him standing," Jerrik called to Drystan. "I want a round too."

The rest of the company gathered around, already betting heatedly. Not surprisingly, Kevlin was given long odds, but not to win. The men were betting on how many seconds he'd last.

Drystan can't be that good.

Drystan raised his spear, and Kevlin attacked with his sword. Drystan easily deflected the blow and returned with a blinding counterattack that had Kevlin backpedaling to avoid being struck in the first seconds of the match.

Maybe he is.

Kevlin circled and attacked again. Again, his Einarri brother easily blocked and swiped the butt end of the spear lightly across Kevlin's ribs to mark a point.

Kevlin fought hard, but Drystan danced just out of reach, like a wraith, always a step ahead. Every time he thought he had worked out a sequence that could reach the lanky warrior, a surprise spin or unexpected twist of the spear left him stumbling on the defensive.

Drystan paused each time to explain what Kevlin had done wrong, what opening he'd left unguarded, or how his balance or the placement of his feet had been incorrect. The breadth of Drystan's knowledge was astounding.

As they dueled, Kevlin thought back to his fight with Dhanjal. Immediately, a drum beat in his soul, reverberating through his body.

Oh no.

Horns blared a fanfare that set his limbs quivering.

He tried to push the song away and, while distracted, caught a heavy blow from Drystan on his leather-armored chest.

"Sorry about that," Drystan said with an easy smile. "I thought you'd see that one coming."

You are weak, a soft but powerful voice spoke inside his mind. *Serve me and fail no more.*

Kevlin lunged, trying to ignore the voice by renewing the contest. Drystan flowed back into the fight without hesitation, striking Kevlin again within seconds.

The drums returned, stronger than before, and with their insistent beat came the mocking voice.

Failed again. Always failing.

Images flashed through Kevlin's mind with the blaring of Savas' horns: Terach, with Dhanjal's scimitar protruding from his back, while his blood burned; Antigonus, lying helpless in the inn while Kevlin dove through the window to escape. . .

Drystan paused and leaned on his spear. "You need to watch your stance," he began.

Kevlin wasn't listening. Rage at his failures burned, and the song of Savas intensified. The drums rumbled through his soul, magnified by his anger, and a wave of sound only he could hear overwhelmed all thought.

Behold victory, the voice declared, and a fighting form flashed into his mind, punctuated by the next beat of the cadence.

He couldn't resist.

Leaping forward, he slashed at Drystan's face.

The lanky captain barely managed to dodge the blow. The crowd of soldiers booed, but Kevlin heard nothing but the beating of drums as he slipped under the spell of Savas' song.

His sword slashed, each blow punctuated by blaring horns, and his feet danced in time with the drums. The two of them battled across the clearing, weapons flashing in the early morning light and filling the air with the sound of the struggle.

Drystan never slowed, and after a minute, Jerrik leaped into the fray, swinging the flat of his huge axe at Kevlin's chest. Kevlin, fully immersed in the Song, laughed as his body twisted around the blow. He struck Jerrik across his armored torso.

Jerrik dropped the axe and grabbed Kevlin's arms, holding him in a viselike grip. "That's enough."

The song intensified, and a new sound joined the melody. Some kind of stringed instrument burst into the song in a striking counterpoint to the original beat. Energy shivered down Kevlin's spine and he *ran* straight up Jerrik's torso and slammed his boots into the big man's head, then thrust himself back and away.

Jerrik lost his grip. He grabbed his axe and bellowed, "Ukko's Beard! I said that's enough, Kevlin."

Kevlin landed back on his feet, but Drystan stepped between them, spear at the ready, "Kevlin, what's going on?"

Victory, the voice called, and the cadence swelled into a battle dirge that swept Kevlin into a new form. Without a word, he attacked.

Drystan blocked the initial strike but Kevlin flowed around Drystan's spear and slammed a fist into the tall warrior's jaw, knocking him back. Kevlin's sword whistled in for the kill.

Jerrik deflected it, then stepped close and grabbed at Kevlin again. Kevlin rolled away and slashed Jerrik's armored torso once more.

The two captains faced him together and he fought them both, all thought surrendered to the song of Savas, all action dictated by it. The three whirled around each other, weapons clashing together in a wonderful din that reinforced the song in Kevlin's soul. It built toward a crescendo where Kevlin would stand victorious over his enemies.

The song drove Kevlin's body far beyond its natural limits, but even as it propelled him to heights of skill greater even than when he had faced Dhanjal, his swordbrothers met his every stroke.

The two captains used vastly different styles. Drystan fought with a grace and speed unmatched by anyone Kevlin had ever seen. Jerrik kept his huge axe whirling in front of him in a constant blur. Despite every form dictated by the song, Kevlin could not touch them.

After a moment, Drystan unexpectedly took a step back and lowered his spear.

Kevlin lunged for the kill, but their eyes met, and he *felt* Drystan's thoughts. A single word slipped through the clamoring song

Brother.

Kevlin stumbled. Jerrik halted beside Drystan and lowered his axe. Kevlin *felt* Jerrik's thought just as he had Drystan's.

Brother.

Serve me, the voice commanded, and the next beat pounded through his soul with fresh intensity. *Destroy them.*

He raised his sword, but it wavered.

Surrender to me, and all victory will be yours.

A new image burned into Kevlin's mind, so startling that he staggered back. In a flash, Savas revealed what he wanted: Oris.

In that second, Savas showed him how to reach Oris's power and surrender it.

Victory everlasting.

Drums beat, horns blared, and strings pulled at him. He wouldn't have to worry any more. Savas would take care of everything.

Brother.

That single word punched through the image, shattering it, and holding back the insistent power of the cadence. Kevlin's mind surfaced and he stumbled away, fighting to regain control.

He looked up, and became aware of two women standing nearby. One was auburn-haired and olive-skinned, with brilliant emerald eyes. The other was slightly taller, with dark hair framing creamy white skin, and eyes like pools of midnight.

A memory crept into his mind, undimmed by the beating of drums. His lips tingled from the memory of a sweet kiss, of soft lips pressed against his own. He blinked, and in that moment awakened fully from the nightmare of Savas' control.

I will not serve you! Kevlin shouted the thought, and pushed the song away. His sword slipped from his fingers.

He willed wobbly legs forward toward Ceren and Indira, who he finally recognized. The two women held their ground. Ceren grasped the hilt of her sword as if on the verge of drawing it.

"Thank you," he said to her.

"What are you talking about, you leech-brained fool?" Ceren exclaimed. "You're making an idiot of yourself."

He threw an arm around each woman and pulled them close.

Ceren punched him in the stomach, but yelped when her fist struck armor. "Let me go," she hissed.

He kissed her on the cheek, then kissed Indira in like manner before releasing them.

"Are you all right?" Indira asked, laying one hand on his shoulder.

"I am now."

Ceren snorted.

He turned away from them to face Drystan and Jerrik, who had approached behind him. Drystan had picked up the discarded sword, but the two stood at the ready.

"Brothers, I'm sorry about that," Kevlin said.

"What got into you?" Jerrik demanded.

Harafin pushed past them, his expression hard and eyes flashing with power. "You have some explaining to do, young man." To Gabral, he said, "Colonel, dismiss your men."

Gabral gave the order and all the other soldiers drifted slowly toward their mounts, talking amongst themselves. The colonel crossed his arms and watched Kevlin with a disapproving frown. In a moment, only he, Harafin, Leander, and Kevlin's two swordbrothers remained.

"Now," Harafin said, peering at Kevlin like a hawk considering a potential kill, "explain your connection to Savas."

"You knew?"

"I saw. When a god grants their influence, their power surrounds the stalwart and is visible to sentinels as particular forms of light. You glowed with the unique hues of Savas, yet you are no Blade Stalwart."

"No, I'm not." Kevlin felt so exhausted he could barely stand. He ran a hand through his hair. "I can't explain it. It started when I faced Dhanjal."

"This is unusual," Leander said.

"I tried to ask Antigonus about it, but we didn't have much time, and all he would say was that I should be cautious."

"You should have heeded his advice."

"You think I wanted this to happen? I tried, but I couldn't stop it. He just took over."

Harafin frowned. "Tell me everything this time."

Kevlin told them about the fight with Dhanjal, and how the voice and cadence had overwhelmed him. Then he described how it had taken control again while dueling Drystan and Jerrik."

"How'd you break out of it?" Jerrik asked.

"It was you and Drystan."

Kevlin tried to explain how he had felt their thoughts and their connection as swordbrothers, and how that had interrupted the song long enough to break free of its domination. He left out the impact of remembering the kiss. They'd think he'd totally lost his mind.

Drystan turned to Harafin. "Is that why you told us to lower our weapons?"

"No. It looked like Kevlin was only partially under Savas' control. I hoped that by removing the threat, his lust for battle would fade and he could break free."

"You weren't sure?" Jerrik asked.

"Not entirely."

"That experiment could've killed me," Drystan complained.

"But it did not. Thank you for trusting me."

Drystan muttered something too low for Kevlin to hear.

"This is an unexpected turn of events," Harafin declared.

"I'd say it's more than that," Colonel Gabral said. "He withheld information from us."

"I didn't think it was going to be a problem again," Kevlin said.

"You endangered our company. As such, you should be executed," Grabral declared.

"No," Harafin said. "No one will be executed today."

"I'm in command," Gabral retorted. "Decisions of discipline are mine to make."

Harafin leveled his steely gaze on the colonel, who backed up an uneasy step.

"Well, it is," Gabral muttered.

"Generally, yes, but this case is unique, and I will overrule you if I must. As a member of the ruling council, I possess that authority."

"We cannot have a steward in thrall to Savas," Leander observed. "It would be disastrous."

Kevlin bit back the urge to tell them what Savas had revealed to him. If they realized what Savas wanted, they'd kill him for sure. The images had begun to fade already, and Kevlin wasn't even sure the revelation would have worked had he tried to follow Savas' instructions.

"No, we cannot," Harafin agreed. "But he was named steward, and Oris has accepted him. We cannot take the stone from him now."

"I don't want to be in thrall to Savas," Kevlin said with a suppressed shudder. He tried to forget the amazing memory of standing against both Jerrik and Drystan simultaneously. He had fought like a god under Savas' control.

That wasn't helpful.

"You are wise to feel that way," Harafin said. "For should you give in to Savas, He could unleash unending war on the empire through you."

"I don't understand."

"You are Oris's steward. Until a bearer again wields it, its power is associated with you. You haven't offered your soul to Savas as a stalwart, yet nonetheless he has attempted to claim you. He has never done anything like that before."

Leander said thoughtfully, "It is possible he seeks to access Oris's power through Kevlin by making him his pawn."

Harafin shook his head. "Kevlin is not actinopathic. He cannot surrender that power even if he wanted to."

Kevlin should tell them. They just about had it figured out, but what would they do to him once they knew for sure?

Then he thought of something. "Wait a minute. I wasn't steward when I fought Dhanjal."

"No," Harafin said, "but Savas may have suspected you would be."

"So the gods *do* know the future," Drystan said.

"I am afraid it's not so simple." Harafin glanced sharply at Drystan and Jerrik. "Kevlin felt your thoughts. Otherwise, he might not have escaped. Without the two of you. . ." His voice trailed off, and his eyes widened in surprise. For a moment he looked shocked.

"What is it?" Kevlin asked, suddenly very nervous.

"You three. . ."

Harafin's voiced trailed off again and he glanced down at Kevlin's hand. Kevlin turned it over, showing his palm. The small swordbrother scar gleamed white in the morning light.

"Life over death," Harafin said in a whisper.

"What is it?" Kevlin asked again.

"It cannot be," Harafin muttered to himself.

"Well, it might be. Why don't you tell us?"

I don't even know what we're talking about!

Was there a school they attended to learn cryptic dialogue?

"I must think on this further," Harafin said, and turned away.

"He's been saying that a lot lately," Jerrik remarked.

"How could I have been so wrong?" Harafin's voice carried to them as he walked toward his horse, head bowed in thought.

"I wonder if he's really as smart as everyone thinks," Drystan said.

"You just worry about sticking that spear into makrasha," Leander said. "Let Harafin worry about the weighty matters."

"With pleasure."

Leander turned to Kevlin. "Know this. With Savas, all will be decided the third time. You have rebuffed him twice, but if you surrender to him the third time, you will never escape his control. He will own your soul."

"How do I stop him?"

"Stay close to your brothers," Harafin said loudly from a dozen paces away.

Gabral said, "I will offer what aid I can."

That was surprising. "Thanks," Kevlin said.

The short colonel raised a hand to Kevlin's shoulder. "I swear this oath. Should you fall to Savas' power, I will strike you down myself. With the Mace, I don't care what power enslaves you. It'll crush your skull just as easily."

"I don't need your oath."

"It is already given, and I won't hesitate to honor it."

"I think that's enough," Leander said.

"We've wasted enough time," Gabral decided. "Let's ride."

Kevlin headed for his horse, ignoring the many sidelong glances from soldiers in the company. They must have thought him crazy. It would be better if it were that simple.

Nearby, Harafin said to Leander, "Ride with me, my old friend. I need your wisdom."

Leander said, "Savas is a crafty one."

"He has far more access to the prophecies than we, and may understand them better."

"Let's just get Antigonus back tomorrow," Kevlin called over the back of his horse. He fought to suppress a shiver at how those old men spoke so familiarly of the gods and prophecies, things he wanted nothing to do with.

Harafin said grimly, "Yes, tomorrow will decide many things."

Kevlin drew Jerrik and Drystan aside. "Look," he began, "I'm sorry about that fight. I didn't plan for that to happen. I just. . ."

The words trailed off. How could he explain it?

"It's all right," Drystan said. "Harafin always talks in riddles, so I don't know what's going on, but we'll try to help. Just try to warn us next time."

"At least it was a good fight," Jerrik said.

"Aye," Drystan said. "Best I've had in years. And since Jerrik and I aren't allowed to fight each other, you turned out to be the next best thing."

"What does he have against you two fighting?"

"Common sense," Gabral interrupted from where he stood by his horse.

"A wager then," replied Drystan, a sly look on his face. "We're both leading identical forces in identical maneuvers against the fort."

"Aye."

"Then, first man to the center of the courtyard inside the fort wins," said Drystan.

"Just a minute," said Gabral. "I will not have you endangering your men to win a bet."

"Then how about this?" Jerrik said. "First to the middle, but with the fewest casualties."

When Gabral offered no argument, Drystan laughed loudly, "Done."

Word of the wager spread quickly, and the other soldiers began eagerly making their own side bets.

Kevlin went over to Gabral, who was working some kind of cream into his hair. "Why not let Jerrik and Drystan duel? You let them fight me."

"I didn't expect you'd be possessed by Savas, or I wouldn't have allowed it. I can't let those two loose on each other."

"Why not?"

Gabral snorted and began carefully brushing his black hair, forming its naturally straight locks into waves. "You really have no idea who they are, do you?"

"I know Jerrik's family. His brother was one of the best soldiers I ever met."

"You've been adopted by two of the best fighters in the empire. When word gets out that you managed to unite them as brothers, it'll create a stir, I promise you."

"Why?"

"Jerrik is the undisputed champion of Donarr. No one's ever come close against him."

Kevlin shrugged. "And Drystan is. . ." His voice trailed off as he finally made the connection.

Gabral nodded when Kevlin's eyes widened in realization. "Took you long enough." He tucked the brush into a saddlebag and surveyed his shining hair in a small hand mirror.

"Drystan Aldacosia," Kevlin muttered. "I can't believe I didn't see it."

Drystan was the great champion, winner of the last five imperial games. His fame had swept the empire after the last games, with many claiming he was the best fighter in imperial history.

Kevlin hadn't paid much attention to the claims. While leading his mercenary troops, he had always had more important things to worry about than who won the imperial games. He considered the games less meaningful, less worthy than the very real battles he'd been fighting for years.

"So what's the problem if Drystan's the champion?"

"That's the question. Is he really? Jerrik's never been free to go to the games and face him."

"Oh. That would be quite a fight."

"Not on my watch," Gabral said. "I can't afford to have either of them killed or disabled. This troop was thrown together when Harafin received a message from Antigonus, and includes elite soldiers from three different kingdoms. Until we galloped out of the city, no one even realized they'd both be riding together under the same command."

Kevlin whistled softly. "Amazing."

"Aye."

Kevlin returned to his mount, his mind full. Becoming swordbrothers yesterday had been enough of a surprise without that added twist.

He'd stood alone against both of them. It was a good thing Savas wasn't in the prize fighting business. He could rake in a lot of cash.

Kevlin thought back to the feeling of awesome power bestowed by Savas, but then forced the memory away. Better to stay in control. All he wanted was for the battle to be won tomorrow and his involvement with gods and talismans of power and stalwarts to end.

Still, it felt good to be part of a company again. Kevlin hadn't realized how much he missed the feeling of riding with like-minded men, united in purpose and preparing for battle. Whatever came next, he was glad he had that opportunity.

"Move out," Gabral ordered.

43

Unexpected Company

The sun hung low over the forest when Kevlin led his horse wearily into a small clearing about a mile from the fort. After seeing to the animal, he sat down in the tall grass and lay back, happy to rest for a few minutes. The woods had been thick. Had it not been for Adalia and the other hunters from Baldev finding the most accessible route, they would never have managed it in one day.

Not far away, Gabral ordered, "No fires tonight. Post a double guard."

Harafin said, "I think I'll check on the men of Baldev and see if they're in position."

"How are you going to do that?" asked Kevlin. "You can't possibly reach them and return before morning."

"Not by walking," Harafin said. "Come, I'll show you."

"First I want to get a look at the fort," said Gabral. "Kevlin, join us."

"Good idea."

They set off into the woods, with the captains, Leander, and Ceren in tow. With Adalia to guide them, and without horses to slow them down in the thick undergrowth, they made little noise. After about a hundred yards, they crossed a wide trail that headed due east toward the cliff.

"Let's keep an eye on this trail tonight in case the Grakonians send out a patrol," ordered Gabral.

"Aye, sir," said Drystan.

"Looks like the trail we followed the first time," Kevlin said to Ceren.

She nodded, and he wondered if she was thinking about kissing him in the darkness nearby. They followed the trail to where it turned north. At that point they slipped into the woods and soon reached the edge of the large clearing.

The fortress huddled against the base of the massive cliff. They spent a few minutes studying the wall and the half mile of open space they'd have to charge across. The enemy showed no signs of preparing their defenses, so hopefully the attack would be a surprise.

Ceren whispered, "I never actually got to see it last time. It makes me shiver to think we walked right up to that wall."

"It won't be so easy next time."

Kevlin asked Adalia, "Still sure you can get in range without being seen?"

"Aye, we kin get close, no worries." She pointed to the sky. "Tonight looks ta be cloudy an dark. Plenty of shadows ta hide in."

Kevlin detailed to everyone the layout of the fort behind the wall and answered a few questions. As darkness descended, torches were lit along the top of the wall. They marked carefully the placement of the guards and Kevlin explained the pattern of their movements that he'd witnessed.

Finally satisfied, they headed back for camp. Harafin lagged behind and placed a hand on Kevlin's shoulder. "It's time I check on our friends. Will you watch with me?"

"Of course. What exactly are you going to do?"

The old sentinel smiled, a flash of white in the gathering darkness. "One major branch of study in the sentinel enclaves is nature. There is much knowledge and power to be found within the natural world. One very useful skill which I will be using tonight is the ability to connect with nearby animals."

"You can speak with animals?"

"Not exactly. It's more like the ability to encourage them to take certain actions, and then accompany them as they do so."

"So, you possess them?"

"No, but I can use their senses, seeing what they see, hearing what they hear, or even smelling what they smell."

"That's amazing."

Harafin smiled again, then closed his eyes and tilted his head toward the sky. Kevlin watched for several long minutes, but the old man made no further movement.

A soft yellow glow concentrated around his closed eyes, illuminating his face. The sentinel remained unmoving for fifteen minutes before taking a deep breath and opening his eyes.

"How did it go?" Kevlin asked

"Our friends are in position and ready. A roving owl was kind enough to fly over and inspect their handiwork." Harafin laughed. "No matter how many times I do that, I always find it amazing to stare down upon the world through the eyes of a bird."

It sounded like an amazing ability, but watching it from the outside was just a little more exciting than watching paint dry.

"Why don't you do it more often?" Kevlin asked.

"It could prove dangerous. Giving in to the temptation to use one's magic unnecessarily is as potentially destructive as giving in to the temptation to drink oneself unconscious every night. Both become addictions that can come to rule one's life and eventually destroy it."

"I hadn't thought of it that way."

Back at camp, the men had completed their final preparations for the morning's attack, eaten a cold meal, and most of them had already rolled into their blankets. Kevlin ate his meal quickly and was laying out his own blankets when Drystan approached and held out a long spear.

"You'll need this for the assault tomorrow," Drystan said.

"Thanks."

A high-pitched shout rang through the night from the edge of the clearing.

Kevlin recognized the voice. "Adalia."

They ran into the darkness toward the source of the shouting. Another voice, deeper, cursed loudly. They reached the edge of the forest and came upon Adalia's small tent pitched by the edge of the trees.

A man was staggering out of it, doubled over, one hand clutching his midsection. His other hand covered his nose. In the darkness, Kevlin couldn't clearly see his face.

"Halt," Kevlin commanded, placing the point of his spear against the man's chest.

The fellow stopped, but growled, "Get out of my way."

The tent flap flew aside and Adalia leaped out and launched herself toward the man. Drystan intercepted her and grabbed her arms before she could stab the man with the arrow she wielded like a spear.

"Stop it," Drystan barked.

"By Jagen, I'm gonna kill him!" she shrieked in rage, struggling mightily against Drystan's grasp.

Drystan said, "No one is going to kill anyone until I know what happened."

Jerrik and several men with drawn swords and torches approached. The additional light revealed the features of the man Kevlin held at spear point. His nose was bleeding.

"Cridan," Jerrik addressed him. "What's going on?"

Adalia shouted, "He attacked me, that's wot. An' I'm gonna kill him fer it!"

She lunged for Cridan, but Drystan restrained her. "Calm down or you're going to hurt yourself. What did he do?"

Cridan said, "The little wench invited me into her tent and then attacked me like a demon."

"Liar!" Adalia screamed, fury pouring off her in waves.

"Silence," Gabral commanded, arriving with Leander, Indira, and Ceren.

Indira took Adalia from Drystan and wrapped a protective arm around her. Ceren joined the two other women, her sword held low and at the ready. Adalia seemed to deflate as she sagged against the healer.

Gabral surveyed them angrily. "Do you plan to announce our presence to everyone within a mile of our position? Are you trying to get us all killed?"

"No, sir," Adalia snarled. "Just him."

"You're crazy," sneered Cridan. He turned to Gabral. "She's been eyeing me for the past two days. I know what she wants, and when I asked her if she wanted some company tonight, she invited me into her tent. But when I started giving her what she wanted, she attacked me."

Adalia stared at him, momentarily so angry she couldn't speak. "I never eyed ye, ye disgustin' pig. Ye showed up with no warnin' an' I told ye ta leave."

To Gabral she said, "He pushed hisself into me tent an' grabbed me an' started pawin at me an' tellin me ta be quiet. But I knocked him off an' hit him with me boot an' kicked him. An' now I'm gonna kill him."

"She's a lying whore," said Cridan. He stepped toward her, but Kevlin stopped him with the spear against his chest.

Their eyes met, and Kevlin said simply, "One more step and you're a dead man."

Part of him hoped Cridan would take that step.

"Let him go, Kevlin," Ceren said. She gripped the hilt of her sword so tight her fingers gleamed white in the darkness. "Let him show *me* how he treats a lady."

"Enough," Gabral warned. "Cridan, I don't like your tone or your words."

"We can summon Harafin," Leander said. "It is a simple matter to cast Truth on each of them."

Without warning, Cridan knocked Kevlin's spear aside, ducked the shaft, and ran for the trees.

"Catch him," Gabral ordered, and several of the men gave chase.

Ceren moved faster.

Before Gabral finished speaking, she threw her sword. The blade spun low and slashed into Cridan's legs, tripping him. He tumbled to the ground with a cry, but surged to his feet again immediately.

Jerrik's fist met him as he rose and drove him back to the ground. The huge Donarri captain hauled Cridan to his feet where he hung limp in Jerrik's grip.

"I believe we have our answer," Leander declared.

"Aye," Gabral said.

"Good throw," Adalia said to Ceren with a fierce grin.

"Thank you." She accepted her sword from one of the other soldiers.

"Execute him," Gabral ordered Jerrik. The big man dragged Cridan away.

"Thank ye," Adalia said to Gabral.

"When justice needs to be done, I see to it." He cast a dark look at Kevlin before turning away.

"Justice was served," Leander agreed.

They returned to the fire where Gabral told Harafin what had happened. "Curse that fool," Harafin said. "I'll see if the shouting alerted the fort." He closed his eyes, and once again a yellow glow gathered around his face.

Only a few minutes passed before Harafin's eyes popped open, and he clutched Kevlin's shoulder.

"Sentinels," Harafin said.

"What?"

"There is a large group of sentinels less than half a mile away. They sensed my presence, and they're coming fast."

"Are they allied with Tanathos?" Gabral asked.

"I do not know."

"Maybe that's what they've been waiting for," Ceren said. "Reinforcements."

"How many?" Leander asked.

"About a dozen," Harafin said.

Ceren gasped. "So many? How is it possible?"

Kevlin hadn't heard of so many sentinels gathered outside of the enclaves since the last war.

"Colonel, assemble your men," Harafin ordered. "Retreat to the south side of the clearing. If they prove hostile, we're in grave danger."

44

KIDNEYS IN THE MIND

The clearing erupted into activity, with Gabral and his captains shouting orders and men scrambling for weapons and armor. Shadows jumped in the flickering torchlight.

Kevlin paced near the forest's edge and peered into the darkness. So many sentinels. Could they really be allied with Tanathos? Rhea and Bajaran were, but could there be so many others? What else could have dragged them into the wilderness?

"Move," Harafin urged Gabral. "Get everyone back." Leander hovered beside Harafin near the central fire, his right hand occasionally clenching at empty air as if grasping for his hammer.

Soldiers scrambled into their saddles and Kevlin breathed a sigh of relief. They were going to make it.

Wrong.

An arrow of white-hot magic shot from the darkened forest and struck one rider in the chest. The resulting explosion catapulted him from the saddle. He tumbled to the ground, a limp, unmoving corpse.

"Go!" Harafin yelled.

Flanked by Leander, he ran toward the trees, but was still fifty paces away when a second bolt of magic shot out of the woods.

The glowing projectile ricocheted off an invisible barrier with a surprisingly musical twang and careened into the night sky.

As Harafin charged through the ranks of soldiers, right hand glowing with power, men scattered out of his way. Two bolts of green magic flashed from the trees toward Harafin, but he deflected them away. A third struck the ground right in front of him, blasting dirt into his face.

While he pawed at his eyes, Leander stepped in front of him and snapped his fingers, calling forth his mighty hammer. He held it at the ready, as if to knock any further bolts of magic from the air like he had done with the Grakonian crossbow bolts in Baldev.

They were out of time. The men were too spread out and Harafin was only a single man. Even he couldn't hope to hold off so many attackers alone until the soldiers were safely away.

Kevlin was only twenty feet from the trees.

Time to spin the Wheel.

He sprinted toward the trees, drew his sword, and shouted a wordless battle cry.

"What are you doing?" Leander shouted.

"I'll slow them down."

I'm insane.

Kevlin ran on, swinging his sword wildly to draw the attention of the hidden assailants.

The ghostly white figure of a sentinel stepped from behind a tree five paces away and raised an arm toward him.

This had better work.

A spear of red-gold magic shot from the unknown sentinel's hand and struck Kevlin in the chest. The magic crackled like dead leaves, flared, and disappeared. The familiar sensation of warmth began spreading through Kevlin as the amulet captured the magic and poured it into him. The scent of clover hung in the air around him.

Kevlin leaped at the surprised sentinel, driven by the thrill of still being alive as much as by the influx of energy. The man reacted too slowly and Kevlin drove his sword deep into the man's chest. Hot blood poured over his hand and its sharp, coppery stench triggered a flood of memories of past battles.

The sentinel shuddered, his face locked into a shocked grimace and his mouth moving wordlessly as he toppled to the ground.

Kevlin stared at him for a double heartbeat, fighting to center his mind and stem the tide of memories that threatened to sweep him into battle rage.

I just killed a sentinel.

For years he'd wanted nothing so badly as to thrust a sword through a sentinel's guts and watch him die. Killing this nameless enemy brought none of the anticipated satisfaction, though. He wasn't sure what he felt.

He tried to kill me. That's enough. . .for now.

Two more sentinels emerged from the deeper shadows under the trees to either side of him, magic blasting from their hands. Light half-blinded Kevlin and his ears rang with an angry buzzing, as if he'd stuck his head in a giant hornets' nest. He raised a hand to shield his face, gritting his teeth against the unnerving sound.

The light faded and he marveled that he still stood, unscathed by the attack.

Thank the Lady for the amulet.

The two sentinels stared, as surprised by their failure as the first man had been. Kevlin embraced the battle fury surging through him and lunged left, captured magic boiling down his limbs and setting his muscles thrumming with power. He swallowed the terror that bubbled through him and slashed the throat of one man who was already raising a hand to cast another spell.

The sentinel fell back with a gurgling cry, and Kevlin spun toward the other sentinel.

A woman.

She stood, glowing hands half-raised to cast another spell, her face a mixture of fear and determination. Their eyes met for a second, then she glanced down at her fallen companions who lay twitching in pools of their own blood.

"If you surrender, I won't kill you," Kevlin said. He'd fought many battles, but couldn't remember ever having killed a woman. He'd rather not, if it could be avoided.

Instead of answering, the woman spun and ran into the darkness.

So be it. Kevlin gave chase.

Sentinel robes might be good for many things, but running was not one of them. Nor was hiding. The woman's white robe seemed to glow in the deep shadows, drawing him like a beacon. He closed on her fast. It would be over in seconds.

Why doesn't she just surrender?

She burst through a screen of bushes and stumbled out onto the trail leading to the fort. There she turned, her face triumphant as Kevlin leaped out onto the road beside her.

He started in surprise, having been so focused on running her down that he hadn't noticed the other four enemy sentinels. Two pairs of white-robed men flanked him on either side, mere paces away. They stared back, appearing equally surprised to have him appear in their midst.

"Kill him," the woman screamed. She raised her hands and light coalesced into her. For a single heartbeat, her entire body blazed like the sun, glowing with every color imaginable. Light shimmered around her in a breathtaking rainbow.

In that second, while she manipulated actinic energy, she was the most beautiful thing Kevlin had ever seen. Time seemed to slow and Kevlin stared, transfixed.

Then she flung open her hand. The same brilliant light blasted out from her palm in a crackling ball of fire that seared the air with its supernatural heat. His lungs burned as he tried to draw a breath, and his face began to blister.

The ball of flame flared blindingly as it struck.

Then it disappeared.

Kevlin stood untouched in the trail, his entire body shivering both with awe at what he'd seen and from the new influx of power he'd absorbed.

The woman shouted a vile curse and raised her hands again.

Enough. Kevlin lunged and slugged her in the side of the head with the hilt of his sword.

She dropped like a stone.

At the same instant, the other sentinels struck. Magic blasted into Kevlin from all sides, blinding him with its brilliant flashes of light. Energy snapped and whipped around him, deafening him with concussive thunderclaps.

He ducked against the light and shouted, a guttural cry of fear. The amulet might protect him, but it couldn't erase the terror of standing alone between four sentinels in the darkness while they tried to rip him apart.

The air crackled with power. Dust blew up from the trail, then blackened to powder as magic vaporized it. The air tasted stale, lifeless, and smelled like a charnel house.

Magic flooded into him, a boiling river that churned through his torso and roared along his veins. His body swelled with power until it nearly overwhelmed him. It felt like drowning, and he couldn't hold his breath against it.

He panicked.

"Stop!" He shouted so loud it hurt. His arms tingled with so much strength that he felt he could throw the accursed sentinels back to Ingolf if he could get his hands on them. He turned toward the pair on his left, threw out his arms, and *pushed* the magic away.

A wave of pure white light erupted from him in a solid wall. His skin burned as the power passed through it, and out of him. A heavy thunderclap shattered the air. He clutched his ears and shouted a wordless howl.

Whatever Harafin's planning, he'd better hurry. I can't take any more of this.

His blast of magic tumbled the two sentinels to the ground, temporarily stunned.

Kevlin spun back to the other pair, who had paused in their attack. One, a heavyset fellow with a florid complexion, pointed at Kevlin and said, "Halimaw tactics, lad."

A bush next to Kevlin ripped out of the ground and slammed into his back. He staggered.

Bushes? Who kills someone with bushes? The thought seemed ludicrous.

The sentinel raised a hand, and fire erupted out of the air around Kevlin, blinding him and blocking his view. The amulet captured magic and, although the flames licked to within inches of his face, they didn't touch him.

The heat did. It seared his skin, and he had to hold his breath to keep it from scorching his lungs.

Something heavy struck him in the side, and he stumbled through the wall of flames. More magic poured into him from the amulet.

The two sentinels turned toward the forest, and light coalesced inside of them as they focused actinic energy. Kevlin glanced in that direction to see what they were doing.

A foot-thick sapling swayed, lifting slowly from the ground. It groaned like a living thing, and its roots thrashed as if fighting against its fate.

That's just not fair.

A slender figure leaped from the forest right behind the sentinels.

Ceren.

She struck the back of the heavyset sentinel's neck, right at the base of the skull, with the hilt of her sword. He collapsed. The other sentinel spun toward Ceren, and she kicked him in the groin.

The impact lifted him off the ground and he fell face-first in the dirt, clutching at himself and writhing in pain. Ceren kicked him in the head and he stopped moving.

Kevlin ran to her. She turned to him, panting, her emerald eyes sparkling with excitement.

"What are you doing?" he demanded. "You could've been killed."

"Oh, so you're the only one who can do something brave?"

"That's not what I meant."

She tossed her hair and gave him that look, as if trying to remind him of his place in the world. "They were too focused on you. I was in no danger."

Another sentinel emerged from the trees ten paces up the trail, behind Ceren. He wasted no time in pointing a glowing finger at them.

Ceren had no protection.

Kevlin lunged past her just as a spear of red-gold magic sprang from the man's hands. Kevlin ran right through it, so far beyond fear that he didn't even cringe when it struck.

The sentinel tried to retreat, but Kevlin closed on him fast and slashed him from shoulder to thigh. Blood spurted from the deep wound and the man tumbled to the ground. Even as he fell, he threw a blast of magic right at Kevlin's face, momentarily blinding him.

When Kevlin recovered his sight, the sentinel lay on the ground, clutching at his wounded side. "What in the name of the seven gods are you?" the man asked.

Kevlin kicked him in the teeth.

With a terrifying *crack* of splintering wood, a large branch snapped from a heavy oak tree nearby.

Shield!

In a heartbeat, Kevlin formed the image of a broad shield in his mind. The magic burning in his chest exploded out of him, forming an amber-colored shield of light just as the heavy branch whisked through the air in his direction.

The branch collided with his shield inches from his head. The shield shuddered from the blow, but held. In his mind, it felt like someone had punched him in the kidneys. He winced. He'd never imagined having kidneys in his mind.

By the Lady, I hate magic.

Voices shouted in the darkness as people crashed through the dense forest. The other sentinels were coming fast.

Kevlin grabbed Ceren's arm and pushed her up the trail at a run, just as trees and bushes began shaking nearby. The sentinels seemed to have realized they needed to attack him indirectly. He and Ceren couldn't get back to Harafin through the woods, so they raced up the path leading toward the fort.

A crowd of shouting sentinels emerged from the woods behind them and gave chase. Bushes, branches and even a few rocks launched through the air after them. Kevlin deflected the debris with his glowing shield, quickly gaining mastery over the mechanics of moving it around as he fought to protect both Ceren and himself.

Magic surged through him and flowed out through his hand to fuel the shield. He'd absorbed a huge reserve of power, and wished he could just push it all away.

It filled him with euphoria, but he hated the false feeling and worried it might draw Savas again. He gritted his teeth and held the magic in, kept it focused, and even admitted it was a good thing Harafin had taught him the spell. Hopefully he'd never have to use it again. He hated every second of it.

More shouts, and several bolts of magic shot from the trees to his left.

Uh oh.

More sentinels. Harafin had said there were a dozen of them, but he'd hoped the others were farther behind. Kevlin tried increasing his pace, but it was hard to maintain his shield and move at the same time, so he settled for a frustratingly slow trot back along the trail.

"Where are we going?" Ceren cried, her face pale and terrified.

"Away."

Bolts of magic pelted his back, and power surged through him in a barely contained torrent despite the energy he was using to fuel the shield. Thank the gods they were all aiming at him rather than Ceren.

He tried to increase the size of the shield, and even to angle it to protect them better, but the effort felt like trying to mold clay with his knees while blindfolded. Sweat dripped down into his eyes as he struggled with the unaccustomed effort.

A sentinel stepped into the trail and pointed at Ceren. A wall of golden light appeared just in front of her.

She couldn't stop, and ran into it. It wrapped around her, immobilizing her.

"Let her go," Kevlin shouted.

The sight of Ceren imprisoned sparked his rage and he could think of nothing but punching the man's face. The energy boiling in his chest reacted.

A huge ball of amber magic, shaped roughly like a fist, shot from Kevlin and slammed the sentinel headlong into the trees.

Ceren's golden prison flickered and disappeared. She gasped and staggered forward. Kevlin caught her arm.

"Thanks," she panted.

A tree crashed to the ground right next to him, shaking the earth and blasting dust-laden air up in a wave. Not a sapling, but a tree. A big one.

Kevlin stared at the massive trunk still quivering inches away, and tried to swallow. His mouth felt parched and his legs shook.

Half a foot, and it would have squashed us into jelly.

Time to go. Really.

Kevlin released the shield, grabbed Ceren's arm, and sprinted as fast as he could up the trail, dragging her with him. The sentinels gave chase and debris rained down on them. One large branch slammed into his right shoulder, and pain lanced all the way down his arm. Magic then rolled up into it, and the pain subsided.

Ceren cried out and stumbled, nearly falling. A rock had struck her thigh. She clutched at her injured leg and tried to run, but could barely stand. Tears glistened in her terrified eyes.

Kevlin swept her up into his arms and cradled her against his chest, barely slowing in his mad dash. He drew upon the magic pounding through his limbs, using its strength not only to keep going but to speed up.

We're going to die, he realized. They couldn't run fast enough. Ceren clutched at him and buried her face against his neck as she shook with fear.

Her terror triggered rage in him. It was his fault. She'd come to help. He couldn't let her die.

Slowing his pace, he concentrated on the raging power in his soul. A little shield wouldn't do. With anger strengthening his will, he cast aside his fears and envisioned a large, bowl-shaped shield resting over him.

Do it, he commanded the churning power. *By the gods, do it.*

It obeyed. Magic poured out of him to form a huge, amber colored shield.

He ran on, with the shimmering bowl over his head, gasping from the effort. His body trembled from the strain, but he growled with determination and forced himself on.

The forest shook and trees groaned. Dust and leaves lifted into the air, making it even harder to see. His shield held as debris rained down.

Please, no more trees. If one of those hit directly, they'd be dead.

The trail turned sharply, illuminated by flashes of light, and he took the corner leaning so far over he nearly lost his footing. The debris subsided, but he didn't slow. Still sprinting, he raced out of the trees and into the clearing. On the far side, hidden in the gloom, loomed the fort.

He slowed. Torches burned all along the wall, clearly visible even half a mile away.

"Tanathos knows we're here," Ceren said in his ear.

Had it been a trap all along?

"We've got to get back to Harafin," Kevlin decided.

He turned back toward the trees, but a bolt of silvery magic shot out from them and struck the shield directly in front of his chest. He winced at the mental jab as his shield deflected the strike.

A long line of white-robed sentinels stepped out of the trees to face him. A woman at the center of the group declared, "It doesn't matter how many souls you've stolen. You can't stop us all."

She talked like she thought *he* was the enemy.

Oh, no.

Could they really have messed things up that badly? He opened his mouth to speak, but the sentinels raised their hands and bolts of white-hot magic shot from every palm.

His shield shattered under the simultaneous impacts of so much magic, and half a dozen bolts slammed into Ceren.

She screamed in terror, and the impact rocked Kevlin backward. Bright light seared his eyes, and magic crackled all around them like lightning, arcing from Ceren to himself, and back again. The sharp scent of ozone burned his nose and set his blinded eyes watering.

Despite the tumult, dazzling lights, and smoky haze that surrounded them, he could feel nothing but Ceren's body trembling against him with fear.

In the next heartbeat, the amulet absorbed all the magic and poured it into him, a torrent of power so vast it nearly lifted him off the ground. He bellowed, his voice magnified so loud by the energy that several of the sentinels clutched at their ears.

Ceren screamed again and punched him in the shoulder. The magic thundered through his soul, a storm of energy with which he could do all things. At the same time it tore at his body, seeking a way out.

It wanted to kill him.

Kevlin threw his arms wide and Ceren dropped to the ground with a squawk of surprise. Magic raced down his arms like liquid fire and exploded out his fingers.

Lightning-like sheets of raw energy shot from his hands and lit the night like the return of the sun. The ground rippled and dirt shot into the air. Trees splintered behind the sentinels as energy whipped back and forth through their ranks.

The sentinels reacted with impressive discipline. Several shouted in surprise, but all reinforced their shields to block the deadly energy.

One of them failed. The man screamed, a long, terrified shriek of mortal agony that rose to an ear-piercing crescendo as fingers of lightning punched through his body. His scream cut short abruptly, and he fell straight to the ground, as if every muscle had been liquefied.

Kevlin hauled Ceren off the ground, slung her over his shoulder, and fled into the clearing.

45

CHOICES

Two hundred feet above Kevlin, an owl floated on silent wings as it stared down at the running figure and the line of white-robed men and women. Movement under the trees drew its gaze and that of Tanathos, who controlled it. Following his mental command, it flapped its wings, and several withered feathers fell away.

The owl coasted over the forest while small cracks formed in its beak and its claws blackened, consumed from within. It stared down at a large company of men running up a narrow path, led by an old man glowing with power.

The owl shuddered and pitched to one side. Suddenly-brittle bones shattered, one wing crumpled under its own weight, and the bird began a silent death spiral. It hit the ground a few heartbeats later, a dry husk that ruptured into a cloud of dust.

\# \# \#

Tanathos reeled when he returned to his body. The owl, its life force sacrificed to his need, had shown him far more than he'd wanted to see. He clutched the top of the parapet and stared toward the edge of the forest where magic flared anew.

Could that really be the man Kevlin standing against so many sentinels? How was it possible? He wasn't actinopathic.

And yet, hadn't Kevlin made him the fool? He still couldn't explain by what power Kevlin had struck him down in the cell.

So many sentinels. . . but that wasn't even important. It was the man leading the other force of soldiers into the clearing whose face burned into Tanathos' mind and filled his heart with terror.

Harafin.

The name was a death knell to any shadeleech, and Tanathos wanted to scream in rage. Kevlin was running *toward* him, alone, bearing with him the prize for which Tanathos desperately hungered.

There was nothing he could do about it.

He had to get away, or Harafin would kill him. Not even the massed power of all the other sentinels drove such fear into his heart.

"What did you see?" Neasa asked, her milky white eyes watching him intently. "What's going on?"

"There are two groups," Tanathos said. "They seem to be fighting."

"No single sentinel can throw around all that power."

"There are at least two." Before the ugly toad of a woman could speak again, Tanathos continued, "Their argument provides the perfect distraction. I will lead the ambush."

Casting out fingers of power, he pulled on the minds of half a hundred makrasha. The creatures came running to the northern wall and began pouring out through a small sally port. One of them fetched Tanathos' horse from the stable.

The Blade Stalwart Dhanjal exited the command building, flanked by his men. The big, dark-skinned fellow approached with his normal confident stride.

"You're coming with me," Tanathos said. "Gather your men."

Dhanjal smiled, a flash of white against his dark skin. "We will dance the song of Savas this night."

Tanathos turned at the sound of a deep growl and grinned at the sight of the halimaw lumbering into view from behind the command building. The monster radiated lethal power as it stalked toward the wall on long-fingered paws tipped with curved claws. Covered in dense blond fur, its limbs bulged with impossibly huge muscles that strained the limits of its thick hide.

It was as beautiful in its new form as it had been as a human before Neasa changed her. Rhea had never imagined she'd serve them so well. As much as Tanathos yearned to rip out Neasa's heart, he had to admit she'd done an excellent job creating the halimaw.

When the monster reached the wall, it reared up on its hind legs and lifted its massive head until its glowing amber eyes came level with Tanathos atop the wall, a full dozen feet above the ground.

It opened its long, heavy maw to reveal row after row of sharp, triangular teeth, and its breath washed over him in a deliciously fetid blast. Its face, a twisted mixture of bear and human, still bore a striking resemblance to the once lovely woman that had been Rhea.

Tanathos placed a hand between the halimaw's eyes, exulting in the sense of power that came with control of such a primal force. Still smiling, he said, "Fetch the sentinel Antigonus."

The monster spun away and raced for the command building. It landed on the narrow porch in three leaping strides, and the entire structure shuddered under the impact. It ripped open the door and squeezed through the opening, disappearing in a flash of blond fur.

"Why take Antigonus?" Neasa asked suspiciously. "He's safest in his cell."

Tanathos chuckled. "Think deeper if you ever hope to lead."

She frowned, and Tanathos hid a smile. The cryptic answer would keep her busy long enough for him to get away. Finally, the white-eyed hag would serve him well.

It was just too bad he wouldn't get to kill her himself.

46

A Friend of a Friend

Sitara hurried through the main halls of the Palace. She rarely ventured so far from the keisara's apartments in the Emperor's Palace, but the keisara wished to be alone, which gave Sitara the perfect opportunity to track down the one contact Bajaran had mentioned before he left.

It took an hour to escape the halls of the Emperor's Palace and reach the far simpler yet very functional Hallvarr Palace. The various palaces that made up the greater imperial complex were linked together above and belowground. She could have taken a shorter route through the Imperial Palace, the Great Dome, and then across the huge central courtyard, but the risk of being recognized would have been much greater. Besides, on this errand she felt uncomfortable walking through open sunlight.

Instead, she descended to the sub-levels that filled the plateau beneath the greater palace complex. Fewer people moved about, and she found the perpetual twilight of the lower levels comforting.

Sitara eventually climbed to the main levels of the Hallvarr Palace, where the diplomats, nobles, and administrators from Hallvarr worked and lived. She stopped before an ornate door on the third floor and knocked. A moment later it was opened by a page who politely inquired after her business.

"I need to speak with Remiel. Please fetch him for me."

"Yes, ma'am." He ushered her into a comfortably appointed sitting room and disappeared from view. They were in a wing of the palace where the ambassador's staff worked.

If this is the wrong name, all is lost.

Before he left, Bajaran had mentioned that if she ever found herself in desperate need, she should come and ask for Remiel. He would know how to contact an ally. She tried to breathe normally and hold together the frayed edges of hope while she waited, for she desperately needed a friend.

The page returned a few minutes later, followed by a very handsome young man who walked with a confident swagger. He paused when he saw her and his eyes ran appraisingly over her figure before focusing on her face. Her heart skipped a beat as she stared into his dark eyes.

He brushed his jet-black hair from his face and approached with a smile that made her knees weak. "My lady." He bowed over her hand and kissed it lightly, as if he were a nobleman and she a lady of the court.

He straightened and added, "I am yours to command."

He was very smooth. He looked no more than sixteen, but she knew that to be misleading. Bajaran had warned her that he was much older than he looked. It had to be the right man.

"Is there a more private place to talk?" she asked.

"Of course."

She gratefully accepted his extended arm, and he led her to a comfortable sitting room with several overstuffed chairs, a long couch, and a fireplace with a large, ornately carved wooden mantel. She seated herself in one of the chairs while Remiel remained standing.

"What can I do for you, miss?"

Sitara opened her mouth to speak, but no words came. She suddenly realized the terrible flaw in her plan. Bajaran was a known traitor. Admitting association with him was tantamount to admitting one was a traitor.

Remiel faced the same risk she did. He didn't know her, so had no motivation to take a risk to reveal his true loyalty. On top of it all, she had kept her relationship with Bajaran secret for so long, the thought of revealing the truth to anyone made her want to cringe.

When she did not immediately speak, Remiel gave her another confident smile. "Relax, angel. I have that effect all the time. You're not the first."

Sitara laughed, which eased the knot in her throat. "I'm glad you impress yourself so easily. I hesitated only because I find myself in a delicate position.

I was referred to you by a mutual friend, but the nature of that friendship prevents me from speaking their name."

"What did she say I could do for you?" he asked, dropping into an overstuffed chair.

"*He* said you could put me in contact with a mutual acquaintance."

Remiel rubbed his jaw. "Angel, you want me to contact someone who's a friend of someone else that I might happen to know?"

"That's about it," she said. "Sounds crazy, doesn't it."

He laughed. "If you weren't so good looking, I doubt I'd be able to help you."

Sitara flushed, which only stoked his incredible ego. "I'm glad I'm so attractive."

"Me too." Remiel leaned closer, his dark-eyed gaze intent. "However, think about this from my perspective. Your secrecy suggests this person I'm supposed to know is currently out of favor with the authorities."

She nodded, her heart in her throat. Even that much admission could get her into trouble, but she couldn't think of any way to avoid it.

"You're asking a lot," Remiel said. "Asking me to trust that you are who you say you are. Yet no code words or other tokens are given to assure me that you're telling the truth and you're not a spy trying to trick me into a confession."

"Code words?"

"Of course. Assuming for a moment that I do know something about what you're talking about, you're nameless contact must have given you some code or phrase so I can know he really sent you."

She thought back to the night Bajaran had left, desperately trying to remember the conversation. She had been so distracted by his leaving, she had barely paid attention to what he told her about Remiel.

"I can't remember any special code word or phrase," she admitted finally in defeat, tears glistening in her eyes as she struggled to hold her composure together. "Nothing."

She couldn't let the man leave without helping. She doubted she could persuade him with words. He seemed far too sophisticated. Her only other option was her best weapon. She settled her face into an innocent mask and pleaded with sweet sincerity, "Please help me."

Remiel slapped his leg. "By the Dark Lord's fiery chains, you're a rare one. Let's assume for a moment I fall for your excellent performance and believe you, that I am the man he sent you to and that I can, in fact, place you in touch with an ally."

She sat forward eagerly, grasping onto the thin hope his words dangled before her.

"And let's assume he either failed to give you a code word, or you forgot it."

She nodded. "Yes."

"Then there's only two things we need to settle. First, you have to say his name."

"But I thought . . . "

Remiel shook his head, his expression hardening. "Say it."

Sitara hesitated. Speaking it would prove her words to Remiel but leave her at his mercy. He still hadn't actually admitted anything, but he demanded she do so.

"Bajaran," she whispered finally.

The name hung in the air between them for a moment. Remiel did not speak for several seconds, and Sitara's anxiety grew with every heartbeat.

"That wasn't so hard, was it, Angel?" Remiel said finally.

"Yes it was," she snapped.

He grinned. "You're right. That's a dangerous name to speak these days."

"I said it. Now help me."

Speaking the name aloud helped ease some of her fear. She had declared her allegiance to Bajaran to another. It reinforced her commitment to him. He would be proud of her.

"One final item," Remiel said. "Surely he told you what payment I would expect for my services."

"Payment?" She blinked a couple of times.

"Of course. You're asking me to take a big risk by agreeing to help you. There has to be something in it for me. It wouldn't be fair if you benefited from the exchange but I got nothing."

"I don't have much money," she began.

He raised a hand to silence her, and stood. "No, I could never take your money, Angel."

"Then what?"

In answer, he slowly let his eyes run down the length of her body and back up again. When he finally looked her in the eye once more, he smiled invitingly. "I am a man of simple needs, Angel. What do you say?"

Understanding struck her like a blow to the stomach. She gasped and raised one hand to her mouth, unable to hide her furiously blushing face. His laughter confirmed her fears and only made her blush deepen.

"You can't be serious," she nearly shouted.

"Sure," he said, still smiling. "It could be a lot of fun."

She jumped to her feet, her embarrassment turning to outrage. "How dare you!" she yelled, not caring if anyone overheard them. "I came to you for help and you demand that I. . ." She paused, trying to collect her thoughts and give adequate voice to her anger.

Before she could do so, he placed a hand to her lips. She struck it aside, but he only grinned wider. "I like your spirit, Angel. I look forward to an arrangement with you."

He walked to the door and, with one hand on the latch, turned back. "You know my price. Were Bajaran still alive and able to guarantee some other payment, things would be different."

"But," he continued in a harder tone, "Bajaran is dead. My price stands."

She could only stare.

"Think about it," he said. "You know where to find me."

47

WITH ALLIES LIKE THESE . . .

Magic slammed into Kevlin and ripped the ground around them. Ceren screamed and pounded on his back.

"Let me go!" she shouted as another bolt struck him next to where her head bounced against his armored shoulder.

Not slowing, he pulled her around and cradled her to his chest. He drank deep from the energy surging through him, pushing himself faster than he'd ever thought possible.

It wasn't fast enough.

The earth boiled like the surface of a giant cauldron and his feet sank into clinging mud. Thunder crashed in ceaseless waves, drowning out whatever Ceren was trying to scream into his ear. He slogged through the mud, his legs churning and kicking up heavy globs of steaming earth in his single-minded drive to get away.

A shimmering wall of blue-green light appeared in front of him. He had no idea what it was supposed to do and, trusting in the amulet, he tucked his shoulder and crashed into it without slowing.

It flared angrily, but the amulet proved stronger, and he punched a man-sized hole through it.

"Kevlin, you're mad," Ceren cried and punched him in the jaw. The blow shocked him out of his panicked sprint and he slowed a little.

Impossibly, the magical barrage intensified. Sheets of multi-hued light shredded the ground and tore the air. Ceren's hair rose from her head and floated around them as he ran, a dark red halo that tickled his nose. Her gentle perfume masked some of the charred smell clinging to the back of his throat.

So much new magic thundered through his soul that it drowned out his thoughts. Howling with terror, he threw magic back at the sentinels in shapeless waves that lit the clearing in myriad colors but did little to help.

"Kill him," the leader of the sentinels shouted. "He cannot be allowed to reach that fort."

I'm really starting to hate that woman.

"I'll deal with it," said an excited young male voice.

"Stay out of it, you fool."

Maybe they'll kill each other, Kevlin hoped, still running. He could run faster if he weren't carrying Ceren, but he couldn't set her down. She wouldn't last half a heartbeat without his protection.

The earth under his feet surged upward, sending him tumbling through the air and tossed Ceren from his arms. He landed hard. She crashed to the ground nearby and yelped in pain. He crawled over to her.

Just as he reached her, the long, straight trunk of a sapling speared into the ground right behind him and drilled several feet into the earth, quivering from the impact.

Something whistled through the air overhead. Kevlin grabbed Ceren and dove to one side. He hit the ground on his shoulder, and she landed on top of him. They rolled together just as a huge oak tree crashed to the ground beside them, its dozens of branches slashing the earth to dust all around. Wood shattered against his armored back, showering them with fragments and filling the air with the sound of screaming timber.

They clung to each other amid the splintered wood, staring wide-eyed at the branches all around. Any one could have killed them.

A tree. Kevlin struggled to process the reality that the sentinels had really thrown a giant tree that far.

More trees, saplings, and rocks rained down all around, shaking the ground and filling the air with the tortured sounds of splintering wood and shattering stone. Dust billowed up to coat Kevlin's face with a heavy layer of grime.

"Come on, we've got to get away," Ceren screamed into his ear. She tried to stand and claw her way past the branches.

"Wait." Kevlin pulled her back down, then shoved her closer to the mighty tree.

"What are you doing?" she snarled, slapping his hands away.

"This is the only cover. If we go out there, we're dead." Ignoring her complaints, he crouched beside her. She jabbed him in the ribs with her elbow.

"Stop it and let me concentrate."

Kevlin formed the image of another bowl-shaped shield in his mind.

Do it, he commanded, then poured the burning energy into it, willing it to be strong, and then stronger.

His body glowed as the magic poured out of him. Ceren gaped as the shield formed, a translucent, shimmering half-sphere of silvery light. It consumed an incredible amount of energy and began swaying drunkenly, on the point of bursting out of his limited control.

Sweat poured down his face. He gasped for breath as he fought to maintain the shield.

Ceren placed a tentative hand on his arm, and he glanced at her. With an awed expression on her face, she said, "You can do it, Kevlin."

Kevlin was such a sucker for a girl with tears in her eyes, even if she had been treating him badly. He gritted his teeth and held onto the shield. It was like wrestling a greased pig, one he could never hope to control for long.

The glowing half-sphere gave the sentinels an excellent target. Magic slammed into it in bolts, waves of fire, arcing lightning, and forms he couldn't identify, shaking it and pounding at his mind. It felt like a dozen midgets had climbed inside his head and started beating his brain with hammers.

The shield held, barely. He threw every ounce of willpower into the struggle. A raging headache pounded behind his temples in time with the midgets' hammers.

Harafin, where are you?

Were he and Ceren being abandoned to die alone? The sentinels would change tactics soon and try something he couldn't stop. Nothing could save him.

Oris.

In the vision granted from Savas, the god had suggested he could unlock Oris's power, even though he wasn't actinopathic. That vision was like a half-remembered nightmare, but he might still be able to figure it out. It might save him, but if he followed Savas' counsel, would he be surrendering his soul to the god?

Would that be worse than letting those betrayers steal the rock?

Something *boomed* from across the clearing, a sound so thunderously vast that it overwhelmed everything else.

The bombardment stopped.

Something strange was going on. Kevlin imagined the sentinels advancing, hidden from view by the piled debris.

He wouldn't die like a caged rabbit, so he released the shield and clawed his way up through the tangle. Wordlessly, Ceren followed.

Peering through the highest branches, he could see the sentinels still in a ragged line, pointing across the clearing toward the fort.

He turned, and stared. "By all the gods. . ."

Lit by dozens of torches and an eerie red glow from an unknown source, a gigantic oak tree reared above the fort, its immense trunk rising from the middle of the command building as if it had been planted there.

The huge tree began to tip. Ever so slowly it toppled to one side, tearing the command building apart in as majestic a fall as Kevlin had ever witnessed.

The shrieking of timbers sounded faintly from across the clearing. The crown, which could easily span an acre, crashed onto the southern end of the outer wall and shattered it. The boom of the impact followed a little late, shaking Kevlin to the bone.

"How. . .?" Ceren whispered as she crouched close beside him.

More trees and boulders plummeted out of the stygian sky above the fortress, a deadly rain of destruction that assaulted the structure without warning and without mercy. Cries of panic and screams of pain mingled with the crashing of stone and wood.

The men of Baldev. It must be.

Kevlin swore. He'd sent the miners and woodsmen from town along the top of the cliff while the army advanced along the base. The plan had been for them to rain destruction down from above in the morning. They must have seen the lights from the sentinel's magic and assumed the attack was starting early.

A shimmering crimson light appeared above the fort and rose until it took the shape of a steeply pitched roof. The barrage of debris struck that light and bounced off, falling to either side of the fort.

How could they sustain such a huge shield? The little one he'd been using had taxed him to the limits. He suddenly felt very small, like a boy with a stick facing a fully armored knight.

A terrible realization struck Kevlin like a physical blow.

"Antigonus!"

That tree had destroyed the command building where Antigonus was held prisoner. Kevlin pounded on the tangled debris in frustrated rage. Everything was falling apart. They had been so close, but he struggled to believe Antigonus might have survived that destruction.

It was all the fault of those sentinels.

Kevlin scrambled from under the concealing branches and turned toward the sentinels, who still stood watching the cascading missiles like children on High Summer Day. His eyes fixed on the woman in the center who had commanded the attack and he growled like an animal, his entire body quivering with rage.

She was responsible. He was going to kill her.

He started forward, but one of the sentinels shouted an alarm, and the group spun to face the forest. Several conjured balls of light that illuminated the area.

The ground began rippling, flowing together into a mound that grew with alarming speed. Within six heartbeats, it reared twenty feet tall and a dozen feet thick. Then the rough column began to shift, forming arms and a head, becoming a giant earthen man standing at the edge of the clearing, glowing faintly green.

One sentinel threw a bolt of silvery magic at the apparition, but the missile deflected away with no visible effect.

"What is that?" Ceren whispered.

"I have no idea."

Kevlin took advantage of everyone's distraction to work his way out of the tangled pile of debris.

"Declare your allegiance," Harafin's voice emanated from the earthen giant facing the sentinels. Kevlin smiled with relief, although he wasn't sure why Harafin didn't just kill all the rogue sentinels.

"What devilry is this?" The female leader of the group called.

"Declare your allegiance," Harafin demanded again through the earthen giant. "Are you in league with the shadeleeches?"

Someone pushed through the group to the woman's side. He looked more like a soldier in the dim light, not a sentinel.

"I'll kill it," he yelled, his eager voice carrying easily. He raised his hand and blue fire burst to life at both ends of the weapon he held. It looked like a bladestaff.

"Shut up, Nikias," the woman ordered.

Kevlin groaned. Nikias. He really was carrying the Bladestaff, one of the Six, the weapon entrusted to Hallvarr. They couldn't be traitors. He refused to believe any of the Six would turn on the empire.

They'd been fighting people who should have been allies.

Apparently Harafin came to the same decision, because the earthen giant collapsed into a formless mound of dirt. Harafin strode out of the forest, flanked by Leander and Gabral. The rest of the company followed in a tight group, weapons held at the ready.

At the sight of the newcomers, the sentinels raised hands glowing with power. Kevlin worked his way around them toward Harafin's company. If it came to a fight, he wanted to be part of it.

"Hold," Harafin bellowed. "We are not your enemy."

"Prove it," said Nikias. He lifted the burning Bladestaff high.

Gabral raised the Mace, and it too burst into blue fire. "I am Gabral, bearer of the Mace, and I order you to stand down."

A ripple of surprise ran through the group of sentinels. Harafin halted a dozen paces from their leader and announced, "I am Harafin."

"Harafin?" she gasped.

"Yes. And who might you be?"

"I am Nikias," the youth proclaimed. "Bearer of the Bladestaff."

He lifted the burning weapon high. Flames licked along its silvered blades and reflected off the intricate inlaid silver runes that ran the length of its polished wooden shaft.

The woman who led the sentinels snarled, "Put that out, you fool, before you set yourself on fire."

"Sorry." Nikias lowered the weapon and the fire winked out.

Kevlin had circled far enough that he could finally see her pinched features. Calling her plain would be a compliment. Her eyes were too big, making her appear half-crazy.

"I am Wayra, adjutant to the gerent of Il'Aicharen, and leader of this company of Kestrels."

"What are you doing out here?" Harafin asked.

"We came to save Antigonus," Nikias said with a wave of the Bladestaff.

"You attacked the wrong group," Gabral said angrily, pointing at the fort. "The shadeleeches are over there, and you've warned them of our presence."

"It's not my fault." Nikias lowered the Bladestaff. "Wayra said--"

"It *is* your fault," Gabral interrupted. "As a bearer of one of the Six, you are in command. You are responsible for the death of one of my men."

Harafin said to Wayra, "Why did you attack before ascertaining whether we were, in fact, allied with the enemy?"

She opened her mouth to reply, but caught sight of Kevlin as he joined the group. Focusing those freakishly big eyes on him, she pointed. "This man killed two Kestrels tonight."

"Just returning the favor," Kevlin responded with a glare.

"Are you a sentinel?"

Kevlin barked a laugh. "Not hardly."

"Then you are an abomination and must be destroyed." She raised a hand that exploded into flames.

Kevlin raised his sword, a snarl on his lips. Perfect. Time to kill her.

"Enough!" Harafin thundered. "Wayra, your rash actions have already caused death and a great deal of trouble tonight. Don't repeat your mistake."

She lowered her hand. "I demand an explanation."

"Explanations can wait. Right now, we must take that fort and see if Antigonus somehow survived this debacle."

"Very well," Nikias said. "I accept you into our company."

"What?" Gabral snorted.

"Like you said," Nikias said with a grin, "as bearer of the Bladestaff, I am in command."

"What makes you think a boy like you could command me? I am a colonel in the elite guard. You will join my company and follow my orders."

"I am on a mission for King Leszek. On his authority, I command."

"And I am the emperor's champion, commissioned directly by him," Gabral spat. "So you *will* submit to me."

"Never!"

"Stop it, you fool," Wayra snapped at Nikias.

"I will not. I'm in charge."

"That does it," Gabral said. He raised the Mace, which burst into blue fire.

Nikias responded instantly, bringing the Bladestaff around, its silvery blades bursting into fire identical to Gabral's.

"Stop!" Harafin's voice cracked like a whip. His eyes flashed with power, and the temperature plummeted until ice formed in the air and fell around their feet in a tinkling cascade. "This will not happen."

The men lowered their weapons and the fires winked out. Harafin scowled. "Never before have bearers of the Six fought each other in anger, and it will not happen tonight. Should you do so, the consequences would be devastating."

"Fine," Gabral said. "Then tell him I'm in charge."

"Never," Nikias shot back.

Harafin raised his hands placatingly. "We don't have time for this. That fort must be taken immediately. May I suggest you both lead your companies in a joint assault? We can come to an agreement on the chain of command afterward."

With one last angry glare, Gabral said, "I accept your counsel, Master Harafin."

Nikias looked from one to the other. "So, I get to lead the charge? Great!"

Harafin turned back to Wayra. "Send some Kestrels to flank both sides of the fort in case anyone tries to escape. The rest of us will attack together."

Pairs of sentinels were dispatched in both directions while Gabral and his captains began barking orders. Most of the other Kestrels collapsed to the ground, exhausted from their efforts to kill Kevlin.

Ceren pulled Kevlin aside and asked shakily, "What happened back there?"

"We nearly died."

"I should have." Ceren stared past him, emerald eyes wide with remembered terror. Her face was streaked with grime and tears, and her hair hung in a tangled mane. In a whisper, she said, "It struck me, the magic. I *felt* it." She met his gaze. "It passed *through* me."

"You were touching me, and through me the amulet protected you too." If she hadn't needed him to carry her. . . Kevlin shuddered to think what might have happened.

He squeezed her shoulder. "Why did you come, Ceren? You didn't know you'd be protected. You could have died."

"I had to prove you weren't the only one who . . ." She trailed off and looked away.

"The only one who could what?" Kevlin demanded, gripping her shoulder. If not to help him, why do something so rash?

She shook off his arm and met his gaze. "You're not the only one who can be Cunning."

"What?"

The words came in an angry torrent. "You're just not satisfied being steward, are you? You have to run off into the woods and single-handedly take on a dozen sentinels? You want to be a hero that bad? You want to be Cunning?"

"Ceren, I--"

She talked right over him. "I'm not going to let that happen." She jabbed him in the chest with a finger. "You're not taking it away from me. *I* was chosen by Antigonus, and I'll do whatever it takes to prove I can do it!"

She spun away, but Kevlin pulled her back around.

"Let me go," she said and threw a punch at his face.

He caught her fist and held it. She struggled against his grip but he said, "Listen to me for a minute. You think I did that because I wanted glory? Because I wanted to take *your* title away from you? Really?"

She didn't look away, but seemed a little less sure of herself.

He blew out a breath. "Ceren, if I could give you Oris and name you steward, I would do it in a heartbeat."

"I don't believe you."

"Believe what you want. I never wanted any of this." He swung an arm around to take in the fort, the sentinels, and the soldiers preparing for battle. "I hate magic and I don't trust the people who use it. The last thing I want is *another* cryptic title from some ancient prophecy only Harafin understands."

"Then why. . .?"

Kevlin shrugged. "I have a job to do." He gestured toward the others. "Those men needed my help. I had the tools to protect them, so I had to try."

Her mouth moved silently, as if she was trying to say something but the words wouldn't come out.

"You look like a fish out of water," Kevlin laughed.

She snapped her jaw closed, but managed a weak smile. "I don't understand you, Kevlin."

"I'm the simplest of men, Ceren."

She snorted. "You're a liar too."

"I need you to believe me when I tell you I don't want your position. We need you." He nodded toward the fort. "Antigonus needs you. He chose you. You're Cunning. I don't think anyone can take that title away."

She frowned, considering his words.

He added, "I knew a man once who claimed he saw his face in a bloodset cloud. He died the next day in battle."

Ceren frowned. "I don't understand."

"He let himself get distracted. Did he really see his face? I don't know. I don't think it mattered. What mattered was that he didn't focus on the job at hand." He squeezed her shoulder again. "Don't let yourself get distracted, Ceren. You won't fail."

He turned and jogged toward the line of horses.

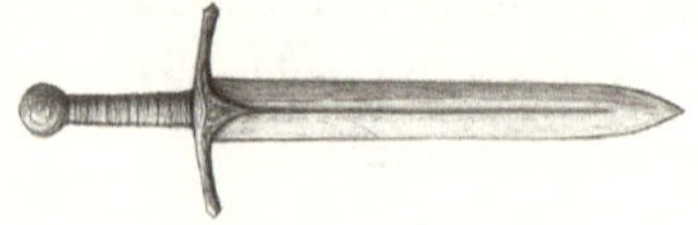

Ceren watched him go, her mind whirling and her heart filled with conflicting emotions. She stood for a moment, staring after him, then slowly shook her head.

That is the most complicated man I've ever met.

Indira approached. "Lady Ceren, are you all right?"

Ceren started to say her leg was hurt, but paused, a frown on her lips, because she felt no pain. She leaned down and probed her injured thigh with careful fingers. It felt whole and strong.

"I'm fine," she said with a smile, and cast another glance after Kevlin. Taking Indira's arm, she headed back toward the trees.

I have a lot to think about.

48

A Taste of Battle Magic

Ten minutes later, they charged.

All pretense at stealth gone, they galloped across the clearing with four large globes of amber light floating overhead like miniature suns.

In the center of the group, Harafin flung open his hand. A bolt of blue-white lightning, thick as his palm, arced across the field and exploded against the closed gates of the fortress. Although expected, it still proved an awesome sight, and dots of light danced in Kevlin's eyes from the after-effects of the flash. Dust and debris erupted into the air, momentarily blocking his view of the gates.

Even before the echoes faded, Wayra and her kestrels attacked in turn. Rippling sheets of lighting, interspersed with individual bolts, ripped the air and slammed into the fortress. Peals of thunder nearly knocked Kevlin from his saddle.

The wall disintegrated.

Thick timbers, engulfed in flames, exploded into the air and covered the scene in a dense pall of smoke. Wood screamed as it splintered, and the entire fort groaned under the onslaught.

Wayra's misguided attack still angered Kevlin, but even he had to admit her force was very effective at their work.

May the gods grant Antigonus is still alive.

It was a slim hope, but he clung to it harder than he did to the saddle of his galloping mount.

Nikias raised the Bladestaff and whooped with excitement.

Gabral glared at him, raised the Mace above his head, and shouted the traditional battle cry, "For the Light and the Empire!"

Kevlin and the Tamarri soldiers in the company all echoed him.

"Kamen Seig!" Jerrik bellowed the Donarri war cry from the left flank where he led a company toward the north end of the wall.

Drystan responded from the right flank where he led an identical company south. "Elu Falas Ke Gairahan!"

Every Einarri soldier responded in unison. "Ke Gairahan!"

Nikias glanced from one group to the next, then shouted, "For King and the Lady!" Then he glared at Gabral galloping slightly ahead of the rest of them. "Hey, I'm supposed to lead the charge."

Gabral ignored him. Nikias spurred his mount harder, but only managed to pull even with Kevlin, who rode just behind the colonel.

The smoke cleared to reveal the damage. Most of the wall had been reduced to piles of charred timber. The two small buildings flanking the gate still stood, forming an alley into the main fort. One side of the gate was simply gone while the other hung open, twisted half off its hinges and engulfed in fire. Behind the gate, makrasha scurried through the charred wreckage.

At that moment, Adalia and her archers rose from their hiding places far ahead of the horsemen and unleashed the first volley from their bows. The hunters had taken a significant gamble by approaching far closer to the fortress than had been discussed, no more than fifty yards from the wall. Kevlin could imagine their terror as they lay in the grass with debris falling all around them from the top of the cliff.

Yet the hardy folk clung to the plan and fired. The first volley dropped half a dozen makrasha, and the second did the same. Although few in number, the archers proved their skill.

With most of the defenders' cover gone, they kept a steady stream of deadly missiles hurtling through the debris, striking down makrasha with nearly every shaft. Even the vaunted archers of Freyarr would have been hard-pressed to do better.

Nikias whooped again and called out to Kevlin, "You're lucky Wayra didn't let me come after you this morning."

If he can fight half as good as he boasts, he'll be unstoppable.

A robed figure carrying a staff of twisted wood stepped in front of the ranks of the creatures massing in the broken gate.

Tanathos, Kevlin assumed at first, but this shadeleech was shorter and their eyes glowed white. After another second, he realized it was a woman.

She pointed her staff at Gabral, who rode at the head of the assault force a couple hundred yards from the fort. A bolt of red energy shot from her upraised staff and streaked toward him.

Gabral was prepared. With a yell, he extended the Mace. Blue light spread from it to surround him in a ghostly nimbus of energy. The red lightning struck with an explosion that blasted the colonel right off his horse.

Gabral hung motionless in the air for a split second before falling to the ground. He landed on his feet, furious but unharmed.

Nikias passed so close that he nearly clipped Gabral in the head with one stirrup. "Serves you right!"

Kevlin and Nikias rode at the front of the company, with Leander just behind. The shadeleech again raised her staff.

Nikias shouted, "I'll show him how to deal with a shadeleech."

Before he could do whatever he planned, a bolt of blue energy flashed so close past Kevlin that it singed his skin. The magic barreled down on the shadeleech, but struck an invisible shield a span in front of her and careened up into the darkness.

"Wait," Nikias shouted. "This one is mine."

I don't think so.

The young man's boasting fanned Kevlin's still-smoldering anger, and he focused it on the new target. Kevlin raised his spear, willed the energy still burning in his veins into the weapon, and *threw* it.

As he released the spear, two more bolts of magic flashed past, cast by the kestrels. The spear shot from his hand faster than an arrow, trailing blue fire in its wake.

The shadeleech cried out, hands raised, as the kestrels' magic struck her shield. It shuddered under the double impact, and for a second became visible as a wall of energy. Instead of bouncing off, the bolts flowed up the shield and exploded. The shield rocked.

Kevlin's spear struck.

It blasted through the weakened shield and drove into the shadeleech's chest, splashing blue fire in all directions. It punched through her torso and protruded from her back.

Kevlin raised a fist in triumph.

"Hey!" Nikias shouted.

Several makrasha rushed forward to help the injured shadeleech, but a dense, black cloud engulfed two of them. They screamed and writhed within the concealing darkness, dim shadows suffering some unknown torment.

When the darkness dissipated, the monsters' skeletal remains collapsed at the shadeleech's feet. She rose again, then amazingly grabbed hold of the spear in her chest, broke off the shaft, and extracted the pieces from her chest and back.

Leander's war hammer streaked past Kevlin. The spinning weapon slammed into her, knocking her back into the gathered makrasha.

The beasts along the wall of rubble and packed into the gate raised their crossbows to fire.

They never had a chance. Multicolored fire roared across their lines. Makrasha howled and collapsed, thrashing in agony or beating at the flames in helpless desperation. The beasts at the gate trampled each other in a mad panic to escape the engulfing inferno.

Unopposed, Kevlin and Nikias closed on the gate and the burning creatures clustered there. The fire winked out just before they arrived.

Kevlin's well-trained warhorse pounded over the charred remains of the beasts, never breaking stride as it closed on the ranks of Makrasha. The still-living beasts re-formed a defensive line twenty feet behind the gate, in the narrow alley that led into the fort. Kevlin's world contracted until it included nothing but his sword, his horse, and his target.

They struck.

Kevlin's mount trampled two of the beasts, and the force of impact nearly unhorsed him. As their bones were crushed, the creatures howled in disturbing, high-pitched screeches. On both sides of Kevlin, soldiers slammed into and through the first ranks of defenders.

Then he was slashing at hideous faces and necks, trying to overpower them before they could strike back. The familiar sights and sounds of battle washed over him. The screaming of men and horses, the clashing of steel, the smell of fear and blood assaulted him from every side.

A line of a dozen makrasha in tight formation stretched across the end of the alley. They all bore huge rectangular shields, wider than a man and just as tall. Half of them carried pikes or spears, while the others brandished twin swords. Behind them another fifty beasts filled the near side of the parade ground.

The makrasha were giants, nearly able to look him in the eye as he sat astride his warhorse. Their helmets were rounded on top, with face guards extending down between the creatures' flat, green eyes as far as their hideous wide mouths. Five short horns protruded from the top. Kevlin's heart sank as he recognized them.

The Hands of Death.

Members of the legendary elite Grakonian force, they were said to be the personal guard of the Sigrun. The empire had always paid a heavy price to defeat them. It was beyond reason to find members of the Hands of Death in the remote fortress.

He had seen none of them the last time. Had they arrived as reinforcements?

There was no time to wonder about it. Raising his sword above his head, Kevlin roared a battle cry older than the empire.

"For Light and life!"

They charged, with more soldiers pushing through the narrow gate behind. They collided with the Grakonian line like a storm-churned wave flinging itself against the shore, and drove the defenders back several paces.

The line held, the makrasha repulsing them. Screams and curses accompanied the flashing of swords and spears that struck wildly from both sides. The fighting raged intense and brutal, with neither side giving quarter.

Kevlin pounded on the shield of a makrasha and barely ducked the return strike.

This is stupid. We can't overpower them this way. The alley is too narrow.

A bolt of blue magic burned past his head and *melted* the creature's face. It shrieked and clutched at its head while its skin liquefied.

Kevlin retreated from the horrible sight but couldn't tear his eyes from the creature as it fell to the ground. As its flesh bubbled away, he caught a glimpse of the white of its skull.

Then Leander arrived.

The Hammer stalwart leaped past Kevlin. Ignoring the ruin of the beast still writhing underfoot, he stepped into the gap and struck two mighty blows. Two creatures crumpled to the ground on either side.

The old man snarled like a wolf, and rage poured off him like a wave of blistering heat. His eyes burned with hatred so fierce that Kevlin hesitated to join him.

Another makrasha attacked, but Leander struck it down. His hammer blurred in the air. Leander then raised the bloody weapon and roared, more a howl of animal rage than a battle cry. The sound reverberated in the tight alley, and man and beast alike cringed away from him.

The enraged stalwart stalked forward and smashed another creature to the ground.

Nikias charged past Kevlin, whooping and trailing twin streamers of blue fire. He leaped into the gap, the Bladestaff whistling around him in dazzling, flaming arcs that shredded makrasha on every side.

Like legends incarnate, he and Leander shattered the left flank of the Grakonian line till monsters began fighting each other in their attempts to flee.

Gabral arrived next, speeding through the ranks of soldiers with the burning Mace held high. Men pressed against the wall to give him room as he charged the right flank of the makrasha line. One stepped forward to meet the little colonel, and the Mace punched through its heavy shield and shattered the creature's chest.

That broke the spell, and Kevlin and the other soldiers launched forward again to rejoin the attack.

The defenders broke.

Makrasha pushed back into the parade ground to get away, but found no escape. Led by Leander and the two bearers, the assault force pushed deep into the enemy ranks and split them into two groups.

A boom from behind the defenders drew Kevlin's eyes. A huge ball of red fire arced over the creatures and fell toward the soldiers. It was so vast there was no way he could ensure it struck him first so the amulet could nullify it.

Glittering gold light intercepted the fireball and shattered it into a thousand shards. Kevlin breathed a sigh of relief. Sometimes it was actually nice having sentinels around.

Kevlin paused and turned to the north, *knowing* that Jerrik and his men were coming. The giant Donarri warrior rounded the corner of what had been the stables, roaring like a berserker. Followed by his men, Jerrik charged into the left flank of the Grakonians, swinging his massive battle-axe with devastating effect.

The Hands of Death's advantage over most Tamerlane soldiers in size and raw power was lacking against Jerrik. Nearly their equal in size, Jerrik wielded his heavy axe in lightning strikes. Inspired by his example, his men attacked ferociously, driving the Grakonians back in a disorganized mass.

At the same time, Drystan and his men swarmed the Grakonians from the right flank. Where Jerrik relied on his size and overwhelming strength, Drystan moved in a deadly blur.

The lanky Einarri warrior descended on the makrasha like a whirlwind. Kevlin had never seen his equal with the spear. Drystan's movements were as graceful as they were fast, as if stepping to a dance whose music he alone could hear.

Drystan's men fought to keep up, and one soldier overextended himself in trying to match his captain's speed, stumbling to the ground at the feet of a makrasha. Without missing a beat, Drystan yanked a javelin from the quiver on his back and hurled it through the open mouth of the beast before it could finish the soldier.

Drystan continued with a spin, using the momentum to strike down another makrasha. The advantage of his unusually long-headed spear became apparent, as he used the weapon equally for slashing and stabbing, flowing from one movement to the next in an unbroken rhythm.

Under the united onslaught, the makrasha lines disintegrated. Soldiers swarmed over them, shouting in victory.

At that moment, the toad-faced shadeleech woman with hideous white eyes stepped through the command building's shattered front door, followed by a dozen makrasha. She raised her staff and shouted a single word of power that slithered into Kevlin's ears and down his spine like a snake.

Fire engulfed them from all sides, searing their lungs and skin.

The amulet grew warm against Kevlin's chest as it captured the magic, but it didn't quench the flames.

There was nowhere to run, no way to hide.

Then it was gone.

The fire lasted but a heartbeat, more like a waking nightmare than something tangible, yet Kevlin shivered with lingering terror. Thank the gods that the sentinels managed to counter that spell before she destroyed the entire company in a single stroke.

"Your evil power will not avail you," Harafin declared. The sentinel had managed to climb to the shattered roof of one of the small buildings flanking the gate.

The white-eyed shadeleech raised her staff, and a bolt of magic flashed through the air toward him. It deflected harmlessly away. Whatever shield Harafin used, it remained invisible.

The sentinel leaped off the building. The air beneath him darkened into an opaque slide which he descended to the parade ground to face the shadeleech. Wayra and her kestrels pushed through the ranks of soldiers to flank him.

"I'll deal with this," Nikias said, charging from the left, but the shadeleech and sentinels all ignored him.

"I am Harafin." The sentinel's voice boomed unnaturally loud, echoing off the walls. "I command you to surrender."

The woman swayed, as if his words had struck her a physical blow. Her face drained of color until its pallor matched her hideous eyes.

"You will not take me," she shrieked, then added, "Tanathos, you betrayer!"

Then she threw her arms wide. A dense black cloud descended over the porch and all the makrasha upon it. Inside the dark mist, the creatures writhed in agony and emitted ear-piercing wails. Three heartbeats later, the cloud dissipated and where makrasha had stood, only piles of withered bones remained.

"Beware," Harafin shouted. In unison, he and the other sentinels raised hands shining with brilliant white light.

Nikias charged past them and leaped for the stairs to the porch where the shadeleech burned with crimson magic.

He reached the steps and vaulted them in a single bound, the Bladestaff flashing down toward the shadeleech.

With a demonic laugh, she exploded.

49

An Unexpected Power of Healing

The blast catapulted Nikias into the air and threw him across the parade ground, where he smashed through the sagging roof of the stables. The Bladestaff flew from his hand and tumbled far out into the field outside the fort.

The shockwave knocked Kevlin and most of the other soldiers to the ground. Men gagged, and some vomited, from the cloying stench of smoke and burned flesh.

Curse magic and all who wield it, Kevlin thought, as he rubbed smoke out of his eyes. *Give me a swordfight any day.*

He stood as his vision cleared, then groaned. The shadeleech was gone, as was the porch. Only shattered, burning wreckage marked where the command center had stood.

The kestrels stood in a line facing the rubble, with Harafin in the center, a shimmering nimbus of light still visible from the shields they'd used to deflect most of the blast.

"Antigonus," Kevlin cried. He stumbled forward until the heat from the burning wreckage pushed him back. No one could have survived.

The huge funeral pyre mocked his failure.

At least now Antigonus was at peace. That didn't help Kevlin much, though. He'd have to keep the rock until Harafin found another bearer. If they didn't find one before the solstice, he was going to drop the rock into the ocean before it blew them all to the next world.

Kevlin's eyes burned from the smoke and his muscles shook with post-battle exhaustion. Antigonus was supposed to be such a powerful sentinel. Kevlin wished he'd known the man before Bajaran's cursed dagger struck him down.

Harafin raised a hand, and the flames winked out. Even as soldiers staggered to their feet, he called, "Colonel Gabral."

"Aye." The short officer trotted over. He looked unaffected by the shadeleech's explosion. He'd already pulled off his helm, and sweat-drenched hair lay matted against his head.

"I sense no shadeleeches in the immediate vicinity, but keep your men on alert for an ambush. Post a double guard, and search the fort."

"Aye." Despite Gabral's insistence about being in command, he saluted before barking orders. He ran a hand through his hair and grimaced.

Some soldiers began searching for wounded, while others moved to defensive positions along the shattered wall, or spread out to search the rubble for any surviving makrasha.

Wayra pointed at the wreckage of the command building, calling to her kestrels. "Move this rubble. Find Antigonus' body. We cannot rest until he is found."

The group, some sagging with exhaustion, approached the wreckage with glowing hands. Debris floated into the air and piled against the base of the cliff.

Kevlin still blamed Wayra for the disaster, but her dedication to finding Antigonus diminished his hatred a little. Pushing aside the dark despair, he moved to join Harafin, who stood surveying the kestrels' efforts.

"We must discover if Tanathos is buried here too," Harafin said to Wayra.

"Do you really think he might be?" Kevlin asked.

Wayra glanced over and glared. "Get back, you fool."

Kevlin glared. "I want Antigonus found at least as much as you do."

Wayra waved him away. "Don't be stupid, man. The old fool's dead. All that matters is finding Oris."

She turned away, and Kevlin stared after her. She was one cold-hearted piece of work.

Harafin placed a hand on his shoulder. The old man looked tired and sad. He shook his head and motioned Kevlin back.

Kevlin turned away from the cascading wave of rubble that swiftly piled against the cliff. Billowing dust covered the area in a light haze that mixed with the sentinel lights, coloring everything in a strange twilight.

Sweeping his gaze across the devastation, Kevlin fought to hold back despair. He noticed Indira exiting the stables, followed by a pair of soldiers carrying Nikias in a makeshift stretcher. They set him down, and she began working on his broken body.

Dawn had not yet arrived and despite the glowing orbs of sentinel magic, deep shadows still clung to much of the fort. In the near-darkness, Indira's creamy skin glowed. Whether it was her healing magic, or a trick caused by the hazy air, the effect was powerful and he couldn't look away.

He hadn't been able to determine any falsehood in her goodness. As he studied her beautiful face, he suddenly longed to understand how she maintained it despite the grim work she was often forced to undertake. She leaned farther over Nikias' unmoving form and her midnight hair fell forward and obscured her face from view.

He decided to talk with her. He could use some peace and she was the only person around who he trusted to ask.

He was just opening his mouth to call to her when a clicking sound caught his attention. It came a second time from the darkness of the shattered stables behind Indira, and there was no mistaking the disgusting noise.

Makrasha.

Two of the giant beasts rushed from the darkness, howling with delight as they descended on Indira.

Instead of screaming or fleeing, she stepped toward the monsters and raised her hands as if to push them away from her patient.

Kevlin had never imagined her simple goodness might stem from being an idiot.

As one of the beasts raised a sword to strike Indira down, Ceren appeared from behind a pile of rubble and leaped forward, shouting, "Indira, run!"

The second beast caught Ceren mid-leap with a backhand blow that smashed her to the ground in a crumpled heap.

The first beast slashed at Indira's head, a mighty blow that could split a person in half.

"No!" Kevlin sprinted toward her. He'd never arrive in time to help. Behind him, warning cries rang throughout the fort, but they were all too slow.

The blade never touched Indira.

A finger's width above her unflinching face, the huge blade bounced back as if it had struck a solid wall.

Kevlin didn't have time to wonder at it. Shouting a wordless cry of rage, he lunged past Indira and plunged his blade through a rent in the huge creature's armor. It sank to the hilt and hot blood poured over his hands.

The makrasha howled and thrashed in pain, ripping the sword out of Kevlin's hand. The second monster aimed a crossbow at him. Only three feet away, it couldn't miss.

It pulled the trigger.

The impact staggered Kevlin back as the small bolt punched through his leather armor and sank to the fletching in his side. Agony shot through him, so intense he couldn't breathe, couldn't scream. Bile rose in his throat, and he tasted his own blood.

He fumbled for his dagger, his hand slow and uncoordinated, but the monster clubbed him in the side of the head with the crossbow.

Darkness took him.

50

THE PATH OF DANGERS

I *can't believe this is happening,* Sitara lamented as she hurried toward the sanctuary of her own room. *The world has gone mad.*

She walked fast, ignoring the people she passed, not caring that many of them turned to stare after her. She was unable to hide the tears streaming openly down her face.

She had to get back to her room, had to be alone. It seemed like an eternity before she reached the Emperor's Palace and the keisara's tower. With a sigh of relief, she made her way toward her own small room.

Just in front of her, the door to the keisara's study opened and Keisara Fideima stepped into the hall.

There was nowhere to hide.

"Sitara," her mistress exclaimed in surprise when she caught sight of Sitara's tear-streaked face. "Whatever is the matter?" She placed a comforting hand on Sitara's shoulder.

"Oh, Your Majesty," she sobbed. It was useless to try to pretend nothing was wrong, and the touch of a hand extended in friendship broke down her restraint. Tears started flowing anew. For a moment she could do nothing but sob into the taller woman's shoulder.

"What's the matter?" the Keisara repeated in a deeply concerned tone.

Sitara wiped her eyes and caught her breath. She could not deny how good it felt to release some of her pent-up emotions, but the fact that it was the keisara's shoulder twisted her gut. She wished she were alone so she could be sick.

"I'm sorry for this terrible display of emotion," she apologized.

"Nonsense," her mistress said softly. "Tell me what is the matter."

"It is a private matter. I should not bother you with it."

"Sitara," the Keisara's voice held a threat of reprimand. "I wish to know what causes you to weep."

"I received word today that my grandmother is very ill," Sitara lied. "She may be on her deathbed."

"I thought you told me you had no family to speak of."

Oops.

Of course she had. The lie had seemed so appropriate at the time. Claiming to have no family was the best way to avoid any future questions regarding them.

If only she had remembered. She should have said she was weeping in sympathy for all the keisara herself was going through.

"I don't," Sitara said, wiping her nose on her handkerchief.

"Sitara, you're not making sense," Keisara Fideima said sternly, assuming that regal look she adopted when displeased.

"How can you have a family and yet not have a family?"

A woman stepped into the hallway behind the keisara. The blonde, blue-eyed woman could have easily been mistaken for one of her majesty's relatives. She stood a little taller than Sitara, with a full figure and clear complexion unmarred by lines or blemishes.

The Keisara turned to the newcomer and frowned. "Sentinel Omolara, you may be here at the command of my husband, but I must insist that you stop skulking around behind me."

Omolara made a graceful curtsy and retreated a step. "I am very sorry, Your Majesty. I did not intend any harm. I couldn't help but overhear your conversation and I find myself intrigued."

The Keisara turned back to Sitara. "Sentinel Omolara has been assigned as additional protection until my attacker is found."

Sitara had not imaged things could get worse.

"A pleasure to meet you," Omolara said with a warm smile. "I am also assisting with the investigation, so I'll want to speak with you privately as soon as time permits."

"First," Keisara Fideima said, "you will explain yourself, Sitara."

Sitara nodded as panic-driven thoughts rang through her mind like a death knell. She used the excuse of wiping tears from her face to buy another second to think. "I must ask your forgiveness, Your Majesty," she said humbly. "I fear I misled you when I first entered your service."

"What do you mean?" The Keisara's expression settled into an unreadable mask.

"You see," Sitara kept an eye on Omolara while appearing to give her full attention to the keisara, "my family disowned me when I left home, so I find them a painful topic to discuss. That's why I said I had no family to speak of. I meant it exactly as I said it. I do not speak of them. I did not mean that I did not actually have a family."

Keisara Fideima regarded her for a moment, but it was the sight of Omolara's face tightening in concentration that set Sitara's heart skipping a fearful beat. She knew that look. Omolara was preparing to use magic.

She couldn't fight the sentinel. Instead, she focused on a mental image of her grandmother lying sick in bed.

There. She felt the tickle of Omolara's mind touching her own. It was a feather-soft touch, but she recognized it. She wasn't sure how much the sentinel could sense with such a light probing, but she forced herself to focus only on the thought of her sick grandmother.

"That's a very convoluted explanation," the Keisara said finally. "I am displeased with you."

Sitara bowed her head and said nothing.

"You have always served me faithfully," Fideima added, "so I find it uncharacteristic of you to do something to warrant your family disowning you. What was your crime?"

"I . . . my parents believed very strongly that a young woman should be a maid when she is married, and I. . .well, I. . ."

Again she felt the touch of Omolara's mind, and she cast about for an image of a young man to create as the partner in her alleged crime.

Remiel.

His image in her mind was so surprising, she nearly cried out, but it was too late to change it. Omolara might have already caught a glimpse of him.

She clothed him in the simple garb of a farmer, and forced herself to generate feelings of affection for him.

The pig.

Then she switched to an image of her parents, her father furious and her mother weeping. It was easy to do. Her brothers had provoked such a scene on many occasions.

"I see," Keisara Fideima said.

Sitara looked up to see an expression of pain flit across the Keisara's face. Her eyes stared off down the hallway, a single tear in one of them.

Sitara hadn't consciously chosen a deed so similar to what she had been tempting the keisara to commit, but she could not have chosen a better one.

The taller woman stepped away slowly. "I am sorry you were so foolish."

"So am I. I vowed never to tarnish the family's honor again, even though they refuse to know anything more of me. While I bear this shame, I do not speak of them."

She watched her mistress carefully as her words had the intended effect. Fideima seemed to shrink within herself, her own pain clearly evident before she turned away to hide her tears.

"Thank you for clarifying the matter for me."

Sitara curtsied to the Keisara's back. "Yes, Majesty."

"You are relieved of your duties for the afternoon to grieve in private. Omolara will attend me."

"Thank you, Your Majesty."

"I too am sorry for your grief." Omolara's eyes shone bright with the reflected light of her gift.

Sitara took her leave, trying not to run.

"Oh, Sitara," the Keisara called after her.

"Majesty?"

"Perhaps this provides an opportunity to repair relations with your family. If you wish to visit your grandmother, I will pay your passage home."

"Thank you," Sitara replied, surprised. "I had not considered that."

"Let me know tomorrow what you decide."

When Sitara reached the safety of her room, she threw herself on her bed as a wave of grief swept over her. It was a long time before she finally rolled onto her back and wiped the tears from her face.

All hope was lost. Bajaran was dead. The cold finality of that thought brought fresh tears to her eyes, but she forced herself to face the reality of it. He was dead. He was never coming for her. They would never rule together. She would never again feel his arms holding her.

That sentinel, Omolara, would be around constantly, searching for clues. How long could Sitara fool her? The initial fear of discovery had just started to dim, replaced by a tiny glimmer of hope that she might remain undiscovered.

That hope was now dashed. Omolara already considered her a liar. One more slip, and surely she would be exposed.

After a time, Sitara roused herself to wash her face. Almost immediately, a soft knock came at the door. It opened and the blond-haired sentinel poked her head in.

Omolara smiled. "I'm glad to see you up and about." She stepped into the room and closed the door behind her.

Sitara suppressed a flash of irritation at the intrusion. Omolara was a sentinel with the emperor's own commission. She could do whatever she pleased. Sitara, a lowly handmaiden, had no right to object.

The woman seated herself at Sitara's small desk, motioning Sitara to perch on the bed. "I have a few questions I'd like to ask you."

"Of course."

"The keisara has been the victim of a very subtle mind attack."

"It's terrible." Sitara adopted a look of innocent terror. "I'm so glad you're here to protect us."

"This suggests a well-trained assailant possessing a deft touch with magic."

Sitara felt a flash of pride at the compliment. Perhaps her training had progressed farther than she'd thought.

"Assaulting a mind is delicate work," Omolara continued. "It is most effective when one knows the victim or can strike from close proximity."

"So the attacker came here?" Sitara glanced around as if someone might be hiding in the room.

"That is what I need to determine. Has anyone unusual visited these apartments lately?"

"No, not that I can remember."

Sitara regretted the words as soon as they left her lips. What a fool! She had just squandered a perfect opportunity to invent someone for Omolara to chase.

"No one else remembers any strangers either," Omolara said. "Which is the most puzzling part of the mystery. How did they approach close enough to strike?"

"I don't know," Sitara replied, then frowned thoughtfully. "The only time we've left over the past few days was to visit the audience hall."

"When?" Omolara leaned forward. "When did she go?"

Sitara managed to look surprised and made a show of thinking. "Several days ago, and then again just the other day."

"Is that unusual?"

"Yes. The keisara rarely goes to listen to petitions. They're so boring."

"Don't you see?" Omolara exclaimed. "That's it! That's where the attacker struck."

"Do you really think so?"

"Of course." Omolara sat back, lost in thought. After a moment, she rose. "I'll check with the office of records. They'll have a listing of everyone who attended on both days. Our attacker is probably on those lists. Thank you, Sitara. You've been wonderful."

Omolara gave her a little hug and hurried for the door.

Sitara beamed. Omolara had taken the bait. She must be new to the palace. Sometimes hundreds of people attended a single audience session, and many of them came to every one. The list of possibilities would be enormous. Omolara was going to be very busy chasing down false leads, probably for weeks.

The door reopened and Omolara popped her head back in. "Oh, I almost forgot. I've been ordered to cast a simple Truth spell on everyone who has spent time with the keisara over the past month, to see if anything has been overlooked."

Sitara's smile fell, dragged down by the burning avalanche of recent hope.

Truth.

That single word resounded like an executioner's drumbeat in her heart.

She fought to keep the look of horror from her face, but Omolara must have noticed something. "Don't worry. I'll explain it to you later. It won't hurt, and it'll only take a few minutes."

"That doesn't sound so bad."

Omolara gave a final wave. "I don't have time for it now, and I expect I'll be busy tomorrow, so let's plan on the day after.

"That will be perfect," Sitara said with forced cheer.

The closing of the door was like the sealing of a coffin. Sitara threw herself back on the bed and pounded on the sheets with her fists.

Two days.

In two days, her life would end. She might have fooled Omolara for now, but had no illusions that her secrets could remain hidden against the power of Truth.

Under its power, Truth denied anyone the ability to speak falsehood. Through its influence, conflicting accounts could be resolved, and spells of darkness dispersed.

Black despair washed over her, and Sitara tugged at her hair in terror. She could think of no good option. If she tried to fight, she would die. She might take Omolara by surprise, but she could never conceal the deed. Other sentinels would destroy her.

No, Sitara was alone and surrounded by enemies. She could not escape.

If you wish to visit your grandmother, I will pay your passage home.

She sat up, fear driven back by a spark of hope. This was her chance. She could depart the capital on the next ship headed for Freyarr. She could leave before the impending interview and not look like she was fleeing. Once she landed in Parthalan, she could disappear. They would never find her.

Sitara sank slowly back onto her pillow as the full ramifications of this plan sank in. If she left, she would be admitting defeat and throwing away everything she and Bajaran had worked so hard to accomplish. Instead of leading the revolution, she would be running from her destiny.

Worse, she could never use her gift again. Ever since she had discovered her gift, it had been a glorious light burning inside her soul, warming and strengthening her. Could she turn away from it forever?

She would have to. She could not return to the sentinels and resume her studies as an accepted. After learning of their evil ways, she could never join them. That meant she could never reveal her powers and risk discovery.

She lay pondering the kind of life she could build for herself, and it was not encouraging. She could never approach any of the seats of power for fear of someone recognizing her from her years at the palace. That meant a life of obscurity in some remote village. The more she considered such a future, the less it appealed to her.

What other option did she have?

Only one. Remiel.

She rose, splashed water on her face and looked in the mirror. Her face was a mess, her eyes puffy and red, haunted by fear and grief. She sat on the bed and for the first time seriously considered Remiel's offer.

That made her punch one of her pillows in frustrated anger. Why did he have to make it so difficult?

He was the only other option available. Doing nothing would guarantee discovery within two days, followed by torture and death. Worst of all, the keisara would know of her betrayal. This triggered such a wave of anguish that Sitara clutched her midsection and moaned.

She could not leave. Tempting though it might seem, she could not accept the life of mediocrity that would result from running. She knew that life and could never return to it.

No, her destiny included greater things. Bajaran had opened her eyes to her potential, and although he lay dead, murdered before his lofty goals could be realized, she could not throw away the destiny he had laid out for her.

He was a great man, but only she remained to see his dream realized. She couldn't turn away from it. She had to reach for it, to grasp for victory. She might die in the attempt, but her soul would die inside her if she didn't at least try.

That meant dealing with Remiel.

At least he was very handsome. Other women would have accepted the invitation eagerly. Still, she hesitated. Bajaran was her one great love. The thought of giving herself to Remiel made her feel dirty. Could she really make such a sacrifice for the good of all?

She lay awake long into the night, steeling her heart for what she had to do.

51

THE PATH TO GLORY

As dawn crept across the world, a crow flew over the devastated remains of the fort. Unlike the other carrion birds hunting for warm flesh, the crow did not slow, but circled low overhead. Its eyes sought the living, not the dead.

As it flapped its wings, feathers began falling away. Its claws cracked, and its beak split. After one final turn, it fell like a stone, landing in a puff of dust just outside what remains of the fort wall.

Only three miles away, Tanathos cursed. That rubble held both the tantalizing promise of glory and the threat of destruction.

The man Kevlin was so close, and with him the prize that would assure Tanathos' seat on the Sigrun council. He yearned to take it. He could taste the sweet power of Kevlin's soul. He would rip it out of the man and suck it dry. It would feed him for weeks. The more powerful and cunning the enemy, the more glorious the victory over their souls.

Kevlin, the man who made him a fool.

To think he had held the man's life in his hand but squandered the opportunity. The memory of falling in that cell seared his mind.

Kevlin was no sentinel, yet he had done more damage than Tanathos could have imagined. He had stolen Oris right out from under their noses, killed Haraz, and taken Bajaran's marvelous amulet.

With that powerful relic, Tanathos could have faced Harafin without fear. Kevlin had singlehandedly destroyed everything Tanathos had worked so hard to gain, snatching it from the jaws of victory.

He'd never longed to annihilate anyone so badly.

Snarling with fury, he took a step toward the fort concealed by the heavy forest. There lay glory.

He stopped. There lay destruction.

Harafin. With that name came fear and a return to reason. Harafin was the most hated of the sentinels. Merely thinking the name filled Tanathos with dread. Harafin, who always seemed to find a way to thwart the Sigrun. Any other sentinel, and he would throw himself into battle, confident of victory.

Such irony that it was that man standing between him and Oris. The quorum of masters had attempted to destroy Harafin many times, yet somehow the sentinel always prevailed.

Even Kyllikki and Nyyrikki, the twin rulers of the quorum, had been defeated by him when they first rose up in rebellion, murdered their teachers, and launched the Great Revolution. They lived by his mercy, marred permanently with skin and hair tinged blue by the after-effects of his power.

Sigrun Zvonko, humiliated after a particularly disastrous attempt on Harafin's life, had hunted the man down alone. He'd left a seat open at the council table as a result.

Tanathos was one of many who yearned to fill it and had plotted and murdered and maneuvered through the past decades to win it. For with acceptance at the table of Sigrun, with passage into the quorum, came unbelievable power.

Tanathos had proven himself so many times, positioned himself with excruciating care to win the coveted seat. He struggled to maintain control. He, Tanathos, who should be preparing to return to Grakonia carrying Oris and glory in his wake, was instead running for his life from the one sentinel he could not defeat.

He took several deep breaths to calm himself. There had to be a way. Facing Harafin was suicide, but returning empty-handed would be worse.

Only half a hundred makrasha, whose souls he could suck dry, remained to him. The halimaw crouched on the ground nearby, emanating raw power even while inactive. As its amber eyes met his, it opened its long maw and growled. Even the power of that mighty beast was not enough.

Antigonus lay bound in a stretcher carried by two of the makrasha, while the new prisoners lay unconscious nearby. Even if he could use them, the risk of facing Harafin was too great.

They could keep Antigonus alive a while longer, but without Oris, the old man was virtually useless. It would be better to kill him.

A sudden idea burned so bright that Tanathos gasped at its audacity. He stood still for a minute, breathing fast. The more he pondered it, the quicker his heart raced.

He threw his head back and laughed long and loud as he gloried in the revelation. If the Sigrun knew what he planned, they would rip out his soul. That made his smile widen. The next time they saw him, they would bow down and worship him.

Glory be mine.

Defeat, an unfamiliar taint, would never threaten him again. His very first command had won an overwhelming victory. He had personally tortured dozens of women and children taken prisoner from the village his force had destroyed.

That day, he had tasted true power for the first time as he glutted himself on their pain and the undefiled essence of those innocent souls. That glory had launched his career, and never had he bettered the accomplishments of that day.

Soon he would rise above even the greatest of the Sigrun.

His first victory had given him a new name. In the ancient tongue, it meant 'Destruction of purity,' and he allowed it to be spoken only as his force's battle cry. The power of that name had never been stained with defeat. With his next conquest, he would assure victory everlasting, and his new name would be revered by all.

His mind raced as he orchestrated the components of the plan and considered how to place his assets. Concentrating, he shielded his mind and cast a thought over the forest. It took a few minutes to find the mind he sought, and every mile his thoughts traveled consumed ever greater amounts of power.

The risk of detection by Harafin or the other sentinels increased equally. Although he would soon be above worrying about them, for the moment they remained a very real risk.

There. The one he sought sharpened into focus in his mind's eye by its unique signature. The connection solidified, and without preamble Tanathos projected a thought down the length of the magical channel.

The plan has changed. Commence your attack immediately.

It is too soon. The shadeleech was cautious, his mind well shielded, and his response exactly what Tanathos expected.

You question me? Tanathos asked.

Never. But can you escape with the prize? Once we attack, the response will be swift. You were supposed to be gone already.

As I said, the plan has changed. Your task is to obey, and to launch the first attack with the rising sun.

It will be done.

Tanathos severed the connection and paused a moment to wipe sweat from his brow. The connection had been taxing. He needed to ration the souls still at his disposal, so instead of destroying one of the beasts, he drew a little power from each of them.

Over the next half hour, he contacted four other shadeleeches to give them new orders.

The board was set and the pieces moving. Only Dhanjal remained. He summoned the Blade Stalwart, and the man approached with his normal, confident stride.

"What is it you wish, son of EnKur?" Dhanjal asked.

"What word of your brothers?"

"There is one in Fiachra."

"What force does he command?"

"Four hundred."

Perfect. "Summon him."

"He cannot arrive in time. Let us go and dance the song of Savas together."

Tanathos waved a hand dismissively. "This battle is of no moment. The plan has changed." He outlined what he needed.

Dhanjal nodded. "I will see it done, but I do not understand why you request this."

"My reasons are my own, but be assured that through this, war will soon consume the Six Kingdoms."

"Too long has the song of Savas been absent from these shores."

"That's about to change. Forever."

Dhanjal spun on his heel and strode back to his men. A moment later, a pigeon shot skyward with a note attached to its leg.

The final piece in place.

Tanathos smiled. Mounting his horse, he spurred the animal north along the narrow path, racing toward destiny and glory everlasting.

52

THE WEIGHT OF POWER

Rhisart, Gerent of Il'Aicharen, paced his large study as he considered the best way to utilize the pitiful number of teachers available to him. The students were holding up well so far, but it would not be long before discipline began to crack.

Why did Wayra not contact him? He had not the time or energy to waste casting his mind over thousands of square miles in search of her. He didn't even have enough qualified sentinels to form a conclave and reach out to the high council.

Rhisart was isolated. Alone.

That thought left him with a deep sense of foreboding. He tried to push it away, but could not. At Il'Aicharen, he not only oversaw the training of accepted and managed the daily activities of the keep, but he protected a vital node of power. That was the main reason so many kestrels were assigned to the remote enclave to begin with. His current forces could not protect it.

He sent for the Keeper of Keys.

The old man arrived several minutes later, leaning on the arm of a young accepted. Rhisart smiled warmly in greeting. The keeper was the oldest person at the keep, and had once been one of Rhisart's mentors.

The keeper thanked the accepted and dismissed him before turning back to Rhisart with a smile. "You can't let an old man get his rest before he tries to teach that gaggle of children tomorrow?"

"I am sorry." Rhisart's own smile faded. "Have you had any foretelling lately, my old friend?"

The keeper frowned, his gaze sharpening at the unexpected question. "Nothing for longer than I care to remember. Why?"

If Rhisart's feeling of dread were anything more than nerves, surely the keeper would have felt it too. Old though he might be, he still wielded tremendous power, and was the only sentinel Rhisart knew to possess even a trace of the prophetic gift.

"We are exposed, our forces too few," Rhisart said.

"No word from Wayra?"

"None." Rhisart took a deep breath. "I need the central tower cleared out."

The keeper nodded gravely, his eyes locked onto Rhisart's. "You are gerent," the old man said. "With that mantel comes many gifts none other possess. Never ignore impressions you receive."

Rhisart smiled. The keeper couldn't help but teach. "I do feel . . . something."

"Then the tower will be prepared at once."

"Do it quietly."

The keeper smiled. "Since when do you need to teach *me* how to perform my responsibilities?"

Rhisart turned to stare into the fire burning low in the fireplace.

The keeper placed a withered old hand on his shoulder, "What else is on your mind?"

Without turning, Rhisart declared, "I am going to seal the heart of the mountain."

53

Continuing The Chase

Kevlin awoke slowly. With a start, he remembered the makrasha and Indira. He reached for his belt dagger, but a shape loomed over him, reaching toward him.

He grabbed it, yanking to overbalance the monster so he could get a grip on its throat. Instead of powerful hengaruk, the shape was warm and soft. It cried out with a woman's voice.

Indira.

Her face came into focus scant inches from his own, an adorable shy smile on her lips. For two pounding heartbeats he stared, mesmerized. Her sable hair had fallen forward to frame her face, and the locks caressed him while her faint alluring scent enveloped him.

He was lying on a cot and had grabbed Indira's cloak just below the neck and tugged her forward over him. He was suddenly and intensely aware of her body pressed against his.

"I'm so sorry," he stammered and helped her to rise. He wanted to say so much more, but could not find the words.

Indira said nothing, and Jerrik called out from behind her. "I tried to warn you, miss."

"I should have listened," Indira said.

"Better just to kick him in the ribs when he oversleeps."

Indira laughed. "Can you imagine me kicking anyone in the ribs?"

"No," said Drystan, stepping into view. "We'll take care of that part."

Indira turned back to Kevlin. "Are you feeling better?"

"Yes, but how. . .are you all right?"

She smiled, and he had to remind himself he hardly knew the woman. That smile influenced him far more than it should. Was she some kind of secret sentinel?

"I'm fine," she said. "You're the one who almost died."

The crossbow. He inspected his side, remembering the pain. They had removed his armor and jerkin, and his skin looked new and clean. A dull ache remained deep in his torso. He stood up and took a deep breath, tentatively swinging his arms and stretching his side.

Her power awed him. "I feel great." He took a step toward her and she backed away.

No kiss.

He bowed low over her hand. "You have nothing to fear from me."

"Be careful," she said. "That wound was deep. It's healed, but your body needs time to fully recover."

"I promise." Kevlin pulled on his jerkin and reached for his tattered breastplate. He stared at it, then dropped it. *Why bother?*

"We have spare chainmail," Jerrik suggested.

"Thanks."

Kevlin noticed for the first time that they were in a long tent full of cots. Most were empty, but a few held wounded soldiers. Nikias slept peacefully on one nearby, the Bladestaff resting underneath. Dried blood covered much of his torso, but his face was clean and unmarred.

Ceren slept on another cot. Kevlin was glad she looked like she was going to be all right. He cared for Ceren. Having shared danger and a common goal over the past days, he felt he knew the strong-willed woman. Hopefully after their last talk, she'd ease up with the attitude and allow them to work together without all the angst.

"How long have I been out?" Kevlin asked.

"About an hour," said Jerrik. "Long enough to get out of most of the work. We'll see you outside." He and Drystan pushed out of the tent.

"How's Ceren?" Kevlin asked Indira. "That was quite a hit she took."

"She'll be all right." Indira tried to step past Kevlin, but her legs gave out suddenly. He barely caught her.

"Indira, what's wrong?"

She muttered something indistinct, then her head rolled to the side.

Kevlin lowered her onto a cot near Ceren. Her forehead was clammy, her breathing shallow. She was a healer. He'd never heard of a healer getting sick.

Before he could rise to fetch Leander, Indira clutched his arm and said in a tired voice, "Please stay."

"What's wrong?" he repeated, kneeling beside the cot. He tried not to notice how good she smelled. Compared to soldiers, her scent was a rare pleasure.

"Just tired," she whispered. "Using my gift drains my strength."

"Are you sure?"

She managed a weak smile and squeezed his hand. He couldn't imagine letting go. He studied her, wondering how she influenced him so powerfully. He'd been around beautiful women, but none of them drew him so strongly. It made him very uneasy.

"I just need a minute."

Kevlin wasn't sure how long he knelt next to her, but it wasn't long enough. Eventually, she closed her eyes and placed her other hand over her forehead.

"Are you sure that makrasha didn't hurt you?"

She laughed, and the sound danced through his heart.

"You have to stop doing that," he muttered. It was too distracting.

"Doing what?"

"Never mind. Are you okay?"

"I'm fine, really. Nothing can hurt me when I'm healing."

Did he really hear that correctly?

"Then why'd you just faint?"

"I told you, I'm tired. That's different. When I'm healing, my gift of Faith protects me."

"Like the stalwarts?"

"Sort of. My gift protects me from physical harm as well as spiritual or magical harm. That's why I didn't fear that makrasha, and why its sword couldn't hurt me. I was using my gift to heal another, so I was protected."

So not an idiot after all. The last excuse he could think of for staying aloof vanished.

Kevlin sat back on his heels. "You can really do that?"

"It is a very rare gift."

"That's amazing."

She nodded, then buried her face in her hands and began to sob.

That was weird. Kevlin never pretended to understand women, but he had no idea how to react.

He touched her shoulder. "I thought you said you were all right?"

She took a deep breath before lowering her hands. Tears streaked her cheeks and glistened in her dark eyes. Her lashes were very long. He wished he hadn't noticed.

She sat up. "There's just so much pain and suffering. I couldn't save them."

Indira drew from a pocket in her robes a well-worn deck of playing cards. She slipped them out of the restraining strap, cut the deck, and expertly shuffled them. Cards flipped between her fingers as she stared blankly at the wall of the tent.

Kevlin sat beside her. "You play?"

Indira glanced at the cards as she bridged them, then snapped them from one hand to the other. She shrugged. "I spend a lot of time around injured soldiers. I picked up a few things."

She held out the cards and he took the proffered deck. The well-used cards were printed with eight different symbols in three colors. These were serious gambling cards, used in the more complex games.

"You ever play for real?"

Indira gave him a hard look and took the cards. "If we had time, I'd teach you a few things. Shuffling helps me relax."

Kevlin grinned. He had never imagined this side of Indira. "Do you cook too?"

She chuckled. "Not for people I care about. The last time I tried cooking, I had to heal everyone who ate it."

"Eating is overrated," Kevlin joked.

Indira slipped the cards back into her robe and her easy smile faded to her normal shy expression. It was as if he had glimpsed a part of her she hesitated to let out, and he was thrilled to have seen it.

He wanted to explore that new side of Indira, but the moment passed.

"I apologize for the outburst earlier," Indira said, once more composed. "I only wish I could have done more. I can't bear to see anyone suffer. I've been given a wonderful gift, and it breaks my heart when I can't help."

"You did more than anyone else could have."

"I'm trying," she said. "When we realized the extent of my gift, Leander accepted me as his ward to tutor me personally. He's trying to learn how to protect others with his faith as I do."

"You protect those you heal too?"

"As long as they don't rejoin the battle, those I heal remain protected by my faith. If they fight again, they're left to their own strength. It wouldn't be fair otherwise."

"So, can you control who you extend your faith to, and for how long?"

She opened her mouth to answer, but paused. "Well, I'm not sure how it works. That's just the way it is."

"You mean it just happens without any control from you?"

"I suppose I must be controlling it at some level, but I never considered how it was done. I just did it."

"So, is it possible you could shield someone with your faith who was not being healed by you?"

She considered the question. "I honestly don't know, but I don't think it would work under normal conditions. I don't think I could bring myself to give anyone such an advantage over another."

"Think about it. You may find a time when it would be justified. It'd be terrible to have the opportunity and not be ready for it."

"Thank you." Indira gave him a warm smile. "I'll consider it. You're a good man." She leaned forward and kissed him lightly on the cheek.

That was more like it.

Kevlin stood, even though he really wanted to try kissing her again. "I'll let you get some rest."

He stepped out of the tent into early morning light. The kestrels still worked amid the rubble of the command building, although most of it had been sifted already.

Wayra threw up her hands, "By the blasted gods, where is it?"

"You have not found the shadeleech Tanathos?" Harafin asked from where he sat on a stump.

"No," Wayra snapped, rounding on the old man. She looked tired, her face dirty, and her skeletal features drawn. "Why are you so focused on a useless shadeleech? We need to find Antigonus. You of all people should know that."

Kevlin approached, intent on asking if they'd found Dhanjal's body. He wanted to spit on the Blade Stalwart's grave.

"I do wish to find Antigonus," Harafin said. "He was a close friend for more than a century and deserves a proper burial. But that is not our most pressing concern. He chose a steward, so Oris is safe."

"What?" Wayra shouted. "You let us dig through that blasted wreckage, knowing it was in vain?"

"Not in vain," Harafin said. "I need to know if Tanathos lies buried there."

"He doesn't. We found no one. Are you satisfied?"

"No." Harafin stared across the wreckage of the wall, "Where is he?"

Wayra crouched beside him, her eyes burning with desperate hunger. "Who is the steward, and where is the stone?"

Harafin, lost in his own thoughts, gestured absently at Kevlin. "He is steward."

"What?" She sounded like she nearly strangled on the word.

"You like saying that, don't you?" Kevlin asked, unable to hide a little smile at her open dismay.

Wayra stared at Kevlin in disbelief. "This abomination is steward?"

Kevlin's smile widened. Her stupid decisions had created this mess.

"Show it to me," Wayra demanded. The other kestrels drew closer, and none of them looked friendly.

"No."

Wayra's mouth opened and closed wordlessly a couple of times. Kevlin watched her, outwardly impassive, but inwardly ready and eager to fight.

She had sent her forces to attack them without determining if they were really enemies first. Kevlin had killed two sentinels who might have lived otherwise. He'd killed before and had figured out how to make peace with himself, but it was a lot harder knowing those deaths could have been avoided.

She turned her back on him and addressed Harafin. "Why did you keep this from me?"

"I kept nothing from you," Harafin said. "This is the first time you asked about it, and I told you."

"You know what I mean."

"Watch yourself," Gabral said, joining the group.

The colonel had changed into a clean uniform. His hair shone with the oils he preferred. "Insubordination will not be tolerated."

"If you'd told me the truth up front," she snarled, "we wouldn't be in this mess."

"If you'd shown a little restraint, instead of attacking us and warning them of our presence, Antigonus would be free," Gabral countered.

Angry murmurs ran through the kestrels and tension crackled in the air around the group. Gabral shifted his grip on the Mace, but made no other outward sign that he cared about the threat of danger.

"Enough bickering," Harafin said. "Tanathos is not dead. Antigonus is not dead. Our work is not finished."

"Very well," Wayra said. "I will escort the steward safely away while you continue your search."

Kevlin laughed.

"My kestrels are best able to protect Oris."

"Then why was it *my* spear that broke through that shadeleech's defenses this morning?" Kevlin said. "Looks to me like we don't really need you."

Wayra glared. "How did you do that? You're not actinopathic."

"No, I'm not."

"I demand to know."

Jerrik pushed through the group and stopped before Gabral. He wore a scowl so deep the sentinels drew back and let him through without argument. Ignoring Wayra's angry glare at the interruption, he announced, "Sir, the scouts report tracks leading north. Fresh ones. The two kestrels Wayra assigned to watch the northern edge of the clearing have not reported in."

Harafin had to raise his voice to speak above the ensuing babble of voices. "Silence." Looking up, he closed his eyes. A soft yellow glow shone around his face.

He's using a bird, Kevlin realized.

For several long minutes, they waited in hushed anticipation until he opened his eyes. With a grave face he said, "Tanathos rides north."

"Is Antigonus with him?" Kevlin asked at the same time Wayra asked, "My kestrels?" and Gabral asked, "How far?"

Harafin raised his hands. "Slow down." To Kevlin, he said, "Antigonus is being carried along, so I assume he is alive."

"Thank the gods," Kevlin breathed. Maybe they still had a chance to salvage the situation.

Harafin turned to Wayra next. "Your sentinels are captive, and Tanathos has a halimaw."

"What's a halimaw?" Ceren asked. She joined the group, stepping gingerly, as if still in pain.

"Did he have more bears?" Wayra asked, her face paler than normal. Whatever a halimaw was, the announcement had set all of the kestrels muttering nervously.

Ignoring the question, Harafin continued. "He is five miles north, moving fast."

"He's running," Jerrik said.

"Coward," Gabral spat.

"I doubt it," Ceren said with a shudder. "That man was terrifying. He knows we have Oris, so I can't see him running."

"No," Harafin said. "He cannot afford to return to the Sigrun empty-handed, and Antigonus has no value to him without Oris."

"Maybe he has reinforcements," Drystan suggested.

"You think there's more of them?" Jerrik demanded with an angry glare.

Drystan ignored the look and shrugged. "Who knows? There shouldn't be any at all."

"Then we catch him before he can reach them." Gabral ordered, "Captains, assemble the men. Prepare to ride."

"Aye." Both saluted and left.

"Do not be so hasty," Harafin cautioned. "A choice must be made."

"What choice?" Wayra asked. "There is little danger. One shadeleech, no matter how strong, cannot stand against my kestrels, and we are trained to fight halimaw."

"That is not my concern," Harafin said. "More importantly, we have but three days before the autumn equinox. In Baldev, we agreed that should we fail to liberate Antigonus, we must make for Tamera with all speed in hopes of choosing the next bearer before Oris's power is broken."

"He's so close," Kevlin protested. "We can catch him."

"And if Tanathos kills him before we catch them?" Harafin asked. "What then? Will you have me risk the fate of the empire on the slim chance that Antigonus will be saved alive?"

"That's why we're here," Kevlin said angrily. "To save him."

"Perhaps Kevlin is right," Wayra said, surprising Kevlin. "Even if we fail to save Antigonus, we should destroy the shadeleech and his halimaw." She met Harafin's gaze and squared her shoulders. "We can reach Diodor if we have to. My master, Ah'Shan, is coming."

Harafin turned north, as if he could penetrate miles of forest with his gaze. Then he glanced back at Kevlin, his brows furrowed in thought.

Kevlin knew chasing Tanathos was the right choice. That assurance *burned* deep in his heart, but how could he convince Harafin to take the risk?

"Listen," Kevlin said, drawing the old man's powerful gaze with a gesture toward the towering cliff face. "Antigonus chose me as steward right here, and I risked my life climbing that cliff to get the rock to you. Now we've returned. He's the old bearer, and he deserves a chance. I mean to keep my oath, even if the path leads into the heart of darkness."

A look of surprise flitted across Harafin's face, but he blinked it away fast. When Wayra started to speak, Harafin waved her to silence without breaking eye contact with Kevlin, who began to sweat under the penetrating gaze. It felt like Harafin was trying to read his mind.

After a dozen heartbeats, Harafin glanced at Leander, who looked equally grave, then announced, "Colonel, we leave in ten minutes."

Kevlin watched after Harafin as the old man strode away. That little speech wasn't nearly good enough. Harafin was playing a game only he seemed to understand. Kevlin was grateful their paths still lay in the same direction, but couldn't shake the feeling that he had just played into Harafin's hands.

54

THE CHOOSING

After ten minutes of frantic activity, the troop stood assembled and ready. With the power of the kestrels augmenting their gifts, Leander and Indira performed miraculous healings so that every man still living could ride.

Nikias emerged from the hospital tent looking worn, with none of his customary swagger. Drystan pulled the young Bladestaff bearer aside and spoke with him for a few minutes. At one point, Nikias started, a look of glee flitting across his face. Eventually Drystan placed a hand on his shoulder and the younger man nodded.

"What was that all about?" Kevlin asked Drystan after the two had separated.

"I explained a few things to him." At Kevlin's quizzical look, he added, "Trust me."

They left the shattered fort and headed north. Indira swayed in her saddle, so exhausted that it looked like she might fall. Ceren moved to her side and rode close, one steadying hand on her shoulder. The young noblewoman met Kevlin's gaze, but her eyes looked troubled and she turned away.

When they reached the outer edge of the clearing, a couple of sentinels turned back and raised their hands. A thunderclap pealed, and a dense pall of smoke billowed out of the fort.

"A fitting pyre for those beasts," Leander said.

Kevlin urged his mount up beside Jerrik, who rode just behind Drystan, frowning.

"Why are you in such a foul mood?" Kevlin asked. "I thought a good fight always cheered you up."

Jerrik grunted. "Aye, that part was good."

"He's just angry he lost," Drystan explained.

Jerrik squeezed the reins till the corded muscles of his arms stood out sharply under the skin, but said nothing.

"Lost?" Kevlin repeated. "But we won."

"It's not fair," Jerrik muttered.

"Stop moping," Gabral called from where he rode beside Harafin. "You're the one who agreed to the wager, and you lost."

"Well, didn't you both reach the center of the fort at the same time?"

"Aye," Jerrik said. "Exactly the same time."

"Your casualties were higher," Gabral said in a long-suffering tone, as if they'd argued the point more than once already.

"What were they?" Kevlin asked, fighting to keep a straight face.

"Three dead and eight wounded in my company," Drystan said.

"Five dead and six wounded in mine," Jerrik growled.

"Drystan wins," Gabral declared.

Drystan smiled, while Jerrik muttered a curse. "It's not fair. The numbers weren't different enough to really matter."

Leander asked, "How many lives would you consider enough to 'really matter'?"

Jerrik opened his mouth to reply, but frowned. With a growl, he looked down at his hands still clenching the reins.

"Hold on a minute," said Kevlin. "Was there an agreement on what 'casualty' meant?"

"What do you mean?" asked Gabral.

"Well, casualty can mean both dead and wounded. I believe that's how you used it after our battle in Baldev."

"So?"

"So," Kevlin continued, "if you total up the dead and wounded together as the casualty count. . ."

Jerrik's face lit with understanding. "We both have eleven casualties!"

Gabral groaned. "Fine. It's a draw."

Jerrik grinned at Drystan. "Looks like you don't get off the hook so easy after all, brother."

"I prefer to beat you man to man anyway."

Kevlin smiled. Jerrik's use of 'brother' might have only been a slip of the tongue, but it was a sign that maybe he was coming around.

They pressed north through the morning, hands close to weapons. Two of the sentinels rode strapped to their saddles while their minds soared above the company, linked to hawks and using the birds' senses to spy out the road ahead.

They covered several miles at a steady canter, but just as the sun finally slid into view over the rim of the cliff at noon, Harafin reined in. The trail split ahead, and one branch turned to ascend the steep cliff in a series of switchbacks that zigzagged all the way to the top.

Leaning far back in his saddle, Kevlin admired the route. If only he'd had that when he climbed up last time.

"Which way did they go?" Harafin asked Adalia. The tiny archer studied the trail for only a few seconds before pointing up the steep slope. Harafin frowned. "This is unexpected."

"I assumed they'd run north for the highway, and try to escape through Diodor," Wayra said. "Or turn west and make straight for the Tamerlane Sea. Why climb the cliff?"

The old sentinel's brow furrowed, but it was Leander who spoke. "There is little to the east. Fiachra is the only large city in that direction, and Il'Aicharen lies northeast."

Inhaling a sharp breath, Harafin hissed, "Il'Aicharen. It can't be."

"What?" Leander asked.

"I've just considered a terrible possibility, but the enclave is well defended. Tanathos could not hope to overcome there, even with a halimaw."

Wayra coughed, staring at her feet and rubbing her hands on her skirt. "We, ah, may have a problem."

"What problem?"

Gesturing at her company, she said, "We all came from Il'Aicharen. It is one of the kestrel centers."

"I know," Harafin said. "The battle prowess of your order is one of the things that comfort me. How many kestrels are still stationed there?"

"Well," she said slowly, "when Antigonus contacted me, I ordered all the remaining kestrels in Il'Aicharen to make haste for Diodor. They have probably already arrived."

"You left Il'Aicharen undefended? I can't believe Rhisart approved your decision."

Wayra refused to meet his gaze. "I ordered them away on my authority alone. I. . .haven't spoken with Rhisart yet."

Harafin turned to glance up the cliff. "Could Tanathos have known? Wayra, you may have doomed us all with your rash stupidity. If Tanathos knows Il'Aicharen is all but undefended, he could attack with impunity."

"I don't understand," Wayra replied, trying not to cringe under Harafin's angry glare. "What's the danger?"

"Tanathos could murder Antigonus there."

Turning his face toward the sky, he closed his eyes. The company silently watched as a silvery glow appeared around Harafin's face.

"What's he doing?" Gabral asked.

"Mindlink," Wayra said. "I believe he's trying to reach the gerent of Il'Aicharen."

Harafin suddenly cried out and his entire body convulsed. With eyes still closed, he pitched from his horse and fell twitching to the ground.

Leander reached him first. The old stalwart placed a glowing hand on his forehead. The sentinel gasped and sat up in one convulsive movement. His eyes popped open, and then he sagged back to the ground. As he tried to rise again, Leander held him down.

"Rest a while, my old friend." Leander began chanting softly, his hands shining with pure white light. After a minute, he trailed off, and only then offered to help Harafin up.

"What happened?" Gabral asked.

"I fear I am right about Tanathos' plans." Harafin took a deep breath. "I tried to reach Rhisart, but triggered a web placed across this entire section of country. I was attacked."

"Tanathos?" Kevlin asked.

"No, it was another shadeleech. I did not discover his name, but he was skilled." He smiled ruefully. "He will not be troubling anyone else."

"We should try to reach the gerent again," Wayra said, her expression more pinched than normal. "With the united power of the kestrels, we could break through."

"No, the web was extensive," Harafin said. "It must be maintained by several shadeleeches. We cannot risk another attack." He frowned. "We must move quickly. The fate of the empire hangs in the balance."

"I still don't understand the danger," Wayra frowned. "Why does it matter *where* Tanathos kills Antigonus?"

Harafin scanned the group, and everyone bunched up close to hear. "What I share with you is knowledge held only by members of the high council, but I believe you need to understand the gravity of the threat we face."

Kevlin shared a glance with Jerrik. The big man shrugged and eagerly turned back to Harafin.

"At the heart of Mount Il'Aicharen lies a node of power. Across the world only a few such places exist, nexuses where the energy of the very planet is concentrated. Should Tanathos murder Antigonus at the heart of the mountain, he would not only shatter the aegis protecting the empire from the Sigrun, but most likely destroy most of Hallvarr in one cataclysmic eruption."

Kevlin wished he could convince himself that the old man was exaggerating. How could such a thing be possible? He could barely imagine it.

"Antigonus' life is bound to Oris," Harafin explained. "He is bearer. Should he be murdered at a node of power, Oris's power would be shattered. The result would kill everyone within a hundred miles of the stone."

Kevlin stared down at his boot in horror. No wonder Harafin was so worried. This was a nightmare, but there was one sure way out of it.

Tanathos had to die. Despite the terror Kevlin felt at the very mention of the shadeleech's name, the solution seemed surprisingly simple.

"Wait a minute," Wayra interrupted. "All of that death and destruction is tied to the risk of the bearer of Oris being murdered at a node of power, right?"

Harafin nodded.

"Then choose a new bearer. The steward is here with Oris, so Antigonus must have understood the danger." Her eyes shone with excitement. She waved a hand toward her company of kestrels. "Choose one of us. Choose me."

"Hold on a minute," Kevlin began, but Harafin quieted him with a glance.

"Wayra is right," Harafin said. "The risk is too great. Bring out Oris."

Kevlin reluctantly cut the stitches holding the rune-covered bag under the flap of his boot and extracted it. While he did so, Harafin directed the soldiers back and ordered the kestrels to assemble in a semicircle close to him.

Kevlin dumped the rock into his palm. He automatically adjusted it so that his fingers curled over the rough edge. The emblem of the flaming sword glinted with flashes of blue light.

At the sight of the emblem, Wayra inhaled sharply. "The flaming sword."

A murmur rippled through the kestrels.

Why am I always the only one with no idea what's going on?

Kevlin stared down at the rock. Even though he'd always known his possession of it was temporary, he felt a wrenching feeling of loss at the thought of handing it over to someone else. The crystal flashed with light, drawing his gaze deep inside of it. His mind began to tumble, as if falling into the rock.

"Kevlin!" Harafin's voice cracked across his thoughts like a slap to the face. He started and pulled his eyes from the emblem. The old sentinel's gaze lingered on him before he turned to the kestrels.

"I am the chooser," he declared solemnly. "The responsibility of identifying the next bearer of Oris has been entrusted to me."

Wayra smiled, her eyes never leaving the stone in Kevlin's hand.

"But. . ." Harafin waited until he held their full attention. "Oris, not I, must make the final decision."

Wayra frowned. "How is that possible?"

"You will understand if you are chosen."

The old sentinel gestured her forward. "Approach the stone, but do not touch it."

She advanced, one hand eagerly outstretched.

"Beware," Harafin said sharply. "Do not touch it unless I tell you to."

Wayra ignored him and snatched for the rock with an exultant look on her face.

Blinding blue light erupted from the stone and a jolt of power staggered Kevlin back a step. The blast flung Wayra ten feet. She crumpled to the ground in a ball, weeping.

Thyra, her second-in-command, rushed to her side and placed glowing hands on her shoulders. A moment later, she helped her leader roll over and sit up.

Wayra's face was white from shock and pain, and she clutched a hand to her chest. Thyra pulled back the sleeve of Wayra's robe to reveal her hand, blackened and twisted like a lightning-blasted tree.

Wayra stared at her mangled hand and wailed.

Indira pushed through the kestrels and dropped to her knees beside Wayra. Taking the injured hand in her own, she bent over it and began chanting.

Oris might have punished Wayra, but Kevlin felt an urge to run her through for attempting to take the stone. He glanced down at the rock, and surprisingly felt no fear for himself.

They all waited until Indira finished chanting. The young healer looked up with tears in her eyes. "I am sorry, but I cannot restore your hand."

Wayra pushed her away, and she stumbled and fell. Kevlin growled and reached for his sword.

Leander crouched beside Wayra and spoke in a deadly soft voice. "Your folly is proven thrice over, and I will not save you from your own stupidity." Leaning closer he added, "Should you lay hands on my ward again, I will execute you myself."

Wayra cringed back, and Leander helped Indira to her feet.

"You are lucky the blast did not kill you," Harafin said to Wayra, his tone disapproving. "The punishment for trying to take Oris by force varies, but is usually fatal. Be grateful for the opportunity to learn from your mistake."

Wayra grimaced but said nothing. Hugging her withered hand to her chest, she began to sob.

To the other kestrels, Harafin said, "Now, who is next?"

When they pulled away fearfully, he nodded in approval. "Better. I had expected Wayra to understand. The choosing of a bearer is a multi-faceted process. One with sufficient power must be available, but they must also have a heart empty of greed, the intention only to serve and to protect. Usually we have more time to prepare candidates for a choosing."

He glanced at Kevlin before repeating, "Who is next?"

"I will try," Thyra offered. She approached Kevlin, but kept her hand by her side.

Harafin placed one palm on her forehead and held the other several inches above Oris. He closed his eyes and his hands began to glow with a soft green light.

After a moment, he reopened them with a shake of his head. Thyra breathed a sigh of obvious relief and withdrew. In like manner, each of the kestrels approached, and in like manner they were all rejected.

"What now?" Gabral asked when the last of them backed away.

Kevlin gripped the rock harder, barely hiding a triumphant smile. They hadn't taken it from him, and he wasn't surprised. They weren't supposed to have it yet. He had no idea how he knew that, but he did.

"Take it to Diodor," Wayra suggested. Her face was drawn and streaked with tears, and her unnaturally large eyes looked haunted. She still clasped the blackened hand to her chest. "Take the stone to Diodor and choose Ah'Shan. He's the rightful bearer."

"We need to chase Tanathos," Kevlin argued. "He's not far ahead. We can catch him."

"You'd leave the empire shattered and defenseless?" Wayra demanded angrily.

"It won't be if we kill Tanathos."

"If Tanathos sees he cannot reach the heart of the mountain," Leander said, "he may kill Antigonus anyway."

"Not if we kill Tanathos first," Kevlin repeated.

"Enough." Harafin held up a hand for silence. "Events are moving too fast and the fate of the empire hangs in the balance."

He glanced again at Kevlin and then down at Oris. "The path of darkness," he muttered.

"Uh, you're being cryptic again," Drystan remarked.

Harafin shot him such a withering glare that even the normally indomitable Einarri captain backed away.

Harafin said, "Wayra, take your kestrels north as fast as you can ride. When you are close enough, call to your force in Diodor and order them back to Il'Aicharen with all speed. Ah'Shan as well, if he has arrived. Warn King Leszek of the danger."

"Shouldn't we escort the steward to Diodor?" she asked. "If all else fails, Ah'Shan could take up the stone. That would kill Antigonus but avert the disaster."

"Wait a minute," Kevlin said. "What do you mean, it'd kill Antigonus?"

"Kevlin rides with me," Harafin said before answering. "Once a new bearer is chosen, Antigonus' life will be forfeit."

Kevlin hugged the rock close to his chest. "Then no one gets another chance to take it. I'm giving it back to Antigonus."

"It is not your place to decide," Harafin said.

"I'm the steward," Kevlin replied defiantly. "So I get a say."

Gabral reached for the Mace. "We can find another steward."

"Try it."

"Relax," Harafin said. "There will be no choosing today. Wayra, you are to ride to Il'Aicharen after reaching the highway. Push on with all speed, for time is against us."

"We will."

"Watch for halimaw."

"We are trained to fight them, but the one you saw is with Tanathos."

"Be cautious nonetheless," Harafin said. "Tanathos has proven wily and dangerous, so do not underestimate him. The rest of us will pursue Tanathos. It is possible I am wrong, so I will not lose the trail. With good fortune, we will overtake him and rescue Antigonus."

"I will ride with you," Nikias declared.

"King Leszek ordered you to ride with me," Wayra protested.

"No, he ordered me to save Antigonus, so I ride with Kevlin."

Harafin surveyed the company, his eyes settling for a moment on Nikias and then Gabral. "Strength and Cunning," he muttered. His gaze moved to Ceren, then Kevlin, and then to Jerrik and Drystan.

"Nikias rides with us," he declared.

"Fine," Wayra said, and with no more farewell, she led her troop north, past the point where the path turned up the cliff.

The two sentinels at the front of the party raised glowing fists. An invisible force smashed trees and brush aside, and the soil flowed back to cover the holes, producing a wide path over which the sentinels galloped north along the base of the cliff.

They disappeared in a moment.

Harafin turned toward the cliff. "Come, we must hurry."

He led the way up.

55

A Point of No Return

Sitara paused, hand poised to knock.

There could be no turning back. She had told the keisara that morning that she wouldn't leave, that she trusted in a positive spin of the Wheel to preserve her grandmother.

She had closed that door.

She needed Remiel's unnamed ally, who she had to believe knew how to thwart Omolara. If they did not, all hope was lost.

So she stood before the door leading to Remiel. At the first opportunity, she had excused herself and made her way here. If he could not help her, Omolara's interview would seal her fate.

Sitara settled her face into a pleasant mask and knocked loudly on the door. It was opened by the same young page who had answered the day before.

"Back already, miss?" he asked with a grin and a wink.

"I beg your pardon." She gave him a hard look.

Mumbling an apology, he backed out of her way, holding the door wide for her.

"Fetch Remiel for me," she commanded.

"Yes, ma'am." He led her to the comfortable waiting room and disappeared from view. Remiel appeared a few minutes later.

"Well hello, Angel," he said warmly. "I didn't expect to see you again so soon."

"Will you accompany me, please?" she asked before turning. Without waiting for a reply, she left the room. He quickly followed.

"Where are we going?" he asked as he caught up to her.

"To somewhere a little more private."

"Well lead on, darlin'," he said happily. "I hadn't thought we'd get right down to business so fast."

"I'm not in a patient mood today."

Encouraged by her answer, he stepped closer and slipped an arm around her slender waist. When she did not object, he said, "I have the feeling this is going to be the beginning of a long and profitable relationship."

"You have no idea."

"I like you more and more every minute." He hugged her closer.

She led him down to the sub-levels of the palace, into an empty corridor lined with guest rooms. As they walked, she carefully explored the rooms around them with her mind to ensure all were empty.

She stopped before a plain wooden door. Remiel eagerly opened it for her. She stepped through into a simple room furnished with a bed, a single chair, and a small closet. His excitement was almost palpable as he followed her in and closed the door behind them.

Sitara turned to him and placed a hand on the middle of his chest. He smiled and reached for her.

Her hand began to glow with an angry red light.

Shocked, he met her gaze, and tensed in fear under her cold stare.

Sitara smiled without warmth and reached into his chest with her magic. She wrapped it like cold fingers around his heart. Her smile widened at the feel of its quickening pulse and on seeing the fear he vainly tried to hide behind his eyes.

She squeezed.

He cried out in pain, but she held him immobile in her power. Unlike her experience with the old woman, holding his life in her hand exhilarated her. The dark power racing through her filled her with strength, and the filth that dragged through her soul no longer bothered her.

In this moment, it felt right.

Had she not needed the pig, she would destroy him and take his life force. She maintained the pressure around his heart for several long seconds as she fought the temptation.

After a moment, she reluctantly withdrew her hand. She needed him, for the moment. Still, she knew how she would kill him when his usefulness ended.

She would look him in the eye while squeezing the life out of him, would take his life force and use it to further her own ends. That would be sweet justice for what he forced her to do next.

He breathed rapidly, all traces of the cocky young man gone, replaced by a far more pitiful, more honest person. He was so far beneath Bajaran that he repulsed her.

"My name is Sitara," she said sweetly.

He cringed initially at the sound of her voice, but regained some of his composure once he realized she wasn't going to kill him immediately.

"You're a sentinel! Why didn't you tell me?"

She raised one eyebrow. "Would you have changed the price for your services?"

"I wouldn't have let you drag me down here to kill me."

"I'm not going to kill you yet," she said in a matter-of-fact tone. "I need your services, for the time being." As he visibly relaxed, she added, "I have decided to allow you to serve me."

"Wait a minute," he protested.

"Listen to me. I will pay your price, and you will serve me. You will reveal to no one the secret that I am a sentinel, and you will take no other woman to your bed until I'm through with you."

"Hold on, that's not the deal we agreed to."

"We *agreed* to nothing. You stated a price for your service. I am accepting that service, and explaining what it will entail.

"And know this," she leaned close and he cringed back against the door. "If you disappoint me, I will kill you."

"I won't," he promised.

She raised a hand once more glowing with ugly red fire. "Should you share your bed with another woman before I release you from my service, you will be privileged to witness her terrible, agonizing death in your arms."

His face paled, his eyes riveted to her glowing hand.

"I think we understand each other," she added crisply before dropping her hand and stepping away. "You will arrange a meeting between myself and the ally Bajaran spoke of."

"I'll see what I can do."

"You don't understand," she said in her sweetest tone. "If I don't meet with that person tomorrow, my secret will become known. Therefore your service to me will be discovered, and your own life will be forfeit."

He exclaimed, "Why would you drag me into this knowing you had so little time?"

"Because I have so little time!" she snarled. "I need that person's help and you're the only one who can help me reach them. Your life is also on the line."

He glowered at her, but did not dare voice the thoughts so clearly running through his mind.

"Enough," she said. "I'm sure you're as good as you claim to be. Now, on to better things."

She took another step back and felt the bed behind her. With a touch of her mind, she pulled apart the back of her dress and let it slip off her shoulders and fall to the floor.

Remiel immediately forgot his anger. Resentment drained out of him as his eyes eagerly feasted on the curves of her body, visible through the thin shift.

Typical man.

"Let's discuss your payment," she said and settled onto the bed.

"Yes, ma'am," he said heartily and began pulling at his shirt.

"One last thing."

"What?"

"I had better enjoy myself."

He grinned. "That, Angel, I can guarantee."

56

DOING MAGIC

"What exactly are halimaw?" Ceren asked as they crept up the steep, narrow trail.

"Abominations spawned by the shadeleeches' power," Harafin replied. "By sacrificing a sentinel, they can merge the life force of the victim with that of a bear. The result is a horrific monster immune to magic and very hard to kill."

"I've never heard of them," Ceren said with a shudder.

"Few have seen them. Since only a sentinel can be sacrificed to create one, they are very rare."

"Tanathos has captured two more sentinels," Leander pointed out.

"Let us pray he does not have the opportunity to use their souls before we catch him," Harafin said. "One halimaw will prove difficult enough. Three would be. . .challenging."

With those grim words hanging in the air, they focused on the perilous trail up the steep side of the cliff. It was not as sheer as the spot where Kevlin had climbed, but still proved difficult. The laboring horses were soon lathered with sweat.

As they rose high above the forest, Jerrik glanced over the edge, then clutched the saddle with eyes closed tight. "Ukko's beard, Kevlin, I can't believe you climbed that with no trail. It would've killed me."

"I don't think I could do it again." Kevlin's hands ached just thinking about it.

Reaching the top without incident, they pushed through the waning afternoon light. When it grew too dark to see, Harafin lit the path ahead and they covered a couple more miles before finally halting in a glade beside a small stream.

After helping hobble and water the horses, Kevlin came across Gabral and Ceren conversing near the edge of the firelight.

"Of course, my lady," Gabral was saying. "I have everything you need."

"Thank you," she said and placed a hand on his arm.

Kevlin withdrew and returned to the fire. He shouldn't be surprised that Ceren would warm to Gabral. They were both noble born, but the sight of her hand on Gabral's arm stirred unexpected irritation. He had thought she had better taste.

She didn't join them for the evening meal, but Kevlin wasn't about to ask where she was.

After the meal, Harafin gestured to the single makrasha they'd captured at the fort, which hovered nearby in a magical cage. "Let us see if our prisoner has any insight into Tanathos' plan."

"I thought you already interrogated it at the fort," Drystan remarked, glancing up from sharpening his spear with a stone.

"We did, but these creatures' minds are rather shallow, so you need to know which questions to ask. We now have a better idea what its master is planning."

Harafin motioned with his hand, and the captive makrasha floated closer in its magic cage.

Kevlin shuddered. "It's amazing the disgusting creatures can even talk."

"It is one of the few human characteristics that the Sigrun have not yet eradicated," Harafin said.

"They were once men?"

"Yes. The makrasha are spawned by the dark powers of the Sigrun. They are the creation of Nyyrikki, one of the twin leaders of the Sigrun."

"I never knew," said Gabral. "How is it possible?"

Harafin surveyed the company. "It's startling sometimes to see how much has been forgotten. During the first years of their uprising, the Sigrun were desperate to increase control over whatever parts of the nation they overthrew. They started sending captives home with broken minds."

"Wouldn't that just make people more determined to keep fighting?" asked Gabral.

"Those men were not innocent victims, but murderers. The Sigrun broke their minds and sent them home to kill. They would murder their own families and neighbors."

"That's horrible," said Drystan.

"Yes, and unbelievably effective. Terror undermined entire sections of the nation."

"How did that generate makrasha?" Kevlin asked.

"It did not until they captured a sentinel. His name was Mokosoh, and he was a close friend of mine. He was betrayed and captured by Nyyrikki.

"They had never captured a sentinel before, and Mokosoh was saved especially for Nyyrikki's sport. We all knew each other in the days prior to the uprising. The pair of them had disliked each other even as students. Mokosoh was a powerful sentinel with a brilliant mind, but he had an unreasoning fear of spiders."

"Well aware of that fear, Nyyrikki devised a cruel torture. Mokosoh was forced to stand naked while hundreds of poisonous spiders crawled over him, biting him, and eventually driving him mad."

"He could not even scream for fear of the insects crawling into his mouth. When he could bear it no longer, Nyyrikki drove the spiders into Mokosoh's flesh, combining their life essences with his.

"The result was unprecedented. Unbeknownst to sentinels at that time, there is a similarity between the most basic elements of arachnids and humans."

"With the dark magic as catalyst, tiny pieces of those hundreds of spiders were embedded into the very core of what made Mokosoh a man. That changed him, twisting and mutilating him beyond humanity, making him into something the world had never known before.

"Makrasha."

The popping of the fire sounded loud in the otherwise silent clearing as everyone stared with fresh horror at the creature floating in its glowing prison.

Gesturing at their prisoner, Harafin continued. "The makrasha proved so successful that it quickly became the favorite punishment for anyone who dared oppose the Sigrun. The fear of being mutilated into something inhuman forced entire regions to surrender."

"It was not long before the fighting prowess of the makrasha became clear, and the Sigrun started tithing the population for men to mutilate into those perfect fighting creatures. The Sigrun have used them ever since as the core of their armies."

Harafin shook his head sadly. "Mokosoh was the first, and there was never another to equal him. Those makrasha formed from sentinels have an innate resistance to magic, which makes them exceptionally deadly. They were used as the personal guard of the Sigrun, and to assassinate other sentinels. That is the service Nyyrikki forced on Mokosoh. As such, Nyyrikki was able to enjoy daily the victory over one of his oldest enemies."

He continued softly, his voice clear in the deep silence. "Even when he died, Mokosoh never regained his mind. He never understood who he was, or realized what had happened to him. It was probably for the best."

"How do you know that?" Kevlin asked.

"I killed him."

"I thought you said he was resistant to magic?"

"He was. By the most ironic twist of fate, it was his final sacrifice that allowed Nyyrikki to escape from me."

"He will not escape the next time you meet," Leander declared.

"No, he will not." Harafin studied them all. "These creatures are living testimony to the cruelty and evil of the men who are their masters. There can be no peace with the Sigrun. Now, let us find out if it knows anything useful."

Harafin raised his hand, and the glowing nimbus surrounding the prisoner's body slowly sank away from its head.

The makrasha came awake and struggled to free itself, snapping its deadly jaws at the air. "Release me," it hollered. Its flat, insect-like eyes roved over the company, showing no fear.

Harafin raised his hand again, drawing the prisoner's eyes. "I want you to relax. I am seeking Truth."

The creature's snarling died away as Harafin's hand began to glow faintly white. Its head settled low on its short, powerful neck.

Kevlin shuddered and looked away. The sight of the monster helpless in Harafin's power stirred boyhood memories of Kevlin's own torture under the influence of Truth. He breathed slowly to suppress them. It took a moment, but he had a lot of practice not remembering.

"Why does your master ride north?" Harafin asked.

The creature spoke in a broken, harsh voice. "Know nothing. Obey. Kill."

"Did you see them ride north?"

The creature threw back its head and screamed.

"Beware," shouted Leander.

Before Harafin could seal up the creature's prison, it looked straight at him, its eyes filled with the same empty blackness that had possessed Merab. Then it howled again.

Harafin staggered back a couple of steps as if struck by a powerful blow. "Cover its eyes!"

Kevlin leaped at the beast thrashing inside its prison. He hoped the magical bonds would hold.

It turned toward him, its face contorted into a mask of hatred. "You will know my vengeance."

It spoke with Tanathos' voice.

"Unless I get you first." Kevlin slammed his hand across its insect-like eyes, hoping Tanathos was sharing its senses.

The amulet hanging around Kevlin's neck grew hot. At the same time, he *felt* the beast's features begin to shrink under his hand as its life drained away. The flesh melted under his touch, and the leathery skin blackened and cracked.

"Get out of the way, Kevlin," yelled Harafin. "I need to restore the prison before it dies."

He could not let go.

His hand remained stuck fast to the creature's face. Without the amulet, Tanathos might have been able to suck his life away too. The horrific cruelty of what was happening filled him with a towering rage.

The energy captured by the amulet strained inside Kevlin, pushing to be released. Meanwhile, under his hand, the life being sucked out of the makrasha flowed to Tanathos like an invisible stream of power, linking the two of them together.

Kevlin envisioned the shadeleech in his mind and, focusing all the energy on that image, cried out, "Tanathos!"

The energy burned up into his hand and through the creature's eyes. For a split second, Kevlin touched the conduit between Tanathos and the creature.

In his mind's eye he caught a glimpse of the shadeleech as power blasted through the makrasha toward its master. He could feel the searing pain and surprise it inflicted, and heard Tanathos scream. The connection severed.

Kevlin staggered back and immediately the magical prison sealed over the creature's head. The beast looked smaller, its skin hanging loose over its skull, its ribs standing out against its shrunken chest.

"Is it still alive?" Kevlin asked.

"Barely." Harafin dropped onto a seat by the fire. "What did you think you were doing? Why didn't you get out of the way? You could have been killed."

"I couldn't let go. My hand was stuck to its face, and Tanathos was trying to attack me through the connection."

"How did you break free?" Drystan asked.

"I'm not entirely sure. Through the amulet I was able to somehow refocus Tanathos' attack back on him through the makrasha. I could feel him, and even saw him for a second." He grinned. "I surprised him and hurt him too."

Harafin regarded him with an unreadable expression. "Your instincts are very good, my young friend," he said finally. "What you did involved very advanced magic."

Kevlin laughed a little nervously. "I didn't really do magic. I just used his own power against him to get him to stop."

Harafin laughed, and Leander joined in.

"My dear boy," Harafin said. "Using a shadeleech's own magic against him, and attacking him through his own conduit of power, is a significant accomplishment. It should have taken you years of training. Trust me, my boy, you definitely did *do* magic."

It seemed wrong that Harafin should be laughing so hard. It wasn't dignified. Kevlin frowned, not wanting to think about wielding magic.

The soldiers around them were all staring. They hadn't witnessed his fight with Wayra's kestrels, nor had they known about the amulet. He should have held his tongue until he could speak with Harafin alone.

"Tanathos is close," Kevlin said. "I could feel it."

Gabral leaned forward. "How close?"

"It wasn't exact, just a feeling, but he's not far. I'm sure he could sense it too."

"I am confident that he could," said Harafin. "He was able to see through that creature's eyes."

"So he knows our numbers," said Drystan.

"Yes. He knows we are chasing him."

"He'll run all the harder now," observed Gabral.

"Have faith," said Leander. "We will catch him."

"Faith I leave to you. I'm looking for something a little more tangible."

Leander only smiled.

57

A New Kind of Journey

Gabral doubled the watch. While everyone retired to their blankets near the fire, Harafin pulled Kevlin aside.

"Come, it is time to continue your training. You have done well in the past couple of days. It is remarkable you are still alive."

"Thanks," Kevlin said dryly.

"I meant it as a compliment. But instinct and luck will not be enough if you wish to survive the confrontation we are racing toward."

"I'm not a sentinel," Kevlin pointed out. Sure, he didn't want to give up Oris, but only until he could return it to Antigonus.

"No," Harafin agreed. "You are something unique. For that reason we need to prepare you for whatever may come."

"I know what's coming. We kill Tanathos. Antigonus gets the rock back. We go home."

"Perhaps, but humor an old man. Oris has taken an unusual interest in you, and has even granted you the tools necessary to succeed in a role never before played by a steward."

"What do you mean?"

"The amulet. . .and the ring."

"What about the ring?"

"That ring has always been worn by the bearer of Oris, just as the bearers of the Six each wear a ring. They are not merely symbolic emblems of their office. Those are important conduits of power that enhance the bearers' ability to convey their commands to their weapons, and for the weapons to protect and influence them."

"I never knew that." Kevlin gazed at the heavy ring and its flaming sword emblem. With so much focus on the rock and amulet, he hadn't given the ring much consideration.

"And the amulet," continued Harafin. "When Oris touched the amulet with its power, it changed into a powerful tool that allows you, non-actinopathic though you are, to wield magic."

"We've covered that already."

"That is only the beginning," Harafin insisted as he tugged at his beard. "Events are moving too fast. We have yet to discuss the significance of the flaming sword, the symbol Oris has chosen for you. The symbol it has chosen for itself."

"Then explain it to me."

"Every time a new bearer is chosen, the symbol on their ring changes, but usually only a little. In rare instances, such changes are dramatic."

"Hold on. I'm only the steward."

"Yet Oris chose a new symbol, the symbol of the Catalyst."

"Who's the catalyst?"

"We will discuss that another time. For today, understand that symbol is significant. We've been waiting for Oris to choose that symbol for over two hundred years, and dreading the day it would."

That doesn't sound good.

"Now that day has come, but manifested through the steward. *This is not supposed to happen.*" The intensity of the old man's gaze scared Kevlin.

"All right," Kevlin said slowly. "Then let's get it back to Antigonus and forget about it."

Harafin barked a laugh. "Understand something else, Kevlin. We have only three more days. I took a terrible gamble today."

"Why did you do it then?"

Harafin regarded him for a moment. "Because I am starting to see that my own assumptions have been incorrect. The events of the past few days have led me to a new conclusion, despite its seeming impossibility. I am trusting in what has been revealed." He scratched at his beard and added, "If I chose wrong, all is lost."

"You chose the right course." It terrified Kevlin to see Harafin unsure. Of everyone in the party, Harafin was supposed to know what was going on. It didn't have to be so complicated.

Kill Tanathos. Just focus on that.

"We'll get him back."

"When we catch Tanathos, leave him to me," Harafin said. "He is not your concern, because you have the most important duty. Even if we all fall in battle, you must not fail."

The old man fixed him with a powerful gaze. "You must reach Antigonus and place the stone in his hand. Nothing else matters. Whatever the cost."

Kevlin swallowed a lump of fear. "I won't fail."

"Tell Antigonus to use Oris's power."

"Wouldn't he do that anyway?"

"No. He is trained to release Oris's power only under very specific circumstances. It is a dangerous power, capable of wreaking terrible destruction if misused."

"In this case, tell him I order him to use it. It is worth the risk, because with that power, he should be able to overcome Tanathos' hold and restore his strength."

"I will see it done."

"See that you do. We are moving into a time prophesied centuries ago, and events are spiraling beyond our worst fears. We can afford no hesitation, and no mistakes."

The fervor in the old man's tone drove home the magnitude of what they were engaged in. Kevlin took a deep breath and faced the task ahead, pledging his honor to it. The moment he had snuck into Antigonus' cell and accepted the old man's charge, he'd cast his lot with him. Hopefully he had chosen well, because there was no way out.

Whatever the cost.

"All right then, what do I have to do?"

"Continue what you have started and allow nothing to get in your way." With a wave of his hand, Harafin conjured the small amber sphere of magic.

"What now?" Kevlin asked.

"You will need Oris tonight."

Kevlin took out the rock. "Why?"

"We are going to try something a little different. I want you to focus on the stone. Let your mind drift into it, and see if you can connect with it."

"That's kind of vague."

"Trust me."

Kevlin bit back a retort and instead focused on the rock, amazed as always by its unusual warmth. Peace flooded through him, washing away weariness from the long day, replacing it with clarity of mind and a feeling of tremendous strength.

He focused on the crystal emblem. A flash of light caught his eye, drawing it into the blue depths where tantalizing hints of light danced beneath the surface. His vision dimmed until he saw only the dark blue light of the crystal, his attention fixed on those mysterious glimpses of light. His mind slipped deeper into Oris and all thought, all concern flowed from him, leaving his soul empty of everything but the rock's magic.

Eventually he became aware that the dark blue world he had entered pulsated to a slow, regular rhythm. Unlike the pounding cadence of the song of Savas, this slow pulse brought only strength and peace, with no sense of fear.

He couldn't guess how long he remained in that state. His mind floated formlessly within Oris, struggling vainly to see more clearly the lights or to understand the rhythm. Eventually Harafin's voice echoed in his mind, like a lifeline calling him back. Reluctantly, he followed it and returned to awareness.

As Kevlin slid Oris back into the rune-covered bag he asked, "How long was I gone?"

"About two hours. Tell me what you experienced."

Kevlin related what he felt, tried to convey the blue expanse that consumed his vision. Harafin seemed to understand, or at least he nodded as if he did.

"So I guess it was all a waste of time," Kevlin said.

"Not necessarily. We will continue exploring your connection with Oris. This is uncharted ground, so we cannot be entirely sure what will happen."

"Have other stewards done this?"

"No steward has ever felt even a glimmer of the stone's power. Now, back to your training. Have you considered what we discussed last time?"

"I've tried to, but something has me a little confused. You said light is magic and the lifeblood of the world, or something like that."

"That is a fair summary."

"When people speak of the Light, they usually refer to some higher power tied to the creator. Some even claim the Light is a god."

"We will have to invite Leander to these discussions. He loves discussing such topics, but be warned, he might keep us up all night with his explanations. For tonight, suffice it to say that light is indeed intimately related to spiritual matters, although it is not in and of itself a sentient being or god."

"At its very core, spirit is really nothing more than light, light that is more refined than our senses can register, but light nonetheless."

"Hold on a minute," Kevlin said. He'd started to think he was grasping at least a little of what Harafin had said, but he found himself lost again. "I thought you said light is magic."

"Yes, it is."

"But now you're saying light is spirit."

"Yes."

"So are you saying that spirit is really magic?"

"In a sense, it is. That is how the shadeleeches are able to steal another person's life force and use its power. That life force is the essence of a person's spirit. But since shadeleeches have the ability to feed on magic and life, they can also feed on spirit."

"That's horrible." Kevlin thought back to what Harafin had said about the spirits of those destroyed by the shadeleeches.

"Agreed. Light, magic, and spirit are closely related. As one's understanding of that relationship deepens, so does one's ability to control and wield those forces. We will revisit the topic later and delve more deeply into it."

"So how do stalwarts fit in? Like Leander's Pallians, or Blade Stalwarts like Dhanjal?"

Harafin chuckled. "Leander could discuss such things for days if you let him. We lack the time tonight." He raised a hand glowing with magic. "Let's test your shields again."

Half an hour later, Harafin released him from the glowing sphere. Kevlin staggered to his feet, dripping with sweat. After the battle with Wayra's troop, he'd felt pretty confident in his shields, but Harafin had pushed him to the limits and taught him new concepts, expanding his skill exponentially.

Kevlin dropped gratefully onto his blankets, but passed an uneasy night. He kept reliving the encounter with Tanathos. Over and over he felt the sickening sensation of the makrasha shrinking under his touch. After each nightmare, his mind returned to that sensation of floating unconcerned within Oris's magic and he was able to sleep for a time.

58

SETTING THE BOARD

"What are you doing?"

Wayra grabbed Keld's shoulder with her good hand and spun him around to face her. "I didn't authorize you to make any mindlink connections."

The dim, silvery halo faded from Keld's head as he dropped the mindlink spell. He blinked fast as he returned to the present.

"Forgive me, I was just checking if it was safe to connect to Diodor."

Wayra frowned. "It is not your place to cast that spell. You could have been attacked."

He met her gaze for a second. "Yes, my lady, I know." After a brief hesitation, he added, "It's just, I've been practicing mindlink recently and wanted to see if I could make it that far."

"And you felt it necessary to hide in the woods to make the attempt?" Wayra asked, her voice soft but menacing.

Keld glanced at the heavy brush concealing them from the rest of the camp.

Only by chance had Wayra stumbled upon the young man in the midst of the spell. The connection had been so heavily shielded that she had been unable to glean any idea of what he was saying.

His face flushed with embarrassment. "Again, I'm sorry. I knew you might not approve."

"Then why do it?"

He shuffled his feet and replied in a whisper, "I knew you'd probably try it, and I didn't want you hurt if the enemy was still blocking the connections."

Wayra paused, swallowing an angry reprimand. She studied the young fellow closely. Everything he said sounded plausible, but something didn't feel right.

She was tempted to cast Truth on him and demand to know everything, but if he had really been motivated by loyalty and concern for her, could she repay him with such a lack of trust?

Too much had gone wrong in the past week, and events were spiraling out of control. She refused to look down at her withered hand. She'd slipped, just for a second. She deserved better.

She would have better. Soon.

She didn't understand everything Harafin said, and that made her nervous. Tanathos could murder Antigonus anywhere. It didn't make sense that he needed to invade Il'Aicharen to do so. But if he did, she'd have failed doubly. It could not be allowed.

"You made a connection?" Wayra asked.

"Yes."

"To whom?"

"You interrupted me before I could complete the link to Ruggiero," he said quickly. "But I could sense his mind, so I know the way is clear."

They returned to the campsite and she considered Keld's words. If he really had reached all the way to Diodor, his powers were greater than she had realized. She would have to test him soon. With that much strength, and with some careful guidance, he could become a powerful helpmate.

The rest of the company sat around a cheery fire stoked high enough to hold back the chill night air. "I will contact Diodor," she said, seating herself near the blaze.

"Do you think that's wise?" Thyra asked.

"Keld made it through."

Wayra closed her eyes and focused her power. Taking great care, she triple-shielded her mind and thrust out with her senses, hurtling northwest toward the capital.

Racing her thoughts across the surface of the land always invigorated her, and the heightened risk tonight only intensified the thrill. In the clearing by the fire, her breath came fast and her face flushed with excitement. The other sentinels watched, ready to leap to her aid if needed.

The land flashed by, a pale shadow of reality. The general shape of the land, trees, and buildings flowed through her mind-sight. Smaller things, like people, were vague, ethereal forms that glowed with subdued amber light.

As she neared Diodor, pinpoints of light appeared in her vision and, as she drew closer, they brightened into flaming beacons which called to her mind. Those were the minds of the actinopathic, ones who could sense her, accept the touch of her mind, and communicate in return.

Sweeping over the capital, she felt growing resistance. The palace was shielded, making it difficult to penetrate. Sentinels assigned to the king's service monitored that space, ready to intervene should any mind draw close enough to pose a threat.

She avoided the palace and swept instead toward the inn where her company had stayed, where a bright cluster of gifted minds beckoned. Each was slightly different, glowing in her mind-sight with varying hues.

Spotting the one she wanted, she closed the distance and touched it. A second later, it responded and the connection solidified.

Who is this? Ruggiero asked, his mindvoice cautious.

Wayra. I have new orders.

His relief flowed back through the connection. *We arrived two days ago,* his thought raced down the link, conveying pride at their rapid journey.

You must leave immediately. Return to Il'Aicharen with all speed.

He could not shield his surprise or his anger. *I don't understand.*

She couldn't allow his valid frustration to interfere. *Do not question. Matters have changed and the enclave itself is now a target. It is at risk, and the enemy is on the move.*

What? Anger gave way to surprise.

We have little time. The enemy is trying to block communication, so it is dangerous to mindlink over any distance. Just obey, and be wary. The road may not be safe.

We will leave at once. Should I notify the king?

After a pause, she said, *No, I will deal with that. Obey and go with all speed. This is the moment we have trained for.*

I will not fail you, he said, his mindvoice strong and filled with confidence.

She cut the connection. When she returned to her own body, she sagged by the fire, exhausted. Thyra brought her a towel for her face and a canteen of icy water while she caught her breath.

After drinking deep, Wayra said, "We ride for Il'Aicharen at first light."

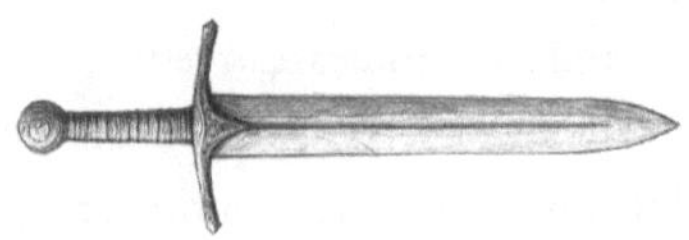

"Come," King Leszek called. He put down the parchment he had been reading and leaned back in the overstuffed chair behind the mahogany desk in his study.

"Sentinel Hathor," the page announced.

Hathor, dressed in sentinel white, entered the room. He was of average height and build, but King Leszek could not hazard a guess at his age. He appeared to be in his fifties, but he had served House Dalagan for the past half-century, so he had to be far older than that. Hathor oversaw the three sentinels assigned to the palace, responsible for security and magical defenses.

"Welcome, my friend," King Leszek said. "What brings you here tonight?"

Hathor approached with a grave expression. "I have news of Wayra's party."

"Good. She's been lax of late."

"It appears there is some threat to the enclave of Il'Aicharen."

The king sat forward, surprised. "What type of threat?"

"I know nothing specific, but I believe the warning to be credible. Apparently Master Sentinel Harafin is involved, and it is he who identified the danger."

"Harafin? He should be in Tamera. Does the ruling council know what's going on?"

The thought disturbed King Leszek far more than he could reveal. If the emperor learned the truth, everything Leszek had worked toward would be destroyed.

Hathor shrugged. "My information is sketchy, but it seems Harafin is also hunting Antigonus. There appear to be enemy forces at large in Hallvarr, and they pose a direct threat to Il'Aicharen."

"I find that hard to believe," King Leszek said. "We have a company of kestrels from Il'Aicharen here in Diodor, do we not?"

"We do."

"Send for them. They must know something."

Hathor nodded and withdrew. King Leszek rang a tiny gong on his desk. A servant entered the room.

"Send for Tekla," the king instructed.

Half an hour later, the grizzled commander arrived and they took seats by the fire.

"How may I serve?" Tekla asked.

"We may have a problem." The king related to the commander what he knew.

Tekla frowned. "It is difficult to make the right decision with so little information."

"I know." The king drummed the arm of his chair. "Everything's falling apart. We can't lose it. We are too close."

A knock at the door interrupted them. "I wish not to be disturbed," the king called, but the door opened and the servant intruded fearfully.

The young man bowed low. "Pardon, my liege, but I was told this cannot wait."

"Very well, but let whoever disturbs me know they bear responsibility if they waste my time lightly."

The man nodded and exited as fast as propriety would allow.

A few seconds later, a tall soldier in mud-splattered clothing entered the room. His face haggard and unshaven, he banged his fist to his heart in salute.

"What is it?" the king demanded.

"My king, I bear grave news. The northern village of Condurso was attacked yesterday at dawn by a large force of makrasha and shadeleeches. They left only a handful of survivors."

The king shared a startled glance with Tekla. "Are you sure?"

The soldier nodded. "My patrol was operating in the area and stumbled upon a survivor fleeing through the woods. We found the village destroyed. Some of the villagers put up a fight. We saw the corpses of two makrasha."

"How is it possible?" King Leszek turned to stare into the fire, his mind whirling as he considered the information and tried to match it with the intelligence he had received from Hathor. Events were moving too fast, and nothing was proceeding as he had been led to believe.

One thought became clear though, as mounting anger burned away doubt and confusion.

"I have been betrayed. Tekla, the time has come to act before all descends into chaos. Mobilize our forces across the kingdom. Issue a general call to arms. Assemble the Outriders."

Even as Tekla saluted, the door was thrown open and Hathor strode in, ignoring the protests of the page outside.

"My king, the kestrels from Il'Aicharen are gone. They left the city not half an hour ago and took the road toward Il'Aicharen at full gallop."

"Then it is true."

"It appears so."

The king turned back to Tekla and placed a hand on the old commander's shoulder. ""Rouse the kingdom. You will ride north with a column of outriders and three Jagen Stalwarts." He glanced over at Hathor, adding, "A sentinel will accompany you. Track down that band of makrasha and destroy them. I ride at first light for Il'Aicharen with the rest of the outriders."

"I swear it will be done." Tekla saluted before spinning on his heel and striding from the room.

"Hathor, prepare your sentinels to ride."

"What is going on, my liege?"

The king grimaced. "A time of trial and testing is upon us. Fire and sword is unleashed in my kingdom, and I will see it stamped out."

After Hathor took his leave, King Leszek glanced at his house banner above the fire. "My rule will not end this way. Time to spin the Wheel."

59

THE PAIN BEHIND THE LAUGHTER

When dawn was but a blush on the eastern horizon, Kevlin and the others had already returned to their saddles, following Tanathos' tracks east. Their breath hung about them in silver clouds, and saddles creaked loud in the cold. They followed the narrow, winding trail at a fast trot.

After the sun crept above the horizon, Ceren drew her horse beside Kevlin's. The trail was a little wider, but they were still forced to ride knee to knee.

"Good morning," she said with a dazzling smile.

She had managed to bathe, and her olive skin glowed warm in the early morning sunlight. Her auburn hair was woven into a complex knot that spilled down in front of one shoulder, glistening with oils that highlighted its vibrant color.

She'd laundered her clothes and wore her original riding outfit. How she had contrived to look like they'd just left a comfortable inn instead of having slept another night in the forest he could not imagine.

Riding beside the scrubbed and radiant woman, he felt like an unwashed barbarian in his travel-stained garments, unshaven face, and borrowed chainmail. The wind blew toward them from the east, so at least she couldn't smell him.

Without saying a word, she had managed to reinforce their respective social positions. Not encouraging.

She spoke above the clatter of the trotting horses. "Kevlin, I want to apologize for the way I've been acting. Will you forgive me?"

She sat her horse with perfect posture, every inch the lady. Kevlin was intrigued. That opening turned his expectations for the conversation on their head.

"Uh, sure. Nothing to forgive."

"Thank you." She gave him another smile and placed a hand lightly on his forearm.

She was trying way too hard. Whatever she wanted from him, it had to be big. He probably wouldn't like it.

He wished she'd just get over her insecurities about being Cunning and do the job. That would earn the respect she wanted better than anything.

"I've been thinking about you a lot," Ceren continued.

"Really?"

He hadn't expected her to be the kind of person who stayed up nights imagining creative tortures for people who upset her. He tried to think what he might have done to set her off lately.

"Yes." She slid her hand slowly off his arm. "You are in a unique position, tied by blood to two powerful noble families."

"Oh." He gave up trying to anticipate where this twisted conversation was about to go.

"What do you know of your new families?"

"I knew Jerrik's brother. He's commander of the first Donarri legion, and a good man."

"Did you know that Jerrik's father is lord of Yochanan, one of the richest holdings in Donarr?"

"No, I didn't."

"What of Drystan's family? Did you know his father is lord of the Chandana, one of the most powerful tribes on the plains?"

"I didn't."

"And his father-in-law is the Einarri ambassador, holding a seat on the ruling council."

"I didn't know that either."

At least when he visited, there would be good food.

"Think about it. You'll be moving in different circles now, and new opportunities are within your grasp." When he said nothing, she leaned closer. "Don't sell yourself short."

She spurred her horse forward to ride alongside Gabral. "Thank you for the soaps and oils, Colonel."

Gabral ran a hand through his own freshly oiled hair. "I use only the best. From Freyarr, as I'm sure you noticed."

"I felt almost like I was back home in my father's palace." She glanced at Kevlin as she spoke.

It was too early in the morning for riddles, and he had always hated deciphering court intrigue. As a legion commander, he'd gotten a taste of it and preferred the honesty of a military campaign. He still had no idea what Ceren wanted.

Leander urged his horse up beside him. "The questions of youth I do not miss," the old man said with a twinkle in his eye. "But don't worry, my young friend, you will sort things out."

"Do you mind if I ask you a question?"

"Not at all, my boy."

"When we were fighting those makrasha at the fort, you looked really angry." Leander's face fell and Kevlin finished lamely, "I was just wondering why."

Leander rode in silence for a moment, staring straight ahead. "That was an old anger you glimpsed, rekindled by the presence of the Hands of Death."

His voice trailed off, and for several minutes he said nothing while Kevlin waited. When he began again, his tone was so soft that even riding beside him, Kevlin had to strain to hear.

"The origin of that anger has roots in a war against the Grakonians almost a hundred years ago. My wife and young daughter were killed in a raid."

"I'm very sorry."

"Thank you," Leander said with a sad smile. "I was a young sentinel and had been away fighting. We were victorious and had driven the enemy out of that part of the land, but a small force slipped past and destroyed our village."

Leander, a sentinel? That was all kinds of interesting. He held his questions, not wanting to risk Leander lapsing into silence again.

"They killed everyone. All were brutally tortured and murdered. All of them. Every building destroyed, every animal butchered."

Ancient suffering shone in Leander's eyes. What a burden to carry for so long.

"Who was responsible?" Kevlin asked, not wanting to know more, but unable to keep from asking.

"It was a company of the Hands of Death, but I never found out who led them." Leander grimaced. "I went quite literally mad with grief, my friend. I can look back and recognize it. The desire, the *need* for revenge, burned so hot that I am still amazed I wasn't consumed by it. I sought vengeance with terrible determination. Alone I tracked the force that murdered my family. I caught up with them just as they reached the borderlands.

"I destroyed them all."

He spoke with a cold finality matched by a look as frightening as anything he had said. It held the coldness of death, the same expression on Leander's face as they fought the Hands of Death the day before. Kevlin began to understand what had motivated the old stalwart.

He reminded himself never to anger Leander.

"I learned that a small group had left the company the day before, and that among the group was the individual responsible for the carnage. All I could learn of them was one word: Abaval"

"Abaval? Is that a name?"

"I don't know. At first I was convinced it was, but I have never been able to confirm it."

"I followed them until they joined a larger Grakonian force engaged in battle with the Tamerlane armies. I joined the fray with a crazed abandon that turned the tide in favor of the empire. I take some small comfort in that, at least. But my family was not avenged, and I pursued that vengeance with single-minded purpose."

He sighed. "I could not be reasoned with, but roamed the borderlands, attacking all enemy forces I encountered. For a full year I fought them. I have no idea how many I killed, but I fear it was thousands, for the uncontrolled wrath of a sentinel in the grip of madness is a terrible thing."

Kevlin struggled to reconcile the crazed sentinel Leander described with the pleasant, kindly old stalwart he knew. Maybe he should give the old man more room on the trail.

"Over time I grew reckless. One day, I came upon a small company and unleashed my magic upon them. But I had ranged far closer to settled country than I realized, and attacked a group of refugees trying to reach safe haven."

Clenching his hands on the saddle horn, he continued in a whisper. "As I looked upon the destruction I had wrought, at the terror and pain of those who had survived, I realized that I had gone too far. That was when I saw the child. Lying beside her murdered mother was a terribly injured little girl."

Tears shone in his eyes, and his voice cracked. "She looked so much like my own daughter, the sight nearly stopped my heart. It was the one thing that could penetrate my madness. I fell to my knees beside her and realized that in my mindless hunger for revenge, my actions had become those of my enemy. With innocent blood on my hands, I was equally guilty."

Kevlin reached out and squeezed Leander's shoulder. He had thought he had guilt issues. The old man seemed to shrink in on himself. He looked at Kevlin, his pain seemed nearly unbearable.

"I tried to save her," Leander said. "I bent all of my will, all of my magic, all of my terrible power into saving that one little child, but I could not. I had focused so long on destruction that I had no gift for healing. All of my powers were useless for saving her. I held her in my arms and watched her die."

He sighed. "She watched me try to save her, watched with the pure innocence and love of a child. She did not blame me for what I had done, she did not hate me. . . She forgave me. That moment is burned in my soul forever. She touched my tears with her little hand, and smiled at me before she died."

For a long moment, he could not continue, but rode staring blankly ahead, lost in the horrors of his past. Kevlin rode silently beside him, trying to imagine how he'd handle killing a child. He didn't think he could have lived with himself.

Finally, Leander sat up tall in the saddle. His eyes cleared and he took a deep breath. "I very nearly killed myself there, holding that little girl in my arms, but I could not do it. That would have been the final act of cowardice.

I could not dishonor her memory and the memories of my wife and child by running from the price I would have to pay for my actions."

"What did you do?"

Leander nodded toward Harafin. "A good friend and mentor guided me through that terrible time and helped me ground myself once more. I travelled a difficult road, but eventually regained a level of control. I still felt a burning desire for vengeance, for justice to be done, but at the same time I felt an overwhelming need to heal rather than destroy. My failure to heal that little girl still haunts me to this day."

Leander smiled. "Harafin introduced me to a stalwart, the head of the Pallians. Suddenly I knew what I had to do, for the Pallians are dedicated to the very two things I wished to devote the rest of my life to: bringing justice to those who deserve it, and mercy to those who need it."

"So you joined the Pallians?" Kevlin asked.

"With Harafin's assistance, I was eventually accepted into their order. On the day I took the vows, I renounced my sentinel powers. They had been used so long for destruction that I feared I could not control them were I to unleash that power again. The only exception was my hammer, but that's a story for another day. Since then I have focused on purifying myself and acquiring the gift of healing. I have known some success in my new life."

"A lot of success, I'd say."

"Thank you. I traveled a long road to where I met you on the streets of Baldev. On the way, I feel I have done some good. I hope to have many more years to serve and heal, for I have found a measure of peace, which is something I thought I would never feel again."

Kevlin hesitated to ask any more questions. He hadn't expected such an outpouring of deep, emotional history from Leander. He liked the old man, but they didn't exactly know each other that well.

"Why are you telling me all this?" Kevlin asked.

"I'm sorry if I'm boring you," Leander said.

"It's not that. It's just. . ."

Leander regarded Kevlin for a moment, his expression serious. "I shared my story with you because I believe you face a difficult choice in the days ahead. Let my story serve as a warning and a guiding light."

"I appreciate your concern," Kevlin said. He did, but he didn't understand the lesson. He didn't have a family to avenge. All he had to do was get a rock back to an old man.

Leander interrupted his musing, gesturing toward Harafin. "Speaking of our old friend, let me tell you of the time when he talked some of the first year Accepted into sneaking out at night. . ."

With that, he launched into a hilarious tale of a misadventure he and Harafin had experienced together. Leander's booming mirth at the end of the story seemed to wash away the horror of his memories.

At least for a time.

60

THE RHYTHM OF LIFE

After dinner, Harafin pulled Kevlin aside to continue their lessons. They settled once more within the glowing sphere, and Kevlin pulled out the rock.

"I still don't understand how this is going to work. Even if I somehow manage to make a connection with Oris, how will that help? I'm just the steward. I mean, I'm not creating magic like you and the other sentinels do. The only magic I can use is what the amulet captures for me." He gestured to his shirt front where the amulet rested against his skin.

"There are different sources of magic," explained Harafin. "Learning to access and wield power what originates outside of yourself is as important as reaching the power within you. I cannot yet answer all of your questions. This is a unique situation."

"So how do you know I can connect with Oris?"

"An educated guess. Now, concentrate."

Kevlin bent his gaze to Oris, amazed anew at the exquisite detail of the raised emblem of the flaming sword on the face of the rock. As he stared in fascination at the crystal, the rock grew warm in his palm and his mind was again pulled into its depths.

As he sank into the deep blue nothingness of the magic of Oris, the faint pulsing rhythm swept through him with greater intensity. It vibrated through his entire being. In the very depths of his soul, he *recognized* it. A dormant sense he had never known awakened.

The next pulse filled him with boundless energy, as if untapped reserves deep within him had been opened. He wanted to spring into the air and shout with the thrill of being alive, so alive his entire life to that point felt like he'd lived it in a half-dream.

Something caught his eye. Any movement within the formless blue expanse was startling, so the flash of light drew his attention immediately.

It began receding. Floating within Oris's magic, he could not feel his body, so had no means to move. But as another pulse of magic washed through him like the wave of an endless sea, he willed himself forward. With a thrill of excitement, he felt it working.

He pursued, and the light began to grow in size. Little by little he drew closer. If he could just catch that will-o'-the-wisp glimmer, perhaps he would finally understand some of the mystery of the rock.

All other thought vanished as he gained slowly on the tantalizing flicker. As he drew close, he imagined he could see something moving within the light, answers just out of reach.

Just before overtaking the light and perhaps answering the mystery once and for all, his mind collided with an invisible barrier. The shock of the impact numbed him.

He hung listless until the next pulse of magic shook him from his stupor. He pushed against the invisible wall with his mind, sliding his thoughts along it like fingers seeking a door, a crack, any sign of weakness. He pounded on it, focusing all of his will on bursting through, but to no avail.

Then he sensed another presence nearby.

He extended his senses in every direction, like questing fingers, but found nothing. Frustrated, he sagged against the unmoving barrier. For a split second something had been there, but where had it gone?

He felt it again, on the far side of the wall, although he still saw nothing but those frustrating flickers of light. He tried to call out, forming words in his mind and casting them forth.

Is anyone there?

Silence.

At that moment Harafin called him back from the stone. As soon as his vision cleared, Harafin said, "Something was different."

"There was something," Kevlin said, trying to make sense of what he had just experienced.

"You connected with it?" Harafin's voice quavered a little.

"Not really."

He tried to explain about following the light, encountering the invisible wall, and sensing the other presence. "Does that make any sense to you?"

"Not entirely. That you felt a presence is a great accomplishment. The presence you felt had to be the essence of Oris."

"You mean it's alive?"

"In a manner of speaking, yes, but not in the same way as you or I."

Harafin held up his hand to forestall Kevlin's next question. "I cannot explain exactly how. You must experience it for yourself. Oris has presented itself to different bearers in different ways, but never before to a steward, so I cannot tell you exactly what to expect."

"Why couldn't I reach it?"

"I do not know."

"There was something else tonight." Kevlin explained about the pulsing rhythm in the magic.

"Very good," Harafin said with a smile. "I'm glad you finally took note of that."

"You knew about it?"

"Yes. Partially because of how refreshed you appeared after submerging yourself in Oris. I imagine you feel unusually good at the moment?"

"Actually, I do." Kevlin hadn't realized the vibrant energy he had felt within the stone had remained with him after he returned. "What is it?"

"It is known as the Rhythm of Life. It flows through everything, and all things recognize it and respond to it. You might say it is the basic rhythm of magic, or the rhythm of light."

"I don't understand," Kevlin confessed. "But I did feel as if I recognized it. That's when I felt the burst of energy."

"Good. Then you understand enough for tonight. I want you to think on this as we ride tomorrow. The rhythm of life is very subtle, but you can see it in the flight of birds, in the cycle of the winds, in the rhythm of the waves of the sea, and in the flickering of a fire. Recognizing it is a key to unlocking tremendous power."

"If you say so. One thing bothers me. In some ways, that rhythm reminded me of the song of Savas. Is Oris going to try to take over my mind like Savas did?"

"No, it will not. The rhythm of life provides a powerful tool for those who know how to tap it, but nothing more."

"That's a relief."

"Savas is different," Harafin said, holding Kevlin with his gaze. "The god of war seeks to dominate you and own your soul. Beware the gifts He offers, no matter how enticing He makes them."

"Don't worry," Kevlin said, unnerved by the old man's intensity. "I don't want anything to do with Him."

"Good. Savas thrives on war, and through you as steward, he could unleash unending conflict upon the Six Kingdoms."

"Then take back the rock."

"You know I cannot. You alone must bear this burden."

Kevlin swallowed a curse and stared up at the curving dome of their little room. Trying to put his frustrations to words, he said, "I don't want this. I feel like I'm stuck in the middle of a magical whirlwind." He blew out a breath. "Does that make sense?"

Harafin climbed to his feet. With a gesture, the sphere of magic disappeared. He placed a hand on Kevlin's shoulder. "You did well tonight." Then he turned and headed for his blankets.

Kevlin stood musing in the chill darkness, pondering what he had learned and wondering what else Harafin was hiding from him. He wasn't sure if he had accomplished anything.

He had always tried to distance himself from sentinels and magic, but a door had been opened in his soul. Despite his fear, part of him was anxious to enter and behold what lay on the other side.

He avoided the group gathered around the fire, seeking the quiet of his own bedroll to try to making sense of his thoughts and feelings. He was not very successful.

Sleep was a long time in coming.

61

POWER RESERVES EXIST FOR A REASON

Rhisart sat back in his chair and rubbed his aching eyes. *Curse all kestrels.*

He stood, stretching his lanky frame to its full six and a half feet. The problems compounded every day they were gone, and Wayra still hadn't contacted him to explain their absence. Despite having sealed the passage to the heart of the mountain, his sense of foreboding continued to grow.

He stepped around the desk and began pacing. Bookshelves covered the walls, and two overstuffed chairs sat close to a cheery fire burning in the large stone fireplace.

Why did I ever agree to post so many kestrels here?

Of course, it had seemed a wonderful boon until they all left. Their sudden departure had thrown the enclave into chaos. The few sentinels remaining were mostly young accepted, with a handful of old-timers, most of whom could barely summon enough power to teach.

The door to the study burst open and the keeper of keys rushed in, still wearing his night robe. The old man usually tottered along, and Rhisart hadn't seen him move so fast in decades.

"Gerent," the keeper exclaimed, "the town is under attack!"

Rhisart threw open a large window and looked out upon a panoramic view of the valley. Nestled in the wide arms of the mountain, the town of Il'Aicharen lay draped in early evening shadow.

Everything looked tranquil.

The keeper leaned against the desk, trying to catch his breath. "You must listen. I have foreseen it."

"You haven't had a foretelling in half a century."

"Never matter." The keeper gave an impatient wave of his hand. "I tell you, I have seen the town burn!"

I was right. The keeper spoke the truth, for Rhisart had been feeling that same truth for two days.

His forces were stripped bare.

An icy trickle of dread slid down his spine.

"Come." He led the way through the keep and up onto the crenellated battlements with their unobstructed view of the valley.

Mount Il'Aicharen reared thousands of feet in sheer cliffs behind the keep, blocking the sky to the north. The keep was a solid mass of stone with five towers, built right against the cliff at the head of the valley.

A dozen smaller buildings flanked it on both sides, and a thick wall rearing twenty feet high protected the entire enclave. Constructed one hundred and fifty years ago with granite quarried nearby, the keep had never seen battle, and many regarded such a formidable structure built so far beyond the farthest reach of the enemy a foolish expense. Perhaps tonight that caution would be proven justified.

Arms of the mountain swept by on either side, enclosing the deep valley in which the local settlement thrived. The valley widened from a mile at the head, to twice that further down. The town comprised half a hundred buildings, near where the headwaters of the Ujutus gushed out of the eastern flank of the mountain, cascading five hundred feet down the cliff in a spectacular waterfall.

The churning waters raced down the mountain, split the town, and tumbled along the western side of the valley as the mighty Ujutus started its long, winding path through the heart of Hallvarr. Two bridges spanned the frothing river, connecting the upper and lower halves of the town. Farther south, farms dotted the central and western side of the valley all the way along the river, while ancient forest sheathed the eastern hills.

Rhisart stared out at the lovely view as he had countless times before. The air was clear, but no sound carried above the distant thunder of the falls. Cold wind sliced through their clothes, and the keeper shivered.

"How long?" Rhisart asked.

A scream echoed up the valley, its faint wail penetrating to his soul and chilling him far more than the wind. They shared a glance, not needing words.

Rhisart cast his mind off the wall.

His thoughts raced down the slope, into the town, and past shadowy, insubstantial buildings. Ethereal glimmers of the townsfolks' souls shone through the walls of their homes. Slipping his thoughts farther, he found what he was looking for in an alley near the river.

The mongrel dog growled at his first touch, then yelped when Rhisart seized upon its mind with more force than wisdom in his haste. He sent a comforting thought to it, then sent it racing down the street, over the bridge, and into the lower half of town.

Another scream rang out, magnified many times through the dog's ears, followed by yet another. Borne along with the dog, Rhisart's mind hurtled around the last corner.

The dog slid to a stop, and Rhisart gasped.

Two farmhouses southeast of town, built right against the forest, burned like giant torches. Silhouetted by the flames, a host of makrasha charged toward the town, led by no less than four shadeleeches. With the dog, Rhisart smelled the sharp tang of blood and fire, and the reek of the onrushing beasts.

The dog began barking a warning, but Rhisart was already gone. Again inside his own body, he stared toward the lower end of the valley, horrified by what he'd seen, and by what it meant.

Grabbing the keeper's shoulder, he said, "Makrasha. . .and shadeleeches. Rouse the keep!"

The old man gasped, rocking back as if Rhisart had struck him a physical blow.

Turning back toward the town and gathering his will, Rhisart amplified his voice until his words shook the valley. "We are under attack. Flee! Flee to the keep. Run for your lives!"

Several screams punctuated his warning.

Many doors opened, but most of the people stood on their doorsteps, staring toward the keep, more confused than afraid.

"Don't delay," he bellowed again. "Run for your lives! Makrasha!"

The screaming intensified as more voices joined in, and several buildings in the lower town exploded into flames. Townsfolk finally began to understand, and started running for the road that twisted up the steep slope toward the keep.

Only a fraction of them were moving fast enough.

Sentinels began to straggle out onto the wall to either side of Rhisart, asking what was going on. He left the answers to the keeper, as he focused again on the town.

Projecting his senses, he concentrated on the bridge. The lower half of the town already burned. Makrasha ran about the streets, slaughtering people as they emerged from their homes.

Returning to himself, Rhisart cursed. He could not allow the town to fall without any defense. If those monsters crossed the river, none of the villagers would make it to safety. Two bridges spanned the river, one old and wide and made of stone as solid as the keep itself. The second, added as the town grew over the past century, was smaller, simpler, and made of wood.

Shapes moved across the wooden bridge, tiny in the distance. Squinting, he could just make out a dark wave rushing onto the structure. The enemy was nearly across.

Rhisart formed an image of fire in his mind and focused his power into a concentrated shaft of pure energy that thrummed in his soul, chafing against the restraints that kept it bound.

He released it.

Liquid heat, invisible to non-actinopathic eyes, leaped from him and flashed across the distance. The distant bridge exploded.

Fire raced down its length, consuming everything in a wave of heat and destruction. New screams echoed across the valley, and he cringed. The bridge had not been totally clear of townsfolk.

It had been necessary, but the cost tore at his soul. The high-pitched wailing of makrasha testified that he'd caught the beasts before they'd made it across.

With the wooden bridge engulfed, he turned his attention to the stone crossing. He could not burn it, and the spells of strength woven into its stonework made it nearly impossible to destroy.

"What's going on?" a young accepted called to him, breaking his concentration.

"See the keeper," he snarled before pointing toward the tide of villagers racing up the slope. "Then open the gates and let them inside!"

A black tide flowed over the stone bridge. They were so fast!

Rhisart hurled a bolt of magic down the length of the valley in an attempt to slow them. The shimmering spear of power lit the night as it streaked from his hand toward the approaching enemy, but it glanced away just shy of the mark, and sailed harmlessly into the air.

Rhisart cursed. The shadeleeches held every advantage. Focusing on one tall building at the upper end of the bridge, he hardened the air around it, then drew the air in like a noose. Timbers splintered under the force of his will, and the building collapsed onto the street, blocking the road.

It would not slow them for long, but every second helped. The keeper, already back on the wall, directed the defenders and sent people to help the villagers into the keep.

"You are in charge," Rhisart said. "I must activate the keep's defenses."

Rhisart rushed from the wall. With his long legs eating the distance, he raced through the keep and up the long flight of stairs to the top of the central tower. The room he entered was furnished simply with low bookshelves, a small fireplace, and a couple of squat padded chairs. A wide window overlooked the valley.

Stopping in the exact middle of the room, Rhisart threw out his hands. Blue-white lightning arced from every finger to strike the walls. Energy crackled through the air and a series of thunderclaps shook the tower to its roots. The air heated until it seared his lungs and choked his nostrils with the smell of ozone.

The lightning didn't punch through the walls, but deflected, rippling vertically up the walls, then splitting, with slivers of energy shooting horizontal. Where the bolts intersected, they split again and then again. Within a double heartbeat, a grid-like pattern of glowing magic covered the room.

Sweat poured off Rhisart's face as he held the spell. He bellowed a word of power, and magic shot back toward him from every intersecting node. Seven hundred and seventy-three bolts of magic collided simultaneously just above his head, forming a brilliant sphere of magic the size of his two cupped palms.

With another shouted command, Rhisart placed both hands around the crackling sphere. The lines of magic disappeared, and the glowing gridlines faded into the walls, leaving the room dim but for the brightly glowing orb clasped between his fingers.

Rhisart intoned the rest of the spell, and as he spoke the sphere shrank until it disappeared. He threw his arms wide as he uttered the final word.

His entire body shook as raw magic surged up, filling him far beyond his normal capacity. Under his feet, the tower thrummed like a giant bell struck with a silver hammer. As the sound reverberated through the keep, runes of power glowed across every stone surface.

Rhisart opened eyes that now shone silver, and sparked with power. The defenses of the keep were activated and under his command. The mighty awakened forces bound his soul to the keep, which acted like an extension of him, giving him control of vast amounts of power.

He spoke with a voice that shook the room, "Let them come."

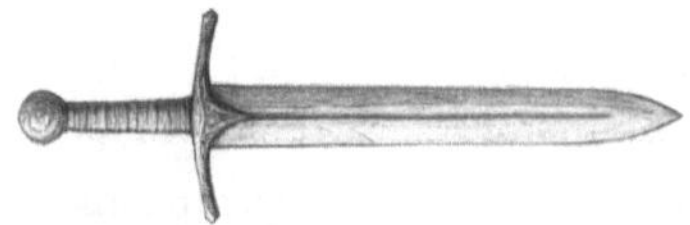

After the gerent left, the keeper marshaled his forces with the vigor of a far younger man. Several of the sentinels began casting energy from the walls, trying to slow the attackers.

Most of them were young accepted with little experience, or else old and tired and far past their prime. Their efforts helped but little, and the attacking horde soon fell upon the straggling villagers.

Screams filled the valley and defenders cursed in helpless frustration as they witnessed the slaughter.

One woman on the path urged her children ahead, then turned to face the charging beasts. With arms thrown wide and a wordless shout of defiance on her lips, she tried to slow them with her body long enough for her children to escape.

One old sentinel, his eyes fixed on that act of desperate heroism, cried out in rage. The keeper glanced at the man, who barely retained enough strength to teach the most basic spells, just as he raised both hands, and his body began to glow with power.

"Don't," the keeper yelled.

Too late.

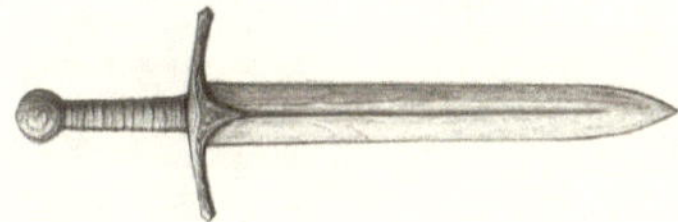

The old sentinel ignored the keeper and drew in the magic until it pounded through his bones and began tearing him apart. He had years of experience managing pain and held on tenaciously, riding the wave of power like a man trying to float the mighty Ujutus standing on a slippery log.

On the verge of losing control, he shouted a single word that rocked the valley and sent stones cascading down from above. A bolt of lightning flashed out of the clear evening sky and obliterated the beast closest to the desperate woman on the trail. The brilliant light seared eyeballs, while the thunderclap knocked people from their feet and shook the distant waters of the falls.

The same lightning bolt bounced up from the scorch mark that was all that remained of the makrasha, and coalesced into a ball of crackling silver energy, half the height of a man. It floated a couple of feet above the ground and drifted down the valley, with lightning arcing out toward nearby makrasha, cutting them down and splashing their carcasses across the road.

It reached the first of the shadeleeches and again arced lightning. The man's shield deflected it and he raised a hand to cast a spell. A second bolt of lightning struck first. That one penetrated his shield and blasted him to bloody ruin.

A second shadeleech threw a bolt of pure darkness at the ball lightning, and it exploded. The shockwave knocked scores of attackers from their feet.

Atop the wall, the old sentinel clutched his head, unable to control the magic still pounding through him and tearing him apart.

Even though his body screamed in agony, peace reigned in his soul.

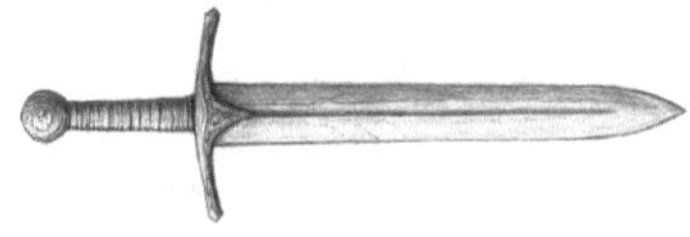

"Tai Pari", shouted the keeper.

The old fool, he thought sorrowfully, and knocked the old sentinel back off the wall with a blast of hardened air.

The veteran, a friend of more than a century, erupted.

Magical energy he'd condensed within himself overwhelmed his capacity and ripped him apart in a cataclysmic blast that knocked two people off the wall and shook the keep. A section of wall nearby cracked and buckled under the impact. The keeper staggered to the edge and stared down at the sagging stones where the old fellow had lost control.

"Be at peace, my friend."

He turned and urged the other defenders to hurry. The old sentinel's sacrifice had given the villagers close to the keep time enough to race inside, and the gate swung shut behind the pitiful few who made it.

The enemy flowed up the slope, while the flames of the burning town rose into an inferno below.

"Prepare," the keeper shouted.

Sentinels and men with makeshift weapons raced to the edge of the parapet to repel the attackers.

The enemy charged the main length of wall. On the eastern side of the keep, the ground fell away steeply all the way to the river. The western wall was built right into the cliff. The central section however, was built back from the edge of the plateau, giving the enemy ample room to form up ranks and charge.

Throwing grappling hooks tied to ropes, makrasha swarmed up the wall with incredible swiftness, using their hengaruk to dig into the stones like giant bugs. As defenders ran to cut the ropes and push the makrasha back, the shadeleeches struck.

The keeper focused his energies on blocking the magical attacks. He extinguished fires that exploded along the wall without warning, deflected bolts of power, and fought to quell the efforts of the shadeleeches who were strong in their evil arts. Shouts and screams echoed across the valley as the battle raged.

A makrasha reached the top of the wall and slaughtered a stable boy wielding a pitchfork. An accepted knocked the creature off the wall with a blast of air, but was then killed from behind by another beast.

As his scattered defenders fought, already on the verge of being overrun, the keeper wondered what kept the gerent. They would all die in minutes if aid did not come.

As if in response, the keep thrummed to life and runes of power began glowing along the wall.

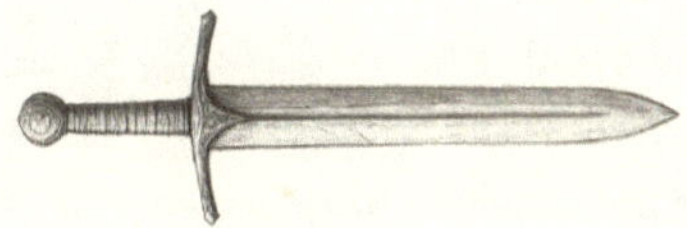

Rhisart took in the situation at a glance. Makrasha swarmed up the wall while shadeleeches kept his sentinels busy. Raising his hand, he called upon the keep's latent magic, and it came to life, surging through him like the rising of the tides.

The stones of the wall's exterior glowed, becoming red hot in seconds. Ropes burst into flame and makrasha fell shrieking to the ground.

Three shadeleeches in unison cast bolts of inky magic toward the highest tower, but heavy, glittering shields rose around the keep, deflecting them easily aside. Rhisart cast a bolt of pure white energy back at them. It shattered the shield of the foremost shadeleech and blasted him into the next world. The other two ran, followed by the makrasha, still numbering at least a hundred.

The defenders on the wall cheered.

Rhisart held no illusion that the fight was over, but still couldn't imagine how it had even begun. When it was clear the enemy didn't plan another immediate assault, he released the power of the keep and returned to the main hall where the keeper waited.

Placing a glowing finger on the keeper's forehead, he said, "I name you second. Should I fall, the keep's defenses will be yours to command."

"What of Wayra?"

"If she returns, the spell will revert back to her." Rhisart dropped into a chair. "Thank you. If not for your warning, they might have overrun the keep and killed us all."

"It nearly happened anyway. They killed many." The keeper dropped into another chair, looking exhausted.

Rhisart nodded, already turning his thoughts to unanswered questions. "If we hadn't just lived through this, I'd have considered it impossible."

"It seems impossible even now," the keeper agreed with an answering frown. "I have heard nothing of war."

"Nor I."

"How they came to Hallvarr undiscovered I do not know, but why attack here?"

"That bothers me the most. They have nothing to gain by destroying the keep." Rhisart paused, a wild possibility coming to mind. He considered it for a moment, then discarded it. Antigonus could not have fallen into their hands. Besides, he'd sealed the heart of the mountain.

"Any word of the kestrels?" the keeper asked.

"None. That is my second greatest worry. How did the enemy know we are so weak?"

"You think they knew?"

"It is the only explanation that makes sense. Had the kestrels been here, we'd have destroyed them all. They must know that."

"I wonder if this is why Wayra left with her forces," the keeper said. "To chase this enemy?"

"Perhaps. But then either they defeated her, or made her the fool and slipped past."

"I fear it is the former, but let us hope it is the latter," the keeper said.

"Let us hope so."

An accepted with a bloody bandage tied around his head entered the room with estimates of the dead, and reports of damage.

While Rhisart spoke with him, the keeper said, "I will try to reach Wayra and call for help."

It took a moment for the words to sink in. When they did, Rhisart turned to the keeper. "I don't think that's a good. . ."

The old man's eyes were closed. A shimmering, silvery halo surrounding his head testified that he was already casting the mindlink spell.

The keeper suddenly cried out, clutching his head, and fell to the floor, unmoving. Rhisart rushed to him and placed a hand on his brow, questing with careful fingers of thought.

The keeper's mind was locked away in an intricate defensive spell. Rhisart couldn't force his way in without causing more damage. Whatever had attacked him had nearly overcome the keeper's defenses, leaving only the hidden core of him heavily shielded.

Rhisart turned to the accepted. "Have him carried to his room and watched. He will awaken when the spell runs its course."

The young man left, leaving Rhisart to stare at the keeper's unmoving form.

He felt desperately alone.

62

A NEW MASTER

Sitara paused at the corner of a hallway to adjust her dress. She used the excuse to glance back to ensure she wasn't being followed. Satisfied, she resumed her journey. She did not want to be late.

She had left Remiel not long before. He had proven reliable. Only one day since sealing their agreement in the lower levels of the palace, she was on her way to meet the mysterious ally.

She'd been surprised when Remiel could only tell her that the ally was a sentinel, but that he had never actually met the man. All Remiel knew was the sound of his voice. Of course, given the risk they all faced if betrayed, she couldn't fault the fellow for taking such precautions.

"He calls himself Masego," Remiel had informed her as she dressed in the small room that had become their regular meeting place. She let her thoughts dwell on Remiel a moment longer, just as her eyes had lingered on him before she took her leave. He hadn't noticed the look, and as soon as she realized what she was doing, she turned away.

She couldn't afford to fall for the lie that Remiel cared for her. He was skilled at physical intimacy, but that didn't change the situation. He had forced her to prostitute herself to save her life. She was willing to endure the man's touch as a necessary evil to see Bajaran's dream to fruition, but Remiel was still a pig.

She maintained her sanity by dwelling on her imminent revenge. As soon as she no longer needed Remiel, he would reap the reward for his evil. She would purge her shame by destroying him, both body and soul.

Outside, the sun had long set and the underground corridors were mostly empty as people sought their beds. Another of Masego's surprises had been the meeting place. She could not understand why he would insist upon meeting beneath Sentinel Tower.

Struck by a sudden fear, Sitara paused in midstride.

Was it a trap?

It was a possibility she could not ignore, but she had no choice but to go on. No one knew she was a secret sentinel, and her simple dress blended in well in the palace. No one would look twice at her. If Remiel had betrayed her, she was already dead.

Sitara was not familiar with the underground passages that led to Sentinel Tower, so she climbed to the main level to exit the Great Dome and cross the expansive central courtyard. She glanced east to where the palaces of each of the Six Kingdoms faced the central palace.

The entire greater palace complex glowed with lights, the glow spilling out over the imperial capital. Tonight the Fire Stalwarts were hosting a gala to honor Akillik, and Freyarr Palace glowed like a jewel that beckoned throngs of people into the huge gambling hall in honor of the god of luck.

Sitara continued south, past the other palaces, toward a stout tower of white granite, flanked by an expansive building of gray stone. She'd never entered the tower. It was foolish to draw close to so many sentinels, but she breathed deep the cool early evening air and tried to instill calm on herself.

Half a dozen white-robed sentinels moved about, just inside the main entrance, but none gave her so much as a passing glance. She hurried down the wide stair of white marble on her left that descended into the lower levels, eager to reach their concealing shadows.

Three levels down, she left the stair and navigated four separate empty corridors until she found the appointed meeting place. It was unmistakable. Powerful magic pulsed around a nearby training room in a permanent shield. She waited anxiously as the minutes ticked by.

No one came.

Her anxiety turned to fear, which soon verged on panic. What if Masego had been captured? The authorities would find out about the meeting place.

What if they were already coming for her? They would find her standing like a lamb waiting to be slaughtered.

Just as she was about to flee, she felt a tickle at the back of her neck and jumped, with a little squeal of surprise. She angrily regained control. The tickle came again, and she recognized it as a Mindlink connection.

That was not what she expected, but she opened herself a little to the communication.

Who is it?

If it were anyone but me, you would already be dead, replied a deep, mocking voice. The tone was powerful, cruel.

Where are you? I thought we were going to meet.

A laugh. *This is all the meeting you've earned until you prove yourself.*

Prove myself? Anger began to replace fear. Who was he to talk to her that way? She was Bajaran's mistress.

Bajaran was a fool. And you are nothing but his pawn.

The mocking tone infuriated her. She had been through too much, lived in fear for too long. She had come looking for a friend and found nothing but another man full of his own importance. It was the final drop that burst the dam inside her.

She reached for the power of darkness, and it roared into her, matching her fury and staining her soul with filth. Swept away by the power of her emotions, she struck at the stranger's mind. In that moment, she didn't care about the consequences of injuring or even killing her sole ally. He would not insult Bajaran's memory.

The man deflected her attack as easily as a mother subdues a flailing child. He responded with the mental equivalent to a slap in the face.

She recoiled, but could not break the connection with his mind. She tried to erect barriers between them, but he crushed the attempt even as the thought formed.

Fear clutched at her heart. She could not stop him!

Is that the best you can do? He mocked again. *I thought you might prove useful. You are nothing but an untrained, undisciplined fool.*

Anger surged through her again, once more overwhelming restraint. She focused her power into a mental dagger and struck once more. He recoiled, and for a split second she connected with him. With an animal snarl, she lunged against his shields again, desperate to inflict pain.

Her victory, if it ever truly existed, lasted but for the blink of an eye. Once more he shattered her efforts and struck back at her exposed mind with a tremendous blow.

Waves of pain seared her mind and something lifted her bodily from the floor and slammed her against the wall. Agony exploded through her, and she cried out.

Silence, you idiot, he snarled. *If someone hears you, I'll kill you myself.*

What do you expect? She shouted back.

I expect discipline and control, he replied in a cold, deadly voice. *If you cannot demonstrate either, I have no use for you.*

The threat broke her anger, replacing it with terror. She drove the magic away and calmed her mind. She could not beat him. She would wait for a better opportunity.

His voice struck again. *Guard your thoughts better. If I were not shielding you, everyone in the tower would be able to hear what you're thinking.*

Fear made it hard to think clearly. Masego was obviously far more powerful than she. She had only ever engaged in a mindlink conversation with Bajaran, and then only on rare occasions. He had taught her the shielding techniques, but she'd had very little opportunity to practice.

If you ever attack me again, his thought seeped into her mind like venom, *people will whisper of your fate for ages.*

She shivered with growing fear.

After a pause he continued. *I will accept you as my servant. You will do my will until I release you or kill you.* The statement so closely paralleled what she had said to Remiel that she shuddered.

Remiel's allegiance to me will always trump his service to you, Masego added, once more reading her thoughts.

Her mind spun as she tried to adjust to the unexpected turn of events. She had known only Bajaran in the revolution and had assumed others would be like him. But where he was noble and kind and generous, Masego was cruel and vicious and frightening.

I don't have time to bed you, girl, Masego said cruelly. *Use Remiel for that if you must. Serving me is simple. Do well and you will be richly rewarded, and hold a position of power when we triumph. Fail me and I will rip your soul from your broken body and consume your life force.*

She took a deep breath. *I accept.* There was nothing else she could say. She could not turn back.

Of course you do.

Sitara collected her scattered thoughts. *I need your help. A sentinel intends to cast Truth on me tomorrow.*

I know. I will deal with it. First, tell me what training you've received. Did Bajaran teach you anything useful?

He taught me to plant thoughts into the minds of others, she said proudly.

Something like this?

An overpowering desire flooded through her, so intense she gasped. A desire for him.

His voice was so powerful. He was everything she ever dreamed of in a man. She needed him! If he would only speak again so she could hear his voice.

Sitara pressed her body against the wall in the direction she sensed his voice coming from, panting for breath as she desperately searched for him. Sweat broke out all over her body, trickled down her neck and between her breasts, and she moaned for him.

She needed him. She would do anything if he would only touch her, speak to her.

Then the feeling disappeared.

It was as if her mind plunged into a bucket of icy water. She was left gasping in shock and horror at what he had done to her, while his mocking laugh rang through her mind.

He had commanded complete control over her will. She would have done anything for him. The thought was terrifying. She felt violated far more intimately than anything Remiel could do to her.

Again he laughed, but an honest laugh. *We will see if you have potential.*

Teach me how to do that, she said.

That brief demonstration only highlighted how naive she had been. She had been so proud of her accomplishment in influencing the keisara, but that had been mere whispers compared to Masego's power. She needed to understand. That was the only way to protect herself.

Whispers sometimes prove more effective than overwhelming force, Masego explained, and for the first time his voice seemed gentler, the voice of a teacher. *The time will come when you will learn more powerful techniques, and when to use them. You are not yet ready.*

But--

No, he cut her off. *Only when you are will I teach it to you. But now, I have an important assignment for you.*

Sitara feared to hear what this brute wanted from her.

You will use your skills to convince the keisara to send you to Hallvarr.

Hallvarr? Sitara couldn't hide her confusion. *What's in Hallvarr?*

Accomplish what I command and I will tell you more.

But, Omolara is protecting the keisara. She watches constantly.

Masego's voice rang in her mind, cold as ice. *That is your first test. Find a way, or I have no use for you.*

Sitara cringed. *I'll do it.*

See that you do. Once you are successful, I will deal with the Truth spell that concerns you so much.

How?

I will explain later. First we need to work on more basic matters, like your complete inability to shield your thoughts.

The lesson began in earnest.

63

A Bit of Insight

Kevlin rolled out of his blankets with a groan in the icy gray light of pre-dawn. He spent the next few minutes stamping his feet and swinging his arms to drive warmth into them.

Winter was fast approaching in the Hallvarri highlands. Frost coated the grass, and mist curled up from the horses' backs. Snow could start flying any day.

The rest of the party looked as worn and tired as he felt. The long days were taking their toll. During breakfast, he jockeyed for position around the fire. Ceren joined him. Her auburn hair hung in a simple braid that morning, and he marveled how different a woman could look just by changing her hair.

"Good morning," he greeted her.

"Good morning," she replied with a dazzling smile. She held her hands out to the fire. "Have you thought about what we discussed yesterday?"

"Not really."

She frowned, leaning close, and he caught a whiff of perfume. That just made him think about how badly he must stink.

Her emerald eyes held him. "Don't be daft, Kevlin. You have to think about your situation. You can't sell yourself short."

That phrase again. She turned, and he followed her gaze to the right. A few feet away stood Indira chatting with Jerrik and Drystan. Behind the trio, Harafin approached the fire, looking grumpy and tired.

Ceren turned back to Kevlin and raised an eyebrow, as if to make sure he got the point.

He hadn't.

She moved away, leaving him muttering to himself about the insanity of understanding women. Was she referring to Indira, his swordbrothers, Harafin, or all of them?

Jerrik and Drystan honored him with their blood oath. Harafin freely taught him magic and trusted him with knowledge only the sentinels usually held. If anything, Harafin was setting him up for something, making him a tool the old man could use in whatever plots he kept locked in that bearded head. Was Ceren warning him against Harafin's influence?

His eyes settled on Indira. Her midnight hair was brushed back from her face, and her cheeks flushed with the cold. She laughed at some comment Drystan made, and the clear sound warmed him in a way the fire never could.

She glanced in his direction and noticed him watching. He looked away, cursing himself for a gawking fool. In her own way, Indira troubled him more than Ceren.

Ceren played with his mind, trying to maneuver him into doing something for her that he'd probably be happy to help with if she just asked. Indira played with his heart and that was far deadlier. Did she even understand what kind of weapon she wielded with those long lashes and shy smiles?

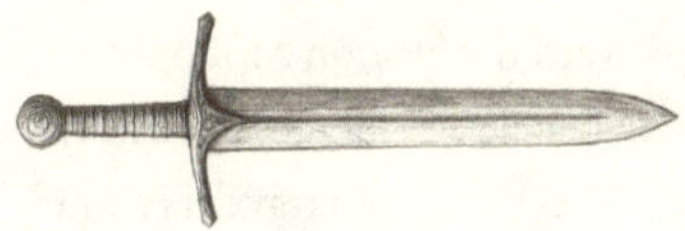

Later that morning, the trail widened into a regular country road, allowing them to kick the horses into a canter. By mid-morning they reached the wide expanse of the Imperial Highway.

After studying its hard-packed surface for a minute, Adalia declared, "They went north."

Harafin nodded, his expression grave. "North, the road splits. One path leads west, back toward Diodor. I do not believe they came so far east only to go west again."

"So they're going north, to Il'Aicharen," Gabral said.

"Yes." Harafin nodded toward the distant mountains rising to the north. At this distance, they were dark shadows on the horizon. "Mount Il'Aicharen lies there. I must contact Rhisart and warn him of the danger."

"Is that wise?" Leander asked.

"Perhaps not, but I can delay no longer."

"I will lend you my strength," Leander offered.

"No, old friend, I should be safe enough. But stand ready in case I am wrong." Without waiting for a reply, Harafin closed his eyes, and a dim, silvery light gathered around his eyes.

A moment later, Harafin opened his eyes and swayed in the saddle.

Kevlin steadied him, "Are you all right?"

Harafin rubbed his temple with one hand. "Yes . . . I got through to Rhisart, and he knows we are coming, but the attack has already begun."

"How is that possible?" Gabral asked. "Tanathos can't be that far ahead of us."

"Perhaps Tanathos has other forces at his command," Leander said.

Harafin nodded. "It seems likely. Regardless, the keep has powerful defenses, and it appears Rhisart was successful in activating them in time. He should be able to hold until we arrive."

They pushed the horses hard, heading north. Miles slipped by and the ground began rising toward the Straton Mountains. Individual peaks, with snow clinging to the higher elevations, became clear. Mount Il'Aicharen towered behind them. They passed no travelers coming south, and Kevlin wondered if traffic was just light, or if Tanathos had killed them all.

At noon, they paused beside a stream to rest the horses and eat a quick lunch. Kevlin dropped onto a fallen log beside Indira and she smiled in greeting.

"How about teaching me one of those card games you know?" he asked.

"Sure."

"Don't do it," Jerrik interrupted. "She'll steal your shirt, Kevlin."

"How do you know?"

Indira said, "Done is done, Jerrik. No whining."

"It wasn't fair," the big man complained.

"I gave it back," Indira said. She caught Kevlin staring, and blushed.

"You sold it back," Jerrik exclaimed. "At twice the price I could've bought a new one."

"You play for clothes?" Kevlin asked, trying to reconcile Indira the gentle healer with Indira the card shark.

Indira shrugged. "He drank away all his money. He insisted he could win for once, and wouldn't listen to reason. Sometimes you have to teach a lesson."

"No cards," Gabral said. "It's bad for morale when you win all the time."

"Are you saying I cheat?" Indira asked.

Gabral stammered under her gaze. "No, of course, not. You're the most honest person I know."

Ceren joined them, grinning. "Indira, you'll have to teach me how you do that."

The two scooted closer together, chatting excitedly. Kevlin's chance to spend private time with Indira was gone. Still, he had enough money in Bajaran's purse that he could stay at the table a long time, no matter how good Indira proved to be. He was looking forward to the chance to play her.

It wouldn't be soon, so he turned to Harafin. "I still don't understand how killing Antigonus at the node of power will cause so much destruction."

"It is because he is bearer of Oris."

"But I have the rock."

"Stone," Harafin corrected out of habit.

Kevlin shrugged. "I have it, so what's the danger?"

The others gathered around to listen.

"The danger lies at the heart of Oris's power. The empire's magical defenses against the Sigrun are extremely complex and require vast amounts of energy. No person can generate that much power."

"That's why we need Oris, right?" Kevlin asked.

"It is more than that. Oris is a crucial element, but the power that fuels the aegis comes from the very fabric of the planet. Mount Il'Aicharen is a node of power, a nexus of the planet's energy."

Harafin waited a second, as if for the import of that statement to settle on him. "It is also a dormant volcano. Similar nodes of power are dotted around the globe, and serve several important functions in balancing and sustaining all life. Il'Aicharen is the closest. If Tanathos gains access to the heart of the mountain, the core of that node of power, and murders Antigonus there, he will shatter the aegis."

Kevlin whistled softly, finally beginning to understand the danger.

Harafin continued. "Antigonus' life is tied to the spell, as is the power of Oris. Not only will the aegis crumble, but Oris will be destroyed, releasing the vast amounts of energy tied to it. Tanathos would be imbued with much of that energy, becoming the most powerful shadeleech on the planet."

Leander interjected, "Nothing we could do would likely stop him. Only the combined power of the quorum of masters might challenge him since the Six could never again unite with Oris gone."

"Now you begin to see my fear," Harafin said into the silence. "If he succeeds, Tanathos could return to Grakonia and wrest power from the Sigrun, then unleash a war upon the Six Kingdoms we could not win."

He smiled ruefully. "And most likely the event would trigger an eruption in Mount Il'Aicharen, burying half of Hallvarr in ash and fire."

"Then what are we waiting for?" Jerrik asked, rising to his feet. "Sounds like a good little fight ahead of us."

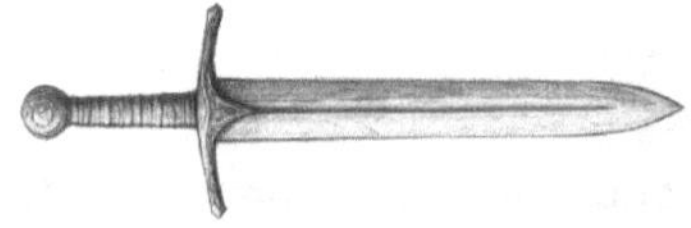

The noonday sun shone warm and bright on the bustling docks of Diodor. The crisp salt air blew in from the Tamerlane Sea, driving the stench of dead fish and rotting waste from the docks up into the city. As the large merchant ship *Ceara* tied off at the dock, the captain and sailors joined together in a great cheer.

"Oy! What be the hollerin fer?" a burly port worker called up to them.

"We beat the record for crossing from Parthalan by a full day," called down the mate. The sailors let out another "Huzzah!" even as a few of them ran out a boarding plank. A powerfully-built sentinel with a heavy mane of black hair hurried across.

"Sentinel Ah'Shan," the captain called. The sentinel paused after stepping onto the pier and glanced back. "May the Lady's favor go with you."

Ah'Shan nodded, and without a word rushed up the pier. To himself, he muttered, "Fastest crossing indeed. Pray it was enough."

If only Wayra had warned him sooner. He grabbed the shoulder of the nearest official and spun the man around. "Tell me where I can buy a fast horse."

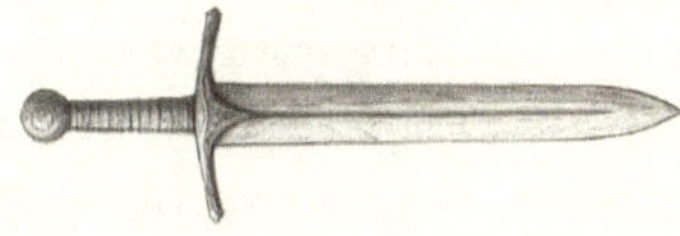

Long after the sun set, the exhausted group finally stopped for the night. Kevlin wandered to the edge of camp, hoping for some quiet time to think, and perhaps avoid another lesson.

"Kevlin."

He turned at the soft voice and was surprised to find Indira standing behind him.

"You getting a game together?" he asked, drinking in the sight of her.

She stepped closer, smiling. "No. I've been thinking about you . . . ah, about what you said." Her eyes dropped and her cheeks flushed, but she took a deep breath and looked up again.

"What exactly did I say?" Hopefully it was something smart.

"About my gift." She took another step closer, within arm's reach, and smiled again, a real, warm smile, not the shy little things she normally gave. Her eyes sparkled. "I think I can do it. I think I can control how I shield people, and when."

"That's wonderful."

She placed a hand on his arm. "Thank you."

She leaned closer, and for a heartbeat he thought she was going to kiss him. His mouth went dry and his heart pounded. She was so close he could feel her warmth and smell the faint fragrance of her hair. Her creamy skin glowed in the dim light, and her full, red lips parted just a little.

She retreated suddenly, chuckling. "Kevlin, you are so gullible. You wouldn't last ten minutes in Tamera." She held his purse in one hand and hefted it a couple of times. "Where does a mercenary get a stash like this?"

"Where does a healer get such quick hands?" he retorted, snatching the purse back. He half hoped she'd try to run so he could chase her, but she relinquished it without a struggle.

"You didn't answer my question," she said.

"Let's just say Bajaran lost a toss of the dice."

"And you got the winnings? You sure you want to lose all that to me?"

"Who are you?" he asked. This was such a different side to her.

Indira's face flushed and she looked down, as if realizing how forward she'd been acting. In a second, she switched from a bold woman, confident in her skills to a shy girl, anguished that she couldn't heal all the world's ills.

"I'm sorry," she stammered. "I don't know what got into me. I just . . . you make me . . ."

Kevlin took a step forward, hoping to coax out the secret Indira again.

She backed away. "I'll see you later, Kevlin."

Indira rushed away without looking back.

Kevlin started after her, but Ceren stepped out of the shadows. "Kevlin, we need to talk."

"Now's not really a good time."

She moved to block his way. "Actually, now's the best time."

"What is it?"

She nodded after Indira. "Be careful, Kevlin. You're messing with that girl's heart."

I'm messing with her?

"You're a nobleman now," Ceren continued "Allied with two very powerful houses. You need to think before you act."

"And you need to focus on doing your job, not mine."

"If you hurt her, I'll kill you myself."

"From everything I've heard, I'm the one who's likely to get hurt playing against her."

"That's not what I mean and you know it," Ceren said.

"I have no idea what you mean. Ever. You're the one who's Cunning, remember?"

Ceren abruptly changed tactics. "Kevlin, I worry about you sometimes."

"Please don't. It gives me a headache."

"You're moving in new circles. I see dangers ahead and I'm trying to help you avoid them."

Kevlin forced down his frustration. "I appreciate it, Ceren. Let's just focus on the mission at hand. We can worry about everything else later. Deal?"

She took his proffered hand. "Deal."

After she left, he considered her words. There was more she had been trying to communicate, but he still didn't get it. She was the most complicated woman he'd ever met.

Not wanting to speak with anyone for a while, he returned to the fire. He tried to see the rhythm of life Harafin had talked about, but to him the flames flickered randomly.

It's hopeless. I can't do all this magic stuff. I just need my sword and a clear shot at Tanathos. With the amulet to help, I'll only need a second to finish him.

64

A Glimpse

The town of Il'Aicharen burned.

Rhisart stood atop the wall and surveyed the valley filled with smoldering ruins. Smoke hung heavy in the air, concealing the lower town in a shifting haze. Makrasha moved amid the rubble, but the shadeleeches were nowhere to be seen. Other than the fifty or so beasts posted at the foot of the road leading to the keep, none of the attackers paid them any mind.

That worried him the most.

Why didn't they attack? With their numbers, they might still be able to overrun the keep. He had expected them to attack during the night, so he'd maintained a careful vigil until dawn. When no assault came, he finally risked getting some sleep.

Still they did not come. The sun had already slipped behind the western spur of the mountain with no movement from the enemy. Were they planning on attacking during the night? It seemed likely. But why wait the extra day and give the defenders time to organize?

He was overlooking something. The enemy must have known that every hour they waited only increased the chances that aid would come.

Above the keep, heavy clouds piled atop each other, brewing a storm like Rhisart had not seen for decades. He wondered if the shadeleeches were tampering with the weather.

Such spells were very tricky and required vast amounts of energy. Working with the weather was difficult at the best of times, and one could never be sure of the result. Why risk it? A heavy downpour would make the keep harder to defend, but it would also hamper efforts to scale the wall.

He needed to figure out the mystery. He feared what would happen if the enemy attacked before he could.

65

ALLIES

The steady pounding of hooves on the hard-packed roadway surrounded the party with constant thunder. Kevlin's body moved in time with his mount, but his mind wandered.

For a while he grappled with Harafin's lessons on magic, but the effort left his head hurting. Hopefully Harafin would grow tired of the game soon and leave him alone. Kevlin wasn't a sentinel and no amount of training was going to change that.

He had given up trying to understand Ceren's behavior. She had treated him with professional courtesy ever since their deal and he hoped to build upon that.

His thoughts turned to Indira, as they often did of late. She fascinated him. The gentle healer side of her attracted him with undiminished force, but it was the hidden side of her that he yearned to learn more about.

First he had to deal with Tanathos. After that, if he could escape whatever machinations Harafin was laying in his path, then he would play a long game of cards with Indira.

Around mid-morning, the highway split. The main road turned west toward Diodor, but they followed the smaller branch north without pause.

The road wound into the foothills of the Straton Mountains. By noon, when they stopped for a quick lunch, they were already past the foothills.

While they ate some jerked beef and flat travel bread, Harafin paused mid-sentence. He closed his eyes and a silvery halo surrounded his head.

"What's going on?" Kevlin asked.

Leander moved to stand next to Harafin. "It appears he has received a mindlink communication."

Nikias and Ceren, who had been discussing the various noble families of Hallvarr, shifted closer to listen. Nikias knew all the women at court and, if his boasts could be believed, was beloved by all.

"I thought mindlink was dangerous right now," said Ceren.

"It is."

They watched in silence for another minute until Harafin opened his eyes. "I was not attacked. In fact, for a change I have good news."

"Tanathos is dead?" Nikias asked excitedly.

"No, not so good as that," Harafin chuckled. "I was contacted by Ah'Shan. He founded the kestrels half a century ago. Wayra was right. He's traveled all the way from Parthalan to come to our aid."

"What size force does he bring with him?" Nikias asked.

"Just himself." At Nikias' crestfallen look, Harafin added, "Ah'Shan is an adept sentinel of the highest caliber, and a force to be reckoned with."

"Where is he?" Ceren asked.

"On the road from Diodor."

"He made incredible time from Parthalan," Kevlin observed.

Harafin nodded. "Sometimes it is possible to manipulate the winds to help speed a ship, if the need is great enough."

Kevlin frowned. "I hope he told the captain what he was doing."

"Why?" Ceren asked.

"Because they can't take credit for beating the record for passage from Parthalan to Diodor if a sentinel tampered with the winds."

"What record?" Indira asked.

"Traveling between cities usually takes about the same average time," Kevlin said. "Those merchants able to make the passage faster win prestige and can command better prices. Using magic disqualifies a trip from getting posted."

Ceren laughed. "I think Ah'Shan had more important things to worry about."

Kevlin said, "Don't make fun of it. It's an important part of a merchant's life."

Ceren raised a hand defensively. "Don't get upset. It's not worth the fuss."

"It is to some people."

Leander clapped Kevlin on the shoulder. "I'm sure things will be sorted out. It is good to know we have another ally on the way."

"Indeed," Harafin said, his expression thoughtful.

They pushed the horses all afternoon, climbing through the hills, ever nearer to the towering bulk of Mount Il'Aicharen. The mountain filled the sky to the north. As the sun slid toward the west, dark clouds began building around the high peak.

"Looks like a storm's coming," Kevlin commented when they slowed to walk the horses for a while.

"The sky's getting hazy," Drystan pointed out.

"We ride through the night," Harafin decided, his expression grave as he looked north. "Time is very short."

They paused late in the day to eat dinner and rest the tired horses again. Kevlin sank to the ground next to the fire and sighed, happy to be out of the saddle for a while to rest his aching thighs.

Indira settled next to him, tucking her legs up under her robe. She pushed her silky black hair behind one ear and met his gaze.

Before she retreated into her shy shell he asked, "Tell me how you can control your gift."

She leaned closer, her eyes glowing with excitement. "I haven't tried it yet, but I think under the right circumstances I could shield someone with my faith even before they get hurt."

He liked her best like that, her eyes sparkling, her cheeks a little flushed, radiating confidence. He wondered why she feared showing the world that side of her.

"Tell me about it." Ceren sat on the far side of Indira. The two huddled together, chatting in hushed tones.

Kevlin decided to leave them be. Indira was inching out of her shell and he was finally reaching a workable relationship with Ceren. He went looking for Jerrik. He needed to learn everything he could about Indira's style at cards.

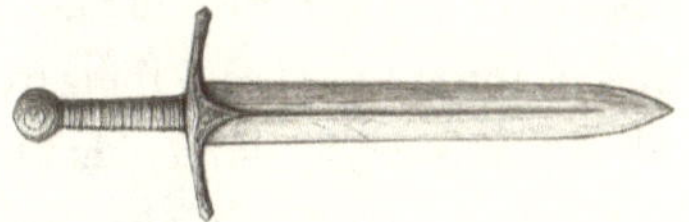

"There's an army camped in the next valley," a scout reported. Adalia stood with him.

"What are their numbers?" Gabral asked.

Jerrik simultaneously asked, "Tanathos?"

"We couldn't tell. We saw many campfires, but did not risk approaching."

"I coulda snuck up on 'em," Adalia boasted before jerking her head toward the soldier, "but he wouldn't let me."

"He was right," Harafin said.

Adalia muttered, "Nobody woulda seen me."

"Perhaps not, but why take the risk? I will investigate." Harafin closed his eyes and a light amber glow suffused his face, concentrated around his eyes.

"He's connecting with an animal," Kevlin whispered.

Probably an owl, since it was nearly midnight. The moon had yet to rise and the clouds blocked all the stars. The darkness was so deep that they had slowed to a walk, a single lantern lighting the way.

They waited several minutes before the glow faded and Harafin shifted and smiled in the wan light of the lantern, "It seems Wayra managed to contact Diodor after all. That's the king's army you saw. Come, I wish to speak with King Leszek."

The king greeted Harafin warmly and quickly agreed to order his forces to push on through the night. As the army moved out, the king rode near the vanguard of the company, calling together a war council of Harafin, Colonel Gabral, and another sentinel named Hathor.

Kevlin rode farther back, amid the main troop, his hopes buoyed by the number of new allies. The king's army was made up mostly of Outriders. Those soldiers were impressive. He'd never met another force so clearly ready for battle.

The company also boasted three sentinels and four Jagen Stalwarts. The combined might of the two forces was a heady thing to consider.

Despite the strength of their army, Kevlin couldn't help but wonder what secret forces Tanathos was bringing to bear. He had proven a wily, dangerous foe. No matter how strong their force, Kevlin wasn't naïve enough to think they'd beat Tanathos easily.

Hopefully the army would keep Tanathos distracted long enough for Kevlin to close. That was all that mattered.

Leander reined in beside him, followed a moment later by the leader of the Jagen Stalwarts. He was a thick-set, middle-aged man named Areli, with a heavy mustache and brown hair.

"Well met, my old friend," he greeted Leander warmly.

The two clasped arms and Leander laughed. "Praise the lady you serve for blessing us to ride together."

The three of them chatted for a while as they rode through the darkness. At one point, Areli glanced up at the sky. "The air is very heavy tonight."

"Aye," said Leander. "It will be a storm to remember."

"Let's hope it holds off until we're finished," Kevlin grumbled. He hated fighting in the rain.

He enjoyed the company of the old men. Areli proved to be friendly, and liked to laugh as much as Leander.

Climbing steadily, they rode through the chill night. Dawn reluctantly came, and revealed a threatening sky filled with ominous dark clouds that roiled low overhead, blocking the view of Mount Il'Aicharen.

The clouds filled Kevlin with a cold sense of foreboding.

"We must hurry," Harafin urged, his face grim.

66

A New Angle

Sitara opened her eyes and looked around. She was in her own small room, alive and, better yet, not imprisoned.

She sat up in bed and noticed a small piece of paper next to her. The inside turned out to be blank. After a moment's consideration, she embraced her power and focused her will on the paper. Gilded letters appeared on its surface.

Omolara is satisfied. Meet tonight at the eighth bell.

Then it burst into flame. With a cry of surprise, Sitara dropped it. The paper disintegrated before reaching the bed.

She was safe. Her relief mingled with confusion while she struggled to recall the events of the day. The morning had passed too quickly. She'd been a wreck, unable to gather the courage to implant new thoughts in the keisara's mind with Omolara in attendance.

Then, as she brushed her majesty's golden hair, the keisara had surprised Sitara with some news. "Crown Prince Lievin is returning to Diodor tomorrow by ship. Omolara, you will transcribe a letter to my cousin Miren, who is still there in Hallvarr."

As the keisara dictated the letter, Sitara's mind raced. Had Masego known the keisara would be sending that letter? He must have. She shivered at the subtle mastery of his power. She needed to make sure she got on that ship to Diodor.

The solution was so simple, she nearly laughed. She needed to take the letter personally, but she dared not touch her gift with Omolara in the room.

If she failed, Masego would destroy her.

With the letter finished, Omolara excused herself to fetch an envelope. As soon as she left the room, Sitara reached for her gift.

It didn't respond.

She wanted to howl with frustration. She couldn't bear to touch the power of darkness during the light of day, not when Omolara might return in seconds.

She redoubled her efforts, trying to calm her mind. Finally her gift came, but weak and hesitant. She seized on it and reached for the keisara's mind.

Those long nights spent breaching the keisara's will had developed in Sitara an affinity for the woman's mind, a deep understanding of how she thought. She easily linked to those thoughts and slipped a single idea into the current. Then she withdrew and drove her power away.

Several pounding heartbeats later, Omolara returned. As she sat down to finish preparing the letter, the keisara declared, "Sitara, I just had a thought. I will send you with Crown Prince Lievin. You will bear my letter and my love to my cousin."

Omolara looked up and frowned.

Barely able to breathe, Sitara managed a curtsy. "Are you sure, Your Majesty? I would hate to leave you for so long."

"Nonsense." The keisara gave a dismissive wave of one hand. "Omolara will attend me in your absence." After a moment's thought, she added, "I will give you another message for dear Miren, one I hesitate to write down."

Omolara seemed to relax, but as soon as they were excused, she pulled Sitara aside.

"Didn't you find the keisara's decision to send you to Diodor rather strange?"

Sitara frowned. "No, why?"

"Has she ever done anything like that before?"

"She has never sent me so far, no."

Omolara frowned again. "I must check the shields around the apartments."

"You're still planning to cast Truth on me later?"

"At the third bell." Omolara smiled. "Have you ever experienced Truth?"

"No, but I hear it's very liberating."

"I'm glad you think of it that way." She lay a comforting hand on Sitara's shoulder. "Don't worry, I won't forget."

Sitara had returned to her room and leaned against the door, so terrified she could barely stagger to her chair before her legs gave out.

Masego touched her mind.

What if Omolara senses this communication? she asked fearfully.

She will not. Now, open your mind to me.

What are you going to do?

You must surrender yourself completely to me. She will cast the Truth spell on you, but I will speak through your voice. I must have complete control to fool her.

There was no alternative. Sitara had dropped her shields and forced herself to allow Masego into her mind. In their recent training, he had repeatedly driven his thoughts into her mind, but that had been different. This time he entered her mind and pushed her consciousness back into a tiny corner of herself.

The experience terrified her, and it took all her self-control to suppress the urge to drive him out. Then it was over and he possessed her.

She could not have regained control had she wanted to. She was a prisoner inside her own body. Panicked, she began to struggle, no longer caring how much she needed his help.

He held her captive and gently said, *You will remember nothing.*

Blackness descended over her.

He was right. A blank hole in her memory was all that remained of the time he possessed her. If only he had removed the memory of those first moments when he took possession of her.

She felt violated more completely than she ever could have imagined. Remiel had already violated her body and now Masego had violated her will with that terrifying spell. They had sullied everything that she was.

Sitara shuddered and hugged herself while cold chills rippled through her body. Masego had possessed her. He'd had access to every thought, every memory, every feeling. He had controlled her very body.

What had he done with it?

She stripped off her clothes, stood before the mirror and inspected herself carefully. There were no visible marks, but she would never be the same.

She dressed again and dried her tears.

Only with great effort did she force herself to slip away that evening to meet him. She didn't want him touching her mind again. According to his note, they had fooled Omolara, and Sitara was grateful for that. She couldn't bear to let him dominate her like that again. Better to die.

Could she stop him, though? She feared that she could not.

She realized then that she had made a mistake. Going to Remiel had been the wrong choice. Bajaran must not have realized how corrupt these co-revolutionaries were. The purity of his dream to salvage the empire was being twisted by Masego and Remiel.

How could such evil men bring about the positive changes she had dedicated her life to? They had violated her at every step, and they would do the same to the empire.

She had to get away, had to find a way to escape Masego's influence. She would learn what she could from him, but only until she found a path to freedom. She could endure any torture they inflicted upon her with that goal fixed firm in her deepest heart.

She considered her plight as she traversed the long underground corridors beneath the palaces. She couldn't escape him here in Tamera, but she had already closed the door on the chance to escape to her homeland.

Sitara stopped abruptly as the answer came. Masego had provided her escape already. She would take that ship to Hallvarr, but she would never return.

Before she reached the sentinel tower and their regular mindlink meeting place, she buried her new plan deep in the recesses of her mind. She couldn't allow Masego in again or he might discover her secret. She held no illusions about how he would react to her planned deceit.

The first part of the lesson again focused on shielding, and she tried harder than ever. It was a painful failure.

She had learned so much, and the shields she placed around her mind were so much stronger and effective than before, but nothing proved good enough to resist him.

He battered her shields down easily and punished her, both mind and body, at each failure. At least he didn't bother mining her thoughts. Perhaps after possessing her completely he thought he knew all her secrets.

You're useless, he snapped in disgust, lashing her with his magic. He seared the inside of her mind and body as if with white-hot iron.

She screamed and writhed in pain, unable to form a coherent thought or rebuild her defenses.

He struck again, leaving her only barely conscious. *I told you never to scream out loud. You have no discipline. I don't know why I waste my time with you.*

Defiant, she roused herself. *What do you expect? No one could hold their tongue under that punishment.*

Then perhaps you should shield yourself better, he mocked.

I'm trying!

You have so little vision. After a pause, he continued, *I will demonstrate something since you are clearly not talented enough to figure it out for yourself. But this is the only time I will give you such assistance.*

Thank you.

A student shouldn't have to beg their teacher to actually teach. Masego's grasp of the principles of instruction made no sense. If he was this twisted in other aspects of his life, she marveled that he could function at all.

Strike at me, he commanded.

Sitara did not hesitate. She gathered her will and unleashed a powerful dagger of magic, hoping to inflict a fraction of the pain upon him that he had just done to her. He deflected her blow easily. It accomplished nothing.

What did you learn?

That you're stronger than me, she said sullenly.

No. Concentrate. Do it again.

Again she struck, but again he deflected the blow.

What did you learn?

When she did not answer, he snarled, *You have one more attempt. I believe you will fail, but I hope you prove me wrong.*

Instead of answering, she struck again. Since her power was so easily defeated when striking in a focused, dagger-like beam, she changed tactics.

This time she slashed at his mind from the side, like a sword slicing across the face of an enemy.

Again her attack was deflected, but she felt something she hadn't noticed before. She reached out again, but not to strike. Instead she extended her power gently to touch his shields like caressing fingers.

There.

Understanding came like a ray of light. It was so simple and yet so brilliant. She altered her own shields to match what he was doing.

What did you learn? he asked again, his voice gentler, approving.

Incredible. I would never have thought to angle my shields like that.

That is why you failed. You must use your imagination.

He struck without warning, but she was ready. Rather than holding her shields like a solid wall in an attempt to stop him with sheer strength, she angled them into a multi-faceted barrier that deflected his assault away.

It worked.

Even as she congratulated herself and reveled in the feeling of victory, he struck again. His second blow was slanted to strike a narrow section of her shield at right angles, thus negating the deflecting effect. Her shield crumpled under his focused power.

Much better, but remember that an experienced sentinel will alter his method of attack. You must be ready to alter your defenses.

I will, she promised.

You had better, because you're not yet strong enough to fight a trained sentinel on equal footing. You must become smarter, more creative, or you will die.

Now, I will teach you two skills you will need for your journey.

67

CHANGING FORECASTS

Rhisart vaulted the last two steps and sped to the edge of the parapet where an accepted, face pale with fear, pointed with a trembling hand. "There."

The haze of smoke from the day before had dissipated. Although the sun had not yet crested the eastern flank of the mountain, dawn was far enough along that he could dimly make out the lower valley. He squinted into the distance, and his heart fell.

Marching out of the forest and up the road toward the lower town came rank after rank of makrasha. The horde advanced at a steady, inexorable pace. The vanguard entered the blasted remains of the town before the rear of the force emerged from the forest.

So many, Rhisart thought. *All here to destroy the keep. How in the truename of the creator is it possible?*

No, he realized with a growing sense of horror. They weren't there to destroy the keep, but to reach the heart of the mountain. As impossible as it seemed, that had to be their intention.

He'd already sealed the passage, so anyone trying to break through would be shattered by the many defensive spells. As he stared at the advancing horde, he wished he'd doubled the number of protective wards.

"I estimate around eight hundred," one old sentinel remarked, his voice calm.

"Look." The young accepted's voice cracked with fear. The advancing horde began crossing the bridge into the upper town.

Rhisart could make out the crimson-robed figures in the vanguard.

"Eight shadeleeches." The old sentinel breathed. "By the creator, there are eight of them."

All along the wall, sentinels and townsfolk alike watched the host with terror. The wall of the keep stood high and strong, but with so few defenders, it seemed insanity to attempt resisting such an army.

None of the townsfolk were trained soldiers, although at least they carried real weapons. A dusty armory had provided swords and spears that had never before tasted battle. Sharpened for the first time, those old weapons had offered the townsfolk the hope of fighting for their lives instead of being slaughtered like sheep. That hope seemed vain in the face of this new army.

"Be strong," Rhisart called, projecting confidence he struggled to feel. "Hope is not lost. They will not find this keep an easy conquest."

The defenders all turned toward him, their faces desperate for any hope he could offer.

"We are not defenseless. Take courage, my friends." Sweeping his arm toward the advancing host, he declared, "The enemy seeks to kill and plunder, but we fight for a better cause. We fight for our freedom, and for the lives of our families. Be strong and of good courage, and we will triumph!"

A weak cheer greeted his words and he raced for the long stair to the central tower. *I should have spent some time preparing something a little more stirring,* he thought. *I should have realized they were waiting for reinforcements.*

If only he'd prepared the keep better.

It is too late for that. He reached the top of the tower and stepped into the simple room. Raising a hand, he called upon the magic of the keep. Runes of power burned along the walls, then faded again. Magic rose through the building to fill him, and his eyes shone silver as he linked his soul to the keep.

Rhisart blew out a deep breath, a little more confident than a moment ago.

Let them come.

The army had begun climbing the twisting road up toward the keep, and Rhisart felt a shiver of fear despite the tremendous power he controlled. He might inspire the hearts of the defenders on the wall, but he could not delude himself. They would most likely all die.

It will not happen, he vowed, defiantly casting away the doubts that threatened to undermine his purpose.

A rumble of thunder from the sky drew his eyes upward. The heavy clouds that had threatened rain all night churned low, spinning directly above the keep. A flash of lightning arced between two of those clouds, and a peal of thunder shattered the early morning air.

At the rear of the advancing army, six shadeleeches stood in a circle, surrounded by two score kneeling makrasha. The six raised their hands in unison, and a dark cloud enveloped them. Tendrils of darkness snaked out to consume several of the kneeling makrasha. The beasts howled and writhed as evil power consumed their souls.

Another flash of lightning arced above, lighting the entire landscape for a second. Thunder shattered the air and the sky opened. Rain hammered down upon the keep in a torrent, concealing the attackers and threatening to knock defenders off the wall. The wind howled, buffeting the keep.

Rain lashed Rhisart's face through the open window. Raising his arms, he called upon the magic of the keep. The stones thrummed in response and the awesome latent power at his command awakened.

He formed an invisible shield of magic that pushed the rain back from the tower. Drawing deep, he pushed the shield farther, extending it over the keep, and then beyond, until it spread over the entire walled enclave.

The rain stopped and the defenders on the wall stared in open amazement at the water pooling in the air high overhead before cascading to the ground just beyond the wall in a giant waterfall. The roar of water and howling of the wind outside the fortress rose until the very ground rumbled, reducing communication to gestures.

Rhisart grunted under the strain of sustaining the spell. The weight of the water was staggering, but he allowed a fierce grin as he stared at the waterfall he'd created. Any makrasha trying to scale the walls would first have to fight through those tons of churning water. He could imagine the rage of the shadeleeches.

Perhaps they were not so clever after all.

The rain stopped.

The water drained off the shield a moment later and Rhisart gaped. The lowering clouds whirled above the keep in a tight circle. As he watched, an opaque funnel descended toward the keep. The wind shrieked to a new pitch, lightning flashing all around the funnel, pealing thunder shaking the entire valley.

A tornado.

Rhisart had never heard of anyone triggering and controlling a tornado. The enemy had not just been waiting, but spent the previous day preparing for this moment. Around the six shadeleeches, makrasha fell in ever-increasing numbers as the spawn of Angrama drained the life force of their slaves and expended that energy to fuel their spell.

The tornado touched down on Rhisart's shield, and brilliant amber sparks flew. The shield buckled under the pressure and the funnel descended lower.

Rhisart drew from the power of the keep until it nearly overwhelmed even his enhanced capacity. Shouting a word of power, he buttressed the shield and reinforced the spell, pouring everything he had into holding the tornado at bay.

A scream of agony startled the defenders. Most of them were staring in open-mouthed terror at the tornado whirling only a couple hundred feet above them. The scream reminded them of their own situation. While they had been distracted, the makrasha had silently rushed the wall. One of the defenders toppled off, clutching a crossbow bolt protruding from his chest.

Grappling hooks whistled up from below, and heavy wooden ladders capped with iron thudded against the top of the wall. Howling for blood, makrasha swarmed up.

Fire and glittering sheets of raw magic knocked the invaders from the wall, but more kept coming. The two shadeleeches not part of the group generating the tornado attacked in turn.

Bolts of magic arced up from below, knocking defenders from the wall, and crimson fire exploded along the parapet. Most of the sentinels were forced to focus on warding off the magical attacks, leaving the townsfolk to fight off the hundreds of swarming makrasha.

With desperate strength, villagers cut ropes and pushed ladders, but there weren't enough of them. As makrasha reached the top, they tore into the defenders and blood sprayed across the ancient parapet.

One old sentinel cleared the wall with a blast of hardened air, but let his guard down against the shadeleeches. A bolt of darkness struck him in the back and knocked him from the wall to his death.

Up in the tower, Rhisart groaned from the strain of holding the tornado at bay. The whirling cyclone continued to grow in strength, expanding both in girth and weight. It bore down upon the shields with the untamable power of nature. Rhisart gritted his teeth and uttered a wordless howl of defiance. He would not relent. If the shield failed, the tornado would destroy them all.

Sparing a glance down at the wall, he stared with growing dread at the makrasha.

We're not strong enough. We're all going to die.

68

ELEMENTAL CARNAGE

High up the east side of the valley, near the headwaters of the Ujutus, a dozen cloaked riders emerged from the woods. Leaving their horses, they descended the slope to the churning waters.

Wayra discarded her cloak and paused to stare at the incredible sight of the tornado whirling above the keep, and the makrasha swarming the walls.

"They won't last long," Thyra said, wiping spray from her face.

"We must hurry." Wayra pointed to the steep slope across the river. "They do not attack from the east side. It's too steep. We'll climb there. Follow me!"

Using a powerful blast of air, Wayra threw herself into the air and across the river. She tumbled in a heap on the other side, landing on a cushion of air that saved her from breaking her neck. She struggled to her feet and turned to watch the rest of her company.

Thyra landed gracefully nearby, making the dangerous spell seem easy. She grinned at Wayra, her face flushed with excitement. The other kestrels landed around them, most duplicating Wayra's clumsier effort, but landing safely.

All but one. The last of them, a young man barely confirmed, misjudged the distance and slammed into a large rock in the river. The impact shattered his body, and the churning current swept the bloody remains under, leaving a crimson smear on the rock that soon washed away under the merciless pounding of the waters.

He was not ready.

This was no time to mourn the loss of one who could not keep up. Wayra glanced down at the glove that concealed the blackened claw of her right hand. *I will not fail again.*

Turning from the river, she considered the steep, barren slope they still had to climb. Coarse grass and scraggly bushes fought for purchase in the rocky slope. High above, the east wall of the keep reared, beckoning them on.

Wayra focused her will and gouged out a footstep in the hard ground, and then another just above it. Leading the way, she ascended the hill, dirt and small rocks flying as she carved a staircase one step at a time.

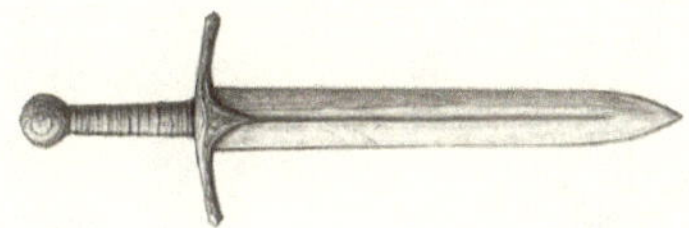

Tanathos surveyed the battle and smiled. Only half an hour into the fighting and victory was close at hand. The defenders would break soon. The pitiful force could not withstand his makrasha with the keep's defenses being consumed by the tornado.

He stared at the whirling vortex for a second and gloried in its raw, destructive power. Perhaps he would choose it as his symbol.

He deserved it.

Turning, he beckoned, and a halimaw rose from where it had been crouching on the ground with two others. The beast towered over him, an impressive specimen at fourteen feet. Covered in dark fur that strained to contain its awesome strength, the monster glared hungrily at the wall, its amber eyes tracking targets constantly. Its huge maw dripped saliva and its body quivered with the need to kill.

Tanathos stroked its flank and pointed toward the highest tower. "Go. Kill."

The halimaw roared, the sound drowning out everything else and sending a shudder of fear through both armies, and raced for the wall. With incredible speed, it hurdled through the ranks of makrasha, trampling any of the smaller beasts too slow to get out of its way.

From the wall, bolts of magic speared down toward it, but the halimaw paid them no heed, and the magic dissipated. A rain of arrows tried to slow it, but it moved so fast most of the bolts missed. A few struck true, doing little more than scratching the thick hide and enraging it further.

The halimaw reached the base of the wall and, gathering itself low to the ground, *leaped*. It soared high, grasped the parapet, and vaulted over the wall.

Ignoring the townsfolk tumbling away in terror, it leaped to the roof of the keep, crossed to the central tower, and began to climb.

Tanathos smiled.

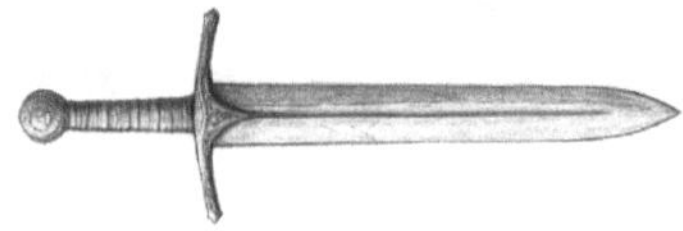

His body trembling with the strain of holding the tornado at bay, Rhisart no longer saw the battle below. Immersed in the effort to defend the keep, he was unprepared for the long, clawed paw that reached through the window and tore into his shoulder. Agony exploded through him and he staggered back.

Above the keep, the tornado dropped lower until it howled just above the highest turret. Defenders cried out in renewed terror, but there was nowhere to run. Through the transparent shield, they could look right up into the whirling funnel that yawed above like the insatiable maw of some giant demon.

Gasping in pain, Rhisart stared in horror at the halimaw clawing its way through the window in pursuit. Even as his mind struggled to adjust to the terrifying sight, his training kicked in. Reaching out with fingers of power, he grabbed the chairs in the room and hurled them at the beast just as it sprang through the window.

The first chair unbalanced it, and the second knocked it back from the window. As it began to fall, a single claw dug into the stone and held firm.

The effort cost Rhisart too much concentration, and the shield protecting the keep, already weakened, slipped from his control.

He fell to one knee, fighting to withstand the agony of his wound and focus the power again to salvage the spell.

It wasn't enough. The shield crumpled and the tornado descended. The huge funnel encircled the keep.

Outbuildings shredded under the onslaught, and defenders threw themselves to the stone floor of the rampart. The combined might of the remaining sentinels was barely enough to shield the people on the wall from the worst of the wind. The tornado roared like a living thing, glorying in its power to destroy.

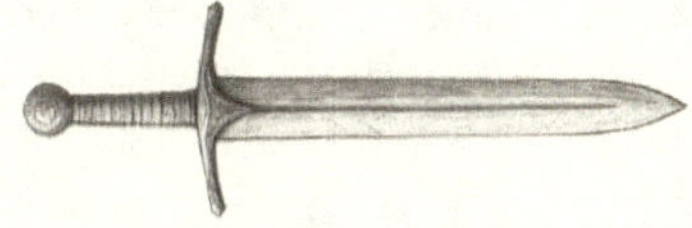

"Victory!" Tanathos shouted.

At that moment, the ground beneath the six shadeleeches controlling the tornado lurched upward a dozen feet. The shadeleeches tumbled into the air amid the shriveled corpses of the makrasha sacrificed to fuel the spell.

The tornado disintegrated.

Wind blasted in every direction, whipping everything behind the wall into the air. Three mini-cyclones spun off the main funnel as it fell apart. They spiraled away, ripping stones from the keep and destroying smaller buildings in their path. Defenders screamed in fear, but the shield over the top of the wall held.

One of the cyclones crossed the wall right at the point where the sentinel had suffered the *Tai Pari*. The wind caught the buckled stones and wrenched them out of place. The wall groaned as huge blocks twisted. The same cyclone ripped through the ranks of the attacking horde, scattering makrasha and whipping their weapons into a deadly barrage.

Even the halimaw roared with impotent rage as the wind tore it from its precarious perch on the side of the tower and threw it across the courtyard.

At the far end of the valley, silver trumpets rang out as an arriving army galloped from the shelter of the forest and charged toward the lower town.

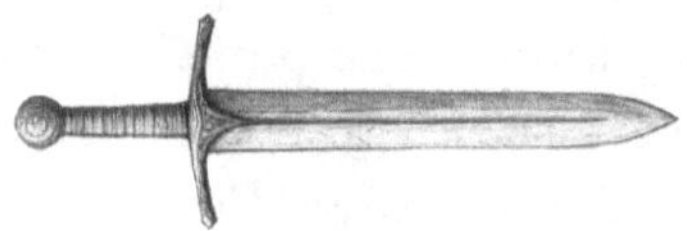

On the eastern slope, Wayra shouted, "Brace!"

She focused her shields to direct the wind away. Below her on the narrow staircase they had carved into the hill, the other kestrels tried to follow her lead.

Two were unsuccessful, and the howling wind caught their cloaks and yanked them into the air. One hardened the air around himself in a counter spiral and used the wind's own power to slingshot him back to the stair. He crashed onto a step and grabbed hold to keep from sliding.

The other, a heavyset fellow, was not so clear-headed. He thrashed and screamed until he slammed into the slope and bounced. His cries turned into howls of pain as he tumbled into the waiting arms of the mighty Ujutus. Its uncaring waters sucked him under.

Wayra could not see what had happened to the tornado. Something had changed, but she had no idea if it was beneficial. "Hurry!"

69

THE MAN WITH THE PLAN

"Harafin," Tanathos snarled. Although he couldn't see the cursed sentinel yet, only Harafin could disrupt his glorious victory.

It did not matter. Harafin was too late.

Pointing to one of the seven shadeleeches, he commanded, "Take three of the others and half the slaves and stop that rabble before they cross the bridge." He pointed to a halimaw still crouched nearby. "Take that one too."

The shadeleech started shouting orders and within seconds the army split, half of it racing down the slope toward the bridge. It was going to be close.

Tanathos turned back to the keep, dismissing everything in the lower valley. The useless attack by the new army didn't matter. Once he reached the heart of the mountain, not even Harafin could stop him. He'd love it if the sentinel tried. Consuming that old man's soul would be a fitting capstone to his victory.

He spared a glance at the unconscious white-robed figure strapped securely to a stretcher at the rear of his force. Antigonus barely lived, but it was enough. Tanathos needed only a tiny spark of life remaining when he slaughtered the old man.

Near Antigonus, a large bear cringed in its cage, silently eyeing the blond halimaw crouching nearby. The hulking monster growled low and tore its eyes away from the walls to meet Tanathos' gaze.

It was beautiful.

He smiled again, and shouted, "Charge!"

The makrasha howled and began racing for the wall like a tide of doom.

70

BRIDGES

Gabral led the charge through the lower town, with the king's army pounding behind him. They raced toward the wide stone bridge and the host of makrasha scrambling into a defensive formation there. Two crimson-robed shadeleeches stood at the fore.

His whole life had led him to this moment of glory when he would prove his worth as bearer. The honor he was about to win would raise his family name to the highest levels.

To his left, Harafin raised a hand and wheeled away from the main host. Most of Gabral's original command followed him, along with about a third of the king's troops.

Gabral exulted at the battle plan that placed Harafin and anyone else who might threaten to steal his glory onto a different path. He alone would lead this charge, he would stamp out the enemy.

Gabral galloped toward the bridge, with the army in tight formation behind him. He extended the Mace like a lance, and blue flame exploded around the weapon, then rolled back over him. Areli and another Jagen Stalwart flanked him, followed by a company of outriders.

They thundered onto the bridge like an avalanche of steel.

In that moment, the bridge exploded with crimson fire. The roar of flames drowned out all other sound, and the sharp tang of sulfur billowed into the already smoke-filled air, making breathing all but impossible. Gabral galloped through the inferna, grateful that he rode a mount trained for battle and unfazed by magic.

Flames concealed everything, and he heard the rest of the army rein their mounts to a skidding halt.

This moment belonged to him alone.

Gabral charged out the far side of the flames, flanked by the stalwarts and a few soldiers of the vanguard protected by a sentinel shield.

"Glory, and the Emperor!" Gabral cried.

Makrasha bared fangs and raised weapons. Gabral's force collided with them with a resounding crash. The warhorses churned the front ranks of makrasha under their steel-shod hooves, leaving a bloody tangle writhing on the ground amidst high-pitched howls.

Gabral smashed down Makrasha pressing forward to rip him from the saddle. Blue fire splashed in all directions and the smell of singed flesh gagged him.

Makrasha on all sides recoiled from the power of the Mace. The two Jagen Stalwarts spurred through the gap toward the shadeleeches.

Gabral cursed. They were capitalizing on his battle prowess. He should be the one to strike down the shadeleeches.

Makrasha tried to block the stalwarts, but a volley of arrows from the outriders of the vanguard cut down their front ranks. Gabral leaped off his charger, landing in the midst of the tightly-packed makrasha with an explosion of blue fire that sent monsters tumbling away.

Bows thrummed by the hundreds. Fires crackled behind him. Men and monsters alike screamed, rending the airs with their cries.

It was glorious bedlam.

Soldiers pressed in the opening behind Gabral to engage the makrasha in close combat. Swords and axes flashed in the early morning sunlight, and fresh screams punctuated the sickening sounds of steel rending flesh.

One of the shadeleeches threw a wave of darkness at Areli as the Jagen Stalwart closed on him, but the spell dissipated around him. Areli slammed his mace into the fellow's face, crumpling him to the ground. His fellow stalwart decapitated the other shadeleech.

The flames blocking the bridge winked out, and Areli raised his fist in victory.

A deep roar drowned out all other sound, and a halimaw leaped the front ranks of makrasha and landed beside the pair of Jagen Stalwarts.

Gabral grinned. This was an opponent whose defeat would catapult him to fame around the empire.

Areli struck the halimaw with his mace, but the heavy weapon left no mark on the monster's thick hide. It plunged one clawed fist through Areli's armor and deep into his chest. He screamed and shuddered with agony.

It ripped Areli's heart out.

His body fell to the ground, still twitching, with his lifeblood gushing over the halimaw's feet. The monster ignored the bleeding corpse and turned toward the second stalwart.

Gabral arrived first.

He smashed the Mace into the monster's chest. Fire splattered in all directions, driving back makrasha and soldiers alike, and staggered the halimaw.

With a snarl, it snatched Gabral off the ground and pulled him into its deadly embrace, as if to squeeze the life out of him. The beast reeked of blood and evil magic.

Gabral increased the Mace's fire. Although not actually burning, the monster cringed back from the flames. Before Gabral could strike again, it threw him over the ranks of soldiers. He crashed onto the center of the bridge.

The monster leaped the other soldiers, who cowered from its fury. It ignored them, intent only on Gabral.

As it arced high into the air and plunged toward him, a lance flew across the bridge and drove half its length through the monster's torso.

"Good shot," Gabral shouted as he climbed back to his feet. At least the sentinel Hathor knew how to deal with halimaw. That wound would slow the monster enough for him to finish it.

The halimaw crashed to the bridge next to Gabral, and he slammed the Mace into the beast's throat. The shock of the impact rattled his arm and numbed his hand. The weapon gashed deep into the monster's neck.

It howled in pain but struggled to its feet despite the lance protruding from its chest and back. Gabral struck again and again, bashing its face repeatedly, puncturing its skin in half a dozen places.

The monster swept him up in its gigantic arms again, and tried to bite his head off. Its gaping maw scraped across the burning shield of the Mace's power, inches from his head. The reek of its fetid breath gagged him. It was so huge, radiating so much raw strength that for the first time Gabral felt a flicker of fear, despite the Mace's protective shield.

That fear enraged him. He would not fear this spawn of evil! This was exactly the type of battle he was destined to win.

Gabral twisted in the monster's grasp, freed his right arm and hit the halimaw again on the head. He punctured one of its eyes, and it reared its head back, splattering Gabral with hot blood.

It overbalanced and fell against the bridge's balustrade. Unable to break free, Gabral hung in its arms over the raging river.

"Why won't you just die?" he shouted, and hit it again.

Men and makrasha battled around them in a desperate contest to secure the bridge, but none ventured close to the titanic struggle between Gabral and the halimaw.

Gabral pulled his other arm free and drove the Mace into the monster's throat with both arms. It fell against the railing again, and with a sharp snap the rail gave way. The halimaw toppled over the edge, dragging Gabral with it.

Even as they fell, Gabral struck it in the throat, then again, and a third time. With the last blow, the Mace ripped into a major artery and blood sprayed far out over the water in a crimson wave.

"Victory!" Gabral shouted into the uncaring wind.

They hit the surface, and the raging torrent dragged them both under.

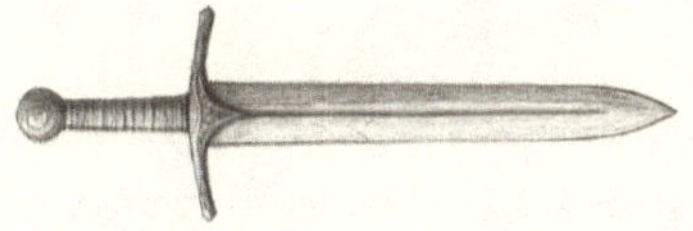

"Did you see that?" Kevlin cried.

"That was Gabral," Ceren said, also staring at the frothing water in horror.

"We can do nothing for him," Harafin said.

Kevlin reined in his mount on the western side of the ruined town and spared a glance at the fighting still raging at the upper end of the bridge.

The king's charge had faltered, and the tight confines of the bridge prevented him from deploying the full force of his army. Screams of pain and flashes of magic punctuated the struggle.

The king's force would win through eventually. All of the makrasha were clustered around the bridge and that desperate battle. None had been spared to watch Kevlin's company since there was no way for them to cross the river at the blackened, broken ruin of what had been a wooden bridge.

Kevlin turned from the raging battle toward the second makrasha army high on the slope above the town. The keep of Il'Aicharen towered over the valley, with makrasha clambering up its walls.

How in the name of the Lady can there be so many?

Harafin shouted, "We make for the keep. Kevlin must reach Antigonus. Nothing else matters."

I will not fail.

There would be no other chance. Everything had led to this final effort. He would get the rock back to Antigonus. Nothing would stop him.

"I can't swim that river," Jerrik growled, pointing at the churning Ujutus. His hand clenched the shaft of his huge axe as he stared at the fighting. He clearly wanted to be a part of it.

"We will not be swimming."

Harafin raised a hand. The air above the river shimmered and coalesced into a blue-green arc of light that spanned to the far bank. Harafin spurred his horse across the bridge of light, and the rest of the company followed close behind.

Kevlin held his breath all the way over and refused to look down. Riding on light was fine for sentinels, but he'd have preferred taking the stone bridge.

On the far side of the river, the rear of the makrasha army turned to meet them. Fifty monsters moved to intercept Harafin as he galloped toward the upper road.

Harafin pointed at them and shouted a word of power. The entire band of monsters halted midstride, as if frozen in place. As they galloped past, Kevlin stared in awe at the monsters stuck in the spell like flies in a spider's web.

Kevlin rode close behind Leander, flanked by Drystan and Jerrik. Behind him rode Ceren, who wore an oversized mail shirt and a look of fierce determination. Indira rode behind her, with Adalia at her side and soldiers crowded close around them both.

Kevlin called to Harafin, "Can't you use that spell on the makrasha by the bridge?"

Harafin shook his head. "I do not have the strength to hold so many."

"Can't you use the latent power all around us?"

Ceren glanced at him in surprise and Kevlin suppressed a smug smile. He couldn't help a surge of pride. Maybe he was starting to retain a little of what Harafin had taught him.

"There is no latent magic," Harafin explained without slowing. "Rhisart sealed the heart of the mountain, and the battle up at the keep is draining away what little there is left."

Kevlin frowned, wondering how badly that would limit Harafin's ability. Hopefully he had enough power to get Kevlin to Antigonus.

Unopposed, they clattered out of the upper town and made for the winding road up to the keep. Makrasha were assaulting the walls and magic flashed between the two forces in a constant barrage. Sounds of the combat drifted down the slope and spurred them on.

71

MEETING YOUR WORST NIGHTMARE

"Come on!" Wayra urged. Another fifty yards and they'd reach the base of the wall. The sound of trumpets generated a cheer from the defenders above. She needed to see what was happening.

"Look out!" Thyra called.

Two dozen makrasha came rushing around a corner of the wall toward Wayra and her company. Even using their hengaruk for extra purchase, the beasts slid as much as ran down the steep hill toward them.

The monsters' roars of bloodlust turned into howls of pain as the air in front of them hardened into invisible blades that tore through their ranks, reducing them to bloody carcasses in seconds.

We are ready, Wayra thought with a satisfied smile as her team approached the wall. Nothing would stop them.

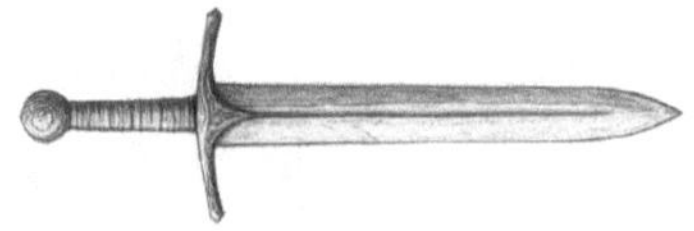

Rhisart staggered to the window and stared out. Below, the battle raged anew, and despite the attacking force being reduced by more than half, there were still too many of them. The defenders barely held back the tide rising against the wall.

He struggled to force aside the wracking pain in his shoulder. He'd have to stop the bleeding soon, or it would weaken him until he was of no help to anyone.

Later. I just need to hold on a few more minutes.

He focused the power of the keep. Ten thousand fiery darts rained upon the makrasha that were clambering upward. The darts tore through faces and limbs, slicing deep and leaving the beasts not killed outright writhing from the searing pain. The entire front line of attackers disintegrated. Makrasha tumbled into heaps at the base of the wall.

The defenders cheered, many shouting Rhisart's name, their flagging spirits bolstered by the reprieve.

A clatter below caught Rhisart's attention. He looked down and cursed. The bloodied halimaw was clawing its way up the roof toward the tower, dislodging slate tiles as it went. Its amber gaze locked on him and it snarled as their eyes met.

It would not stop.

One of them had to die.

Rhisart raised his good hand and focused his will. All the recently dislodged tiles whipped into the air and battered the halimaw, slicing into its thick hide and beating against its skull. The monster howled and swiped ineffectually at the objects whirling around it.

Then it met his gaze again and roared louder, its fanged maw wide. It leaped thirty feet, vaulting the cluster of whipping tiles. Even as Rhisart redirected the tiles, it leaped again, clawing at the tower and climbing with amazing speed.

Rhisart's mouth went dry as he fought to unseat the beast. Tiles slashed at it from all sides, but it ignored them and pulled itself higher.

I need something stronger.

He cast his eyes out across the devastation littering the interior of the keep. A pile of metal poles in one corner of the courtyard caught his eye. He grabbed one with fingers of power and yanked it up toward the tower.

Glancing toward the halimaw again to direct the new missile, he cried out in fear.

The monster clung from the ledge just below him.

It's so fast, he thought as a clawed hand grabbed his robe and yanked him out the window.

It opened its huge maw to rip his head off.

Rhisart drove the metal pole into the halimaw's back. The beast shuddered under the impact and lost its grip on the wall.

The two fell together and, for a terrifying heartbeat, hung weightless in the air. The screams of battle, clanging of steel, and heavy breathing of the monster seemed to hold them aloft. Its foul, heavy stench nearly gagged Rhisart.

They slammed onto the roof, and it shuddered under the impact. That entire section of tiled roofing broke loose.

The halimaw landed on its head, the impact temporarily stunning it. Its huge torso cushioned the fall a little for Rhisart, and he popped out of its grasp.

As they tumbled around each other, he managed to kick off against the roof and climb onto the monster's back. The two slid fast toward the edge on the wave of loosened tile.

The halimaw growled as it recovered from the shock. It clawed at Rhisart, but its bulging muscles worked against it, preventing it from reaching around its back. It struggled to turn over, thrashing in an attempt to gain purchase on the loose tiles.

It was like riding a bucking stallion, one with claws and fangs to rip him to pieces if he fell off.

As they shot toward the edge of the roof and the forty foot drop to the cobblestones below, Rhisart could do nothing but fight to keep the beast from grasping him with those terrible claws.

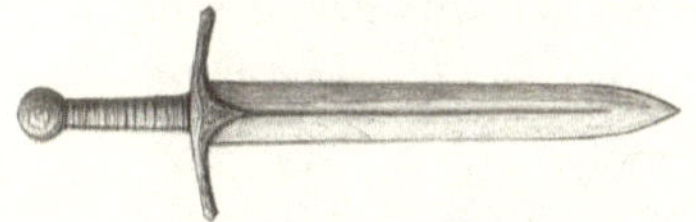

We made it.

Wayra placed one hand against the eastern wall. The rest of the kestrels were only a few paces behind.

A deep growl whipped her around. Not ten paces away, a halimaw crouched. Although covered with blond fur, the monster looked feminine. Wayra stared into its amber eyes and, with a terrible shock, recognized the vestiges of a once lovely face.

"Rhea!"

The halimaw roared, its fanged jaws wide, and leaped.

Wayra cried out in alarm and scoured the ground with magic, seeking a weapon to hold the beast off. Finding nothing, she froze in fear, watching helplessly as the halimaw that had once been Rhea plummeted toward her, claws reaching to rend her to pieces.

Out of nowhere, a boulder slammed into the halimaw's shoulder, knocking the monster aside. It tumbled twenty yards down the slope, deeply gouging the hardened earth with its claws in an effort to stop.

Thyra stepped up beside her. "You're welcome."

The blond-furred halimaw arrested its slide and clambered back up the hill toward them, grunting with the effort, but closing the distance fast. Wayra and the other kestrels rained stones and dirt down upon it. They were trained to kill the monsters, but there was nothing on that barren slope heavy enough to do the job.

"Up!" Wayra shouted, pointing toward the wall. "We'll fight it there."

The kestrels raced for the wall. Wayra formed a pillar of air beneath her feet that whisked her up the vertical stone surface in a matter of seconds. As she stepped over the parapet, a nearby man with a pitchfork shouted in surprise and raised his weapon.

She snatched it from him with her good hand. "Can't you tell an ally from one of those monsters?" She waved him aside. "Go do something useful. You're in the way."

Not waiting for a reply, she turned back to peer over the wall. Two other kestrels arrived over the parapet, but a terrified scream rang from below. It ended in a wet gurgle.

The halimaw had caught the last kestrel and ripped him apart.

Even as Wayra looked down, the monster leaped again, landing in the middle of the remaining kestrels preparing to lift themselves up the wall. It grabbed two men and crushed their heads even as they tried to hit it with stones. It leaped upon a third and buried its snout in the man's belly, ripping him open and showering the hillside with entrails and gore.

The other kestrels lifted simultaneously from the ground. The halimaw leaped after them, catching a woman with red-gold hair. She screamed in terror and beat at the monster with her fists as the two plummeted toward the slope. When they struck the ground, the halimaw raked its claws down the victim's torso, ripping until all that remained of the once-lovely woman was a shredded mass of dripping flesh.

The halimaw raised its bloody maw toward where the remainder of the party stood, then leaped, grasping with its gore-covered claws.

Wayra hurled the pitchfork, propelling it down with all her actinic strength. It met the ascending halimaw and the tines buried deep in its chest.

The monster missed the top of the wall by scant inches and tumbled back to the ground. It staggered to its feet, wavered, and ripped the pitchfork out of its chest.

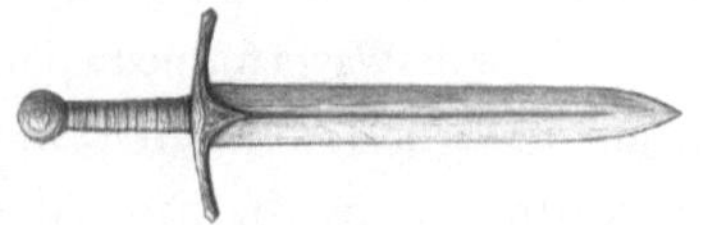

Rhisart and the halimaw shot off the edge of the roof in a graceful arc toward the cobblestones below. The beast managed to grab one of his legs and it dug its claws in deep, trying to pull him around so it could kill him. Rhisart held on with all the strength left in his good arm, shouting a wordless scream of defiance as the ground rose to meet them.

A dozen spears whisked across the courtyard, stopping directly under them, standing on end with their blades pointing up to meet them. The monster fell onto the weapons with a meaty splat. Its legs shredded and several spears punched deep into its torso. It bellowed with pain, then slowly toppled to the ground.

The impact knocked Rhisart free of the monster's grasp and tumbled him across the courtyard. He came to a painful stop, gasping for breath, trying to hold onto consciousness.

His body shuddered with pain. One of his legs stuck out at an odd angle, and breathing was agony, as if he'd broken many ribs. Blood trickled into his eyes, and he couldn't gather his thoughts sufficient to call upon his magic.

The halimaw clawed at the stones, its eyes shining with desperate hunger as it tried to pull itself toward him. A heavy boulder floated into the air above its head, paused, then crashed down.

The monster shuddered one more time, then lay still.

Rhisart managed a weak smile, staring up at the scattered clouds. His ears didn't seem to be working, and peaceful silence encircled him in its gentle embrace as he drifted toward sweet insensibility.

72

INTO THE BREACH

T anathos smiled. *Victory is at hand.*

Makrasha fought along the top of the wall against a pitiful force of defenders. Tanathos' shadeleeches battled four sentinels who had only recently joined the fighting.

The sentinels clustered together and fought well as a team, but it wouldn't be enough. The mighty defenses of the keep had trickled to nothing. That could only mean his halimaw had been successful. With the gerent out of the fight, victory was guaranteed.

As one defender leaped atop one of the battlements to knock over a ladder, Tanathos reached out with fingers of power and *yanked* the man off.

What a waste. He hated throwing away good souls, but war demanded so many sacrifices. Still, he would soon slaughter Antigonus, or what was left of him, in the heart of the mountain. Then he would have the time to properly destroy all the souls he wanted.

As was his right.

One of the sentinels stumbled onto the buckled stones of a weakened section of wall. Tanathos flung a bolt of crackling fire at another of them. Impressive to look at, it posed little real threat to the sentinels. It moved too slow and gave ample warning of its approach.

It wasn't meant to kill. He nearly laughed when the fool dodged the bolt of fire and joined his companion on that weakened section of wall. The pitiful sentinels thought themselves so mighty, but he could make them dance to his will.

Time to finish it.

He threw out grasping tentacles of power that fastened onto the life forces of three makrasha slaves kneeling around him, *and pulled*. It took only a single heartbeat to drain their souls.

Tanathos threw his head back in ecstasy, glorying in the influx of strength as the beasts shriveled to dry husks. The only thing sweeter was feeding on the life force of a true innocent, or ripping the soul out of an adversary. But this was good. So very good.

He laughed. This was true power. It was his right.

Tanathos pointed toward the buckled stones and unleashed the force of those three lives. A thick coil of magic, so black it sucked light out of the surrounding air, arced over his force and slammed into the base of the wall. It crawled up the wall, tracing the stones and sinking deep into its fractured joints.

Tanathos lifted his hands, then twisted them down, as if snapping a twig. The stones groaned and shifted. The groaning rose to a shriek, and the entire section of wall shattered.

Giant slabs of shaped granite exploded outward, raining onto his own troops and cascading down the slope. Borne along with the tumbling stone, the two sentinels were ground to bloody smears.

A billowing cloud of dust obscured the shattered wall for half a dozen heartbeats. Screams of pain and panic reverberated across the valley. Undulating in the breeze, the dust cloud clung to the sweating makrasha, forming a sticky mud on their hides. The dust finally parted to reveal a jagged crack two spans wide.

The wall was breached.

His laugh of victory died on his lips though as he glanced back at the battle in the town. The king's forces were pushing his host back into the upper town, and soon soldiers would begin sweeping the horde before them. It did not matter. They had served their purpose.

It was the mounted force galloping toward the road to the keep that drew his attention. In their lead rode a white-robed sentinel.

Harafin!

A twinge of fear cracked his confidence, but he drove it away. Harafin would not win the day. Tanathos just needed a few minutes.

Pointing down the hill, he turned to the three shadeleeches still throwing magic at the defenders.

"Slow him. Take a hundred makrasha." He nodded toward the blond-furred halimaw crouching next to Antigonus' stretcher, licking its bloody flanks. "When you have his full attention, use the beast to kill him."

Tanathos left them to their duty and spared a glance at Antigonus. The old sentinel barely lived. The front of his robe was blood-soaked, and thick crimson drops trickled off his sleeve.

Soon he would know true pain.

To half a dozen makrasha crouched nearby he commanded, "Guard him. Bring him when I call."

He turned and strode toward the breach while his army overran the wall.

73

Well-Timed Faith

Howling for blood, makrasha charged down the slope in a dark wave. Behind them came three shadeleeches.

"Bout time," Jerrik said with a grin.

"A wager," Drystan said. "Man with the most kills gets the first shot at the next halimaw."

"Done!"

While the beasts were yet fifty yards away, a huge slab of masonry that had been part of the keep lumbered up into the air and hurtled down toward the men. The makrasha fired their small crossbows, and some unseen power drove the bolts at twice their normal speed. At the same time, fire erupted into life out of thin air all around the force of humans.

Kevlin started in surprise, but the amulet absorbed the magic, trickling a little bit of power into him as fire licked at his clothes. Around him, people beat at the flames and shouted curses.

Then the fire disappeared. The flames lasted no more than a heartbeat. All down the line, soldiers cast grateful glances at Harafin for saving them from the near-broiling.

The wave of onrushing crossbow bolts struck an invisible wall and deflected away. The heavy stone falling toward the company tumbled to one side, barely missing the last man.

"These three are good. They work together better than most shadeleeches." Harafin let out an explosive breath, his face set in a mask of concentration. "It will take me a little time to defeat them."

Leander hefted his hammer. "Maybe I'll get to them first." He threw the hammer, and it smashed a distant makrasha off its feet. "Charge!"

The old Pallian Stalwart spurred his horse toward the advancing horde.

Raising his sword, Kevlin added his own battle cry to the others, but he hung back a little, scanning the slope for any sign of Antigonus.

Nothing.

We have to get past these monsters.

Kevlin spurred his mount forward, focused on one of the beasts leaping toward him. His hand tingled with the rush of strength that always came at the onset of battle, and he shouted a second time.

The two lines collided with a resounding crash. Screams and curses mingled with clashing of steel and tumbling bodies as the two forces hacked at each other.

Kevlin stabbed and slashed with all his might, fighting monsters that stood as tall as he did astride his horse. They fought with brutal strength, and companions fell screaming, their bodies rent by the monsters' savage blows.

But soldiers outnumbered makrasha, and the men were experienced fighters. They fought in four-man squads to bring down each monster, and slowly began driving the makrasha back up the hill.

As Kevlin fought, distant drums began beating in time with his heart.

The song of Savas.

I will not yield! He resisted the song and, amazingly, it faded.

I'm getting better at this.

Bolstered by the success, Kevlin pressed ahead to help a squad fighting a particularly huge makrasha.

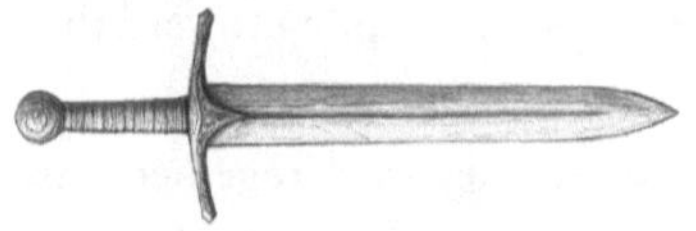

Drystan and Jerrik fought on either side of Leander, and around them makrasha fell in heaps, slashed by precision strikes of Drystan's spear or torn by jagged wounds from Jerrik's axe.

The two could barely keep up.

Leander plowed into ranks of the makrasha, his hammer trailing blue sparks as he smashed them down. With single-minded intensity, he pounded through the ranks, roaring a continuous battle cry and closing inexorably on the shadeleeches.

Motivated by his example, the soldiers redoubled their efforts. The coppery stink of blood mingled with the stench of death and exposed entrails in a reeking cloud. Shouts and high-pitched wails punctuated the constant ringing of steel, assaulting the ear and drowning out all speech.

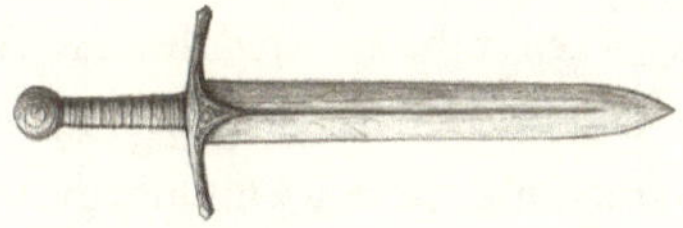

Harafin sat his horse, unmoving, focused on the three shadeleeches, fighting to deflect their spells. Magic arced above the combatants in white-hot bolts and black clouds, coloring everything in shifting hues of light and giving the battlefield the surreal air of a nightmare.

The battle was draining his reserves at an alarming rate.

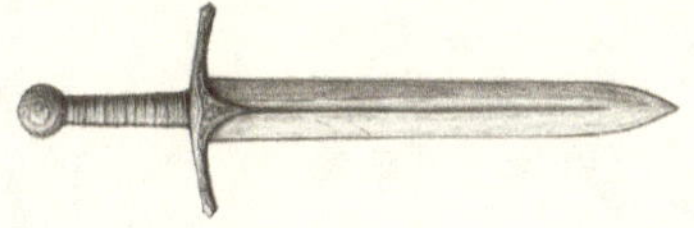

Ceren fought to hold down the bile threatening to spew from her stomach, and to shut out the terrible sights and sounds of pitched battle. Beside her, a soldier fell screaming, his armor rent and his body pierced.

The makrasha that killed him barreled past the rest of the squad and lunged at Ceren. A second beast pushed into the gap and launched itself at the soldiers. They would not be able to save her.

Panic set her hand shaking, and the sight of the huge beast nearly made her scream.

I can do this!

She slashed at its face, and her sword sliced across two of its eyes. It shrieked in pain, and battle rage swept aside her fear.

Spurring her mount forward, she slashed again. The monster caught her sword on one armored forearm, and the shock of the blow rattled her.

It was so close, its heavy, musky scent clung to her mouth. Before she could strike again, it grabbed her with its hengaruk.

She screamed and hacked at the monster's head as its disgusting stubby fingers clawed at her waist through her chainmail, trying to gain purchase. It beat her sword aside and drove one heavy fist into the side of Ceren's head, knocking her from the saddle.

She slammed into the ground, the impact jarring her teeth and jingling the unfamiliar bulk of mail that dragged at her shoulders. Her head rang from the blow, and her sword caught under her. Before she could pull it free, the makrasha lunged, its poisoned fangs snapping for her throat.

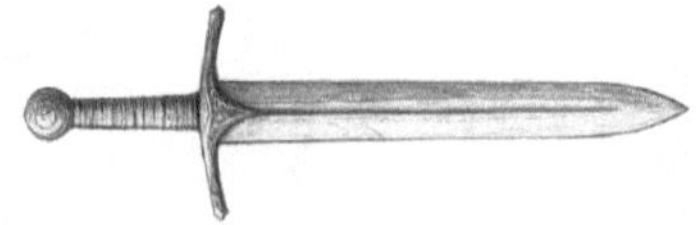

"Ceren!" Kevlin yelled.

He'd seen her fall, and watched in horror as the makrasha lunged toward her fallen form. He couldn't turn his mount against the press of soldiers.

Rising to a crouch in the saddle, he leaped off, and ran across the backs of two horses to reach hers.

Ceren screamed as the beast's jaws opened wide around her throat. She struggled to bring her sword around, but it was pinned underneath her.

It was all happening too fast.

The monster's jaws snapped shut.

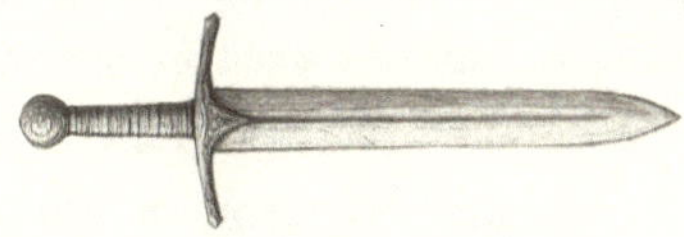

Ceren gagged at the makrasha's fetid breath. Its wicked fangs quivered half an inch from her exposed throat. She stared into its gaping maw and knew she was going to die.

The monster growled and sawed its deadly teeth back and forth, as if some invisible barrier prevented it from reaching her soft flesh. She recoiled against the ground, unable to escape.

Angered by its inability to kill her, the makrasha reared back and raised a sword. Ceren was so shocked that she didn't seize the chance to roll away.

Then someone crashed into the beast, and the two tumbled to the ground. The pair of them rolled over each other, stabbing and growling in animal fury.

Shaking off her stupor, Ceren surged to her knees and plunged her blade into the monster's back. It convulsed, and her rescuer slashed its throat.

"Kevlin!" she cried when she saw who it was.

"Are you hurt?"

"No." She stared into his hazel eyes and whispered, "I should be dead." She fought the sobs that threatened to burst forth and make her look the fool.

I will not be weak. He will not see me cry. Why doesn't he hold me?

Then Indira dropped to her knees and threw her arms around Ceren's shoulders. Ceren returned the embrace as powerful emotions overwhelmed her.

I did it. I really fought that monster.

"I did it," Indira said, echoing her thoughts. "I knew I could do it."

"You?"

Indira grinned. "I told you how I thought I could, and it worked." She pulled Ceren to her feet. "Come."

"Well done," Kevlin said to Indira, placing a hand on her shoulder.

Indira hugged Kevlin tight. Then she flushed and retreated.

Ceren pulled her from the battle frenzy, fighting down a flash of irritation that Indira dared hug him, while she had hesitated. Adalia joined them, arrow nocked and bow half-drawn, her eyes locked on the fighting.

"Glad yer safe," said the diminutive archer. "Ye be brave ta fight them brutes close up." She drew her bow and released the arrow in a single, fluid motion.

Ceren turned to see the shaft punch through the eye of a makrasha that had been gripping a soldier in its hengaruk. She trembled to think how close she had come to dying.

"Thank you," she said, turning back to Indira. "You saved my life."

"You are welcome." The healer pointed toward the bridge where the king's forces were driving the makrasha back. "Come help me. There will be many wounded."

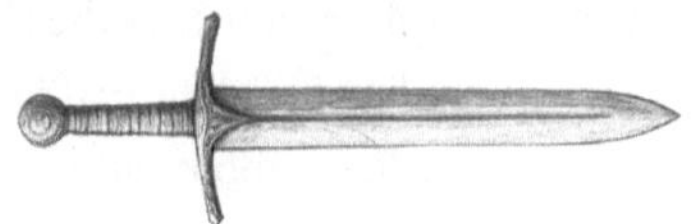

Kevlin waited until the three women were safely away. His heart still pounded with fear at how close Ceren had come to dying. He cared for the fiery noblewoman. Not many women he knew would have tried to take part in such a battle.

Chayah would have. He pushed thoughts of that betrayer out of his mind and considered how Indira had saved Ceren. There was more than one kind of strength.

Before rejoining the fighting, he paused to study what he could of the plateau at the base of the keep's wall. The fighting still raged, although it looked like the enemy was pushing through the breach. By the time Kevlin's company fought through, Tanathos would have won.

A flash of white caught his eye, and he squinted, still unable to make it out. He grabbed a nearby soldier by the collar and handed him the reins of a couple of horses. "Hold them steady."

Kevlin climbed up and stood on the animals' backs, focusing on the spot he'd seen the flash.

A bear?

It looked like a bear in a cage, and his heart sank. Shadeleeches made halimaw from bears. Beside the bear lay a figure in white.

Antigonus. It had to be.

The sentinel was so close. Kevlin just needed a little more time. He spotted a narrow path leading off the road, barely a rut where water ran across the mountain, but it led in the right direction along the edge of the steep slope.

Kevlin jumped down and headed for the path, leaving the fighting behind. Moving as fast as he dared, he edged out over the steep slope until he judged he was positioned directly below Antigonus.

It looked like only a few makrasha guarded Antigonus. If he could get the rock into the hands of its bearer, Antigonus could do the rest. Kevlin would need to hold off the makrasha until Antigonus triggered Oris's power.

Regardless of the cost.

The slope was steep, but not as bad as the cliff he'd scaled to escape the fort. Kevlin sheathed his sword, reached for promising handholds, and began to climb.

74

HEROES COME IN ALL SIZES

Trailing twin streams of blue fire, Nikias pivoted between two makrasha and whirled the Bladestaff in dizzying arcs, slashing the creatures half a dozen times.

"Follow me," he shouted before rushing through the gap in the enemy line.

Outriders surged behind him and engaged the makrasha flank, rolling it back and opening the way for more soldiers to cross the bridge. Nikias left them to it and circled the enemy to engage the last two shadeleeches ensconced at the rear.

He whooped another warcry, riding the current of battle fury that drove him on. He had only been chosen as bearer months before, and many scoffed at him, calling him untrained and reckless.

Today he would prove he was worthy.

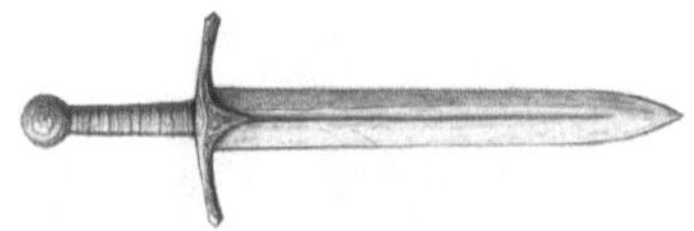

Sweat beaded Harafin's brow. *These three are very good.*

He'd rarely faced such tightly coordinated attacks. The trio of shadeleeches deployed a wide portfolio of spells, challenging him more than he had been in a long time. Under different circumstances, he would have enjoyed the contest, but today every second lost could prove fatal.

Just as serious, every second spent battling these three expended more of his waning reserves. He'd never experienced such a dearth of latent magic. It was just gone, spent by the battling sentinels, leaving nothing for him to draw upon. With the heart of the mountain sealed and the sun's rays blocked, no reserves flowed into the area.

A fresh attack began eating through his shields. As he worked to nullify the new threat, a blond-furred halimaw leaped out from where it had been concealed among the makrasha.

Harafin grinned at the rush of fear and excitement. It had been too long since he'd engaged in such a challenge. He was a man of peace at heart, but when the moment called for it, he easily donned his battle persona. He excelled at it.

As the monster launched itself down the slope, Harafin lifted four nearby makrasha corpses into the air and *pushed*, using them to catapult the halimaw overhead. It was an awkward throw, but with a little luck the monster would land in the river.

With the halimaw at least temporarily out of the way, Harafin finished nullifying the latest shadeleech attack. Then he conjured a wave of flaming darts to pelt across the enemy lines. It did little real harm, but distracted them for a second while he completed preparations on a much more complex spell.

There. He grinned. *Time to end this.*

Looking to the sky, he breathed a word of power and threw most of his remaining energy up toward the clouds.

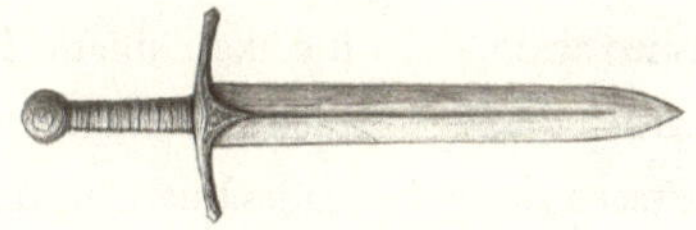

"What is that?" Ceren gasped, her voice squeaking with fear.

A blond-furred halimaw fell from the sky and slammed into the ground twenty paces downslope before tumbling toward the river. For a second it looked like it would roll right into the raging waters, but its impossibly muscled arms dug its curved claws into the ground. They gouged deep furrows and slowed its headlong rush just short of the bank.

The monster turned and fastened amber eyes on them. It opened its long snout and roared, showing a mouth full of sharp teeth.

An arrow slammed into the center of its chest.

"That'll teach it," Adalia said with a satisfied smile. The smile faded when the halimaw rose to its full twelve-foot height and yanked the arrow out of its fur.

"We be in trouble," Adalia decided, but even as she spoke, she drew another arrow, nocked it, and took aim.

The monster lunged onto all four legs and charged, tearing at the earth in its hunger to reach them.

Ceren raised her sword, but her hand shook with terror. It wasn't fair! She hadn't just survived death by makrasha to die by this horror.

Adalia let fly the second arrow and caught the monster in the face, just missing an eye. The shaft grazed its skull, leaving a thin crimson gash.

"By Jagen, that ain't right," Adalia cried, already drawing another arrow.

The monster barreled toward them, its terrifying gaze fixed on Adalia's tiny form. Unfazed, she nocked the third arrow.

"See how ye like this," she snarled, drawing the bow with a rock-steady hand. She would get only one more shot.

Nikias arrived first.

In a blur of blue flame, he intercepted the monster and slashed its torso with the burning silvery blades of his staff.

The monster skidded to a halt and grasped at the puny human, but Nikias danced aside and slashed again, shouting like a lunatic. His blades sliced across the monster's arms, cutting its thick hide but not penetrating the dense muscle beneath. Fire raced along the blades but seemed to have no effect on it.

The monster lunged at him again, but again he danced aside, twirling behind the beast and stabbing at its back, again just scraping through the tough hide. The monster spun after him, but he dodged its grasping claws, slashing again.

Ceren watched in amazement as the two lunged and ducked, slashed and clawed, spun and dodged in a deadly dance punctuated by the beast's frustrated roar and Nikias' incessant whooping yells.

Then Nikias misjudged a dodge and one huge, furry arm clobbered him in the side of the head. He tumbled to the ground, and the monster pounced. Ceren gasped with a spike of fear, but an arrow slammed into the base of its throat, punctured the softer skin of the neck, and sank several inches into the flesh.

The beast grunted, clutching at its neck, and tore the arrow free. It turned back to Nikias, but the young Bladestaff bearer was already back on his feet, striking a gallant pose and grinning like a fool.

"Turn off the fire," Adalia shouted as she drew another arrow. "It be distracting me."

Nikias dodged the monster again and spared a glance at Adalia. "But the fire's the best part."

Adalia stared, mouth agape. With a scowl, she shouted, "Be ye daft, man? If'n what yer doin' don't help, get rid of it."

Nikias slashed again, looking a little crestfallen. The fire winked out. The monster lunged, its dozen bleeding wounds not slowing it.

Nikias whirled closer, and for a second it looked like the monster was going to encircle him in its crushing arms. Nikias slashed a blade across its throat before ducking and rolling under its arms. It opened its mouth wide and roared.

"Perfect," Adalia whispered.

Her next arrow shot into the beast's mouth and buried itself in the soft tissue at the back of its throat. The monster gagged and staggered, tearing at the shaft with its claws. Another arrow punched through a huge, amber eye. The monster clutched at its wounded face, roaring in agony.

"For King and the Lady Jagen," Nikias shouted.

Moving around the monster, he hacked with both blades of the Bladestaff, twirling the weapon so fast it blurred into a silvery cloud.

Fur exploded from the halimaw's body and drifted around the combatants. Strips of muscle and flesh shredded from its limbs and torso. Blood fountained from a hundred wounds as Nikias carved the beast from neck to thigh, peeling it layer by layer to the core.

It convulsed in agony and tried to swipe at him, but the wounds were beginning to slow it, and Nikias had found his rhythm. It staggered as Nikias carved through its bulk. It shrank in size as its flesh billowed away in crimson clouds.

Ceren gagged and wanted to turn away from the grisly sight, but could not. Nikias drove one blade of his weapon up through the monster's bare midsection, plunging it deep and sinking half the length of the wooden shaft up under its ribs to pierce the heart.

Blood sprayed from the monster's mouth as it convulsed a final time. Then it toppled, a ruined shadow of its former terrifying might.

Nikias withdrew the Bladestaff and stood panting, his face drenched with sweat and covered with gore.

"Wow," Ceren said, glancing at Indira, who nodded and said, "the way is clear. I have to reach the wounded."

"Nice blade work at the end," Adalia said.

Nikias beamed and made an extravagant bow. "Thank you, my beautiful young archer!"

"Took long enough," she said, and turned to follow Indira and Ceren toward the bridge and the ranks of wounded. Ceren bit back a chuckle at Nikias' crestfallen expression.

The young hero shrugged, grinned, and let out another wild cry. Turning back to the main conflict, he rushed toward the fighting.

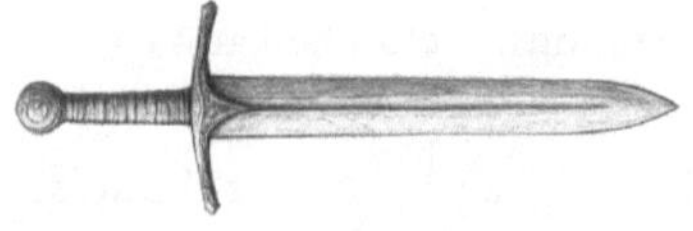

The lowering clouds above the valley roiled as if shaken by a giant hand. Half a dozen jagged bolts of lightning ripped the air, striking around the three shadeleeches confronting Harafin. Thunder pealed in an overwhelming rumble that shook men and monsters alike to the ground and reverberated off the cliffs.

Leander shook his head to clear the after-effects of the blasts. Leading the charge, he'd been closest to the shadeleeches when the lightning struck. A makrasha groaned nearby, and he dispatched it with a blow to the head.

The shadeleeches were simply obliterated. The surviving makrasha howled in fear as the men charged in to finish the fight, some shouting Harafin's name as they brought the monsters down. Harafin joined Leander a moment later.

"You always finish things with a flair," Leander said with a weary chuckle. "Had you waited a few seconds, you would have blasted me to the eternities with them."

"Trust me."

Leander laughed, and pulled himself onto an available horse.

"We must help Rhisart," Harafin said as he also mounted.

"Jerrik, Drystan," Leander called. "Wrap this up and join us when you're done." The two captains saluted and turned back to the last pocket of fighting.

"I'm at eleven," Jerrik's voice drifted back to Leander.

"Same," Drystan replied.

"We'd better hurry then," Jerrik said, "before there's none left."

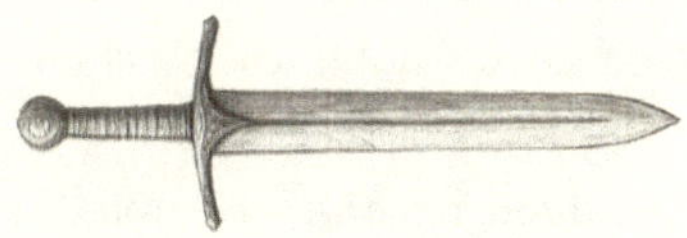

Wayra banged the heel of her hand against one side of her head, trying to stop the ringing. Debris covered the courtyard inside the wall, and a thick haze of dust choked her lungs. All along the still-standing sections of wall, the fighting had resumed. The defenders, led by two kestrels, were about to be overrun.

We're out of time.

She turned to Rhisart. She'd managed to impale the halimaw as it fell, but hadn't managed to cushion Rhisart's fall. One leg was badly broken, and his chest had been ripped open by the monster's claws. She laid a hand on his pallid face, searching for the spark of life.

She felt a distant glimmer, but it disappeared before she could fan it back to strength.

Rhisart, Gerent of Il'Aicharen, was dead.

She prepared to compress his heart with her power. At times that had been proven successful in reviving the recently deceased. She paused with her will gathered, struck by a new realization.

As Rhisart's second, she was the new gerent.

She ruled Il'Aicharen.

She turned from the fallen man, filled with an exultant feeling of triumph. She ruled! It was a bitter irony that her keep was on the point of destruction.

Then she gasped, eyes wide, as power thundered into her. The ecstasy of it stunned her for several heartbeats, and she threw back her head and moaned with pleasure.

This feeling was everything she had ever dreamed. Her senses extended, sliding along every surface, from the wall to the still-standing buildings, and on to the passages into the mountain. Her soul became linked with the keep.

You are my second.

Rhisart's words resonated in her mind and she laughed, finally understanding what that meant. The keep's vast defenses were hers to command. She spun to focus on the breached wall and the enemy she sensed approaching.

A shadeleech stepped through the haze. He stood average height, and dust dulled his crimson robes. He met her gaze, and even imbued with all the power of the keep, she shuddered at the roiling blackness covering his eyes.

Tanathos! It had to be.

He snarled and raised a hand.

I am ready.

With a single thought, she unleashed a blast of raw power.

She was stronger than she thought. The wave of magic struck Tanathos, shattered his shields, and catapulted him backward, high over the wall. He tumbled out of view, leaving behind a vile curse.

Wayra laughed, then headed up onto the wall. With her newly acquired powers, she would eliminate Tanathos and destroy his army. She would not allow these invaders to tarnish this first day of her rule.

75

The Song of Savas

"Drive them into the river," King Leszek shouted with a wave of his sword.

His army surrounded the enemy horde on three sides. Hathor had killed one of the last two shadeleeches and had the other completely on the defensive. The outriders advanced, and the makrasha fell back. Another hundred yards and they could throw the monsters into the churning Ujutus.

Victory is ours.

Already the king began considering the best way to turn the unexpected attack into an opportunity to launch the next phase of his plan.

The coarse blatting of brass horns, unlike any used by his armies, turned him in his saddle. An army of men came running out of the woods below the town, charging toward his rearguard.

Frowning, King Leszek squinted at the new force. They came on foot, dressed in leather armor, like a muddy wave.

Mercenaries.

More poured out of the forest until they filled the lower valley, at least five hundred men.

Running at the head of the approaching army in long, loping strides charged a dark-skinned man. His scale armor shone in the morning light, shifting through various hues.

A Blade Stalwart, one already in full battle rhapsody.

Leszek wheeled around and shouted an order. A column of outriders turned back toward the bridge, while the others continued hacking at the remaining makrasha. The king led his men over the bridge to the lower town to meet the onrushing force.

"Your orders?" his captain asked.

"Stand ready. I'll know their intent in a moment."

The mercenaries continued their advance, and soon the king recognized Dhanjal in the lead, his bald pate glowing with dozens of tattoos. The man ran confidently, head held high and shoulders back.

King Leszek relaxed. He had been wishing Dhanjal would show up. The stalwart had dropped from all contact after leaving on his mission to assist Piran. If the king had thought even for a moment the chore would have taken so long, he never would have authorized it, no matter how much he owed Piran.

For one who worshipped war, the stalwart was running late. He had better have a good reason for bringing such a force into the kingdom without prior authorization.

Another Blade Stalwart joined Dhanjal at the head of the mercenary company. A huge brute, also dark-skinned, he stood half a head taller than Dhanjal, his massive shoulders making the other stalwart look skinny by comparison. He ran with twin maces in hand, and his scale armor also shifted through muted hues of light.

Dhanjal slowed to a stop a dozen paces away from the king's lines. The mercenary company halted behind him. He folded his arms across his chest and, all along the length of the king's army, men obeyed the powerful impulse to sheath their weapons.

King Leszek ignored the impulse. "You're late. Where have you been?"

Dhanjal swept his gaze along the ranks of outriders marshaled around the king. Raising a hand, he spoke, and his surprisingly gentle voice carried easily to everyone.

"I salute you all, chosen to fall on the field of battle. May Savas guide your souls to your gods and deliver you with honor."

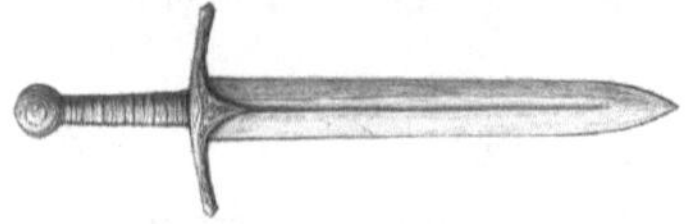

Kevlin shifted his feet as he tried to find solid purchase on a narrow protrusion. He crouched ten feet below the summit, directly below Antigonus.

Six makrasha stood near the sentinel, but they hadn't noticed Kevlin. Instead they watched the battle rage along the walls of the keep, or stared toward Harafin's force climbing the road.

Antigonus looked to be sleeping, and that could be disastrous. Kevlin could get the stone to him, but wouldn't have time to rouse the old man. He'd be too busy fighting off makrasha.

A man tumbled into view high overhead, his crimson robes snapping in the wind as he fell toward the ground.

Tanathos.

A cloud of darkness appeared around one of the makrasha. The beast howled as it shriveled and died, its life sacrificed to Tanathos. The shadeleech slowed his descent.

He'd land close to the makrasha.

Kevlin finalized his plan. Get the rock to Antigonus. Kill Tanathos.

He crouched to spring, but the blaring of distant brass horns caught his attention. He turned to see a large force of men moving up through the lower valley.

Kevlin focused the tiny amount of magic the amulet had captured earlier, and willed his eyes to see. Despite the distance, the mass of leather-armored men came into sharp focus. At the head of the new force strode a distinctive figure whose armor shone with shifting hues of light.

Dhanjal.

Drums beat in Kevlin's soul, trumpets blared loud in his mind, and a crescendo of strings stirred his heart. The song of Savas blasted all thought from his mind and set his muscles quivering with the need to obey.

My chosen, the soft voice whispered with such power that he felt his skull would crack. *Fight for me.*

No. . .I'm so close, Kevlin tried to shout, but the thought was barely a whisper in his mind.

Instead his body obeyed the pounding cadence. In a tiny corner of his consciousness, Kevlin struggled to defy the command, but the song usurped control.

Releasing his hold on the slope, Kevlin spun and sprinted headlong down the hill. His legs pumped in time with the beating drums, driving him in a terrifying rush.

Reaching the narrow path, he sped back to the main road. There he yanked a wounded soldier from his mount. Vaulting into the saddle, Kevlin spurred the animal toward the bridge. Horns blared in time with the thundering hooves, and he laughed with bloodlust.

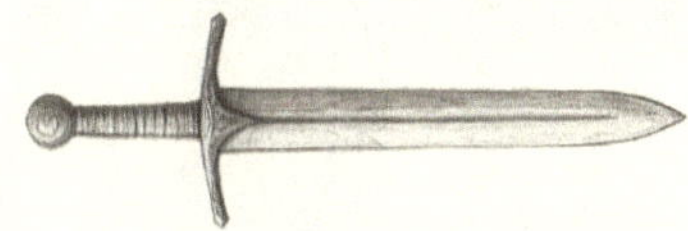

"That's Kevlin," Drystan called, pointing to a figure hurtling down the steep slope in a reckless dash.

"What's he doing?" Jerrik asked. "And how'd he get way up there?"

Harafin followed their gaze, and gasped. "Savas! I'd hoped He wouldn't interfere." He glanced up the slope, and then again at Kevlin. "This couldn't be worse timing."

"We have to stop him," Leander declared.

"No," Harafin said. "You and I must get to the keep before Tanathos wins through."

"If Kevlin gives in to Savas, he could destroy everything," Leander protested.

"I know." Harafin frowned. "Time to spin the Wheel."

"Don't bring that fool-headed Akillik into this."

"Just an expression." Harafin turned to Drystan and Jerrik. "You two go after Kevlin. If I'm right, you are the one chance he has of breaking free."

"And if you're wrong?" Drystan asked.

"Then you have to kill him."

At their shocked looks, Harafin added, "Know this. If Kevlin surrenders to Savas, all is lost. Either help him escape Savas' control, or kill him."

"How do we do it?" Drystan asked with a frown.

"Just be yourselves."

"How will that help?" Jerrik asked.

"Trust me."

The two spurred their horses. Drystan's voice carried back to Harafin. "I hate it when he says that."

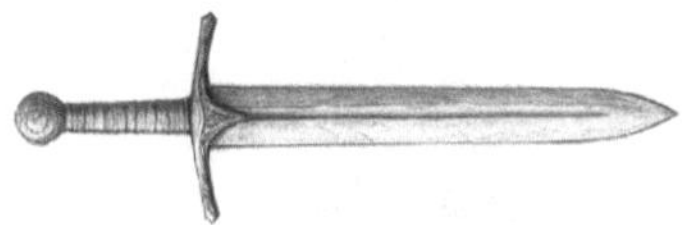

"I get the other Blade Stalwart," Jerrik called to Drystan as they galloped down the road after Kevlin.

"We're tied." Drystan pointed toward the mercenaries. "Besides, looks like they're already in battle rhapsody."

"Bout time," Jerrik laughed. "A real challenge. I get him first."

Bent low over the horses, and still arguing, they raced for the upper town.

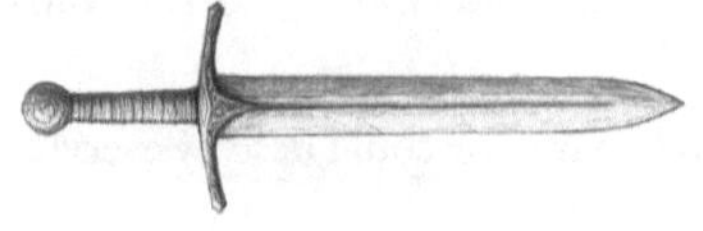

"What is the meaning of this?" King Leszek demanded, hoping he had misunderstood Dhanjal's intent. "You are under contract with me."

Dhanjal took one step closer. "The contract is canceled. I will bury you with yew and stone, as a favored son of the Lady Jagen."

The king gasped, and a ripple of anger ran through the outrider ranks.

Dhanjal reached over his shoulder and drew a pala from its sheath on his back. Raising it high, he proclaimed in a ringing voice, "Behold the will of Savas!"

He threw the sword.

The slender blade glinted in the morning sun before slamming into the center of King Leszek's chest. It punched through his armor. The tip of the blade drove out his back and clanked against his armor, setting the entire weapon quivering.

A wave of pain so intense he could not comprehend it flooded the king's mind.

Then it disappeared. . .and he felt nothing.

He stared at the hilt standing out from his chest. Thought fled as he opened his mouth, but only blood spilled out, running down his chin. Darkness descended over his mind and drove him into oblivion.

The king of Hallvarr toppled slowly from his saddle.

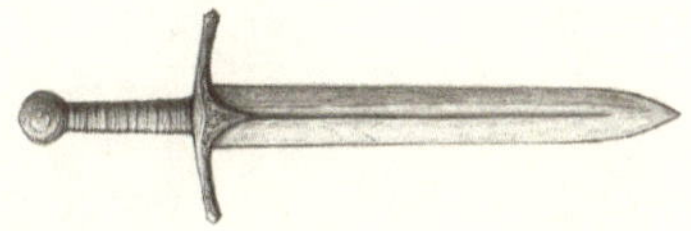

Elite warriors though they were, the outriders watched in horror as their leader fell to the ground with a clatter of steel. Nor did they react until the mercenary army shouted in unison, drew swords, and charged.

Outriders fumbled for swords sheathed under Dhanjal's influence and struggled to focus their minds. Shock turned to rage, and they screamed for blood.

Weapons flashed in the morning sun as men struck at each other. Blood spurted in sheets from hundreds of wounds, and screams drowned out the din of battle.

The mounted outriders fought for vengeance, rage driving them at the mercenary infantry. Word of the king's death spread quickly, and soon outriders veered off from the other battle and raced for the bridge, howling for the blood of the murderers. Within minutes, the mercenaries were outnumbered two to one.

The outriders never stood a chance.

Dhanjal and the other Blade Stalwart decimated their ranks. Outriders crowded around the pair, hungry for a chance to avenge their king.

They all died.

Corpses piled up around the stalwarts as the big men cut through the ranks, their multi-hued armor glowing brighter with every kill. Dhanjal's heavy scimitars sheared through armor and bone as easily as flesh, while the other stalwart's maces caved in chests and crushed skulls.

Men fought to get away from the onslaught, and the center of the king's army collapsed as outriders ran for their lives.

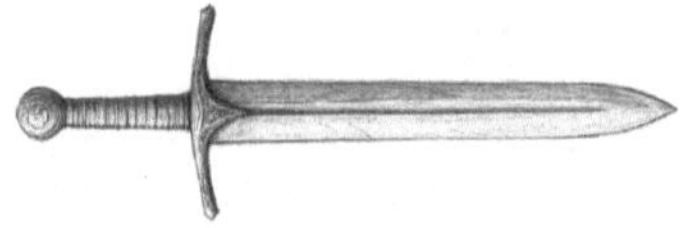

Howling like a berserker, Kevlin charged through the thinning ranks of the outriders. Dhanjal and the other stalwart were fighting some distance apart as they chased the king's men.

"Dhanjal!" Kevlin bellowed so loud his vocal chords burned.

The Blade Stalwart turned to face him, and a wide smile cut through the blackness of his face. He beckoned, his arm dripping with other men's blood. "Come, trueson of Savas. Let us finish the Dance."

The song of Savas swelled in response, and the cadence overwhelmed the feeble thoughts of protest Kevlin tried to form. He leaped from the horse, raised his sword high and launched himself at Dhanjal.

The clear ringing of their swords vibrated through Kevlin's soul as the song swelled louder. Stringed instruments that sent shivers down his spine joined the next beat, and his soul exulted in the pure joy of battle.

The two fought each other alone, surrounded by the corpses of the dead, while on all sides men from both armies disengaged to stare at the spectacle. Dhanjal, his armor glowing so bright that men couldn't look directly at it, rained heavy blows on his smaller opponent.

Undaunted and unafraid, Kevlin whirled around the bigger man like a sparrow attacking a crow. Again and again their swords clashed, and the valley rang with the echoes.

The other Blade Stalwart paused to watch the fight. Then, after Kevlin scraped his sword across Dhanjal's armor, the man hefted his twin maces and began to advance on the combatants.

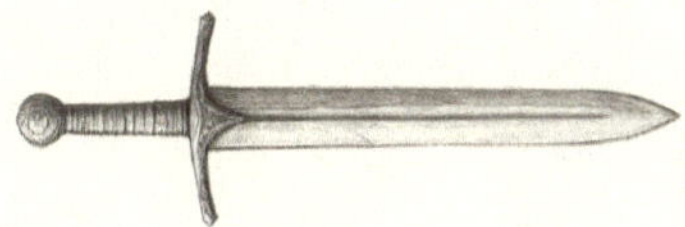

"Hey, pick your own fight!" Jerrik shouted as he leaped from his mount.

The big stalwart turned as Drystan joined his swordbrother. The unknown Blade Stalwart smiled. "To you who dare compete for Savas' favor, I salute you."

"Are they always like this?" Drystan asked as he moved to flank the big man.

The Blade Stalwart beckoned. "Come, let us dance the song of Savas."

Jerrik hefted his axe. "I hear Savas sings like a girl." To Drystan he added, "I get him first."

The two giant warriors came together, axe crashing against crossed maces. Their heavy weapons whirled, clashing in counterpoint to the staccato ringing of Kevlin and Dhanjal's swords.

The four battled amid the dead while the living looked on in wonder.

76

A Name For Death

Nikias, bearer of the Bladestaff, ducked under a bolt of magic and leaped, the silvered blades of his weapon trailing streamers of blue flame. He landed close to the shadeleech and removed the man's head and lower legs with a single twirl of his weapon. The shadeleech fell, his mouth still trying to utter a final word of power.

"Ha," Nikias shouted, pumping his weapon overhead. "See if Drystan can top that!"

He glanced over the bridge and noticed the fighting on that side for the first time. Drystan was down there, and Blade Stalwarts.

Without hesitation, he ran for the bridge.

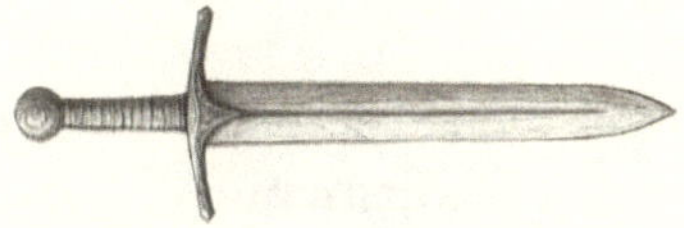

"Indira, look!" Ceren pulled the healer to her feet and pointed at the blazing forms of the Blade Stalwarts fighting on the other side of the river.

Kevlin fought alone against Dhanjal.

Seeing Dhanjal again brought back the terror of the morning in the clearing when he had first attacked. Even together, Kevlin and Terach hadn't been able to beat him.

Terach. The image of him struck down by Dhanjal's blade brought a fresh wave of devastating grief. He had been an honorable man, and Ceren had come to depend on him. His death still tore at her. Watching as Kevlin fought Dhanjal alone, fear nearly overwhelmed her.

She couldn't lose him too. Kevlin was a complicated, difficult man, but she didn't want him killed.

He was about to become a central player in the empire. His family connections and appointment as steward would open doors he could not yet fathom. Ceren planned to help, to guide him. As Cunning, she was best suited for it.

She clutched Indira's arm. "You have to help him. Protect him like you did me."

"I'll try."

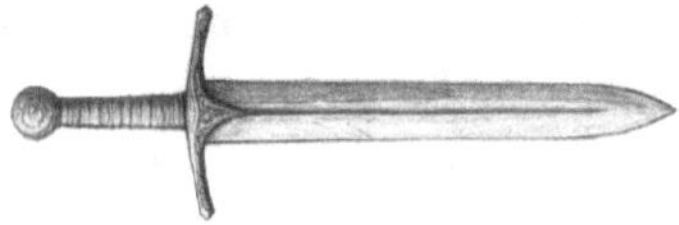

Tanathos landed hard. The life force of the makrasha he'd sacrificed gave him the power to slow his descent, but not stop it altogether. How many souls would it take to fly? When he ruled the world, he would have to find out.

He turned back to the keep in time to see a blast of air shred his makrasha fighting atop the wall and hurl their shattered corpses away. The ragged knots of defenders cheered as if they had a chance at victory.

Fewer than two hundred makrasha remained of his host. Glancing down the valley, Tanathos ground his teeth in frustration. Both hordes were destroyed. At least the mercenaries had finally arrived to engage the king's forces. That would slow the bulk of the enemy army.

Harafin was coming up the slope. The sentinel was more than halfway up the road from the upper town, and moving fast.

Tanathos snapped a mental command at the makrasha, recalling them back to surround him. The fools wanted to challenge him? They would suffer the same fate as everyone else he'd chosen for destruction. Casting out a wide net, he began sucking the lives of his slaves. A dark cloud descended over his force.

One makrasha died in writhing agony.

Then a second.

Then a third.

Tanathos exulted in the glory of their life forces sacrificed at *his* command, to fulfill *his* destiny. Drawing in the life of a fourth slave, he smiled.

Time to end this.

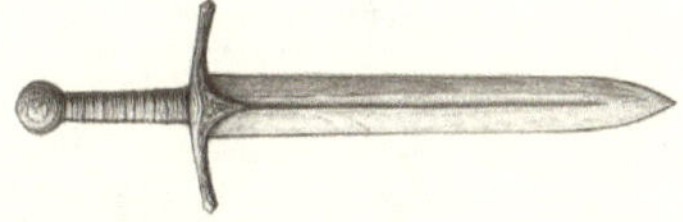

Wayra stepped to the edge of the parapet and surveyed the carnage. Corpses of men and makrasha littered the ground as far as she could see. Blood streaked the hills, and carrion birds circled overhead by the hundreds. Far down in the lower valley, soldiers still fought, but a menacing silence had settled over the upper slope.

Atop the wall, the few who remained standing cheered her arrival. Bloody, haggard villagers leaned on weapons familiar from desperate use. Only two of her kestrels survived, but they saluted her with pride.

Tanathos huddled on the eastern edge of the plateau, just above where the land fell away toward the river. His makrasha circled him, a last, desperate bodyguard.

Harafin spurred his horse up the road from the upper town. In a matter of minutes it would be over, and it looked like Tanathos realized it. His attempt to hide from Harafin was laughable.

As she watched, a dark cloud descended over the makrasha. One died screaming, then a second, and more. It looked like Tanathos was preparing to make a final, pitiful attempt at taking the keep.

I am ready.

Drawing upon the vast power at her command, Wayra raised impenetrable shields of shimmering light up the wall and higher still, until they reared a hundred feet over her head. Staring toward Tanathos through the rainbow hues, she smiled.

Let him come.

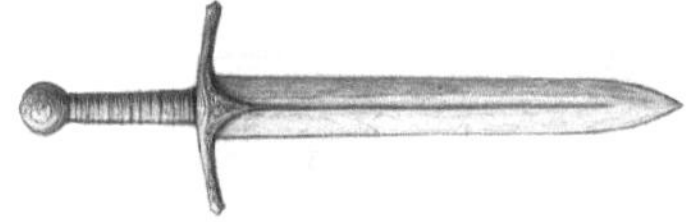

Lightning-like magic arced between Tanathos' open palms. The energy of four lives surged through his body, straining his restraints. So few could ever enjoy that experience. It verged on the sacred.

He exulted in the exquisite joy, and spoke a single word.

Half a mile from the eastern wall of the keep, the mighty Ujutus falls thundered out of the face of the cliff. They plunged in an uncaring torrent over five hundred feet before dashing against the roots of the mountain in an eternal battle of primal forces.

Near the bottom of the cascade, the air shimmered. The glistening mist boiling around the falls began to dim and turn opaque.

The water tumbling out the bottom of the dark cloud slowed, then stopped altogether.

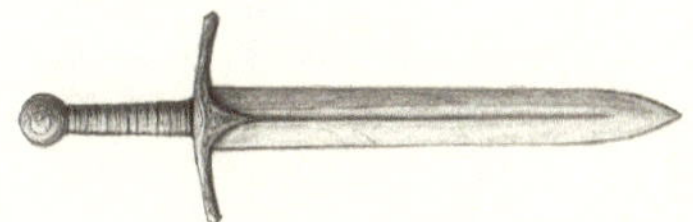

The air high above the keep shimmered and flexed, casting light in widening arcs like a shifting prism.

Wayra looked up and cursed.

Her shields were in the wrong place.

With the sound of a thousand linen sheets ripping in unison, the sky sundered and a torrent of water plunged out of the nothingness. On the wall, men and women had two or three heartbeats to comprehend the titanic wall of water cascading down on the enclave.

The waterfall struck the center of the keep, and the impact shook the entire slope. Smaller buildings disintegrated under the unimaginable pressure. Doors, windows, and entire sections of wall ripped from the keep. The water roared like a million lions, consuming everything in its path.

When the torrent struck the outer wall, the gates shattered and chunks of timber blasted all the way across the valley to rain down on the forest across the river. The magically enhanced stones held some of the wall together, but the water blasting through the breach ripped more stones free, shooting them hundreds of feet. Within seconds, the gap yawed fifty feet wide, and the wall to either side bowed out under the pressure of the flood.

Elsewhere, the wave crested up over the wall, rearing above the tallest tower before crashing back outside the wall and plunging down the slope in a roiling flood. The tide flung screaming townsfolk and sentinels alike off the wall.

Wayra alone withstood the first barrage. Drawing the shields around her in a tight column, she barely deflected the tidal wave. The water splashed up and over the upper rim of her shields. The conjured waterfall cut off, but the backsplash crashed into Wayra, knocked her off the wall and into the turbulent waters inside the enclave.

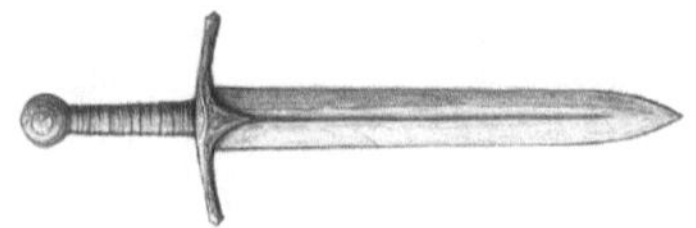

Tanathos shouted and raised a fist in triumph.

Water cascaded close by his small force, but he'd placed himself perfectly. The tidal wave blasted down the slope, scouring the ground to bare rock and wiping the road off the mountain. The churning flood tumbled directly toward Harafin, who stood a quarter of a mile downslope.

With arms outstretched, Tanathos commanded in a ringing voice, "Now, my slaves, release the power of my new name. Kill for me!"

A score of makrasha had been sacrificed to fuel the spell, but a hundred remained. More than enough to announce to the world the name of the man about to rule all things.

All the beasts, except the six tasked with guarding Antigonus, brandished weapons and chased the waters down the slope. As they ran, they raised their inhuman voices in unison and began chanting his new name, the battle cry that would sweep the entire world.

"Abaval! Abaval! Abaval!"

77

MESS WITH ONE BROTHER, MESS WITH THEM ALL

Jerrik caught a mace on his axe. He panted, lungs blasting like a bellows, and grinned like a madman.

This guy's incredible!

Why hadn't he ever thought to fight a Blade Stalwart before? He poured every ounce of strength and skill into the battle, and the Blade Stalwart matched him stroke for stroke. The swarthy stalwart nearly matched Jerrik's size, and was unbelievably strong.

The stalwart drew his twin maces to the left in an odd move that exposed his right flank. Jerrik struck without hesitation.

The stalwart struck at the same time.

The full force of both maces caught the flat of Jerrik's battle-axe and shattered the great blade. The shock rattled him and knocked him off-balance. He dropped to one knee and shook his head to clear it.

The stalwart stepped in for the kill.

Drystan moved faster.

The lanky Einarri leaped and, using Jerrik's broad shoulder as a springboard, vaulted a full ten feet off the ground. He sailed above the Blade Stalwart's maces and slashed at the dark-skinned man's face with his spear.

The stalwart stumbled, and the spear tip skidded across one shoulder, scraping the scale armor with a shrieking of steel. Drystan landed and rolled, rising to his feet in a single, fluid motion, spear at the ready.

The Blade Stalwart turned back, and Jerrik was ready, one mighty fist cocked back.

Jerrik punched him in the jaw. The blow rocked the stalwart back, and Jerrik wrapped his massive hands over the stalwart's on the mace handles. The two struggled for control of the weapons.

The stalwart's armor shifted with a flutter of glowing scales. Jerrik's shoulders and arms swelled with power, and he threw all his strength against the stalwart's, trying to drive the maces away.

For the first time in his life, Jerrik wasn't strong enough.

His eyes widened in surprise as the stalwart stopped the movement of the weapons. And then, his face set in a mask of concentration, the dark-skinned man very slowly pushed Jerrik back, bending the maces toward the Donarri warrior.

Drystan approached, spear raised to strike.

"Back off," Jerrik growled between clenched teeth. Sweat poured down his face. His arms burned with the effort as he drove his body to the edge of strength. "Get your own. This one's mine."

Drystan frowned. "Ungrateful." Then he turned and headed for Kevlin, who battled Dhanjal twenty paces away.

Their faces only inches apart, the Blade Stalwart said, "I will cover your body with stone in honor of your strength that will soon be mine."

He pushed even harder.

"Don't. . .celebrate. . .too. . .soon," Jerrik panted. His wrists burned as the maces tilted toward him. A little further, and the stalwart would have the advantage.

Then Jerrik would die.

The two men locked gazes as they struggled, and Jerrik realized he couldn't win this test of strength.

"You got good arms," Jerrik said. "How strong are your fingers?"

Jerrik squeezed.

Drawing from his deepest reserves of strength, he poured everything he had left into the effort. The stalwart grimaced and tried to pull back, but Jerrik held him and squeezed harder. The dark-skinned man grunted and the brilliant glow of his armor began to fade.

Jerrik's hands and wrists felt like they were immersed in living fire, but he did not relent.

The stalwart howled with pain, and Jerrik shouted as he drove his body to its uttermost limits and crushed the other man's hands against the handle of his own weapons. The stalwart's left hand twitched, and his fingers cracked audibly. The scale-clad warrior threw his head back and screamed.

Yanking the mace out of the man's broken fingers, Jerrik smashed the weapon into the Blade Stalwart's face, crushing his features and shattering his skull. Blood and grey matter sprayed across Jerrik's face. He spat a gobbet of flesh.

Stepping back, he struck again, and then a third time.

The stalwart crumpled to the ground, his head a formless, bloody mass.

Jerrik threw his arms wide and roared his victory. He wiped his face and let out an explosive breath.

"Ukko's Beard, that was a good fight!"

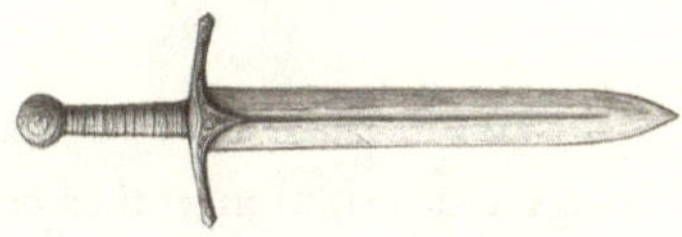

Drums beat in Kevlin's soul and power raged in his limbs. Horns never heard by mortal man rang in counterpoint, stoking the flames of that power. A dozen different strings trilled complex scales that set his mind ablaze with possible forms.

The voice spoke, soft but undeniable.

Lost in the song of Savas, Kevlin's body moved to the beat and danced through the forms, his sword ringing against Dhanjal's scimitars. The clashing steel provided a perfect harmony to the song in his soul.

Time ceased to exist. Thought was irrelevant. Only honoring the song mattered.

Serve me, the voice said in his head. *Surrender all to me and I will give you victory everlasting.*

With the next form, his sword slipped past a scimitar, drove through a scale on Dhanjal's glowing armor, and scraped into Dhanjal's flesh.

And Kevlin could think again--just a little. Enough to answer the voice. *I want victory.*

You will have it. You will shatter armies, destroy nations.

The song rose to a crescendo and visions of conquest and glory rained down upon his flooded brain. *You will bring justice to the world. You will rule all things.*

The glory of the vision pounded at him and filled him with joy. He could destroy evil, subdue all enemies. What could be wrong with that?

A dim corner of his mind protested, but he couldn't form a coherent thought as the song of Savas thundered through his soul. Again his sword slipped past a scimitar, and his heart sang with the glory of impending victory.

Pushing the whispered fears aside, he threw out the thought, *I can do this!*

It is well, the voice said with another trilling of strings. The drums beat faster, and his body responded, increasing its pace and moving through the forms in a blur.

Surrender the power of Oris to me, and victory is yours.

The whispered warnings returned, stronger than before, almost understandable, a rip current of danger that tried to pull him back.

It was not enough.

I don't know how, Kevlin said.

Behold, the way.

As it had once before, a vision opened to his mind even as his body flowed through another form, battered aside Dhanjal's blades, and slashed the big man across one arm. The armor parted and his sword bit deep, coming away streaked with Dhanjal's blood.

In his mind, images flashed so quickly that he could not consciously understand them. *Release the power and be thou mine,* the voice commanded with a clamor of horns that resonated to the deepest corners of his soul. The image of a wall appeared in his mind. A solid, ancient wall.

Shatter the wall. Will it so. Then thy soul shall know power and glory beyond imagining.

A second image flashed with the next beat, and suddenly Kevlin knew how to tear down the wall.

He focused his will.

A new voice spoke into his mind, a familiar voice foreign to the Song.

Victory through slavery is a lie.

Drystan?

Kevlin shuddered mentally, and part of him awoke, struggling to rise above the torrent of the song of Savas.

The price is too high.

Drystan spoke into his mind, calm and confident. And somehow Drystan was there, lending his strength to Kevlin along with his iron discipline. The half-heard whispers of warning rang clear.

I will be no pawn. Slavery is not victory, Kevlin shouted the thought.

The drums pounded harder and the horns blared so loud they shook his skull.

Serve me and inherit glory forever, Savas commanded, driving all other thoughts away. Again the wall appeared in Kevlin's mind, and everything else faded to whispers.

Savas sings like a girl.

Jerrik's deep voice rumbled in Kevlin's mind, and the big man's incredible strength flowed into Kevlin, forming a bedrock upon which he could anchor. Drystan's calm discipline buttressed his own thoughts, so that again his mind rose above the song.

Be thou mine, or be destroyed, Savas whispered.

The cadence slowed, and became ominous, threatening. Fear replaced the burning sense of power, and Kevlin's body shook with terror.

I defy you! Kevlin cried out, throwing every ounce of willpower into the thought.

So be it.

The voice disappeared. The strings and horns stopped instantly.

A single drum beat. Once.

The sound rang through his soul like a death knell.

All of the power, all of the strength, departed with it. Kevlin gasped, once more in control of his body. His arms, his hands, his feet, his head, were again his.

The agony was his alone.

His body screamed for respite. He barely held onto his sword as his limbs quivered with exhaustion. He staggered, and his vision blurred, only to focus a second later. . .

On Dhanjal's scimitar.

The heavy blade slammed into his chest, rending his chainmail and slicing into the flesh beneath. The force of the blow tumbled Kevlin to the ground, where he lay stunned.

Another scimitar slashed toward his throat, but his strength was gone. His body refused to respond. He couldn't even blink as the blade descended.

Drystan slammed the butt of his spear into the ground beside Kevlin's neck, and the heavy scimitar struck it, biting deep into the dense wooden shaft.

Dhanjal wrenched the blade free, and the shaft broke.

Drystan lunged past Kevlin and plunged the head of the broken spear into Dhanjal's left shoulder. Dhanjal grunted in pain as the spear penetrated his armor and sank into his meaty shoulder.

Dhanjal did not fall. He dropped one scimitar and slashed at Drystan with the other. Drystan rolled out of the way, leaving the head of the spear sticking out of Dhanjal's shoulder.

Drystan drew his long-knives, their shining steel reflecting Dhanjal's glowing armor like rainbow flames.

Kevlin struggled to his feet, but Drystan said, "My turn. Jerrik wouldn't share, so I hope you don't mind."

"Go ahead," Kevlin said with a weak wave of one hand.

Drystan lunged.

Dhanjal met him with a heavy stroke clearly meant to drive past the much smaller long-knives and smash Drystan to the ground. But Drystan deflected the heavy blade and whirled around Dhanjal in his trademark spin.

Dhanjal struck again, but Drystan proved faster. He stabbed at the base of Dhanjal's neck, where the scales ended in a metal collar. The blade punched through the seam and plunged to the hilt into Dhanjal's chest.

Dhanjal shuddered and spat blood. He wobbled and the brilliant glow of his armor started to fade. He tried to strike with his scimitar, but lacked the strength. Drystan slashed the heavy weapon to the ground.

Dhanjal sank to his knees, his breath shallow and his skin fading to gray.

Kevlin stepped to Drystan's side, and Jerrik joined them, his heavy broadsword in hand.

Dhanjal met Kevlin's scowl. "I am defeated." He dipped his chin in a little bow. "Burn my body, brother, and bear well the honor of Savas."

"Savas does not own my soul."

Raising his sword overhead, Kevlin declared, "For your murders, you are sentenced to death."

He brought the sword down.

A collective groan from hundreds of throats surprised Kevlin. He had forgotten the mercenaries. The leather-clad army stared in disbelief at their fallen leader.

Then they ran.

As one, they turned and bolted for the forest. The outriders pursued and began cutting down the stragglers.

An inhumanly fast blur raced past Kevlin, trailing twin streaks of blue fire. Nikias charged through the mercenary host, the whirling Bladestaff dropping anyone who didn't jump out of his way. He reached the trees first, and spun.

Nikias lifted the Bladestaff high. "Surrender, or we will cut you down like dogs!"

Many of the mercenaries threw down their weapons and dropped to their knees, pleading for mercy. A hundred or more changed course and ran for the trees on either side of Nikias.

"King-killers," Nikias shouted, charging after them.

Drystan nodded toward Nikias. "You know, that lad's got promise. He might just make a decent soldier someday."

Kevlin clasped wrists with his swordbrothers. "Thank you, brothers. Without your strength and discipline, I wouldn't have survived today."

"I wish you hadn't exhausted him," Drystan said. "There wasn't much left for me to finish off."

Jerrik chuckled. "You just hate admitting you lost."

"I didn't lose," Drystan said. "I helped you and Kevlin both."

"Aye," Jerrik said. "You did that. But you just admitted Kevlin did most of the work on Dhanjal, just like I did on the other."

"That's not fair. I was just being polite, letting you go first."

"Doesn't change things."

The entire valley shuddered, and the three turned to stare up at the keep.

"Sherah's Teeth," Kevlin breathed at the sight of the waterfall that suddenly appeared above the keep. The torrent washed over the walls and tumbled down the slope toward Harafin.

A terrible dread sank into Kevlin's heart as he remembered what he was supposed to be doing.

Antigonus.

Dhanjal was dead, but the price might be Antigonus' life.

"Come on," he shouted. "We have to get up there."

He ran for the nearest horse with his brothers at his heels.

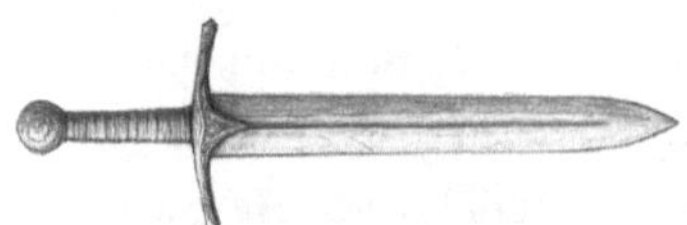

Harafin reined his mount. Soldiers cried out in fear as the floodwaters tumbled toward them, drowning out all sound with its rumbling menace. Borne along in the torrent, all manner of debris churned to the surface only to disappear again.

He recognized some of it as the tumbling bodies of people. He blew out a tired breath. This assault was proving far more difficult than he had hoped.

Carefully crafting the spell to minimize its cost in magic, Harafin formed a gently curving shield across the slope. The raging water glanced off the shield's shallow angle, followed its curve toward the river, and thundered off the edge of the slope in its mindless rampage.

Harafin set a line of curved shields just in front of the leading edge of the water, forming the barrier like a series of long teeth. Water poured through the openings while debris caught on the teeth and catapulted into the air out of the water.

Each time a body tumbled into view, Harafin pointed and, using a gentle blast of air, *pushed* it beyond the churning waters to fall onto a cushion of air.

Some of the people screamed and windmilled their limbs, while others hung limp in the air and lay unmoving where they landed. One Sentinel changed course on his own.

The flood subsided after a moment, leaving the steep slope scoured down to bare rock. The road was gone. Harafin was only a quarter mile from the plateau, but he did not have the strength to throw himself or Leander that high.

Climbing would take at least an hour.

They didn't have that much time.

Leaping down that denuded slope came a hundred makrasha howling for blood. In reckless abandon, they slid from one ledge to the next, their massive bodies absorbing impacts that would have splintered men's legs.

They chanted a single word. "Abaval!"

Harafin gazed from the monsters toward the shattered wall where Tanathos was no longer visible. Several pieces of information clicked together, completing the puzzle.

One fact drowned out the rest.

Leander's long-time quarry had just made a fatal mistake.

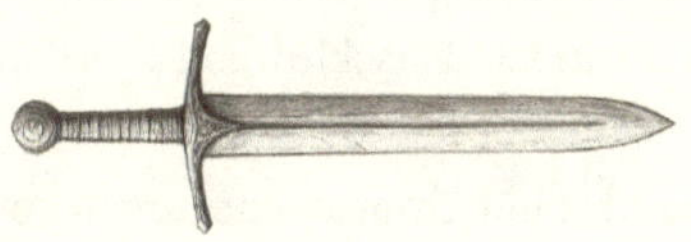

Leander rocked back in his saddle as if struck a physical blow. His face drained of color and he stared at the onrushing creatures, eyes wide with disbelief. The shock only lasted a heartbeat, a heartbeat that thundered through the old stalwart with more force than the recent floodwaters.

"Abaval!"

The chant ripped through his mind, uprooting long-suppressed memories and parading them past his mind's eye.

"Abaval!"

He saw again the bodies of his wife and daughter, tortured and mutilated.

"Abaval!"

His heart beat again and, with it, rage shook him with uncontrollable fury. He vaulted from the saddle and scrambled up the slope toward the makrasha. His war hammer appeared in his hand, already burning with brilliant blue fire.

"Abaval!"

Memories he'd carefully shuttered for more than a century blasted away all restraint and seared his mind, driving his fury to white-hot intensity. His eyes blazed with madness as he charged toward the monsters, hammer raised to kill.

The makrasha came on, oblivious of the danger. A score of them fired crossbows at the lone attacker.

Leander extended his hammer, and a sheet of blue flame exploded from it to consume the approaching missiles. Howling a wordless cry, Leander threw himself to a wide ledge thirty feet up the slope where he met the first group of monsters.

He shattered them.

Howls of bloodlust turned into death cries, and every makrasha that ventured within reach fell to the old man's fury. Blood fountained around him in crimson sheets as he flung broken corpses aside to reach the enemy. The air around him sparked and crackled, and jagged fingers of light crawled across his skin.

The makrasha leaped at him from all sides, trying to surround him and bring him down. He never slowed, and his howling battle cry echoed back from the mountain, a death dirge that drove fear into makrasha hearts.

Soldiers in the company struggled up the hill to Leander's aid, attacking the fringes of the makrasha force, though most of the beasts clustered around the lone old man.

Leander fought on, driven beyond the brink of madness. He was soaked with blood, and it dripped from his beard. His face contorted in a mask of rage, and his eyes blazed. He struck and spun, and struck again, every blow killing yet another makrasha.

He moved through the ranks of creatures like a cyclone, shattering monsters and flinging aside the bloody ruin of their corpses. Makrasha fought each other to get away. Dozens leaped off the ledge and fell to the waiting ranks of soldiers below.

When the last makrasha crumpled into a bloody mass at his feet, Leander stood panting, hammer raised and eyes wild.

Harafin called up to Leander from the foot of the blasted slope. "Come, my old friend. I need your mind as well as your hammer to win this day."

Leander spun, a snarl on his face. He hovered on the brink of the precipice, the control gained over the past century barely holding madness in check.

Finally, he blinked and slowly lowered his hammer to his side.

He wiped blood from his face. "It's Tanathos. I know my enemy now. He cannot escape me."

Justice, not vengeance, will be done.

"If he reaches the heart of the mountain, he'll have nearly enough power to rival the six accidental gods," Harafin said.

"It will not stop me," Leander said. "The gods will die in the days to come. Tanathos dies today."

Harafin frowned. "Speak not of the death of gods yet. We are not ready."

"The time is upon us, whether we are ready or not."

"I know, but not today."

"Very well." Leander blew out a breath and surveyed the slope. "I'm not a great climber. Get me to the top."

Harafin dismounted, looking tired. Soldiers helped him climb to Leander's ledge. The next fifty feet rose in a sheer, vertical slope.

"My power is all but spent," Harafin said.

"We need to get up there," Leander said.

He could feel the dearth of latent magic. He'd exhausted the flicker of actinic gift still available to him in his fight with the makrasha. The lack of magic didn't affect his shield of faith, but he lacked any way to get them up the cliff.

"Let us hope the heart of the mountain is well sealed," Harafin said. "It will delay Tanathos."

"I hope it's enough," Leander said.

Harafin pointed at the steep rock face. Stone chips flew up, as if invisible pickaxes chopped at the slope. In seconds, he carved a wide step in the rock.

"This is going to take too long," Leander growled

"Let me know when you think of a better idea."

Harafin pointed again, and another step appeared.

78

ONE GOOD SHIELD

Kevlin pushed through the soldiers and joined Harafin and Leander at the front of the company. Harafin worked at carving a ladder out of the rock so the party could ascend. After that first stretch, they would be able to climb the rock itself until they neared the top, where another section of sheer cliff blocked the way up onto the plateau.

Movement at the summit drew his attention. Half a dozen makrasha were lifting Antigonus' stretcher from the edge of the plateau and placing it atop the cage that held the bear.

Harafin also noticed the movement. He raised one hand and a bolt of silvery magic leaped from his palm up the slope toward Tanathos. It struck an invisible barrier and glanced away.

Harafin sagged wearily against the rock, and Leander moved to support him.

"This doesn't look good," Jerrik said.

"Is he doing what I think he's doing?" Kevlin asked.

Leander nodded gravely.

"I need your strength," Harafin said to Leander.

Leander grimaced. "You are welcome to what little remains." Under the blood and gore still coating his face, he looked tired and old. He closed his eyes and his hand, already supporting Harafin, began to glow with white light.

Harafin stood taller under the influx of that new strength. His blue eyes sparked with fresh light and he took a deep breath.

Tanathos appeared beside the cage above them, hands raised high.

"Do something," Kevlin begged, his heart pounding with anxiety. He wanted to look away, but couldn't tear his eyes from Antigonus' prone form.

We're so close. We can't lose him now.

Harafin mouthed a word Kevlin didn't understand, but it sent a shiver through him, and he took a step back. Light flared from Harafin's hands.

A royal-blue nimbus formed around Tanathos, swirling in the air. It collided with an invisible shield protecting Tanathos, Antigonus, and the group of makrasha. The light flowed around the shield as if seeking an opening.

Kevlin's heart fell. Even he, unschooled in the ways of magic, had managed to deflect tremendous amounts of energy with a shield.

"Hit him from underneath," Drystan suggested.

Harafin grunted. "He's standing on solid rock."

The light flared, and the shield began to shrink around Tanathos.

Kevlin held his breath. Harafin was doing it!

Leander collapsed. His skin was pale and his breathing shallow. Then even Harafin staggered and dropped to one knee.

As the blue light faded away, a distant shout of victory sounded from the plateau. A dark cloud descended over one of the makrasha, then another. . .and then a third.

"No," Kevlin shouted. "Stop this!"

In his soul sounded a single drumbeat, and he heard the echo of soft laughter.

Harafin, panting, face covered in sweat, met Kevlin's gaze, and shook his head. "I have nothing left with which to fight."

Amber light flashed bright around Antigonus. The bear huddling in its cage roared as if in pain. The light intensified until Kevlin had to look away.

Antigonus screamed.

The sound echoed off the mountain and grew into a throat-wrenching shriek. Kevlin dropped to his knees and banged his fists against the uncaring ground. For once, he wished he were actinopathic. Anything to stop it.

He dredged his body for any vestige of magic he could summon or lend to Harafin, but found nothing. He yanked the amulet from under his shirt and clenched it until the edges bit into the palm of his hand, as if he could will it to capture magic for him.

It did nothing. He should have known. Magic was a curse. Kevlin threw back his head and shouted, a howl of animal rage until his throat burned with pain.

It didn't help much.

Atop the cliff, the screaming stopped.

Harafin whispered, "It is done."

The brilliant light around Tanathos dissipated, revealing a ten-foot monster where Antigonus and the caged bear had been. Covered in white fur, it stood on massively powerful limbs. Raising its heavy maw to the sky, it roared a deep ringing challenge.

"No," Kevlin whispered. He stared at the monster that had been Antigonus, and wanted to punch something.

I failed.

After everything he'd done, he'd failed. Again.

He watched in impotent rage as Tanathos turned and headed for the shattered keep, the new-formed halimaw lumbering in his wake.

79

An Open Door Is An Open Invitation

Wayra groaned. Her head hurt, and so did her abdomen, like a horse had kicked her in the stomach. She opened her eyes and stared at a red blur only an inch from her face. She tilted her head back and the blur resolved into a brick. Beside that brick was another, and another.

It took a couple of seconds for her to realize she was looking at a brick wall. She glanced around and cried out in surprise, scrabbling for purchase. She was hanging out a second-story window of the keep. Finding a handhold, she dragged herself up and back in through the window.

And nearly fell to her death.

She gasped. The inside of the keep was little more than a shell. Doors, windows, and entire rooms were just. . .gone. There was no second floor. Along the back wall, the stair that led up to the central tower remained standing, but it was the only recognizable feature. So many holes gaped in the walls it was a miracle the entire structure didn't buckle. Out in the courtyard, scattered debris floated in calf-deep water.

Wayra reached for her power and frowned. The magic of the keep responded, but weakly, as if her connection were failing. Still, it was enough to wash away the pain and clear her mind.

She looked around the devastated courtyard that stood empty as a tomb. From where she straddled the window, she couldn't see over the wall, nor through any of the gaping holes. She had to get higher, had to know what was going on.

Leaping from inside the window, she hardened the air and slid down to the first floor. She then slogged through the standing water to the stairs and raced up toward the room at the top of the central tower.

She didn't notice the crimson-robed figure striding into the blasted shell of the keep, followed by a lumbering halimaw.

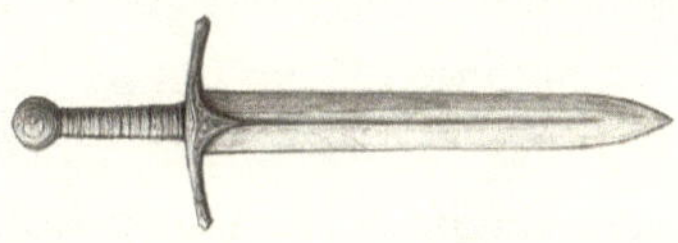

Ceren stared at the brilliant light burning on the plateau near the keep wall, and then glanced at the slope where Kevlin and the others struggled to get up the slope.

Antigonus had chosen her for a reason, and it was not to be a nursemaid. Turning to Indira she said, "Come on. We need to help them."

"But there are so many who need my help."

"You've already saved the critically wounded," Ceren insisted. Despite exhaustion, Indira had kept applying her amazing gift to heal as many as possible. "If Tanathos wins, we'll all die."

"What can we do?"

"We won't know until we get up there."

"I couldn't help Kevlin."

Ceren frowned. Indira had tried to protect Kevlin, but she'd said that something had blocked her gift. Ceren pushed away doubt.

"Let's get up there. I'm sure you'll be able to do some good."

Pulling Indira to her feet, she led the healer to a row of horses. The two mounted and galloped toward the keep.

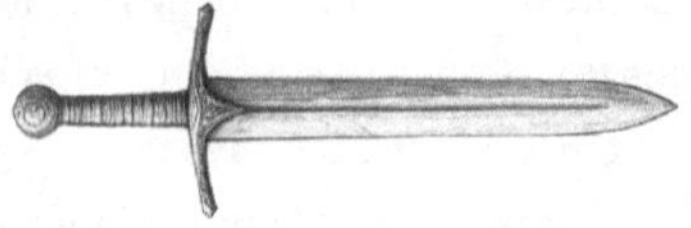

Dripping wet and battered, Gabral hauled himself out of the river. He dropped to the earth and lay panting for several minutes. He released the Mace and rubbed his aching fingers.

At least he was alive. Even with the Mace's power, it had been a near thing. His body felt like one giant bruise, and he'd swallowed so much water that he'd thrown up twice. The river had swept him at least two miles downstream.

Staggering to his feet, he ran a hand through his sodden hair and frowned. Killing the halimaw had been a great victory, but they would need him at the keep. That was where the ultimate glory of the day would be won.

80

THE RACE IS ON

Kevlin helped Leander up another step, barely holding his impatience in check. Leander's body trembled with fatigue as he leaned heavily on Kevlin. Still, the old stalwart kept his glowing hand on Harafin's shoulder, loaning what little strength he had left to aid the work of creating steps.

Harafin swayed on the next step, looking like he could topple over any second. He worked at a feverish pace, carving three steps out of the rock face in the same time it had taken him to carve one earlier.

In his heart, Kevlin knew it wouldn't be enough.

Over the past ten frantic minutes, they'd scaled the first rock face and then scrambled up sloping ramps of stone, or climbed rough sections of the cliff, dropping ropes down to the men behind.

Only one sheer face of stone blocked their path. Another hundred feet and they'd reach the edge of the plateau. Once they reached halfway up this next stretch, Jerrik could probably throw a grappling hook to the rim so they could climb the rest of the way. Harafin only needed to hold on a little longer.

Kevlin had no idea exactly where the heart of the mountain was situated, but every second gave Tanathos more time to get there, murder the monster that had once been Antigonus, and kill them all.

Not if I kill him first.

The initial despair at seeing Tanathos transform Antigonus into the halimaw had been replaced by a renewed resolve to destroy the shadeleech. He'd been stunned to learn that Tanathos was Abaval, so he'd have to move fast to beat Leander to the quarry.

One way or the other, Tanathos was a dead man.

"Harafin, is there any way to reverse the spell and restore Antigonus?"

Despite an impatient growl from Leander, Harafin paused to lean against the stone of the cliff, his face covered with sweat. After a few seconds, he panted, "I do not believe anyone has ever tried. It would take great power, though. More power than any one sentinel commands."

Kevlin kicked at the step in frustration. There had to be a way.

"Master Harafin!"

They all turned at the shout. A soldier pointed back down the valley to a lone rider wearing sentinel white galloping toward them. The rider dismounted at the first stone ladder, but instead of climbing, he threw himself up the cliff face.

"Ah'Shan," Harafin said, surprised. "He made very good time."

Leander glanced at Kevlin and then back down the slope at the advancing sentinel. "If you are to choose him, now would be the opportune moment."

"No," Kevlin protested. "I can catch Tanathos."

"We will kill him," Leander said, "but Antigonus is unable to bear Oris any longer."

"There must be a new bearer before sunset," Harafin said, "or Oris's power will be broken."

"We are running out of time," Leander pointed out.

"Then stop wasting it," Kevlin retorted. "We have to stop Tanathos first. At least give me that chance."

Ah'Shan was closing fast, and Kevlin could now see his features. He was powerfully built with a heavy mane of black hair. The man looked up and their eyes met.

Kevlin frowned. Shouldn't he feel something from Oris if that man was destined to be its next bearer? He felt nothing, and turned back to Harafin, who was regarding him closely.

"Just give me the chance to catch Tanathos," Kevlin said.

Harafin looked from Kevlin to Drystan and Jerrik. "Together you broke free of Savas' control, did you not?"

"Aye, but what does that have to do with anything?"

"Everything. It is manifest beyond a doubt. The Three have been declared."

"The Three?" Leander asked. "*These* three?"

Harafin said. "I still don't understand how it can be so, but I am convinced it is."

I can't deal with this, Kevlin thought. *Tanathos could reach the heart of the mountain any minute, and Harafin starts talking in riddles?*

"I have no idea what you just said," Kevlin said. "But if it helps, I agree."

"Agree to what?" Ceren asked as she and Indira joined the group. She looked fully recovered from her near-death experience. Indira looked tired, but just as lovely as ever.

"It had better help," Harafin said. "All hope rests on your shoulders."

"Are you sure?" Leander asked.

Harafin said, "Kevlin, seek the lower levels under the keep. The door is in the innermost wall. That is where Tanathos is going."

"Well, get me up there and I'll catch him."

"Indira, lend me your strength," Harafin said.

"I don't have much left," she said.

"I need only a little."

"I told you," Ceren told Indira. "Of course you can help."

Indira placed a glowing hand on Harafin's shoulder and bowed her head in concentration. She sagged in exhaustion and Ceren slipped under her arm to prop her up.

Harafin stood taller, a little less exhausted. He blew out a breath and squared his shoulders. "Brace yourself, then."

He made a sweeping gesture with one arm. An invisible force caught Kevlin around the waist and *threw* him up the face of the cliff.

Kevlin kept his head enough to grab for purchase when his rapid ascent slowed. He caught an outcropping of rock at the top and pulled himself over. Not looking back, he scrambled up the rest of the slope and raced for the gaping hole in the wall where the gate had once stood.

A hundred feet below, Harafin collapsed.

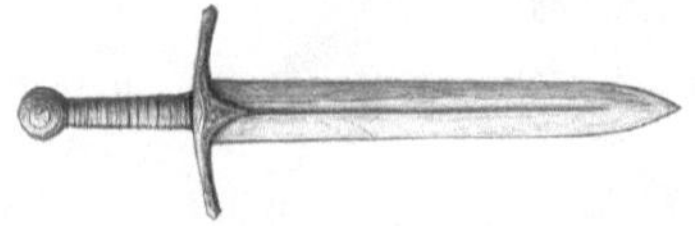

At the rear of the keep, only one ancient stone wall remained, in which was set a heavy oak door banded with iron. Tanathos pointed at the door, and the halimaw ripped it from its hinges, revealing a wide stone stair descending into darkness.

The passage was nearly filled with water from the flood. Smoke hung heavy in the little air remaining, and the walls were charred as if by fire. They plunged into nearly boiling water that should have been icy cold. The halimaw powered through the liquid, dragging Tanathos behind.

Tanathos smiled. He had almost decided against spending the effort to transform Antigonus. The decision was proving key to finalizing his victory.

If only Antigonus could understand that he was facilitating his own destruction. The halimaw was slave to Tanathos' will and he doubted the remnant of the once-powerful sentinel was conscious enough to understand what he was doing.

After a moment, they reached a set of steel double doors intricately carved with runes of power. The runes looked dull and faded, not glowing with silver light the way they should.

Tanathos tentatively laid a hand on the doors, and grinned. It was not sealed. The runes were not active. How could the fools not think to seal the heart of the mountain?

Then he understood, and laughed. All things were working together for his good. The floodwaters had triggered the defensive spells, so the powerful wards had been wasted before he even entered the keep.

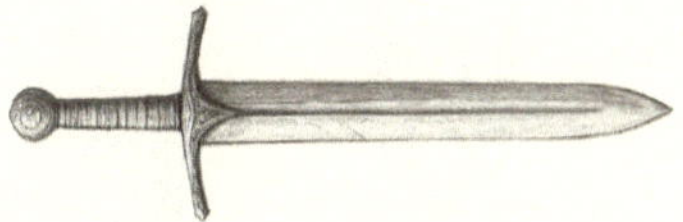

Panting, Wayra entered the small room at the top of the tower. Her tower.

Silver runes flared to life around the walls as if in greeting, and the power of the keep welled up through her like it had the first time she'd touched it. So much power! She gasped with the ecstasy, threw back her head, arms wide, and exulted in the moment.

This was what she had sacrificed so many years, and one hand, to achieve. She deserved it.

Extending fingers of power down through the keep, she explored the extent of the damage. The keep was completely gutted. Had the defensive magic not been activated, the structure probably would have collapsed.

She reached farther, and gasped in horror at what she found.

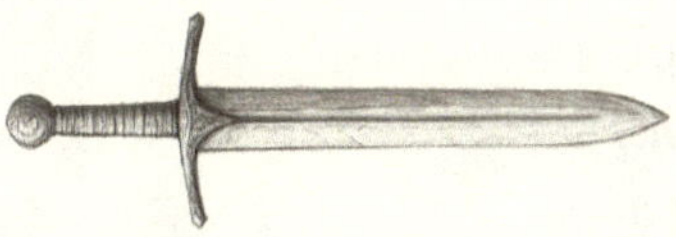

The halimaw bashed its heavy paws into the steel doors. They rang from the impact, the sound reverberating through the deep water. The monster's paws left a dent in the steel, but the doors held.

It struck again, and then again. The solid steel panel slowly caved inward and the door began to split.

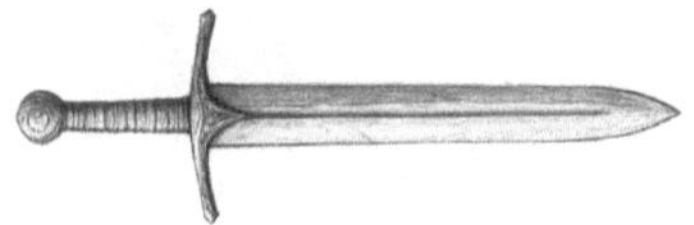

Drystan and Jerrik carried Harafin down the partially completed stair and laid him on an outcrop of rock. The old man breathed shallow, face pale as death, and did not stir.

Leander sat beside him, but lacked the strength to restore Harafin's vitality. Indira hovered nearby, but Leander motioned her to wait. He did not want her to exhaust herself with help on the way.

The sentinel Ah'Shan pushed past the soldiers. "What is going on here, Leander?"

"Welcome," Leander said. "If you would be so kind?" He motioned toward the unconscious Harafin.

Ah'Shan placed a hand on Harafin's forehead and closed his eyes in concentration. Several seconds later, Harafin shuddered and came awake. Ah'Shan helped him sit.

"You overtaxed yourself, my old friend," Ah'Shan said in a deep voice.

"I'm glad you came," Harafin said.

"Where is the stone?" Ah'Shan asked. "You must choose me, quickly."

"It is not yet your time."

"Don't toy with me, Harafin. I will stand for my right to be chosen this time."

Leander held his peace. This choice belonged to Harafin alone, and he did not envy his old friend the decision that lay before him.

"Loan me your strength," Harafin said. "We must finish this."

Ah'Shan stepped back and folded his arms. "I do nothing further until the stone is in my hand."

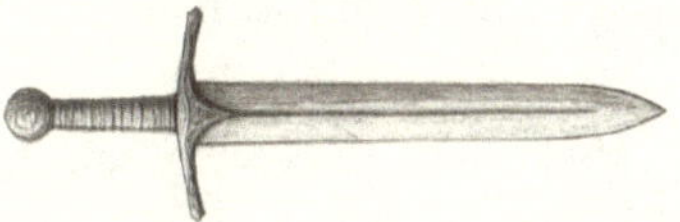

This can't be happening!

Wayra tried to activate the wards protecting the lower levels of the keep, but the water had triggered them all. Their incredible destructive force had spent itself in the floodwaters.

She didn't know how to create new ones. Channeling her power, she instead formed a superheated spear of energy in the center of the keep and drove it through the heavy stone floor.

If she couldn't block them, she would kill them like rats.

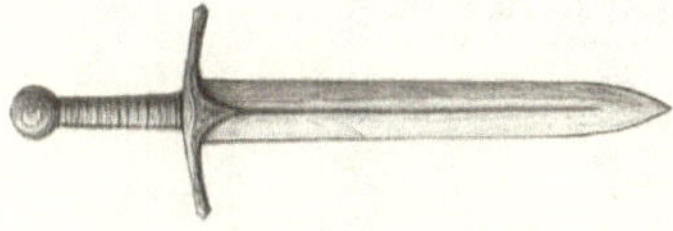

The halimaw kept beating on the doors, bending them in little by little. The sharp metal tore at the halimaw's paws, leaving them ripped and bleeding.

Tanathos smiled. No matter. The creature only had moments left to live.

The roof groaned overhead. A spear of silver light punched through the ceiling and plunged into the water beside him.

Water exploded into steam that seared Tanathos' face. He ducked his head below the water and frantically swam away from the super-heated shaft.

It began twisting toward him.

He pressed himself against the steel doors, but there was nowhere else to go.

Oblivious of the danger, the halimaw slammed the doors again.

They buckled.

Water surged through the breach, sweeping Tanathos and the monster along as it cascaded down a long, smooth corridor carved into the mountain.

The empty halls of the keep reverberated with the thunderous flood.

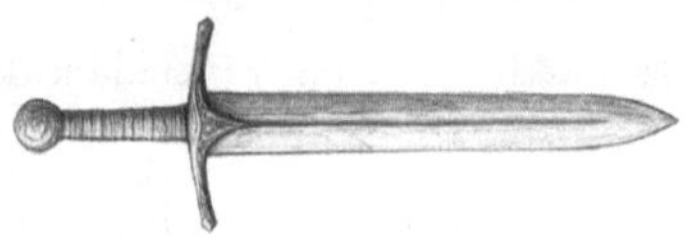

"No!"

Wayra ran to the window and stared toward the cliff rearing thousands of feet above the keep, as if she could see through the solid rock.

Tanathos had breached the mountain.

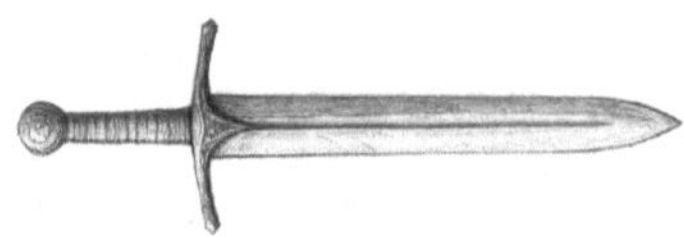

Harafin, who had been drooping with weariness, suddenly straightened and seemed to shed decades. Beside him, Leander jumped to his feet with his normal vigor.

Leander glanced up the mountain, the import of the new rush of latent magic all too obvious.

"What happened?" Drystan asked.

"Tanathos has breached the seal," Harafin said, confirming Leander's fears. "The heart of the mountain is vulnerable."

Ah'Shan grabbed Harafin's shoulder and spun him around. "Choose me," he growled. "You must."

Harafin seized a heavy rope and tossed it to Drystan. "See that the others get up safely."

"Wait--" Drystan started. Harafin threw him up the cliff face, just as he had Kevlin moments earlier.

Harafin turned to Ah'Shan. "The choosing must wait until the day is won." He threw himself up the slope. Ah'Shan spat and rose up the slope after Harafin at a slower but steadier pace.

"Not a very pleasant fellow, is he?" Jerrik said.

"Not really," Leander agreed. "But he is a very powerful sentinel. I wish he'd arrived sooner."

The end of Drystan's rope dropped beside him.

Leander took up the rope. "We'll need at least one more line set up. Who's the best climber?"

"I am." Ceren tied a second rope to her waist and, without another word, began pulling herself up the steep cliff face.

"She's very good," Jerrik admitted, tilting his head back to watch.

Leander slapped his shoulder. "Stop staring. When she ties off the rope, it's your turn."

He took hold of the rope and pulled himself up the cliff after Ceren.

Jerrik sighed. "I hate climbing."

81

PERFECT TIME FOR A BIT OF DRAMA

Kevlin paused just inside the wall to stare at the devastated enclave. The keep barely stood, while all the other buildings had been reduced to scattered debris floating in the standing water. Sloshing his way into the courtyard, he made for a wide gap in the wall of the devastated keep.

"Kevlin."

He looked up. It took a few seconds to focus on the figure waving to him from a window of the central tower. Was that Wayra?

"Where is Rhisart?" Harafin's voice, magnified several times, boomed from the shattered gate behind Kevlin. Harafin looked refreshed, like he'd slept for a couple of days.

"Dead," Wayra called. "I control the keep now."

"Where is Tanathos?"

"He just breached the passage leading to the heart of the mountain."

Ah'Shan strode through the shattered gate beside Harafin. "Why didn't you stop him?"

"I was unconscious until just now, master. Time is short. Harafin must choose you."

"Agreed." Ah'Shan looked to Kevlin. "Give me the stone."

"I don't think so." Kevlin dashed toward the door.

If Tanathos had just breached the passage, it didn't sound like he could be too far ahead. Kevlin wasn't about to stop. The desperate hope that somehow he could free Antigonus' soul from Tanathos' spell drove him on.

"Stop," Wayra and Ah'Shan shouted simultaneously.

Kevlin ran harder.

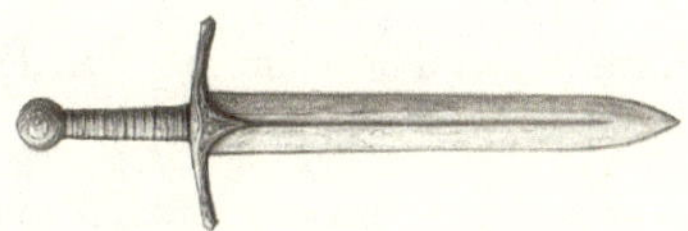

In the tower, Wayra cursed and drew upon the power of the keep. The man Kevlin was an abomination, and he'd gone too far. She was master of Il'Aicharen, so she dictated what happened within the walls of the keep. She had every right to execute him for disobeying her command.

She intended to do so.

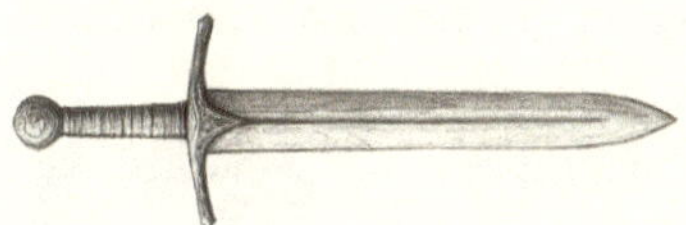

"Wayra, stop!" Harafin yelled.

He could feel the latent power of the keep coming to life. What was the rash young woman planning? Several ideas came to mind.

All of them worried him.

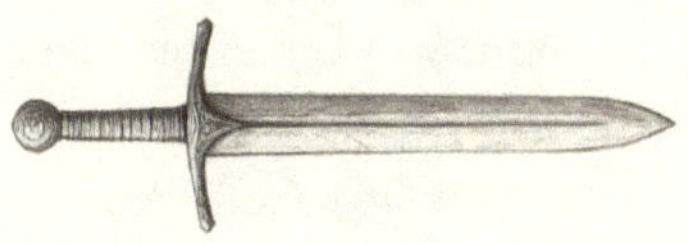

A heavy bolt of blue-white magic, as thick as Kevlin's waist, shot from the central tower and struck him in the center of the chest. The heat of the magic boiled standing water into a cloud of steam that seared his exposed skin.

The amulet absorbed the magic and poured it into him, a wild torrent of power that burned away exhaustion from the day's fighting. It filled him with unimaginable strength and churned inside him, hungry for release. His muscles quivered with the need to act.

The cloud dissipated and he wiped moisture from his eyes.

"What are you doing?" he shouted up at the tower.

Wayra was insane. Really.

He hadn't trusted her since that first night when she'd wrecked their plan and caused the whole mess. This was the worst time to be proven right about her. He lacked time to deal with her. He had to catch Tanathos.

"Stop!"

Ah'Shan plowed through the courtyard, sending up a wide spray of water as he raced toward Kevlin. "Just give me the stone, you fool!"

"No."

"Give it to him, abomination," Wayra shouted.

Kevlin wished he knew how to magnify his voice like Harafin did. He sounded like a child arguing with adults.

"Leave him," Harafin commanded. "We must stop Tanathos first."

"*This* is how we stop him," Ah'Shan retorted. "Now, give me the stone."

"I said no," Kevlin repeated. For a powerful sentinel, Ah'Shan seemed hard of hearing. "Leave me alone."

Not slowing, Ah'Shan raised a hand glowing with power. "You have no right to deny me, steward. I will take it."

Ah'Shan punched Kevlin in the stomach.

Magic blasted into him with the punch, but the amulet absorbed it. Kevlin staggered back a step. Ah'Shan was a formidable man. Even without magic, his punch carried a lot of weight.

Ah'Shan cursed and shook out his hand. Hopefully he'd broken something on Kevlin's armor.

"What are you?" Ah'Shan asked.

That does it.

All his pent-up frustration burst free, with Ah'Shan as the target.

"My turn," Kevlin growled. Focusing all of that burning energy, he willed the magic into his fist and punched Ah'Shan in the jaw.

The sentinel's jaw snapped.

His head whipped back so hard Kevlin was amazed the man's neck didn't break. The magic blasted out of Kevlin, striking Ah'Shan in the head and torso in an explosion of red-hot energy.

Ah'Shan had enough shielding in place that he wasn't ripped apart by the blast. Instead it catapulted him backward across the courtyard. He slammed into the exterior wall and fell onto a pile of rubble where he lay, unmoving.

Kevlin stared down at his hand.

That felt really good, though he might have gone just a little too far. He raised his clenched fist and decided that was how he would kill Tanathos.

"You killed him," Wayra shrieked in a voice so loud Kevlin had to cover his ears.

"Wayra, stop," Harafin called, running forward. "Kevlin, beware!"

Kevlin ran for the door.

He only made it two steps.

A dozen bolts of crimson magic shot from the top of the tower. The impact staggered Kevlin and he fell to the courtyard. The water was gone, evaporated by the tremendous heat.

The amulet burned against his chest as it drank in the magic and poured it into him, a torrent so vast he barely comprehended it. It pounded through him, a wild maelstrom boiling through every muscle, bone and fiber. It raged through his body, seeping deep down into the smallest particles and pulling at the very fabric of his soul.

It began to tear him apart.

He struggled against it, tried to bend it to his will and command it to obey, but he could not. It boiled out of control.

In a panic, Kevlin tried to flee, but he couldn't move. He lay on the dry, cracked cobblestones, his body rigid and unmoving, with blue light streaming from every gap in his clothing. He tried moving his legs, his face, his head, but all to no avail.

He focused on blinking an eye.

Nothing.

In the depths of his mind, he screamed. The amulet on his chest burned into his flesh.

Will it explode?

Or will I?

82

DESPERATE CHOICES

Harafin stared in horror. Kevlin's prostrate form glowed with so much magic that Harafin wondered that the young man wasn't screaming. In the tower, Wayra was shouting something incoherent.

She's going to hit him again, Harafin realized. Had the woman lost her mind? They were wasting precious time. He had to stop her. After pausing for a triple heartbeat to reinforce his shields, he raised his hands.

This is insane.

He spoke a word of power.

A bolt of pure white energy shot from his hands and slammed into Wayra's shields with explosive force. His missile shattered and showered the courtyard with shards of fire.

Harafin ignored the fear that fluttered in his stomach. Wayra commanded vast amounts of power, so attacking her was next to suicide.

He had no choice.

Kevlin still didn't move. He'd better get up soon, because Harafin could only buy a little time. If Kevlin stayed down and if he couldn't help Wayra see reason, they were all going to die.

Half a dozen bolts of raw power blasted from the tower toward Harafin, drilling through the air with the promise of absolute destruction. The thunderclaps ripped the air and reverberated from the cliff.

The volley struck his shields and ricocheted. The impact staggered him and he grunted in pain. It felt like being hit in the head with a hammer. He couldn't take many more of those.

"Stop, or I will destroy you," Harafin shouted. "Tanathos is the real enemy. We need to join against him."

She did not need to know the truth. If she continued attacking, she would overwhelm him all too soon.

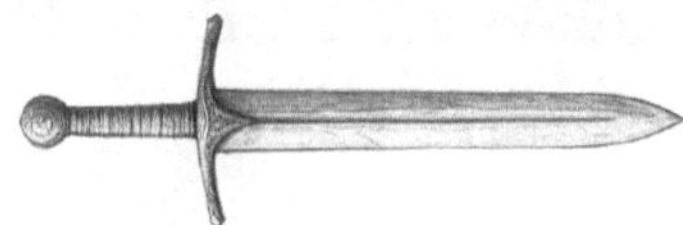

In the tower, Wayra cursed.

How can he do that?

The old man was so frustrating. She was beyond listening to his counsel. She now held the power over Il'Aicharen and she alone would choose how it was spent. Anyone standing against her deserved their fate.

A glance at Ah'Shan's prostrate form reinforced her resolve. She had trained and sacrificed decades to reach this point. Everything she was or hoped to become boiled down to this moment. She would cement her rule over Il'Aicharen, take the stone from the abomination, and present it to her master. Nothing else mattered.

If Harafin continued to challenge her dominance here or to thwart Ah'Shan's rightful choosing as bearer, then she would remove him.

She shoulted, "Stand down, old man. Choose my master and stop these games."

"Wayra, listen to me," Harafin shouted. "You don't understand."

She understood. He wished to remove her new rule, wished to keep Ah'Shan subjected to him, a pawn for another century. She was done obeying.

Drawing even more deeply from the vast power at her command, she unleashed a fresh wave of fiery magic at Harafin.

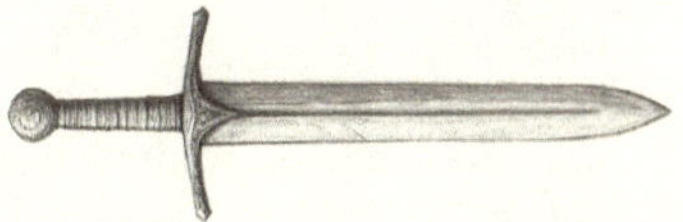

Black motes danced in Harafin's vision and magic pulsed against his constraints, nearly bursting free of his control. Then strength flooded into him, augmenting his own and buttressing his shields.

"You should learn to choose your fights more wisely," Leander remarked. The Pallian Stalwart stood beside him, one glowing hand on Harafin's shoulder, pouring strength into him.

"Thank you, my friend."

"She's lost her senses. Why?" Leander asked.

"Actinic addiction. It's the only explanation."

Leander muttered a curse, reflecting Harafin's dismay. If he was right, there would be no reasoning with Wayra. Some sentinels, either from lust for power or lack of discipline, suffered a rare mental breakdown when infused with too much magic.

The influx of so much light dazzled the mind and set it adrift, often wandering far afield. When that level of power could be drained away, they often returned to themselves, but Harafin could think of no way to do that with Wayra in this situation.

She struck again and, even with Leander's strength augmenting his own, the contest taxed Harafin to the limits.

He couldn't hold on much longer.

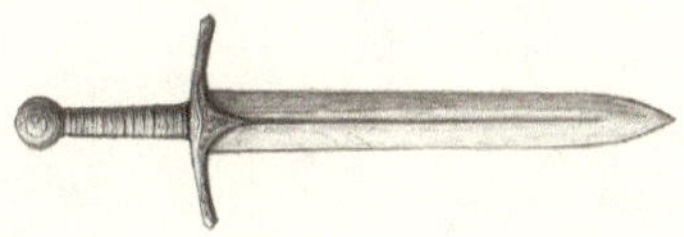

Ceren raced through the gaping hole that had once been the gate and stared. Harafin and Leander stood nearby, a shimmering sphere of magic surrounding them as they battled someone in the tower. How had the enemy gotten up there?

Then she spotted Kevlin. He lay unmoving across the courtyard, surrounded by blinding blue light, as if he were burning with indigo flame.

She stepped into the courtyard just as the attacker in the tower shouted, "You cannot defeat me, Harafin. I rule this keep. Choose my master and bow to me!"

Wayra?

Ten spears of magic blasted down and slammed into Harafin's shield. It held, but wobbled as if on the verge of collapsing. Harafin looked exhausted.

"Ceren, wait."

She turned as Indira raced through the shattered gate. The healer was surprisingly fast. Behind her, Jerrik had just finished ascending the rope, and he and Drystan were busy overseeing the effort of getting the forces up the cliff.

"Kevlin's in trouble," Ceren explained. "Can you help him?"

Indira frowned in concentration, staring at Kevlin's unmoving form. After several heartbeats she stamped her foot in frustration.

"I can't. Something's blocking me." Indira grabbed her arm. "I think he's dying."

"I've got to do something."

"Wait." Indira lifted a hand that glowed pure white with her power. She touched a single finger to Ceren's forehead, and a shiver ran through her.

Indira's dark eyes glowed with her gift. "I will do everything in my power to keep you safe."

Ceren spun, and raced for the keep, and Wayra. She wasn't actinopathic, but she knew one thing about magic.

Kill the sentinel, and their spells died with them.

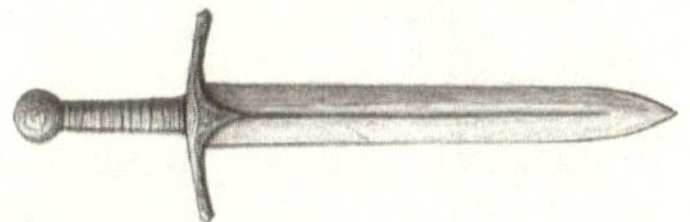

The flood swept Tanathos forward at a breakneck pace. The rounded stone passage descended sharply at first and the flood picked up speed, tumbling him around like a doll in its grasp.

Sharp detonations reverberated through the water, the sound slamming painfully into his ears. Varicolored lights exploded ahead of him, and the leading edge of the water sizzled and boiled into steam.

Wards, he realized. *The water triggered warding spells.*

It saved his life. He barely kept from laughing underwater. No one had ever expected to have to ward against a flood. Instead of triggering a wall to block the floodwaters and drown him, the wards appeared set to trigger destructive blasts that would shred any invader but proved ineffectual against tons of water.

The shape of the passage remained constant and smooth, eight feet in diameter as it bored into the mountain. Soon the slope eased, and the waters slowed in their rush toward the heart of the mountain.

His head broke the surface as they subsided. He wanted to shout with glee. Everything was working together for his victory.

A moment later, he slid to a stop. Climbing to his feet, he pushed ahead through the knee-deep water and almost complete darkness.

The halimaw followed, shambling on all fours, a sodden mass of silvery fur. Its heavy odor filled the passage and its rasping breath drowned out the splashing of their footsteps.

A few minutes later, Tanathos rounded the passageway's first turn and grinned. A faint glow of silvery light outlined another corner perhaps a hundred paces ahead. He jogged to the corner and stepped around it. The passage widened until its ceiling reared fifteen feet and the walls stretched twice as wide. At the limit of his vision, the passage turned again, with the light glowing bright from somewhere beyond.

As they approached, that light pulsated with the unmistakable rhythm of life. A faint thrumming vibrated through the stones under his feet. His skin began to prickle as if from a faint breeze, even though the air remained deathly still.

Magic.

The mountain was heavy with it.

83

THE POINT OF NO RETURN

Ceren entered the keep through a hole in the wall. The ground floor of the building yawed open, an empty shell that seemed ready to collapse in on itself at any moment. A single iron-banded oak door hung open in the innermost wall, leaning on broken hinges. She ignored it, and ran for the staircase set against the rear wall.

The stairs were mostly intact, although many stones were missing from the supports. Despite the risk of a collapse, it was the only way up to the tower. Inside the building was strangely quiet. She glanced back toward the courtyard where Kevlin lay unmoving, surrounded by that blue halo.

I can do this, Ceren told herself as she ran for the stairs. *I must.*

She raced up, taking steps two at a time.

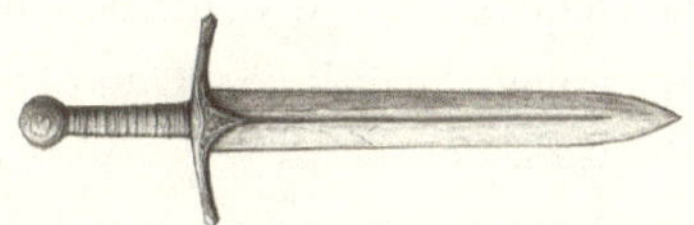

Another bolt of magic struck Kevlin like a sledgehammer to the chest. Bursts of light exploded behind his eyes and his vision blurred. His world swam with agonizing pain. His eyes refocused, but slowly, and he half-expected to find himself rolling toward the river instead of lying motionless in the courtyard.

He wanted to scream, to run, to do anything to rid himself of the magic, but he couldn't move, couldn't even breathe. The magic held him immobile. He was helpless against its power, a slave to its whims.

Again.

Under the onslaught of Wayra's magic, the terror of that memory when he was tortured by magic as a boy returned, undiminished. Kevlin fought to scream, but again was held captive to the magic. His thoughts scattered and for a second he wished desperately that he'd given the shade-cursed stone to Ah'Shan. The thought only lasted a second before he drove it away.

He would escape this torture. He would save Antigonus. He would prove to Wayra and to the faceless sentinel who still tortured his memories that they could not control him. That determination held him above the panic-driven madness that threatened to overwhelm his soul. It was all he had left to cling to.

He tried to push the wild magic away, to will it to obey him, but his efforts were as ineffectual as if he were trying to divert the course of the Ujutus with his bare hands. The magic pounded at him, striving to destroy him and escape the cage of his body.

Despair tempted him to give up. Even if he caught up with Tanathos, Harafin had said no one had the power to reverse the spell. He'd have to kill the halimaw to end Antigonus' torture.

Wayra had enough power, but she would never do it. The woman had gone mad. He would gladly kill her. It would be a mercy.

Oris *was* powerful enough, he realized. Hadn't Harafin said it gave its bearer access to limitless magic?

Antigonus was its bearer, but Antigonus couldn't do anything with it. In his current form, he'd probably just try to eat it.

I could do it.

The thought struck like a thunderbolt. Despite the magic gnawing at his soul and threatening to destroy him, Kevlin focused his scattered will.

Savas had shown him how to do it. Did he dare?

Was he insane? He had hoped that saving Antigonus would help reconcile his issues with magic, but embracing that power was a totally different plan. Could he really do it?

The magic surged to a new intensity, assaulting his mind, the last bastion of his control. It boiled through him in an unstoppable wave, and his grip on consciousness weakened. His vision went black as the last spark of thought was uprooted and pushed deep into the depths of his soul. Like a man drowning, he struggled against the current, but it was no use. His mind was about to be overrun.

He had no choice. If he failed, he would die.

So would Antigonus.

And Indira.

And everyone.

When Savas had tried to steal his soul, he'd shown Kevlin an image of an ancient wall. Now Kevlin formed that image. As soon as he did so, he felt it, there in his mind.

Time to spin the Wheel.

Releasing all restraint, he cast his mind free into the magical torrent roaring through his soul. The magic swept his thoughts into the flood and slammed his mind into the wall. The impact rocked him and searing pain threatened to overwhelm him.

How can it hurt? I can't even feel my body. It seemed terribly unfair that he could feel pain but nothing else.

He attacked it again, and this time the wall began to buckle. Agony beyond anything he'd imagined assaulted his mind like a dagger.

Savas had lied to him.

He yearned for the promised oblivion of death.

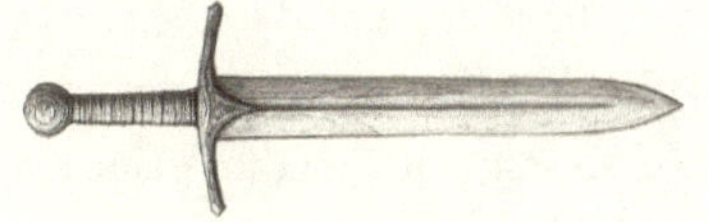

Gasping for breath, Ceren pulled herself up the last step and staggered through the threshold of the small room at the very top of the central tower. She paused, wiping sweat from her face and trying to calm her breathing.

Why does Wayra have to be at the top of the tallest tower?

She peered into the single room and with a glance took in the rune-covered walls, bookshelves, and fireplace, before focusing on the sole occupant.

Wayra stood at the window with her back to Ceren. She glowed with magic that crackled along her arms and through her hair.

I'm crazy, Ceren thought. *She's going to kill me.*

Ceren allowed herself one more deep breath, then pushed the terror away enough to move.

I am Cunning. I will do my duty.

Raising her sword, Ceren slipped forward, trying not to make a sound. The fifty-foot span to Wayra seemed a mile, but she only needed a few seconds.

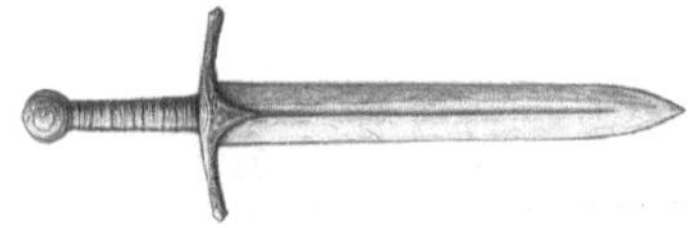

Tanathos rounded the third corner and stepped into a gigantic cavern. Not the room he expected, this cavern was the hollow core of the long-dormant volcano. Silver runes covered the walls and spilled soft light across the flat, smooth floor that extended at least a mile until passing beyond the limits of his vision. The ceiling reared so high that shadows concealed it.

The air glowed with that pulsating silver light, and the entire cavern thrummed with power so vast that Tanathos gasped in wonder. He began to pant with unrestrained lust for it, threw back his head, and shouted in triumph.

He'd made it to the heart of the mountain. All that power was his! Shivering with anticipation, he threw tentacles of power into the cavernous room to draw the magic in.

He screamed.

Magic ripped along his senses, searing him to the bone. His legs convulsed and he collapsed. Rolling on the smooth stone floor, he clutched his head and fought to block the magic of the cavern before it overwhelmed him.

For a second he hung by a thread, barely holding the torrent at bay, while oblivion gaped wide. With a final effort, he cut off the flow of power and shielded his mind.

Whimpering with terror, he lay panting until the agony subsided. He finally managed to stagger to his feet and look around the vast open space.

He couldn't corrupt this magic.

He'd thought he understood the nature of the nodes of power, but he'd been so wrong. The magic thrumming around him was part of the very foundation of the world. The lifeblood of the planet flowed through it, light so concentrated his skin prickled. He could leech the life away from individual beings but could not challenge the power of this place.

Not yet.

He shouted a curse, and the obscenity echoed back and forth across the cavern. He *would* dominate it. He had but one more thing to do.

Murder.

Summoning the halimaw, he strode into the cavern. Perhaps he should continue on to the midpoint, but impatience won out. Turning to the halimaw who had been Antigonus, the shattered remnant of a man still considered bearer of Oris, Tanathos drew a heavy, black-bladed dagger from his robes.

Raising the dagger high, he shouted, "Today, Abaval rules the world!"

He plunged it toward the monster's heart.

84

FIRES OF CHANGE

The wall in Kevlin's mind collapsed.

The next wave of magic pushed him through, and beyond. For a second there was only grinding pressure, as if his mind were being squeezed through a crack in his skull and pushed outside the physical confines of his body, expanding in a way he'd never imagined possible.

Then he was falling, propelled by the unstoppable force. All thought, all concern, all fear vanished. He didn't even know if he still lived.

One word defined him, all that remained: Oris.

Driven by that single word, his consciousness expanded, reaching out with a finger of thought as he plummeted toward oblivion.

He touched it.

Plunging into Oris, his vision changed from the perfect blackness of his sightless mind to the deep blue of the rock's magic. He hurtled past the will-o'-the-wisp lights until he sensed another presence.

This time, no wall blocked him. His mind connected with the presence, and it enveloped him. He reeled from the impact of that touch.

The *other* presence was so fundamentally different than anything he'd ever experienced, he couldn't fathom it. For a split second, he touched a power so vast it stretched away like a never-ending chasm. His mind refused to comprehend it, and he pulled back from the brink to preserve his sanity.

Then there was nothing but the deep peace of Oris. It flooded through him, pulsing with the rhythm of life.

It *changed* the raging magic. That presence within the rock, that *other* being, absorbed the power, and somehow made it part of him.

Was it Oris? Even its full name of Oris, The Fatebreaker seemed inadequate, but he couldn't say why. His vision cleared and he could see again, although the deep blue of Oris tinged everything. Still lying in the courtyard, filled beyond capacity with magic, he was once more master of at least part of himself.

The vast presence joined him in a corner of his mind. The magic filled him with life and unfathomable power. Still lacking control over his body, in his mind he threw back his head and laughed with joy, tears of pure magic coursing down his face.

The presence in his head pushed a thought to him and he blinked, suddenly enlightened. He knew how to release the magic. It was so simple, as if a light had come on in his head. He focused, his thoughts magnified by Oris, and formed a command.

Fire.

Magic thundered out of him, and a column of fire erupted out of the air around the highest tower of the keep. Even though he'd commanded it, the spectacle awed him.

Dense flames a hundred feet thick and rearing twice as high concealed the tower and roared like a living thing, a ravenous giant. The column swayed a little as it ate at the tower.

The gigantic flame consumed the magic at a terrific rate, but there was so much that it could burn for half an hour.

Wayra struck again even as the tower burned, a rippling sheet of magic that slammed into Kevlin's torso. The amulet seared his chest with its heat.

The presence of Oris *changed* the new magic, making it part of him. It illuminated his understanding, pouring knowledge into him. He mastered concepts he couldn't have grasped on his own. Next time, he could change the magic himself, without Oris's help.

This is incredible!

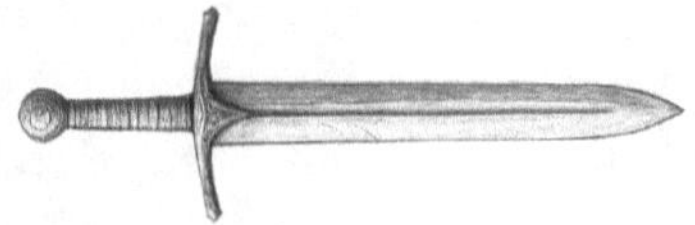

The halimaw howled and thrashed in agony, knocking Tanathos back several paces.

He hadn't stabbed it yet.

Tanathos frowned at the glowing runes covering the cavern walls. The node of power had already tried to kill him once. Was the beast trying to break free of his control?

It didn't matter.

"You will die as I will," he snarled and leaped at the still-thrashing halimaw. Slipping between its massive arms, he plunged the dagger through the monster's thick hide.

It penetrated only an inch before the beast knocked Tanathos away. He rolled back to his feet and circled the monster. It continued to thrash around as if some other power was attacking it.

He only needed one good strike to reach its heart.

Seeing his chance, he lunged.

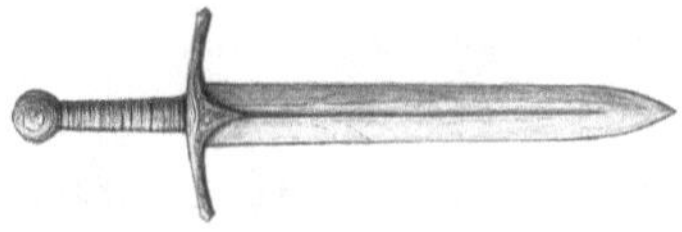

Flames poured into the room through the open window, consuming the bookcases and licking the rune-covered walls.

In the midst of the inferno, Wayra broke off the attack on Kevlin and shifted her focus to her failing shields. In a heartbeat, she dropped everything except a shield around herself. The flames burned with supernatural heat and ate through her barrier, forcing her to pour more and more power into buttressing her defenses. The power of the keep began to wane.

How is this possible? Had some new sentinel joined the attack? She could see nothing but orange flame.

Gathering her will, she struck one more time at the abomination known as Kevlin.

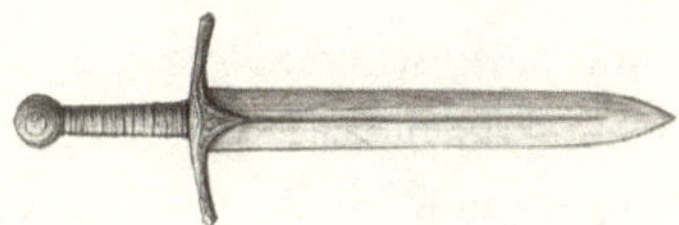

Ceren screamed and beat at the flames all around her. It took a moment to realize through her panic that she wasn't dead. She wasn't even hurt.

She slowly lowered her hands from her face and stared in awe at the inferno that burned everything but her.

How am I not dead?

Indira!

How long could the healer protect her from such a blaze? She had to focus. Fighting to quell her panic, and trying not to breathe too deep, she pushed through the flames.

She had to find Wayra.

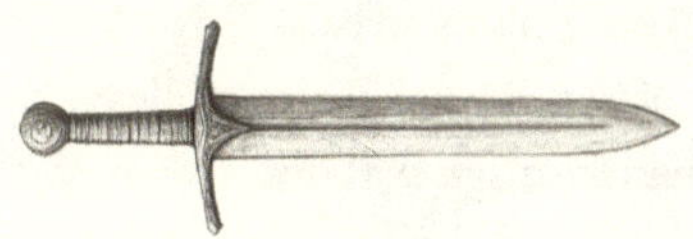

More impressions came from the presence that was Oris, and Kevlin obeyed. He modified the stream of magic fueling the fire, expanding it to compensate for the greater force pouring into him from the amulet. It was as if he were standing in a raging river of fire roaring into, through, and back out of him.

It was the most awesome experience of his life.

The magic—*his* magic—filled him with power, with strength, and with light. The prior agony faded into shadowy memory as magic soothed and healed his body. He let part of his mind flow with it, savoring the new knowledge he gained.

Another bolt of hostile power slammed into him. With his newfound understanding, and with subtle guidance from Oris, he mastered the process of taking the power from the amulet and making it his own.

He poured the magic out as fast as it came in, a torrent fueling the flames which rose until they enveloped the entire keep. It burned so close to him that its heat blistered his skin, and its roaring pounded his ears.

The inferno melted the very stones of the keep, straining the limits of his control. Kevlin held on grimly, focusing every ounce of will to hold it in place.

Someone grabbed his arm and began dragging him away from the keep. He couldn't even glance around to see who it was.

An invisible force suddenly tore at the column of fire, trying to rip it apart. The fire swayed, tilting dangerously as it pushed Kevlin's fledgling mastery to the uttermost limits.

Wayra. It had to be.

The presence of Oris sent new promptings to him. He tried to obey, but could not. The instructions made no sense. Or rather, they seemed impossible, like trying to bend his leg up at the knee to touch his toe to his stomach.

Even as he tried to obey, his mind balked. To obey the prompting would alter the very nature of how he thought, to challenge the core of his identity. He would have to embrace magic without reservation and without malice. He would have to accept it as a force with which he could do much good, yet acknowledge the risk of abusing it just as so many others had.

The price of wielding the magic terrified him.

The column of fire sprayed flames, gyrating wildly. It would burst from his control in a moment.

He tried again to follow the new promptings, to bend his thoughts in new directions, but a stubborn core of his soul resisted the change. It was more than his distrust of magic. He needed to sail with a new tide, embark on a life where magic was part of him. To do so meant altering his identity at a fundamental level.

Could he really trust this presence that he couldn't comprehend, or was it going to enslave him like Savas had tried to do?

Thou has the knowledge requisite for thine action. Thou must choose.

The voice in his head, barely a whisper, rocked him to his core. Savas had spoken in his mind, and the similarity made him shudder, although the voice of Oris carried no threat, no hint of domination.

Holding to that thought like a shield, he fought down his fear of magic, the distrust and resentment toward those possessing the actinopathic gift. He cast aside his terror and long-festering thirst for vengeance.

He felt numb, hollow. Then new emotions rushed in to fill the gap: the thrill of magic, excitement of knowledge, and hunger to learn more.

Making a choice, Kevlin stepped out of the realm of the familiar and into the shadows on a path he couldn't yet understand. He cast himself onto this new tide, knowing his choice would change him forever, but unable to turn back. He would carry the burden until the new bearer of Oris was chosen by Harafin.

With that commitment, he finally managed to follow Oris's instructions. His mind shifted and expanded, and it amazed him to find just how *right* it felt, as if he had lived with a handicap all his life without knowing it.

As his control improved, the column of flame slowed its gyration, but did not entirely settle. Something fundamental within the flame had been damaged by Wayra's blow.

New promptings came and he let his thoughts ride the river of magic toward the inferno. Immersed in the flames, he became one with them.

Then he understood.

The blaze wasn't one giant, unbroken flame, but countless tiny tongues of burning energy that together formed the huge column. It pulsed with an internal rhythm that took those tiny flames and combined them into one body, but not all of them burned with the ebb and flow he had dictated. Some flickered to a different tune and threatened the whole with instability.

Harafin's words finally made sense. Each tongue of fire pulsed with the rhythm of life, all in harmony with it even though they danced at different times. The individual pulses were masked by the overall flame, which explained why he had never noticed it before.

Those tongues of fire that threatened to break from his control had lost the rhythm, so he pulled them back into harmony. His control became complete, like a maestro conducting a mighty orchestra, all burning in harmony in their individual pulsing rhythms, all obeying his command.

It was a moment he would never forget.

As he pulled his thoughts away from the well-controlled flame, he extended his senses and drank in what they found: the excited breathing of soldiers massing on the lip of the cliff, the stirring of individual blades of grass that had survived the flood, the tug of hot wind from the fire, the very texture of the air.

He had mastered the magic and he could do anything with it. All he had to do was think it and speak it, and it would happen. The possibilities were endless, and exciting.

And terrifying.

Then he remembered: Antigonus!

Help me. Kevlin cast the thought toward the presence in his mind. *How can I save Antigonus?*

The measure of Antigonus' life is fulfilled, and his fate complete. Be at peace.

The authority of the voice was such that he couldn't help but feel the peace it commanded, although part of him raged against it.

If only he'd acted sooner.

It was Wayra's fault. She had delayed him, kept him from catching Antigonus.

He made the fire hotter.

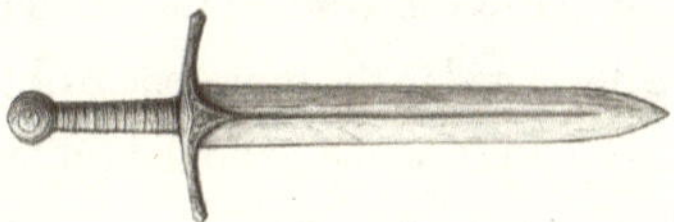

Indira slumped to her knees, hands clutching her temples. Sweat matted her midnight hair and dripped from her chin. The strain of protecting Ceren threatened to drag her into unconsciousness.

Panting for breath, she held on. She'd never used her power this way to maintain the shield. Like exercising muscles never used, the strain soon turned painful.

I will not let her die.

"Are you all right?" Drystan asked, dropping to one knee beside her.

She clutched his arm and whispered, "Take me to Kevlin."

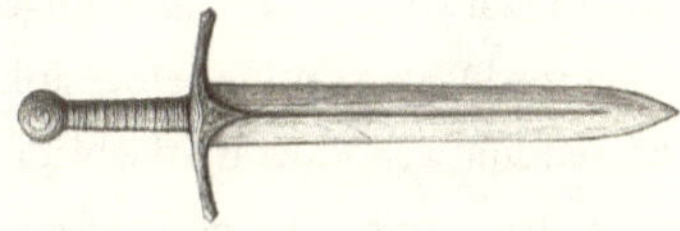

Wayra tried to marshal the rapidly fading power of the keep. For a few heartbeats, it had looked like she was going to shatter that gigantic column of fire. But then she'd been rejected, and the flames burned hotter than ever.

She pushed against them, but couldn't gain purchase. Whoever summoned the inferno controlled it with an iron hand. She'd never felt anything like it before. Her shields barely held, but the rest of the keep was succumbing to the flames. She could feel the slate roof tiles cracking and melting. She couldn't shield it all.

Such unexpected helplessness infuriated her. It could not be happening!

Expanding the shield across the window, she sealed the upper room from the flames. As the fire dissipated in the room, she grunted in satisfaction, savoring the small victory. She just had to hold the inferno at bay until it petered out. No one could sustain a spell that massive for long.

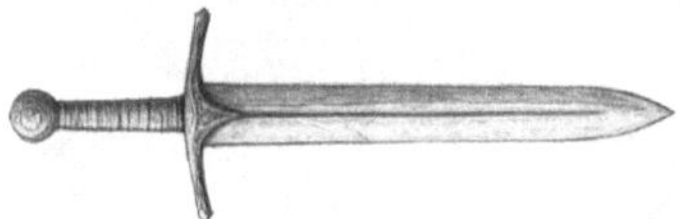

Ceren crouched four paces behind Wayra, trying not to breathe. Wayra hadn't notice her.

Her hand began to shake as she stared at the other woman's unprotected back. She'd never killed anyone before. Her mouth went dry, and she felt cold despite the stifling heat.

Taking a deep breath, she raised her sword and lunged.

The tip of her blade scraped Wayra's spine before sinking to the hilt. Wayra screamed and twitched, sending a shudder up the blade to Ceren's hand. It was all she could do not to let go of the weapon and back away with a shriek.

Ceren held on, and twisted.

85

UNLEASH THE HOUND OF JUSTICE

The keep shook violently above Kevlin. Then it collapsed.

Towers, roof, and walls imploded into one gigantic heap. The collapse shook the ground, and fear clamored along the outer edges of his magic-soaked senses.

Clouds of smoke and dust billowed up, obscuring everything. Kevlin's column of fire settled over the broken remains, and stones melted from the supernatural heat.

Nothing could survive the inferno.

Kevlin stared wide-eyed at the spectacle. What a mess.

When the raging fire consumed all but a fraction of the power he controlled, he cut off the flow, keeping just enough rippling through him to keep him from collapsing.

The fire winked out, leaving a deep silence behind. Harafin was kneeling on the ground nearby, panting with exhaustion.

Kevlin glanced up to see who had dragged him away from the keep. It was Leander, but before he could thank him, the stalwart raced for the pile of rubble.

He's going after Tanathos.

Antigonus was dead, beyond Tanathos' power. Kevlin stared at the sheer cliff looming above the ruins of the shattered keep and struggled to understand.

His connection with Oris faded as the presence of the stone withdrew from his mind. He wanted to pull the rock from its rune-covered bag and connect with it again. A final thought floated up to him from the stone, the reassurance that it would come to his call again when he needed it.

Then it was gone.

He was left wondering what it all meant. How could he, the steward, ever summon Oris again? Who was going to be bearer since Antigonus was dead?

He'd failed--and yet, perhaps he hadn't.

"Kevlin."

Drystan's voice snapped him out of his reverie. The lanky soldier settled Indira on the ground nearby. She was glistening with sweat and shook like she had a fever. Her face was deathly pale and haggard.

"What happened?" Kevlin rolled over, and nearly fell on his face. Every muscle ached as if he'd been beaten with a stick for a year. Only the sight of Indira gave him the will to move. He crawled to her and gently wiped her sweat-streaked face.

She opened her eyes and murmured, "Ceren."

He glanced around but didn't see the auburn-haired noblewoman. "Where is she?"

"The keep."

Kevlin blinked in shock and turned to stare at the clouds of smoke marking the devastated keep. Ceren was in there? The thought struck him like a hammer. How did Ceren get in there? What was she doing?

Indira clutched his arm. "Not dead. My shield." She paused, then whispered, "Not much time," before sagging back to the ground.

"We have to find her," Kevlin shouted.

His gallant words failed to motivate his body. Kevlin barely managed to stand, and Drystan had to support him as he stumbled toward the still-burning rubble.

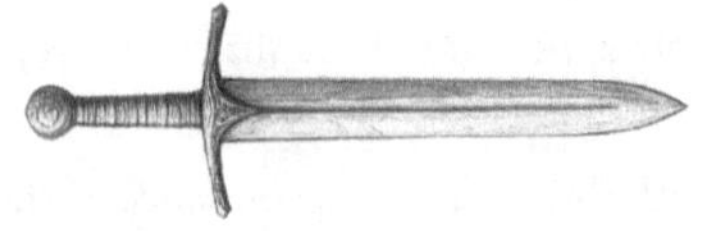

Despite the intense heat, Leander vaulted onto the pile of rubble. He reached for a gift he'd renounced a century ago. Weak from disuse, the power came slowly. This magic, so different from the pure light of faith granted him as a stalwart, seeped back into his soul and rattled him with remembered insanity.

Abaval. The murderer of his family. He was close.

Memories laid bare by the identification of his family's murderer burned with undiminished clarity.

Breathing hard, he drank in the power and let the pain augment his strength. A desire to see justice done tempered his rabid need for vengeance, lifting him just a little from the roiling madness.

He pushed air away from his body, creating a void between him and the searing heat. He filled that void with water to protect his skin, and scrambled over the rubble until he reached the sheer wall of the cliff. Lifting his hands high, he focused his will and released the magic.

Debris fountained up and away from him in a showering cascade as he tore through the debris with fingers of power. Dust heavy with ash clogged his nose and coated his throat with the taste of cinders.

The clattering of rocks and splintered wood drowned out the calls of his companions as they approached. Piles of slate, brick, charred timbers, and twisted steel grew around him and he sank through the shifting debris.

Within seconds he disappeared into a deepening hole.

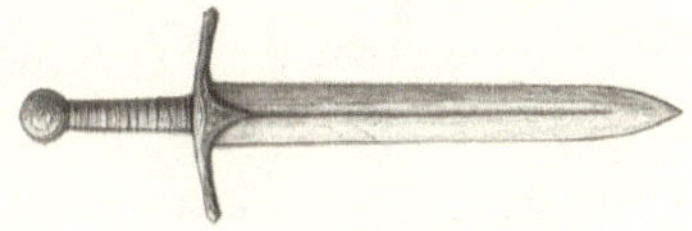

Tanathos howled.

Kneeling on the dead corpse of the halimaw, he raised his hands and shouted until his voice cracked. The echoes bounced around the cavern, amplifying his frustrated rage and mocking him again and again.

Yanking the dagger from the halimaw's chest, he plunged it in again and again, driving the blade with all his anger until his crimson robes dripped a deeper red from the monster's blood.

A loud boom rolled out of the passageway from the keep, and the stone floor vibrated under some heavy impact. Dust drifted into the cavern a moment later, tasting like ash.

Tanathos rose to his feet and forced control over his emotions. From behind the roiling blackness of his eyes, he considered the fallen monster. It lay dead, its heart pierced, but the aegis had not shattered, nor had titanic waves of magic been released through him.

That could mean only one thing. Oris's next bearer had taken up the stone.

He'd been so close! He wanted to scream again with impotent rage and shred the corpse to assuage his anger.

The next bearer had to be a powerful sentinel. Surely they had been in Tamera or the distant sentinel island of Il'Marinen. How had Harafin gotten the stone to them so quickly? Tanathos should have had plenty of time.

He wanted to race back up the passage to the keep and unleash deadly vengeance on those who had thwarted his victory, but he could not. Something had changed, and that meant his life hung in the balance. He would wreak vengeance on his enemies, but not today.

Today he needed to live. To live, he needed to run.

He couldn't escape the way he'd come. That way lay danger. With a bit of focused energy, he magnified his sight until he could pierce the surrounding gloom. He spotted a shadowy doorway in the opposite wall. It offered the only other way out.

Abandoning the bloody ruin of the halimaw on the floor, he ran for the exit. The echoes of his footfalls chased him across the vast, empty cavern.

He reached the doorway, panting from the unfamiliar exertion without the reinforcing strength of his slaves' life forces. Glancing back, he saw no movement, but a sixth sense of danger clamored that time was short.

He strode through and followed a squared passage upward. It curved in an ever-ascending spiral. The silver glow of the rune-covered cavern gradually faded behind him until the darkness pressed so deep that even he had difficulty finding his way.

He raised a hand and summoned a ball of crimson light that pushed the shadows back like a bloody curtain. He climbed for what seemed like hours until he emerged into another huge cavern that must have lain directly above the heart of the mountain.

Although smaller than the lower cavern, this one still extended hundreds of yards into darkness. No runes covered its rough obsidian walls, but a faint light shone from above. He smiled, and for a moment stared up at the great chasm of the dormant volcano's cone.

To his right, a rough stair with no rail rose above the jagged floor. Carved into the wall, the stairs spiraled up into the shadows.

Tanathos began to climb.

86

A Devious Quarry

Kevlin limped toward the mountain of debris that had been the keep. How could anyone have survived such a disaster? Even with Indira's help, was it possible?

Heat shimmered above the still-glowing rubble and forced him to slow. Drawing closer was like walking into a giant oven, and soon sweat dripped down his face. Dust hung heavy in the air, obscuring his vision. Smoke choked him and ash irritated his throat.

He didn't have enough magic left to cool it down. The little power left to him barely kept him on his feet.

Indira couldn't hold out for long, so they had to find Ceren fast. Even shielding his face, he couldn't get to within ten paces of the debris.

"Hold," Harafin called out, raising a hand toward the rubble.

Silver mist congealed out of the air, thickening until Kevlin could barely see the mound. It settled over the smoking ruin and the red-hot stones hissed like a giant, angry cat. Clouds of searing steam billowed up, forcing Kevlin and Drystan back.

The wind picked up, and within a few heartbeats it whipped his clothing and nearly knocked him to the ground. It cut through the clouds of steam, and in less than a minute, the air cleared.

"It is still hot," Harafin warned, "but it should be passable if you use caution." The old sentinel retreated and leaned against the broken wall.

"Thanks." Kevlin and Drsytan approached the mound, followed by more soldiers as the word of Ceren's plight spread. The rubble shifted and rolled treacherously underfoot as they scrambled up. Drystan left Kevlin near a section of unbroken gable and moved on, scampering across the rubble like a deer.

Kevlin circled the gable and caught sight of a partially intact piece of roofing. It looked like part of the central tower. He extended his sense and slipped them under the closest edge to probe the cavity underneath.

Ceren.

"Here," Kevlin yelled to the others. He clawed away the debris so he could worm under the edge and into a pocket of air underneath.

Ceren lay inside, unmoving. He called her name, but she made no response. He crawled to her, wiped the grime from her face, and placed a finger on the side of her neck, feeling for a pulse. It beat, but only faintly.

As impossible as it seemed, she still lived. The plucky noblewoman didn't seem hurt, but she also didn't respond when he shook her. She clutched the hilt of her broken sword so tightly that he couldn't pry her fingers loose.

No one else could fit under the rubble to help him retrieve her. The effort of passing Ceren's limp body to the others left him trembling with exhaustion. Jerrik finally managed to get one beefy hand on her mail shirt and drag her free.

As soon as he saw they didn't need his help, Drystan ran for Leander's hole amid the rubble. Gabral followed him, and the two disappeared from view.

Kevlin stared after the colonel. "Didn't he fall into the river?"

"He came back." Jerrik lifted Ceren into his arms and carefully picked his way back across the rubble, with Kevlin following as best he could. They bore her from the shattered enclave and lay her down next to Indira.

Kevlin dropped to the ground between the two women. Indira was panting, her cheeks flushed and hot. He stroked her face gently with one hand and her eyes fluttered open.

"We found her. Ceren is safe."

Indira closed her eyes again with a great sigh of relief. Someone brought over a couple of cloaks with which Kevlin covered both women. He didn't have the energy to move, so remained seated between them.

Indira slid her warm fingers into his free hand. He was content to sit beside her like that. His thoughts moved sluggishly. He tried to make sense of everything, but failed. He couldn't even decide exactly what he felt for Indira.

Ceren was safe. Despite how confusing she could be, he cared for her. They'd shared danger and a common goal. He didn't want to lose yet another companion today.

Indira's hand in his felt so good it made him nervous. Even covered with sweat and with her hair matted to her face, she was achingly beautiful. He couldn't fight the attraction any longer. He would get to know this gentle healer and let tomorrow decide how deep his interest grew. He wasn't even sure she'd welcome his attention.

Well, he'd find out.

Antigonus was dead. A heavy weight of grief settled over him. Under Oris's influence, it had seemed right that Antigonus was dead, but he couldn't understand how. Too many things had changed, and all the emotion had been burned out of him.

Harafin knelt beside him and placed a hand on Ceren's forehead. He closed his eyes in concentration, and Kevlin *felt* Harafin molding magic.

Several heartbeats later, Harafin sat back. "She will be fine with a little rest."

Indira smiled and closed her eyes. In seconds, she started snoring softly.

"What just happened?" Kevlin asked Harafin.

"You connected with it?"

"Aye."

"Choices were made today that will shape the destiny of the empire."

"I don't understand."

Harafin smiled ruefully. "Neither do I, but we will. We must."

The sentinel climbed to his feet and gazed out over the valley. "We will speak again soon." He headed for Ah'Shan, who had been dragged out of the enclave and lay unmoving under a cloak.

With his ears still supernaturally sharp, Kevlin clearly heard Harafin say to himself, "Two hundred years of study, and still we walk in darkness."

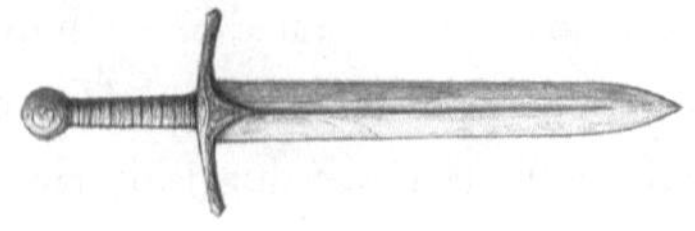

Leander paused just inside the huge, vaulted cavern. The soft light from the silver runes on the walls gently illuminated the slaughtered halimaw.

Nothing moved. The cavern appeared empty. Leander strode to the carcass of the monster and sighed. "May the light grant rest to your soul. Goodbye, my friend."

The sound of running feet spun him back to face the passageway just as Drystan and Gabral charged into the room. Drystan said, "We came to help."

"Then come," Leander said. "But Tanathos is mine."

With the two men flanking him, Leander ran for the doorway in the far wall. As they entered the square passage, Leander raised his hammer and it burst into blue fire to light the way. They pounded up the spiraling passage until it emptied into the rough cavern under the volcano's cone.

High above, a stone rattled. Several seconds later it clattered to the floor nearby.

"He's up there," Gabral said, pointing up the shadowed cone.

Leander leapt for the stairs and took them three at a time.

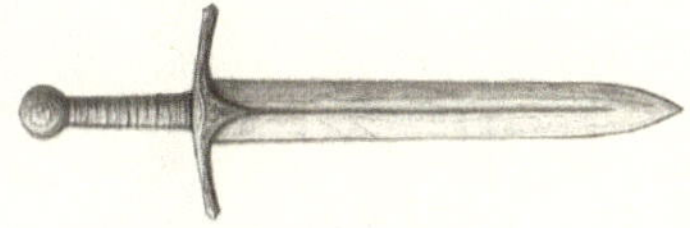

Tanathos stepped into sunshine high on the northern slope of Mount Il'Aicharen, where the air bit into his exposed flesh with icy fangs. At this altitude, winter already held sway.

Snow clung to the rocks and lay in drifts on the narrow ledge that led toward a small, round stone observatory with an open roof. The building clung to the edge of a fold in the mountainside. Low clouds hung around the mountain below, obscuring its base. Several peaks of the smaller Stratton Mountains pierced the clouds to the north. The cone of Mount Il'Aicharen reared yet thousands of feet higher.

The shadeleech glanced back into the darkness of the passage. A clatter of stone echoed up from below. Someone was chasing him.

The temptation to wait for the unknown pursuer, rip their soul from their body, and consume their life force held him a moment. But fortune had turned against him, tarnishing the glory of his name with defeat. It might be Harafin. He couldn't take that risk.

He pushed through the drifted snow while icy wind tugged his crimson robes, trying to dislodge him and send him tumbling a thousand feet to his death. He managed to cross to the observatory without incident.

The one-room structure protruded from the face of the mountain, a single wide window on the far wall looking out over nothingness. He stepped to the window and stared down the steep slope. The ground fell away in near-vertical tiers. Scrub brush and twisted trees clung to the slope amid the boulders and snow. It was a harsh, barren landscape.

No path led down the mountain.

A guttural shout of animal fury spun him back to the narrow path. A man carrying a flaming hammer hurtled out onto the ledge, followed by two others.

Servants of Ophisurus knew and feared that indomitable old man.

Leander, the Hammer Stalwart.

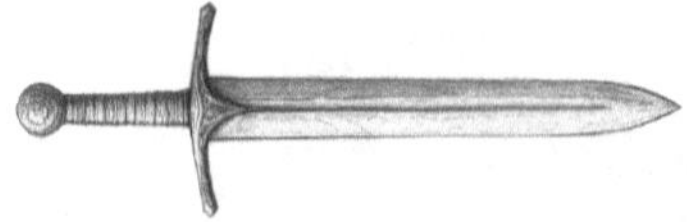

Howling with the need to crush his enemy, Leander charged onto the narrow ledge and plowed through the snow despite the precipitous drop. His eyes never left his quarry.

Abaval. Trapped.

The shadeleech raised a hand, and the snow whipped into a blizzard. Leander never slowed, but dragged his hammer along the cliff face to keep from straying off the ledge. The creature of darkness could drop all the mountain's snow onto the path and it would not stop him.

Justice would be done.

Vengeance would be dealt.

The blizzard dissipated when he'd traversed halfway across the ledge. Abaval stood not a hundred yards off, both hands raised to cast another spell.

Leander snarled. Nothing the shadeleech conjured would stop him this time.

Tanathos threw his hands wide and shouted a word of power that whipped away in the wind. Stones high above the ledge shifted and cracked. Snow slid down, and then the boulders. More stones shifted, and within seconds a broad section of slope began sliding down.

"Look out!" Drystan shouted as the ominous rumbling grew.

Leander tore his gaze from his hated enemy. Raising his hammer, he channeled magic to form a slanting shield above his head.

The stones thundering down slammed into the shield, and the impact nearly drove him to his knees. He held on as the stones bounced off, tumbling out over the edge and plunging down the steep slope.

Step by step, he pushed forward through the landslide as tons of rocks cascaded down on either side. The entire face of the mountain shuddered, and he had to clutch at the cliff wall to keep his feet. Snow and dust billowed around him, turning the scene into a surreal nightmare.

Rubble piled up on the ledge. He couldn't both hold the shield and clear the path, and was forced to halt. The landslide only lasted half a minute, but every heartbeat seemed to drag on forever.

It finally began to ease. Through an eddy of the icy wind he caught a glimpse of the observatory just as Tanathos leaped out the window.

Hardening the air in front of him like a plow, Leander cleared the path, and a minute later stumbled into the observatory. The small, circular structure stood empty.

He peered out the single window at the steep, barren slope. Tanathos was gone. Blackened vegetation, shriveled by the shadeleech's power, stretched down the length of the mountain until low clouds obscured it.

Leander didn't hesitate. Backing up a couple of steps to get a running start, he raised his hammer high. It again burst into blue fire.

"Justice will be done."

He ran forward and dove out the window.

87

GROUP HUG

Ceren coughed and stirred as Kevlin pushed a lock of hair from her face. She opened her emerald eyes and smiled.

"Kevlin, you're safe."

He helped her sit up, relieved to see her awake.

Indira, who had been sitting beside Kevlin said, "Ceren, you did it."

"No, you did it," Ceren said. Then she laughed, "I guess we both did."

Two women hugged each other, laughing and crying simultaneously. Kevlin wrapped his arms around them both. They hugged him back, and for a moment all was well with the world. His worries melted away under the simple embrace.

Ceren drew back. "What happened?"

"I'm not really sure," Kevlin said.

For some reason, they all found that incredibly funny.

88

THE DEVILS WE SERVE

A wide-winged hawk fought the turbulent air currents high above Il'Aicharen, driven by Sitara's will. An unexpected gust threw it toward the sheer cliff face above the wreckage of the keep. It clawed at the air, its wings cracking under the strain. A few feathers fell away and crumbled to dust in the wind.

Sitara growled in frustration as she struggled to maintain her tenuous connection with the great hawk. From where she sat on her bunk in the tiny cabin assigned to her for the journey to Diodor, she caught glimpses through the hawk's eyes.

The view triggered a sense of vertigo. Flashes of vision from high above the devastated battlefield superimposed themselves every second or two over her view of the gently rolling sea through the tiny porthole.

She nearly lost the connection entirely as the hawk changed course and let the wind carry it up and over the cone of Mount Il'Aicharen. Sitara muttered a curse and re-established control.

The spell Masego had taught her for controlling animals was similar to the one Bajaran had taught her for bleeding away their life to feed her own soul. It was subtly different, however. Instead of leeching the animal's life and drawing it into herself, she used that power to fuel the conduit she used to control it.

The animal still had to die.

Sitara shuddered as she felt the hawk decaying beneath her spell. Every muscle in her body quivered from the strain of holding the far-distant connection. She had consumed the life force of another bird prior to commencing this attempt, but even with that energy bolstering her strength, she couldn't maintain the effort much longer.

Tears stung her eyes as she forced herself to re-establish control. Masego had been clear in his directive, and she couldn't risk failing. The hawk's vision swept her away from the ship as her connection solidified. Before she could direct it back toward the battlefield where she expected to find her quarry, something caught her attention.

On a remote corner of the mountain, a small circular building clung to the edge of a barren cliff. A long black streak marred the otherwise white expanse of snow.

A man, glowing brilliant white, suddenly leaped from the window and fell through the air, barely cresting the edges of the long steps of stone. Sitara watched in astonishment as the figure in the unbleached woolen garments of a stalwart descended in a graceful slide that somehow kept him from slamming fatally into the rocks.

The hawk circled far above, but its beak cracked and two of its talons crumpled and fell away. As it began its final death spiral through the cloud bank hugging the mountainside, Sitara noticed something new. At the terminus of the black streak, a crimson-robed man was running through the forest.

Sitara focused the bird's dimming vision on the figure and confirmed her suspicion. He was a shadeleech.

The hawk disintegrated into powdery bits of ash as Sitara returned to herself, rubbing at the deep chill that had settled into her limbs. She could still feel the hawk's indomitable spirit, its love of high places, and its fierce hunger. She very nearly screamed its final cry for it, and only barely swallowed the impulse.

Wiping tears from her eyes, Sitara whispered, "I hate you, master."

She had been tempted to ignore his order and flee when she reached Diodor, never looking back. Curiosity got the better of her. She wanted to see the shadeleech.

She yearned to fulfill Bajaran's goal of restoring the Tamerlane Empire to greatness and establishing peace finally with their neighbors to the west. How better to do that than to begin a dialogue with the shadeleeches?

Despite her loathing for Masego, she applauded this attempt to begin the process. She had no idea how he knew to find the shadeleech in Hallvarr, didn't understand how the shadeleech's presence there tied to the gruesome battlefield, but she would contact him.

She prepared her mind for yet another spell as she took a tawny cat out of its box and set it in her lap. It purred as she stroked its flanks. Sitara kissed it gently while fresh tears dripped onto its head.

"Fulfill the measure of your creation," she whispered, her throat dry.

After a long moment, she closed her eyes and reached for the cat with fingers of power. The animal shivered at the touch of her magic. She hushed it with a gentle thought and filled its mind with feelings of love and contentment. It was the least she could do.

Another moment, and the cat would feel nothing.

Sitara had practiced her shielding for hours while she sat in her cabin. Masego had urged her to use her imagination, so she did. She had taken the revelation he shared with her about multifaceted shielding and reinforced it until she felt it would withstand her master's next assault.

If only she could shield her emotions so well. Applying her newly enhanced shields, she threw her mind out into the air. Reinforced by the strength of the cat's life force, Sitara left the ship and whisked north toward Diodor with the speed of thought.

The sea appeared to her as a vast amber plain, teeming with life, while the shoreline looked black, flashes of ethereal life forms glowing upon it like subdued candles.

Eventually, Diodor blazed on the horizon. As Sitara's mind raced closer, the concentrated population appeared like a giant, writhing flame. She avoided the lure of the city for there, glowing brighter than the rest, brilliant points of light identified the presence of sentinels. Masego had warned her of heavy shielding around the palace. She wouldn't risk approaching, but needed the beacon only as a landmark.

Turning east, she flashed across the dense forest toward the mountains, then followed the rising peaks toward Mount Il'Aicharen. On the far side of its bulk, at the limits of her strength, she detected two bright points of light, gifted souls heading westward.

Sitara approached the first and reached out to touch it.

A brutally powerful hammerstrike of magic slammed into her. Her multifaceted shields deflected most of the impact, but its intensity rattled her. She threw out a thought.

I am not the enemy that pursues you. I am an ally.

She didn't want to open dialogue for peace by fighting, but she couldn't let the shadeleech destroy her before getting her message out either.

She reached again toward the soul and made the most tenuous of contact. That brief touch felt like plunging her mind into a boiling cesspool. Hundreds of miles away, Sitara's body fell back onto the cot, covered with a sheen of cold sweat.

The horrifying mind spoke to her. *I am busy. Do not waste my time.*

Sitara shook from the contact. She should have known Masego wouldn't send her to a good shadeleech, one seeking peace. He was an evil man, so would collaborate with like-minded men. He had somehow found a shadeleech as corrupt as himself. She shuddered to think what they might be planning.

Despite her loathing, she cast out the next thought. *I bear a proposal from my master. I know you, Tanathos and I am to tell you--*

Tanathos struck with unbelievable force at her shielded mind from three directions at once. Sitara's shield, which she had been so proud of a moment before, shattered under the blow, and he drove into her mind.

Sitara screamed in her cabin as sickening tendrils of thought burrowed into her mind, tearing out her secrets, digging for the core of her being, threatening madness. She struggled to flee, but he held her prisoner with shackles of thought. She tried to force him out, but he shattered her feeble attempts.

I'll have to thank your master for sending me a much-needed soul. His mindvoice laughed with sarcasm. *Who is this master of yours?*

He was going to destroy her. Had Masego sensed her rebellious thoughts despite the care with which she'd tried to conceal them?

Tanathos tore at her mind and she writhed with fresh agony. Impatient with her delay, he tore the name from her mind.

The pain stopped.

Masego? What does this master look like?

I don't know, she wailed. *I've never met him.*

Through the conduit connecting them, she could sense his fear of an approaching threat, his desperate hunger to consume her life force just as she had consumed the cat and the hawk. He hesitated, curiosity holding back the death blow.

What is your master's message?

Sitara didn't know. Masego had implanted it into her mind, a seed surrounded by a form of shielding she had never experienced before. She had feared to tamper with it. Now she cast that seed at Tanathos.

Very well, he said a moment later. *I will spare you until we meet again.*

She would kill him the next time they met. She had vowed no one would again violate her, but he had done so with impunity.

Tanathos drove a dagger of pain into her mind again, his mindvoice laughing. *Study hard, slave. Perhaps you'll put up more of a fight next time.*

Then he released her.

Sitara's thoughts reeled as her mind snapped back to her body. A pounding headache left her groaning on her bunk, and cold sweat broke out across her skin. She didn't understand why the shadeleech had spared her, and she felt defiled by the touch of his filthy mind.

She held the still-warm body of the cat to her chest and sobbed.

"Oh, Bajaran", she whispered. "Whatever is to be done?"

How could he have embraced a cause so filled with evil men? She couldn't believe that he had known the caliber of the other revolutionaries, and yet how could he not have known?

As the steady rocking of the ship slowly eased her clenched innards, she finally understood. Of course Bajaran had known they were evil. That's why he never introduced her to them. He had been shielding her.

The purity of the revolution had been corrupted in both countries. If she fled now, the evil conspiracy might well succeed in overthrowing the government, replacing it with a new rule just as corrupt.

Bajaran must have been planning to cleanse their ranks. No other explanation made any sense. With him gone, it fell to her to restore the purity of their cause. She must seek out other like-minded patriots, just as he had found her.

Sitara considered the challenge. Where would she find people committed to freedom, untainted by the evil of the current regime? They must possess the strength of character to withstand the lure of corruption that had pervaded the cause of the revolution.

She would never find them in the wilds. She had to return to Tamera. There she could leverage her position in the shadows of the emperor's wife to bring about the change the nation so desperately needed.

She would learn Masego's plan, she would pretend to embrace his plotting. When he struck, in the moment of his victory when he toppled the head of the empire, she would strike in turn. She would turn on him and let the emperor's subjects tear him to pieces.

Sitara would rise to take the reins of a leaderless nation.

In the meantime, she had to work on her shields.

89

FATES AND CHANCES

Kevlin groaned with weariness as he dropped to the ground beside a roaring fire. The heat drove back the chill, and his eyes drooped. The little magic he still had left was nearly gone, and he wanted nothing more than to sleep. Instead, his mind wandered back to the momentous events of the morning.

After the battle, much work had been done. Wounded soldiers were scattered all across the valley, and they numbered in the hundreds. Indira and Ceren had worked through the day, along with the Jagen Stalwarts and sentinels to save as many lives as possible. Both women now lay sleeping.

Hathor had excavated huge pits in the ground, and the captured mercenaries had been put to work burying the thousands of dead men, women, and children in mass graves. Giant bonfires burned through the afternoon, cremating makrasha and shadeleeches.

So many dead. Most of the villagers and many soldiers had fallen in that valley. The toll was high and images of corpses flitted behind Kevlin's eyes. He sighed. The burdens of survival never got easier.

A king had died. Although Kevlin hadn't known King Leszek personally, he still mourned the monarch's passing. It shouldn't have happened. Kings weren't killed lightly, and there would be dire consequences of some sort. Kevlin was too tired to hazard a guess what those might be.

He had too many other questions to resolve. Above the rest, he wondered what had really happened. What was that presence he'd found in Oris?

Even more important, with Antigonus dead, who would be chosen to bear Oris? Dusk had fallen, so Harafin should be desperate to finish the choosing, but Kevlin had barely seen the old sentinel since before noon.

Had Kevlin somehow broken Oris when he connected with it? Even though it had saved his life, and it felt right at the time, maybe it was still the wrong thing to do.

Kevlin stared into the fire, worry gnawing a hole in his stomach. Physical exhaustion combined with emotional exhaustion left him yearning for sleep, but he had to know. He rose and left the others who huddled around the fire's warmth. He stopped near the shattered wall of what had once been a home in the upper town.

A soft step turned him around.

Indira.

She drew close, and he couldn't help staring. They had sat comfortably together waiting for Ceren to awaken, but now it was suddenly hard to breathe. Specks of dirt marred her alabaster skin but didn't diminish its radiance. He marveled at the graceful contours of her face and neck.

"I thought you were sleeping," he managed.

"I was." She leaned against him and he slipped an arm around her shoulder. "Drystan and Jerrik are starting a card game. I thought you might like to join us."

"Sure." That would be a great way to take their minds off the horrific day.

She took his hand and led him toward another fire. "Just be warned. They're both broke, so I think they're planning to ask you for a loan."

Kevlin caught sight of Harafin standing with Ah'Shan at another fire. Harafin gestured for Kevlin to join them.

"I'll meet you there in a minute," he said.

She noticed Harafin too. "Don't keep me waiting too long."

"I promise."

Harafin had better not try keeping him practicing for hours. He was not about to let Indira down.

Kevlin approached the two sentinels with heavy steps. This was it. Harafin would finally choose Ah'Shan, and Kevlin would have to give up Oris.

He needed to do it, but hesitated anyway. Once Ah'Shan took up the stone, Kevlin would never connect with that presence again.

He had made peace with his past. He had embraced magic to a degree he never would have imagined even the day before. Would he now have to leave all that behind? Could he return to life as a non-actinopathic mercenary?

What a waste of effort. What alternative did he have?

Ah'Shan glared. Kevlin tried to hide his own dislike, but wasn't very successful. He would submit to whatever choice Harafin made, but he didn't have to like Ah'Shan. He'd done what he had in good faith.

He'd tried to overcome his fears and help protect the empire. He'd tried to save one old man's life.

"Give me the stone, steward," Ah'Shan spat in a tight, angry voice. "It is my right."

Before Kevlin could reach for the rune-covered pouch in its hiding place in his boot, Harafin said, "Not yet."

Ah'Shan glared. "Do not trifle with me, old friend. It's nearly sunset. A new bearer must be chosen."

"A new bearer has already been chosen."

"What?" Kevlin and Ah'Shan spoke simultaneously.

"Who?" Ah'Shan asked.

Harafin pointed at Kevlin.

Kevlin stared at the finger, then looked around to see who was standing behind him. The ruins of the town lay empty.

Ah'shan barked a humorless laugh. "Impossible. This is a poor time to jest."

"I jest not. Kevlin is chosen bearer of Oris. I ratify the choice Oris has made."

As Harafin spoke, a tingling sensation began in Kevlin's right boot where Oris lay hidden. The feeling rippled up through his entire body. It drove away the weariness and filled him with a peaceful exultation the likes of which he'd never known before.

Ah'Shan stared from Harafin to Kevlin, growing angrier by the second.

"Listen, my old friend," Harafin said. "This is unexpected. If it were up to me--"

"Enough!" Ah'Shan backed away, his face livid. "You spoke the same lies the last time you denied me my right." He stormed away, but after only a few paces, spun back. "Know this, Harafin. You mock me at your own peril."

Ah'Shan turned on his heel and disappeared into the gathering darkness. Harafin watched him go for several long seconds, his expression sad.

"How is it possible?" Kevlin asked. His voice sounded thin, scared. He wasn't sure what to think.

Harafin placed a hand on his shoulder. "I know you must be confused. I cannot explain how it happened, but it has happened. You said so yourself. You, the steward, touched Oris's power, and it responded."

"So that hasn't happened before. I get that. Let's not jump to conclusions."

"There is only one conclusion. Only the one chosen by Oris as its bearer can unlock its power. That one is you."

"I'm not even a sentinel," Kevlin protested. Sure, he'd embraced a soul-altering change in connecting with Oris, but he wasn't actinopathic. He couldn't become the bearer of Oris.

"I know." Harafin ran a hand through his white hair, dislodging fragments of rubble and bits of dust. "It is unusual."

Kevlin wanted to scream at Harafin that it was far from *unusual*. The old man really meant to shackle him to this stone? He'd suspected Harafin had plans for him, but had never imagined anything so drastic.

"Now we know why Savas was trying to possess your soul," Harafin added. "He could see what we could not."

Kevlin shook his head. "This can't be right."

"There is no doubt, although I should have realized it sooner. There were several clues, but I did not want to accept them."

"You knew?"

"I suspected."

Kevlin frowned. "That's why you tossed me up the cliff first."

"Yes. I believed you would succeed."

"I was trying to save Antigonus, and you were setting me up as your pawn. We could have all died. Antigonus did die!"

"We faced many risks today. I did not put you in danger lightly."

"But you did it anyway."

"Yes, I did." Harafin's eyes bored into Kevlin's. "A time of strife and trial is upon us, prophesied centuries ago. Oris's name as The Fatebreaker is not because times of ease are coming. No, we will all be tested, and many will be consumed.

Kevlin said nothing, his thoughts on the thousands who had been consumed in the recent battle.

"Know this, my young friend, I will do everything in my power to help you, but you must understand that there is no time for hesitation. No time for second-guessing."

Kevlin looked out into the gloom softening the destruction of the ravaged valley, and shivered.

"This is just the beginning," Harafin continued. "The empire will face its greatest threat. Kingdoms may fall, and powers now considered immovable and eternal will be shaken to their roots. Faith will be shattered, fates will be rewritten, and chaos will threaten to engulf the world. If we fail, it will be the end of all things."

Harafin's eyes blazed with an unshakable resolve. "I have battled enemies of freedom for two and a half centuries. The cost is always high, but the alternative is worse. I will see the empire shattered if I must. I will see the very gods thrown down if that is what it takes. We will not fail."

Kevlin looked away and had to fight to keep from snatching up the rune-covered bag and hurling it at Harafin. Maybe then he'd take it back.

No, he wouldn't. . .but what *might* the old man do?

As Kevlin considered the thought, a single drumbeat rang through his heart. He started, eyes wide, as the echoes faded away.

"What's wrong?" Harafin asked.

"Nothing." He turned from the sentinel's penetrating gaze to stare toward the setting sun.

"Tell no one of the choosing," Harafin instructed.

"Why?"

"Trust me."

That was a rotten way to end a conversation.

As Harafin strode away, Kevlin watched him go, not sure what to think. He began to walk. He moved among the many campfires, but didn't stop, filled with restless energy.

A soft voice turned him around. Indira approached in the shadows.

"Why didn't you join us?" she teased. "Afraid I'll take all you have?"

"Sorry, I've got a lot on my mind."

Indira took his hands. "You spend too much time with cryptic old men. That'll mess with anyone's head."

"I didn't have much choice."

Her hands were warm in his and he found himself smiling.

She stepped closer. "I've spent most of my life around Leander and Harafin. You need to find other things to do to keep a balance."

"What do you suggest?"

"Usually I play cards."

"What if that's not enough?" He stared into her dark eyes and his worries eased under her steady gaze.

Indira smiled. "Then you need to take a chance."

Kevlin drew her close and she slipped her arms around his waist. They held each other for a long moment, her face pressed against his neck, her gentle scent in his nostrils.

Indira pulled back just a little. With so many knots in his stomach, Kevlin could barely breathe, he leaned down and kissed her full lips.

This time she kissed him back.

<<< End >>>

ABOUT THE AUTHOR

Frank Morin loves great stories, great food, and great humor. He is an outdoor enthusiast, and loves to travel for inspiration.

Frank is the author of fast-paced adventures with quirky humor including:

- The Petralist – epic YA fantasy series

- The Facetakers – Urban fantasy thriller series

- *Bacon Master of the Apocalypse* – humorous epic fantasy

- Nexus Runner – litRPG fantasy adventure

He and his wife are often found hiking, camping, Scuba diving, or traveling to research new books. Find out more about his novels and his shorter fiction, or join his readers group at: https://bio.to/authorfrankmorin.

Afterword

I hope you enjoyed Oath & Shadow!

I love this book. Sure, I love every book I've written, and I work very hard to ensure each book is the very best it can be.

This one, though. This book was my first.

Even though I've published quite a few other books first, this was the first one I wrote, so it holds a special place in my heart. For several years, it languished on slush piles at major publishers, and I had two different publishers tell me they loved it, but it didn't fit what they were looking for at the time.

By that time, I was thoroughly distracted writing other books, so this one sat a while longer. Finally, it's time has come!

I have huge plans for this series. Book 2 is already finished, with more outlined. I hope you'll take a moment to post an honest review on Amazon and Goodreads to help boost this series.

If you want to know when future books are released, go to my bio page and follow the link to join the reader's group:

https://bio.to/authorfrankmorin

And, THANK YOU for reading!

OTHER WORKS BY FRANK MORIN

Find all books on www.frankmorin.org
and at: bio.to/authorfrankmorin

The Petralist Series
(Epic YA fantasy)

Set in Stone, Book One
A Stone's Throw, Book Two
No Stone Unturned, Book Three
Affinity for War, Book Four
The Queen's Quarry, Book Five
The King's Craft, Book Six
Blood of the Tallan, Book Seven
When Torcs Fly, A Petralist Origins novella: Tomas and Cameron
Game of Garlands, A Petralist Origins novella: Anika
Builder of Intrigue, A Petralist Origins novella: Ailsa
Sweetbreads, A petralist short story collection.

Bacon Master of the Apocalypse Series

(Humorous fantasy)
Bacon Master of the Apocalypse, Book one
Pawn of the Pantryon, Book two.

The Facetakers Series
(Urban Fantasy Time-Travel Thrillers)

Saving Face, Book One
Memory Hunter, Book Two
Rune Warrior, Book Three
Aeon Champion, Book Four (release in September 2020)

Books to Read Online One Chapter at a Time

Nexus Runner – litRPG fantasy on Royal Road

Short Stories

"Odin's Eye," included in A Game of Horns: A Red Unicorn Anthology
"The Essence," included in the Dragon Writers: An Anthology
"The Seventh Strike," included in Cursed Collectibles: An Anthology

9 781946 910370